Also by Sam Sykes from Gollancz:

The Aeon's Gate
Tome of the Undergates
Black Halo
The Skybound Sea

Bring Down Heaven
The City Stained Red
The Mortal Tally
God's Last Breath

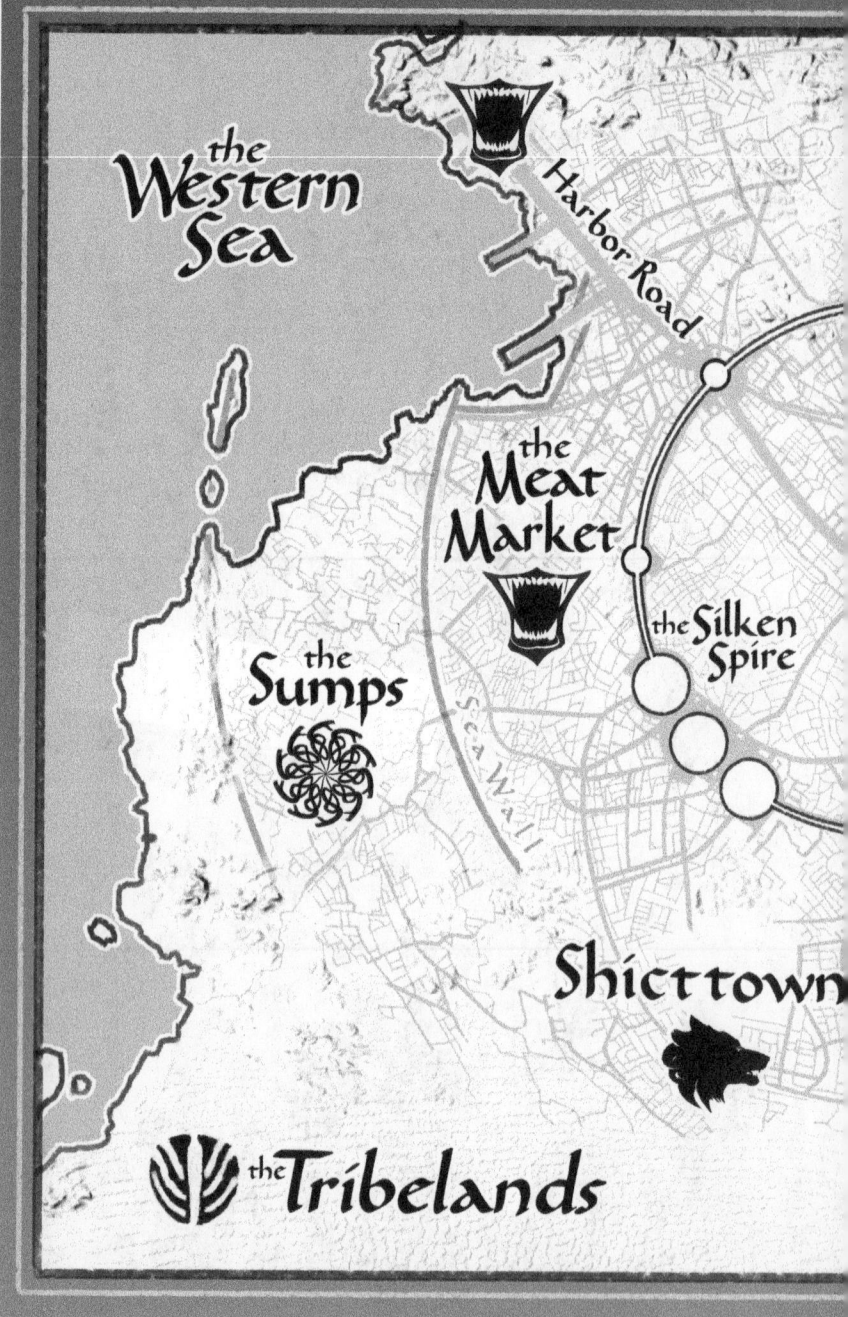

GOD'S LAST BREATH

Bring Down Heaven, Book Three

Sam Sykes

To my mom, who never doubted.

This edition first published in Great Britain in 2018 by Gollancz

First published in Great Britain in 2017 by Gollancz
an imprint of the Orion Publishing Group Ltd
Carmelite House, 50 Victoria Embankment
London EC4Y 0DZ

An Hachette UK Company

1 3 5 7 9 10 8 6 4 2

A CIP catalogue record for this book is
available from the British Library.

ISBN 978 0 575 13227 6

Printed in Great Britain by Clays Ltd, Elcograf S.p.A.

www.samsykes.com
www.gollancz.co.uk

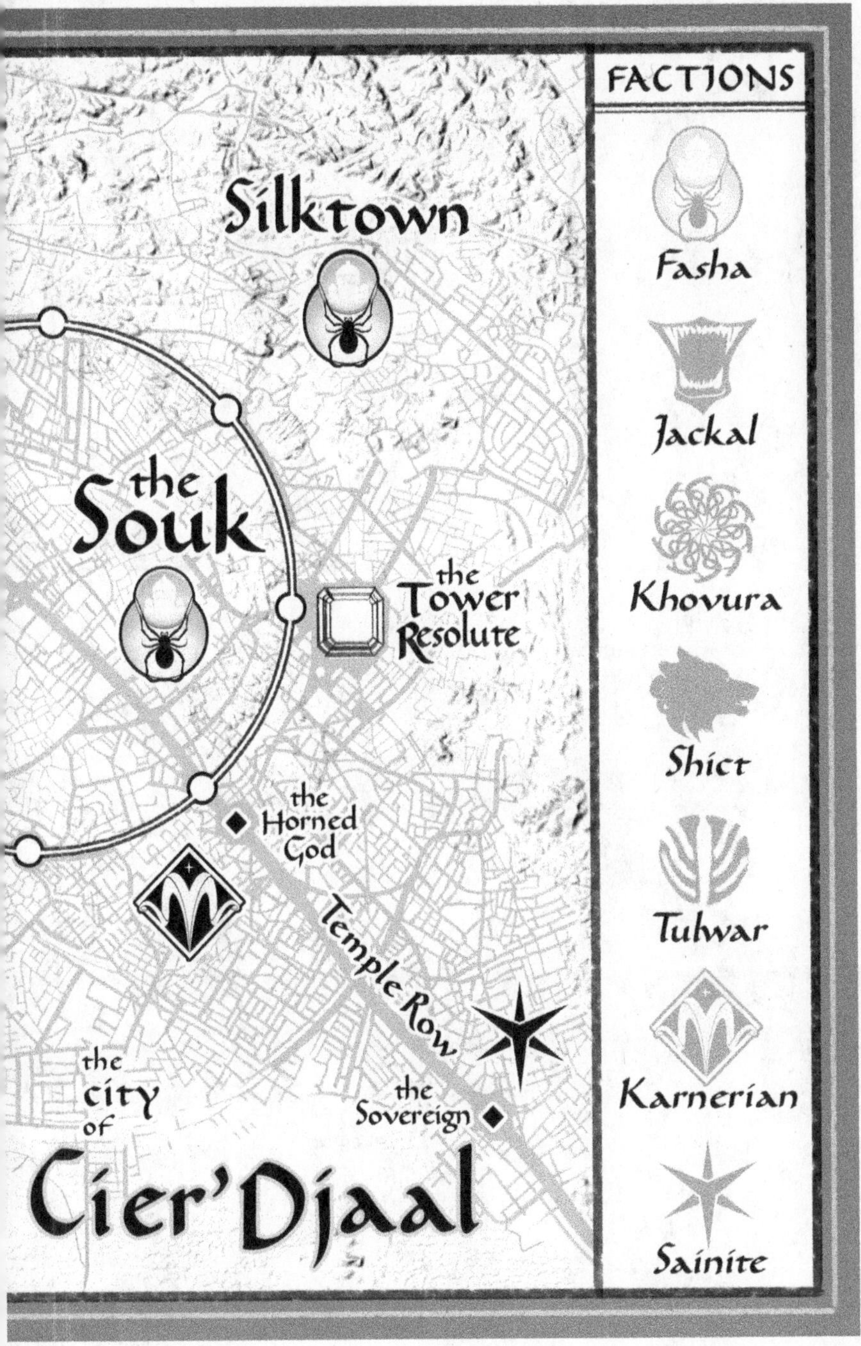

Silktown

the Souk

the **Tower Resolute**

the Horned God

Temple Row

the city of **Cier'Djaal**

the Sovereign

FACTIONS

Fasha

Jackal

Khovura

Shict

Tulwar

Karnerian

Sainite

ACT ONE

A SERMON
OF STEEL

PROLOGUE

For the eyes of His Revered Holiness Who Sees All That Is Worthy and
  Unworthy,
Scion of Heaven, Line of Daeon, Speaker of Speakers,
Herald of the Red Sun and Sword of the Righteous Path,
Lord Emperor of Karneria Amarexes III,

Your humble servant, scholar in pursuit of truth for the greater glories of the
Empire of Karneria, writes you with regard to a subject of immense impor-
tance, and it is with a burden so great as to bend her back that she reports
to you that we are well and truly fucked.

Pardon the coarseness, Holiness, but I fear that this message shall be sani-
tized so thoroughly by your advisers that profanities must be heaped so that
at least some measure of the severity of the situation should reach you.

My correspondence regarding events unfolding in Cier'Djaal and the
status of the holy garrison, Fortress Diplomacy, you have charged has been
thorough, but permit me to squander a moment of your precious time by
reiterating.

Our original charge, under Speaker Careus, third of his order, was to
stymie Sainite efforts to secure economic and military dominance in the city
while furthering Imperial interests.

And for years I dutifully reported that we did exactly that. Even with the
added complication of interference of the local ruling elite known as fashas
and the escalation of criminal warfare between rival criminal organiza-
tions, Jackal and Khovura, our orders were carried out. With permission
from the capital, we escalated our garrison into full warfare with the hated
Sainites.

I regret to inform you, Holiness, that this was a huge fucking mistake.

We were able to topple the Sainite garrison quickly, but the mobility of
their scraws meant that most of their manpower and matériel were evacu-
ated to hidden bases around the city. Attacks from local shict tribes meant

that our reinforcements did not arrive as scheduled. The conflict with the Sainites was long and bloodied and left us in poor condition for what occurred next.

You will doubtless receive many reports on what happened. Your humble servant of the Empire has included her own breakdown of numbers—loss of matériel, soldiers, arms and armor, and so forth—in the pages to follow, but permit me to be frank about the reality of the situation we are facing.

The Sainites can no longer be considered the greatest threat to the Empire.

It was foolish to think that the tulwar clans would remain disparate. Our history tells only that we broke them once, sparing no words for how many legions were killed trying to do so and the fact that three emperors died over the course of their subjugation. The success of their attack on human holdings in and around Cier'Djaal can only confirm that we are looking at a unification we did not think possible.

They are led by a creature—a dragonman, I am told—that has brought the ruling clans under his guidance and has led them to dozens of victories, compounding with the horrors that resulted in the catastrophic failure at Harmony Road.

Further, shictish incursions have reached an all-time high. While we considered them mere nuisances on Imperial roads, it is evident that their designs are stronger, their ambitions are greater, and their machinations deadlier than we considered.

Your servant understands if the following blasphemy requires a swift and immediate execution, but she would be no servant of the Empire were she not to point out that Karneria's hubris has led to this disaster.

We were fools to think we could hold the reins of humanity forever. Fools to think that no other race could challenge us. Fools to think that the shicts would always lurk in the shadows and the tulwar would dwell in their caves. Fools to think that our empire would keep growing.

And, if you do not consider the . . . event that occurred in Cier'Djaal to be evidence enough that we are grossly unprepared for the trials that lie ahead, Holiness, you are a fool, too.

The war has yet to begin. Defeat is not yet assured. And while there are serious doubts as to our preparedness, there can be no overlooking the bright side.

The subject of previous letters, a priestess of Talanas of no previous note, now known as the Prophet, proves an excellent opportunity. Somehow, she orchestrated the salvation of our mission. Somehow, she managed to unite us, as our foes united. Somehow, she is the reason your servant can write to you now.

She has emerged from the ruin of our charge with a message.

And we would be fools not to listen.

Humanity can no longer stand divided.

Our foes can no longer be dismissed.

Heaven is watching.

> With utmost humility and urgency,
> Glory to Karneria, May the Conqueror Forever Watch Her Walls,
> Haethen Caladerus,
> Foescribe of Arda Scriptis

ONE

HIS GLORIOUS REIGN

The barest choke of a gasp whistling through a ragged hole.

Chains rattled, shook flakes of rust free to fall as red motes in the rising light of dawn.

Her jugular shifted beneath the emaciated stretch of her flesh, laboring to push another breath out through the jagged tear in her throat.

And a drop of blood oozed out.

It traveled downward, staining a red path across the length of her jaw. It slid affectionately across her cheek, past her temple, and down a strand of tangled hair. The thick red droplet hung there for a moment before falling upon the scale-and-feathers of one of the two great wings that hung limp from her back. It hung from the tip of emerald plumage, quivering, as though reluctant to leave her.

⊷ ⊷⊱⊰⊶ ⊷

But, like all the others, it finally fell.

And, like all the others, Lenk watched it disappear into the pristine blue waters over which she hung. And when he could no longer see it, he looked up into her face.

If she was in pain, the emotionless silver mask that was her face did not betray it. If she could beg for reprieve, the choked noises she made did not sound like it. And if there was anything he could have done to stop her agony, he could not think of it.

Or perhaps he wasn't trying hard enough.

In the days since it had all happened—since he had been betrayed by Kataria, since had betrayed Shuro, since he had released hell upon the earth—he had often come to this spot. For a dead city, Rhuul Khaas had become noisy of late, and the reservoir at its eastern edge was one of the few places that was still relatively quiet.

One would have thought that, by now, he would have known more about the poor creature that hung over it.

Her name was Kyrael. She was an Aeon. Once, both those names had meant something. They were the names of a trusted adviser, a friend, a lover. They were the names of a herald of the gods, sent to shepherd men and watch over the earth. They were the names of one who had betrayed heaven and duty and been betrayed by the same.

But to Lenk, she still looked like a corpse.

She was tall and slender, even chained upside down as she was, and the elegant musculature of her naked body was still apparent, if withered. She hung with long arms and long wings drooping down over the reservoir. And even the way the chains wrapped about her ankles, holding her over the great pool of water from four cardinal pillars, was almost dainty, like jewelry rather than shackles. And her face—that pristine polish of silver carved in unfeeling, tranquil expression—was still unmarred by time and strife.

She was probably beautiful before Mocca had torn her throat out.

Punishment, Lenk had been told, for her betrayal. In the last days before Mocca had been cast down by the armies of heaven and thrown into hell, she had done him a final kindness by leading his worshippers away that they need not be caught in the battle that would see him thrown down. And, denied the masses that had adulated him, Mocca had responded by condemning the immortal Aeon to forever bleed into the waters.

He'd had another name back then. Mocca might have forgiven her. But Khoth-Kapira, the God-King, did not suffer betrayal.

She had loved him, Lenk had been told. She would have done anything for him. She had given up the bliss of heaven and the love of the gods for him.

And he had still done this to her.

Perhaps Lenk just came here every day only to remind himself of the fate of those who stood at Khoth-Kapira's side.

And yet, in all the days he had watched her blood feed the waters, he had yet to leave. He was still here, watching another cold dawn rise over the dead city. She was still here, bleeding out as she had done for centuries now.

And they had no idea how to help each other.

Kyrael, the perpetually bleeding angel from beyond the stars, was the closest thing to a kindred spirit he had.

And that probably said something about him.

Too damn late to do anything about that now, though, he thought with a sniff.

A sudden tang of acidic reek hit his nostrils. And above the rushing waters of the reservoir, he heard the sound of heavy feet dragging on stone. Behind him, a wet, guttural hiss boiled out of a mouth thick with saliva.

That had once alarmed him. Less so, these days. But as he turned to see his newfound company, he feared he would never get wholly comfortable around the creatures with whom he shared this city.

The man's back was bent, weighed down by the mass of tumorous flesh growing out between his shoulder blades. His arms hung so low that they scraped the stone floor. One leg was limp and dragged behind him; the other was thicker than his arms and hauled the great mass forward.

His face was a mass of molten flesh. One eye had sealed shut; the other was wide and unblinking. His lips had split open to make way for a serpentine snout that burst out of his mouth. A long, slimy tongue flicked out between two jutting fangs.

Lenk cringed. The man did not seem to notice.

"The master commands you to—" the creature began in a thick, slavering voice, but caught himself. "The master *requests* your…your presence. Urgent. Come. You must come."

Lenk sighed, knowing the statement to be a farce. Mocca hadn't requested he come. God-Kings did not "request" anything.

"Come," the man insisted again. "Come, come…you must—"

"I heard you the first time," Lenk said.

He trudged to a nearby pillar. His sword was right where he left it: leaning against the stone, the dawn's light glinting off its hilt and catching him right in the eye. Almost like it was staring at him expectantly.

Remember when you wanted to get rid of me? it seemed to ask.

Remember when you were going to leave me behind and go off and live a peaceful life? Remember how you were going to settle down with a nice young lady and stop surrounding yourself with bloodshed?

Lenk glanced over his shoulder at the abominable creature staring at him. Then he looked back to the sword. And the sword looked back.

How's that working out for you, champ?

"Shut up," Lenk muttered. Ordinarily, talking to a sword might seem crazy. But given his circumstances, it didn't feel quite so bad.

He hefted the scabbarded blade and buckled it over his shoulder. It settled with a familiar, comfortable weight that galled him. He *did* remember wanting to leave this weapon behind.

If only he could remember what it felt like to not have it on his back.

The abomination stalked away. Trying his best to ignore the sound of Kyrael forever choking on her own blood, Lenk followed.

The gray streets of Rhuul Khaas wound their way through rising buildings and sprawling courtyards. Towers and homes stared down at him through empty window eyes, their doors open in gaping yawns. Statues of learned robed men smiled upon him as he passed. Fountains long dried up sat beneath frescoes of weathered tiles depicting scenes of bustling markets and people bowed in worship.

Aside from a few marks of age here and there—loose stones and the occasional foundational crack—Rhuul Khaas was in remarkably good shape for a city dead for centuries.

Kyrael's doing, Lenk knew. When the city had fallen to the mortal armies, she had evacuated the people to spare them the slaughter. The city had escaped the ravages of war. When Lenk had first arrived here, it had stood empty and silent, a massive tomb for only a handful of people.

Not so anymore.

A flicker of movement at the corner of his eye. He didn't bother looking. He was never quick enough to see them.

But he could hear their throaty hisses slithering out from the mouths of alleys and empty doorways. He could feel their unblinking eyes peering at him from the shadows of windows and rooftops. On occasion, he could see a serpentine tail or flaccid limb being dragged around a corner, or the shadow of an emaciated, spindly body slip away.

Abominations? Horrors? Sins against heaven and mockeries of men?

Lenk had no idea what to call them. He could barely stand to look at them. Their own names, they had given up long ago, and any word he might have had for them seemed somehow insufficient to describe them.

Except the one leading him.

He had decided to call this one Jeff.

It just seemed polite.

"Wait," Lenk said as he looked up at suddenly unfamiliar buildings. "This isn't the way to his quarters."

"Not quarters," Jeff hissed. "Not today. The master is in the square. He has something you must see. He has something he must show. We must watch. We must know. We must..."

The creature's voice trailed off into a witless burble that Lenk strove to shut out. He hated listening to these fiends, hated looking at them, hated being reminded what they were.

And what he had done to aid them.

Their path wound them through the city streets, up a long staircase and into the city's upper levels. A stone walkway circled a great plaza. And what lay within it, surrounded by great statues of benevolent robed men, Lenk could not ignore so easily.

A wound in creation, a scar that could never heal, a hole that stretched below the streets of Rhuul Khaas, beneath the earth itself, and into some place much darker. It stretched across the plaza in a jagged scar, a gaping black hole around which the dawn could not touch.

Lenk could not look at it.

And Lenk could not look away from it.

Every time he looked upon it, his mind slipped away from him, back through the days to the fateful night he had stood before it. Back to the night when it had bled a red light and stained the black sky. Back to the night when he had looked into a woman's eyes, as blue and deep and full of fear as his own, and made his choice.

His choice that had made Shuro try to kill him.

His choice that had summoned these abominations here.

His choice that had freed the beast trapped in that dark scar.

He turned away, hurrying to catch up with Jeff as the creature shambled across the walkway and between nearby buildings. But he could not outrun his thoughts.

Often, he wondered if Shuro had escaped, if she had made it out of Rhuul Khaas. Only rarely did he wonder if she hated him for his choice.

He already knew the answer to that.

But he could not think on this for long. For it wasn't long before he couldn't think over the noise.

A distant burble. A formless wail. A verbal poison that seeped past his clothing and into his skin, echoing in the deep sinew.

Voices. Hundreds of them. Straight ahead.

"Ah," Jeff murmured as he led Lenk down another staircase. "They have come."

They emerged out from between two buildings and into a great, sprawling square. The buildings here sat lower than in the streets, giving way to the towering stone statues of the same robed man with elegant features and a warm smile, arms extended out in benediction over those gathered below.

And they were many.

Hundreds. Maybe thousands. It was hard for Lenk to tell how many there were. They boiled together in a stew of deformed flesh and black cloth, each face running together, each body melding into one another.

Some had misshapen limbs: spindly, desiccated legs and arms hulking with bloated, tumorous tissue that erupted out their back in flesh mountains. Others had eyes that did not blink or move of their own volition, mouths with jaws that hung all the way to their knees, tongues that slid out between jutting fangs and coiled around their necks. And many more had scales, tails, black claws, and yellow eyes.

Men and women. Young and old. Large and small and hale and infirm and desperate and scared and writhing and squealing and wailing and screaming. Whatever they had been before, Lenk didn't know. Whatever monsters they were now, Lenk finally had a name for.

Reverent.

Their eyes—mismatched, misshapen, many—were all turned in the same direction. Their limbs—hulking, withered, flaccid—all reached toward the same spot. Their voices . . .

Their voices...

"—*it hurts. It hurts so much, master, please*—"

"—*I came so far, all for you, please help make it*—"

"—*look upon me, master, bless me, help me*—"

Their voices were everywhere.

"Come," Jeff gurgled, shambling forward. "Come with me. He wants you. He needs you to be here...he needs you to see..."

Lenk glanced over his shoulder, as if wondering if he could flee from this. But he knew he could not. This city was not his home. And one did not reject an invitation from its master.

And so, keenly aware of the sword on his back, he followed Jeff into the crowd.

He lost his guide within moments, the misshapen creature disappearing into the hundreds of other misshapen creatures as their fleshy throngs closed in around him. Yet for all the glistening flesh and molten deformities pressing in on him, there were deeper horrors.

"—*master, please, master, help me*—"

They groaned.

"—*it hurts! Oh gods, what have I done, it hurts so*—"

They wailed.

"—*told me I was foolish, I was insane, they never listen, they NEVER*—"

They screamed.

Their words clawed at his ears, at his flesh, burrowed into his sinew. Their every letter was racked with agony, with fear, with desperation. It hurt to listen to, hurt to be around, like their every word poisoned the air around him and made each breath like agony.

And in the space between each word, he could hear his thoughts.

You did this.

Between his ragged breaths, he knew.

You brought them here.

And when he shut his eyes, he heard it.

You let him *out.*

"Children."

A single word, spoken softly. Yet it rang out over the square as clear as a note from a glass bell. And the reverent and their wailing fell silent at it.

"Stand aside."

And in a shuffling, awkward mass, they did. A great curtain of flesh parted, leaving a long wake of stone that stretched between Lenk and the center of the square where a dais rose.

Lenk wasted no time in hurrying down it, keeping his ears shut and his eyes down at the street. He only knew he had reached it when he saw the shadow stretching out upon the stones before him.

The shape of a stately robed man.

"You're late."

Whose beard writhed.

"Did my child find you all right?"

Lenk looked up and the first thing he noticed was Mocca's smile.

Set beneath gentle eyes and framed in a face with elegant, dark-skinned features, it was a warm, fatherly smile. The kind that perfectly complemented the soft white robe that Mocca was garbed in and matched his thin arms outstretched in benediction. Still, Lenk thought it odd that he should notice that first.

As opposed to the beard of serpents coiling out of Mocca's jaw.

"It's not your child," Lenk replied.

At this, the serpents hissed, offended on behalf of their host. Mocca merely smiled and shook his head.

"Do they offend you, my friend?" he asked.

Lenk stepped up onto the dais beside Mocca and turned and gazed over the assembly. And they, with their thousand terrified eyes, stared back. It wasn't long before Lenk cringed and turned away.

"They're monsters," he said.

And they're here because of you, he added.

"You lack respect."

An ancient, rasping voice reached Lenk's ears. A darker shadow loomed over him.

He looked up into eyes that were black, as though someone had scribbled over them with coal. An old man's face, skin gray and fraught with wrinkles, scowled down at him from its position in an elongated head. Withered limbs ending in black claws stretched out as its old man's body, flabby and emaciated all at once, leaned forward. In lieu of legs, a great serpent's coil brought the demon closer to Lenk.

"It is the burden of the layperson," the Disciple hissed, a long purple tongue flicking out of its withered mouth. "Come, let us show you what we have sacrificed."

"Enough."

Mocca raised a hand. The demon froze, inclined its massive head, and settled back upon its coils. Lenk shuddered—it hadn't been so long ago that he was killing demons like these, wiping their stain from the earth. Now he stood alongside them.

And their God-King.

"I suppose they are hideous to you, as they are to me," Mocca said, looking over the crowd. "But then, I suppose you only see the flesh: the twisted muscle and jagged bone."

"Do you *not*?" Lenk asked. "Can't you hear them? They're in pain."

"They were in pain long before my Disciples changed them into what they are now," Mocca said, gesturing to the demon. "The ugliness I see here is the fear and desperation that drove them to this. The ugliness is the city that cared not a bit for the mother whose children were killed in a thieves' war, the people who would not lend a man a shovel that he might bury his father." Mocca's expression grew cold. "It's the world, Lenk. It's the fear and hatred and terror they were given that drove them here, to me."

He spread his arms out wide over the crowd. And they raised a hooting, gibbering, wordless screech at his gesture.

"And it is I who shall cleanse it."

Admittedly, Lenk didn't intend to snort. It wasn't a good idea to back-sass a man with snakes growing out of his face.

Yet it wasn't rage that painted Mocca's face when he turned to look at Lenk. Rather, it was a decidedly unamused frown.

"I've had centuries to rehearse this, Lenk," Mocca said. "Don't rob me of the drama."

"You just make it sound so simple," Lenk replied, shaking his head.

"Is it not?"

Lenk stared at him flatly for a moment. "Not a week ago, you crawled out of a hole to hell. I'm standing in the middle of a city that shouldn't exist, surrounded by ungodly monsters who look at you like a god, hanging around a demon and, if that wasn't fucked up enough, you've got snakes growing out of your face. There is no part of this that is fucking simple, Mocca."

"Khoth-Kapira," Mocca said, correcting him. "And do not forget why you are standing here, why you helped me out of that pit. You know as well as I do that this world is ill. Its plagues are wars and violence. You have seen them up close."

Lenk could only nod weakly. So many weeks later, so many miles away, he could still remember it all: the battles between the Karnerians and Sainites that had driven him here, the brutality of the shicts and the tulwar in the tribelands that had harried him. Just thinking about them made the sword on his back feel heavier.

As if to remind him that this was not a world where it could be dropped so easily.

"Mortality is defined by its brevity, Lenk," Mocca continued, folding his hands behind his back as he looked over the crowd. "By its very nature, it is in a headlong rush to end itself. The wars you have seen, the wars that will yet come, are but a symptom of a base plague that wracks this world."

"You sound so certain," Lenk said.

Mocca hesitated. "Should I not be? When I speak of a war of wars, a time of strife and of suffering so great and so vast as to boggle the minds of gods, do you truly believe such a thing could never come to pass?"

Lenk closed his eyes. His scars ached. His shoulders sagged with the weight of his sword and all the weight of the blood it had spilled.

"The people I will save here, Lenk, are nothing compared to the people I will save by preventing this cataclysm. So many will owe their lives to you, Lenk." Mocca paused, glanced over his shoulder, and regarded Lenk out of the corner of his eye. "Or perhaps you would be satisfied with just one?"

All other pains in Lenk's body fled at the sudden chill that swept through it. Mocca's words sank into him deeper than the abominations' ever could. And as they settled in Lenk's flesh, he knew what Mocca spoke of.

Kataria.

She was still out there, somewhere. Somewhere in that wasteland, filled with its countless people and their countless bloodthirsts. Wherever she had disappeared to, Lenk did not know. But he knew she needed his help, as he needed her.

He needed her to live. And Mocca was the only thing in this world that could make that happen. That was why he had to be freed.

He told himself this.

He shifted his feet. The weight settled on his back.

The sword didn't believe him.

Something touched his shoulder. Mocca squeezed his arm gently. With a hiss, his beard of serpents slid away, retreating back into his flesh. What was left was just a man with dark eyes and a gentle smile.

"We will save her, Lenk," Mocca said. "Her and so many others. I have the power to help them, to prevent so much bloodshed. But I cannot do it without you."

"A God-King shouldn't need my help," Lenk replied.

"Gods are nothing without faith." Mocca shook his head. "And I am nothing if you do not believe in me." He fixed his eyes intently on Lenk's. "Do you?"

Dark eyes. A gentle smile. A neatly trimmed goatee and perfectly manicured fingernails.

Funny, Lenk thought. *Look at him in the right light, he looks just like a man.*

And in the golden rising dawn, Lenk could almost believe it. He could almost forget that there had just been a beard of vipers a moment ago where flesh was now. He could almost pretend he hadn't seen this man crawl out of a pit so dark that light feared to tread there.

Almost.

But this was not a man. And this was not Mocca. This was Khoth-Kapira, the God-King, cast down from heaven to earth and from earth to hell for sins ancient and countless. This was a demon. Foe of man. Enemy of the gods.

And yet . . .

Man was intent on killing himself and everything around him. And the gods did not answer their prayers.

And when gods were silent, demons spoke.

Lenk placed a hand on Mocca's. He felt flesh. Warm and alive.

"I do," Lenk said.

Mocca smiled, nodded. "Then let me show you."

"Show me what?"

Mocca released him and turned back to the crowd. "How I will fix this." He leveled a finger at the crowd. "You. Child. Step forward."

Somehow, they knew to whom he spoke. The crowd of abominations shuffled aside with a murmur, revealing a misshapen creature. No more horrifying than the others, Lenk thought; this one had thin spindly legs, a long flaccid arm that dragged behind it, a mouth rimmed with fangs, and a single unblinking eye focused on Mocca as it shuffled forward.

A man? A woman? Lenk couldn't tell. Not even when it approached the dais and sank to its knees before Mocca.

Mocca sighed, then laid a hand on the molten scars of its brows. He stroked its head, pity playing upon his features. The creature leaned into his touch, a pet deprived of attention.

"You poor soul," Mocca whispered. He shut his eyes, breathing deeply. "I see them. Your family. I feel your hatred." He shook his head. "But you mustn't hate them, child. Their cruelty was driven by their fear. The same fear that drove you to the embrace of my Disciples." He ran his fingers down to the creature's gaping jaws. "Alas, they are but pupils. Their methods are . . . inelegant."

The abomination loosed a sound halfway between a groan and a whimper. Mocca simply smiled and took its face in both his hands.

"In such a short life, you have felt so much pain. I can ease it." Mocca tilted his face toward the sky. "If only you accept . . . just a little more."

A single breath. His eyes snapped open. And the light of the dawn paled before the golden light that burst from Mocca's stare.

That same light poured out of his fingertips and into the creature. It let out a squeal, struggling to escape Mocca's grasp. But his fingers sank deeper into its flesh, white smoke sizzling off his knuckles as the golden light seeped out of his digits and into the creature's flesh. A dark voice from a deep pit tore free from Mocca's mouth.

"A little more," he said. *"Witness my miracle."*

The creature's shriek was lost, as was its form, bathed in a light so bright that Lenk had to shield his eyes from it. And when that was insufficient, he shut them tight and looked away, trying to ignore the terrified wails of the crowd.

Only when they stopped did he dare to open his eyes. The light was gone. The screams had quieted. And in their wake, Lenk's curse seemed woefully insufficient for what he saw.

"Gods..." he whispered.

"No," Mocca said. "Me."

The creature was gone. No, not gone. Changed. It no longer stooped, but stood tall and proud. Its molten flesh had tightened across the broad muscle of a body, hale and whole. Its flesh was dark and warm, its hair was black and lustrous, its face was square and handsome and terribly human.

It was...

He was a man.

No, more than a man.

Lenk saw it in the length of his fingers, the strength of his naked body, the height and the hair and the bright yellow eyes. His face was angular and beautiful, too much for any normal human. This was...he was something else. Something more. Something powerful.

The man looked down at himself, at his long fingers and his thick legs and his nakedness. His face brightened with a childish disbelief as he took himself in. And when he finally found breath to do so, he screamed. Not the terrified, agonized scream of the damned, but the joyous, bright wail of the living.

"Master!" he screamed, falling to his knees before Mocca and coiling around his feet. "Master, you have saved me!"

"I have, child," Mocca said, nodding. "And I have so much more work to do." He stepped over the man, toward the crowd, and extended his arms. "And who among you shall also witness?"

They let out a feral, animalistic screech. In one surge of glistening flesh, they rushed forward: monstrous limbs outstretched and mouths gaping in wails.

And once more, Lenk had to cover his ears. But it did no good.

"*—master, save me! Save me! I have been faithful! You promised—*"

They screamed.

"*—it hurts so much, master! Make it stop! Make it stop, please, I beg—*"

They wailed.

"*—let it end! LET IT END! OH, MASTER, I WANT SO BADLY—*"

Their every word was racked with such agony that it was poison in

Lenk's ears. He could stand it no longer. He fought his way through the throng of monstrosities, who ignored him in their rush to the dais.

And when he was finally clear of them, he cast one final look to the center of the square.

And there he saw Mocca, his arms outstretched, his beard of vipers writhing, a hundred misshapen hands reaching out toward him.

And a look of ecstasy scarred across his face.

TWO

TEN POUNDS OF FLESH

In the right light, Cier'Djaal might look like a beautiful city.

As dawn turned to morning proper, its light—still too early to beat down as a desert sun should—fell over the city like a blanket. And nowhere did it shine brighter than the Silken Spire.

A breeze heralded the sun, sending ripples through the great sheets of spun silk that clung between the three pillars overlooking the city. Their colors, a riot of crimsons and violets and silvers and midnights and indigos and oceans, all took on a heavenly glow as the sunlight seeped through them.

And against the bright golden glow, the Spire's tailors could be seen in eight-legged shadows upon the silken sheets they wove. The spiders, each one the size of a horse, crawled lazily across their haphazard tapestry of a web. Idly, they spun their webs, adding another strand of color to the wild rainbow if the mood took them. Frequently, they fed on whatever food had been left out for them that day. Upon their gorgeous miasma of a web, they seemed quite content.

And Asper couldn't help but wonder if they ever looked down.

Did they ever look down on the Souk and see that its many market stalls and stands now stood empty, its merchants long fled? Did they ever look long to Cier'Djaal's neighborhoods and see the smashed windows, caved-in roofs, burnt-out husks of homes? Did they ever glance down to the streets and see the cold bodies of wives and husbands and soldiers and merchants and let their eight eyes linger there, if only to wonder if those carcasses might be good to eat?

Did they ever wonder what had become of their city?

Don't be stupid, Asper chided herself. *The view's probably great from up there.*

Indeed, she thought as she turned away from the Silken Spire, in the right light, Cier'Djaal might seem like a beautiful city.

Just so long as one didn't look down.

And, especially, so long as one didn't venture into a neighborhood like the Thicket.

Thickets being relatively unknown in the desert, the small collection of dark houses with their peaked roofs and wooden doors had been named for its once-thriving foreigner community. Adventurers, journeymen, and merchants from places like Karneria, Nivoire, and Muraska had all come to Cier'Djaal to seek their fortunes and found themselves in the dingy little neighborhood where the houses were made of subpar wood and the shadows of Cier'Djaal's walls seemed to cling just a little bit dimmer.

The foreigners had mostly fled now, as anyone with sense or luck had when the war between Karneria's black-clad Imperial Legion and Saine's rowdy bands of bird-riding warriors had broken out. Months later, looters and squatters and thieves had had their fill of the Thicket and left behind decaying houses stripped of any goods, a neighborhood spared the violence that had wracked the rest of the city only because it seemed too shitty to fight over.

And when foreigners, thieves, and armies alike had turned up their noses at such a place, what manner of creature moved in?

This was what Asper was intent on finding out.

"This is a bad idea."

No matter who protested.

"A *really* bad idea."

Or how right they probably were.

Asper didn't look over her shoulder. Such an action would suggest doubt to anyone who might be watching. She had walked into enough shitholes in her life to know that one didn't timidly creep in. If she had to dip her toes into shit, she might as well dive in with both feet.

"We should turn back," someone said from behind her.

"Feel free," she replied, continuing to stride through the Thicket's shadowed streets.

"The boy's right," another person grunted. "This place didn't have the best reputation when the city was still safe. We used to send Jhouche here in teams of six."

"We don't have six," she said. "We have three. I'm happy to do it with one, if you're scared."

"It's not a matter of being scared," the second voice protested. "It's a matter of being sensible. And coming to a place like this based on an anonymous *tip*? That's just madness!"

Only at this did Asper bother to turn around. She took in her companions with a hard-eyed glare. The young dark-skinned, delicate-featured Djaalic man in his blue priest's robe looked hardly fit to be here, eyes darting about nervously from beneath his hood. And even the middle-aged man in the polished armor of a guard with the thick beard streaked with gray looked ill at ease in these dark streets.

"And who else am I to ask for help, Dransun?" she demanded of the guard. "Who is left?" She gestured to the houses, to the empty windows. "The war has bled the city dry. There's no one left to save it *but* us."

"Our intelligence suggests that the Karnerians and Sainites have retreated to their bases." The young man in the robe spoke up. "It's been months of fighting now. They've got casualties of their own to worry about."

"And ours outnumber theirs twenty to one, Aturach," Asper replied. "And even with all those dead and wounded, there's still so many more people that could stand to die." She narrowed her eyes. "Or had you forgotten there's an entire tulwar army just a few days from Cier'Djaal?"

Both Dransun and Aturach flinched at that knowledge. And, Asper admitted, it felt cruel to remind them. At least in the Thicket, they could have pretended for a few moments that their biggest concerns were bad neighborhoods.

But things in this city had a way of getting out of hand.

Months ago, Asper's sole concern was getting paid along with her companions. Weeks ago, her attentions were on saving Cier'Djaal's people from the foreign armies of Karneria and Saine tearing each other apart in its streets. And now, after a few mere days, her thoughts were for the army of savage tulwar, simian and barbaric and brimming with steel and flame, lurking out in the tribelands beyond the gates. The savagery of the tulwar, thousands strong, would dwarf any foreigner's, she knew.

Because she knew who led them.

"Suffice to say," Asper said, "we are not at the point where sensibility is an option. Lest you forget."

"I can't forget, priestess," Dransun said with a sneer. "I was there to see you get your ass kicked."

At his words, the pains returned: the creak of her fractured ribs, the ache of a jaw that had been nearly broken, the throbbing pain of her left arm in its sling. She felt all the bruises on her face and on her body beneath her robe flare up. Somehow, in all the hustle and bustle of trying to keep from dying horribly, she had almost forgotten she was close to dying horribly.

She forced herself not to blink. Every time she closed her eyes, she could see Gariath in her head: his teeth bared in a snarl, his fist hammering into her jaw, his clawed fingers twitching as he so effortlessly snapped her arm. And if she wasn't careful, she could hear his voice as he swore to burn Cier'Djaal to the ground.

The memory aggravated the pain. Every breath suddenly felt ragged and her body screamed in shapeless agonies. And in response to the pain, something inside her burned: a profound agony, a more eloquent pain, that spoke pointedly as it stirred inside her broken arm.

They will die, the pain purred through a voice laced with white heat. *You can't save them all.*

She gritted her teeth, drew in a deep breath that felt like swallowing rusted knives, ignored that pain, ignored the other pains. Or tried to.

Deep breaths, she said. *Once. Twice. Again. Until it's bearable. You can handle pain. You can handle this.*

And at this, the pain inside her laughed.

"Turn back if you want," she suddenly said, turning around. "But if we're going to save this city, we've got only one chance." She started stalking into the shadows of the Thicket. "And it's in here."

She never stopped. Never looked behind her. Never gave them a choice to do anything but follow her.

They traveled in silence through the Thicket. Their eyes occasionally darted at stray shapes moving between the shadows. And though Dransun occasionally reached for his sword and Aturach often muttered a prayer, Asper did not so much as blink.

After all, what left in this city could possibly threaten her?

She came to a halt in front of a building. She glanced at its doorframe, then pulled a piece of parchment out of her sling and unfolded it with her good hand and her teeth.

House 117.

As it was written on the parchment, so was it burned into the doorframe. *Knock three times*, the parchment read. *Then wait. Then two times. Password is "oil-based landscape."*

She glanced at Dransun and Aturach. They took up positions behind her, their eyes on the alleys and street. Marching into danger was quickly becoming routine for them.

Asper rapped on the door, as instructed. Three times. A brief pause. Then twice again.

A long silence passed. Long enough that she had just raised her fist to knock once more when a muffled voice spoke from behind the door.

"No solicitations," someone mumbled.

"I'm here about purchasing a painting," Asper replied.

"Nothing sold here. Go away."

"I was really hoping to buy a . . . an oil-based landscape."

A longer silence passed. And when there was no answer, Dransun muttered under his breath.

"Don't like this. Silences this long mean he's talking to someone."

"You think he sold us out?" Aturach asked.

"'Sold us out?'" Asper grinned. "Listen to you, all shady and roguelike."

"I'm not joking," Aturach snapped back. "We're in a dangerous place where dangerous people usually dwell. My tone is totally appropriate." A moment passed. "So . . . like, dashing roguelike or dangerous roguelike?"

"Dashing," Asper said. "Definitely."

Aturach sighed. "How come no one ever thinks I'm dangerous?"

She would have laughed at that, if it didn't hurt like hell to do so. And in another moment, the door creaked open. A Djaalic man, dark skin mapped with wrinkles and dark hair streaked with gray, peered out.

"This isn't a good time, *shkainai*," he whispered. "The couthi are preparing to leave."

"This'll just take a moment," Asper said.

"No, I mean they're preparing to leave Cier'Djaal. Things have gotten *that* bad. They wonder if they can ask to forward you their new address and offer you a modest discount on your next purchase."

"No. Tell them I need to see them."

"I have been authorized to offer an *extremely* generous modest discount."

Asper leaned forward and jammed her boot through the door. Before he could pull away, she leaned in and seized his collar with her good hand.

"Ordinarily, I'm happy to play these games," she growled. "I say a bunch of mysterious passwords, we negotiate, you eventually let me in. But I have spent the last few weeks dodging Karnerians and Sainites, pulling corpses out of the muck, and getting the shit kicked out of me. I am sorry to both you and your associates, but if you don't let me in right now, I will be happy to break down the door and persuade you."

The man eyed her left arm in its sling. "Your arm is broken."

"That leaves me three good limbs to shove up your ass."

The man cleared his throat, eased the door open, and brushed her hand away. He sniffed as she stalked in. The interior of a humble home, sparsely furnished but clean, greeted her.

"In the back," the Djaalic muttered, gesturing toward a door wedged between two bookshelves at the rear of the house. "And don't touch anything, please. I don't know where those three limbs have been."

Dransun and Aturach fell in behind her as she pushed the door open. The back room was dimly lit by a candle. Several crates had been stacked in the corner. Atop them, a mess of black rags and a portrait of an elegant woman in demure, smiling repose sat unmoving.

But not for long.

As she approached, the black cloth suddenly straightened up and fell down into the shape of a well-cut black robe bearing four sleeves. Two large clawed hands slipped out from the top; a pair of smaller, delicate hands folded pleasantly in front of a long torso. From a height of six and a half feet, the portrait inclined down as whatever eyes lurked behind it focused on Asper.

For a moment, it held her gaze. Then, all four limbs extended in a welcoming gesture as the creature inclined its portrait-covered face low in a long, sweeping bow.

"Pleasantries and clarified surprises of a genial nature are heaped upon your face, *shkainai*," the couthi said in a droning monotone. "This one confesses he had not expected to see you so soon."

"It's been months, Man-Shii Kree," Asper replied.

"Apologies are offered in suitably modest amounts, *shkainai*. This one was hoping to avoid bringing to your attention the unfortunate implication that this one did not expect to see you again, suggesting that he had anticipated an unpleasant and likely painful demise had been visited upon your person."

Man-Shii Kree straightened up, folding his four hands in front of him. His portrait betrayed no particular emotion.

"This one hopes it is not necessary to indicate his appropriate relief to learn that your fluids remain internal, but this one does so, anyway, in hopes of soothing previous conversational offenses."

Asper stepped toward Man-Shii Kree. "I'm not here for conversation," she said. "I've been told you and your associates have something I need."

"It is with immense regret that this one must inform you that Man-Shii Kree's Curios and Wonderosities, Safe for Human Consumption (Oral), is temporarily unable to provide assistance as relocations are underway. Suitable replacements can be recommended for a modest fee of—"

"I'm not looking for you, specifically. I need you *and* your associates." She leaned forward. "I need the Bloodwise Brotherhood."

Man-Shii Kree stood completely still. For a moment, Asper wondered if he was pretending to be dead in hopes that they would leave. When he spoke again, his monotone took on a chilling quality.

"This one does not wish to so swiftly destroy the doubtless carefully constructed web of intrigue woven by established enigmatic phrasing, *shkainai*, but this one must inquire as to who, exactly, has offered such information on the dealings of the Brotherhood?"

"The only ones who know about the Brotherhood are the ones who need to know about the Brotherhood," Asper replied. "That's the saying, isn't it?"

"Your aphorism is noted, discerned as charming, and met with apology, as this one would normally demonstrate adequate politeness by indulging it. Immense lament is heaped upon your face, *shkainai*, as this one must regretfully inform and implore that those who know about the Brotherhood are carefully selected and given such information."

Even as his smaller hands remained delicately folded before him, Man-Shii Kree's immense upper arms unfolded and hung at his sides. His long fingers popped as they flexed, the long black claws at their tips glistening in the firelight.

"It is with even greater regret that this one does not recall you being such a selection, *shkainai*."

She heard Dransun reach for his sword. She heard Aturach whisper a curse. She raised a hand to calm them before reaching into her sling. She produced another folded letter, sealed with wax, and handed it to the couthi. The creature's smaller hands took it gently, unfolded it, and held it up before his portrait.

Another moment passed, this one not nearly so long, nor so quiet. Man-Shii Kree made an unpleasant chittering sound behind his portrait. While it had no emotion that Asper could deduce, she guessed it probably wasn't anything good.

"I see," the couthi said.

Without another word, he swept to the far end of the back room. He pulled back a thick rug and reached down, hooking a long finger into a knot in the wooden floor. Hinges creaked as he pried up a hidden door, revealing a dark hole with a ladder leading down.

"Follow me, *shkainai*," he said, abnormally curt. "Your associates will wait here."

"The hell we will," Dransun said, stepping forward.

"Dransun." Asper fixed him in place with a glance and kept him there with a hand on his shoulder. "I'll be fine."

The guardsman glared from her to the couthi, lips trembling like he wanted to say something particularly fierce. But if he had any idea how to threaten a four-armed freak with a painting for a face, it didn't come to him. He stepped aside and watched her as she followed Man-Shii Kree down the ladder.

They continued into a basement below the house, winding their way through stacks of crates in the darkness. It was only until she noticed that they had been winding for quite some time that she realized the basement went deeper than she imagined. She reached out a hand and felt a stone wall instead of a wooden one.

"Tell me something."

Man-Shii Kree's voice echoed in a suddenly bigger space. His monotone ebbed away with each word, leaving behind a rasping, guttural sound punctuated with harsh clicking noises.

"Where did you get that letter?"

"It doesn't concern you," Asper replied.

"Subjects that concern the Brotherhood concern me a great deal, *shkainai*. What you ask for is not something we give away lightly."

"But you *will* give it."

"The couthi honor their debts."

The rest of the trip continued in silence but was mercifully short. Man-Shii Kree came to a sudden halt. She narrowly avoided bumping into him as a door creaked open ahead, releasing a soft green light.

Asper entered a cramped room and glanced around. A hundred eyes looked back at her.

Beakers, vials, jars of various sizes; her reflection stared at her from countless containers. The room was alive with glass and the substances they contained. Red fluids, blue sludge, green slime that oozed and bubbled, various fetal creatures floating in embalming fluid—some still and some still twitching. The reek of low-burning flames and chemical stink filled her nostrils, made her gag.

But she swallowed her bile back down. It wouldn't do to vomit in front of one's hosts.

Especially those that thrust knives in her face.

In one fluid motion, a figure hunched over a nearby table looked up, saw Asper, and whirled on her, a long blade clenched in one of its four hands. The couthi turned its portrait upon her, the tasteful landscape in its frame at stark odds with the weapon thrust in her face.

"Calm yourself, Yun." Man-Shii Kree stepped in front of her, placed one of his larger hands on his fellow couthi's, and guided the blade away from Asper. "She is permitted here."

"We did not discuss interlopers," the other couthi growled in the same guttural clicking voice as Man-Shii Kree. "You should have warned me, Kree."

"I won't be long," Asper said, taking care to take an extra step out of the couthi's reach. "I'm simply here to pick up a delivery."

"Delivery," the other couthi hissed. "The Bloodwise Brotherhood does not make 'deliveries,' *shkainai*."

"You will have to excuse Man-Khoo Yun," Man-Shii Kree said,

stepping past his associate. "He was returned to our company in rather poor condition." The couthi glanced over his shoulder at her. "Though he was returned. Thanks, in part, to your companion."

Asper blinked. "What?"

"The shict. What was her name? I can't remember. They all look the same to me."

"Kataria?" Asper looked to Man-Khoo Yun. "You saw Kataria? Where? Is she all right? What about Lenk?"

"Dead," the couthi replied. After a moment, he shrugged with all four limbs. "Or not. Maybe wounded. Maybe sick. Maybe eaten. I have no particular desire to know, one way or the other. I last saw her in a camp full of her wretched kin and have no desire to know her fate."

"Still," Man-Shii Kree said as he busied himself at a nearby table. "It is thanks to her that the Brotherhood did not lose a member. It hardly forgives the sins of her vile race, but a debt is a debt."

"And the couthi honor their debts," Man-Khoo Yun said.

Asper barely heard them. The sound of her heart thundered in her ears. Kataria was alive, or at least, she *had* been. Lenk might be, too. It had been months since they separated. Lenk and Kataria had left the city in pursuit of an end to the war. Dreadaeleon and Denaos had left her in pursuit of their own ends. And Gariath had simply left. She had feared to wonder at their fates—almost all of them, anyway—but the thought of them brought old fears rushing back to her.

A sudden stab of pain returned her to her senses. Her chest began to tighten, as though the excitement was simply too much for it. She forced herself to calm down, to breathe deeply.

Lenk and Kataria might be alive. They might not be. They might need her help.

But so did thousands of people.

"Your delivery, *shkainai*."

She looked up. Man-Shii Kree extended to her a square object wrapped in brown paper and secured with red twine. A box, she surmised, no longer than a hand across and half a hand tall.

"This is it?" she asked.

"This is what the letter specified. All components are accounted for."

"I was just expecting something a little...bigger."

"Your letter was very specific. Did you not read it yourself, *shkainai*?"

"Er, yes. Of course I did." She reached out, snatched the package from him, and tucked it under her free arm. "Thank you, gentle..." She fixed the two couthi with a puzzled look. "Men?"

"We clear our debts with you and your associates with this," Man-Khoo Yun growled. "And with this wretched city, as well. I cannot wait to be rid of it."

"The situation has become more unstable than profitable. Our fleet of merchant ships shall be making its way to Cier'Djaal on the route to Muraska," Man-Shii Kree said. "We and our assets shall depart with them."

"Hence, if you are dissatisfied with your deal, do not come looking for us," Man-Khoo Yun said. "And do not seek our services again."

"Unless," Man-Shii Kree added, "you should be ready with fair compensation."

"Gods willing," Asper said, "we'll never have to see each other again."

She turned and headed toward the door when a voice caught her attention.

"Priestess."

It was neither the guttural clicking sound nor the chilling monotone; Man-Shii Kree spoke in a voice that was shaky, unused to softness. Yet it sounded plaintive, almost piteous. Enough so that she stopped in her tracks and faced him.

"Do you think you can save them?" he asked.

"What?"

"We know, priestess, about the tulwar." His portrait betrayed no emotion, yet his voice quaked. "Is it true? Are there thousands at the gates?"

She opened her mouth to say something to reassure him, to soothe his fears, as she had soothed the fears of so many before. But something inside her just didn't see the point.

"Not at the gates," she sighed. "Not yet. Nor do we know how many there are, exactly. But there are many." She closed her eyes. "And they are coming."

"And if they come..."

"Then they'll burn Cier'Djaal to the ground and kill everyone inside its walls."

"You are certain?"

She was, if she knew Gariath. She had seen the look in his eyes. She could still feel his claws around her throat.

"What's it matter to you?" Asper asked with a sneer. "Aren't you leaving?"

"We are, priestess. However..."

His larger hands slid up inside his hood. His smaller hands slid the portrait away from his face. Asper held back a gasp at what peered out at her.

Against bone-white skin, fist-sized eyes the color of coal shone brightly against the fires in the lab. His mouth was separated at the bottom into a pair of mandibles that clicked anxiously. And yet all the horror of his features was nothing compared to the map of twisted, hateful scars that covered his face. She knew scars like those, knew the kind of hands that made them.

And she shuddered.

"We couthi," he chittered, "have experience with seeing our homes burn."

"The shicts took everything from us," Man-Khoo Yun added, sliding off his portrait to reveal a similarly flayed face beneath. "Our maidens, our armies..." He gestured to his scars. "Our very flesh. We who were not fortunate enough to be killed by their arrows were treated to their knives."

"Only when they had painted our homes with blood did they see fit to burn it all," Man-Shii Kree said. "We have nothing left but this." He gestured to the beakers and vials around him. His smaller hands held up the portrait. "And these."

"Then stay with us," Asper said, stepping forward. "Stay here and fight. I have a plan. It can work." She held up the package. "This is a part of it. We can survive this, if we only stand together. Stand with me. *Fight* with me."

Man-Shii Kree exchanged a glance with his companion. After a moment, he sighed and shook his head.

"Long ago, I would have, *shkainai*. In the days when I was young and had a taste for blood, I would have grabbed my spear and charged with you. But I see their knives in my dreams, I hear the screams of our maidens still, and when I feel a breeze, I stiffen, waiting for the arrow to follow. I have given so much to war. I have nothing left to give."

"Without our maidens, the couthi are left to dwindle," Man-Khoo Yun said. "We cannot waste what few lives we have left."

There was some part of her that wanted to scream at them, to call them cowards, to demand what made them think they were above this in hopes that, maybe, she could just scream loud enough and make them do what she wanted.

But another part of her, an older and exhausted part, heard them all too clearly. That part of her also heard screams in her sleep and had held too many men's hands as they went limp in hers. That part of her couldn't smell soap without thinking of washing blood from her hands.

That part spoke for her.

"I understand," she said, sighing. "The city is dangerous. I can't send anyone to help you out."

"The couthi survive," Man-Khoo Yun replied as he replaced the portrait over his face. "The couthi endure."

"And, of course, we have every faith in your ability to succeed, priestess." Man-Shii Kree did likewise. "But, should you not..."

"Fight to the last," Man-Khoo Yun said, his voice slipping from its guttural growl. "No one ever survives the war, even if they live through it."

"And should ultimate tragedy befall you"—Man-Shii Kree's voice resumed its droning monotone—"this one hopes you will consider leaving instruction with dearest loved ones to seek us out for preservation of your corpse. All due information has been included with your package. Reasonable rates."

<hr />

"And you're all right?" Aturach asked as they made their way through the streets.

"For the last time, yes," Asper growled.

"They didn't...*do* anything to you, did they?" the young man pressed. "I've heard tales that the couthi take samples of people's flesh as a price and they put them in vats and—"

"I was down there for less than half an hour," she snapped back. "And as you can see, I'm perfectly fine."

"It's just that you're walking a little slower, is all, and—"

"Fuck's sake, Aturach, would you let it *rest*?"

The moment she raised her voice, she knew that was a mistake. Or maybe it was when she suddenly fell against the wall of a nearby building, breathing heavily. It was hard to tell, harder to think. Pain flashed through her body, ran up to her skull on explosive legs, robbed her of sight and sound.

She had overdone it.

"Asper!" Aturach called out, rushing over to steady her.

"Easy, boy," Dransun said, holding him back. "Give her some room." He fixed a glance at Asper. "You shouldn't do things like that."

"Really?" she replied with a sneer. "Thank goodness you told me. I'd never have guessed on my own."

"I just mean that—"

"I know what you mean." She nodded, waved him away. "I'm sorry. It's fine. I just..." She chuckled; it hurt. "I guess I got my ass kicked worse than I thought."

"It's not fine, priestess." Dransun's voice was as dire as his face. "People saw you get your ass kicked, but they saw you get back up. They believe in you. They rely on you. And the only way we're going to fight off the tulwar is with you. We can't have you going off into shady deals with four-armed miscreants like the couthi."

"The couthi are the only way we're going to win," she replied. "Trust me on that. And this city will need more than just me. It needs all of us." She looked intently at Dransun. "It needs you, especially. Go back to Temple Row. Make sure preparations are under way. I'll catch up with you later."

"Catch up?" Aturach asked. "We can't leave you here."

"I'll be fine," she said. "You need to be there, too. We have people ready to fight, but we need them to be ready to run, if the time comes. You two make sure that happens."

"But—"

"If she says she's fine, I believe her." Dransun waved the young man over, guiding him away from her. "And so should you." He cast one final glance at her, frowning. "Precious little left in this shithole to believe in."

She managed a weary smile as they took off. She watched them round a corner, waited until she couldn't hear their footsteps anymore, then waited a few moments more.

Only then did she allow herself to collapse.

The pain wrapped itself around her spine. She would have screamed if she had any breath left to do so. As it was, everything inside her came out in a hacking cough as her body shuddered. She wiped her hand across her mouth. It came back red.

Blood.

She was coughing up blood.

Oh my. Inside her, a voice not her own purred. The voice of the pain. Of the curse that fed. *That doesn't look good, does it?* Her left arm burned as something stirred inside her body. *Yes, things are rather a mess in here. I suppose your friend treated you a fair bit more poorly than you thought, didn't he? But don't worry.*

She looked to her left arm. Beneath her sleeve, her skin glowed a faint, dull red. And within her flesh, she could feel the curse inside her look at her and smile.

I will take care of everything, Amoch-Tethr, her perpetual pain, the curse that ate flesh and bone and spirit, hissed.

"You ain't lookin' too good."

Asper immediately shot to her feet, despite the pain, and whirled around. A tall, thin woman stood before her. Wrapped in dusty leathers, she stared at Asper with a sneer through a long face. She shifted the massive crossbow strapped across her back, snorted, and spit on the street.

"Course, you're lookin' better'n most."

"You took your time," Asper muttered, stalking toward the woman. "I was told you'd have given me a signal to let me know you were coming."

"I'm here, ain't I?" the woman grunted. "Don't get much clearer'n that."

"I had thought the Jackals would be a little more professional, is all."

Only at this did the woman's face deepen into a scowl. "Ain't no more Jackals. Not anymore. Just us left. Just Sandal…" She tapped her chest. "And Scarecrow." She glanced over Asper, looked to the package tucked against her sling. "That it?"

"Yes. It took some doing, but I managed to—"

"Give it here."

Asper muttered a curse but obliged, handing the package to Scarecrow. The woman tore open the packaging, revealing a square satchel of hardened leather beneath. She pried its flap open, looked through the assortment of vials within, most of them a sickly green-and-yellow color, and nodded.

"Everything's here," she grunted. "Just like he said it would be."

"Who?"

"Ain't pay me to tell you shit." Scarecrow let her fingers run across the vials before she selected a thin one filled with blue liquid. "This one's for you. Be at the Karnerian garrison tomorrow to use it. We'll take care of our part tonight."

"You think it'll work?" Asper asked.

"The shit the couthi gave us?"

"The plan."

Scarecrow snorted. "Ain't pay me to think. But if I had to lay odds..." She secured the satchel at her belt. "I've heard a' worse plans'n this." She pointed at Asper. "Karnerian garrison tomorrow. Later, the better. Sainite garrison after that. We need you, we'll be in touch."

"Who will be?" Asper asked. "Can't you give me a name? I'm already trusting you enough by agreeing to this plan."

"There's your first mistake, lady. Trust is for idiots." She grinned. "I hear you ain't an idiot." She turned and stalked off. "You want to save Cier'Djaal, you better hope I hear right."

"Wait."

Scarecrow let out a snarl of irritation, but she did come to a halt. Asper was aware how she was reaching out, as if to touch the woman with trembling fingers.

"If the Jackals aren't..." She paused, swallowed something cold. "Tell me, what about Denaos? Is he... is he all right?"

Scarecrow chuckled blackly as she resumed her walk. "Take a look around, lady. Ain't none of us all right."

And within a few moments, she was gone. And Asper was alone.

THREE

THE LANGUAGE OF VIOLENCE

"The key to any advance upon the city is the Green Belt."

"Right."

The old tea scent of parchments, rolled up and unrolled, shuffled across the table.

"Cier'Djaal doesn't lend itself well to defense. The walls are low, the gates are open. Makes the city more inviting to trade. Once we get the city in our sights, it's as good as ours."

"Uh-huh."

The copper pungency of ink stains, smeared across paper before it was dry in greasy thumbprints.

"The city receives much of its food from the Green Belt, situated in a shallow valley here. The dunes form natural walls around it, into which there are only three entrances. They are wide, to accommodate cara-vans. The Djaalics don't keep these guarded, usually, but we can assume that's changed since we made our intentions known."

"Mm."

The perpetual stink of pipe smoke, stale embers dying in the air and filling his nostrils with the odor of old hair.

This was not what Gariath imagined war would smell like.

He knew the scents of battle: the white-hot reek of fury, the blood-clotted stink of fear, the heady smells that made him dizzy just before he tightened his hands around someone's throat.

He imagined war would be like that, only greater. And maybe it would, after all the planning, tactics, and strategy.

Assuming that part ever ended.

"Are you listening to me?"

The pipe smoke became particularly pungent. Gariath looked up into a pair of eyes ringed by dark circles. Above a long beard, a wrinkled, simian face looked back at him through two yellow eyes beneath a furrowed brow. The creature's apelike features—long nose, sloping brow, scars of thick flesh across its face—were softened by age and weariness, though annoyance shone through quite clearly.

"Is it important?" Gariath grunted.

"Assuming you would like your attack on Cier'Djaal to end in something other than all of us being killed?" Mototaru puffed thoughtfully on his pipe, then exhaled a long cloud of smoke. "Possibly."

"For that to happen, we would have to be fighting something stronger than humans." Gariath waved a clawed hand. "I have fought many, killed many. I am not worried about humans."

"Oh, good," the old tulwar said. "For a moment there, I thought declaring war on an enemy that outnumbers us greatly and crushed us decisively in the past might be difficult. But thank goodness, you're not worried. I'll go inform the soldiers that they need not fear never seeing their families again."

Gariath's lips peeled back, baring sharp teeth at Mototaru. He drew himself up and loomed over the old tulwar, letting his wings and earfrills spread and his claws sink into the wood of the table.

"*You* were crushed," the dragonman snarled. "Because *you* were weak. I don't have that problem."

"Mototaru is right, *daanaja*."

Gariath swept his scowl to the other side of the table. A younger tulwar, the gray lean muscle of his body adorned with silver fur and the orange-and-red cloth of his half robe, looked back. The thick knots of flesh across his face grew with color, reds and yellows and blues flooding his face as he furrowed his brow.

"No one doubts that you're stronger," Daaru said. He bared his own simian fangs—pitiful against Gariath's, but still broad and sharp. "No one doubts that the tulwar are stronger. But if your attack is to succeed, we must have strategy."

Gariath rubbed a sore spot beneath his left horn. "When did this become *my* attack? We're taking Cier'Djaal for the tulwar."

"The tulwar will follow you," Daaru grunted. "But the humans are entrenched. They know their land and they are rooted deep inside it. It's not a simple matter of going in and burning them out."

"They are *weak*," Gariath growled.

"They are many," Daaru replied.

"So are we."

"So we were," Motataru added, "when we tried to first take the city so many years ago."

Gariath's eyes narrowed to slits so thin he could barely keep the two tulwar in his sight. He clenched his fist, felt a snarl boiling behind his throat. He held on to it for only a moment before it evaporated into a sigh.

There was a time when this argument would be over by now. He would punch them both, break one of their hands—probably Daaru's, he was younger—and then start breaking things until everyone agreed that his way was best.

Perhaps he was getting too lenient.

Or, he thought, perhaps he was only now realizing the weight of things.

The map looked like such a flimsy thing on the table. He could tear it up in an instant, smash the table to pieces, light them both on fire. But the more he looked at it, the heavier it seemed.

There was the Lyre river in blue, a long jagged scar running along the north. Below it to the east was their position, the city of Jalaang they had killed so many to take. Farther west was the valley wall to the Green Belt, as Mototaru had said. And then, where the Lyre met the ocean, there was a big red dot.

Cier'Djaal.

The city he had left behind, the city he had sworn to destroy, the city he had beaten one of his companions—former, he caught himself, *former* companions—half to death over.

And there it was. Just a big red dot. A smudge of ink on a piece of paper.

But the more he stared at it, the more it seemed something bigger. He could see the people in it, all the people he had vowed to kill in all the buildings he had vowed to burn. He could see the long march between Jalaang and the Green Belt. And if he strained his eyes just so, he could almost see all the graves that would be filled with tulwar bodies because of him.

One here for Mototaru. One here for Daaru. Maybe a few hundred or so here for the ones he had killed back in Shaab Sahaar...

His nostrils quivered, suddenly filled with phantom scents of burning buildings, of flesh and hair cooking, of rank fear in the skies as fire rained from above and sent tulwar screaming into the streets to be cut down by humans.

All because of him.

He staggered suddenly, leaning hard against the table. His head suddenly felt like an iron weight, his neck like a blade of grass. The scents overwhelmed him, swirled inside his skull.

"Are you all right, *daanaja*?" Mototaru hummed.

"Stop calling me that," Gariath growled. He shook his head, straightened himself. "I'm fine. I just need some air." He snorted. "The reek of your pipe is giving me a headache."

"Just as well." Daaru nodded. "Not all the leaders are here. We should gather everyone and return to planning in an hour."

"Not an hour," Gariath growled as he stalked toward the door of the small house.

"Two hours, then."

"No."

"Then when do we—"

"When I say," the dragonman snapped. "If this is my war, we win it when I say we do, how we say we do."

"You sound confident," Mototaru noted.

Gariath shoved the door open so hard it nearly flew off its hinges. Bright sunlight stung his eyes. He snarled.

"I got you this city, didn't I?"

"True. You led. We followed. You won Jalaang and the trust of the tulwar." Mototaru puffed his pipe thoughtfully. "They will follow you, *daanaja*." His next words came sternly on a cloud of gray ash. "Anywhere."

⊷⊶⋈⊷⊶

Anywhere.

That last word hadn't seemed so meaningful until Gariath had left the small house they had made their command room. And if he didn't believe it before, it was hard to deny as he walked the streets of Jalaang.

Barely half the size of Cier'Djaal and nowhere near as wealthy, this city had originally been built as an outpost. After the failed Uprising, in which the tulwar attempted to storm Cier'Djaal and were brutally beaten back, Jalaang had been built as a precautionary measure against future aggression. Over the years, it had gone from a fortress to a city to a glorified trading post. Tulwar attacks had failed to manifest. The fashas of Cier'Djaal, thinking their backs broken, abhorred the waste of valuable trading space that Jalaang was using for guards and moved in more merchants.

Gariath supposed that Jalaang's fall at the hands of tulwar clans would be considered "ironic."

Lenk would have called it that, Gariath thought as he stalked through the streets. *The pointy-eared human would have called it funny. The tall human woman would...* He paused. *What did she call it, again? Barbaric? Cruel? Unthinkable?*

It was hard to remember. He had been too busy beating the life out of her to listen.

Whatever Jalaang had been, it was his now.

Or rather, it was his army's. For whatever they had been, that was what the tulwar were now.

The streets were alive with them. Tall, powerful, long of arm and leg, they hurried throughout the city. Though they came from many different clans, the tulwar looked like one people here.

Tho Thu Bhu clansmen, their fur flecked with sweat, pulled red-hot blades from forges. Rua Tong warriors, muscles glistening, sharpened their weapons. Chee Chree hunters carefully fletched arrows with long simian fingers. All of them, their faces were alive with color. The tulwar "war paint," the reds and blues and yellows that came into their gray skin when their blood was up, was on full display as they sparred and practiced drills in the yards of the barracks.

Once, they had been many. Now, they were one army.

His army.

A distant shriek caught his attention. At the far end of the city, gaambols hooted, shrieked, and hopped in their pens. Massive beasts, resembling red-faced baboons that stood taller than a horse, they eagerly stomped their feet and slapped the earth, baring large fangs eagerly as their Yengu Thuun clan handlers tossed them chunks of raw meat, which they eagerly tore into.

It wasn't hard to imagine those simian noises intermingling with the screams of dying humans. It wasn't hard to imagine the gaambols feasting on a different kind of meat.

And it was even easier to imagine them lying dead on the ground, bleeding out on the sand among hundreds of tulwar corpses, their eyes glassy and staring up at the sky, mouths wordlessly whispering with dying breaths…

You led us here, daanaja. *You led us to die.*

He shook his head, pushed out the thoughts, drew in a deep breath.

And he could still smell the reek of burning flesh.

He growled, locking his eyes on the ground as he stalked through the streets. He ignored the tulwar who noticed him and hailed him by raising their weapons and howling: "*Rise up!*" Ignoring their crowing and excited howling was easy. Ignoring the reek of their rage, that was much harder.

Since the humans had attacked their city of Shaab Sahaar, he had smelled nothing else. The march to Jalaang had been rife with the odor of their anger. He couldn't blame them; half their city had been burned down that day.

He wondered what they might do if they knew he was responsible for it.

Within a few more steps, his nostrils filled with plainer scents: the reek of filth and offal, of dried blood and old wounds. Only then did he look up.

Right into a broad, yellow smile.

"Hello, *daanaja*. What brings you to our little side of paradise?"

Chakaa stood before him, tall and muscular. Her skin was black as pitch, her fur grew in sparse patches on her arms and legs, giving way to knots of old scars that mapped a body left generously bare by her tattered half-robe. She had no color on her face like other tulwar—that is, except for the ugly yellow of her sharp-toothed smile—but then, there wasn't much about her like other tulwar.

The intricacies of tulwar society were still a mystery to Gariath, but he had learned enough to know that Chakaa and her clan, the Mak Lak Kai, were *malaa*: creatures who existed outside the Tul that governed all tulwar life.

While the tulwar had lengthy explanations as to why this made her and her kin undesirable, they had fought well to help take Jalaang, and Gariath would not cast them out of the city. Still, he had yielded to their demands to keep the Mak Lak Kai far away from the other tulwar.

And Chakaa didn't seem to mind jail duty.

"I'm here to see the prisoner," Gariath said.

He glanced up. The large warehouse at the edge of the city was already showing signs of its Mak Lak Kai occupation. Shit and blood were smeared on its side. Gaambol offal lay where it had fallen. If the other Mak Lak Kai noticed, they didn't mind. They gathered in small clusters around campfires, gnawing undercooked meat and sharpening rusted blades.

Gariath couldn't help but wonder if they had been branded *malaa* because they were so disgusting or if they had been called that first and simply decided to live up to the title.

"Where is Kudj? He and his kin were supposed to be helping you guard."

Gariath glanced to an empty spot where a two-ton creature resembling a very drunken night between a gorilla and a rhinoceros should be. Kudj's vulgores, the hulking creatures who had been called to the city once it fell, were nowhere to be seen.

"Apparently, the vulgore's delicate senses were offended by our presence." Chakaa laughed, spraying spittle from yellow teeth. "You would think two-ton beasts wouldn't mind a little stink."

Gariath's nostrils twitched; whatever words one would use to describe the scent of the Mak Lak Kai, *little* was not one of them.

"He and his cousins are loitering at the other end of the city, discussing economics or tea instead of readying for battle. Flagrant disregard of your order." She reached over her shoulder to the filthy leather-wrapped hilt of a very large blade strapped to her back. "Should I punish him for you, *daanaja*?"

Gariath might have said yes, were he not certain that Chakaa's definition of *punishment* likely began with decapitation and ended with defecation.

"You have your own mission to look to," he grunted.

"As you say. We leave tomorrow morning. Would you like me to bring you back a present? Maybe a necklace of ears? Or a nice bouquet?" She slapped her forehead with the heel of her hand. "But where are my manners? You were on your way to see the prisoner." She stepped aside, gesturing to the door of the warehouse. "I beg your forgiveness; if we knew you were coming, we would have cleaned the shit out first."

Gariath spared a moment to let his glower linger on her before stalking past and pulling the massive door open. The reek of ancient gaambol offal assaulted his nostrils immediately. The warehouse had been used as a stable for the Mak Lak Kai's mounts—the other clans' gaambols found their presence upsetting. But Gariath had had it repurposed when he decided the barracks serving as the previous prison was a bit too comfortable.

There was a moment, as he stalked into the reek-ridden darkness of the warehouse, flies buzzing at his ear-frills and roaches scattering away, where he wondered if he had been too cruel.

But once he saw his prisoner, he wondered if there was anywhere worse he could stash him.

"How are you getting on?" he asked.

Chains rattled. At the end of the warehouse, an immense shape stirred. Ten feet tall, roughly the color, size, and shape of a great stone, a creature rose up. As much as he could, anyway. A great, reptilian head, its snout dominated by a rhinoceros-like horn, swung toward Gariath. A single black eye took him in.

Kharga said nothing. Not with words, anyway. His scent was clear, though: a reek of rage and contempt and hatred that overwhelmed the stink of gaambol offal.

"Can't complain," a deep voice boomed back.

Gariath glanced at a nearby pile of shit before looking back at Kharga. "No?"

"Nah," the other dragonman rumbled. "Chained up, covered in flies, surrounded by shit." He snorted, dispelling a cloud of insects from his face. "Could be worse." His scaly lips peeled back, revealing sharp teeth. "I could be stuck outside with your monkeys."

Gariath growled. "The tulwar are warriors. They are strong, fierce, proud."

"Make good rugs, too," Kharga grunted. "Back during the Uprising, I stomped sixty of them into the earth. Felt like walking on air. Must have been the pride. Makes them nice and soft."

"They took this city," Gariath snarled. "They took *you*."

Kharga straightened up. Through the shafts of light pouring through the broken slats of the roof, Gariath saw the dull shimmer of his gray, armorlike scales. And over them, the great iron chains that bound him. The dragonman let loose a long, low sigh.

"I should be dead, *Rhega*." He spit the word, the name, let it lie limp and glistening on the ground in the shit. "It should have been you and me. No monkeys. No others. A real fight. A real death. You disgrace yourself with these chains."

"You don't deserve death at my hands, *Drokha*," Gariath replied. "I thought you did, you and the rest of your cowardly people, but I changed my mind." He stalked forward, looking up at the bigger dragonman. "Before you die, I want you to see."

"See what?" Kharga snorted.

"See what you people sold yourselves for. The *Drokha* are supposed to be brave, strong, proud. And you sold yourselves to the humans, giant dogs to bark and bite at whatever scares them." Gariath sneered, baring his teeth. "The *Rhega* would never—"

"The *Rhega* are dead."

Gariath paused. Kharga spoke the words plainly, with only minimal contempt. It was a fact, not an insult, and Gariath knew it. The *Rhega* had once been numerous. But if there were others out there besides himself, he had never met one.

And when he spoke again, it was with that knowledge in his throat.

"Everything the humans built with your strength," Gariath said, slowly, "all the enemies they drove back with your claws, all the stone houses they raised with your protection . . . I will burn to the ground."

Kharga stared back, his expression unreadable. His scent betrayed nothing that Gariath could smell over the shit.

"Every wall, every home, every palace. The pubs where they eat broken meat and drink piss, the big homes where they make each other slaves. Everything with the stink of human on it will be gone, and only the scent of ash will remain. And when it's gone"—he leaned forward—"we'll sift through the embers to see if we can find the blood you sold to build it."

Kharga blinked. "You think you can burn it down. You want to destroy Cier'Djaal."

"Cowards think, *Drokha*. Weaklings want." Gariath narrowed his eyes. "I destroy."

The two dragonmen stared at each other. Gariath's nostrils opened, inhaling the reek of offal and flies. He searched between the stenches, looking for a scent more profound: the odor of fear, of shame, anything that would betray Kharga. It had to be there, he knew, the stink that would show him that Kharga knew now just how far his people had fallen and for nothing.

A long silence passed and Gariath smelled nothing but shit. In the darkness, Kharga betrayed no shame, no fear, nothing.

No scent, at least.

His chains rattled as his body shook. A deep, low chuckle emerged out of the darkness.

Not a haughty chuckle, nor a desperate attempt to appear brave in the face of his captor. Kharga's laughter was something bitter and black, the punch line of an ugly joke with several foul verses.

And in the heat of his breath as he laughed, to Gariath's fury, there was not a single whiff of fear.

"Yeah," Kharga grunted. "Good luck."

"Wood burns. Stone breaks. Humans die," Gariath snarled. "This city will fall."

"I'm sure you're the only one who's had that idea before," Kharga said. "You're not even the first dragonman. Hundreds of years ago, when Cier'Djaal was just a village of oxshit and logs, we *Drokha* thought to come in and knock it over. And we did."

"You did a shit job of it."

"No, we were thorough. We were huge. And we did it. Over and over. And every time, they would just rebuild it bigger than before. Until finally, we came in and saw that their houses stood bigger than us."

"A tall house burns the same as a small house," Gariath replied. "It just has a longer way to fall."

"Idiot *Rhega*." Kharga slumped back against the wall, his chains settling against his scales. "Your breed was always stupid. You look upon something and think only of how you can break it. We *Drokha* looked upon their city and saw something else."

"Weakness."

Kharga did not reply.

"Cowardice."

Kharga remained silent.

"Coin you'd sell your blood for, boots you'd eagerly lick, your own stupid shame reflected back at you." Gariath rushed toward him, snarling through bared teeth. "*Tell me.* Tell me what you saw."

"It'd be hard to explain," Kharga replied. He smiled broadly. "Maybe you should ask your monkeys what they saw when they entered it."

Gariath narrowed his eyes and snorted. He turned around and stalked away, ignoring Kharga as he called out after him.

"Even better, ask them what they saw after we painted the city with them," Kharga bellowed, laughing. "Are they trying for another Uprising? Did they tell you how it ends?"

Gariath stalked to a nearby stake that had been used to tether a gaambol. He seized it in both hands and pried it out of the ground.

"I don't want to spoil anything for you," Kharga said as Gariath turned around to face him, "but after we sent their little rebellion running, I was picking pieces of them out of my toes for—"

Bone cracked. Splinters flew.

The hide of the *Drokha* was legend. Thick, armored scales that could turn aside blades, arrows, and the harsh sun of the desert. Some might have found it hard to believe that a large stick could hurt them.

But just as legendary was the philosophy of the *Rhega*. Which stated that nothing was impossible, just so long as one hit it hard enough.

Admittedly, as Gariath struck Kharga again and again with the stake, he knew this might not be seen as the most graceful argument. And as it splintered with each blow, leaving shards of wood embedded in the *Drokha*'s face, he knew he had not refuted any of Kharga's points.

But Kharga was no longer talking. And in a few moments, Kharga was no longer conscious. And that, Gariath figured, still counted as a win.

But when the last few splinters fell from his hand and Kharga lay on the ground, unmoving, Gariath felt no better. And he couldn't get the sound of Kharga's laughter out of his head.

Nor his words.

Ask your monkeys what they saw.

He stalked out of the warehouse.

Are they trying for another Uprising?

He walked into the setting sun of Jalaang.

Did they tell you how it ends?

And he trudged through the streets. The tulwar raised their fists to him, the reek of their anger peeling off them, their chants booming from their voices. Gariath couldn't smell them, or hear them. And he did not dare look up at them.

He knew he would only see corpses.

FOUR

A GIFT FOR A DEAD CHILD

Thua had always been an honest boy.

He had no talent for lying, like his sister. He did not like to play hiding games and often cried if he went too long without finding his playmates. He did not like to be teased, either, though, so he often tried to play them.

But he had no head for deception, no tongue for lies, no patience for sitting still and waiting. Whenever it was his turn to hide, he would find it too much to sit still and would frequently come out of hiding with an explosion of nervous laughter, happy that the game was over, even if he had lost.

And as his father looked down at him, lying so still and peaceful beneath the blanket, he was tempted to lift the cloth and look under. There was some part of him that thought, if he did, his son would still be there, giggling that he had been able to sit so still for so long.

There was some part of his father that made his fingers brush against the cloth. But it was not enough to make him raise it.

Sai-Thuwan knew what he would see underneath.

He stepped back from the pyre. He saw the heaped, dry sticks beneath the swaddled body. He saw the still, motionless shape beneath the cloth. He saw the small bundle resting at the top where the head should have been, separate from the rest. Sticks and cloth; he tried to tell himself that this was not Thua, that this was not his son.

That he didn't have to do this.

That he hadn't caused this.

But Sai-Thuwan had been trying to tell himself that for days now, and the lies tasted more bitter in his mouth each time.

He walked wearily to the nearby bonfire. The sand crunched beneath his feet. Wind wound its way through the dunes of the desert, moaning softly to herald the falling of the sun. He pulled the torch from the fire and began to walk back to the pyre.

Halfway there, the wind kicked up. The torch's light sputtered out in his hand. He sighed and went back to the fire, lighting it once more. And when the wind blew it out again, he sighed deeper and went back. But by the third time, when it began to blow again, he was weeping.

"Please," he whispered to the wind. "Please. I don't deserve it. But he does. He is such a good boy. He never did anything to deserve this." Tears stung his eyes, were blown away by the wind. "Please. Let him have this. *Please.*"

The wind did not hear him.

But someone did.

A shadow fell over him. An arm draped across his shoulder. He looked up. A woman's face looked back at him: middle-aged, wrinkles tugging at the corner of her eyes as she smiled. Her long, pointed ears quivered—four notches in one length, five in the other.

And he felt his own quiver in response.

And Sai-Thuwan knew this woman, this shict.

Shekune. Spear of the Ninth.

The torch rekindled to faint life, shielded by her body. Together, they walked slowly to the pyre, keeping the torch alive. Together, they stood beside Thua's pyre. And when Sai-Thuwan's hand faltered, Shekune took him gently by the wrist and together, they set his son to the flame.

As the sun sank in the distance, they stood together and watched. Thua's pyre glowed brighter as the sun disappeared. And when it had fallen behind a distant dune, he was one more bright star in the night.

And only then did Sai-Thuwan speak.

"It's my fault."

He had thought that finally saying those words, after so many days of thinking them, would feel a little better. He was wrong.

"Every parent says that about their child," Shekune said. Her voice was vast and deep like a river. "And every parent is right."

"He was such an honest boy. Too honest for this world and its monsters. When he was little, he would always try to tell me things, but he spoke so plainly, without a thought, that I never listened." His head sank. "I never listened to him."

Shekune, her long and hard body wrapped in furs and leathers, did not move. She only barely looked at him. Her eyes were on the pyre.

"Thua was so unlike his sister," Sai-Thuwan said. "She was always causing trouble, always picking fights, always making life hard for her mother. He was always so quiet, always wanted to play by himself. We didn't look at him enough...we didn't..."

The tears came once again, sliding down his cheeks. He tasted salt at the corners of his mouth.

"But he cried," Sai-Thuwan said. "He cried so easily. Whenever he fell down, he would cry. And his sister would tease him for crying and he would cry more. I worried he would grow up weak. And so when he cried for me, I pretended I didn't hear him and...and..."

He looked to Shekune. For what, he didn't know. Absolution, maybe: some assurance that it wasn't his fault. Or at least damnation: some assurance that it was. She didn't look at him. But her ears, long like spears, were aloft and open.

She was listening.

"But even as she teased him so much, he loved his sister." Sai-Thuwan looked back to the pyre, could barely see it through the tears. "I remember...when they were growing up, we found his sister in a tent with Janashi, our neighbor's daughter, under a blanket, in each other's arms. His mother was furious, said there was something wrong with her. And I didn't know what to do. But Thua...

"Thua came to us. He begged us to listen to him. He told us about his sister and how she...who she loved. His mother was still angry, but I listened. I tried my best to. And somehow, after a long time, we all understood."

Sai-Thuwan looked at his hands. "His mother died fighting the humans," he said. "Back when we were building Shicttown. I was so scared of losing him and his sister that I tried to make peace with the humans, even after all they had done. His sister hated me for that, but I thought that was fine. She could hate me, so long as we had peace and I did not have to lose her. And then she ran away. And we did not have peace. And the humans took..."

He looked at the pyre as the fires crackled. Was his son still somewhere in there, he wondered?

"And now...I have lost them all. It's my fault."

"It is not, Sai-Thuwan."

Now Shekune spoke. Now her dark eyes were upon him. Now her ears were flattened against her head and her overlarge canines were bared.

"You tried to protect your children, your family, your tribe," she said. "Any shict would have done the same. You thought you could have peace with the humans and their city."

"I was a fool."

"You were a father. You were a chieftain. You were trying to protect your people. That is not foolish, Sai-Thuwan."

"But they attacked us. They killed us, burned down Shicttown, sent my tribe scattering and—"

"And they were always going to attack us. They are *humans*." She hissed the words. "This is what they do. They build their cities and tell us that they own our land. They hunt our game and tell us that they own our meat. They push us into the desert and tell us that we belong there. And they will not stop until we are all dead. Or until they are."

Sai-Thuwan felt his ears rise up, open up, let in a sound. No earthly sound of wind and voice and sand. He heard something dark, something furious, something born from a hard place from Shekune's heart that filled his ears with all her anger and all her hatred and found his buried beneath his sorrow.

Her Howling. The true language of the shicts, unspoken and impossible to ignore.

"You have lost a wife, Sai-Thuwan. You have lost a son. How much more will you lose? Your people? Your land? Your daughter?"

He shook his head. "My daughter is already lost."

"She is gone. But she will come back, Sai-Thuwan. She waits for you to be her father again, to protect her."

Shekune extended a hand to him. He stared at it, his ears full of Shekune's words and his heart full of her anger.

"How?" he asked. "How do I protect her?"

"Your tribe knows Cier'Djaal. Your tribe knows these lands. Find them. Gather them. Add them to mine. Show us the ways into the city. And we will make this world safe for them once more. Safe for her."

Sai-Thuwan looked into her eyes. Dark and wild, like a beast's, Shekune stared at him without blinking. And like a beast, there was no lie in those eyes. And what she said, he wanted so desperately to be true. And what her Howling spoke, he could feel so keenly.

And as he reached out and took her hand in his own, the sound of her rage brought him to his knees.

—•—◦◦◦—•—

From all the way up here, they no longer looked like people.

The color had drained from their faces, along with their fears. Their screams had been torn from ragged throats until their mouths simply hung slack. Whatever had been in their eyes had along faded, leaving behind glassy, vacant stares.

They no longer looked like people. Merely corpses who hadn't realized they were dead yet.

Kataria was not so far away that she could not see that.

Far below, down the sloping dune, the tulwar knelt amid the wreckage of their caravan. Their wagons were shattered into splinters; their gaambols lay bleeding out on the sand. Those few that remained were on their knees, silent and empty, patiently waiting for what happened next.

The khoshicts seemed no more hurried. Short, slender, dark of skin and hair, they walked silently among the wreckage. Their long, pointed ears trembled as they spoke to each other in their own Howling. Their faces were hidden behind leering grins of the wooden masks they wore, visages twisted in silent laughter as they poked through the rubble in search of what had survived their attack.

A few trinkets, a few bars of raw metal, a nice bow or two.

This, they decided, was all that was worth preserving.

And, with that settled, they quietly took their knives out and began cutting.

No begging or crying. When the khoshicts' blades slid across their throats, the tulwar simply slumped over. They seemed less like bodies and more like bladders, air leaking out and leaving a deflated skin behind. They did not make a sound more than their bodies hitting the sand.

What good would it do? Kataria wondered. *Not like khoshicts would listen.*

It was hard to tell, what with their masks and all, but even the khoshicts seemed to be finding this routine. The desert had always been alive with trade before, and shict raids on tulwar and human caravans were not unheard-of. But these were not raids. Raids left people alive.

What the khoshicts were doing—what Shekune was doing—could not be described in so tame a word.

She meant to cleanse this desert of every nonshict. Too long had her tribe suffered in the shadows of human cities, at the blades of tulwar warriors. Too long had she indulged ideas that they might one day share this land. Too many of her people—Kataria's people, all shicts—had died in pursuit of that farce.

Shekune knew this. Many shicts did.

But not many shicts knew what would happen afterward.

It seemed as though only Kataria realized just how many more humans there were than shicts. It seemed as though only Kataria knew what humans would do once they considered the shicts more than mere raiders. And it seemed only Kataria wanted to stop the massive retaliation that would inevitably follow Shekune's war.

Not like khoshicts are interested, she thought bitterly.

As if in response to that, a khoshict's ears twitched far below. A wooden grin looked up toward her position. She quickly ducked back behind the dune and held her breath. When she heard no sounds of pursuit, she slid down the dune's slope.

Her boots, bow, and quiver lay in a heap at the base of it. She collected them up and went treading lightly across the sands, balancing on her toes as she did. Wind and darkness would conspire to make her tracks harder to distinguish from those of the roaming yiji packs.

Or so she desperately hoped.

The desert, of late, had little room for things that weren't desperate.

She made her way across indigo sands, careful to keep to the shadows cast by the dunes beneath the rising moon, lest there be eyes upon her that she hadn't noticed. Though the possibility of that diminished with each step—after all, any eyes cast her way would likely have been followed by an arrow.

And it wasn't like a shict with skin as pale and hair as blond as hers would be particularly hard to pick out in the darkness. But with each breath that passed out of her mouth and not out of an arrow wound in her lungs, she ran a little faster, left a few more tracks, until she was outright sprinting as she rounded the corner of a dune, where the dying embers of a campfire greeted her.

"We can't stay long." Kataria dropped to her rear and began pulling on her boots. "There's a war party not far from here. I don't think they saw me, but they'll find my tracks, eventually."

At the edge of the halo of fire's light, a figure lifted its head.

"They attacked a tulwar caravan. Heading to Jalaang, I think. This is the sixth one I've seen destroyed." Kataria clambered back to her feet, dusted sand from her leggings. "Shekune's getting bolder. Humans, tulwar, soldiers, or peasants; she's attacking everything."

The figure lowered its head again and cast unseen eyes back to the fire.

"It's worse than I thought. The tulwar are gathering. They've been leaving their villages in droves. If Shekune draws them into her war, every shict is going to be in danger. Humans are one thing, but fighting humans *and* tulwar?" Kataria attached her quiver to her hip and slung her bow over her shoulder. "The yijis are nearby, right? We've got to get out of here if we're going to—"

"Who cares?"

The figure spoke in a muted voice, as though from some place in a deep ocean, lungs filling with salt water.

"It doesn't matter."

The fire crackled. The glow illuminated Kwar's face: dark eyes that had once not sunk so low, sharp dark-skinned features that had once not been so dull, lips that had roared instead of whispered into the fire.

"It doesn't matter, Kataria."

She was not the woman Kataria remembered: the woman she had met so long ago in Cier'Djaal, the woman who had loved her, cursed her, kidnapped her, begged her for forgiveness. That woman was wild. That woman roared.

That woman had died when her brother had.

That day, she had watched Thua's blood paint the sand, heard his last words. That day, her face had been painted with horror. And in the days that followed, she had screamed her voice dry and her throat raw. But sorrow and fear, these were precious to shicts, something they did not spare often and had too little of to begin with.

And they had drained from Kwar's heart and her face and left her stare as numb and empty as the masks her people wore. The hollowness of her eyes seemed to reach out and Kataria found herself turning away, just to avoid being sucked in.

That was the lie she told herself, anyway, to avoid telling herself that it hurt too much to look upon Kwar's face and not remember what her smile looked like.

"Tulwar have always killed shicts, shicts have always killed humans," Kwar whispered, looking back to the fire. "And humans have—"

"Fuck, I *know* that," Kataria snarled. "I'm not out to make people sit down and exchange coy kisses, I'm trying to stop our people from getting *wiped. Out.* Do you not get that? Shekune's war, what she's doing, it'll make the humans retaliate against our people, they'll come after us and—"

"They're not your people."

A few words. Empty and numb. Yet they cut Kataria all the same, made her cringe as though she were bleeding.

"You are a stranger to them," Kwar said. "You have their ears, but they can't hear your Howling. You talk the same language, but they can't understand you. They don't know you or anything about you." She stared at Kataria blankly for a moment. "Except that you lay with a human."

"Don't." Kataria's voice came out a chest-born snarl. "Don't you even fucking *try.*"

"But it's true."

"Yeah, it's true. And he's gone now. You took me away from him and now he's gone."

"Dead, probably."

"Not dead," Kataria replied, firmly. "Not him. But gone. And I'm here. And so is Shekune. And so are you." She sighed. "And I lay with you, too."

"And forbade me from touching you."

"Don't—"

"Don't what, Kataria? What could I do? I have lost you. I have lost my father. I have lost Thua." Kwar looked off into the night, let her voice escape on a breath that should have come from a dying woman. "What could I do? What would it matter?"

Kataria stared at Kwar, eyes as hard and sharp as an arrowhead. "There's always more to lose."

Kwar simply pulled her knees up to her chest, lowered her head, and closed her eyes. Whatever there was left to lose—if there was anything left—she looked as if she would simply sit and wait for it to go.

"What are you going to do?" Kwar asked. "How are you going to stop it?"

Kataria didn't know. And so Kataria didn't answer. To say the words aloud, to admit she wasn't sure how one person could stop a war, would make everything too real. Everything she needed to do—stop Shekune, stop the war, stop the retaliation—required her to keep running far ahead of reality.

And she couldn't do that staying here.

"I'll think of something," she said. She moved about the campfire, collecting what supplies remained in haphazard piles and stuffing them into a satchel. She attached it to her belt. "Or you can. Stay here and contemplate how many more people are going to die." She stalked past Kwar, toward the distant dunes. "Let me know if you think of something."

She had taken only two steps when she stopped. Warm fingers curled around hers. A soft voice whispered.

"Don't," Kwar said. "Don't leave me, too."

She closed her eyes, felt Kwar rise up behind her. Those warm, dark fingers intertwined with her own. A hand slid around her shoulder. The voice in her ear was something soft and weak, sand disappearing on a cold breeze.

"Please," Kwar whispered. "I know it's bad. I know I'm not helping. But I've just...I've lost..." The words she sought were lost in a choked, sobbing plea. "Please. Don't go."

Kwar's hand slid down around her waist; she felt its desperate warmth in her belly. The sweat of Kwar's palm made her own slick as her fingers gripped even tighter. She felt the khoshict's breath as Kwar drew her tighter, laid her chin upon her shoulder, and wept softly.

"Please."

If Kataria closed her eyes, it was almost easy to pretend that this was how it always was: this warmth, this softness, this need that reached out of Kwar's fingers to pull at hers. It was almost easy to pretend they were still in Kwar's tent, forgetting the world beyond its walls, forgetting everything but the sweat of their skin, the crook of Kwar's smile, the way her breath left her.

And she could almost pretend that this hand around her wrist had never cruelly bound her, that this hand around her belly had never viciously struck her, that this voice whispering in her ear had never spoken so many cruelties, accused her of so many villainies.

Almost. But not quite.

Kataria pulled free of Kwar's touch. Part of her ached to feel chill where warm skin had just touched. But another part of her, a small and angry part with sharp teeth, pushed her away.

"Not now," Kataria snarled. "Not ever again."

She wasted no more words, stalking away toward the dune where they had left their yijis. She had made her decision; never again would Kwar touch her. And whether the khoshict stayed or left, that would never change. So she kept walking toward the dunes, never looking back, even as she heard the crunch of sand as Kwar followed her.

And, if she closed her eyes, she could almost pretend she didn't care.

FIVE

A Fair Price from a
Black Butcher

Dreadaeleon's eyes snapped open and beheld a dot of orange light. It moved back and forth and his stare, unconsciously, followed it.

"Both eyes intact," a voice behind the light muttered. "And in good condition."

"Mm-hm," someone else said, their voice followed by scratching of pen on paper.

There were stories of wizards. Dreadaeleon knew them, same as anyone: tales of crotchety old men with long flowing beards high up in towers, or slinky enchantresses raiding forbidden libraries beneath the earth, and they always had something like big poofy robes with stars and moons. The stories had delighted him as a child.

"Ten fingers, all intact. Slight bend to the left little finger."

"Got it."

And then he had become one.

"Ten toes, likewise."

"Uh-huh."

No wands and crystal balls. No laboratories of alchemical formulae and bubbling crockpots. No pointy hats, poofy robes, long beards, curly-toed shoes, eyes of newt, or whatever. And, definitively and disappointingly, no slinky enchantresses.

There was a ripping sound as a pair of shears rent his shirt in twain. A chill crept over him as his sweat-slick torso was exposed. He closed his eyes again.

"Torso looks mostly intact," the voice said. "I'd put the weight at maybe...ninety-five, ninety-seven pounds."

"I'll cut the difference and say ninety-six."

There was magic, of course. Wizards had it in their blood, along with their bones and their skin and their hair and every other piece of him that was currently being cataloged. And absolutely none of it could ever go to waste. But beyond that, there wasn't much to being a wizard except for an awful lot of bureaucracy, record keeping and—

Another shearing sound as his trousers were torn apart and hung at his ankles.

And whatever this is, he thought.

"Genitalia looks fine," the first voice said. "Legs seem a little atrophied."

"Could probably put that down to the imprisonment," the second voice said.

"Or maybe he's just skinny, I don't know. Put down both, so they can't say we weren't thorough." The first voice sniffed. "Right, then. All that's left is the teeth. Hey. Hey, wake up."

A tap on his naked chest. He opened his eyes again and glanced down at the man standing before him—short, stout, bald, and wrapped in the simple clothes of a clerk. Behind a pair of spectacles, his eyes looked huge as he looked over Dreadaeleon's naked form.

"Yeah, I'm not enjoying it any more than you are," he said. "But I guess they don't tell you about this part of being convicted of heresy, do they? Before your execution, we need a comprehensive list of what we'll be harvesting afterward. That includes what's behind this."

He reached up and tapped the contraption of leather and steel strapped over Dreadaeleon's mouth whose metal clamps kept his lips pinned shut. A Seen-And-Not-Heard: an inelegant device for an inelegant solution to the problem of wizards speaking their spells.

"I'm going to take this off to get there. Bite me, spit on me, speak a single syllable of a spell and we'll have trouble. You're not going to make any trouble for me, right?"

Dreadaeleon glanced to either side, where his arms had been stretched out against the broad table and manacled. He looked back down at the clerk, as if to ask what he could possibly do while chained to a table deep beneath a tower swarming with wizards who wanted to kill him.

Eventually, the clerk seemed to catch on. He glanced over his shoulder to the other clerk—a skinny, dark-haired young man scribbling things down on a clipboard.

"Keep your pen ready," the bald clerk grunted. "I don't want to do this any longer than I have to."

He got up on a stool and reached around, unclasping the Seen-And-Not-Heard. It fell off and clattered to the floor. Dreadaeleon took a moment to stretch his jaws, lick his lips, all the things he had been deprived of these past few days. After a moment, the clerk reached up to his mouth. His fingers hesitated just shy of his lips, a look of concern crossing his face.

And Dreadaeleon couldn't help but smile.

"You seem nervous," he observed.

The clerk shot a glare at him but didn't dispel the observation by reaching forward. His hands remained a fair distance away.

"Makes sense," Dreadaeleon said. "They told you what I did to end up down here, didn't they? The men I've killed?" He chuckled. "I overheard someone saying Palanis isn't doing too good. Are you going to visit him after me? Are you going—"

His tirade was cut off by the clerk shoving his fingers into his mouth, prying his jaws apart.

"I said no talking," the clerk growled.

"You actually didn't," the second clerk noted.

"Well, I meant to," the first said. He muttered as he peeled back Dreadaeleon's lips. "Yeah, I've heard about what you've done. The civilians you murdered are bad enough. But you killed members of the Venarium, brothers and sisters who swore the same oaths as you. I was sick enough at that before I heard you brag about it." He glared hard at Dreadaeleon. "I'm going to enjoy watching you burn, heretic.

"Teeth are all here," the clerk said over his shoulder. "Tongue's in good condition, unfortunately. The rest of him..." He paused, pulled back a bit more of Dreadaeleon's lips. "Blackening around the gums. Some withering of the rear molars." He raised his eyebrows. "Signs of the Decay?"

"Doesn't seem likely," the second clerk noted. "The Decay kills."

"In most cases," the first clerk said. "Write it down, regardless. I don't want the wizards getting up my ass if they harvest him down and find out he's damaged." He hopped off the stool and collected the Seen-And-Not-Heard. "External analysis looks satisfactory. They should get some good parts off this shitstain."

"It's the internal you have to watch out for," Dreadaeleon said, sneering. "The brain, especially. Full of dangerous thoughts, that one. Thoughts like 'maybe this organization is nothing more than a treasonous, tyrannical crock of—'"

That thought, and the thousand more profanity-laced ones he had been brewing, went unheard. The Seen-And-Not-Heard was reattached in an instant, secured at the back of Dreadaeleon's head.

"We'll find out in four days," the clerk said. "They've got you scheduled to go onto the slab right after you're executed. They said they want you gone quickly." He sneered at Dreadaeleon. "For my part, I hope they don't go so quickly that you can't feel it."

He turned and pushed past the second clerk and out the door to the tiny cell. "You coming?"

"Yeah, soon," the second clerk said, still scribbling on his clipboard. "If there's a sign of Decay, I need to be absolutely clear that it wasn't our fault. That means a *lot* of fucking notes."

"Do it later. Come to lunch."

"Do it later." The second clerk looked at the first blankly. "The Lectors made it clear that this fucker's going to burn for what he did. And if I mess up the notes, I'll burn with him." He waved off his companion. "Go on. I'll catch up."

"Yeah, sure." The first clerk hesitated at the door, looking back at Dreadaeleon. "Listen, not that you were going to, but... keep that thing on his face, all right? The Lectors don't trust him even to speak."

"I don't look for conversation with heretics." The second clerk chuckled, waving his companion away. "Go on. You're distracting me."

The bald clerk grunted and left, shutting the door behind him. The second clerk continued scribbling in silence for another few moments before glancing up. He shot a meaningful look to Dreadaeleon before creaking open the iron door and peering out into the hallway beyond. He glanced left and right, then quietly lit a candle ensconced in the wall beside the door.

He eased it shut and then set his clipboard aside. Hurriedly, he rushed over to the table Dreadaeleon was strapped to and undid his manacles.

The boy slid off the table to land rudely upon the ground. He muffled a curse behind the device on his mouth as he fussed with it.

"Hold on, hold on," the second clerk said, reaching behind Dreadaeleon's face. "They make these things so you can't get them off by yourself."

There was a click as the straps on the Seen-And-Not-Heard fell off. The clerk winced at the sound, but nonetheless reached into a satchel at his hip and produced a small loaf of bread and some mostly fresh meat wrapped in paper. He thrust them at Dreadaeleon.

"Hurry up and eat," the clerk said. "No one but us *should* be down here, but that doesn't mean others might not come."

Dreadaeleon took the food and lifted it to his mouth before hesitating. He glanced askance at the clerk. "You didn't bother to wrap these? They've just been stewing in your pocket?"

"Just shut up and eat."

Dreadaeleon shot him a grudging glare before taking a bite. But once that happened, it was hard for him to stop himself from almost inhaling the food. These pilfered meals came too infrequently for him to resist devouring them. And while it wasn't luxuriant, it was better than what he got regularly. The watery slop his jailors gave him was only enough to keep him from dying before they could have the pleasure of killing him.

That was the Venarium's conservation at its finest: Why bother expending decent food on a heretic when they were just going to have him executed? Why bother giving him a trial, hearing *his* side of the story, when they had already made up their minds?

Cowards, he thought. *Hypocrites. As though it's my fault their precious concomitants are dead.*

In fairness, he replied to himself, *you did kill them.*

But they *sent them after me! Annis, the other Lectors, the Venarium . . . they could have left me alone! I wasn't hurting anyone. But their stupid oaths, their stupid rules, their stupid . . . stupid . . . STUPID!*

He was grateful to have merely thought that. Words were not his strong suit lately. He supposed having spent the majority of these past weeks with a pound of metal around his mouth, strapped to a table or otherwise locked in a cell, would do that.

But there was nothing left in him for clever words. Behind his eyes, he could feel his magic burning like a fever. The Venarie, the power that flowed within all wizards, boiled at the thoughts of the indignity and humiliations that had been heaped on him by his captors. His palms itched, eager to explode into flames. His breath turned hoary in his mouth, ice forming on his lips.

It was only discipline that kept him from storming out of his cell and casting spells at anything that moved.

Well, discipline and the fact that he had had his ass magically kicked just a few days ago. He couldn't imagine the outcome would be any different this time, save that he would be naked and they wouldn't bother to simply capture him this time.

There was a knock at the door. He froze with a mouthful of food. The clerk stared at the door with eyes wide. After two breaths, there was another three quick knocks. And finally, two more knocks a moment later.

The clerk got up and pushed the door open. A pair of wizards—tall, stern-looking, wearing elegant brown coats and broad-brimmed hats—walked into the room and took up a position on either side of the door. Librarians, Dreadaeleon recognized; the elite seekers of the Venarium.

A Lector never traveled with fewer than two.

A moment later, she came in through the doors herself. A tall, thin woman, as elegant as could be in the drab confines of Venarium uniform. Her coat was clean and pressed, her leggings and shirt loose, her boots brightly polished, and a thick spellbook hung by a gold chain at her hip. Framed between dark curls, Lector Shinka looked down a long nose toward the sweaty naked boy sitting on the floor with a mouth full of partially chewed food.

And somehow, Dreadaeleon got the impression that she was regretting choosing him to help her destroy the Venarium.

"So." Shinka glanced at the clerk. "Did no one think to get him some clothes, or is this display purely for my benefit?"

"There was no time," the clerk said. "You told me to get him free and fed. You said he needed his strength."

"Yes, yes." Shinka sighed and placed a finger to her temple. "I suppose it's my fault for not telling you my needs. For future reference, though, they don't include a skinny naked boy."

Dreadaeleon thought to protest but suspected that doing so with a mouthful of food wasn't likely to raise her opinion of his dignity.

She wandered over to the clerk's clipboard and glanced it over. "How is our little champion doing, anyway? Everything on the up-and-up?"

"Yes, Lector." The clerk caught himself, coughed. "Well, *mostly*."

Lips pursed, Shinka did not so much shoot the clerk a look as impale him with it. "I do not like 'mostly.'"

"All his external functionalities are intact," the clerk said, shrinking away. "But...there's slight evidence of—"

"The Decay." Shinka looked from the clipboard to Dreadaeleon. "You did not think to mention this to us?"

Dreadaeleon finished chewing, swallowed. "A past condition. Long since healed."

"Wizards rarely heal from the Decay," Shinka replied. "And its conditions rarely stay in the past." She narrowed her eyes. "Too much relies on you being able to perform, concomitant. If you can't—"

"I can." Dreadaeleon's voice was a low growl. "I can bring down Lector Annis. I can bring this whole fucking tower down and everyone in it, given the chance."

Shinka's lip curled back. "I'll remind you that, given the chance, Annis did to you what you did to that meat." She pointed to the mess of crumbs and grease on his fingers. "And I'll further remind you that I have no desire to bring down this tower and every desire to spare as many lives beyond Annis's as possible. I will need them if I'm to save this city."

"Ah, yes," Dreadaeleon replied, licking his lips. "You're still on about that, I see. Thinking you can drive the foreigners, the thieves, the cultists out of Cier'Djaal with just a wave of your hand."

"I can't drive them out." Shinka's eyes glowed red. Electricity danced across her fingertips in cobalt arcs. "But with a wave of my hand, I can make their bowels erupt out their anuses. So that's a start."

Dreadaeleon grunted, took another bite of his meal.

"The Venarium has stayed neutral for too long," Shinka continued. "Wizards were trusted with both power overwhelming and the insight and reason with which to control it. It's reckless to allow archaic traditions to shackle us when foreign armies run rampant through our streets and violence plagues every quarter."

"How very noble of you," Dreadaeleon said, swallowing. "Centuries of protocol be damned, I'm certain the Venarium will see the error of their ways and heed your keen insight of 'war is bad.' After all, all good reigns begin with assassination, don't they?"

Shinka was a wizard in every sense of the world: clever, calculating, and conservative right down to her expressions. And when Dreadaeleon spoke, she did not snarl or spit or glare. She merely regarded him with the slightest coil to the corners of her mouth and spoke softly and easily.

"Annis's dedication to a cause he believes in is admirable, but unfortunate. If his intervention hinders the efforts to secure safety in this city, then it is with a heavy conscience that he must be removed from his position as Primary Lector."

As easy as though she had been filling out a form. Not a single word fumbled or a single breath out of place. How long had she been rehearsing that speech, Dreadaeleon wondered? And whom did she intend to tell it to once she killed Annis?

Well, let's not be unfair, old man, he told himself. *It's when you kill Annis that she'll tell it to someone.*

That was his role in all this, after all: the dangerous heretic who would inexplicably break free of his restraints and bring down Annis, thus allowing Shinka to assume control and use the Venarium to save the city. Annis would be an unfortunate martyr, Shinka would be a triumphing heroine, and Dreadaeleon would be forgotten.

Free.

Stricken from every Venarium record. Expunged from every history. A brief footnote in a long, rambling diatribe that would be ignored by every dull-eyed, barknecked reader until he was long dead.

He smiled bitterly at the prospect.

"Regardless," Shinka said, "you should know there's been a change in plans."

He looked up, eyes twitching. "You can't go back on this. Not now. Not after—"

"Calm yourself." She held up a hand. "I was hoping to persuade Annis to delay your execution by a few days to allow you to get your strength back." She cast a glance over his skinny, naked form. "Unless that's as big as you get."

"I'm slender. *Lots* of men are—"

"But we have no time," she interrupted. "There has been an incident in the desert. The tulwar clans have assembled into some manner of army. Jalaang has already fallen. They've got eyes on Cier'Djaal. There's some kind of red lizard-thing leading them."

Dreadaeleon's brows shot up. "Gariath?"

"I don't know what they call it and I don't care. A bunch of backward savages is just that, no matter what kind of army they pretend to be. But I'd rather have Cier'Djaal secure before I deal with them."

She held up a hand and extended four fingers.

"Your execution is going forward as planned. Four days. On the third, at midnight, you'll be freed from your cell. Annis's study is on the top floor of the tower. We'll do our best to make sure our people are doing the patrols that night, but it's up to you to get there."

"Fine," he said. He rose and brushed crumbs from his flesh. "And when I succeed..."

"You'll get what you want," Shinka replied. "Two days to collect whatever you need and leave the city. Once you pass out the gates, no one will so much as speak your name."

"Are you certain? The man who brought down the Venarium would be the subject of some talk."

"The *boy* who proved useful to progress will be of small concern compared to what we'll have to accomplish. We have thieves to smoke out of their holes and foreign armies to drive away. Cier'Djaal will be a very busy place."

"Someone's coming," one of the Librarians beside the door muttered. "I can hear them."

Shinka glanced at Dreadaeleon, eyes alight with red power. She waved a hand. Invisible force roiled from her fingertips. An invisible grip seized him, raised him, and pressed him against the table in short order. The manacles clasped around his wrists of their own accord. He barely had time to grunt, let alone protest, before one of the Librarians was gathering up the Seen-And-Not-Heard and preparing to reattach it.

"Four days. Midnight. You'll continue receiving visits until then," Shinka said. She turned to move out the door. "And then you'll be gone from my city."

"About that," Dreadaeleon called after her.

She hesitated, but did not look back.

"You seem to have forgotten about the people. What if they don't support your rule? This *is* all about protecting them, isn't it?"

Shinka remained silent before slowly turning her head to regard him out of the corner of her eye.

"As a rule," she said, "I do not consider advice when given from men with their cocks flopping about."

Dreadaeleon's mouth hung open a fraction of a moment before the Seen-And-Not-Heard went back on. Just as well.

It wasn't until well after she and her retinue had departed and the door slammed shut that he had even remotely come to think of a good retort for that.

SIX

A FEAST FOR POOR GODS

It was the moment that the last drop of liquid from the waterskin hit his tongue that Lenk noticed it.

He glanced to his left, to the man walking beside him.

He had once been broken—stooped of back, withered of limb—but one wouldn't know it by looking at him anymore. Mocca's power had changed him, as it had changed all the others.

It had made him tall and strong, straightened his spine, and sculpted his muscle into the creature that now towered over Lenk. Black hair shimmered in the desert sun; his skin glistened as he strode through the same sands that Lenk stumbled over. And where Lenk squinted against the glare of the sun, this man, this perfect creature, stared straight ahead with bright yellow eyes.

"Do you need any water?" Lenk asked.

The man did not look down, not at first. He didn't even blink. So Lenk cleared his throat and spoke again.

"Hey. *Hey.*"

At this, the man stirred, as if from reverie. He looked down at Lenk. His features, though handsome and sharp, displayed a kind of distance that was swiftly shattered as a broad smile of perfectly white, even teeth flashed.

"Yes, my friend?" he asked in a voice that had not been his own.

"Water." Lenk held up the waterskin, dangling it. "Do you need any? I drained this one, but..." He gestured over his shoulder to the caravan of goods hauled by oxen toward the back. "I can go back and get some more, if you want."

The man looked away, puzzled. "I... don't think so."

"You don't think so." Lenk shaded his eyes with his hand and glanced up at the sun blazing down. "Feels like you probably ought to know by now."

"I know I should." The man looked down at his broad hands. "When I was . . . imperfect, I was so terribly thirsty. No water could slake it. But now, I feel like I could walk forever on a single drop." He smiled back at Lenk. "The master's touch. It cures every pain, heals every wound, slakes every—"

"Yeah. He's a peach." Lenk tucked the waterskin back into his belt and turned away. "If you'll pardon me."

The man did—or at least didn't protest. He just went back to staring straight ahead, continuing to walk.

Just like the thousands of others.

Silently, their eyes turned up toward the sun, they walked in singular purpose. Men and women who had once been shattered, twisted, torn apart, and fused back together. Now they were tall and strong as trees behind scanty silk garments and their faces were painfully beautiful to behold. Those few moments Lenk caught a glimpse of them, he realized they looked remarkably similar: all of them bearing similar sharp features, pointed chins, long noses. And all of them had those big, bright eyes the color of a waning moon.

They couldn't possibly all have looked like that before they were changed. Yet if any of them missed their old bodies, they didn't show it. And if Lenk felt like asking, he was sure they wouldn't be up for discussing it. As it was, he found looking them in the eye uncomfortable. And not merely because they towered over him.

So he kept his eyes down as he wandered through their ranks. They idly stepped around him, smiled at him, but said not a word. They kept their eyes toward the west and their stride moving as he made his way back toward the oxen.

A few raggedy beasts found at some abandoned farms when Mocca's "Chosen," as he called them, had made their way down from the mountains and into the desert. The oxen were tasked with hauling what few possessions they had, mostly just food and water.

Yet as Lenk tossed his waterskin in and produced a new one, he realized that the supplies had only dwindled insomuch as he had taken from them. No one else had so much as touched the food or drink in the days since they had been traveling. And none of them seemed so much as winded from the long march, even though Lenk could still see the spots where he had napped in the wagon.

It worried him.

"Hello there!"

Then again, considering the company he kept, he suspected worry was reasonable.

He glanced up. Amid the sea of towering dark flesh, Mocca stood out like a ghost. His robes fluttered about him in the warm breeze, pristine white despite the sand and heat. He, short and fragile-looking among his creations, waved at Lenk with the carefree whimsy that somehow didn't befit a demon lord.

The two Disciples, serpentine and withered and tremendous, that flanked him, though? Those *quite* befitted a demon lord.

"Hello," Lenk replied.

He did his best to ignore the scribble-black eyes of the demons as they came slinking up, preferring instead to focus on Mocca's gentle smile. Yet somehow that smile was just as unnerving, given that Lenk knew the demon that lurked behind it.

"You look ill at ease." Mocca laughed. "Is the pilgrimage proving arduous?"

"I'm not complaining," Lenk said. He glanced pointedly at the Disciples. "And I've been through worse."

Mocca quirked a brow. He glanced up at the Disciples. "I believe you are making my friend uncomfortable. Would you mind going on ahead? Your brethren will be close by now and seeking us out."

The Disciples exchanged glances through their withered old-man faces. When one of them spoke, it did so with the lash of tongue.

"Is it wise to leave you with this child of woe, master?" it asked.

"Our tongues are free of lies, our minds clean of doubt," the other added. "But the world is sparse of one of the learned owing to this one's unclean hands."

Lenk bristled at the accusation, though he wasn't sure why. It was true, after all, that he had slain one of these creatures before. Perhaps it was just the idea of being called *unclean* by something so foul as a demon-snake-old-man-thing.

"There is no creature so learned as to be free of mistake," Mocca replied, wagging a finger. "The instant he achieves perfection of thought is the instant he is no longer part of this world and all its tragic beauties." He glanced at Lenk and smiled. "We will be fine on our own, will we not?"

Fine.

Fine was a word that did not belong here. A demon was free by Lenk's hand, walking the earth among an army of people changed. And though those people were happy, as this demon swore he could make the rest of the world, Lenk could not feel easy among them.

It was for a good cause. The best cause, even, he knew. The wars that had wracked Cier'Djaal would spread to the rest of the world, kill it slowly over a thousand years. The gods were deaf, they did not listen, they could not stop it. But Khoth-Kapira could. Khoth-Kapira listened.

Khoth-Kapira could save Kataria. He was the only one who could.

Lenk knew this, but he could not shake the memories: the people he had betrayed, the blood he had spilled, all for this desperate hope that the thing that had crawled out of hell would save the world.

No. He was not fine.

Yet he nodded, all the same.

At this, the two Disciples bowed low and then slithered away. Their ancient, withered grayness made them look like decaying statues among the Chosen, who did not look at them.

"Not that they aren't charming," Mocca said. "But I fear that the Disciples merely learned to regurgitate, rather than orate."

"I'd just as soon they not open their mouths for either." Lenk shuddered. "I've seen what comes out of them."

Mocca laughed, beckoning Lenk to follow him. "They weren't always the twisted creatures you see now. I counted them once as precious company, learned minds that at least tried to keep up with what I was telling them."

"You talk as though they didn't succeed."

"To sound perfectly arrogant, who could?" He led Lenk farther away from the caravan and the crowd, in the direction of distant cliffs to the south. "Mine is an intellect formed in the wonders of heaven, shaped by the pleasures of earth and tested by the torments below it. One does not experience the entirety of creation and come away unchanged."

"Feels like you'd have a lot in common with demons," Lenk muttered.

Mocca cast a glower over his shoulder. "A term I don't find endearing. We were branded that name by fanatics. Fanatics who took exception to the flaws we discovered with their masters' creation and sought to slay us for it. We gazed upon this earth and saw its illnesses, its wars, its famines. They could not deny this, so they branded us, cast us out, and called our truths *blasphemy*. Fanatics are not useful to me."

Lenk glanced over to the crowd. What, then, he wondered, did Mocca see in these Chosen who could not speak his name without going wide-eyed and breathless?

When he looked back, Mocca was standing not a foot away, his eyes locked on Lenk's. The beard of serpents had returned, their beady stares fixated on him in a way that made his legs go cold beneath him.

"What I need is a champion."

"What?" Lenk took a step back.

"We've been in each other's company for weeks now, Lenk, and I've spent much of that time as a passenger inside your head." He tapped his own temple. "With all my power, all my grace, have you never thought it odd that I never once attempted to control you? To exert my will over you?"

Lenk opened his mouth but found no words. Now that it was spoken, it *did* seem odd that a demon should be so restrained. He had fought them before, knew their urge to dominate well.

"I would not be so arrogant as to say I could have tortured you, broken you down to madness and reshaped you as I saw fit." He pursed his lips. "But I could have tried, Lenk. Just as I could have shattered this world, marched on it with a horde of demons at my back and brought it to its knees until they gazed up at me and begged me for mercy."

There was something in Mocca's voice, a coldness that slid off his tongue. He spoke in bitter poisons, his face coiling up in disgust as the serpents of his beard twisted and writhed excitedly.

Lenk felt that itch in his palm that went away whenever he gripped his sword. He fought to keep his hand at his side.

"So why didn't you?" he asked. "Why are we walking to Cier'Djaal with this rabble?"

Mocca let out a sigh. His eyes closed shut. The serpents receded back into his flesh.

"I cannot shepherd them as a conqueror," he said. "Were I to descend out of the sky on fire, they would only speak my name so that they could avoid being burned. Faith taught through fear only yields fanatics. For this to work..." He gestured out over the desert. "For me to be able to save this world, they must believe in me." He looked at Lenk intently. "*You* must believe in me."

"I let you out of hell, didn't I?" Lenk asked. He silently congratulated himself on only feeling *slightly* disgusted with himself for saying it this time.

And, as though Mocca could see that revulsion coursing through him, he spoke. "You believe that I tell you a war is coming, but you've seen it coming for weeks. You believe that I can save your shict, but you'd do anything to save her. You believe me, but do you believe *in* me, Lenk?"

Lenk stared at him for a long time. And, after a long time, he whispered a single word.

"No."

Mocca frowned. If God-Kings could weep, he might have. But there was no denying it—whatever miracles he promised or sicknesses he could cure, Khoth-Kapira was merely the means to an end. To Lenk, it had been a simple bargain: the God-King's freedom for Kataria's life and safety. Everything else was just a bonus. And apparently that was not enough.

Mocca inclined his head low. "You are no fanatic, Lenk. But you are no believer, either. You trust only what you can see, what you can touch."

He turned and looked long over the desert. Across the sands to the south, cliffs rose up in the distance.

"And that's what I intend to give you."

＊＊＊

The moon was already peering over the cliffs when Lenk arrived. The roar of the hot afternoon wind had become a frigid moan. It felt refreshing for all of a moment before the chill made his sweat-ridden clothes all but freeze to his skin.

The journey had taken an entire day and two waterskins to trek from the caravan to the cliffs. His skin, burned a bright pink, tingled as he pulled his sweat-drenched shirt away from his body.

"Fucking outstanding," Lenk muttered, peering down his shirt.

"Half my body is sweated away and the other half is cooked." He inhaled deeply. "I smell bacon. Do you smell bacon?"

He looked around. Mocca stood several feet away, his back turned to Lenk, silent as a grave. As he had been for the entirety of the trip.

Their journey had begun pleasantly enough—Lenk had been pleased to be away from the Chosen and their empty, grinning faces.

But as they trekked farther into the desert and the wind and sun took their toll, the two of them had fallen quiet. Lenk because he had been presently sweating his balls off, but Mocca's reasons were…less apparent.

As a demon, he had no need to eat, to drink, to adhere to the mortal limitations that bound Lenk's weary muscles. But every step farther away from his Chosen, his words had come more sparsely and his face had grown darker. After a few hours in the desert, Mocca's eyes were locked on their destination and unblinking, as dark and empty as the Chosen he had left behind.

"Not that you're not riveting company," Lenk said, approaching the man in white. "But if you've hauled me through a day of baking sun just to show me a bunch of rocks, I'm going to jam this somewhere soft." He patted the hilt of his sword.

"I thought you said you wouldn't complain," Mocca replied. His tone was flat and soft.

"That wasn't a complaint," Lenk replied. "That was a threat. Very different."

Mocca said nothing for a moment. "You would, wouldn't you?"

Lenk flinched. He wasn't used to words like that.

Words like that—soft words, dying words—they belonged in the mouths of grandmothers and weeping women. The last time Lenk had heard words like that, they had come from lips he had known the taste of beneath green eyes rimmed with tears.

To hear them coming from a demon, to think the God-King could sound so vulnerable as…as…

As she did, Lenk thought, involuntarily.

The thought made him shiver in a way the wind could not.

"It's not your fault," Mocca whispered. "Just one more tragedy of this world." He raised a finger and pointed toward the cliff face. "A very long, very old one."

Lenk peered into the darkness. The moon had climbed over the peaks into a cloudless sky, painting the cliffs indigo. And through the jagged shadows cast by the crags, Lenk could just barely see a rock he would call most peculiar.

After all, he had rarely met a rock that had stared back at him.

He pushed past Mocca and hurried across the sand to the cliff face. As he drew nearer, he saw more and more: a head, an arm, a torso. And, at the level of his face, a singular stone eye, wide open and staring directly at him.

From the neck down, the statue looked like a robed man. Carved from the rock, as though it were reaching out from the cliff face itself, a single hand extended with the palm raised. But instead of a face, it had just one massive eye. And though it was stone, it seemed to peer directly at Lenk.

Like it knew him.

"I've seen this before..." The words escaped his lips without him realizing. "Somewhere..."

A past adventure. Or maybe just in a dark dream he had once buried long ago.

"What do you suppose was the first face you saw?"

Mocca appeared beside him, looking gravely at the stone statue.

"Like when I was born? How would I know?" Lenk shrugged. "I don't know. My father? My mother? The village midwife, I guess."

"That would be accurate for most children," Mocca said. He reached out, fingered a lock of Lenk's silver hair. "But then, most children were not as unusual as you. They are all dead, yes?"

Lenk flinched away. "What?"

"Your mother? Father? The midwife?"

"Yeah." Lenk's voice turned dark. "All dead." His hands clenched into fists at his side. "By my hand."

It had been Shuro who told him. The woman with hair like his, eyes the same cold blue as his. The woman who, too, carried a sword she could not put down and left corpses in her wake...starting with her family. Whatever had made them this way, it began with that: the murder of their families by their own hands.

"You had a reason for bringing that up, I assume," Lenk said. "But if you dragged me all the way out here just to be an asshole, I'm not going to stop at chopping off your head."

"The first face you saw when you were born"—Mocca gestured to the statue—"was this."

"So you brought me all the way out here to be cryptic? That's... better?"

"I brought you here"—Mocca raised a hand and pressed it against the statue's—"because I need you to see for yourself."

His fingers interwove with the statue's stone digits. And suddenly the statue returned the grasp. Dust fell from its fingers as it clasped Mocca's hand and held it tightly.

"Magic," Lenk gasped.

"Not the kind you know," Mocca replied. "The power of this place is older than any wizard's."

As if in agreement, a low and distant rumble shook through the cliff's face. The statue released Mocca's hand and, with the grinding of stone, began to slide backward, disappearing into the rock. In its place, a lightless gap in the stone stood.

Mocca glanced at Lenk, offering the barest of smiles as he gestured to the new doorway. "It's quite safe, I assure you."

"I have only a few rules I abide by in life," Lenk said, glancing at the gap. "And if I don't have one about going into a dark hole in the middle of a desert, I can make one up *real* quick."

Mocca shrugged and walked into the gap. "I suppose I can't blame you." While it was small, it easily accommodated his size. "Were I you, I wouldn't want to know what lay inside here, either."

"What? Some kind of monster? Demons?" Lenk called after him as he disappeared into darkness. "I've killed plenty of those."

"Oh, no." Mocca's chuckle came back as an echo from inside. "A demon could merely kill you. This is much worse."

There probably also should be a rule about never following demons who said shit like that, either, Lenk thought.

And, as he followed Mocca into the darkness, he knew that the demon spoke true. Whatever was down here, he would regret. His life, of late, left little room for anything but regrets: for freeing Khoth-Kapira, for betraying Shuro, for every corpse and bloodstain he had left in his wake.

All for her.

He felt his way through the darkness, found the walls of the tunnel no more than an arm's length to either side. The ceiling hung low, only a foot above his head.

The passage was choked with dust, his feet the first to have seen it in ages. But as he pressed on, a pinprick of light appeared. It grew brighter, silver moonlight pouring into the tunnel, illuminating walls that had been carved smooth, torch sconces that now hung empty. People had once been here.

But that was a long time ago. And the only thing that greeted him as he stepped out of the tunnel was wind and shadow.

His feet crunched on sand-covered stone as he stepped into a courtyard. The moon hung high overhead, casting a singular great shadow from a singular great shape presiding over all.

A statue. Just like the one he had seen in the cliff's face, except much bigger.

Tremendous, towering, it rose over the courtyard like a god. But unlike any other god, its hands were not extended in benediction. It raised a single hand outstretched in warning. In lieu of a face, it bore a single, unblinking eye. And though its stare was stone, Lenk couldn't help but feel like it was looking at him with the cold familiarity with which one regards an unwelcome relative.

It knew him.

"They called him Darior, back when he was worshipped."

Mocca appeared at Lenk's side, staring up at the statue. Upon the demon's face, despair tugged at the corners of his lips, and scorn burned in his eyes.

"That was the closest thing he had to a name, at least," Mocca continued. "He had more than a few, most of them scornful. Some called him the Judge. A precious few called him the God of Gods, long ago."

"Long ago..." Lenk whispered.

"One can't ever say if a god truly dies," Mocca said. "But when no one speaks their name, when their statues no longer stand, when no one thinks to cry out in the night for them...well, that's the closest thing to a true death they might ever know."

"What was he the god of?"

A moment's hesitation before he answered. "Justice."

"I've seen the inside of a few courthouses. They always invoke their own realm's gods."

"Not your concept of justice." Mocca waved a hand. "Yours is merely a fancy word for revenge. Darior saw something…grander."

He held out both of his hands, palms up.

"Mortals view justice as a scale. They stack virtue on one plate and weigh it against corpses stacked on the other." He mimed the motion of a scale balancing before flitting his hands, casting both corpses and virtues aside. "Darior saw it not as a balance to be kept but an inevitability. All actions demanded responses; all responses demanded more actions. Justice, true justice, was not a question of sin answered with atonement. It is a conversation that continues forever with many unpleasant words."

Lenk looked thoughtfully at the statue looming over them before he casually spit on the sand.

"Sounds like a cock."

Mocca said nothing. He extended a hand to the western wall of the courtyard. He closed his eyes and, one by one, braziers that had had been hidden by shadow burst to life. Without wood to fuel them, they burned an eerie green flame that cast the courtyard into an unnatural light.

And Lenk would have thought that odd, had he not seen what they illuminated.

A mural, its paint dry and flaked away in places, and all of it covered in dust. It stretched across the entirety of the wall, depicting a scene of darkness. Humans, women all, their heads bowed and backs turned, knelt in rows in the blackness. And at the center of it, a painting of Darior, his unblinking eye turned upon them all, seemed to leer out and stare at Lenk.

"It was our sins that made Darior take notice," Mocca spoke from behind. "We were still called Aeons, then, though only barely. Our desires to guide mortality had turned to a need to herd them, to control them. The mortal armies marched against us, but to no avail. Our powers were greater back then, our sight endless. Darior alone could see that mortality required a new weapon.

"And he made them. His forges were the wombs of the desperate and sorrowful mothers who were too merciful to bring life into this dark earth. His metals were their tears and their agonies. Their service was compulsory…"

The green fires sputtered to brighter life, illuminating more of the mural. The mothers lay hacked and bloodied, empty eyes and sad frowns looking up at the children that had been born from them: naked babes with heads of silver hair and clenching blades in their hands.

"And brief," Mocca said.

Lenk's mouth fell open. Unconsciously, he mouthed the words. "Family, home, faith..."

"All three must be lost before they can realize their potential," Mocca said. "Darior instilled the barest of his essence into these children, these weapons, and in doing so commanded them to fulfill their purpose."

"A god?" Lenk whirled on Mocca, eyes incredulous. "I have...a *god* in me?"

"No." Mocca smiled. "The fraction of a power that you can contain couldn't even qualify as part of a god. Yet Darior's strength was such that even that fraction was enough."

"Enough for what?" Lenk demanded.

Mocca closed his eyes. The flames died away. Yet just as swiftly, he pointed to the eastern wall and more braziers sprang to life.

"For their duty to be done."

Another mural sprawled across the wall. But where the former had been black, this one was red. And silver. It showed the children with the silver hair, now grown and marching upon hordes of twisted creatures. Demons, Lenk knew; some he recognized, some he did not.

Their faces were alive with fear, their bodies hewn and hacked and bursting with bright red. Their corpses lay in sheaves upon the mural. And the people with the silver hair showed no emotion. Their eyes, each one the same cold shade of blue, betrayed nothing as they waded into the horde and slaughtered with impunity.

"And this, they did," Mocca said, sighing. "When we fell from Aeon to demon, we lusted for the things that mortals would grant us: devotion, fear, hope. These creatures for which we had no name, they gave us nothing but steel. And slowly, we fell beneath their blades. Darior's will drove them, Darior's power fueled them, and they drove us to the edge of the shadow."

Mocca's voice grew soft. His eyes grew distant.

"I remember them," he whispered. "In the darker days of the war, when the mortal armies marched upon Rhuul Khaas, I heard my Disciples scream as these nameless ones tore them open. Yet they themselves said not a word. Even when I was cast below and their victory was won, they never so much as smiled."

Lenk stared at them for a long time, their empty faces and cold eyes. After a while, the question leapt to his mouth without him knowing.

"Are there songs?" he asked.

"What?"

"Songs." Lenk turned and looked to the demon. "There are always songs about war. That's how you remember them. The heroes, the villains, the massacres...if it's worth remembering, there's a song about them."

"Lenk," Mocca replied, "this is history lost to every mortal race—"

"But not to you," Lenk said. His voice cracked slightly. "You were there. You saw everything. Did they sing about them? Did anyone tell stories about them?" He felt his voice choke inside his throat. "Were they people?"

Mocca stared back at him for a moment. His face grew long and brimmed with sorrow.

"There is only one story of them." He turned to the northern wall and closed his eyes. "And you are reading it."

More braziers lit. One more mural was illuminated. And it was bright white.

Humans, these ones with eyes wide with fear and mouths alive with screams, gathered at one edge of the mural. They flew banners of bright colors, sigils of gods that Lenk knew well: Talanas, Galatrine, Daeon...

An army, he recognized, but only by their colors. To look upon them, he could see little difference between them and the demons. Their weapons were bloodied and their faces were bright with terror as they swarmed toward one edge of the mural, where the brightness gave way to an endless dark.

And there, he saw them. The nameless warriors, their hair the color of their steel, their faces empty and their eyes unflinching.

Even as the humans pushed them into darkness.

Like hail, they fell into the gloom, fading the lower they went. And at the bottom of that great black pit, a single eye stared up, so dim it was barely there.

"Darior," Lenk whispered. "What happened to him?"

"Gone," Mocca said. "As gone as a god can be, at least. His essence was spent forging his living weapons. And when they had fulfilled their function, the remaining gods and their mortal vessels feared what he might do next. Darior represented inevitability, all that rises and all that falls. And as he cast down the Aeons, heaven feared that they would be the next to fall.

"And so they were hunted. They were executed. They were slaughtered. They faded from the world, the last of Darior's name. And as their memory of him disappeared, so, too, did he."

A hand fell upon Lenk's shoulder. He looked up into Mocca's smile, a warm light amid the cold flames of the courtyard.

"But he was still a god. His essence was not so easily extinguished. And though they appear but rarely, his children still are born into this world."

Lenk looked around him, at the murals, at the history of these people…

His people.

"No," he whispered to himself. "Not people."

"Pardon?"

"Not people. Not children. Not *born*." He tore away from Mocca's grasp and stalked to the mural. "Forged. Made. Wrought. I wasn't born. I was *made*. Like them." He gestured wildly to their empty faces. "I slaughtered my own family. I've left nothing in my wake but bodies since the day I left home. I wasn't born. I'm not a person."

When he whirled back to Mocca, only then was he aware of the tears streaming down his face.

"I'm a *weapon*."

Mocca's face was as stone: as silent, as cold. He stared at Lenk, his expression betraying nothing.

"Aren't I?" Lenk asked. He stormed toward Mocca. "Aren't I just like them? Aren't I just a weapon that can't stop killing because what else does a weapon do?" He seized the man in white by his robes and shook him. *"Aren't I?"*

And yet, even grabbing him roughly as Lenk did, Mocca felt too solid to be moved. Lenk felt as though he gripped a statue. Mocca would not move. Mocca would not even blink as he looked upon Lenk and whispered.

"I cannot answer that," he said. "But I came here to find out."

"No," Lenk all but screamed. "No more cryptic bullshit, no more games, no more of this." He tried to shove Mocca away but succeeded only in pushing himself off the man in white. "I want to know."

"As do I," Mocca replied. "I have wanted to know nothing else since I first contacted you."

"Talk sense!"

"Listen to sense." Mocca's voice rose barely an octave, yet the sands shook beneath him. "All I have told you is true. All you suspect is true. Yes…" His face hardened. "You are a weapon. And you are a weapon designed to kill me."

Lenk felt the sword on his back grow heavier, as though it heard a conversation it yearned to be a part of and leaned in. And his hand ached, as if begging to hold it once again.

"And that is why I approached you, Lenk," Mocca said, "that is why I guided you to Rhuul Khaas. That is why it *had* to be you." He held his hands out. "All I have planned, all that I can do for this world, all the lives I can save…it will mean *nothing* if I cannot convince you that I am worth saving."

Lenk froze, staring at the man in white blankly.

"You were made to kill me. You were made to end what I have planned. But you haven't yet." He stepped toward Lenk. "You haven't slain me. You haven't condemned all those who would die in the wars to come should I be unable to stop them. Weapons are designed to kill, Lenk. You could kill more than any one man in history, forgotten or otherwise, with just one stroke of your sword."

He held his hands out wide and gestured to his chest.

"Run me through. Cut my heart out. Or hack off my head. *Kill me.* And send them all to their deaths, including *her.* Fulfill your purpose."

And Lenk wanted to.

Despite everything, all that he knew and all that he feared, he wanted to tear his sword from his scabbard and plunge it into Mocca's chest. He wanted to stain the sand red and watch the life leave Mocca's eyes. He wanted to keep hacking until he was too tired to stand, too tired to think.

Because that was what he knew. That was what killing was. It was quick, it was messy, and then it was over. It made sense.

And he wanted so badly for this all to make sense.

And his hand slid up to the sword on his back. And his jaw clenched. And the tears on his face grew cold. And, despite all that he knew and all that he feared . . .

He let his hand fall. And his head followed. And soon, his body slumped to the earth.

"I can't," he whispered.

And he felt hands on his shoulders, guiding him back to his feet. And when he looked up, Mocca's eyes were bright and his smile was warm.

"You could," the man in white said. "But you won't. A weapon fulfills many purposes." He nodded slowly. "And this one . . . is not yours."

Lenk had fought demons before. Not just demons but those depraved few who came to bow at their altars. In all the bodies he'd left behind him, both from earth and from hell, he rarely stopped to consider what would make a mortal bend the knee to a creature from hell.

Not until now, when he looked intently at Mocca's face. For when he looked into Mocca's eyes, they sprawled with a vastness that could never be contained in a mortal frame. And in his stare, Lenk saw a knowing-ness, a certainty that was so broad and so deep that Lenk could not help but listen to Mocca when he said he was more than a weapon.

And he could not help but believe him.

And yet that comforting knowledge lingered in Mocca's stare only for a moment longer. The stare of the man in white was drawn up, toward the statue of Darior, and the darkness of his stare went alight with fear.

"What is it?" Lenk asked.

Mocca took a step backward and drew tense.

Lenk's sword came to his hand as he whirled about and stared up. There, upon the shoulder of the great statue, a stare more hateful than that of the dead god's eye fixed itself upon Lenk. A shadow stirred. A blade flashed. A pair of eyes, cold and blue as a winter that claims an infant, looked down upon him.

"Shuro," he whispered.

She was draped in shadow, but he didn't need to see her to know her. He could feel her stare as keen as any blade. And though she said not a word, he could almost hear the hatred in her breath as she raised her long, thin blade.

And leapt.

She landed on the sand soundlessly and took off toward him. Her face betrayed no emotion, as pale and rigid as a corpse, as she rushed toward him. Yet her eyes were alive with anger.

"Shuro, wait!" he cried out. "Let me explain!"

How exactly he planned to explain betraying her to release a demon she had been training her entire life to kill, he wasn't quite sure.

But, then, he didn't suppose any of that really mattered.

After all, it wasn't like he could talk faster than she could eviscerate him.

She picked up speed, bent low as she rushed toward him. She took her blade up in both hands, narrowing her eyes upon him.

He slid his feet apart and planted them on the earth, ready to take her charge.

Watch her, not the blade, he told himself. *Watch her, not the blade. She'll tell you how she's going to strike.*

He watched her rush. He watched her close the distance between them in another breath. He watched her body tense, her arms draw back, her legs leave the earth.

NOW!

He swung a vicious chop, aiming for her torso.

And he probably would have hit her.

Had she been going for him, anyway.

She didn't look at him, she looked *through* him. And as his blade went arcing, she darted below it, past him, behind him, faster than he could blink.

In fact, he had just gotten around to blinking when he heard the scream behind him.

Funny, he thought, but he always expected demons to die with a lot of fanfare—corpse turning to dust on his blade, flesh burning away in a bright flash of light, that sort of thing.

But when he turned around, all he saw was a dark patch on Mocca's robes blossoming as Shuro jerked her sword out of his side and he slumped, motionless, to the ground.

His body acted before his mind could catch up. Before he could even stop to think about how badly he was outmatched, he tore off running in a spray of sand. She whirled on him, raising her sword. Not high enough to keep his shoulder from barreling into her, though.

He bore her to the earth—trained as she might be, she was still small and he had at least twenty pounds on her—and seized her by the throat with a fury that he hadn't expected to feel, his sword driven by a panic that wasn't there this morning.

The thought of Mocca dying—of all that he promised dying with him—made him raise his sword high and bring it down upon her.

Shuro barely twisted out of the way, her hand lashing up to catch him in the chin. In the moment that he reeled from the blow, her leg shot up and her knee caught him in the belly, knocking him off.

They scrambled to their feet, blades held high. But when Shuro found her footing, there was something off about her. She stood a little too unsteadily, her sword was held a little too tightly, and her anger was plain on her face.

"What have you done?" he asked.

"I killed a demon." Her voice was cold, straining to smother the rage boiling in her throat. "As I was meant to do." She flicked Mocca's blood from her blade. "As *we* were meant to do."

"He was going to fix it," Lenk said, voice hysterical. "He was going to fix *everything*!"

"Is that what he told you? Six words?" She narrowed her eyes. "Is that all it took for you to betray me?"

"I...I didn't..." He let that thought die; there was no way he could deny it. "It wasn't supposed to happen like this. I was ready to kill him, like you were, but then he said—"

"He lied," Shuro interrupted. "Demons lie, Lenk. Demons *always* lie."

"No, he wasn't."

"It is in their blood. As it is in our blood to kill them for—"

"Will you shut the fuck up and listen?" Lenk gestured out, away from the square and toward the distant desert. "You've been up in a monastery this whole time, so you have no idea what's going on out there. There's a war. A big one. One that'll take more lives than any demon could. He could have stopped it," he roared. *"He could have saved her!"*

The words came to him without thinking, ugly and desperate things that tumbled out of his mouth and lay twitching on the sand. And when Shuro heard them, her anger became something soft, something wounded. But only for a moment.

"Not for lies, not for promises, not for a woman can you trust a demon," she hissed, raising her sword. *"Not ever."*

She came rushing toward him, swift as a shadow chased by firelight. He barely had his sword up in time to block her as her blade lashed out. And he barely missed her blade when she twisted away from him and slashed at him, catching him at the arm and drawing a deep cut.

He snarled, swung, found only empty air. She was twisting again, darting behind him, thrusting. He leaned over, avoiding her blade more out of clumsy luck than skill, and she punished him for it by lashing out again, drawing another wound on his leg.

He whirled, backed away from her, tried to put distance between them. She was too quick, too nimble up close. But even as he moved away, he could feel it, a tremor coursing through his body. His sword felt heavier, and his leg trembled as he put weight on it. Her cuts had sliced something out of him, left him a little weaker.

She wasn't trying to kill him. She was trying to disable him. Out of mercy, maybe. Or maybe she just thought a quick kill was kinder than he deserved.

Either way, keeping her at a distance was his best chance, he knew. And so did she. Her blade struck like an asp. He kept backpedaling, blocking what he could, suffering her cuts when he couldn't. She lunged for him; his sword came up to block but only succeeded in driving her blade away from his shoulder and up toward his brow.

Skin split. Blood wept into his eye. And as he staggered backward, he saw her through a haze of red.

Even as furious as she was, her stance was strong, her movements effortless, the sword merely one more part of her body. They had lived together, trained together, spent years becoming one in that monastery of hers.

And that was when his eyes widened.

She came darting in again, blade ready. But he let his eyes drift away from that sword, slick with his own life, and looked down to her legs. She came in close; he felt the wind of her blade as she lashed toward him. And then, he lashed out in kind.

Though not with any blade.

He shot out a foot and let the hard toe of his boot crack against her shin. She let out a cry, the kind of pained shriek that came from people who had never been hit before. Her gait stumbled and she came crashing into him.

He seized her by the collar with one hand, trapping her sword with the other. And by the time she had regained enough sense to look at him, all she would see coming was his forehead as he smashed it against the bridge of her nose.

It felt almost refreshing to have blood on his face that wasn't his own.

She dropped her blade, tearing away with a scream as she darted back from him. It wasn't that she was delicate, he knew. She was simply surprised. She had trained for battle all her life, doubtless read every book, studied every form, learned every lesson she could on the subject of the sword.

But some lessons were best taught in back alleys and tavern brawls. Some lessons were best learned from scars from dirty knives and broken bones setting from sucker punches.

And Lenk had been learning these since he could first hold a sword.

And yet when she staggered away, holding her bloodied nose, she did not return to press her attack. She did not even raise her blade against him. He wasn't so stupid as to think he had beaten the fight out of her with one dirty trick.

Certainly not after she looked at him with tears in her eyes.

"Even now," she hissed, voice quavering. "Even after everything that happened, I wanted to forgive you, Lenk. I wanted to believe that you were tricked, that it could be fixed."

"It's going to be fixed," he said, lowering his blade. "It *was*, anyway. Shuro, understand—"

"That's why I asked them to let me come first," she said. "That's why I asked them to give me a chance."

His blood ran cold. His eyes widened. "Who?"

He didn't have to ask.

Not as he heard feet crunching on sand behind him.

He whirled about. And there they were. Leaping from the walls, landing lightly on the sand, sweeping toward him. Blades bared, their steel the same color as their hair, their eyes all the same shade of piercing blue.

Like his.

Men. Women. Boys. Girls. About a dozen of them. Most of them young, with faces both fresh and hard, free from scars and full of harsh angles, like blades fresh from forges. They came sweeping up to him, arraying themselves in a semicircle. Their blades were raised high as they all slid into the same fighting stance that Shuro had held, but they approached no further. They merely fixed their cold gazes upon him.

"Khetashe," Lenk whispered.

"No," Shuro said from behind him. "We have no gods, Lenk. All we have is our duty. And each other." He glanced behind him and saw her staring at him. "We can…it's not too late. We can try to make this work."

Swords.

Somehow, it always came down to swords. No matter how hard he tried, he could never put it down. And now, knowing all this—about Darior, about himself, about Shuro—even if he did put his weapon down, what good would it do?

He would still be one.

Better to just give in, then. Better to just go with Shuro and these people. Try to do some good as a weapon, do what he did best, do what he was made to do.

"*NO!*"

He all but tore the word from his mouth and thrust it into the ground. His blade was up, held out before in a show of defiance as he turned to face them all, meeting each of their cold stares with one of his own.

"I'm not one of you," he snarled. "I don't fucking know what you are, what you call yourselves, but I'm not one. I don't give a fuck what god died for me, and I don't give a shit what he intended for me. I'm not a weapon. I'm not a sword." He held his blade up above his head. "*This* is. And I will use it to tear each and every one of you fuckers apart, and no god alive or dead will be able to fucking help you!"

As far as threats went, that had to be one of his better ones, he thought.

And it was rather polite of them to allow him a moment to appreciate it as they simply stared at him. But as time went on, and he came to consider just how small his single blade looked against so many of theirs, he began to wonder what they were waiting for.

And then he realized they weren't staring at him, but up toward the sky.

In one breath, a great shadow fell upon Shuro. In one more, it had swallowed the entire courtyard. And in one more, she was flying through the air.

A great flash of bronze and emerald. The sound of the earth shaking. A great cloud of dust as something fell very quickly from very high up. Lenk shielded his eyes from it as the sand blew past him.

And when it cleared, he wasn't sure what to call what he saw. Except its name.

"Oerboros," he whispered.

The creature rose up, his magnificent ten-foot height diminished by the withered stoop of an emaciated and scarred body. In spindly arms, he clutched a massive piece of metal vaguely resembling a sword. Blood wept from his arms, his chest, his legs, wounds that would never close.

Yet even the ruin of his body could not tarnish the glory of his wings: ivory feathers and emerald scales glistening with a light that wasn't there. They twitched around him, still alive and full of vigor. His face, a bronze mask cast in an expressionless stare, looked down on Lenk impassively.

Oerboros. The last living Aeon.

"Mortal," he said, voice distant and chiming like a brass bell. "My apologies for my lateness."

"What are you doing here?" Lenk asked.

"Oh, let's not pretend you don't know."

With one tremendous stride, Oerboros walked over Lenk's head and waded toward the warriors. They backed away, blades held up defensively; they might have been trained to fight otherworldly horrors, but actually seeing one in the flesh, however withered, was something else entirely.

But that fear was only momentary. In another moment, in a sound-less charge, they found their nerve and rushed toward the Aeon, blades bared and thirsty.

His mask betraying nothing, Oerboros raised his massive weapon and began his bloody business.

Lenk saw it only in fragments: blurs of metal as he swept his blade back and forth, bursts of dark red as their blades bit at his withered flesh, crimson staining the magnificence of his wings. And over the screams of the dying and the roars of his agony, he almost missed the sound of feet on sand as Shuro rushed toward him.

He whirled, saw her cold gaze narrowed not on him, but on Oerbo-ros's back. Without thinking, he lunged to impose himself between the

Aeon and the woman. His sword caught hers, tangled each other up as she pressed close to him and he tried to shove her back.

"After everything, you still fight," she snarled. "The demon is dead. This one will follow. It is *over*, Lenk." She broke their deadlock with a savage kick to his belly, driving him backward. "There's no point in fighting further."

The quaver in her voice almost made him think that was a plea. Or maybe a threat? It was hard to tell, what with his breath having been knocked out of him.

Either way, she was right. Mocca was done. Oerboros couldn't stand against so many. There was no sense in fighting just to spit in a long-dead god's eye.

His body, though, didn't seem to believe him: the hands that tightened around the grip of his sword, the feet that took off at a rush, the lips that hurled the last roar he would ever take.

Those parts seemed to think this was a fine thing to die over. And they were speaking quite a lot louder.

Who was he to argue with them?

He came at her with his fury, his scream, his muscle. She met him with silence, with swiftness, with steadiness. He swung in vicious arcs, each one more than enough to kill her. She darted away, ducked low, stepped to the side, barely moving at all.

Even when she brought him down.

Three strokes was all it took: one at his wrist to weaken his grip, another at his calf to slow him down, one more across his hand to knock his sword away. He barely even noticed what had happened before she leapt and delivered a kick to his chest that knocked him to the earth.

He glanced to his sword, moved for it. Her boot slammed down on his chest and drove him to the earth. Her blade was at his throat. When he looked up it, he saw no tears, no sorrow, no regrets. And he knew that she saw the same in his eyes.

There was no room between them for that. No room for anything but three feet of steel and a single breath that Lenk held as he waited for it to plunge into his throat.

Her blow was lightning fast, barely a twitch of her hand. And yet it still was not fast enough to kill him.

A blur of motion, a great shadow, a scream; he wasn't sure what happened, or what was happening. Not until he saw a tremendous hand wrap around Shuro's body and pluck her from the earth.

And then, it became all too clear.

The battle ceased all at once. Oerboros and the cold-eyed warriors alike turned their eyes skyward. Mouths and blades dropped alike in awe as a shadow darker than night, vaster than sky fell upon them.

He loomed over the courtyard as a colossus of naked flesh, growing larger with every breath until Shuro looked like an insect in his grip. Beneath his jaw and above his brow, a halo of serpents writhed, hissed, shrieked in anticipation as he let them loose. His stride shook the earth as he stepped forward and gazed down upon the battle below through eyes the color of a pale moon.

Mocca.

No, he thought, correcting himself. The man in white was gone. This colossus, this *thing* left behind, had a different name.

"Khoth-Kapira," Oerboros said. Blood fell from his wings as he rose up into the sky and made a long, courteous bow. "You do take your time, master."

"Have you not learned?" Khoth-Kapira's voice boomed, sending the sands trembling. *"In all your years of violence, have you not learned? Have you seen any fruits of your labor beyond bloodstains and broken metal? Have you known anything in your lives but violence?"*

The cold-eyed warriors said nothing—or if they did, they were far too small for Khoth-Kapira to have heard.

"All your potential," he rumbled. *"All your wasted years. You never stopped to realize..."*

He raised a massive foot.

"That it all ends the same way."

Some ran. Some screamed. Some merely stood and stared, silent, muttering prayers to gods they didn't believe in. All of them ended the same way.

His foot came down. The earth shuddered. A cloud of dust erupted to smother the stars. For one brief, merciless moment, Lenk could hear Shuro scream.

And when he drew his foot back up, nothing remained but broken swords and greasy smears upon the earth.

Lenk should have fled right then and there, he knew. He should have screamed. Failing all of that, he should have prayed.

But he did not.

He knew who would hear them.

"I am sorry you had to see that."

He looked up. Khoth-Kapira's baleful stare was upon him. All of the serpents blossoming from his face looked down upon him with keen curiosity. Shuro hung limp in his hand, eyes wide with horror, the color gone from her face, as though she had also died down there.

"I am sorry that I had to resort to it." He shook his head with a long, ancient sigh. *"I was meant to stop all this. And here…"* He looked to Shuro in his hand. His eyes narrowed. He began to squeeze. *"It seems I yet have gruesome work to do."*

"NO!"

Lenk's own voice sounded small and insignificant against the rolling thunder of Khoth-Kapira's. He almost didn't believe that his words would reach a creature so high up.

And yet the great demon paused and looked down at him.

"Don't," he said. "Please."

"I spared her once before. And she nearly destroyed this world," he said. *"Is that what you wish, Lenk? That she should ruin all the great works I will accomplish? That she cost so many precious lives with her shortsightedness?"*

"No," Lenk said. "But you can't kill her."

"I beg to differ." Oerboros, wings slowly flapping, hovered beside Khoth-Kapira. "From here, it looks like it would take hardly a flick of the wrist."

"Gods damn it, *NO!*" Lenk roared. He held his sword up, though against such a creature it seemed more an act of petulance than defiance. "No! No more of this! No more blood, no more death, no more massacre! The more you do it, the more you'll need to keep doing it!"

Khoth-Kapira's face was unreadable from so high up. His eyes, along with those of his serpents, were locked upon Lenk.

"Whatever you want to do," Lenk said, "whatever you want from this world, you're not going to get it by killing."

A long silence.

And then a longer sigh, a dark and ancient sound, like a mountain settling upon the mountain of the world. And despite the thunder that was his voice, when Khoth-Kapira spoke, it was with tenderness.

"As you have so often shown me."

He drew a deep breath and, with it, seemed to diminish. And with each successive breath, he grew smaller and smaller. Until finally, Khoth-Kapira was gone and Mocca, naked and small, stood before him once more, the limp form of Shuro in his arms.

The serpents disappeared, slithering back into his flesh. What remained was a soft smile.

"For all my centuries, I still have so much to learn," he said. He looked down at Shuro, frowned. "But I cannot let her threaten me again."

Mocca glanced skyward. And as though this were enough to summon him, Oerboros descended to land in a flutter of wings and a cloud of dust beside him. His empty bronze face looked over the paralyzed woman in Mocca's arms. Then, slowly, he looked to Lenk.

The Aeon's stare, empty and black in his mask of bronze, betrayed no emotion. So perhaps it was just Lenk's imagination that he suspected the creature was smiling at him.

"Curious," he said, in his chiming brass voice, "how often the master seems swayed by mortals." He glanced to Mocca. "One would expect you'd learn."

"If we are to spare mortals the agony of their deaf gods," Mocca replied, "we must strive to show a better example." He offered Shuro up to Oerboros. "Let ours be a portrait of mercy and hope."

"Of course." Oerboros took the woman in one arm, cradling her like an infant. He glanced to the bloody mass of broken bones and shattered swords upon the sands. "Such fine examples we are setting tonight."

His wings stretched out, bearing him and his prisoner aloft. He ascended into the night sky and took off, flying in the direction they had come from, back toward the camp of the Chosen. Lenk felt a pain in the back of his head.

"He's not going to hurt her, is he?" he asked.

"The Aeons, for all their gifts, were cursed with a desire to be loved," Mocca replied. "Even when he wished me dead, Oerboros never had a desire to disappoint me."

"And he did hate you," Lenk said. "I heard him say it. Yet here he is." He glanced to Mocca. "What happened?"

Mocca offered him a smile. "Perhaps I have a talent for persuading people to see things in a larger perspective." He laid a hand on Lenk's shoulder. "You, for example, did more than you realize by standing up to her."

Lenk looked to the empty sky where Oerboros had flown. "She'll be all right, won't she? I have your word?"

"She will. The entire world will, thanks to you." Mocca's smile grew broad, almost ecstatic. "You found your purpose tonight, Lenk. Weapons are used for many reasons. If yours can save more lives, then that is a noble goal, is it not?"

Lenk returned the smile, though it felt heavy and tired on his face, like it might slip off at any moment and land with a thud on the bloody dust. He believed Mocca, for what Mocca said was true, yet a part of him felt worse for hearing it.

After all, no matter whom it saved or killed, a weapon was still covered in blood at the end.

SEVEN

PROPHECY, FRAUD, WHATEVER

At the height of his reign, the sixtieth Emperor Karner claimed that Karneria's strongholds numbered as countless as the stars across the face of the sky.

Of course, after many years of shict raids, slave uprisings, tulwar incursions, and Sainite offensives, the seventy-fifth Emperor Karner brought that number down to something a little more reasonable.

While Karneria was still strong, the Empire's designs for their out-posts switched from quantity to quality. And when it came to quality, the Karnerian definition consisted of being big, black, and imposing as shit.

Such as the one Asper stood before.

Fortress Diplomacy, as it was officially deemed by its occupants, was built not so long ago as an embassy in Cier'Djaal in what was then Temple Square. When the Sainites moved in across the street in what had become Temple Row, it had quickly built up: a tasteful iron gate being replaced by wooden palisades, then by stone walls, then towering iron-reinforced ramparts. And from behind it, construction had begun on the massive statue that now scraped the sky far overhead.

Asper craned her neck, looking up at Daeon the Conqueror. Tower-ing, muscular, clad in dark armor with a pair of horns thrusting from his imposing brow, the stone god had seen better days. Sainite attacks had scorched his face clean off, shorn one of the horns from his head, and broken off his left arm and shoulder.

Still, she thought as she looked to the pile of rubble across the way, he wasn't doing as bad as the Sainite garrison.

The war between the two armies had left Cier'Djaal scarred. Its citizens today lived in constant terror, wondering when the next clash between them would occur and who would be killed in the crossfire.

Asper, as she looked up at the towering metal doors of Fortress Diplomacy, had a different question in mind that day.

"So," she said aloud, "do I just knock or..."

She glanced to her side.

"Or what?"

Her companion offered her an unhelpful look. Or what Asper assumed was an unhelpful look, anyway; it was hard to tell from beneath the hood. But she could clearly make out Scarecrow's unpleasant sneer.

"Ain't our problem," she grunted. "We took care of our part *ages* ago." She glanced around the square warily. "Ain't even supposed to be here. Ain't supposed to be seen together."

Asper cast a look around Temple Row. Where the cobblestones had once thrived with priests, penitents, and the faithful of a dozen different deities, all that remained was rubble, scorch marks, and bloodstains painting months of warfare across the roads.

"I doubt that'll be a problem." She quirked a brow at Scarecrow. "Why *did* you come, anyway?"

"They wanted t'make sure ya got here all right." Scarecrow sniffed. "And ya did, so I'll be on my way."

"Wait, who's 'they'? You never said—"

Asper was cut off by the sudden thrust of a skinny finger in her face.

"Ya just worry about yer part. We did ours." Scarecrow pulled her cloak tighter around her body, turned, and began to stalk away. "Stick to the plan. You're good at that, I hear."

"But what if it doesn't—"

"Then it was nice knowin' ya."

Scarecrow rounded a corner and disappeared before Asper could call out again. She fought the urge to go chasing after her. Not that she expected Scarecrow would provide any more answers, but...

She glanced back up at the looming walls of Fortress Diplomacy.

Just how the hell am *I supposed to do this?*

She closed her eyes and drew in a deep breath.

Calm down. You know the plan. This will work. You can make it work.

There was a pause as she held her breath. Usually, this was the part where she offered a prayer to Talanas. But this time, she refrained.

On the off chance anyone in heaven was listening, she didn't want them to see this next part.

She raised a hand and rapped an echoing knock upon the iron door. A long moment of silence passed. She glanced around the ruins of Temple Row, glancing at shadows, looking to the alleys and corners. With every passing moment, they seemed to stir of their own volition, seemed to creep a little closer every time she took her eyes off them.

Her paranoia was interrupted by a creak of metal, then deafened by a great, rusted groan. The doors slowly eased open, pushed by three Karnerian soldiers—dark-skinned, fine-boned youths in black armor.

As the door swung open, they released the handle. With rehearsed order, they immediately drew swords and swept toward her. She almost turned to bolt when they swept past her, forming a protective ring around her. Their eyes were on the shadows and alleys, just as hers had been.

"Priestess! Madam! Thank you for coming!"

Her attentions were seized by another soldier who came rushing toward her. He stumbled to an awkward halt, fired off an even more awkward salute, and flashed an unbearably awkward grin at her.

"Marcher Pathon, at your service!"

His voice was too shrill, Asper thought, cracking on the last syllable. He was too skinny for his armor, too gangly for the sword at his hip. But it was his grin, so broad as to threaten to burst out of his helmet, that brought a frown to her own face.

Too big, she thought. *His smile's too big for a soldier.*

Only when he started shifting uncomfortably did she realize she was staring.

"Marcher Pathon." She thought to ask him how old he was but realized she couldn't bear the answer. "Your garrison called for me?"

"Ah, yes, priestess. Thank you for coming." He paused, blinked. "Oh, shit. Sorry, I already said that." He coughed. "Not that it's not true, madam. Priestess. Madam."

"Right." She shot him a peculiar look. "What's this all about, then?"

As if you don't already know, she thought, scolding herself inwardly.

"I was sent by our Foescribe, madam," Pathon said. "I'm not permitted to speak casually on the subject." He glanced to the three other soldiers. "All clear?"

"Clear," they grunted, one after the other.

Slowly, they backed away, ushering her into the interior of the fortress. Together, they seized the door and hauled it shut with a massive crash of metal. They swiftly ran to the side, two of them sliding a great metal bar across the door to secure it while the third started hauling what appeared to be heavy sandbags in front of the gate.

Lot of security, Asper noted inwardly. *More than I'd expect, even for soldiers at war.* She swallowed hard, winced. *They did it. Son of a bitch, this might actually work.*

"Priestess?"

She glanced over at Pathon, who made a gesture to follow him. She reached down to her medicine bag and gave it a brief jostle; it weighed exactly as much as it did when she left the temple.

All up to you now, she told herself. And with that, she nodded toward Pathon and followed him as he led her through the courtyard.

With conquests as widespread as theirs had been, there were more than a few legends about the Karnerian Empire: their ferocity, their fanaticism, and their absolute disregard for the rights of anyone outside their empire chief among them. But it was their discipline, the iron machine of their great marches, that was the most renowned.

Asper had often wondered what it might be like inside one of their fortresses. She had always imagined them as bristling with activity: phalanx squares running drills beneath the gazes of bellowing commanders, archer squadrons firing relentlessly into targets, forges belching smoke into the sky in an attempt to slake the Empire's endless thirst for steel.

Funny, she thought, never once had she considered that a fortress full of warriors would look more like people who had just seen war.

The courtyard of Fortress Diplomacy might very well have once held endless drills and marches. Of course, it probably looked a *lot* different before three months of warfare.

The forge had gone cold but for one haggard-looking Karnerian wearily tending to a pile of damaged armor. Whatever straw targets had been used for archery had been broken down to be used as kindling for impromptu campfires. The stones were seared with scorch marks from Sainite fireflasks, the barracks had been consumed by flame, and the soldiers…

Well, there were still plenty of soldiers, at least.

Far from the disciplined squares she had been expecting, the Karnerians huddled around their fires. Some wore bandages that had been soaked through, some lay unmoving on pallets, and even the most hale-looking among them looked like they hadn't slept in days. Only a few wearily looked up as she and Pathon passed, sparing no more than a grunt for Pathon's enthusiastic salutes.

"Talanas," she whispered. "What happened here?"

"Hm?" Pathon glanced over his shoulder. "Ah. Right. Well, the battle to secure safety for the people of Cier'Djaal remains...difficult. We struck a mighty blow in the early days of the war, taking the enemy garrison and bringing low their cliff god. Many of us thought the pigeons would crumble shortly after."

"Pigeons?"

"The Sainites, madam," Pathon replied. "We called them that for those birds they ride. Kind of ironic, isn't it? We didn't even think they'd use them to mount a counterattack."

He gestured to a pair of nearby burnt-out buildings, blackened by long dead fires.

"They dropped a heap of fireflasks on our barracks, burnt us out."

He pointed to the far end of the courtyard, where a marble building rose up, scarred by scorch marks.

"Their fires couldn't get our temple, fortunately."

"So why not put the wounded in there?"

Pathon shot her a queer look. "The wounded? In a temple to the Conqueror?" He shook his head. "We sons of Daeon are hardy. We made do."

He gestured to the various pallets and bedrolls around the courtyard. She didn't doubt that Karnerians were a hardy lot—she had seen them fight, after all. But many nights of sleeping on the cold ground would hinder anyone, even people who weren't living with the fear of fire falling from the sky.

"With all respect, Marcher Pathon," she said, "your optimism seems a bit...misplaced."

"Not at all, madam!" He cast a grin over his shoulder. "Daeon watches over those who march in his name! I myself survived a shict raid on our convoy not two weeks ago and managed to make it to my post here. What do you call that but divine providence?"

"How many were in your convoy?"

"Two hundred fifty-six, madam."

She lofted a brow. "And how many others made it to the garrison?"

"Thirteen," he said with unnerving cheeriness.

She glanced around the camp again. A few tired eyes followed her for a few tired steps but quickly turned back to their campfires. She had seen wounded Karnerians before; she had seen tired Karnerians before. But this was the first time she had ever seen demoralized Karnerians.

The Karnerian belief in Daeon was such that *fanatic* could be used to describe those few casual worshippers. The speakers, their battle-priests, were a constant presence in any Karnerian regiment. Which was when Asper thought to ask…

"All my dealings with your soldiers have been through Speaker Careus. May I ask where he is?"

At this, Pathon froze. And when he turned to face her, the grin was gone from his face.

"The speaker is…" Pathon glanced away nervously. "That is, madam, we didn't know who else to call. The soldiers have heard of you, they say you're the best of the few healers who remain in the city. We would leave this to the medic, but…"

She stared at him intently. "But?"

He paled. "The speaker has been—"

"Marcher Pathon."

Another voice cut through the air with such authority that it might well have impaled Pathon on the spot. He certainly froze in place as though he had been skewered. He turned, slowly, to face who had spoken and Asper peered around him. Her eyebrows rose in appreciation.

She hadn't expected such a booming voice could come from such a small woman.

She, like her fellow Karnerians, stood dark-skinned with dark hair done up in a businesslike bun. Unlike the soldiers surrounding her, though, she stood smaller, slighter. Her draping black garments left her shoulders and arms bare, making her look almost too delicate for this sort of surrounding. Upon the bridge of a delicate nose, a pair of spectacles did little to shield the intensity of the stare she fixed on Pathon.

"Foescribe." He snapped to a stiff salute. "As you commanded, I have—"

"I did. And you have," the woman replied with a voice just as stiff. "Kindly return to your phalanx."

"Yes, but, madam, I—"

"Marcher."

Her voice like a bone breaking, the command came out swiftly and sent Pathon scurrying away just as quick. The soldier spared a brief nod for Asper, his grin all but gone, as he disappeared.

"Asper. Priestess."

As the woman approached her, Asper could see that she carried something. Clutched in the crook of her arm with the sort of protectiveness one might cradle an infant was a thick scroll bound with a thin black chain. She quickly unclasped the chain and unfurled it, glancing it over while casting fleeting looks at Asper.

"Northern descent, strong chance of Muraskan origin," she said. "Just short of six feet of height, approximately short of one hundred and…" She glanced back up at Asper, removed a quill from her sash and made a quick notation. "Fifty pounds."

"Hey!" Asper protested.

"Faith: Talanite," the woman continued, ignoring her. "Position: Priestess. Seventeen complaints lodged from various commanding positions in the Imperial Legion describing persistent meddling in areas of Empire-Sainite conflict. Eighteen complaints lodged describing unwarranted profanities and invectives launched at them—"

"Oh, that's oxshit—"

"Nineteen." She made another little note in her scroll before furling it up, clasping the chain over it, and returning it to the protective crook in her arm. She then looked at Asper, taking in her incredulous stare with a flat expression. "Is something amiss, priestess?"

"Yeah, something like that." She furrowed her brow. "I didn't even know there *were* women in the Karnerian military, let alone ones who have an unnerving fascination with me."

"All Imperials serve in the Divine Mandate, priestess," the woman replied. "Men have their duties. We women of the Arda Scriptis have our own. Knowing thoroughly potential dangers to the Mandate is one such duty." She looked down at Asper, somehow, despite being half a head shorter. *"Not* a fascination."

"Women of the what?"

"To the layperson, such as Marcher Pathon, the Arda Scriptis are commonly known as Foescribes. Such a term will suffice, if it's easier for you."

"All right." Asper rubbed the back of her neck. "*Or* I could call you by your name?"

The woman arched a brow, as though this were a novel concept. "If it is necessary." She inclined her head in a bow. "Haethen Caladerus. Thank you for answering our summons, priestess." She eyed Asper's left arm in its sling. "Are you capable of performing duties so incapacitated?"

Asper adjusted her arm slightly. "More than capable. Is that what this is about?"

"I..." Haethen paused, glancing around. "This is not the place to discuss it, priestess." She made a beckoning gesture and started walking toward the rear of the fortress, where the looming temple stood. "Please, come with me. All will be explained in time."

"Of course," Asper said, making certain to sigh just loud enough so that Haethen would be certain to hear her.

She didn't want the Foescribe realizing she already knew what she was needed for.

Within moments of entering the Temple of Daeon, Asper began to see why Pathon had scoffed at the idea of housing the injured here.

After what seemed like an hour of waiting here, Asper began to wonder how, with so much devotion for the Conqueror here, there was any room for his faithful.

From the entryway to the central chamber to which she had been led, every room was less a place of worship and more a place of war. Every wall bristled with displays of crossed spears, shining shields, and tapestries scrawled with Imperial oaths. Every floor was crowded by tables laden with charts, maps, logbooks, and manifests. And those few spaces that were not dedicated to waging war were dominated by the horned god who demanded it.

At the center of the chamber, towering over her in a suit of black iron armor, the statue of Daeon watched over the room with a scowl beneath sweeping horns. He leaned heavily on a massive blade, as though ready to spring to life and decapitate any who might displease him.

Far from intimidated, Asper looked over the armored effigy with a sour indignity.

For just a fraction of the wealth that had been used to decorate this statue, she could have bought supplies to save at least a hundred lives.

But then... She looked up into the statue's scowl with a sigh. *You don't go looking to a war god to save lives, do you?*

That was probably why Haethen had excused herself, bidding Asper to await her here, she reasoned. She knew enough about Karnerians to know that they valued displays of power as much as power itself. Keeping her waiting was obviously an attempt to make it clear that Asper was here at the Empire's pleasure.

And while she had endured several such shallow displays of power in her time at Cier'Djaal, it was only with this one that she started to worry.

This was a mistake, she thought, glancing around the chamber. *They know. How could they not know? This is the Empire of fucking Karneria you're trying to fuck with, not some backwater dimwits. They've brought you here to have you killed. This was the dumbest thing you've—*

Something caught her eye. And in another moment, self-abuse no longer seemed like the most productive thing in the room to do.

Besides the war god himself, the largest thing in the room was a sprawling table with an elaborate map of Cier'Djaal and the surrounding regions upon it. Asper wandered closer and saw several small wooden icons dotting it. Black icons dotted Temple Row and the surrounding area while several blue icons remained scattered around Harbor Road.

Troop positions, she thought. *Black for Karnerian, blue for their Sainite enemies, and...*

Her eyes drifted away, down toward the end of the sprawling table, across the long map. Over Cier'Djaal's paper walls, across the parchment desert, down the roads of ink to a small drawing of four stone walls and a collection of huts.

"Jalaang," she whispered, reading the inscription.

The city she had just come from. The city someone she had once called friend had conquered. The city whose walls held an army he was building to burn down Cier'Djaal.

On this map, with all its grand designs and icons like a great game board, there was nothing on Jalaang: no icon, no game piece, not so much as a single note of "reminder to self: lots of hideous ape-men that want to kill us hanging out here."

They don't even know, she thought. *They're so paranoid about the Sainites, they have no fucking clue that the tulwar are going to come raze this city. Those stupid pieces of—*

She paused, drew in a deep breath.

Easy. Anger won't help here. Remember the plan. She stared down at the map of Cier'Djaal and all its parchment towers. *Remember why you need the plan. Remember that this—*

"Priestess?"

She whirled a little more swiftly than she intended to at the sound of Haethen's voice. And when she beheld the woman, the welcoming smile from before was gone, replaced by the iron glower and tightly pursed lips from before.

"Something has caught your eye, I take it."

"Your war looks as though it will continue to drag on," Asper observed. "There's a lot of blue on this map."

Ire flashed across Haethen's face for a moment. "It was my understanding that Talanites took no side in this conflict."

"Talanites are here to save lives," Asper replied. "The side we take is against any who raise blades against the helpless." She eyed the troop formations across the map with a sneer. "Turns out neutrality does fuck-all for that."

"I sympathize," Haethen replied in a tone that suggested *sympathy* and *contempt* were synonyms to her. "The battle has been more protracted than we expected. Sainite mobility has proven detrimental to nailing down their location." She inhaled sharply, then drew herself up. "Still, we have no doubts that the war will end in Karnerian favor."

"Yeah?" Asper glanced over her shoulder. "So you called me here merely to reassure me of that?"

Haethen's face twitched ever so slightly. "The Empire does not seek consult from outside sources. The logistics of the Arda Scriptis are such that—"

"Because even if you defeat the Sainites, you'll still have a ravaged husk of a city and a people you've slaughtered for the past month."

"That, too, can be dealt with. Once the Sainite threat is conquered, we can move toward reassuring—"

"And what then? After the Sainites, what about the tulwar in the lands beyond the walls? What about the shicts? What about the—"

"*I can handle it!*" Haethen suddenly snapped. Anger did not so much flash as flood across her face. She swept past Asper, thrusting a finger toward the troop formations on the map. "I have studied *every* treatise, *every* manual, *every* historical account in the Imperial Library. I can choke the Sainites, I can fend off the savages, I can save Cier'Djaal. And if Careus were here, he'd—"

She stopped suddenly, whirling on Asper with her horror in her eyes as she realized what she had just said. Asper fixed Haethen with a scrutinizing glare. The woman's mouth hung open, still trying to hold on to the words she had just so carelessly blurted out.

Her face twisted into a cringe, then a grimace, and then, finally, it all but melted off her with as she released a very long, very low sigh. When she removed her spectacles and looked back to Asper, it was as though she were staring at a different person.

The Imperial sternness and rigidity had disappeared, leaving behind a woman who looked almost too young to be here. But the youth of her face was starkly at odds with the deep, sleepless rings beneath her eyes that her spectacles had so gallantly hidden.

"Understand, priestess," Haethen began, her voice softer, "that a Foescribe is a highly specialized role. We memorize, we study, we plan. Our duty to the Empire is to learn, not to lead. I'm…" She rubbed her eyes. "We lost all our commanders to Sainite strikes. Everyone but Careus. I'm the last one remaining and I wasn't… I'm not supposed to…"

Asper reached out and placed her hand on Haethen's shoulder. She felt tension radiating out of the woman, a weary stress that she recognized quite keenly. The widowed mother, the ailing man, the boy with the limp; she knew that tension of a strong person ready to snap. And when Haethen looked up at her, she offered her no comforting smile. Strong people didn't need that. She merely looked at her and spoke simply.

"Haethen," she said, "where is Careus?"

—•—⊷⊶—•—

Dilation of the pupils. Involuntary muscle spasms. High fever. Symptoms common enough to a variety of illnesses; ones she had expected.

The paling of flesh to the point that the veins of his body shone black and ragged through his skin, though?

That, she hadn't expected.

When Asper had first met Speaker Careus, dark-skinned and shorn of hair, he had looked more statue than man: muscles carved of dark stone and wrapped in black armor, a face unflinching in its sternness and a voice unwavering in its forcefulness.

Now, as he lay upon the cot in a back room of the temple, his blankets black with sweat and the air sick with the scent of pain, he looked frail. His piercing eyes were shut tight in trembling agony. His bellowing voice was a soft whimper with each staggered breath he took. And his muscular body was a ruin. His dark skin was so pale that his veins were visible and pronounced beneath, an ugly map of the illness ravaging his body.

Just like they said he'd be, Asper thought.

"It began days ago," Haethen said from behind her. "One moment, he was reviewing our deployment, the next he just..." She gestured to his twitching, prone form. "Dropped."

Asper nodded. She made a show of glancing around the room, noting the water jug, the washbasin, the numerous field medical textbooks— all grossly out-of-date, she noted.

"Has he slept at all?" she asked, like she didn't know. "Or has he just been twitching this whole time?"

"He hasn't responded to us, nor has he stopped moving." Haethen rubbed her eyes. "Our medics are useless. They're trained for stitching wounds and treating whorehouse diseases. They couldn't even begin to guess what had happened to him."

Asper pursed her lips, staring intently at Careus for a long moment.

"Priestess."

She felt Haethen's urgent, heated gaze upon her before she even turned to face her. But when she looked upon the woman, she didn't anticipate seeing someone who looked like she was ready to fall to pieces.

"The medics urged me not to call upon you," she said. "It would be severely compromising for anyone to learn of the speaker's condition." She glanced over the rim of her spectacles. "The risks I took to bring you here... That is, if I brought you here and you can't..."

Haethen left her words hanging; she had neither the force to make a threat nor the strength to finish that thought. But she didn't need to, Asper knew. For there was more at stake here than Haethen suspected.

And so much of it depended on what Asper said next.

"Do you believe in gods?"

Haethen looked at Asper as though she had not so much asked a question as hitched up her robes and urinated on Careus's face.

"I am loyal to the Empire," she said, "as the Empire is loyal to Daeon. It is through the Conqueror that Karneria was forged in red fire, through him that its glories spread beyond its—"

"I didn't ask if you could recite scripture," Asper said. "I asked if you believed in gods."

"Yes," Haethen answered softly, after a moment. "I do."

Asper nodded, then looked back to Careus, twitching and sweating upon the cot.

"Everyone does, don't they?" she whispered. "No matter how awful things get, no matter how many people die, everyone still believes the gods will fix things."

Asper knelt down beside Careus, knees creaking with a familiar pain. With a wince, she pulled the strap of her medicine bag over her head, cringing as it brushed her broken left arm. At the touch, something within the shattered bone stirred. She tried to ignore it.

"Did you pray for him?" Asper asked.

"We held a beseeching service to Daeon," Haethen replied, "assembling all viable soldiers for—"

"Haethen."

Asper looked over her shoulder.

"Whatever happens next, happens not because of what you think the gods want, but because of what you did." She fixed the woman with a long gaze. "Did you pray for him?"

Haethen met Asper's stare. "I did."

"How long?"

A pause. She spoke more softly. "Every moment I could spare."

"And how many was that?"

A bleak silence hung between them. The answer was painted in the despair creeping in at the edges of Haethen's face. Asper nodded slowly.

"There comes a point when it's too much, isn't it?" she whispered. "There comes a point when you realize that the longer you pray, the deeper the silence will be when the gods don't answer you."

Asper slid her free hand into the sling around her broken arm.

Beneath her fingers, she could feel the flesh of the damaged limb tremble and quiver. At the back of her head, she could hear a dark voice whisper.

"What did you expect to happen, I wonder?"

Asper pulled free from the cloth a silver pendant: a Phoenix, sacred symbol of Talanas.

"Don't answer that," Asper said. "I think everyone expects the same thing: The clouds part, the heavens open up, and something happens, right? Fire rains from the sky, a divine light reaches down, maybe a big bearded guy looks down and smiles on you. Something like that."

Asper delicately wrapped the chain of the pendant around her wrist, holding the pendant tightly in the palm of her right hand. She studied it, looking over its dull and tarnished metal, noting the jagged tear where one of its wings had been broken off.

"I think I always expected that, too," she said. "It took me a long time to realize that the gods never send fire or light or anything like that." She wrapped her fingers around the pendant and closed her eyes. "You pray hard enough ... the gods send someone like me."

Her hand snapped out. Something inside her quivered with anticipation. She pressed the pendant to Careus's brow as though it were a branding iron. He let out a shuddering breath. Behind her, Haethen let out a cry.

"What are you—"

Asper did not hear her. Asper could not hear her over the sound of her own voice. She began to chant in an old tongue, a tongue she had pored over in dusty texts in lonely libraries on dark nights when her sole company was a dark whisper. The same dark whisper that spoke to her now.

Fraud, Amoch-Tethr whispered.

She spoke louder, raising her voice to fill the room and send the lights of the candles quivering and the beads of sweat trembling upon Careus's flesh.

You cannot save them, he hissed.

She let her voice rise until her chant was a thing unto itself, a living creature tearing itself out of her throat, reaching out to shake the windows and send the shadows creeping as the candlelight quivered.

And still, it was not enough to silence him.

You know how this will end.

Asper shut her eyes tighter, raised her voice louder. She pressed the symbol of Talanas against Careus's collarbone. Beneath her hand, the man twitched, then jolted. His mouth craned open in a scream as she pressed the symbol closer against him.

"What's happening?" Haethen demanded. "What are you doing to him? *STOP!*"

She said other things, Asper knew. And she knew that only because she could feel Haethen's hands around her, trying to pull her off. But she steeled herself, leaned into Careus, pressed the holy symbol more violently against him until the jagged edge of its broken wing cut his flesh.

Her chant, the old Talanic tongue, was little more than a scream now, a formless howl into which she poured everything, every breath and every sound and every last bit of her strength.

And when it was done and Haethen pulled her away, she all but collapsed to the floor.

"I knew it," the Karnerian woman whispered. "I knew I should have listened to the medics. Imperial business should be taken care of by Imperials, but I thought..." She shook her head. "You were supposed to be the best healer in the city."

"I am," Asper replied, voice hoarse. She looked up at Haethen through heavy-lidded eyes. "I thought you said you believed."

"I believe in gods," Haethen said. "But I *know* that four hundred men are relying on me to see our mission through to completion. We *needed* Careus and all you did was..."

"Foescribe."

A voice, ragged with pain and exhaustion, but not enough to weaken its depth. The two women looked up to the cot to see a body rising on trembling legs, standing sweat-soaked and twitching, looking as though it could barely stand.

But he did.

Speaker Careus stood.

His breath came slow, deep, pained. But with each inhale, the color returned to his flesh. The dark lines of his veins slowly faded. And though his face was long with weariness and his body quaked, he stood, hale and whole and alive.

"Careus."

Haethen rose and approached him slowly, as though wary of what had brought him back. Or perhaps just leery of the fact that he was totally nude, Asper thought. It didn't matter now. She had done what she had come to.

"How did..." She looked from the speaker to Asper as the priestess rose to her feet. "What did you do? What magic—"

"*No.*"

It hurt to speak, let alone to shout, but Asper found the strength to do so, to force fire into her voice and iron into her scowl.

"No magic. No scripture. No prayers." She stiffened, rising high. "Heaven does not speak through words. I know that now. It speaks through actions, it speaks through miracles." She narrowed her eyes. "It speaks *through me.*"

She gestured toward a window, to some far-off place.

"I have come not at your behest, but at the command of a power higher than you could dream of. I have come to deliver you from darkness, and you, in your petty squabbles and the misery you sow, have been blind to it. A storm approaches, one that will raze the ruin you have made of this city and make into meat the people you claim to liberate."

She regarded the Karnerians coolly.

"And I have come to stop it."

Haethen stared at her not with the shock she expected, but with a cold scrutiny, as though she could narrow her eyes so thin as to slice through Asper's words and flesh and see what lurked beneath.

Careus did not stare. Careus staggered forward on shaking legs. Careus loomed over her, staring down at her through eyes that had seen the slaughter of thousands and had never blinked.

And, slowly, dropped to a knee.

"Careus—" Haethen caught herself. "*Speaker.* It is highly improper to—"

"It came to me swiftly, Foescribe," Careus replied, his voice black and ragged. "One moment I was standing, speaking, whispering. The next, I was..." He lowered his head, closed his eyes. "I have told myself that I am ready to die in Daeon's name, all this time, to join the Eternal Army. But when it happened, when I fell... I saw only darkness.

"All that we have done for the Conqueror," he whispered, "it has not been enough. He has brought us here, to this moment, to show us our true task."

When Careus looked up at Asper, his eyes were as dark and foreboding as ever. Yet beneath all the sternness and iron of his stare lingered something bright, something Asper had not seen for a very long time.

"Tell me what we must do, prophet," he said.

The sound of iron was in her ears. And the feel of a hundred eyes was upon her.

She did not turn around as the gates of Fortress Diplomacy slammed shut behind her. Nor did she turn around to see the dozens of soldiers upon its battlements.

Perhaps a priestess, humble and desperate, would want to see them looking at her with all their fear and all their awe.

But a prophet? A prophet did not need to look to know.

And so, without turning around, she turned and walked away, wearing their astonishment like a cape with no end.

It wasn't until she had rounded the corner that she allowed herself to collapse against a wall. She barely felt the cold stone of the wall through the heat that was roiling through her.

Her left arm was searing with pain, bursting with so much heat she thought her sling would catch fire. Within the broken limb, she could feel it, even if she couldn't see it. A red eye opened wide and stared at her. A wide smile opened and revealed black teeth. A voice of smoke and flame spoke inside her.

Amoch-Tethr.

Ah, you were cruel to remove us from that place, he purred inside her. *I could all but taste their desperation. Their war goes poorly. Their dead grow each day. Fortunate you came along to feed them that lie, hm?*

"Not a lie," she whispered. "Not where it counts."

Of course not. Your motives are just stainless, aren't they? You'll send them to die fighting that lizard you called a friend and praise your deaf gods for the blood spilled. Maybe they'll erect a statue of you.

"Shut up," she hissed. *"Shut up."*

But it's all for naught, isn't it? It's not like you're going to live to see it. He chuckled blackly. She felt something shift inside her. *I could feel it, you know. How you screamed that nonsense to keep them from realizing how much pain you were in. Something's broken inside you, my dear. Something I can fix.*

"No."

All you need to do is listen.

"No!"

All you need to do . . . is let me help you.

"NO!"

"No what?"

She opened her eyes. A figure stood over her.

Hands on skinny hips, Scarecrow stared down at Asper with a quirked brow. Behind her, another figure—a squat man in soot-stained leather armor with a thick burlap cloth wrapped around his head—peered at her through a wooden visor.

"Thf fhck fh mfttfr whth hfr?" He muttered something unintelligible.

"Aw, lay off her," Scarecrow grunted. She grinned down at Asper. "She's probably havin' a vision or some shit like that. She's a prophet now. Or ain't you heard?"

Asper clenched her teeth, forcing herself to ignore the pain and the voice inside her alike. She staggered to her feet, glaring at Scarecrow through weary eyes.

"How did you know that?"

"We were on a roof nearby," Scarecrow said. "Heard you screamin' through the damn windows. The Karnies looked impressed." She waggled her eyebrows. "Plan went good, I'm bettin'."

Asper reached into her sling and removed her pendant. Scarecrow's hand shot out and snatched it from her. She turned the trinket over, revealing a small vial attached to the back with wire, a thick needle sticking out of it. She glanced over it, totally drained but for a few droplets of bright blue liquid.

"I hope this is empty because you stuck him with it," she grunted, "and not because you drank it."

"Wfsn't fhsy pfhsfnfng hfm," the shrouded man said.

"Yeah, it wasn't easy sneakin' the poison into his tea," Scarecrow said. "Damn place was crawlin' with scalps. And the couthi said he needs to take the *whole thing* to be cured."

"He took it all," Asper said. "I was there."

"And no one saw you slip it to him?"

"As you say, I was screaming," Asper replied. "The Foescribe...I think she might have suspected something."

"If she does, she ain't suspectin' the right thing," Scarecrow said. She pried the vial off the pendant and tossed the trinket back to Asper. "Far as I can tell, whole plan went off like a rich man in a whorehouse." She glanced to her shrouded companion. "Hey, Sandal."

"Thft's nft mh nhmf."

"I ain't care." She tossed him the vial. "Take this back to the boss. And make sure you ain't seen."

"*Whftfvhr*," the man grunted, tucking the vial into his armor. *"Lfkh yfh frh thf hpfthmf hf stfhlth."*

He stalked off, disappearing around a corner.

"Who's this boss you're speaking of?" Asper asked.

"Ain't important."

"We just poisoned a man," Asper replied, glaring at Scarecrow. "He looked into my eyes like he believed everything I was saying."

"Means you're better at lyin' than you thought."

"It *means* everything we're doing is important. If we're going to do this, I need to know—"

Scarecrow's hand shot out, clapped over Asper's mouth. She sneered, revealing yellow teeth, many of them missing.

"Ain't. Important." She released Asper, turning to stalk away. "You got few enough friends in this city to go shittin' on the ones'll help you. Boss wants to meet you, he'll meet you. Not before. Besides, I were you? I'd be worryin' 'bout bigger things."

She loosed a black chuckle as she turned and walked away.

"You done good with the Karnies. Now let's see if you can trick the Sainites half as well."

EIGHT

WHERE WE BURY OURSELVES

Poison, maybe?

Kataria idly scratched an itch on her belly. She sniffed, staring at the sunlight shafting through the fronds of the tree overhead.

Shekune wants to poison the entire city of Cier'Djaal, right? She wouldn't ever expect someone to poison her. *One sip of water from a tainted cup and* bwong! *She's dead, the shicts don't attack, the humans don't retaliate, no one dies.*

She chuckled to herself.

Yeah, it's just that easy. All you have to do is find where she's heading through hundreds of miles of desert, sneak through her thousands of warriors without being seen, poison what you hope *is her cup, wait until you* hope *she drinks from it and . . .*

She sighed.

She doesn't drink from it. She slaughters Cier'Djaal. Humans retaliate. Everyone dies.

She shut her eyes.

Okay, so more straightforward. You call her to a duel. Make this quick. Her pride won't let her turn it down. You just track her down, again, through hundreds of miles of desert and . . . She clicked her tongue. *She kicks the shit out of you, force-feeds you your own tongue, slaughters Cier'Djaal, humans retaliate, everyone dies.*

A hot breeze picked up, sending the fronds of the tree swaying. She raised her hand to shield her eyes from the beam of sun that came shooting through.

Okay, so what else is there? Trigger a yiji stampede on her? Drive her into a tulwar ambush? Hit . . . hit her with a rock? A big rock?

One by one, she ran through the options. One by one, she ran through the scenarios.

She sees the yiji stampede coming a mile away, goes to its source, then kills you. She kills the tulwar, like she's killed all the other tulwar, then kills you. She finds you trying to lift a big rock, watches you hurl it, like, a foot, then kills you, then laughs at you because what the fuck kind of plan was that?

And one by one, with a weary sigh, she ran through the outcomes.

She slaughters Cier'Djaal. Humans retaliate. Everyone dies.

Everyone dies. Everyone.

That word did not so much echo inside her head as it did embed. It jabbed itself into her skull like a knife, twisted itself around and around.

Everyone dies. Asper dies. Gariath dies. Kwar dies. Sai-Thuwan dies. Denaos dies... well, no, he'd probably survive somehow. Dreadaeleon dies. The thought twisted itself, tore something open inside her. *Lenk dies.*

If he's not already dead.

Maybe he is. Maybe they all are. Maybe this is just how things go and you're fucking stupid for even trying, you stupid piece of shit. Why are you even acting like you can do this? You abandoned Lenk, you let Thua die, you couldn't even... you can't...

She clenched her teeth, pressed the heels of her palms against her eyes, tried to force hot tears back inside her eyes. Failed.

You can't. You can't. You can't. You can't. You can't.

Her heart raced inside her chest. Her breath came out in short, ragged gasps. Her skin split as she dug her nails into her forehead.

Her ears folded themselves over, pressed flat against her head. Everything went quiet. For a long time.

The wind shifted again. The shade returned to her. She opened her ears. Water lapped nearby. She let out a long breath.

Okay?

She nodded to herself.

"Yeah, okay."

And she got up.

She brushed sand from her breeches, then trudged across the earth toward the edge of the oasis. One of a few hundred that dotted the desert, this one wasn't so large as to be suitable enough to build a village on like the others were. This one was barely large enough to support a few trees and clusters of scrub grass.

But for their purposes, it would serve. Their yijis certainly didn't seem to mind. The beasts looked up as Kataria retrieved her boots and bow from the shore, then returned to lazily lapping up mouthfuls of water.

They had been roaming the desert for a few days now. It had begun, in theory, as an attempt to track the movements of Shekune's army across the desert. But shicts did not move like armies should, and as the days dragged on, it became clear that trying to track hunters who knew every side of every dune for four hundred miles was an idiot's errand.

And so, their search had turned to mostly aimless wandering as Kataria had tried, and failed, to think of something better and Kwar had...

Kataria muttered a curse under her breath. She tugged her boots on, nearly falling over as she did so. She strung her bow over her shoulder, fixed her quiver to her belt, made a quick count of her arrows.

Ten. She turned over the number in her head, clicked her tongue. She looked up toward the crest of a nearby dune. *Figure you'll have to shoot her with... what? Maybe two to make her move? So that's eight to hunt with tonight.*

She sighed, started trudging toward the dune.

Or maybe I'll need to use the knife today.

She rounded the dune and was greeted by a chill. They had—or rather, she had—built camp in the shade of the dune to protect from the sun. The fire had long since gone out, leaving cold ashes behind. The waterskin lay drained and empty nearby. The desert hare she had killed had gone cold over the fire, barely any of it eaten. The tent lay in a mess of canvas and sticks.

None of this seemed to bother Kwar.

The khoshict was exactly where she had been since last afternoon: the same spot in the same dirt that she had fallen in after another day of riding in numb silence, like any other day. She lay on her back, staring up at the sky through glassy eyes. Just a husk of skin and hair and cloth.

Kwar was gone. Kwar was left in tears drying on the sand, in screams emptied into the night, in long and mournful Howling that disappeared in the dawn. Of the woman Kataria had left Cier'Djaal with, there was nothing left.

"You going to get the fuck up today or what?"

Granted, Kataria wasn't sure spewing curses at her would help that. But the days were becoming hotter and her ideas were becoming fewer.

And still, Kwar said nothing.

"Because you've been lying there for hours and nothing seems to be changing," Kataria grunted, glancing around the camp. "Fire's out, tent's down, food's not even eaten. Do you think you're helping?" A snarl crept into her voice. "I'm out there trying to stop a massacre and you're just—"

Kwar didn't cringe at her words. Kwar didn't so much as blink. Yet Kataria caught herself, all the same. She shut her eyes tight, held her breath, forced her voice lower, soft as she could make it.

"I've turned it over time and time again in my head, thinking there was something I missed," Kataria said. "That there was some way I could end this all, make Shekune see reason, make the other shicts listen, something. I don't know, maybe there still is. But I can't think of it. I can't think of anything that doesn't end with someone dying.

"And if it has to be that way, then it has to be Shekune," she said. The words fell out of her mouth, heavy with impossibility. "Kill her, the tribes lose their leader, their will to fight. That's all I can come up with. But I need to find her, first. If that's the way to do it, anyway. If I've missed anything, if there's another way I'm not seeing, I . . ."

She looked down at her hands, at the calluses on her fingers from bows drawn and arrows fired. She'd killed many creatures before today: for food, for protection, sometimes for fun. This shouldn't be any different. Just one more death.

Yet somehow, it felt like much more.

"Kwar," she whispered, "get up."

Kwar didn't get up.

Kwar didn't move. She barely breathed. Her ears hung limp from her head, lying in the sand. Her eyelids twitched slightly. And that was it. Maybe she hadn't even heard Kataria.

Or maybe it's time for the knife, Kataria thought.

"I don't think I can."

Kwar was not speaking to her. Not directly. She spoke to the sky, as though she were simply breathing and words just came out with her breath.

"My head feels heavy," Kwar said. "Like it's filled with iron. And if I try to move, I might break my neck."

She fell silent for a long time. When she spoke again, her words were so soft that Kataria strained to hear them.

"I don't know what I did," she said. "I just sit here and I keep wondering what I did wrong. I don't know if it was the time I made my mother cry or the time I hit Thua or…something. I don't know. But everything…everything I had, I lost. And I don't know why I did."

"Kwar…" Kataria began, but Kwar did not seem to hear her.

"When my mother died, all I could think about was killing humans. I kept thinking that if I could just kill enough of them, I'd make it better. But whenever I tried to think of them, of the humans that killed her that I had to kill, all I could see was her face. And now…whenever I see her face, I see Thua's face with her. I see him crying, I see him laughing, and I…he just feels like a dream, like he was never there, so I try to get up and move and…I fall down."

Her body shuddered. As though it were trying to shed tears she didn't have, loose a scream she lost long ago.

"I don't have a name for it, when I know things are okay. I barely know what it is, just that I know when I have it and when I don't. I can never hold on to it. I only get it for a few days and then it's gone. And I can't figure out how to get it back or what I did to lose it and I wonder if I lie here…will everything just be easier if I stop trying to find it?"

Kataria had never thought of herself as stupid. Far from it, she was the one who was clever enough not to waste time on stupid conversations and stupid ideas. She was made for shooting arrows, stabbing knives, and generally beating problems to death.

Not…this.

Whatever this was, this thing happening to Kwar, to her, she couldn't shoot it, she couldn't kill it. All she could do was stand there, like an idiot, staring at the empty air Kwar's words disappeared into.

Which was probably why she started cursing.

"Fuck that," she snarled. "*FUCK THAT.* We didn't come this far to hear that! We didn't see so many people die, with so many more to come, to hear that! I can't…I can't *use* that, Kwar!" she all but roared, her voice carrying across the dunes. "I can't stop Shekune by myself! I can't save everyone if you don't get up! So get up."

Kwar did not get up.

"Get up, Kwar."

Kwar did not move.

"Get up."

Kwar closed her eyes, let out a breath, and lay still.

There were more words she could have said, Kataria thought. Tender words she had whispered in dark places, ones that had moved Kwar before. But she clenched her jaw tight, ground those words between her teeth, spit them onto the ground in a thick phlegm as she turned around and left.

She wouldn't waste anything more on the woman who had kidnapped her, who had made her abandon everything, who now lay as useless and limp as a dead fish on dry earth. No more breath, no more words.

Words weren't arrows.

Words couldn't kill anyone. Words couldn't save everyone. Words couldn't stop Shekune.

She would solve this with arrows. With poison, with yijis, with rocks, with whatever she had to use to stop Shekune, to save the shicts, to save the humans, to save Asper and Dreadaeleon and...

And Lenk.

And if she had to do it without Kwar, then so be it.

She stopped by the oasis pool, gathered up what supplies and water she had left there, and hitched them to her belt. She glanced up and saw that the yijis were gone. Perhaps they had heard that outburst and left, or perhaps they saw some prey to chase. Kataria didn't care.

She snorted, spit, and stormed off.

Her storming turned to a stalking turned to a weary trudging as she put more tracks behind her and the oasis grew distant. While she might not have had any words to waste on Kwar, she found that she had quite a few thoughts to spare on her.

Most of them angry.

Stupid fucking idiot, she snarled inside her own skull. *Stupid fucking idiot with her stupid fucking... whatever. Does she not see what I'm trying to do? Or does she just not care? Does she think I'm doing this for the humans? For Lenk?*

Aren't you?

"No!" Kataria snarled aloud.

Not just for them, anyway. I'm not saying we need to live in peace with them. We just... can't fight them this way. There are so many of them and they'll kill us all. Can't she see I'm doing this for us? Our people? She won't even help. I'm the one who has to save the shicts.

Those thoughts grew heavy in her skull, made her feet sink deeper into the sand, made her head bow itself under the weight until she stopped and stared down at the earth. And the realization bore down on her like the heat.

Save the shicts, she thought. *When you can't even save one.*

Words were not arrows. Words couldn't kill. She had severe doubts that words could do much of anything. But some of them felt very satisfying to say.

"Fuck."

Like that one.

She ran her hands over her face, turned around, and started stalking back toward the oasis.

She kidnapped you, she reminded herself.

She hadn't forgotten.

You told her never to touch you again.

She had meant it.

So why bother?

She didn't have an answer.

Not one in her head, anyway.

The sun had just begun creeping low in the sky as she drew closer to the oasis. The sands were painted orange and the scrub grass looked like jagged shadows across its face. The dune where they had made camp still loomed and she knew she'd find Kwar on the other side, still.

The plan hadn't changed. She would find new yijis. She would find Shekune. She would stop her plan, her war, and the slaughter that would follow. She would save everyone.

Starting with Kwar.

Just as soon as you think of what to tell her to make her get up, she thought.

"Fuck," she whispered breathlessly to herself as she drew nearer to the oasis and the scrub grass loomed large. "No, that didn't work last time. Maybe 'Hey, listen, could you maybe put this off, whatever you're doing, until I can kill the leader of our people?' Probably not." She snorted. "I'm going to have to apologize, aren't I?"

"Did you say something?"

Her ears shot straight up. Her feet froze in their tracks.

"I don't know. Have I said anything to you for the last six hours?"

"No."

Voices. Two of them. Gruff, angry, unfamiliar.

"No?"

And she was moving again.

She went low to the ground, creeping swiftly toward a hedge of scrub grass. She pulled her bow from her back, an arrow from her quiver, and nocked it as she ducked behind the foliage and peered through its branches.

"Then what makes you think I'd have anything to say to you now?"

Tulwar.

Two of them. One male. One female.

Kataria murmured a curse under her breath; she had been so consumed with thought she hadn't heard them until she was this close.

They stood at the water's edge, tall and lean, their skin and hair black beneath the ragged leather armor they wore. Their faces were painted with a chalky white dust, their belts sagging with what looked like pieces of metal that someone had started shaping into blades and got bored halfway through.

Nearby, a pair of gaambols stood. The massive simians had buried their faces in the water, lapping eagerly. None of them seemed to have noticed her; the gaambols were too involved in slaking their thirst and the tulwar were too consumed with ...

"You always get like this on journeys," the female grunted. "You always get *snippy* if you don't kill something."

Whatever this was.

"I do not get *snippy*." The male sneered, baring long yellow fangs. "I just had nothing to say and I didn't say anything like you thought I did."

"You're bored with tracking shicts all day and not getting to fight them," the female replied. "That is why you're snippy."

"I just *said* I wasn't—" He snarled suddenly, throwing his hands up and turning away from her. "It just doesn't make any sense. The *daanaja* said he wants to march on the humans soon, and he sends the Mak Lak Kai out to track *shicts*?"

Kataria's ears twitched at the name. Mak Lak Kai. She knew them. She had fought them.

It hadn't gone well.

She kept her breathing shallow, forced herself still. With any luck, they would stay only long enough to water their beasts and then be on their way. No sense in betraying her position before then. Not when she had only ten arrows and need for all of them.

"It's a long way between the two cities," the female replied. "The *daanaja* wants to make sure the way is clear for his march." She reached into her belt, produced a rolled-up hide scroll, and waved it. "And there are *many* shicts these days."

Kataria's eyes narrowed on the scroll. But before she could even begin to guess what it might be, the female tulwar returned it to her belt.

"Then why not send the Chee Chree or some other clan to do it?" the male snarled. "The Mak Lak Kai are made for *war*, not scouting."

"The other clans are weak. Stupid. They whine to the *daanaja* about having us *malaa* in their city. So he sends us out on these little errands to placate them. Do not worry. We will be there at the slaughter."

"They cast me out of my clan because I was *malaa*," the male grumbled. "They cast me out of the city because I was *malaa*. Why would they not cast me out of the battle because I am *malaa*?"

"Because they need Mak Lak Kai more than they hate *malaa*." The female shot him a yellow, toothy grin. "If they cast you out of the battle, it will be because you're snippy."

The male roared, tore his crude blade from his belt, and brandished it at her. She laughed, tearing her own weapon free. They tensed, as if to rush each other, when a third voice cut through the air.

"And what is this?"

From a nearby dune, another gaambol came loping down. This one was bigger, fiercer-looking, its face and hands the color of blood and its fur and eyes black as pitch. Yet for all its ferocity, it seemed a pale sight compared to its rider.

Another tulwar, her long and lean body covered in black fur, sparse in patches where knotted scars protruded. Her armor was tattered and damaged, yet it was clear no effort had been made to repair it. The sword on her back, a massive wedge of sharpened metal, looked almost too big for her to wield. And though she wore white paint on her face, there was no substance on earth thick enough to cover the wild red of her eyes and the manic yellow of her fanged smile.

"Chakaa," the female said. "Come and see. I am about to cut him open."

"No, Chakaa," the male snapped. "We are simply settling an argument."

The creature known as Chakaa glanced between the two tulwar. She offered a shrug and slipped off her gaambol, walking nonchalantly between the two.

"I am not convinced that there is much difference between the two," she said. "And I am even less convinced that you two would be interesting to watch kill each other." She patted the male on the head, as though he were a child. "You may kill each other when we are done or when the idea seems a little funnier. We'll see which comes first."

The tulwar muttered something but sheathed his sword, the female following. Kataria held her breath, watching Chakaa carefully. The leader, no doubt. Somehow the tulwar always seemed to elect whoever looked like they chewed glass for fun as their leadership.

Chakaa turned to her gaambol. The great beast scowled down at her through a pair of black eyes. She made a clicking sound with her tongue before delivering a fierce slap to the creature's face.

"What are you looking at me like that for?" she chided. "You are always so cranky when you don't eat. Go. Find your dinner."

Kataria wasn't sure what was more amazing: the fact that the beast didn't strike back or the fact that it seemed to understand her. Casting an indignant stare at her, and being sure to flash its bright red buttocks at her as it turned, it took off loping into the dunes. The other two got up and followed it, shrieking as they did.

Fuck, Kataria thought.

However slim her hopes had been for the tulwar to be on their way were damn near starved to death now. Chakaa pulled something that was either clumps of meat or clumps of hair from her belt and began to chew on it.

"Typical," the male snorted. "Even the gaambol get to kill something before I do."

"If you want to go chase down horses, go right ahead," Chakaa said. "Just be sure you run faster than I do. I do not like your snippiness."

"*See?*" the female said.

"Otherwise, be patient," Chakaa continued. "They will be back before long and we can go kill a shict, if it will make you happy."

"It would make me happy to kill *many* shicts," the male snapped.

"There are enough, aren't there? What are they all moving in such big numbers for? Are they going to a party?"

"Rude of them not to invite us." She popped another piece of flesh and hair into her mouth, chewed for a moment, then spit out what appeared to be a bone. "But then, what do shicts know of good manners?"

Kataria's sense of revulsion was overwhelmed by her curiosity. They were tracking the shicts. They knew where they had gone. The scroll. That had to be what was written on it.

"Either way, the *daanaja* wants to know where they are. If you'd like to tell him you didn't have the patience to learn, you may do that, too, once he is done killing the others."

"If he even *is* a *daanaja*," the male spit. "I have heard of no *daanaja* like him. What did Mototaru call him? A drag…drago…"

"Dragonman," Chakaa replied. "Different word, same thing."

Kataria's blood froze. And for the first time since she had met him, she wished there were more dragonmen in the world so that she *might* have reason to believe that Gariath wasn't involved with these creatures.

"What are we to do for our food, Chakaa?" the female asked. She eyed the bits of meat in Chakaa's hands. "Will you share?"

"What example would I be setting for you, then?" Chakaa laughed, spewing bits of hair and flesh everywhere. "If you are hungry, go search for something."

Kataria tensed as the female cast a gaze around the oasis before settling on the scrub grass she was hiding behind. She held her breath as the tulwar drew close, drew her bow, aiming for the heart as the tulwar drew within twenty paces and—

"Wait."

At Chakaa's voice, the female glanced up and looked back. Chakaa glanced to the male, gesturing with her chin.

"You do it."

"What? Why me?" the male replied, indignant.

"I would be a poor *Humn* to my clan if I did not seek to improve attitudes wherever I went," Chakaa said. "You think too much of your needs. Doing a good deed for your fellow Mak Lak Kai will improve your attitude."

Kataria breathed a sigh of relief as the female hurried back toward the other two tulwar.

"But this is all scrub!" the male complained. "There won't be anything here!"

"True." Chakaa glanced to a nearby dune and Kataria froze once more. "Go see the other side of that dune, then. There is probably a yoto den or something."

The male glanced toward the dune, the very dune Kwar hid behind.

And without thinking, Kataria's bow was up. Her arrow was drawn. And there was the sound of wind whistling.

And by the time the male looked back, three feet of wood was quivering where his left eye was.

He blinked, as if not quite sure what had happened. The two female tulwar looked at him, as if they didn't quite recognize him anymore. Then, without a sound, he collapsed to the earth.

"He's dead," the female tulwar observed.

"Isn't that typical," Chakaa sighed. "Give him a little criticism and he goes and gets shot in the face."

Whatever reply the female might have offered was lost in the shriek of wind and the punch of hard flesh. The female staggered two steps backward, head contorting as she tried to look at the arrow shaft jutting from her throat.

She turned a bewildered stare to Chakaa, who stared back, blankly. She opened her mouth, but whatever she intended to say came out as only a wet gurgling sound buried beneath the crunch of sand as she fell to the earth and did not rise.

Chakaa stared at the corpse for a moment. She popped another morsel of meat into her mouth. She chewed thoughtfully.

"Huh."

The third arrow came shrieking past. She stepped out of the way with an almost insulting casualness, then glanced toward the hedge of scrub grass. She peered through the foliage and her eyes found Kataria's.

And she smiled a broad, yellow smile.

Fuck.

Kataria thought it rather than spoke it. She needed that breath as she drew another arrow, drew it back. She held it as she closed one eye, took aim for the span of a single heartbeat. She released it and the arrow as one.

And by then, *fuck* seemed no longer sufficient a word for the situation.

Chakaa was already rushing toward her. She did not so much as slow down as the arrow struck her in the collarbone. The only sound she made was the sound of sand crunching under her feet, of leather tearing as she pulled her massive blade free from her back and the wind screaming as she closed the distance and swung.

Kataria threw herself to the earth, felt the sand grate against her skin, felt her hair pulled by the wind of the tulwar's swing, felt branches and leaves fall upon her back as the scrub grass was swiftly decapitated.

All of this compared to the feeling of her heart pounding as it bid her rise and run.

She leapt to her feet and took off at a sprint, struggled to pull and nock another arrow. Her ears quivered, listening for her foe. And when she was sure she had put enough distance between them, she whirled, aimed, and fired.

Chakaa had not taken a single step.

Chakaa did not so much as move as the arrow hit her.

She merely looked down at the shaft of wood quivering in her side. She looked back up at Kataria. Her simian nostrils twitched briefly.

"Rude," she said.

And she took off running again, taking her weapon in both hands as she narrowed her eyes upon her prey.

Kataria pulled an arrow, nocked it, never got the chance to fire it. Chakaa was upon her in the span of three breaths. The fourth breath was robbed from her. The air seemed to be sucked out of the sky with the force of her massive swing. Kataria leapt backward and turned to run.

She had taken a single step before she felt simian fingers seize her by the hair and haul her backward. She let out a cry as they threw her to the earth, a cry swiftly cut short by a hairy foot connecting with her side.

Breathless, she tried to scramble to her feet—a task she found much easier when a hand wrapped around her neck and hauled her up. Had she any breath left, she might have spared some for the ease with which Chakaa hoisted her with one hand. As it was, breath and sense had both been beaten out of her and shriveled up in the desert air.

She could but grope at Chakaa's grip and struggle for breath as the tulwar hoisted her off her feet and fixed her with a queer look.

"Huh." Chakaa thrust her blade into the earth, reached out, and pinched the tip of Kataria's right ear. "Pointy ears, like them." She squinted as Kataria's lips peeled back, revealing her canines. "Pointy teeth, like them. But you're..." She furrowed her brow. "Pink."

"Let *go*," Kataria snarled. Or tried to snarl, anyway. It was really hard to make any sort of sound outside of a choked gurgle with Chakaa's fingers around her throat.

"How strange." The tulwar hoisted her up higher. "I didn't know shicts came in different colors." A long finger extended and gave Kataria a curious prod to her belly. "I learned something new!"

Her ears flattened against her head. Her teeth clenched together. Her eyes shut tight. And, as the fingers tightened around her throat and she had no more breath to give, Kataria screamed with another voice. Something deep inside her head opened its mouth wide and howled into the sky.

Chakaa didn't notice. Chakaa merely smiled broadly.

"So, are there purple ones, too, or—"

There was probably more to that sentence, lost in the clack of teeth as Kataria's foot shot up and smashed beneath her jaw. Chakaa didn't cry out but dropped her regardless, and Kataria lay gasping upon the ground.

"What a shame," Chakaa hummed, jerking her sword free from the earth. "We could have learned so much."

"Stay back," Kataria gasped. She kept her eyes on the tulwar as she crawled away, groping blindly for her bow.

"But I have sung this song many times over many years." Chakaa's voice was accompanied by the hiss of sand as she dragged her blade behind her like a child dragging a stuffed doll.

Kataria found enough strength to haul herself to her feet. And just as quickly, it was knocked from her as Chakaa's fist shot out, catching her in the side and sending her back down. She hacked out a spittle-laden cough, squinting up as Chakaa loomed over her, the setting sun glinting off the blade high above her head.

"You will be just one more verse," the tulwar said, "however unusual."

Some people, including Kataria, had wondered what the last thing they would say before they died would be. No one, including Kataria, ever wondered what the last thing they would ever hear would be. And when Kataria shut her eyes and her ears, all she heard was the beating of her own heart.

But only for a moment.

In the span of an instant, in one great burst, her ears filled with a sound. It reached through her skin, into her skull, into her heart. It filled her body with a sound, something long and loud and torn from a mouth filled with teeth on a dark night. A howl.

One she had heard once, long ago.

And then, all she could hear was feet.

Feet on sand, leaving sand, flying. Screaming, roaring, colliding. To the ground, two bodies, two snarls. All in the span of an instant.

When Kataria opened her eyes, Chakaa was down, struggling, flailing.

And there was Kwar.

Alive. Awake. Roaring.

Her hand was wrapped around Chakaa's throat, bearing the tulwar to the earth. Her other was wrapped around a hatchet, hacking wildly at her prey. Chakaa snarled, screamed, flailed. Kwar didn't flinch, not as fists struck her, not as spittle spattered her, not as the screaming filled her ears.

The onslaught ended as Chakaa managed to seize her by the arms and hurl her off. Kwar tumbled with the force of the throw and sprang back to her feet. A knife leapt from her belt to her hand to join the hatchet. Her eyes were locked on Chakaa as the tulwar sprang to her feet, her fur parted by the dark cuts across her flesh.

Yet her eyes were wild with something other than fear. And her smile only grew broader as she plucked her massive blade back up.

"Oh," she cackled. "I *knew* today was going to be special."

No roars, no threats, just laughter as she rushed toward Kwar. She swung, and the khoshict swept beneath her blade and jammed her dagger into the tulwar's side as she emerged behind her. Chakaa whirled, swinging her blade as she did, heedless of the weapon stuck in her side. Kwar was already out of reach, already rushing forward again.

Her hatchet was up, coming down in an angry arc. Chakaa's blade shot up, catching it in a spray of sparks. The tulwar's fist shot out, trying to catch Kwar as she drew closer, too close for the tulwar to use her blade effectively. The khoshict seized her dagger, tore it free from

Chakaa's side. She found a new space of flesh, stabbed. And again. And again. Over and over, shrieking with rage as she did, until Chakaa's foot lashed out and drove her away. Her hatchet fell from her grasp and her dagger was left lodged in the tulwar as she staggered away.

Her side all but open, her body painted in wounds, arrows quivering from her body, the only sign that she had even felt it was a slight diminishing of Chakaa's smile.

"This was exciting," she said. "I learned something special today. I only wish I had been able to share it with—"

Chakaa spasmed suddenly. She blinked. She looked down at the arrow in her chest.

"Ah."

And fell.

Kataria came trudging forward, her fingers still humming with the feel of her bowstring. Her body ached, her breath came back to her shyly, forcing her to gasp with each breath she took. But she was still alive. And Kwar...

"Kwar?" she asked.

The khoshict stood, breathing heavily, rigid with tension, but unmoving. She stared at Chakaa's lifeless body, mouth agape, hands trembling.

Tentatively, as though she were scared to do so, Kataria reached out and laid a hand on her shoulder. Kwar started, then turned a gaze wild and wide and fearful upon her.

"I'm fine," she gasped. "I'm...I'm fine." She licked her lips. "We need to go. We need to get out of here."

"Right," Kataria said. "They had gaambols. Just give me a moment."

She rushed to the corpse of the female tulwar and rooted around in her belt until she found the hide scroll. She tucked it back into her own belt, then hurried back to Kwar.

"Got it," she said. "Now we can..."

She didn't finish the sentence. She lost all words, all thoughts as something reached out and seized her by the hand. She looked down, saw Kwar's dark fingers tightening around her own pale ones.

She had forgotten Kwar's touch. Just as she forgot, then, that she had told her never to touch her. This barely felt like a touch, barely felt like it should be a shict's. It was alive with something, something wild and screaming, a sound that reached through Kwar's fingers and into hers.

And she looked up into Kwar's dark eyes and whispered.

"You got up."

"I heard you," Kwar replied, voice trembling. "You spoke to me and I..." She looked down, saw her fingers around Kataria's, immediately released them. "Sorry, I forgot. I...I didn't think..."

"No, it was..." Kataria tried to finish that sentence, couldn't think of the words to. The sound was still echoing in her skull, that long and wild roar that tore through her and raced through her body with heavy breath and sharp teeth.

The Howling. Kwar's Howling. How long it had been since she had heard it. It consumed her, made her tremble as Kwar did. And through it, she could barely hear anything else: her breath, her heartbeat...

The sound of sand shifting behind her.

"That was exciting."

A guttural chuckle. A body rising.

Kataria whirled around, nocking an arrow. Yet at the sight of Chakaa, standing there, breathing and hale and whole, the blood left her fingers.

"But I still feel a little insulted." The tulwar's smile was just as big as it had been. Her eyes were just as wide. And it was only now that Kataria noticed that the sands around her were completely dry. "You came to kill Chakaa Humn Mak Lak Kai, and you only brought three arrows, a knife, and a hatchet?"

Chakaa seized the arrow in her neck. Ungently, she pulled it free of her flesh. Not a single drop of blood left her body. And, with a big and broad smile, she looked to Kataria.

"Who do you think you're fucking with?"

There was no word sufficient for what she was seeing. No curse blasphemous enough, no god powerful enough to hear whatever invocation she might say. Words only returned to her when she saw the two other tulwar begin to stir, begin to rise, as though awakening from a bad dream.

One word, anyway.

"Run," she whispered.

And turned.

And fled.

"Run!"

She tore off without a thought for camp or supplies. She cast only a single glance behind her to make sure Kwar was following. And then she could see that the tulwar were in pursuit, as though they hadn't even been injured.

If they couldn't die, she wondered, could they tire? Could she ever outrun them?

That thought became more pressing as her injuries acted up, as her breath faded, as the tulwar closed in.

Kwar rushed past her, seized her by the hand, kept her moving. The khoshict looked to the hills and let out a shout of shictish words that flew into the sky. And was answered, moments later.

Baying, the great crested shape of a yiji came loping over the dune, skidding down and rushing toward her. Slavering, it bounded over, coming to a halt just long enough to let Kwar clamber atop it. The khoshict looked down at Kataria and held her hand out.

Kataria looked at it for but a moment, like she could barely recognize it, before reaching out and taking it.

She felt her feet leave the earth. She felt the yiji's back beneath her legs as she was hauled up to it. She felt Kwar's arm wrap around her and hold her tight as she kicked the animal's flanks and sent it charging forward.

The sound of tulwar faded. The sound of her breath faded. And, in time, so, too, did all sounds.

All Kataria could hear was the sound of the woman behind her—her heart, her breath, her Howling—as the sun set behind them and gave way to night.

NINE

The Law of Creation

First, nothing.

And then...

"Ah."

Mundas did not know a term more elegant for it. For him, it was simple: One moment he did not know something, the next he did. Mortals did the same thing, save with books and words and time.

All things he had left behind.

<hr />

He stood up. He was on top of a roof of a building in a ravaged district of the city. The sun was setting over a horizon of ruined homes and shattered roofs. He walked to the edge of the building, tiles cracking under his feet until he stepped out over nothingness.

And then he was somewhere else. The sky was dark with night, the moon peering over distant dunes. The city and its ruins were one shadow among many, somewhere far away. The desert stretched out far before him.

One moment he was somewhere. The next, he was somewhere else. He was exactly where he needed to be when he needed to be there exactly. Mortals had more complicated terms and explanations for what he did.

They were simply more things he had left behind.

He walked up the dune where his companion was waiting, as he knew he would be. At the crest of the dune, an old man in a white robe turned and regarded him through a face of what Mundas assumed to be grandfatherly kindness. A breath later, the old man's skin twisted and stretched and shrank and he became a small, finely dressed man with a painted face.

"You're late," Azhu-Mahl said.

Mundas saw no reason to reply to that. It was impossible for him to be late.

The skin across Azhu-Mahl's face rippled like water. He sneered, lips peeling back and exposing teeth as long as nails.

"You could at least indulge me, Mundas," he said. "It wasn't easy getting out here."

"I find that hard to believe." Mundas began walking down the dune, toward a distant hill.

"It wasn't easy getting out with any delicacy, at least," Azhu-Mahl hissed, following. "The shadows are alive, Mundas. Every alleyway holds a thousand eyes. The air is filled with the screams of the people."

"Expected."

"The city has gone mad."

"The city was born mad, along with the rest of this world."

"And our intention was to cure that, no? To bring order and hope to this filth?" Azhu-Mahl gestured toward the distant city. "This war continues to drag on. The Jackals are scattered, but the damage they did cannot be undone. The Khovura are boiling up from below the city."

"Expected."

"I *expected* your pawn to be of more use than she has been," Azhu-Mahl said. "I have been in Teneir's house. She speaks to no one, babbles and whispers to the night, dreams of the powers she believes she will be given."

"Not unforeseen," Mundas said. "Fanatics, above all else, are pliable."

"Above all else, they are unstable, and her especially. The Khovura were intended to be a tool. They were intended to expose the rot of this city and make its people ready to accept a savior. But they follow Teneir like hounds, liable to devour those we meant to save."

"They are not without need of salvation themselves," Mundas replied. "The Khovura were chosen because the gods would not answer them. But, like every mortal, they yearn to be heard. They have heaped their hopes and their fears upon Ancaa. When he comes, in whatever form he chooses, they will fall into line behind him."

Azhu-Mahl let out a low, unpleasant hum. "And what will surprise them more, I wonder? That their goddess is male or that their savior is a demon?"

Mundas chose not to protest.

There was no such thing as a complete record of the time that produced the Aeons, or even of the divine creatures themselves that ultimately were cast from heaven. But of all the fragments and myths and poems to have emerged from that era, only those on the God-King were of any particular use.

And while they had made no attempts to hide his shortcomings—his cruelty, his tyranny, his lust for worship—they had also venerated his ideals—his mercy, his attentiveness, his need to create. These were attributes that could salvage mortality from the dark earth from which they had crawled, even if they came with a burden.

The concept of ultimate benevolence only existed in gods.

And gods had long ago ceased to be an option for the Renouncers.

"If there are problems," Mundas said, casting a sidelong glance at his companion, "I trust you can handle it."

There was a wet popping sound, the creak of skin stretching and snapping, the thick squish of it re-forming. The small man with the painted face was gone. Walking beside him now was a saccarii woman, tall and regal in elegant robes. From ochre eyes not his own, Azhu-Mahl looked at Mundas and flashed a fanged smirk.

"I have considered it," he replied in a feminine voice. "Though, once he arrives, I expect my talents will be needed many places."

Mundas looked toward the top of the dune. At its crest, against the rising moon, a shadow was painted: small, slender, a delicate reed growing from the sand.

And his mouth curled into a thick, deep frown.

"Sooner than that."

At the top of the hill, the three of them met. The last time this had happened was several hundred years and many more bodies ago. Azhu-Mahl had looked very different back then. Mundas himself had not left quite so many of his burdens behind. And Qulon . . .

"Mundas," a shrill song of a voice chimed out, "how good of you to crawl out to see me."

Qulon never seemed to change.

Short, barely coming up to Mundas's chest, she looked delicate and austere, an heirloom passed through several generations of a petty and spiteful family with many dead relatives.

Mundas had never seen much purpose in clothes—he didn't feel cold, let alone shame or modesty—and so Qulon's elegant silk leggings and long, collared tunic always struck him as ostentatious. But that decadence seeped into every part of her being. Her left eye was shut coyly, her right bright and observing. Her black hair was done up in a braid so long she wore it draped around her neck like a scarf. Even the long scar on her face, she wore like jewelry: a deep line running down from her eye that pulled the right corner of her lip up into a crooked grin.

"One never comes to *see* you, Qulon," Azhu-Mahl said, sneering. "One only comes to see what damage is done upon your arrival."

"And...*you*." She turned that crooked grin, dripping with contemptuous false sincerity, upon him. "You've changed since I saw you last."

"What is it you wish, Qulon?" Mundas asked before Azhu-Mahl could retort.

She looked to him with her one eye. "That's it? Straight down to business? No pleasantries? No questions as to what *I've* been up to all these years? I'd ask what you've been up to, of course, but..." She glanced toward the distant shadow of Cier'Djaal. "By the bodies in your wake, I think I've an idea."

"What a very clever way to demonstrate that you have *no* idea what we're doing," Azhu-Mahl replied. "Did you come all this way just to try to lecture us?"

"Lecture you?" Qulon placed a hand to her chest in mock shock. "Perish the thought. But if my presence is interrupting your *delicate* work, I can come back later. Say, when you've killed the entire city instead of just half?"

"As though *anyone* would listen to you, of all people, on matters of life, you selfish—"

"The oath."

Both Azhu-Mahl and Qulon turned glares upon Mundas for disrupting their spat. He did not acknowledge this.

"Really," Qulon sighed. "Is it necessary? We all know it. No one *forgot* it in the past thousand years. Must we—"

"Nothing is true until it is spoken, nothing is a lie until it is spoken," Mundas replied. "We did not come out here to argue." He fixed a steady stare upon her. "The oath."

Qulon looked to Azhu-Mahl, who folded his arms over his chest and shrugged. She sighed, rolled a single eye.

"If you insist." She made a gesture toward Mundas. "You're senior. You begin."

Mundas inclined his head and spoke low into the wind.

"There is no law but mortal law."

"There are no gods but deaf gods," Azhu-Mahl continued, bowing his head.

"There are no answers but the answer," Qulon replied, likewise bowing.

"We who renounce do so to find the answer." Mundas raised his head. "Let them be spoken."

Qulon raised her head. "Death is not eternal."

Azhu-Mahl raised his. "Flesh is not a prison."

"Time," Mundas said, "means nothing."

He let out a long breath. These oaths had seemed more glamorous long ago. They had carried more weight, it seemed, took longer to speak. Or perhaps there had simply been more of the Renouncers back then.

In some quiet moments between so many years, he almost forgot why they needed them. But then, on nights such as these, he would remember the bloodshed that had made them necessary. And suddenly the oath seemed heavy again.

"Your presence here is unwarranted," Mundas said. "The pact does not require us to disclose our pursuits toward one another. We all agreed that we would pursue our own ends toward the answer."

"The pact *does* forbid interference," Azhu-Mahl added, coldly.

"*Direct* interference." Qulon held up a finger. "I am violating no agreement by stopping by." She wielded her smile like a weapon, brandishing its saccharine insincerity at them. "Really, all this parroting of laws and oaths at me makes me think you boys don't trust me."

Emotion was something that Mundas recalled fondly. Much in the way, he supposed, a mortal would recall fondly a toy from their childhood. He had left much of his behind much in the way they would leave theirs behind.

And just as the sight of a ragged doll or a dusty wooden horse would anger a mortal at the reminder of time's cruel passage, so too was Mundas annoyed that he could feel ire forming at the corners of his eyes.

"We are doing good work here, Qulon," he said. "We have found our answer."

"Indeed? And your work is *so* good that you have not seen fit to share it with the other Renouncers?" Qulon let out a shrill laugh. "Or were the rest of us to simply take you at your word that you've solved the problem of mortal frailty?"

"We simply thought not to bother you," Azhu-Mahl replied. "One would hate to strain such narrow perceptions with so vast a vision as ours. Especially one such as—"

Mundas held up a hand. Azhu-Mahl slid into a sneering, contemptuous silence.

"It has been many years since we gathered," Mundas said. "Many wars, many plagues, many famines; surely you have not been blind to it. Surely you have heard the screams they offer to heaven."

"As I have heard the silence heaven offers them," Qulon replied, coldly. "Do not presume to speak to me as though I am sympathetic to gods. I search for the answer, just as you do." She shook her head. "But what you plan to do . . ." Her lips curled up in a cold grimace. "You would offer them slavery and call it salvation."

Mundas regarded her carefully. "What do you think you know?"

"More than you believe I do," she replied. "I know you have engineered two wars in this city. I know you have driven the people to despair. I know you intend to bring about a god for them to worship." She cast him a sidelong look. "But more importantly, I know *you*, Mundas.

"You have always believed that the answer lay with gods, even as you agree that they are worthless. You have always sought to give them a savior. And, after so many years and deaths, you've never *once* considered that mortals need no shepherd."

"It is precisely because of those deaths that I see no other way," Mundas replied, more heatedly than he intended to. "Mortality is a curse, a two-headed hound that fights itself for scraps while it starves to death. The best and brightest among them still do not seek anything but power for themselves. They *need* guidance. If heaven will not grant it to them, then I shall."

"By delivering them to a demon," Qulon snapped.

"By giving them someone who will listen," Mundas retorted. "By giving them someone who has the power to save them. The God-King was so named for—"

"I have read the records," Qulon interrupted. "Though perhaps not the same as yours. What *I* read was the tale of a cruel tyrant who craved absolute control over his subjects and was cast into hell for it."

Mundas stiffened. "He has had time to reflect upon this. He has had time to learn."

"No one ever truly learns, Mundas. A demon's mind is expanded, but it remains finite. It only means his penchant for savagery is that much broader than a mortal's. You may try to temper him, you may try to guide him, but he will not be commanded. Sooner or later, he will return to what he knows."

"If we are to believe that gods are deaf, we must also question their judgment," Azhu-Mahl chimed in. "And if they saw reason to cast him into hell, that is reason enough to question whether he deserved it. We all knew that the answer, when we found it, would never be perfect." He cast a sneering smile toward Qulon. "*Ours*, at least, has a lower body count."

Only at that comment did Qulon's serenity crack. Her mocking confidence slipped away as her lips curled back, baring her teeth. The scar on her face seemed to grow into a chasm as her face screwed up in anger.

"It remains," she snarled, "the *only* way."

"The only way to a mass slaughter," Azhu-Mahl scoffed.

"You have always looked down upon the mortals," Qulon snapped. "You, with all your powers, think them simple and weak, sheep that must be herded. I see creatures destined to be strong, to need *no* gods, let alone demons posing as them. They are burdened by such reliance, held back by their own fears of a heaven that doesn't exist. Once they shed these..."

"And you intended to make them do this through murder."

"Through *nature*," Qulon retorted. "They are born in conflict, spit out upon an earth that tries to kill them. They think, they endure, they survive, they master. They merely need to figure out how best to do this." She sniffed, trying to force her composure to return. "They are creatures of conflict. Let them embrace it."

"You advocate *slaughter*," Azhu-Mahl snarled. "A world where the weak are killed for no other reason than because someone could kill them."

"If they are to master this world, they must discover what works. That which doesn't must be left behind."

"This indifferent savagery is why we renounced the gods in the first place!" Azhu-Mahl all but roared, his voice shrill and angry. "What good do we do them if we sit back and let them murder each other?"

"Perhaps it's not as charming as your tale of a god descending from on high and delivering them," Qulon replied, forcing her smile saccharine once more. "But it at least treats them as more than beasts to be herded."

"You have seen what we've seen," Mundas replied. "The wars that burn within Cier'Djaal's walls are nothing compared to what the mortals can accomplish. They *need* guidance, they *need* a shepherd."

"A shepherd never comes without a sty and filth to roll in," Qulon replied. "There is no worship that is not slavery, there is no god that is not a tyrant, there is no miracle that comes without a cost."

Shame was not something Mundas recognized, let alone felt. It was a mortal construct, designed to herd the others into obedience. And, for the irritation he felt at Qulon's smug smile, he felt no shame.

Merely regret.

Regret for the precious time wasted in coming out here, regret for thinking that Qulon could ever be convinced of the answer, regret for believing that he would be needed here.

He exchanged a brief glance with Azhu-Mahl, the same conclusion reached between them without words. And as he looked back to Qulon, and as she regarded him through her eye, he saw that she, too, saw no more reason to expend words. And so, with the briefest of nods sparing the briefest respect she was owed, he turned to go.

And that was when he saw it.

A flash of movement, the barest twitch of muscle, out of the corner of his eye. For the briefest of moments, Qulon's crooked smile had become one immense grin of profoundly unnerving joy.

He had seen that smile once, long ago.

He could still recall the smell of the corpses cooking in the sun.

And that was when he knew why he had come here.

"What is it?" Azhu-Mahl asked as Mundas halted.

"You," Mundas spoke, an edge of fire in his voice.

"Me?" Qulon replied, voice lilting like a cracked bell.

"You are plotting something," Mundas said. "What is it?"

"Are we all not plotting something?" She shrugged, smiling. "The Renouncers were formed to plan, after all."

"If you are intent on interfering with our answer, you will reap nothing but carcasses and misery," Mundas said with what might have been a snarl, had he the capability to do so. "Step away from this, Qulon. Pursue your own ends. In time, you will see we were correct."

Her smile faded. She looked at him through her eye and spoke slowly. "Is that a threat?"

"It…" He caught himself. "We maintain the pact. We do not interfere directly with one another."

"Nor do I intend to," she replied. The smile came creeping back. "Directly."

"What is this?" Azhu-Mahl swept forward. "What are you scheming?"

"Scheming? A Renouncer does not scheme. A Renouncer seeks truth, as you have done." She turned away, folded her hands behind her back. "I really do admire your plan, gentlemen. Create enough misery that mortals will crave whatever savior you give them, even if it's a demon. Really, I can't see how that might go wrong." She paused. "Unless, of course, they find a different savior."

"Qulon…" Mundas began.

"Spare me, Mundas," she replied. "The answer is never a monologue. It is a debate, forever going on, an argument in which everyone has a chance to voice their views."

And she turned. And her smile was slow and soft as a porcelain knife.

"All I've done," she said, "is offer my rebuttal."

TEN

THE PLEADING KNIFE

What concerns me are the scraws."

"The what?"

"Those giant birds they ride."

Words passed through a cloud of pipe smoke. Scents of confusion, of fear, of anger through the reek of tobacco. Spilled ink and cold meals and hours upon days in the same small, stinking, sweltering room.

These didn't bother Gariath. Not anymore.

"If they were capable of striking at us," Daaru muttered, "they would have by now, wouldn't they?"

"Not necessarily," Mototaru replied, chewing on his pipe. "We drove them from Shaab Sahaar, but we didn't get all of them. We can assume that their wars in the city have occupied them. That doesn't mean they couldn't turn on us when we marched."

"It's not a quick march to Cier'Djaal." Daaru let out a low hum. "Birds flying over our head, dropping fireflasks, shooting arrows for that many miles..."

"Just so."

"What do you suggest?"

Gariath stood over the same map as they did, staring down at the same parchment they had been staring down at for so long. And for all that time, they had been talking of strategies and casualties and acceptable losses and other terms that, if they came from human mouths, Gariath would smash their teeth in for speaking.

But still, he could only barely see the map. He could only barely hear their voices.

"Send a secondary force up the river." Mototaru drew a finger across the Lyre, toward Cier'Djaal on the map. "Tho Thu Bhu river barges. We can cover them with green fronds that won't burn. Force them to send their forces to intervene them."

"That will divide us." Daaru shook his head. "Our original plan was to storm the three openings to the Green Belt. To send a force of any size up the river, we would abandon one of those openings."

"It divides them, as well." Mototaru tapped the map again. "If they focus their forces on the Green Belt, they won't have enough troops to counter our warriors from the river. If they deal with our barges, then we don't have to worry about those troops at the Green Belt."

Daaru let out a low, frustrated growl. He glanced to Gariath, but only for a moment. Mototaru didn't even bother. Both of them, over the course of hours, had learned that whatever he was thinking, he was not willing to impart to them.

Just as well.

If they knew, he thought, they would just quietly pack up and go home right now.

His mind was somewhere else, somewhere across a hundred sweltering hours and miles of hot sand. There, he couldn't hear anything but the moan of a hot desert wind mingling with the screams of the dying as it blew over blood-soaked sand. There, he couldn't see anything but a road of tulwar flesh and tulwar blood, leading right to the gates of Cier'Djaal. When he closed his eyes, when he opened them, it didn't matter; he couldn't see anything else.

Lesser minds might have called it a vision.

Gariath would have called it annoying.

And he would have said so, but every time he was tempted to open his mouth, his mind went somewhere much closer, to the darkness of the warehouse and Kharga chuckling in the dark. And no matter what he wanted to say, he could only hear seven words.

Have they told you how it ends?

"What if the humans have torn each other apart by now?" Daaru asked. "What if there *are* no . . . bird . . . things?"

"Brilliant." Mototaru puffed on his pipe. "Inform the soldiers to prepare for any sneak attacks by giant ox-women that walk on two legs and spew fire from their twenty nipples."

Daaru blinked. "W-what?"

"Yes, now imagine hearing something that stupid every sixteen breaths. This is what it is like discussing strategy with you." Mototaru snorted, expelling great clouds of pipe smoke from his nostrils. "In war, fortune favors whoever feeds it the most bodies. We would be idiots to gamble on something we have no reason to believe.

"Scraws." He thrust the tip of his pipe at the drawing of Cier'Djaal. "Phalanxes. Legions. Dragonmen." He glanced at Gariath. "*Big* dragonmen. We must assume all of them are present in Cier'Djaal, all of them want to kill us, and all of them will be *very* hard to kill."

Daaru sighed and ran a long hand across a long face. The barest hints of color rose into his complexion but quickly died as he slumped against the map table. He waved at Mototaru to continue.

"We must have a plan for *anything* the humans can do to us," Mototaru said. "The barges we send upriver must have enough warriors to come at the humans from behind. I suggest no less than twenty barges, each one with a dozen warriors or so. Enough for a full contingent. That will—"

"How many will survive?"

Mototaru almost choked on his smoke. Daaru looked up suddenly. Both of the tulwar looked at Gariath as though they just now noticed him. The dragonman himself hardly noticed it when he spoke, the words falling from a numb mouth like so much drool.

"Mm?" Mototaru grunted, when he had cleared his throat.

"How many of them will die if we send them upriver?" Gariath asked.

"Impossible to predict."

Gariath took a breath. He drew in the scent of blood in water, of air bubbles bursting as they fled mouths wide in screams, of sodden lumber dragging flailing bodies to a sandy riverbed.

"Try," he said.

Mototaru sighed and knuckled the small of his back, thrusting his prodigious belly forward. "If the scraws do not take the bait, there is no reason to assume that any of them would die. Without knowing what the scraws' numbers are, we should plan for losing up to half of them and still having enough to put up a stiff resistance."

"Resistance," Gariath muttered, staring at the blue line of the Lyre on the map. "Resisting until they're dead."

"The plan would be to put pressure on the humans to allow the main force to overwhelm them," Mototaru said. "Or draw the scraws out." He puffed on his pipe. "Either way, not an easy job, no."

"To sacrifice themselves to ensure victory," Daaru grunted. "Any tulwar of any clan would answer the call. The Tul will return them to us, in another life, stronger and wiser for their sacrifice."

"And what of their families," Gariath said, more to himself than the others, "their starving children, their broken husbands and wives…"

Daaru glanced between Gariath and Mototaru, quirking a hairy brow. Mototaru, though, kept his eyes squarely on the dragonman.

"Daaru," he said, "how long has it been since you wrote to your family?"

"I haven't," Daaru replied.

"Do that. Make it long. And thorough."

Daaru opened his mouth to protest. But his stare lingered on Gariath, staring numbly down at the map, eyes blank and ear-frills folded, and he sighed. He shot a nod to Mototaru, collected his sword, and left their tiny war room, shutting the door firmly behind him.

Mototaru walked to the window, propped open its shutter long enough to empty his pipe of ash, then shut it and barred it. He plucked a small pouch of tobacco from his belt and began to pack his pipe anew as he walked slowly around the room, barring each window, checking the door to make certain it was locked.

Only when he had walked the entirety of the room did he produce a twig from his belt and light his pipe. He took several deep puffs as he casually strolled back to the map table and blew a long cloud of smoke across the painted cities and rivers.

"They don't need you to save them."

Mototaru didn't even look at Gariath, staring off to somewhere far beyond the walls of their room.

"Even before you came into their lives, they were ready to die for this," the old tulwar said. "It would have been useless, of course. They'd throw their lives away, wait for the Tul to return them, then throw that life away, too. They dream of their next lives being better. They know the one they have now is destined for suffering, for bloodshed."

"Everyone thinks they're ready to die," Gariath said. "Until they do."

His claws unconsciously dug into the table, tearing the map slightly. "Then, when your heart's about to give out and your last breath is in your throat, you realize what else you still have to do."

"They have much to do," Mototaru agreed. "They have crops to harvest. They have meat to hunt. They have children to hug, mates to fuck, swill to drink." He blew a long breath of smoke. "None of that is as important as what we are doing here, now. They don't need your sympathy. They need your leadership."

"They have you."

"Yes. The *Humn* who led them to ruin and ran away, leaving them to be hacked apart by dragonmen. They tolerate me as much as they do the *malaa*." He snorted. "Speaking of which, the Mak Lak Kai have sent word back on the shicts. We should review it at the next—"

"Shicts," Gariath growled. "On top of everything, there's shicts."

"I know. They get everywhere, don't they?"

"Like bugs."

"Exactly. They—"

"They are meant to be broken easily," he said. "They are small, tiny, weak. And you tell me we must have a plan for them, too? Even *they* can kill so many…"

Mototaru's stare might as well have been carved from stone. "Unsurprisingly, a creature as large as you is not very good at dancing around a subject. Speak your mind."

Gariath looked to the old tulwar and he could feel something in his eyes, something weak and quavering that seemed to flinch under Mototaru's stare. Something he dreaded to ask, and yet…

"When you led the Uprising," he said, "you climbed to the top of the Silken Spire. You came back down and left. The tulwar were slaughtered in your absence." He paused. "What did you see?"

Mototaru looked at him very carefully for a very long moment. He drew in a long breath of pipe smoke and let loose a cloud that covered his face.

"It's not important," he said.

"It is to me," Gariath replied.

"Not to you," Mototaru said, "not to me, not to anyone."

"Tell me."

Mototaru said nothing, looked somewhere else.

"*Tell me*," Gariath growled.

Mototaru drew in another long breath.

"*Tell me, you old fuck.*" His roar was punctuated by the sound of a table leg splintering as his fist came down on the map. "If we're to fight this war—"

"If we're to fight this war, then the answer is not important," Mototaru interrupted. "What's begun cannot be stopped. Regardless of what I saw, regardless of what I did, many tulwar will die. Maybe all the tulwar will die. You can't stop that. Knowing won't stop that."

"I *need* to—"

"I know what you need. I know what you *think* you need. You're looking for a reason to stop, to walk away." Mototaru gestured to the door. "Daaru's dumb as a brick and even he can smell the cowardice coming off you. We're lucky he's not dumb as *two* bricks or he might tell someone else.

"I don't claim to know who you were before you came to Shaab Sahaar, but I know you fought with only your own life in your hands. You feel unworthy to hold the others who have given you theirs. So you want me to tell you what happened, the one thing that'll stop this all and make everyone go home.

"It doesn't exist," Mototaru said. "Nothing can stop this. If we run now, the humans will come for us. The tulwar know this. The tulwar know that this is where we die. It's too late for this all to go back to the way it was. The only thing it's not too late for…"

Mototaru sighed. The weight of his years seemed to bend him lower. The breath of pipe smoke came out a little more ragged.

"Is whether you want to be here when the first blood is spilled."

Through the clouds of smoke covering it, Gariath stared at the map. His eyes fixed on the small red crosses painted on the parchment, the areas where they would strike. He could see them now: their high canyon walls, their long and lonely roads, their hot sand under hot feet.

He could see the blood fall upon them.

First, a drop.

Then, oceans.

And, without a word, he rose up and walked out of the room and into the night.

The *Rhega* did not bother to keep many historical records. Outside of a few common stories and a few choice words of contempt, the *Rhega* didn't see much of a point. The primary reason being that nothing ever really changed.

Humans liked to write down the rise and fall of their empires, shicts liked to pass down songs of bravery and merit, tulwar liked to muse about their stupid past lives. They all liked to pretend they were important by calling it *history*, but they weren't.

No matter what had happened in the past, humans were still weak, shicts were still cowards, tulwar were still stupid, and the *Rhega* would have to put up with it. This would never change.

And nothing has *changed*, he reminded himself.

As he had been reminding himself for the past hour he had walked through the night-quiet streets of Jalaang.

"Rise up!"

Or almost night-quiet, at any rate.

Even as the moon hung high in the sky and the majority of the warriors had gone to their rest, the city's conquerors were still active. Forges continued to ring out with hammer blows. Gaambol pits were still alive with hoots and gibbers. Fires lit the activities of elders as they traded stories of the previous Uprising while fletching arrows for those who were about to fight their own.

More were coming.

Sometimes they would arrive in hunting parties of six or seven. Sometimes they would come in their own war bands of a hundred or more. Sometimes it would be just one lone warrior with a grudge to settle from the Uprising. But every day, there were new tulwar in the city, new voices rising up as he passed, calling him *daanaja* like it was a compliment.

And still, nothing had changed.

The tulwar were still morons obsessed with their weird ideas of returning to life after death. They were still smelly, rude, and foolish. And, even if they were stronger than a human, they were still weak: Their bones broke, skin split, blood wept like anyone else's.

Nothing changed. Nothing ever changed.

The tulwar had fought countless wars before, wars that had seen them dead by the thousands. This one was no different, he told himself. Just another war, like so many others, nothing different, nothing changed.

No reason for him to feel this way.

Like his legs were made of water and his bones were made of twigs, like his blood had all surged out of his limbs and welled up in his throat, like the scent of rotting meat was so thick in his nose that he couldn't breathe...

He couldn't breathe.

He took a sharp turn and hurried down an alley. The windows went dark and the shadows pressed closer as he went deeper into the city. Its unoccupied areas were dwindling by the day as warehouses were converted to barracks, but there were still a few points that were mercifully free of anyone who might see what happened next.

He fell against the wall of a nearby building. His nose was filled with the acrid scent of his own breath, his head full of the pounding of his heart. He felt like a pond struck by a stone, quivering and weak as he looked around for someone who might have seen him.

No one. Just shadows and the empty dirt of the alley.

He could leave now, he knew. The gate was not far. No one would see him. There would be confusion over the next few days, but then someone would elect Daaru to lead and they would go back to their fights. Whatever choices they made, then, would be theirs. They would be fighting for themselves, as they should be.

And it would be as if he'd never dragged them into this war just so he could take revenge.

A long, deep breath left him.

Nothing ever changed.

And no matter how many times he told himself this, the end thought was always the same.

You did this, he told himself. *You started this war. And when they die, it'll be you that killed them.* He saw the road of flesh and sinew before his eyes. *All of them.* He smelled the stink of flesh and blood drying on the sand. *Because of you.*

No.

He started moving on bloodless legs, trudging in the direction of the gate. He couldn't breathe. He had to get out of the city, into the open air, keep walking until he could breathe, even if it took miles. He tried to draw in a breath, gasped for air, but choked on the stink of blood and death and...

Anger. His nostrils quivered. *Hair.*

Someone was behind him. Another tulwar. He couldn't go while someone was watching.

Deep breath, he told himself. *Straighten up. Turn around, growl a little, chase them off. Then start running.*

"This had better be good," he rumbled as he turned around, "if you don't want me to rip you—"

He saw the blade rushing toward him in one breath.

And he felt it the next.

His breath came back in a great gulp. His nostrils were filled with the scent of his own blood. His life splashed against his face in a dark red wash as a serrated edge tore through his shoulder.

A small part of him was able to appreciate how, if he hadn't been turning around, it would have gone into his neck.

That small part, of course, was overshadowed by a larger part that was able to appreciate how it would feel to rip someone's limbs off and beat them to death with them.

A roar tore from his throat. His hand lashed out. He felt cloth catch on his claws, heard it tear. But he felt no flesh splitting or blood spilling on his hand.

Through the blood dripping from his brow into his eye, he scowled down the alley at the shadow standing before him.

He didn't know what else to call it.

It stood upright, had a body, but he wasn't sure what else. It was wrapped in black, cloth hanging off it in tatters. A hood was drawn up over its head, nothing but a black, gaping hole where a face should be.

And though Gariath could see no eyes, he knew it was staring right at him as it raised a long knife dripping with his own blood and made a brief, mocking salute with it.

And then, it turned and ran.

And so did Gariath.

As thought left him, blood returned. His legs grew strong, and his heart beat with rage instead of fear. He tore off in pursuit as the shadow turned a corner.

Through the stink of his own blood, he could barely smell his assailant. It was as if it had no scent. No, he thought as he drew in a deep breath, it just smelled of hair and anger and shit, like any other tulwar.

Had Mototaru sent an assassin after him? To punish him for his weakness? Or had Daaru finally decided to take control?

Important questions. Gariath hoped he would remember to not crush the shadow's throat so he could get some answers.

He turned a corner. Another alley stretched before him and already, the shadow was almost at its end, so far ahead of him in so short a time. It was as though it flew instead of ran.

But Gariath had killed lots of things before. Some of them had flown, too. Didn't help them in the end.

He fell to all fours, letting out a roar as he charged after the shadow. He only barely felt the earth under him as he quickly closed the distance, the scent of the shadow's stink growing stronger as he drew up on it, the reek of hair, of anger, and of ...

His nostril quivered.

What was that? Alcohol?

No.

He saw the bright orange of a spark out of the corner of his eye.

Oil.

It fell from the rooftops and shattered on the streets in a spray of glass. A fireflask exploded on the dirt and immediately a wall of fire erupted in front of him, rising up from a stain of oil soaked into the earth.

Gariath skidded to a halt, snarled. On the other side of the fire, the shadow had come to a halt.

He heard the sound of a flint striking steel overhead, the whisper of flame catching. He looked up and saw a squat figure in leather, head wrapped up in cloth, holding a fireflask. Gariath braced to leap, but the figure turned and hurled the fireflask down the alley, away from him. It struck the earth and exploded into another wall of flame behind him.

A trap.

He scowled up. Through a wooden visor, the figure looked down at him and offered him a coy wave.

"Hfvf fhn, fshflh."

He turned back to the wall of flame.

And the shadow was in front of him.

And the blade was in his face.

He twisted out of the way, though not enough to keep the blade from biting into his side and ripping blood from him. He roared and leapt forward, into the blow, and reached out.

His hand wrapped around what he thought was a throat. He snarled, squeezed, and the shadow…

Simply disappeared.

Cloth crumpled in his fingers. The shadow stood away from him, out of his grip, out of his reach. He looked down at his empty hand for just a breath. And when he looked up again, the shadow was there.

And so was the blade.

It lashed out at him like a serpent; he narrowly avoided it. He snarled, swung for the shadow, and caught nothing but cloth and air as the shadow disappeared out of his hand and reappeared at his side, stabbing again, forcing him to dart away.

And again and again. Everywhere Gariath swung, clawed, struck, the shadow was gone. Everywhere Gariath looked, the blade was there, stabbing, biting, carving. Blood stained the sand, the walls, the blade; everywhere but his own claws. He would have convinced himself he was fighting a bad dream, were it not for the blade.

And as he felt the blood weep down his arm, it came to him.

He turned back to his foe, stopped watching the shadow, started watching the blade. Suicide, normally, but he only needed one blow. The blade lashed out, thrust right for his throat. His hand shot up, fingers wrapped around the serrated edge, and pulled hard.

He ignored the pain as the blade cut into his palm. All he felt was the weight of the shadow as he jerked it forward along with its blade. His free hand shot out in a fist and—

The crunch of bone. The impact of flesh. A groan of pain.

So it *was* real.

He let out a laugh, swung again. And the shadow was gone. The blade was still in his hand, but his foe had vanished. He caught movement out the corner of his eye and found his attentions drawn to the roof.

The shadow peered over the edge for just a moment before turning and disappearing.

"No," Gariath snarled. "You forgot your knife."

He leapt at the wall.

"You'll remember it when I jam it up your asshole."

The walls of Jalaang were rough, hewn from second-rate stone and sealed with cheap mortar. It was not hard for him to find crooks to scale the wall of the building and haul himself onto the roof.

He was breathless by the time he arrived. Breathless, bloody, and fading. But he didn't think about any of that. He hardly even noticed. His nostrils were full of the reek of his own life, his tongue tasted the sharpness of his own teeth, and every part of him was straining, holding on so tightly to the anticipation of the pain and the flesh tearing under his claws and the blood dripping into his jaws...

There was simply no more room for anything else.

The shadow was running, leaping from roof to roof. It barely even looked like it was there as the moonlight struck it, a hazy thing like a candle flickering in a strong breeze. But Gariath could still feel the echo of bone on his knuckles, the weight of the dagger in his hand.

It wasn't a bad dream.

It wasn't a candle.

It was real, flesh and blood.

He knew this because he needed to kill it.

He roared and took off running. He drew closer, his heart pounding. He saw the shadow slowing, his blood pumping. He leapt across a gap and landed on the same roof as the shadow, claws stretching.

He reached out. He caught something solid. He pulled hard, drew the shadow toward him, opened his jaws wide and lunged.

And that was when his leg gave out.

He fell to the roof first, heard the meaty smack next, felt agony lancing through his thigh last of all. He looked down at the crossbow bolt jutting from his leg. Across many roofs, so far away, he could barely make out the sight of a human—a human woman, tall and skinny with a massive crossbow.

He saw her wave at him as she disappeared off the edge of the roof.

When he looked back at his hands, they were empty again. The shadow was at the edge of the roof, staring at him as he lay there, crippled. Its arms slid out of the black cloth. It stretched them wide.

And made a dramatic, sweeping bow.

"The Prophet sends her regards."

A deep voice. A male voice.

A *human* voice.

And then, the shadow was gone. Like it had never even been there. He might even have believed that were it not for his wounds and his pains and the knife in his...

He looked down at the knife in his hand. Like a sheet of paper, it crumpled up and folded, turning to ash in his hand that blew away in a strong breeze.

And Gariath was left with the sound of his blood pattering on the roof as it wept from his body and the cries of alarm growing louder as the tulwar rushed toward him.

ELEVEN

THE BENEFICENCE OF TYRANTS

It didn't look like an army.

At least, not like any army Lenk had ever seen.

There were no long, orderly rows of soldiers awaiting orders. There was no structure to the camp at all, truth be told. They all gathered down in the valley in loose clusters, chatting away and dancing as though they were at a social ball and not in the middle of the desert.

There were no armories, no weapons, not even a single tent. The Chosen didn't seem to need tents; they barely even seemed to need the few fires they had lit. The cold of the night didn't bother them. They danced, they sang, they laughed. They were happy, they were free.

Shuro's wrong.

And that thought came creeping up into the base of his skull on cold, cold legs.

She's wrong about them.

He looked at them now, as he had been doing for the past hour. In the valley, the Chosen looked no different from most humans. They were taller, to be sure, and perhaps a little too... perfect. Their skin was clean and soft, their musculature lean and graceful. But they had hair, eyes, arms, and legs, like any other human.

And they used them.

Every day seemed to be new for the Chosen. They greeted each sunrise with gasps of delight. They heralded each night with a song. They clung to each other with no regard for who might be watching.

And why wouldn't they, Lenk thought. It wasn't so long ago, after all, that they couldn't do that. They were monstrosities: malformed and twisted with eyes that hated the sun. And before that? They were

Khovura, deranged and desperate. And before *that*? The dregs and filth of Cier'Djaal from which the Khovura had plucked them.

Why shouldn't they dance? Why shouldn't they sing?

Why was it that when Shuro had looked upon them, she had sneered and called them abominations?

Because she's wrong. That cold thought needled him again. *She doesn't understand yet.*

And again, he thought, *why would she?*

She had grown up in a monastery, surrounded by rhetoric and cloistered away from the wars, the diseases, the murderers.

She hadn't seen what he had seen. She hadn't known what he had known. How could she understand?

And why, he thought, could he never think of her without feeling like an iron spike was being jammed into the back of his skull?

It didn't matter, he told himself. What she understood or didn't understand, what she believed or didn't believe, that didn't matter. He knew the truth that she would someday understand. He knew the war that was coming that could only be stopped by the actions he had taken.

Lenk had made his decision.

And that thought brought him comfort.

And that comfort was colder, still, than the night.

He set off down the dune and into the valley. He felt an uncomfortable lightness on his shoulders. It was harder to walk, it felt, without the weight of his sword on his back. And despite the fact that he was in friendly territory, the absence of it was still keenly felt.

And no more keenly than when he entered the camp of the Chosen.

A shriek filled his ears. He tensed up, fighting the urge to reach for a blade he knew wasn't there. All he could do was steel himself as they came rushing toward him.

Long legs carried them in a writhing swarm. Long arms reached out for him. Mouths twisted into smiles and poured out formless squeals of excitement that writhed into each other. Within a moment, he was surrounded and their hands were upon him.

They reached out toward him. Some grabbed his hands and pressed them to their foreheads. Some tried to embrace him as he tried to step out of their reach. Some simply were content to lay hands upon him and let out a delighted shriek.

He tried to laugh as they did, tried to offer a congenial smile. Failing both of those, he settled for just trying not to look so horrified.

Since their return from the Temple of Darior, word had spread of how he had saved Mocca from Shuro's attack—largely because Mocca had spread it. The Chosen made their gratitude known quickly. He couldn't get within twenty feet of one of them without them swarming over, shrieking and squealing, and the rest of them following like a herd of swine following the scent of filth.

So many bodies so close to his set him on edge, yet he found he could tolerate their affection.

So long as he didn't look at their faces.

Even catching glimpses out the corners of his eyes unsettled him. Their smiles were a little too wide, showed too much teeth. Their eyes grew too big, blinked too infrequently. Their expressions trembled with elastic enthusiasm, made their skin shake and their cheeks grow too bright.

Like children, he thought. Big, excited, wild-eyed children who couldn't hear a damn thing outside their shrieking.

And if they got just a little too excited, if they reached out toward him with one of those big hands with their long fingers just a little too swiftly, grabbed him just a little too hard, and pulled...

No. He shook his head angrily. *They're* not *like that. She's wrong. She's wrong!*

He pushed his way out of the crowd of Chosen. They let him pass with little more protest than a few dejected moans. And within a few breaths, they had found something else to distract them: a fire to dance around, a new song to sing, another ferocious copulation to join...

Just as well, he wasn't keen on them following him as he trudged away into a corner of the valley. He had told Mocca to keep them away from this part, and he had no reason to doubt that Mocca could do just that.

He came to a halt. In the shadow of a looming dune, a small tent rose.

Whether Mocca *would* do just that, though, he had his worries.

He glanced over his shoulder to make sure the Chosen were still busy with their jubilations. Satisfied, he reached toward the tent flap. His hand lingered there, unwilling to pull it back. After a moment, he snorted.

Come on, he said. *It's not like she's going to hurt you.* He paused. *That is, it's not like she's physically capable of hurting you.* He pulled the tent flap back. *Unless she got loose, that is.* He stalked inside. *But if she has, it's not like you'd see it coming before she killed you.*

The tent flap closed shut behind him, bathing him in a darkness the oil lamp overhead didn't do much to counter. Several breaths passed and he wasn't dead, so he suspected she hadn't escaped.

And that was pretty much confirmed once he felt the cold, seething resentment settle around him like a cloak.

She didn't struggle as he approached her. She didn't curse his name. She didn't demand to be released, didn't threaten him, didn't vow vengeance against him.

Shuro didn't so much as move.

Her eyes were closed. Her head was lowered. Her hair hung around her still face in thick silver strands. Her blade and armor were gone, leaving her in simple leggings and a half shirt, exposing lengths of pale skin. It seemed, for a moment, that she was only held up by the chains that raised her arms above her shoulders, each one secured to one of the tent's support poles.

To look at her, one might have thought her dead. It'd be certainly less awkward if she were, Lenk thought—or if he were. Either of them, really; he wasn't picky.

But as he approached, he could see small signs of motion. The slight quiver of tense muscle as her body held itself rigid. The slow curl of hands into fists.

And that was to say nothing of the cold.

She seemed to drink in the warmth of the tent, of the sand, of the lamp. As if she were drawing inside her every little bit of heat to stoke a fire fierce enough to burn the chains from her wrists.

And as she held her breath at his approach, the night did the same. He was left standing before the woman he had betrayed twice, granted no sound or warmth to distract him from her hatred. And in that silence, he could almost hear her hatred being forged inside her, sharpened to a fine point and aimed right at his skull.

He shook his head to dispel that thought.

The thought departed, but the chill remained.

"Are you thirsty?"

Not the most graceful way to start, but he had to break the silence. And that seemed better than *Hey, sorry for betraying you and forcing you to watch your friends get crushed under the heel of a demon.*

Not that it mattered. Shuro didn't answer.

"You haven't had a drink since yesterday," he said. "I told Mocca to keep the Chosen away, so I'm the only one who's around to give you water, so..." He cleared his throat. "If you want any, I've got some. You know...here."

He found his eyes drifting to the dirt, as if to avert her gaze, even though her eyes were shut.

"Mocca wants to move tomorrow, to head toward Cier'Djaal," he said. "He doesn't anticipate much trouble. We'll go slow. And there's an ox cart you can ride, so you won't have to..." He looked to her chains, frowned. "Yeah."

She said nothing, did not move a hairbreadth. But still, he could feel her anger. He could feel the razor-thin spike of her hatred, boring into the base of his skull, forcing his eyes to the ground. And with each cold breath, he could feel it growing heavier, until he thought he might collapse under the weight of her fury.

"I'm sorry."

Her anger, that cold spike, knifed through his neck, pushing the words out of his mouth until they fell and lay cooling on the dirt, lifeless and impotent.

"I should have thought of some other way," he said. "I should have tried harder to convince you to...or Mocca not to...or..." He shut his eyes and tried to ignore the sounds of bone crunching in his head. "I wish it had ended differently. I wish I weren't even here. I wish I hadn't ever been made into..."

He looked at her with pleading eyes. She didn't look back.

"Don't you?"

Every word he spoke, she seemed to grow harder, colder. And he felt himself grow heavier, weaker. Until he thought he might collapse right then and there if he breathed too hard.

"I just want it to end," he said. "I want the killing to stop. I want people like you and me to be able to do something else." He swallowed something bitter. "I know you don't believe me when I say that. But you'll be safe until you see for yourself, at least. Mocca promised me that—"

"Listen to yourself."

Her words came softly, yet they made him take a sudden step backward.

"Giving it a name like that."

Her eyes opened, looked toward him. And beneath her gaze, cold and endlessly blue, he could feel something inside him wither.

"Like it's a person."

He could but look at her for a moment, barely able to meet that stare. But something inside him drew in a long, dark breath, forced him to look at her. And when he spoke, he was surprised to feel the heat in his words.

"He *is*," Lenk said.

"He's a demon."

"He can't be both? You only know what you've read about him. I've *spoken* to him. I know what he thinks, he feels, he regrets."

"And when did you learn this?" Something strained at the edges of her voice, a single crack across a sheet of ice. "When you were walking with me in the jungle? When were fighting alongside each other in Rhuul Khaas? When you claimed to be like me?" Her hands clenched into fists, sent her chains rattling. "How long have you been *speaking* to him? How long has he been twisting you?"

"Twisting *me*?" He took a step toward her, snarling. "You and I come from a dead god who built us to *kill* things. I'm not okay with that and *I'm* the one who's twisted?" He shook his head. "Whatever that monastery did to make you think that, it fucked you up *fierce*."

"*That is my home!*"

He took a sudden step back as she roared, lunging at him. Her chains snapped taut, holding her back. But her face was a mess of anger, her eyes shining with such heat that he feared they'd melt.

"Those were my *friends* you killed!" she said. "I grew up with them. I *learned* with them. And you and your fucking demon *killed them*!"

"*I didn't!*" he shouted back. "I *told* him to spare you back at Rhuul Khaas! You could have told them not to pursue! You could have gone anywhere, done *anything* and just left it alone!" He thrust a finger at her. "*You* came after us. *You* refused to listen. *You* attacked *us* and I wish you could have just fucking *stayed away*."

His breath tasted cold on his tongue. Her gaze hadn't softened in the least. He could still feel it in his back, keen as any knife, as he turned away from her.

"I'm sorry," he said. "I don't give a shit if you don't believe that, but it's true. I'm sorry."

"Sorrow means nothing," she spit at his back. "Your sorrow, even less. We didn't stay away because it was our duty not to. And because of *you*, my friends are dead and this world will suffer in a way thought possible only in stories."

"And what stories have you read?" His voice was heavy, dragging his shoulders down as he looked at her. "How many murders have you seen in stories? How many books talk about famines? On the page, they're just a number. Out there, they're bone and flesh." He gestured to the tent flap. "They're people killing each other for coin, people watching their homes burn. There isn't a poet born who could tell a story that would tell you even half the suffering that goes on out there."

He sighed, rubbed his head. It felt painful to the touch.

"That's why I had to do it. Mocca's going to fix that. Or try his best."

"How?"

The word came without force or malice. There was so little anger in it that he had to turn face her to make sure she had been the one to speak it. But she stood there, staring at him, right through him.

"How is he going to fix it?"

"He has a plan," Lenk said.

"What kind of plan?"

"A plan. He'll . . . he'll make them stop."

"How?"

"We'll find a way."

"How?"

"He'll figure something out."

"HOW?" When he didn't answer, she shook her head. "The demons are full of empty promises, Lenk. That's how they ended up in hell. We put them there because they sought to rule mortals, not help them. It's our duty to—"

"I AM NOT A WEAPON!"

She was struck mute by his roar, recoiled as though he had struck her. When he spoke again, all the wounds and all the scars and all the years came out with it.

"I'm not," he said. "I don't care about duty, what god gave it to me or who died to make me this way. I'm *not going to do it anymore.* I'm not a weapon. Not anyone's."

It wasn't a softness that crept into her face. Her eyes grew no warmer as they looked at him. But it wasn't the same piercing chill that stared at him. Rather it was something quiet, something heavy, the last snowfall on a dead tree.

"You're not a weapon, Lenk," she said. "He is."

His face twisted in confusion. "What?"

"You and I, we have duty. We do things no one else can. Whether we choose to do it is up to us." She looked toward the tent flap. "But the demons were created for a purpose. This is how they came to resent mortals. They were given all the power to rule us and were forced to use it to serve, instead."

He shook his head. "I've heard the same legends. I've *fought* demons. I know what they think and he's not like that."

"I don't doubt that at all."

Her reply nearly knocked the wind out of him. "Then how—"

"Other demons see us a prey, as obstacles, unworthy creatures tainting their earth," she replied. "But I've seen the way he looks at us, at *you.*"

"He doesn't see us as any of that."

"He doesn't. I don't know what he sees us as, but he doesn't see us as what we are. He sees us as he wants us to be, as he needs us to be." A flash of pain creased her face. "When he looks at you, Lenk, what do you think he sees?"

All the insults, all the accusations, all the curses she had spoken or could have spoken didn't hit him quite like that question. It knocked his mouth open, hanging dumbly for a reply.

He probably could have thought of a better one than storming out of the tent, if he tried.

She's wrong.

SHE'S WRONG!

They kept coming to him, the retorts that would make the cold pain stop and make her see. A dozen times, he turned back to the tent to tell her. And a dozen times, he stopped at the tent flap and turned back around.

They all sounded weak, words that limped out lamely and died on the dirt. And any time he tried to speak them, it was her voice he heard.

When he looks at you, what does he see?

Like a hammer, pounding that cold spike into his skull. He had to silence it. He had to make her see.

He had to know.

The Chosen were still in full revelry when he came back through their camp. And they were no less excited when they saw him. But he pushed through them. Beyond a few disappointed moans, he encountered no other resistance.

In fact, he noted, there were quite a few less than before.

He could see them at the edge of the camp. A few dozen simply standing there, arms hanging at their sides, staring out at some distant spot, swaying in the night wind like some kind of fleshy forest.

Freaky bastards, he thought.

Not freaky enough to deter him, though, as he hurried to the very tall dune at the edge of the valley and hauled himself up its slope, coming to a stop at its very peak.

A painted shadow framed in the light of a sinking moon, Mocca looked almost delicate. He was seated cross-legged, his eyes out at some distant point. The serpents of his beard stretched out from his chin, writhing as black stalks, twisting up over his head, their eyes tiny pinpricks of light in the night. He looked a little like a macabre flower in bloom, forever growing.

Yet as Lenk took a step closer, the writhing stopped. The serpents looked toward him and, with an almost resentful hiss, slid back to disappear into Mocca's skin.

Mocca, for his part, didn't seem to notice.

"You seem troubled."

"Getting in my head again?" Lenk muttered, stalking toward him.

A smile crept across Mocca's face. "You're always troubled. It's part of your charm."

He spoke without looking away and Lenk stared out over the dunes, trying to follow his gaze. And though he could see nothing but sand and dust ahead, he knew what the demon's eyes were fixed upon.

What was happening in Cier'Djaal right now, he wondered?

How many people had died since he had departed it? How many

shops had been burned to the ground? When they returned, triumphant, to save the world, would they even find anything left to save? Or would the only people to greet them be the legions of dead with their empty eyes and mouths?

And among the dead, Lenk wondered, would he see her carcass? Her fair skin thin with rot, her hair thick with grime, ears wilted like flowers in winter, and glassy eyes staring at him as if to ask if it was all worth it?

He shook his head. The thought left him, but another one crept in.

You would know, wouldn't you? His gaze drifted toward Mocca. *You can see everything in this desert if you want to. You could tell me if she was still alive.*

You'd tell me if she wasn't.

A breath. Cold.

Wouldn't you?

"I spoke with Shuro," he said.

A stony moment passed before Mocca spoke. "Not what I would have done, were I you."

"I know."

"But then," he sighed, "what is a mortal if not prone to spitting in the eye of logic?" He glanced out the corner of his eye toward Lenk. "I take it this is why you are troubled?"

Lenk folded his arms across his chest. "She still hates me."

"Unfortunate. But understandable."

"Understandable?"

"A mortal can only ever see a grain of sand or the entire desert, nothing in between. Whatever you did or did not do, she will only remember the blood of her fellow pawns on the dirt you stood upon. She may never again think of you without also seeing their bodies, broken and twitching."

He paused, then looked at Lenk with a sheepish smile on his face.

"Ah. Apologies. I expect you wanted to hear something more reassuring. Shall I try again?"

"How are you going to stop it?"

The words just came out, without him even trying. Mocca raised a quizzical brow, but he couldn't stop.

"How are you going to stop the war?" he asked. "How are you going to save everyone?"

Mocca's stare lingered on Lenk for a very long moment. Slowly, he looked back out over the dunes. Slowly, he spoke in a voice soft and ancient.

"Save everyone?" he asked. "Or save her?"

Lenk's mouth went dry. He found that he dreaded to hear the answer. And yet.

"Both," he said. "You said you could save them all. That includes her."

"I did, didn't I? That is why you delivered me from the pit, I suppose." There was a note of contempt in his voice, however brief. "To save her."

"Do you have a plan?"

"I do," Mocca said. "I will watch. I will listen. I will act."

Lenk blinked. "That's it?"

"I'm sorry to disappoint." Mocca cast him a sidelong smirk. "Would you have preferred something more dramatic? Making the heavens open up so that I may descend from a throne of clouds? Or perhaps arrive in a chariot pulled by seventeen white stags? And should the chariot be on fire? Mortals do seem to love fire."

"Stop that," Lenk said, voice hot. "You don't get to joke."

"No? Then take me at my answer," Mocca replied. "I will do what no god has yet been able to. I will see the hungry combing through the filth and I will give them food. I will hear the sick whisper their prayers to me and I will bring them a cure. I will not be blind, or deaf. I will simply... be."

Lenk stared out where he thought Cier'Djaal might be, squinted as though he could see, somewhere in all that desert, where Kataria might be.

"It all sounds so simple," he whispered. "It can't be that easy."

"Simple, yes. Easy, no. There will be work to do, of course. Some of it will come slowly and with great difficulty." He smiled. "But we cannot fail, Lenk. For we are needed."

He shut his eyes. The smile on his face grew broader, serene.

"I can hear them now. I can hear them praying in the dark. I can hear them whispering my name."

"Your name?" Lenk asked. "They don't know your name."

"They do. They simply call me something else there." He cast a glance at Lenk. "You doubt me."

"It's just...I've *seen* it. I've seen what kind of work we have to do out there. I sometimes wonder if even you can do it."

"Perhaps I can't. Perhaps this will all end in failure, somehow." He rose and placed a hand on Lenk's shoulder. "But, as someone close to me once said, I have to try."

"Yeah," Lenk said. "I did say that."

"And did you mean it?"

He met Mocca's gaze. "I did."

"Then cling to it."

Lenk hadn't read enough of them, but in so many stories, it seemed like there was always a moment where someone described a great weight being lifted from their shoulders. In Lenk's experience, it never happened as easily as that.

It got chipped away, that weight. Bit by bit, it fell from people and landed at their feet. And sometimes it followed them and hopped back on. Lenk was sure he'd feel that weight again, someday, feel it crawl back onto his shoulders and settle there until his back broke.

But, for the moment, he felt like a little bit of it had fallen away in just such a way that he could stand a little taller and breathe a little easier.

And yet, as he watched Mocca begin to walk away...

"How does it begin?"

Mocca paused, didn't turn around. A silence hung between them, as if giving Mocca a chance to pretend he hadn't heard, and Lenk a chance to pretend he hadn't spoken. And yet...

"The war that ends it all," Lenk said, "how does it begin?"

Mocca's figure trembled slightly, like a lake with a stone through it. He spoke a cold shadow of a word.

"How," he asked, "do you think it begins?"

"Armies," Lenk said. "Swords. Fire. Stones flying through the air, horses on the ground. Same as any other war."

"Of course." Mocca's voice was low, harsh. "Your stories are filled with such tales, aren't they? Romantic poems about men giving their lives to a glorious cause interspersed with dread tales of shock and horror, each one fighting for the control of the imagination."

"Are they not true?"

"Not this time. Not this war. Mortals are obsessed with death. They can't help but be. And so they build their great stone cities and carve their stone idols in hopes of denying that they will one day be forgotten. But creation, for a mortal, is simply a talent. Not a gift.

"The gods gave you one gift. Not fire. Not story. Not medicine. They gave you a need to destroy. And it burns so brightly within your blood that you can't help it. And it makes it so that, for all the creations and all the wonders in the world, just one person with a big metal stick can destroy it all, if they feel the need to."

Mocca's form was twitching at the edges. His skin was rippling. His robes billowed with a breeze that wasn't there. And his voice burned with a heat that made Lenk feel sick with fever just to hear.

And still, he asked.

"Tell me," he said, "how it begins."

"If we don't stop it," Mocca said. "It begins as all great wars begin." He continued down the hill. "With three words."

TWELVE

WIZARD'S DIPLOMACY

A_w, for fuck's sake, put some pants on. You can't fucking kill a man with your cock flopping about like a dead chicken."

And with those words, the plot to assassinate a Lector was under way.

Dreadaeleon staggered backward as the clothes were thrust into his arms. The woman who had brought them to him spared just a moment to cringe at his nudity before glancing at her companion.

"You couldn't have dressed him before you undid his bonds?"

The other Librarian, a tall Djaalic fellow, glanced up from the table he had just freed Dreadaeleon from.

"We're trusting him with the fate of the entire Venarium. I think we can trust him to dress himself." He glanced at Dreadaeleon and echoed his companion's cringe. "Seriously, though, put some pants on."

Dreadaeleon returned their sneers as he began to dress himself. "You're late. I expected you hours ago."

"It's barely midnight," the woman replied. She leaned out the door to Dreadaeleon's cell, glanced up and down the hall. "Annis has been working late these days. I hear he's trying to figure out the Venarium response to the war."

"That's what you wanted, right? The Venarium to be involved?"

Dreadaeleon cinched up his belt around his trousers, noting with a frown how far he was able to draw it around his waist. The food sneaked in by the conspirators had given him back some weight lost during his imprisonment, but as he looked down at his own scrawny body, he still thought himself not nearly the heroic figure he should have been.

Of course, you've never been one for bulk, have you, old man? He sighed, reached for his shirt. *Chin up. They'll remember you for what you did, not how you looked.*

"Not the way Annis wants," the man said. "He'd have us march out there, say a few words, and go back to the tower. We want freedom." He looked down at his feet. "I want to see my family again."

"He wouldn't do anything to help the city, anyway," the woman muttered. "Shinka's right. Our powers weren't meant to be cloistered up here. We're meant to be out there, helping people."

"And where is Shinka, anyway?" Dreadaeleon smoothed the shirt out and began to pull on the brown coat. "Call me crazy, but I feel like this would go more smoothly if I had another Lector fighting beside me."

"I'd call you worse things than crazy, personally," the woman said. "But Shinka is anything but. If you fuck this up, she wants to be far away. If you can pull it off, though, she'll be there when you need her."

"How reassuring."

Dreadaeleon hadn't meant to sound quite so sarcastic. Rather, he had meant to sound quite a bit more angry. After all, it was bad enough to be used as a tool *without* the implication of being left to die if he didn't do what he was supposed to.

But then, he thought with a sigh, *what else would you do with tools that don't work? It's not like you've got a hell of a lot of other choices, old man.*

That much was true.

Trusting his life to the aid of Shinka, who very clearly valued him only so much as his ability to harm a man who quite likely could kill him, was not good.

But staying down here to rot until he could be executed, harvested for his organs, and have the remainder of his body summarily incinerated or made into a Charnel Hound wasn't much better.

What *would* be good would be escaping, fleeing the tower and disappearing down some hole with someone warm and a voice like silk...

But you fucked that one up, didn't you?

He had tried not to think about Liaja. Because he couldn't remember her dusky skin, her flowing black hair, the curve of her lips without remembering that he couldn't see her. And he couldn't remember that he couldn't see her without remembering how badly he had fucked everything up.

He shook his head, forced her from his thoughts.

Not like she would do much good for him now.

Not like he had ever done much good for her.

As he buttoned the coat around himself, he noticed one more garment on the floor: a long, broad-brimmed hat. He picked it up, felt its weight in his hands.

"This is a Librarian's hat," he said. He glanced up. "Are these a Librarian's clothes?"

"It'll look less conspicuous to have a Librarian out at this hour," the woman replied. "Why? Is that a problem?"

He shook his head.

There was probably a poet out there who could find the words to voice the irony in him, the man who was to assassinate a Lector of the Venarium, wearing the iconic headgear of the Venarium's own champions, the Librarians.

Hell, he could probably have taken a stab at it himself.

But he was smiling just a bit too broadly to try.

"There's one other thing."

The man approached Dreadaeleon and reached into his pocket. He presented Dreadaeleon with a wooden box, small enough to fit neatly in the palm of his hand. He prized the lid open, revealing a soft velvet interior with a small gray thing that vaguely resembled a pebble sitting in it.

But Dreadaeleon knew all too well what it was, and his eyes widened at the sight.

"Broodvine," he whispered, in the same breathless manner in which a starving man slavers over a dead animal.

Instantly, he could feel the pains returning: the haziness of his vision, the crawling of his skin, the distant ringing in his ears. Just seeing the thing was enough to make the addiction come crawling back, skittering up his back on skinny little needle legs and latching on at the back of his skull.

"After your incident, Annis went on a rampage, getting every sample he could find outside the tower and locking everything up. We risked a lot to get it."

The man thrust it toward Dreadaeleon. Instinctively, he cringed away from it.

"You're quite sure"—he paused to wet lips that were suddenly dry—"you want to give that to me?"

"No chances. If you can't win with this, then we were fools to put our trust in you. What's the matter?" the man asked. "This is the thing you used to defeat Lector Palanis, isn't it?"

Dreadaeleon opened his mouth to speak but found no words. What could he say?

No thank you, the last time I used that stuff, your friend Shinka used it to drive me insane and kill a fasha?

So he had found the words but no voice to give them.

"It was a mistake," the woman said. "He can't handle it."

Something hot lit up behind Dreadaeleon's eyes. Without his even realizing it, his hand shot out and snatched the box up, then slid it into his pocket.

"I can handle it. I can handle anything. That's why you're trusting *me* to do this, isn't it?"

"Trust isn't the right word," the woman said. "I wouldn't *trust* you to piss yourself if you were sixty cups deep and strapped to a chair."

"It'd be more accurate to say that your intervention, we believe, yields the highest probability of the accomplishment of our goal." The man offered a stiff nod.

"Oh, good," Dreadaeleon replied with a sneer. "Just so long as we're all friends at the end of it."

The woman spared him a glare but said nothing else. She leaned out the door, peered down the hall once more, and stiffened up. She gave a nod down the hall, then glanced back to her companion.

"Yalva just gave the signal," she said. "Annis just left his study. We've got to move now."

The man looked to Dreadaeleon. "Same plan as before. Are you ready?"

Dreadaeleon stared at the hat in his hands for a long moment. Back when he was a child, one apprentice of many inducted into the Venarium, he occasionally wondered if he would ever wear this uniform. Granted, when he fantasized about it, he always imagined actually *being* one of the Librarians, rather than simply wearing their clothes.

But even then, he barely ever had a thought for the responsibilities that came with it, the dangerous tasks and most malignant heresies that only the Librarians were charged with solving. Rather, whenever he thought about wearing this uniform, his thoughts were always on the people.

The people who would look at him with fear and admiration: the barknecked peasants who would quake and shutter their houses at his passing, the swooning maidens who would quiver at the sensation of power radiating from him, the fellow wizards who would salute and stand at attention in his presence.

The apprentices, just as young as he had been, who would one day fantasize about being him...

And where are you now, old man? He could taste bile on his tongue, held back by a bitter smile. *So many years you've given them, so much of your life to their laws, their rules, their priorities, and what are you? A heretic to be persecuted, a tool to be used... when have any of them looked at you with anything but contempt?*

His fingers tightened around the brim of the hat until they shook.

No more, old man. No fucking more.

He raised the hat and placed it on his head. It settled down upon his head, perhaps a little bigger than he would have liked.

Just like any old dirty hat.

"I'm ready," he said.

⊷—══✦══—⊶

If there were two things wizards prided themselves on, they would be efficiency and the ability to render the typical barknecked mud-grubbing idiot sodden-trousered and jelly-legged with awesome displays of power.

If one asked them to choose between the two?

Well, Dreadaeleon supposed it varied from wizard to wizard, but whoever had been in charge of the design of Tower Resolute was likely more fond of impressing the rabble.

The tower stood tall over Cier'Djaal, dwarfing the two stone gods in Temple Row—or one, now, since the other one had been destroyed—and rivaling the Silken Spire itself for height. A typical wizard tower had to supply room enough for lodging, kitchens, laboratory, library, and chamber for its chapter of the Venarium.

And since Tower Resolute only had about two hundred fifty wizards, that meant there was a lot of empty space dedicated to meandering hallways such as the one Dreadaeleon found himself in.

It was fairly spacious, as hallways went—maybe wide enough for fifteen men to walk abreast and tall enough for three of them to stack on top of each other. Great sets of double doors were on either end of it. Tall pillars, such as the one Dreadaeleon was concealed behind, marched its length.

Ideal place for an ambush involving a magical duel, he noted dryly.

And, with significant less dryness, it was so wide that he could almost hear his own thoughts echoing as he ran through the plan for five hundredth time.

Easy, old man, easy. Breathe in. Breathe out. Steady. Keep your power under control or Annis will sense you a mile away.

He shut his eyes, breathed himself calm.

Any moment now, Annis will come through those doors there. He glanced toward the western doors. *And he'll head toward his study through those doors there.* He looked to the eastern doors. *There are two Librarians there already to hold the doors shut. Two more behind Annis to hold the western ones shut. They'll try to mask the magic you use here. It'll be just you and him.*

He felt something moving, looked down, saw it was his own hands shaking.

Stop that. He breathed in and out. *You can do this. Annis will be tired, weary, he won't be expecting you. A few quick lightning bolts, a bit of fire and you're done, old man. You're free. You can leave the Venarium behind. You can go wherever you want.*

If you don't die, that is.

Stop it. STOP it! He snarled, clenched his teeth. *You're going to succeed. You're going to escape. If the lightning and fire doesn't work, you can always...*

He could feel like it a weight in his pocket: barely the size of a pebble, yet it felt like a boulder. It weighed him down, telling him that all he had to do was take it out, pop it in his mouth, let the smoke come and the visions come and...

Careful. Broodvine's how you get into this situation in the first place. He shook his head. *It's how you wound up here. It's how you became a pawn. It's how you... how you lost...*

His vision grew hazy at the edges. She danced in the shadows of the hall: the scent of her skin in his nose, the flutter of her hair brushing against his cheek, the whisper of her voice in the stillness of the hall.

"Northern boy."

You don't need it, old man. He shook his head. *You don't need it. Don't use it. Don't you dare—*

He paused.

A sudden sensation pricked him: fluctuating temperature, a steady pressure on his temple. The sound of footsteps reached him shortly afterward as someone approached. He had barely enough time to register them before he heard the western doors creak open.

Here we go.

He tried to keep his body still, his breath shallow. He wound up tensing up so tightly that his legs ached and held his breath so long his lungs strained. How did Kataria always make this "ambush" thing look so easy, he wondered?

He heard the sound echoing through the hallway. Footsteps approaching quickly. One after another...and then another after another. His pulse quickened. His heart began beating.

Too many footsteps, he realized. *Annis isn't alone. They said he'd be alone! They lied to you. Betrayed you, old man! They set this whole thing up so—*

Easy. He took a breath. *Easy.* He swallowed bitterness. *Not like it matters much now, does it?* He clenched and unclenched his hands. *No matter how many are in here, the only way this ends well for you is if only one leaves.*

The footsteps came past his hiding place. So close, he was able to count them as they passed him. Three sets of feet, two of them slightly more hurried than the other. He waited for them to pass him, waited for them to reach the eastern doors, waited for them to stop and...

"What's the matter?"

A young voice, shrill and irritated.

"The doors won't open. They're stuck."

Another voice, still young, more worried. Neither of them Annis's. Had he even come?

"You're a wizard," the first one said. "If you can't figure out how doors work, you're in the wrong damn line of work."

"If you're so smart, *you* try them. Blast them open or something."

"No."

Dreadaeleon's ears pricked up at the sound of a third voice.

"That will not help."

Deep, rolling, bitter.

"They've been sealed shut."

Annis.

Blood hammered through his veins, a forge that made his breath burn in his mouth and his heart hammer against his chest. The power came bursting into him, rising up inside him to leap to his eyes, his hands.

Now or never, old man.

The power leapt to his mind, the word leapt to his lips. He spun around the pillar, fingers pointed out like a spear. The hall filled with a bright blue flash as the lightning raced down his arm, into his fingers, and into the air with a sizzling crack.

He could see it streak out from his fingers, flash across the room. He could see Annis as the Lector whirled about just in time for the lightning to reach a jagged arc right toward his chest. And he could *almost* see it pierce the bastard's heart and end it all right then and there.

Almost.

But then, things had never been easy for him before. Why should they start now?

The air shimmered. The lightning dissipated out into a dozen tiny rivulets of electricity, dancing across an invisible shield. Annis's face, a perfectly harsh order of hard angles crowned by a well-groomed scowl, hadn't so much as flinched.

His bodyguards, at least, looked a little frazzled.

Librarians. One man, one woman. The former was still gawping in wide-eyed shock, not certain what was going on. It had been just dumb luck, Dreadaeleon assumed, that the other one had managed to put up a shield. She stood beside Annis, her palms outstretched, eyes ablaze with the red glow of Venarie.

"The heretic!" the man gasped. "How…how did he…"

"Is it not obvious?" Annis muttered. "We have a traitor in our midst."

"In your midst?" Dreadaeleon chuckled. "The traitor is far from here, Lector." He smiled. His teeth were painted red as the Venarie's crimson light poured out of his eyes. "In your midst is something far more dangerous."

"We need help," the woman said, looking to her companion. "Go. I'll protect the Lector. Find the others and—"

"No." Annis's voice was a harsh rasp. His foot slid forward as he eased into a disciplined, steady stance. "There's only one way out of this." He narrowed his eyes at Dreadaeleon. "Isn't that right, *concomitant*?"

"Technically two, Lector," Dreadaeleon replied. He wiggled his fingers, letting the electric sparks dance across them. "Whether you want to leave as a carcass or a pile of ashes, though, I'll let you decide later."

"Do not fear him," Annis said. "A heretic is nothing to a true wizard. With me, members. One, two..."

Dreadaeleon wasn't about to let him finish. He thrust his fingers out, calling the power to them once more. Again, the lightning raced down his arm and out his fingers and sang a thunderous note as it rushed toward Annis.

Or so he assumed.

Really, it was hard to tell, what with all the lightning that followed.

In one fluid motion, the two Librarians mirrored Annis's stance, stretched their own fingers out, and called their own power. Their eyes, all six of them, burst with red power. Their fingers, all three of them, erupted with blue lightning. And in the time it had taken for Dreadaeleon to make one note, the three of them answered in a staggering, cobalt cacophony.

Dreadaeleon narrowly had time to duck back behind the pillar. And he had even less time to fall to the floor as he felt the hall shudder from the blow. Their lightning, all three jagged bolts, sheared through the pillar, gnawing off chunks of stone and spitting them out on the floor and leaving behind smoldering plumes of steam behind.

He heard electricity crackle again. He heard their feet sliding on the floor.

Move, old man. MOVE.

He called the spell to mind, to hands. He threw his limbs out behind him, felt the invisible force erupt from his fingers, propelling him forward with its energy.

He sailed across the floor just as the lightning came again, punching through the remnants of the pillar. It chased him, three tongues of a hungry snake, lashing at the floor and digging deep gouges in the tile as he hurled himself toward the next pillar. He slid behind it, taking cover as their lightning dissipated behind him, their limit met for the moment.

"Spread out," the woman snarled. "Flank him!"

"Do not," Annis replied. "Do not let him trap you in his desperation. Unity is our strength. With me."

Footsteps. In near perfect unison. They were moving toward him. He couldn't stay here, he knew, couldn't be defensive. If necessary, they'd simply blow up the pillars one by one until he had nowhere left to hide.

But what else can you do? he asked himself. *How the fuck are you supposed to handle* three?

He felt his hand drifting unconsciously toward that pocket, toward that weighty little thing in his coat. That thing that cost him everything.

He snarled.

You don't need it, old man. You don't! He looked around. *Think quickly. Three of them all moving together. They'll be slow. Just be faster.*

He looked to the floor, the seemingly impossible distance between his pillar and the one across the hall. An idea came to him just as quickly as the power did. He drew in a deep breath, felt his body go cold, felt the saliva freeze in his mouth.

He blew out a great cloud of white. It raced across the floor like a serpent, leaving a trail of slick frost behind it. And no sooner had it left him than he forced the power back into his arms, threw them out behind him, let the invisible force ripple out and propel him forward.

The momentum carried him out onto the frost. The ice carried him the rest of the way.

He slid across its slick surface, sailing effortlessly across the tile. Too quick for them to get an eye on him, let alone a spell. But he was ready, his power was prepared, and when he caught sight of them, the electricity was already dancing on his fingers.

He let out a shout, let the lightning fly from his fingers. It streaked toward Annis, veered suddenly toward the man. Librarian he might have been, he didn't see it coming in time. His eyes went wide. He let out a scream.

A scream so loud, Dreadaeleon didn't even hear Annis's spell.

The air rippled around the man, an invisible force shoving him out of the way. Dreadaeleon's lightning crackled through empty air, bit at the floor, brought him nothing but a few fragments of stone. He snarled and launched another bolt toward the man. Out of the corner of his eye, he could see Annis's hand pull back, drawing the Librarian back to his side.

Another bolt, this one from the woman, lashed toward Dreadaeleon.

But his momentum was too great. He skidded off the ice, across the floor, and ducked behind the next pillar.

Damn it, he thought as he ducked behind. *Gods* damn *it*.

"Concomitant Arethenes," Annis called out. "This is folly. You could not best me at your full strength. No matter what aid you've received, you'll not best me here."

He's right, you know, he thought. *Anything you can do—any fire, lightning, force, ice—he's had years more training and a hundred more battles than you have. He knows everything, can do anything.*

A thought, like an errant itch at the corner of his eye.

Except one thing.

No. Not that. You can do this, old man. You can beat him.

Footsteps. They were advancing on him again.

He glanced around. The hall was dimly lit by lanterns, each one glowing with a magical light. Not enough light here to bend to create a true illusion, but perhaps...

He reached out with the power, drew what tiny traces of light he could to himself. He bent it with his mind, shaped it into something new before him: a vague image of himself, a skinny fellow in a dirty coat. Hazy and shadowy, he thought, but it would have to do.

And, with that same power, he cast it out.

The shadowy image of himself stepped out behind the pillar. He heard lightning crack, saw a bright flash.

They took the bait.

He whirled out around the other side of the pillar, palms outstretched. He screamed a word. Smoke burst from the palms of his hand.

Fire followed.

In a crackling laughter, gouts of flame erupted from his hands, so bright that he had to shut his eyes. He saw the three of them turn his way, but nothing more as the flames washed over them. But the scream he heard—an agonized, womanly screech—told him he had hit.

No male screams followed, though. Rather, he could hear Annis bellow out a hasty word of power, draw in a deep breath.

What happened next, he felt.

The temperature dropped suddenly. He felt the sweat on his brow freeze. He felt the plumes of steam brush across his face as his fires hissed impotently.

When he opened his eyes, he saw nothing but white.

A great cloud of frost rolled toward him, extinguishing his flames and rendering them into tiny wisps of gray, swallowed and consumed in the cold. Crystals of ice formed inside, reaching out toward him like frigid fingers.

He turned to run back to the safety of the pillar.

He had taken maybe three steps before the ice took hold. It reached out from beneath him, seized his ankles and pulled his feet to the floor and held them there. He tried to pull at them, to no avail. He tried to call fire to his hand to melt them, but the cold seemed to reach inside him and snuff the flames out before he could even make them.

He growled, spread his arms out wide. The power welled up inside him, rushing from his chest to his arms to his hands. He brought his hands together in a great clap.

And the sound was thunder.

The cloud of frost split apart with the reverberating force, its crystals shattering.

Dreadaeleon drew in a breath, found it ragged and coppery on his tongue.

Too much magic, cast one spell after another, too soon. He wasn't strong enough to manage that. His muscles ached, his heart beat too quickly, his breath was ragged.

And still, it had not been enough.

The air shimmered with a rippling shield, the last vestiges of his flames sizzling off it. The male Librarian was sweating; the shield had been hastily erected, cost him a lot. The female was on the ground, clutching a blackened patch of flesh that had once been half of her face.

But Dreadaeleon's eyes were on Annis.

Annis's perfect stance, now slightly crooked. Annis's perfect breathing, now heavy and rapid. Annis's perfectly composed face, now glistening with sweat and marred by genuine surprise and anger.

Son of a bitch. Dreadaeleon couldn't help but smile. *That caught you off guard, didn't it? That's why your cloud was so big. You panicked, you old shit.*

"He burned me," the woman moaned. "That little shit burned me." She turned a single wild eye upon him. "Kill him. *Kill him!*"

"Lector?" The man glanced nervously to Annis. "What do we do?"

Annis didn't answer. No easy retort, no put-down. All the composure had fled from his eyes, replaced by a wild, desperate searching. Was he surprised by Dreadaeleon's power, he wondered? Or was he simply still processing the fact that he had been betrayed?

Dreadaeleon wasn't about to give them a chance to decide.

You can do it, old man. Finish it. Finish it now.

The thought came, the word followed, the power answered.

He drew in a great breath. The frigid mist of Annis's cloud came rushing toward him. His lungs burned with the effort, but he didn't care. He blew outward, sending the cloud toward his foes, little more than a thick blanket of slightly cold fog. But that was fine.

He didn't need it to be anything else.

He spoke a word, swallowed it, sent it deep inside himself. And something answered.

He felt himself burning inside, a furnace stoked. The ice melted from his boots, turned to water at his feet, turned to steam in his wake as he rushed forward through the mist. His blood boiled, skin trembled. His hands flexed, fingers spread wide open. Light blossomed upon his palm.

And hell followed.

Rivers of flame poured from his hands, devouring the freezing mist. He swept them up, driving the fire like a stampede before him.

He heard them scream in surprise, heard their hasty words as they struggled to put up shields to ward off his flames. And though the fires roared, they were not so loud that he could not hear the desperation in their voices, the sound of their footsteps as they retreated before the onslaught, step by step.

The flames cavorted, they writhed, they sang and sprang and tumbled over each other in their rush to get to the three piles of meat and kindling before them. Dreadaeleon pushed them farther, brighter, louder. He poured all that he had into them—his thundering heart, his rushing blood, the throbbing pain in his head. He had to burn them, he had to end it.

And they grew louder at his command, brighter. So much so that he hadn't even heard Annis's spell until the sound of thunder followed.

A rippling wall of force. Wide and tall as a tidal wave, it seemed to fill the entire hall. It drove the mist away before it, snuffed out the flames in an instant, cast aside the debris and stones and rushed toward

Dreadaeleon so fast he hadn't even had time to scream by the time it hit him like an invisible hammer.

And when it did, he had no breath to scream.

He sailed through the air, the tails of his coat fluttering behind him. He struck the floor in a tumble, skidded like a dying fish on a dock's edge until he collided with the doors.

The impact made him ring like a bell, sent it echoing through his blood. He didn't even think to try to stand, to breathe; he had not even the strength to think how impossible that would be. Yet he still had enough in him to think.

Power.

Too much, too fast, too big. Annis had expended so much to make a spell like that. He could still feel the reverberation of magic in the air, taste its crackling power with each breath. It had to have taken a lot to create something like that.

And, somehow, he found the breath to chuckle.

Gods help you, old man, he told himself. *If nothing else, you're the only man on this dark earth who could make Lector Annis break a sweat.*

He held on to that breath, that chuckle, however meager it was. He forced it into his lungs, his body, his legs. Bones ringing, muscles like jelly, he slowly clambered to his feet as he stared down the hall.

The woman was clutching the smoldering ruin of her face. The man was still terrified, trembling, his fear costing him as much power as anything. And Annis—tall, proud Annis—was breathing hard, draped in sweat, eyes ablaze.

And yet they all stood.

And yet they all advanced upon him.

However slowly, however warily, it didn't matter. They would be on him soon. And he felt he had barely the energy to stand, let alone face them. His head thundered with pain. His legs were numb beneath him. His heart felt like it was trying to punch out of his rib cage.

This was it, then. After so many times he had cheated law, death, and fate, this was how it ended. Incinerated, electrocuted, frozen, and smashed to icy shards; it didn't matter. No Harvesting this time; Annis wouldn't leave a trace of him left. There was that small comfort, at least.

He tried to come to peace with that, in the small time he had left.

No.

But some part of him refused.

No!

Some small part, drowning in the pain and numbness creeping through his body, spoke out. And though its voice was small, too, it was a pain all its own, a pain deeper than his aching bones and pounding blood.

Not this way.

It wormed its way into his chest, his limbs. It drove his hand into his pocket. It wrapped his fingers around the tiny little seed.

They can't kill you, old man. They can't use you. They can't stop you.

The barest flicker of power. The barest burst of fire in his palm. The seed was ignited in his hand.

Show them, old man.

His hand rose to his mouth.

Show them who they're fucking with.

And he slid the broodvine into his mouth.

First, nothing.

And then, a breath.

The smoke blossomed inside his mouth, great purple plumes that rushed down his throat and filled him, his bones, his blood, his skin. The pain melted away with every breath. The energy felt alive inside him, bursting so bright that the dim light of the hallway seemed clear as daytime and banished the shadows. The hallway stretched wide as a plain ahead of him. And at the end of it...

His foes looked so small.

He smiled. He drew in a deep breath. And, gaping wide, he blew it out.

The broodvine's smoke sang from him, a soundless symphony whose notes were the coils of its plumes and the writhing of its hazy cloud. The three extended their hands, put up the shields. But it was no use. The smoke slithered around their barriers, coiled up their ankles, reached out to fill their noses and their mouths and show them such beauties as he had seen.

"Cover your noses, fools!" Annis shouted out. "Don't breathe it in!"

His voice sounded faint and muffled to Dreadaeleon's ears. And because of that, he knew the Librarians hadn't even heard him at all.

To a common barkneck, the broodvine was just another hallucinogen, however potent. But to a wizard, it was a tool more powerful than any spellbook or relic. Magic could merely shape reality, but the broodvine erased it entirely and replaced it with something else, something driven by will.

His will.

He narrowed his eyes. He focused.

He disappeared.

Or so it seemed. One moment he was there, the next he was gone. The Librarians immediately thrust their hands out, fire and lightning dancing at their hands as they searched for him.

"Stop that!" Annis shouted. "Conserve your energies, you idiots. He's trying to trick you!"

He could hear Annis. They could not. He could see them. They could not. He knew how Broodvine worked. They could have only read about it.

"Where is he?" the man muttered. "Where did he go?" He glanced at his companion. "Do you see any—"

His voice turned to a shriek. When he turned to face the woman, she was no longer there. What stood in her place was a towering ghoul, as tall and black as any shadow. Skin hung from its body in charred strips. The flesh around its mouth was melted into thick globules that dripped over its teeth. Eyes wide and white and unblinking were turned upon him.

He fell to his rear. Through the screams, he somehow found the clarity to find a word of power upon his lips. He thrust his hands out toward the creature, his palms erupting with light.

Great torrents of flame swept from his palms and washed over the ghoul. It held up its own hands in a futile defense, or perhaps a futile plea, as it tried to beat the flames from its charred flesh. But the fires kept coming, bore it low to the ground where it lay, shrieking in a distinctly feminine voice.

"ENOUGH!"

Annis swept a hand out. A rippling force followed his gesture, struck the man, and sent him flying. He collided with the wall and fell to the floor, unmoving. Annis made a gesture toward himself. The pulverized stones and debris of the shattered pillars flocked toward him like graceless birds. They gathered together in a massive fist of rock.

Another gesture sent it flying, hurtling at a huge speed toward the wall of the tower. It punched a hole through the wall, opening it to the night air. Annis drew in a deep breath and the coils of broodvine smoke came to him. He made another sweeping gesture toward the hole and the smoke went flying out of it.

What was left behind was the mass of ashes and boiled blood that had been the woman Librarian, the unconscious body of the man, Annis's burning eyes, and...

"*No!*"

Dreadaeleon's voice, raw and scratchy. He could feel his power slipping away as the smoke left. The pains returned, raw and throbbing. His energy left him. The shadows seemed deeper, reached out toward him.

And when the air blew in, mercifully cold and clean, Dreadaeleon felt it as though he were naked.

"I should have killed you the first time I laid eyes on you."

And Annis's gaze, he felt like a blade upon his flesh.

"Shinka was right," Annis snarled. "I let devotion to protocol blind me. I let myself be convinced that you were just another heretic, like any other."

Annis came forward slowly, staggering with each step. So many spells, cast so quickly and so desperately, had taken much from him. Yet his weariness seemed only to make him more determined, his pain something entirely different from Dreadaeleon's.

After all, Dreadaeleon realized, *he* could still walk.

"Shinka was right about more than you know, old man." Dreadaeleon took a step forward to meet the man, felt his leg almost go out from under him. Without the smoke, everything felt so fragile, so agonized. "She told me—"

"*No.*"

His word was punctuated with the sound of thunder. Dreadaeleon barely had time to throw his hands out and put up a wall of force as the lightning bolt shrieked out and cracked against it, driving him back a step.

"I am through with you, heretic." Annis's fingers crackled with electricity as he advanced upon Dreadaeleon. "I am through with humoring your pettiness, your childishness, your insults."

Another word. Another bolt of lightning. Dreadaeleon's shield shimmered, straining to hold it back. He fell to his knees, could feel the muscle of his legs burst with agony, burning themselves up to feed his power.

"No more, heretic." Annis fired again. "No more words." And again. "No more of this shit."

And again.

And each time, Dreadaeleon recoiled. Each time, his shield shimmered. Each time, he felt a fresh pain rise up as something else burned to keep the power going—the muscle of his left shoulder, his right shinbone, the hearing of his right ear.

"Wizards built this tower, heretic." Annis drew close, so close that Dreadaeleon could smell the storm on his skin. "It is not a place for weak-minded cowards." He thrust his fingers toward Dreadaeleon. His eyes burned bright enough to fill the hall. "And not for petulant, whining little *boys*."

A single word.

A bright blue flash.

The smell of electricity cleaving the air and skin sizzling and hair curling into thin gray coils of ash.

And Dreadaeleon fell.

The bolt shattered his shield, pierced through his power, and struck him square in the chest. That power had been all that kept the bolt from killing him outright. The smell of his own flesh burning and the agony of his wound was all that kept him awake as he lay on the floor. His body begged to sleep, to simply stop and slide into darkness.

And, truth be told, Dreadaeleon couldn't think of a good reason why it shouldn't.

It was always delusion to think he could defeat Annis. Really, it was a miracle that he had delayed him as much as he could. Three wizards to one malnourished and weakened heretic was impressive odds to have even started a fighting chance.

Really, he thought, it was a miracle he was still breathing.

He once observed this phenomenon in his former companions: in the way Lenk would pull himself back up to fight, in the face of clearly overwhelming odds. He had once asked after such an occurrence and Lenk had explained it as a state at which the mind ceded to the body and the body simply refused to die.

Dreadaeleon had always suspected he meant that some people were simply too stupid to die when they ought to.

And, up until now, he never thought that was actually the case.

And yet...

"I'm not weak."

His voice, ragged in a throat scraped raw, the taste of his own blood on his tongue. But somehow, still speaking.

"I'm not a coward."

His legs, burned and boneless and bloodless beneath him, withered to twigs. But somehow, still standing.

"And I'm not... I'm not..."

His power, blazing brightly, burning inside him, hot with fury and cackling in anticipation. Erupting out of his eyes, out of his hands, out of his mouth as he turned all of them on Annis.

"I'M NOT A BOY."

Fire. Everywhere. Everything. Fire. From his hands, from his fingers, from his mouth. In great rivers and in great storms and in great plumes. Cackling, laughing, roaring, snarling, alive and eager and hungry.

So very hungry.

He sensed Annis's power, though only barely. The Lector reacted quickly, reaching down and pulling the very stone from the floor. It rose up in a coarse, crumbling shield in front of him, barely holding back the flame.

The fire poured out of him, flowed out of him, as though it were the true being and he was merely an inconvenient cloak of flesh and blood that it was currently disentangling itself from.

It burned with such furious intensity, yet he could barely feel it. His body temperature dropped; everything poured into his flames. He could feel his body going dark as the light left him in great, ruinous bursts. The power to fuel it demanded everything from him and, one by one, it took it: his liver, his sinew, his blood, his toes.

But he couldn't stop.

He refused to.

Never again, he told himself. *Never going to be used... never going to be defeated... never going to be humiliated...*

The shield of stone crumbled and flew away in smoldering chunks. Annis held his hands out, his words lost in the roar of the fire, the air rippling around him as he put up a flimsy shield. But the fire ate everything, ate the very air. Annis's shield shrank, forcing him back.

More. MORE.

And Dreadaeleon could not stop it. He gave the fire his heat, felt himself go cold. He gave the fire his breath, felt his lungs wither. He gave the fire his voice, his rage, his very being.

Almost... you can do it... you... you...

Until he could give no more.

The fires did not die easily. They shrank as they had nothing left to feed on, retreating, dissipating, leaving behind nothing but smoke. And when the last of the sparks hissed away, they did so almost resentfully, cursing Dreadaeleon for not giving more.

He would have apologized, had the fire not taken his voice, too.

As it was, breath was all he had left. The rest of him lay on the floor, a limp and flaccid husk, unable to move, to speak, to see. But slowly, as the fires faded, the brightness blinding his eyes did, as well. The shadows returned and so did his sight.

And he could see that, despite it all, Annis was still standing.

Only barely, only just, but he was still there. His clothes had been seared away, and much of his hair had gone with them. His skin bore red and black marks from where the fire had started to gnaw on him. But he still drew breath, however ragged, and he still stood, however shakily.

Dreadaeleon had failed.

He had given everything, and he had still failed.

Annis, at the very least, looked as though he had nothing left in him, either. There was nothing left for hatred or anger as he looked down at him. Only a long, weary appraisal, wondering how the hell it had come this far. He had nothing left for spells. The task of killing the young man lying on the ground, even weak and limp as he was, seemed beyond him.

That was fine, Dreadaeleon thought. He was quite capable of dying here all on his own.

He heard a distant sound from beyond the eastern doors. A few dramatic words shouted, a few thunderous crackling sounds, a few forced shrieks.

He didn't even need to look up when the doors came swinging open to know it was Shinka.

"Annis!"

She came rushing through the doors, followed by a trio of Librarians. She charged up to him, arms extended as if to invite him to collapse into her embrace. But he remained standing, swaying precariously. She swept a wild gaze about the ruin of the hall, a convincingly dramatic expression of shock and horror across her face.

"What happened?" She looked to Dreadaeleon, mouth agape. "Is that the heretic? How the hell did he get loose?"

"Traitors..." Annis's voice was a weary croak. "In the Venarium..."

"What?" she gasped. "How is that even possible? Annis, come, sit down, tell me everything." She pointed to one of her Librarians. "You! Bring water for—"

"Spare me."

Though he could barely stand, Annis still found the strength to cast a long, ugly sneer toward Shinka.

"I know..." He snarled through clenched teeth. "I...know."

The manufactured shock drained away from Shinka's features like perfume from a porcelain basin. Left behind was the cold, appraising stare of a wizard, emotionless and distant.

"I see," she said, folding her hands behind her back. "Shall I ask how?"

"Who...else?" Annis grunted. His body shook, as though he were trying to find the strength for a spell to hurl at her. Or, failing that, simply to strangle her. He could find the power for neither, though, and so he simply gasped. "Why? For...power?"

"Power has always been the pursuit of men like you, Annis," she replied. "The names change, of course. Sometimes it's magic, sometimes it's gold, sometimes it's women. But people like you, they simply hoard it, keep it out of the hands of those who could use it for good."

"Liar..." He managed a weak step toward her. *"Heresy!"*

That was just a bit too much. He collapsed to his knees, trembling, still refusing to fall down completely. She sighed, kneeling down to meet his eyes.

"I won't waste what little time you have left with speeches trying to convince you of the righteousness of what I'm doing, Annis," she said. "Had I thought there was another way, I would have done it. But too many people have died while we've been held prisoner by antiquated laws."

She rose, turned away from Annis, and looked to the western doors. She called out a word and they came open. Another trio of Librarians entered, sparing a glance for Dreadaeleon before joining Shinka and their companions. The Lector let a firm look linger over them a moment before speaking.

"I was stirred from my studies on the lower level shortly after midnight by the sounds of carnage," she said. "I departed to investigate."

"You called the three of us," one of the Librarians said, "to come accompany you once you sensed magic was being expended at great rates."

"We sensed it, too, on the upper level," the other Librarians said. "We arrived too late to help."

Shinka nodded. "Unfortunately, it seems the heretic escaped. His restraints had been applied improperly."

"The clerks that tended to him last," one of the Librarians said, a trace of black humor in his voice, "will be punished accordingly."

Shinka searched the chamber and saw one of Annis's bodyguards—the male one—lying unconscious on the floor. She strode toward him and, with a flick of her wrist and a word of power, sent her flames out. The man's screams were wretched, but brief, as the flames hungrily ate away cloth and flesh until naught was left but a nondescript pile of molten flesh.

"Annis fought bravely, having tried to stop the heretic," she said, once the screaming and the fire had both died down. "Though he succeeded in nearly incinerating the heretic, the madman's desperation allowed him to fight well beyond his abilities."

She muttered a word, let out a breath. A cloud of cold frost poured from her lips, ice crystals dancing within. At her gesture, they drew together, forming a thick icicle as long as a sword. It hovered in the air, dancing at her fingers, following like a particularly vicious puppy as she returned to Annis.

He glared up at her, breathing heavily, unable to do anything else. Though even as weak as he was, the hatred boiling off him was enough to fill the room. And yet Shinka did not so much as blink.

Not as she flicked a finger at him.

Not as she sent the icicle toward him.

Not as it plunged through his chest.

"Unfortunately, he succumbed to his wounds during the fight," she said.

Annis's face contorted in agony. But no scream followed. She had aimed the icicle perfectly, driving it through his chest so that it perforated his left lung. He had no breath to scream, to gasp, to do anything but collapse onto his side and begin the long, agonizing process of choking on his own blood.

"A true hero of the Venarium," one of the Librarians said. "He will be remembered."

"He died in my arms, gasping for air," another added. "His last words were begging me to remember his legacy."

"It remains my greatest shame to this day," a third muttered, "that I arrived too late to save him."

Shinka watched as Annis twitched on the ground. She watched as blood dribbled from his mouth. She watched as the anger and hatred on his face slowly uncoiled into the wide-eyed emptiness of death. And when he finally stopped moving, she turned away and offered a shrug.

"It's not perfect, I suppose," she said. "There are a few holes in it. But we've enough support in the Librarians that the concomitants and apprentices will accept our version of the story." She narrowed her eyes ever so slightly upon the assembled conspirators. "Assuming no one is having second thoughts."

"Just one . . ." A Librarian looked toward Dreadaeleon and gestured with his chin. "What about him?"

Shinka glanced at Dreadaeleon with a quirked brow, as though she had only just now noticed him. She went to his side, leaned down beside him, studied him coldly.

"Dreadaeleon," she said, "can you hear me?"

He couldn't imagine what his face looked like—for he couldn't feel his face anymore. But he guessed from her deepening frown that it didn't look good. She picked up his hand and raised it—he couldn't feel that, either. His fingertips were black as pitch, dark veins creeping down into his palm.

"Decay," she muttered. "Too much magic, too quickly. It must have taken everything you had to fight Annis." She looked to him and sighed. "I suppose it'd be too much to hope that you simply believed in our cause that much, hm?"

"It'd be kinder to kill him," one of the Librarians said. "He's served his purpose." She glanced to the incinerated carcass posing as him. "Besides, *this* guy is a little too tall to be the heretic."

"No," Shinka said. "I made an agreement with him. We are forging a new Venarium this night and its first act will not be one of dishonor." She sighed, lowered Dreadaeleon's hand. "Find a way to get him out of the tower. Take him to my rooms at the Golden Lotus, at the edge of the Souk."

"And do what?"

"Nothing." She rose up. "Make him comfortable. Give him water if he'll take it, food if he asks for it. Though I think his vocal cords were burned away. Tend to him for a few hours."

She looked down at him and offered him one more frown. Though there was no pity in her face, no lamentation for his fate in her eyes. Rather, hers was the fleeting sorrow of farmers who saw their tools broken before the harvest. It was weary, it was weak, it was brief.

And she turned away from him and walked through the ashes of the hall, leaving him as just another pile of debris among many.

"It won't take long."

THIRTEEN

An Echo Unspoken

How long had they run, she wondered?

It seemed an eternity ago that they had started. The yiji had been so swift beneath them, and yet the tulwar had still chased them. Even when it had all but keeled over, panting, they couldn't be sure they had lost their foes. And so they had sent their beast to roam in another direction while they fled south.

The moon had been high in the sky, dropping like a stone, when they were finally so far that they could be certain they had shaken pursuit— or so tired they hadn't cared. It had taken more time still to find the giant rock formation towering out of the dunes, to find the small cavern scarring its stony face. By the time the fire had been made, the fur had been laid out, the water had been drunk, there was no blood left in her limbs and no breath left in her lungs.

They had run so long, so far, so swift that she felt she might simply collapse.

And still, Kataria could not sleep.

Or rather, it would be truer to say she *would* not sleep.

Not while she still had to save everyone.

⁌ ⚊✦⚊ ⁍

Her fingers were trembling—whether from exhaustion or from anticipation, she couldn't tell—as she raised the scroll before her. A piece of dried hide bound by a simple twine, a patch of dark red where the tulwar that had carried it had bled out on it.

A simple thing. A dirty piece of leather. And yet she almost had not the will to open it, not the hope to lose if it was not what she needed.

Her mouth dry, she didn't think of water. Her body aching, she didn't think of sleep. She pulled the twine free, let it unfurl.

A map—crude lines in coarse charcoal on dirty hide—but it was unmistakably a map of the desert. Here was a marking of a destroyed village, there a drawing of a canyon, there the oasis they had fled from. And through it all ran a thin red line of dried blood. Alongside it, numbers, crosses, markings she didn't recognize at first.

Yet the longer she stared at it, the more it came together: the map, the words the tulwar had spoken before she had fought them, the lines and the markings.

"Shekune."

Her lips trembled as she whispered the name.

"This is it," she whispered. "They've been tracking her."

It hardly seemed like a thing that could be done, tracking a shict. But still, Shekune moved with an army. Armies moved slowly, left signs. And if any tulwar could have done it, it would have been those tulwar who had risen from the dead as though rising from a rough night's sleep.

Even the unnaturalness of that encounter seemed so distant, so insignificant, compared to what she had found.

"Look! They actually did it!"

She looked over her shoulder, beaming. Kwar wasn't looking at her. Her back was turned to Kataria as she stood at the cavern's mouth, staring out over the rolling desert. She was breathing heavily, leaning on a nearby stone.

Probably still exhausted, Kataria thought. And who could blame her? She had seen what Kwar had done to that female tulwar—all that rage, all that blood, all that screaming. It was hard to imagine that just that morning, the khoshict had lain still as a corpse.

But that, too, seemed distant and insignificant. As did everything before this map, this chance.

She studied it further, stared at it carefully. The markings that seemed alien at first slowly began to take shape. She could see crude symbols depicting pointed ears, arrows marking directions, crosses marking stops. Slowly, a pattern began to emerge.

"It's a loop," she whispered to the map almost reverently, as though she expected it to smile with leather lips and nod knowingly. "Shekune makes a pattern around the desert. Setting traps, maybe. Talking to troops? Securing lines?"

She shook her head. Her heart thundered inside her.

"Doesn't matter," she muttered. "We know where she goes." She narrowed her eyes and studied the pattern a little more closely. And it dawned on her. "They mark the number of times she's been at one of these places. Where's she going to be next?"

And then she saw it.

A crude little drawing. A tiny blotch of black coal on the hide marking a rocky pass. Just a little north of the oasis they had been at, in fact. Barely a day's ride.

Nothing more than a little smudge of charcoal on a dirty piece of hide.

That was all that she needed to save everyone.

A tiny dirty smudge was going to stop a war.

"We did it."

She didn't want to laugh. She knew it wasn't going to be that easy. But she couldn't help it. She laughed, despite the aches in her body and the hoarseness in her voice; she laughed so hard it carried her to her feet.

"We know where she's going to be next!" she laughed. "We can stop her! We can save everyone!" She turned toward Kwar. "We can..."

She looked up from the map.

Kwar was looking at her.

The khoshict stood at the mouth of the cave, staring at Kataria. Her arms hung limp at her sides. Her mouth hung open, numbly. Her body shook with breath so ragged, Kataria thought she might keel over and die.

But Kwar was alive.

In the burning of her dark eyes, a lightless fire that brimmed with warmth. In the tremble of her skin, glistening with sweat. In the sound of her heart beating so fiercely Kataria could feel the sound of it in her own ears.

Kwar was alive.

"I killed them." Kwar's voice was soft, painfully so, the hush of a knife sliding out of a leather sheath. "I stabbed them. They just got up. I stabbed them."

"They were weird, yeah." Kataria shrugged. "But we lost them. There's nothing to—"

"I killed them." Kwar didn't seem to hear her. She looked down at the ground. "I was lying there, on the dirt, and I couldn't feel anything and I couldn't move and I couldn't hear…" She shook her head, swallowed hard. "But then I did…I heard…"

She looked up. And Kataria felt the khoshict's eyes upon her. And then, she felt the khoshict's eyes look through her, peer past her clothes and past her skin and her hair and see something inside her that made Kataria's belly clench.

"I heard you." Kwar's ears twitched, living and trembling and excited. "I heard your Howling." She reached up, laid a hand across her own chest. "I heard you here."

"You saved me." Kataria was only barely aware of her own voice, which sounded so clumsy by comparison. She was only barely aware of how her own ears trembled. All she could feel was Kwar's eyes, searching through her, beneath her, into her. She looked away. "Thanks. Thank you for that."

Kwar shook her head, giving no sign that she had heard Kataria. "And I…I didn't think anymore. I wasn't thinking about anything, about how heavy my head felt or about Shicttown or about Thua or…or…"

She suddenly swept toward Kataria with such swiftness and such purpose that she almost backed away. Something inside her, that thing that clenched her belly and made the hairs on the back of her neck rise up, shouted at her suddenly to run.

And something else inside her made her stand still.

"And I don't know if that makes me bad for doing that or for not thinking, but I felt…I felt *good*."

Kwar's eyes were wide, wild with the fire burning in them. Her breath was heavy and hot on Kataria's skin. And still she stayed.

"I could feel my legs again. I could feel my breath. And I couldn't think of anything…" Kwar shook her head. Her lips twisted into a snarl, baring her broad canines. Her eyes narrowed upon Kataria. "I couldn't think of *anything* but…but…"

She swept forward. Her hands shot out, seized Kataria by her arms, pinned them to her sides. Kataria saw big, broad canines rush toward her. Inside her, something let out a long, loud sound.

There was no softness in the kiss.

No gentleness in Kwar's lips, no tenderness in the way her tongue slid past Kataria's own. There was only a hungry need, a growling, trembling energy that poured out of her mouth, out of her skin as her belly pressed against Kataria's. And it shook so hard that she might just explode.

And still, the sound of her snarl, of her skin against Kataria's, of her sweat sliding down her body, was not so loud as the Howling. The long, endless sound that rose up inside Kataria's head and raced into her chest and echoed there. Long. Loud. Screaming.

Alive.

She broke away just as suddenly, almost shoving herself off Kataria. Her eyes were still wide and her body still shook, but this time with a sudden fear, just as primal as her hunger had been. Her mouth fumbled over her words before she found one to latch onto.

"Sorry!" she said. She shook her head. "Sorry. Sorry. You told me not to touch you and I didn't mean to...I just couldn't...I had to...I felt..."

Maybe she found more words. Kataria couldn't tell. Kataria couldn't hear. The noise inside her, Kwar's Howling, only grew louder. And inside her own head, rising from somewhere deep inside her, she could hear another sound, the same one she had heard when she had almost died at the hands of the tulwar earlier that day.

Maybe it was that noise that made her reach forward. Maybe it was something else that made her grab Kwar's hand. Maybe it was something she had buried deep enough that she had forgotten she had it that made her pull Kwar toward her.

Kataria couldn't tell. Kataria couldn't hear.

Feet tangling, tripping over each other as Kwar slid into her, pressed her back. Cold stone on bare flesh, the chill of sweat mingled with dust as her back pressed against the cave wall. Teeth at her neck, closing down on the tender skin just beneath her earlobe. Hair in her fingers, braids twisting in her hand as she pulled her closer.

They found the furs laid out somehow, when their legs wouldn't carry them anymore. Kataria looked up as Kwar straddled her waist, saw a silver drop of sweat peel off her brow and fall, splashing cold upon her collarbone. The khoshict's eyes, wild and dark against the firelight, stared at her.

"Are you...are you sure?"

Her body twitched. She seized Kwar by the hand, pulled her down toward her. They tumbled across the furs until Kataria rose up over her. She leaned down on her hands, her hair brushing across Kwar's face as she felt a smile spread across her own.

"Trust me," she whispered.

Her hand found Kwar's cheek, just as Kwar's hand found hers. The khoshict closed her eyes, smiling as she sought to hang on to that hand as it slid downward. Kataria felt the trembling, twitching anger in her body—the roar that spoke so loud inside her that it drowned out all the sorrows and all the hates that had come before.

Kataria's fingers brushed lightly across her neck, trailing down over her collarbone, sliding between her breasts. Her stomach tensed, fine hairs rising in a halo around her navel as Kataria's hand fumbled at the knot of her sash, tore it free. The cloth of her kilt fell away in folds. The muscle of her leg tensed, as Kataria's hand slid down it, over it, between it.

She leaned down closer. Kwar looked up at her with eyes that she had thought she had never seen, an impish curl of a smile that she once thought was gone. And she felt her own smile grow broader as she closed her eyes, leaned down, and pressed her brow to Kwar's.

"I missed you."

Her fingers wandered up, found soft skin and the shudder of a breath drawn quick and held. Kwar's hand slid around her, pulled her close. She felt the dust and sand that covered Kwar mingle with her sweat, the coarseness of the mixture on her own skin as she pressed herself against the khoshict. She felt the curve of her back as she arched her neck for sharp teeth to find. She felt fingers curl around her arm, draw her close with such desperate need that it ached more deeply and sweetly than all the agonies that had come before.

If there were words, she did not have them. They were lost in the sound that rose up. No mournful cry, no savage roar, no anger or hate or sorrow behind their Howling. Just two wordless voices, two tuneless songs, meant only for each other and silent to the world.

Until the nails drew red across the pale skin of her back. Until Kwar's belly pressed up as her back arched and she let out a soft cry into the night. Until Kataria fell upon the furs, hair matted in damp locks against her brow, and her body would barely find the strength to draw breath. Until they lay there, Kwar's head against her chest, her arm around Kwar's waist, and their Howling went so soft it was just another breeze across the desert.

She didn't want to say anything. Words felt so clumsy now, dumb and useless. But still, they clawed their way up her throat and into her mouth. She tried to keep them there, hidden behind her teeth.

It should have been easy to forget that they lived in a world where they needed clumsy words. It should have been easy to forget that they lived in a world that would be torn apart before too long. It should have.

But times like these, when she felt someone warm and brimming with life beside her, were too rare.

And this world would never be so kind as to let her forget that.

"I have to stop her."

They hung in the air, in the smoke of the dying fire, so long that she thought Kwar hadn't heard her—or wouldn't.

"I have to kill her."

Kwar stirred beside her, shuddered. She closed her eyes, let her hand slide away from the khoshict's waist.

"I won't ask you to help," she said. "I won't even ask you to come with me. But I . . . I have to, or else she'll—"

Kwar let out a long groan. "Oh, for fuck's sake, do you have to be so dramatic about it?" She drew herself closer, wrapped her arms around Kataria, and pulled her tight. "You're talking about killing the greatest warrior the desert has ever seen, averting a war that would kill us all. You're going to need someone terribly clever to help you."

She laughed. Weak, breathless, Kataria laughed. "Well, great. For a moment, I was worried it was going to be hard."

"Impossible, even," Kwar said.

"It could be." She had no breath to sigh. No energy to frown. She stared up at the roof of the cavern and the shadows dancing across it as the fire crackled nearby. "It could all go to shit."

"It could," Kwar said. "But it won't."

"What makes you so sure?"

Kwar's hand was at her cheek, pulling her face toward her. Her eyes, dark and wild and still so alive, glimmered in the dark.

"I trust you," she said.

FOURTEEN

BACK ALLEY GODS

Back in the north, there was a saying.

The gods can't tell you how to make money, how to win a woman's heart, or how Saine is still a nation.

Roughly after a century of struggle—all the wars of conquests, the uprisings, the trade disputes—diplomatic policy as to how northern nations dealt with the Kingdom of Saine hadn't amounted to much more than that particular saying.

And having been this close to them for months, Asper could see why.

Karnerians might have been a lot of things—intolerant, expansionist, closed-minded, and belligerent—but at least they were ordered, at least they were predictable.

Sainites, by contrast, were rowdy, aggressive, loud, and, above all else, fiercely independent.

Originally, they had been formed out of several smaller kingdoms, their perpetual wars ended only when scraw-riders brought them to heel. But even then, the only way the kingdom functioned was by adhering to the old clan laws that allowed them far more self-rule than most armies would allow.

This had, in fact, been what had brought them into conflict with the Karnerians. With a strong desire to be free of the fate that the Karnerians had inflicted on other nations, the Sainites repulsed the Imperial Legions, liberated the conquered territories, and then quickly reconquered them so that they might also experience the joys of Sainite freedom.

Asper agreed with a lot of Sainite philosophy. But even the parts she didn't agree with, she could understand the reasoning behind.

"Listen, if you didn't hear me, you little shit, you need to pull your head out of your fuckin' god's feathered arse. The wing-sergeant ain't seein' anyone."

And, truth be told, she perfectly understood why this particular Sainite—a young woman in a dirty blue coat with a tricornered hat pulled low over her eyes—was being a particularly sharp pain in the ass.

"I heard you just fine," she replied. "And you'll notice I'm not going anywhere, despite your vulgarities. I have urgent business with Blacksbarrow. You can either let me in or explain it to her yourself when she breaks your jaw for not letting me." She sniffed. "You shithead."

Just as she understood why that particular word at the end there was necessary.

Sainites, she had learned, responded only to three things: strong beer, strong language, and strong fists. Most of the time, they could be persuaded by at least one of those things.

Most of the time.

But today was different.

She could almost smell it on the smoke that carried through the air. Today, there was an air of nervousness that didn't befit the Sainites.

Today, words weren't going to be enough.

The fall of their garrison had only barely inconvenienced the Sainites, mobile as they were with their avian scraws. They had set up a makeshift base on Harbor Road. With the sea as their wall to the west, and a row of taverns and bathhouses to the east, they had formed walls to the north and south with whatever else they could find.

The young woman that blocked Asper's way stood in front of a small gap in a barrier of debris—shattered chairs, pieces of ship's hulls, crates and carriage wheels and nails and anything else they could salvage from the harbor—a greatsword draped across her shoulders. Atop the wall, six other Sainites stood with crossbows drawn and loaded.

And in their itching hands, Asper could see the same rigid tension that the woman before her carried.

"It's not worth the fight," a weary voice sighed from behind her. Dransun cleared his throat. "Just let us through, madam."

"Or what?" the woman guffawed. "Planning on forcin' your way in?"

She pointed a finger upward. Asper didn't need to look to see what she was looking at. In another moment, a deep shadow fell over her and an avian screech reached her ears.

The scraws, the great monsters of the sky, flew in lazy circles over-head. At least two dozen of them, letting out disgruntled squawks as they wheeled about. Whatever they were looking for, they would certainly take the six breaths needed to eviscerate her if this woman called them down.

"If she was expectin' you, I'd have heard something," the woman snapped back. "Seein' as I haven't heard shit, I can only assume that you haven't got shit to say." She spit on the ground, gestured with her chin. "You can either fuck off or get fucked up if you're so—"

"That is enough."

Aturach was not what she'd call a brave man. Not on his own, any-way. And, judging from the sneer the soldier shot him as he swept for-ward, no one else would call him a brave man, either. And yet he stood, boldly as a man as exhausted as he was shouldn't be able to.

"I don't care who you *think* is talking to you right now," the priest growled, thrusting his finger at the soldier. "But we're not beggars, we're not thieves, we're not the people who would come here if we had any choice in the matter. You speak to Asper—"

"You get that finger out of my face," the soldier snarled, "or I'll break it off and—"

"The Prophet."

They weren't necessarily impressive words. Nor did soft and gentle Aturach say them in a particularly stunning way. And yet everything froze. The soldier's twitching movement, the crossbowmen on the wall, even the stale smoke in the air seemed to dissipate at those two words.

"The..." The soldier mouthed the last word. The anger melted off her face. She stared past Aturach, looked at this woman with one arm in a sling and dirty robes and grime on her face, with eyes that wanted to disbelieve but couldn't quite convince themselves. "Her?"

Asper merely stared back at the soldier, silent.

The soldier glanced up to the crossbowmen atop the wall. Their weapons lowered, they exchanged nervous glances between each other before looking down at the woman standing before Asper. She doffed her hat, scratched her head, and let out a heavy breath.

"Yeah," she said, her voice suddenly heavy. "All right, yeah. Go on in. The W.S. is in her quarters in the Mysterious Stranger, last bar on the right." She stepped aside. "Don't...you know, don't try anything."

Asper said nothing. She spared a respectful incline of her head for the soldier and nothing more. Head held high, the sound of her companions' footsteps behind her, she walked into the Sainite garrison and ignored the awed stares that followed her.

"Reckless," Dransun shuffled closer to her to mutter. "That was fucking reckless what we did." He shook his head. "We should have done like I said, sent a messenger beforehand. You could have been killed."

"I wasn't," Asper replied.

"Yeah, I guess you're the real patron saint of dumb fucking luck, aren't you?" he growled. "Or am I supposed to believe heaven's looking out for you?"

Asper didn't reply to that. Prophets were beyond such things.

And, as far as anyone in Cier'Djaal was concerned, she was *the* Prophet.

At least, that was what they said on the streets.

Word of her actions in the Karnerian fortress had spread quickly—Scarecrow and a team of well-paid street gossips had seen to that. Legends of the crippled woman who had healed the blaspheming commander with a touch had run far and wide. And the past few days had been enough to make sure that the tale had time to reach the Sainite garrison a hundred times over.

And that was more than enough time to let the rumor spread that the Prophet was coming to visit them, as well.

⸻

"I don't like it," Dransun muttered. "This whole plan, any of it. I don't like it. Shouldn't be running around with the likes of those fucking thieves, shouldn't be making plans like this fucking—"

"Language," Aturach interrupted.

"Don't fucking try that shit on me," Dransun growled. "I know what she *really* is."

"And yet you don't know where we *really* are. People are listening."

Dransun opened his mouth to argue but quickly shut it once Harbor Road sprawled out before them, every hairbreadth of it brimming with blue coats.

Makeshift barricades had been erected at ordered intervals in the road, made of the same debris as their wall, but the Sainites were not manning them. Makeshift archer towers had been built on the roofs of the taverns, but the Sainites were not in them. There were well-worn treads where soldiers had stood in formation, but none were standing there now.

But the Sainites weren't gone.

The Sainites were everywhere.

In loose cadres, in huddled circles, in rowdy mobs. Trading flasks of whiskey, trading harsh words, trading fists in some cases. Brawls broke out like fires—except in those spots where fires had broken out—and circles of cheering, screaming soldiers formed around them.

Asper knew she should find this lucky. Among the thrown punches, swilled whiskey, and copious amounts of public urination going on, few Sainites bothered to notice one northern woman and two Djaalic men walking through their garrison. And yet she found her thoughts drifting back to the Karnerians.

They had looked dejected, demoralized, almost defeated with the silent, rueful way they had carried on around their fortress. The Sainites had taken beatings just as hard in this war, yet they looked like they had fight to spare.

Of course, she thought as she spotted a Sainite soldier with his trousers down around his ankles, *at least the Karnerians still bothered to use a toilet when they urinated.*

She hadn't known what to expect. Order, probably, like any military. Maybe even reverence. A thousand men and women watching in awe as the Prophet walked among them?

Careful, careful. A voice chuckled inside her skull; she couldn't say whose. *You're starting to sound like you actually believe this.*

She tried not to respond to that thought. To respond to it would be to debate it. To debate it would be to concede she didn't know how she was going to pull this one off. The Karnerians were fanatics—they believed what their god told them. The Sainites were a coalition, functional at the best of times, and she hadn't expected…

"You fuckin' cunt!"

…whatever this was.

A screaming brawl tore its way across her path, forcing her to stop to let it and the ensuing crowd of cheering onlookers pass before she continued.

The Sainites were like wild dogs now. This garrison was their pen. Once they got out, they'd spread all over the city and rip it apart and leave no one to fight the tulwar and—

You can solve it, that voice purred. *You can solve all of it. Let me help you.*

She forced her mind still. She forced her ears shut. She forced her eyes to the ground.

It wasn't going to be like the Karnerians. Dransun was right; this time, she had pushed her luck too far. This time, she had chosen the wrong people. This time, the plan was going to—

A noise disrupted her train of thought. The clicking of bootheels on cobblestones filled her ears. She couldn't say why she noticed it, or why she looked up at it.

What had Dransun called it? Dumb fucking luck?

A Sainite, a woman soldier, just one more out of several hundred, came walking her way. Asper glanced toward her. She glanced back. And from between the high collar of a blue coat and the low-slung tip of a tricornered hat, a face peered out at Asper.

A familiar face.

And not a Sainite one.

She opened her mouth as if to say something, then forced it shut. The soldier merely tipped her hat, pulled her collar up a little higher around her face, and disappeared into the crowd.

And, as an iron despair settled upon her shoulders, Asper knew everything was going to work.

She pushed her way through the rest of the chaos until she spotted a sign dangling from rusted hinges depicting a thin man in a cloak, bent over. Attached to it was a building that looked like it had seen better days—such as the days before the Sainites had moved in. Asper shoved her way to a door bearing numerous gouges and scratch marks. She glanced over her shoulder at her companions.

"Stay here," she said. "I need to speak to her alone."

"Stupid," Dransun muttered, glancing around. "Fucking stupid."

"Use the time to try to think of something new to complain about."

"He may be right this time," Aturach said. "Something's wrong here."

"No more wrong than we expected," she replied.

"Right, we knew it was bad, but..." He cringed as a bottle flew over his head and shattered against the building. "It'd just be more sensible to have us in there with you."

"I agree." She pushed the door open. "But no one's going to believe that the gods are looking out for me if I go acting sensible, are they?"

If they had other objections, she didn't hear them over the sound of the door closing behind her. The stink immediately assailed her—the stale reek of emptied bottles and half-eaten food. The tables and chairs were all gone from the tavern, likely requisitioned to serve as material for the wall. Just as well.

That all left room for the Sainites who all suddenly whirled on her, swords drawn.

About a dozen of them, all clad in blue coats, murder in their eyes. One of them, an older-looking man, stormed forward, blade held high.

"Who the fuck let you in here?" he snarled.

"The door was open," she replied, pointedly not looking at his blade. "If you invested in a lock, you wouldn't need so many swords."

"Oh, aye? Did they know you were a clever little shit when they let you in or were you just—"

"Back off her and let her by, mate." A familiar voice spoke from the center of the room. "I know her damn voice."

The man went stiff for a moment but sheathed his sword. He snorted at Asper, then grudgingly stalked away to rejoin the crowd. Slowly, they parted to reveal the woman she had come to see.

Funny, she thought, but every time she had seen Wing-Sergeant Blacksbarrow, she always remembered the woman looking bigger than she actually was. Her wild blond hair, the wild anger in her stare, the scars on her face, and the heavy saber she carried always seemed to conspire to make her seem less a woman and more a wolf in Asper's memory.

A wolf that had learned to walk and strolled right into the nearest tavern and got hammered on whiskey, but still.

The woman who sat in the middle of the floor, cross-legged and stripped to the waist, looked nothing like the woman in her memory.

Except for the bottle she cradled in her lap like an infant. That part was pretty on point.

"Well, well." Blacksbarrow looked up with a weary smile that pulled at the scar on her face. Instead of fury, something soft and dark lurked in her eyes. "Didn't I tell you boys I'd get absolution before I went?" She held the bottle of amber liquid high. "And here we are, the Prophet herself come to deliver it. One of my ancestors must have given a god a *great* ass-tonguing."

An excited murmur went through the crowd of Sainites.

"That's her?" one of them asked. "That's the Prophet? But her arm is..."

"Aye, that's what makes her a miracle worker. Wouldn't be nothin' special about her if she had *both* arms, would she?" Blacksbarrow downed a swig of the liquid, then wiped her mouth with the back of her hand. "Well, Your Holiness, what the fuck brings you to my door?"

"I came to seek the aid of the Sainite army on a matter of importance. I had heard there was strife within the ranks and—" Asper paused as a loud scream erupted from outside, followed by the sound of something exploding. "And I came to help."

"Strife? No, no." Blacksbarrow shook her head. "What you're seeing here is good ol' Sainite military order, madam."

Asper blinked. "Harbor Road is half-destroyed, you're drunk, and I walked past a man urinating on a fire as I came here."

"Aye. Like I said."

"What about that is supposed to be—"

"For fuck's sake, you don't get it, do you?"

Blacksbarrow made an attempt to leap to her feet, then settled for staggering to them instead.

Standing up, Asper could see that the Sainite stood a bit shorter than herself. But with her torso exposed as it was, she could see the lean muscle from years of soldiering, the scars carved across her flesh from bad luck and good victories. Even as drunk as she was, Blacksbarrow's entire body was bristling, begging for a fight.

But what spread across her face was not the same kind of energy or even the same fury Asper had seen from the woman before. Hers was a sloppy anger, the anger of the drunk and the ready to die.

"I fucked it up," Blacksbarrow growled. "I fucked *everything* up." She took another swig. "When the last W.S. died, they put me in charge because they were convinced I'd sack the Karnies."

"And you did," one of the soldiers grunted.

"Hundreds of 'em," another agreed.

"Yeah, but my orders weren't to kill a lot of Karnies, were they?" She spit on the floor. "They told me to make this city safe. They told me to make these *people* safe." She chuckled darkly. "Months later, and what? The whole fuckin' thing's on fire. People leavin' in droves. I failed you, boys. I failed everyone."

"You're not going to solve that by getting drunk here," Asper said.

"The time for solving that is over, priestess," Blacksbarrow grunted. "Today's not for solving, today's for settling."

"Settling?" Asper quirked a brow. "Settling what?"

"The *Carrach-an-Cral*," one of the soldiers muttered.

"The what?"

"Means 'Iron-for-Words' in old Sainic," Blacksbarrow replied. "Old clan law from before the Sovereign united us. It was made into military law once the armies formed, to keep the traditions alive."

"Uh...okay," Asper said. "I trust it explains why you're drunk and half-naked?"

"It sure as shit does." Blacksbarrow took another long swig. "If the campaign's going badly, if the commander doesn't know her shit, if the losses keep stacking up, the next rank of officer has the right to challenge for leadership. It's supposed to make sure the best of us are in charge."

"I still don't—"

"What'd I just say? I fucked it all up. I lost too many soldiers. I lost our garrison. I lost the city. Then our supply convoy got into a skirmish with a bunch of fucking savages in the desert and we didn't get enough men and scraws to take it back."

She upended the bottle into her mouth, leaning so far back to drain it that the muscles of her body creaked. She finished with a gasp.

"One of the field commanders, big fucker named Vraefen, has issued a challenge against me."

"And you have to accept?"

"I don't. Not in the middle of a campaign. But because I didn't, his boys are calling me a coward." She gestured to the door. "And they're out there, fighting my boys, until I do. So..."

She hurled the bottle against the floor.

"Right." Asper grimaced. "Should you really be drinking, then?"

"I said he was big, didn't I?" She shook her head. "It's too late, priestess. I'm not going to win this one. I haven't given my kingdom the victory they needed, I haven't given my boys the W.S. they should have had." She ran a hand over her face. "This is how it has to be."

She might have grown up in a temple, but Asper had lived a life not too dissimilar from many other children. She had heard the same tales of brave warriors and their codes.

Honor, valor, noble sacrifices, and unyielding vengeances: They had been her very favorites to hear. Trapped as she was among the priests, she yearned to have such adventures and uphold such traditions as the ones she had read about. She had always dreamed of one day meeting one of these great warriors and seeing one of these great codes.

Honestly, until this day, she had never realized how stupid they really were.

"This is insane." She strove to keep the anger out of her voice—anger would be unseemly in a prophet—and so settled for mere ire. "The city is in flames, the world is falling apart around you and you choose *now* to take up a fight with one of your own men?"

"Insane, aye," Blacksbarrow said. "Like all good traditions."

"A tradition you can't afford!" Asper took a step closer, as if to shake sense into her, but was stopped by two soldiers moving to intercede. "Blacksbarrow, listen to me, there is a force marching on Cier'Djaal that will dwarf the fights you've seen so far. Thousands of tulwar are—"

"Not my concern." Blacksbarrow sighed and stalked back to the center of the room. "Sainites solve Sainite problems first. Whatever pack those monkeys have formed up, they won't threaten Cier'Djaal."

"You're not listening!" Asper all but shrieked. "They already took Jalaang and—"

"I'll make you a deal," Blacksbarrow replied. "Come and talk to me after I win this or talk to my grave after I lose this. Either way, I'll have plenty of time for you, then."

Asper was tempted to say more—or at least, to yell a lot louder—but held her tongue. She had known warriors before, she had seen their pride—in Kataria, in Lenk, in Gariath. And she fully intended to beat the shit out of at least one of those people.

Besides, she told herself, sighing inwardly. *You know how this is going to end.*

Blacksbarrow held out her hand. One of her soldiers obliged, bringing her a bowl of some kind of bluish-black paste. She daubed her fingers into it and began to smear a messy pattern across her face until she looked much more like the walking wolf Asper had always imagined her to be. She must have worn her shock plainly, for Blacksbarrow looked to her and grunted.

"*Wolad,*" she said. "In the old ways, we wore this so that the scraws would know us the same as the skies."

When the bowl was empty, she offered it to one of her soldiers. Another came forward, brandishing a long blade in an ancient sheath. She pulled it free and laid its naked steel in her hands: old, but strong, like an oak branch.

"The family blade," Blacksbarrow muttered. "My father settled a hundred arguments with this one, as his mother did before him."

She held the sword high above her head, stretching both arms up. Another soldier came forward and began to wrap a thick white cloth around her chest, binding her breasts down.

"And is this another tradition?" Asper asked with a sneer. "Do the ancestors demand some weak modesty in battle?"

"Yeah. This is the tradition of not whacking myself in the face with one of my own tits when I fight." Blacksbarrow snorted, spit on the ground, and hefted her blade over her shoulder. She glanced to one of her men. "Head outside. Tell them we're ready."

He nodded in return, pulled a bugle from his belt, and pushed past Asper to head outside. His trumpeting tore a warbling note across the sky, and the sounds of chaos died down, replaced by a funerary silence. She could hear the rush of bodies as the soldiers hurried to assemble.

Blacksbarrow, her sword draped over her shoulder, her men in tow, stalked past Asper and pushed out the door. The priestess hurried to keep up, ignoring the aches and pains in her body as she did so. Aturach and Dransun fell in line behind her, their eyes on her, their mouths shut.

Outside, the chaos had stopped—or at least lulled. The fires burned unchecked and the place reeked of smoke and urine, but at least the soldiers had stopped fighting. They clustered down the road, forming orderly lines along the edges of Harbor Road. They remained silent and at attention as Blacksbarrow came walking through, many of them offering crisp salutes as she did.

"Blacksbarrow!" Asper cried out as she hurried up to the woman's side. No one tried to stop her. "Blacksbarrow, listen to me. We can work this out. Let me talk to this other fellow."

"Talking's done," Blacksbarrow growled. "Vraefen wasn't much for talk to begin with, either." She smiled, patting Asper on the shoulder. "I like you, priestess, really. I respect what you do and what you've done. But this isn't something you can solve."

Oh! The black voice inside Asper's skull let out a shrieking cackle. The shock of it sent agony coursing through her body. *Oh, if only she knew. If only you'd let me show her...*

She clenched her teeth, shut her eyes, forced herself to ignore the pain.

And failed.

It was harder now. Harder with every passing day. The old aches never went away, and new ones seemed to come with every hour. Sometimes she hurt with every breath. Whatever Gariath had knocked loose inside her, it pulled everything else with it.

Still, she could almost deal with that, were it not for Amoch-Tethr. He goaded her pain and the pain responded, laughing and screaming and shrieking until her body was noisy with agony.

She couldn't think through the pain to make words. All she could do was force herself to put one foot in front of the other, to keep walking at Blacksbarrow's side.

Until she realized that Blacksbarrow had stopped walking.

She opened her eyes. The lines of Sainites had turned into a ring, a crude arena of uniforms and tricornered hats, with a vast expanse of space for the two combatants. At one end, beside her, was Blacksbarrow and her loyal soldiers. And at the other end...

Vraefen, she assumed the giant was called.

Damn near seven feet tall, bristling with muscle left bare by the open coat straining against his arms. The hair of his massive body grew so thick it was almost indistinguishable from the heavy hair of his great beard. And behind the dense thicket of facial hair, a craggy face with eyes as cold and dense as stone looked out over her.

"You ready?" He barely raised his voice, but it boomed so that it carried across the square.

"If you've made peace with your ancestors, you hairy shit," Blacksbarrow called back.

"Don't embarrass yourself," Vraefen replied. "It'll be over quick enough."

He held out his huge arms. Two Sainites, doubtless loyal to him, rushed forward and helped him shrug free of his coat. Beneath, his body was a mess of hair and scars layered over muscle dense as rock. Asper cringed; he must have weighed three times as much as Blacksbarrow. Her prospects looked slim.

And that was before she even saw the sword.

To call it a greatsword wouldn't have been enough. There hadn't been a prefix invented yet to describe the massive blade leaning against his thigh. In his other hand, he had another bowl of that thick blue-black paste.

The *wolad*.

Asper's eyes remained on that bowl, staring at it intently as Vraefen took one massive handful out and smeared it across his face. He spread it on so thick and dense that he didn't even look like a man anymore once it had all been applied—and he had only barely looked like a man to begin with.

He stepped forward, picking up his sword. Blacksbarrow stalked forward to meet him, her snarl bright enough to shine through the paint on her face. They held their blades up as they rushed toward each other.

"*WAIT!*"

But not fast enough.

Asper rushed between them, holding her hand up high. A chorus of hushed gasps ran through the crowd of Sainites, amid a few cries of indignation and general cursing. And though the latter certainly was louder than the former, it wasn't enough to keep Asper from catching one word, repeated from mouth to mouth, over and over.

"*...Prophet...*"

"What's this?" Vraefen rumbled. "Not enough that you've led us to disgrace against the Karnies, but now you've got a crippled woman to fight for you?"

"*Heaven is watching!*"

Asper roared to be heard over his rock slide of a voice. And at it, both he and the Sainites fell into an attentive, if leery, silence. She took a moment to let the echo of her voice sink into their skulls, to draw all eyes upon her. And, after it was clear no one was going to throw anything at her, she continued.

"I hear in your voices that some of you know me," she continued, loudly. "And I see on your faces that some of you do not. Whatever titles you call me are irrelevant, for *none* of you know what a mistake you are about to make here.

"The enemies of mankind unite behind the walls of this city, as you yourselves fail to unite even here. And as you wage your petty battles and squabble over the scraps of a dying city, the great maw of your enemies stretches so wide as to swallow you whole, scraps, bones, and flesh. The gods watch you battle among yourselves and sigh to see their creations squandered.

"Let it be known that heaven calls for unity!" she roared. "The gods demand an army to answer the great threat! The heathen! The savage! The monster at your doors! Those who indulge in vendettas..."

She cast a meaningful glare at Vraefen. The giant looked impassive, flinching only as a mosquito flew down and settled on his face.

"...shall stand in judgment. And those who do not recognize judgment shall suffer the verdict." She looked back out to the crowd. "I do not grant you a chance to atone. I beg you, I *plead* with you, to set aside your arms and—"

"Aw, stuff it, shithead!"

Something struck her cheek. A thick, wet glop of a sound cut her off. She said nothing else—it was rather difficult to keep track of a speech with the smell of shit filling her nostrils. She looked down at the pile of scraw dung that settled at her feet before looking back at Vraefen's side of the ring.

His loyalists jeered at her, making rude gestures and barking nonsensical slurs. The giant himself seemed caught between a smirk and a sneer, his contempt even thicker than the paint on his face.

Paint so thick, Asper noted, that he didn't even seem to notice the small band of flies that crawled across it.

"So be it," she said, just loud enough for those who mattered to hear it.

She stepped back.

She held her breath.

She counted the steps.

One. Two. Three.

Vraefen took huge, lumbering strides forward. He hefted his sword up in both hands. His grin split his painted face in two. Six more flies buzzed down and landed on his face.

Four. Five.

Vraefen pulled a hand free to swat at the flies, now dozens of them, that buzzed around him. He snorted, tugging them out of his hair. Eight mosquitoes appeared on his face, as if from nowhere. Someone in the crowd cracked a joke about bug salve.

Six. Seven. Eight.

His eyes were locked on Blacksbarrow as she advanced on him, but he squinted as insects—now well over thirty of them—crawled all across his face. The drone of large wings filled the air. Something large and bulbous landed on his neck. A few Sainites called out to him.

Nine.

A hecatine thrust its proboscis into his throat and latched onto his skin. His roar was heard over the gasps from the crowd as he pulled it free, drawing blood. He pulled the second one free, too. But not the third.

Ten.

And he took not another step forward.

His sword fell from his hands and clattered to the ground. The crowd of Sainites was screaming, suddenly. He roared and snarled and spit angry, vicious curses.

And none of it could be heard above the violent droning sound of a hundred insect wings beating in horrific, relentless harmony.

Long-limbed mosquitoes. Flies as big as pebbles. Roaches of brown and black. And at least six fist-sized hecatines. Asper couldn't bear to count them as they swarmed over Vraefen's face, but she forced herself to watch. Cold, impassive, as though she knew this would happen.

She owed him that much.

Vraefen fell to his knees. His screams went unheard as he clawed at his face, pulling off insects in great fistfuls of writhing, red and black masses. But for each one he removed, more swarmed upon him. More biting bugs, more droning wings, more hecatines thrusting their long, needle proboscises into his flesh.

A few rushed forward to help him but were quickly chased away by the ever-increasing horde of vermin. His loyalists shrieked out impotently to him. All others simply stared and tried to get away.

He kept clawing. He kept shrieking. He kept tearing. But his hands came away with fewer and fewer insects and more and more red-stained fingers each time. Maddened with pain that none could hear, he finally took to swinging his great fists at his own head in an attempt to crush them.

He threw punch after punch, hammering his own skull. But each time, the blows came weaker and weaker, slower and slower, until finally, his massive arms hung limp at his sides.

And the rest of him followed.

It would be some time before the swarm dispersed, flying away in slow, aimless circles, bloated with flesh and drunk with blood. It would be some time later before anyone had the courage to approach Vraefen's carcass and gaze upon the glistening ruin of red and black that was his face. It would be some time before, as wild panic turned to cold-blooded terror, all eyes slowly went to her.

And Asper said nothing.

Not until the entire Sainite army gazed upon her. Not until Blacksbarrow stared at her, all drunkenness fled from her face and replaced by wild, naked awe. Not until the insect wings had silenced and no one dared utter a word.

Only then did she speak.

And all of creation listened.

"The verdict," she said softly, "has been served."

—◆◆◆◆—

"That went well."

Asper didn't bother confirming or denying that. It was late afternoon when she left the Sainite garrison. Her departure had been marked by awed stares, crowds parting before her, and hushed whispers. And even now, as she left with her companions behind her, they were chased by gaping mouths and unblinking eyes as the Sainites crowded around the wall to watch them go.

Even the scraws overhead followed them, the riders unable to turn away, yet fearful to get too low.

"Only one person dead," Aturach continued as they headed down the road toward the gates to the Souk. "It could have been much worse."

"I would have preferred it if no one died," Asper said. "That man was a beast. I would have liked to have him on our side. He could have killed a hundred tulwar with just one hand."

"But you must have known that this would happen. Otherwise, why bother sabotaging the—"

Asper held up a finger. He obediently fell silent. They continued walking until the shadows of the scraws no longer fell over them and the sounds of the garrison were far behind him.

And even then, she would have preferred not to talk about it.

At least, that way, she could pretend she hadn't had a part in it.

Scarecrow and Sandal had been thorough in their research. They not only knew about the internal strife in the Sainites—and likely did their fair share of antagonizing it—they knew how Sainites resolved it. From there, it hadn't been hard to put a powerful attractant—made of chemicals and other, fouler substances only the couthi knew the names to—in Vraefen's *wolad*.

It probably hadn't taken much effort at all. Maybe just a few drops, if that.

And just like that, a man had died in agony so deep she couldn't even begin to think of it. All so that she could send even more men, and women, to their deaths.

It shouldn't be that easy.

And she knew it wouldn't be. She had convinced the Sainites and the Karnerians to fear her, but it would take more to convince them to work together. But that was a different problem.

"We need to get them together," she said. "In the next day, while they still remember what we've done."

"What *you've* done, you mean," Dransun muttered. "You are the Prophet, aren't you?"

"He's trying to be facetious, but he's right," Aturach said. "If the two armies are going to follow your lead, we need to make sure they're following *you*, not a council or anything like that. The Prophet will lead them to victory, not us. We'll not say a word otherwise."

"I trust those shit-eating scumbags you call associates won't, either?" Dransun growled.

"They've helped us this far, haven't they?" Asper asked. "If there were something better in it for Scarecrow, she could have betrayed me a hundred times by now."

"And why is she helping you, anyway? Out of love for her city?" Dransun laughed bitterly. "Back when I was a guard—back when this place still *had* a guard—I put away scum like her daily. Even if they were all blind, deaf, and limbless, I wouldn't trust them not to try to kill me, let alone—"

"I get it, all right?" Asper whirled on him with a scowl. "If I had a better idea, I'd have done that. And if *you've* had a better idea, I fucking well hope you had a great reason for keeping it from me." She gestured out toward the walls of Cier'Djaal. "Do you not fucking get it? Did you not fucking *see* the number of tulwar? They can only have grown since then. And they'll strike soon."

"There are ways we could fight them," Dransun replied, stiffening up. "Better ways. Ways that could—"

"I'm listening." She stared at him in stony silence for a moment. When no answer was forthcoming, she sighed. "I don't have many options here, Dransun. If thieves are the only help I can get, I'm going to take it." She snorted. "Besides, it wasn't that long ago that you were clamoring for us to go fight the Karnerians and Sainites single-handedly to drive them out."

"That…that was still a good idea," he said.

"We'd have been killed," Aturach replied, shaking his head. "Every one of us."

"I…I know, it's just…" Dransun sighed and rubbed his face. "It shouldn't be you that has to do this. It's a lot to ask for a city that isn't yours. You're a foreigner, you're a healer, and you're…you're a…"

She regarded him carefully for a moment before she noticed the skittish way he looked her over and then pointedly looked away.

"Ah," she said. "That's it. If I were a man, this would be noble and resourceful instead of treacherous, is that it?"

"Not entirely," Dransun replied. "But if it were someone else who had to sully themselves—"

"If it bothers you that much, Dransun," she said, "pretend I have a cock."

She turned away and, head held high, began to walk.

"And if it still bothers you, pretend to suck it."

FIFTEEN

CHIEFTAIN

Gariath found he could still recall the day he met them all, right down to their scents.

There had been the short one, smelling like worry and fear poured over a roaring bonfire. There had been the tall one, a rat that walked on two legs and smiled like he didn't smell like treachery. There had been the pointy-eared one, twitching and snarling like her teeth were impressive. And then, of course, there had been Lenk, who simply smelled like Lenk.

And then, there was the tall female one.

She hadn't looked too different from the other humans. They all looked the same to him, back then—most of them still did, today. He could remember parts of her: her tall, straight spine, the tremble of her lips as she tried to smile nervously, the shrillness of her voice as she lectured the others.

But mostly, it was her smell he remembered.

He had heard of gods—it was impossible to learn the human tongue, however simple it might be, and not learn of their imaginary sky-things. Those who spoke their names in prayer always smelled of the same ripe stink of fear and hypocrisy.

Except for her.

She had a hard scent to her, a scent of old stone and dust, a reek of earth that had gathered around feet planted firmly. He recalled this. He had never before smelled conviction before meeting her.

And if he closed his eyes, he could *almost* remember her name.

"The Prophet?"

He glared through a cloud of pipe smoke across the room.

"That's what she's calling herself?"

Mototaru puffed his pipe and shrugged. "This is what our scouts tell us, anyway."

"And who told them?" He rose from his chair. His body protested. The wounds carved into his flesh still ached. And with every movement, he could still feel the steel of the assassin's blade.

Almost as keenly as the humiliation of having almost been killed.

"Farmers," Mototaru replied. "Traveling merchants, fleeing refugees … what humans call 'common people.'"

"And they just offered this word in conversation?"

"I informed our scouts to start looking for certain pieces of information after your…" Mototaru gestured to the many wounds dotting Gariath's body, the ones bandaged and unbandaged. "Incident. They ran a few humans down, interrogated them at length."

"And let them live?" Gariath growled.

"I didn't tell them to kill anyone, no."

"They should have killed them." The dragonman stalked toward the map table. "We should have sent them a message."

"What message would that be?" Mototaru let out a low hum. "'Don't be poor and afraid'? Or perhaps you wanted to send a message to their leadership? 'Don't cross us or we'll kill a couple of defenseless farmers and maybe their chickens, too'?"

"Why not?" Gariath snarled. "They killed yours, didn't they?" He cast a glare toward the old tulwar. "They burned Shaab Sahaar."

"And many innocent people died there." Mototaru nodded. "If the guilty could be punished by hurting the innocent, justice would be a strange thing."

"Then we send the message that no one is innocent."

"An animal would think that." Mototaru let out a long, smoky sigh. "Or a monster."

Through the cloud of pipe smoke, the old tulwar's eyes blazed, challenging Gariath to reply to that. The dragonman met his stare just long enough before looking back to the map.

"I agree with your sentiment, at least," Mototaru said. "We can't have it known that assassins can walk freely in your fortress."

"Freely." Gariath ran a claw across the map, from Jalaang to Cier'Djaal. "And whose fault was that?"

"You stormed out of the war room," Mototaru said. "You will recall the last time I sent someone to check up on you after you did that, you sent him back to me with a broken arm."

"Why were there no guards in the streets?" Gariath growled, tapping his finger on the map. "Why did we have no warriors out training? Why were there no archers on the roofs?" His hand curled into a fist and slammed down upon the table. Inkwells spilled, cups toppled. "How did they just *get in here?*"

He hadn't meant to roar quite that loudly. It wouldn't do for the warriors outside to know what had happened, to know that their commander had almost been killed by a coward's blade.

And so damned easily, too, he thought, spitefully.

His mind drifted back to his fight with the Shadow—he had no better word for the creature he had faced—and all he could remember was his own weakness. The way his hands had reached out and grasped nothing, the way the blade bit at him from all sides at once, the way he had landed only one pathetic blow and the Shadow had simply ... simply ...

Let you live, he snarled to himself. *That piece of shit could have killed you, if he wanted to. She sent him to send a message, to prove she doesn't need you, to prove she could kill you anytime.*

"If you want to destroy the map," Mototaru said softly, "please let me find a scribe who can make a copy first."

Gariath looked down. His hands had uncurled without him noticing; his claws had sunk into the table, digging deep gouges into the map. His heart was thundering in his chest and his mouth tasted dry. He seized a cup—the only one he hadn't knocked over—and quickly drained its contents.

And his mouth still tasted dry.

"You're upset," Mototaru said.

"I don't get upset."

"You're worried, then."

"I have killed monsters as tall as mountains. I have torn giant serpents apart from the inside. I have broken necks by breathing too hard." Gariath turned and stalked toward Mototaru. "I tear armor like paper, I break shields with my fingers, I punch people so hard I force-feed them their own *chins*. I am *Rhega! I DO NOT GET WORRIED!*"

His roar shook the shutters in the windows and chased the smoke out of the room. But Mototaru did not blink. Mototaru didn't even look at him. The old tulwar merely took a long inhale of his pipe and spoke softly.

"You should."

He rose out of his chair with a groan, hefted his weight, and knuckled the small of his back. He trudged past Gariath without looking up, moving toward the map.

"You are brave. You are strong. You are ferocious. And you were almost killed."

"Whatever assassin she sends against me is—"

"Is not your greatest concern." Mototaru leaned on the table, humming. "Not anymore." He drew a circle around Cier'Djaal with his finger. "We have been preparing for eventualities, unforeseen circumstances, but this…this, I didn't even think of."

"Think of what?" Gariath moved to join him.

"The war between the humans was something we always knew would work in our favor," Mototaru hummed. "But there are limits. We knew it would buy us time, allow us to call our forces, but perhaps we have waited too long."

"I was in that city." Gariath folded his arms over his chest. "I saw them tearing each other apart. They are humans, stupid and weak. They won't—"

"They will."

Mototaru's voice was the sound of a sword breaking. His glare was a fire dying. And when he turned toward Gariath, he did so with more weight than his frame could hold.

"Whatever posturing you did to convince yourself they didn't mean anything, you *cannot* be so stupid as to not see what they've accomplished." He gestured to their room. "This room, they built. This city, they made. This *world*, they conquered. We scurry under tents while their cities reach across the land like living things, forever hungry.

"They did *not* make these by being stupid. They did not drive us into the desert by being weak. They have grown so large that they have no other enemies to fight but themselves, but that will not last. Once they realize what we plan to do, once they realize the threat we pose, they will act against us. They will bring their weapons to bear. They will empty their armories. They will…"

Mototaru's voice trailed off. Gariath took a step closer.

"They will what?"

"Unite," Mototaru said. "Behind *her*."

"Impossible. I broke her."

"Prophets are not known for having small ambitions." Mototaru sneered at him. "Or do you think she calls herself that just to get a discount on curry?" He shook his head. "If even farmers, so far from the city, are calling her by that name, we can be certain that everyone in Cier'Djaal knows it, as well."

"That means nothing except that she talks a lot," Gariath snarled. "It doesn't mean that they've united behind her."

"She sent an *assassin*," Mototaru spit. "And, whatever you may have heard, assassins do not simply volunteer for things out of the goodness of their hearts. She had money to do so. Where did she get it? Who gave it to her?"

"That doesn't mean the Karnerians or Sainites—"

"No? And if not, that means there are even *more* unforeseen circumstances. That means we understand even *less* about the enemy than we thought we did." Mototaru shot him an iron look. "That means we are out of time."

Gariath held his gaze for a moment longer before his eyes drifted down to the map across the table. A stupid piece of paper smeared with ink. He had almost destroyed it just by touching it.

Yet to stare upon it now made his heart turn to stone in his chest and his blood freeze in his veins.

Because in that tiny smear of ink marked *Cier'Djaal*, he could see her. She was in there, behind those walls, with all those humans. He had seen but a fraction of them, and he could still remember the way they teemed like a tide, so many more than the tulwar. Who knew how many more were in there? How many forges were churning out swords? How many soldiers were mustering to march?

How many people, right now, were looking upon her, raising their hands, and screaming her name?

Hundreds. Thousands. Tens of thousands. However many humans were in the world could be ready to fight him and his tiny army of a few thousand warriors.

He stared at the map. This time, he did not see many little ink graves where his soldiers would be buried. This time, he saw a tide, moving out from Cier'Djaal and scourging the land of anyone they thought stood against them.

Against her.

"Prophet," he muttered wordlessly.

Mototaru was right.

They were out of time.

Maybe they had been for a long time now.

His nostrils quivered suddenly. A familiar reek of anger and desperation reached his snout. But only for a moment. Hot behind it, and growing stronger, was an odor of confidence, stale meat, and an *awful* lot of shit.

The door flung open. Daaru appeared within, his expression severe and color in his face.

"We have a problem," he said.

He had neither time nor need to expound on that. A black-furred hand appeared behind him and shoved him out of the way. Chakaa came swaggering into the room, heedless of either her reek or the jagged arrow shaft jutting from her chest.

Behind her white-painted face, red-rimmed eyes grew wide and her smile split her face with yellow teeth.

"Gentlemen!" she bellowed. She caught herself, blinked, and fired off an awkward salute. "Or are we generals now? I always think we are done playing war, since we are not fighting at the moment, but it's very hard to tell these—"

"What happened to you?" Gariath interjected, eyes gone wide at her.

"I'm late, yes." She waved a hand. "But I was delayed. It's very hard to get anyone to look after my gaambol, and—"

"No, what happened with the…" Gariath gestured around his chest.

"What?" She blinked, running her hand around her breasts until it found the arrow. "Oh, this!"

She seized it and jerked it free with a sickening sound. Daaru and Mototaru cringed and looked away. Gariath couldn't help but stare as it left nothing more than a scratch behind.

"Some very rude person shot me," she complained.

"Do we…" Gariath glanced to Mototaru. "Do we get her a healer?"

"What?" Chakaa tossed the arrow aside. "For this? Don't be insane, *daanaja*."

"She was ambushed," Daaru said. "Her and the other Mak Lak Kai we sent out."

"Ambushed?" Gariath growled. "By who?"

"Shicts."

"I *think* it was a shict, anyway." Chakaa scratched her head. "Usually, the ones you see crawling around the desert are brown. This one was all . . ." She blanched. "Pale and pink. Hair like corn. *Terrible* smell."

Gariath narrowed his eyes and let out a low growl.

The pointy-eared one.

Separated from them by miles and mere days away from killing them, his former companions continued to find ways to annoy the piss out of him.

"We sent the Mak Lak Kai out to track the shicts," Mototaru hummed. He looked to Chakaa. "Did you?"

"A little," she replied.

Mototaru rubbed his eyes, looked to Daaru. "Tell me what she means."

"We've had several scouts return," the young tulwar said. "As we suspected, the shicts avoid both Cier'Djaal and Jalaang. They're aware of what's going on and there aren't enough of them to challenge either us or the humans." He sighed. "And, as we suspected, they're taking advantage of the chaos to attack tulwar villages."

Mototaru hummed, nodded. "How many?"

"Six? Seven?" Chakaa shrugged. "I lost interest after I saw a very fancy shict with a very fancy spear. I was hoping to see it up close, but she never stayed in one place for very long. So we started tracking her and—"

"I don't fucking care," Gariath growled. "If the shicts are staying out of our way, then they're not as stupid as I thought."

"They *are* raiding a number of villages," Mototaru said. "Those villages could produce more warriors. And if the shicts are out in force, then—"

"*No.*"

Gariath spoke loud enough to silence that thought, and any further thoughts. They turned toward him, attentive.

"We are out of time," he snarled. "Out of time for shicts, out of time for scouting, out of time for waiting." He scowled at the map and thrust a clawed finger at it. "Is our plan in place?"

He looked to Mototaru, who nodded slowly.

"Are our warriors ready?"

He glanced to Daaru. The young warrior sighed.

"We can make them ready."

"How long?"

"Two weeks."

"One." Gariath stalked to the window. "As many swords as can be forged, as many boats as can be sent, as many warriors as can be called back. We march for Cier'Djaal. We move through the Green Belt. We destroy everything. We burn their city to the ground."

"Ha!" Chakaa clapped her hands. "I like this plan! Destroying! Fire! All the hallmarks of good leadership." She scratched her chin. "Send us out again, *daanaja*. Let us do to the humans what the shicts have done to us. Let them *know* we are coming for them."

Gariath tensed. A surge of rage flooded through him, coursing from his nose to his heart and into his fingers. He could feel it in the way they curled up and into his palms, the need to hurt, to wrap around a farmer's throat and choke the screams from him.

To show her, to show this Prophet, that he could inflict upon her the same cold fear he had felt that night.

Perhaps he wore his anger too plainly on his face, for a flash of a scent, something old and terribly dark, caught his nostrils. He glanced to his side. Mototaru stared at him expectantly.

He drew in a hot breath of smoke. He let out a long, cold sigh.

"No," Gariath said. "Call the Mak Lak Kai back. I'll need your clan."

"Then let us destroy a few things on the way back," Chakaa offered.

Gariath slowly shook his head and spoke softly.

"We are not monsters."

Chakaa's face screwed up in confusion before she shrugged helplessly. With another, even more awkward salute, she turned and left the house, slamming the door behind her. But her presence was still felt, in the reek of shit and the lingering tension radiating from Daaru.

"It would have been smarter to send her out," he said. "The warriors get nervous when the Mak Lak Kai are around."

"Good thing they'll only be here for another week, then," Gariath muttered.

"Still, when the time comes to march, keep them in the back. Away from the—"

"How did she do that?"

Daaru blinked at Gariath's interruption. When the dragonman turned around to face him, his own expression was one of bafflement.

"There was no blood," Gariath said. "She tore the arrow out of her like it was a tick. It's not the first time I've seen her do something like that. If she can take an arrow to the chest and not feel it, I want her and her clan in the *front*."

Daaru and Mototaru exchanged a glance whose meaning was lost on him. When Daaru looked back, he shook his head.

"That is ... not a wise idea," he said.

"Why not?"

"The Mak Lak Kai are *malaa*."

Gariath snorted. "And here I was hoping tulwar would have less made-up bullshit words for idiots than humans. Yet every time I ask about them, I get more made-up bullshit words for idiots." He shifted his scowl between the two tulwar. "Will I get a straight answer if I ask first? Or do I have to start beating the shit out of you?"

It was Mototaru who spoke, albeit only after a long moment of emptying his pipe bowl out the window and packing a new one.

"We are made by our Tul," he said. "Our god is dead, and so we can never die."

"You've told me all this before," Gariath growled.

"I've told me part of it." He lit his pipe, took a long smoke. "I am *Humn*. My Tul is long, old." He tapped his head. "It remembers all its previous lives." He gestured to Daaru. "Daaru is *saan*. His Tul dedicated itself to the art of war. It remembers nothing else but the blade. When he dies, his Tul will emerge in another body, another warrior."

"And the *malaa*?"

"When the *malaa* die ..." Mototaru began.

"Their Tul doesn't go anywhere," Daaru said. "It simply ... leaps back into their bodies. The *malaa* never bleed. The *malaa* never die."

"They're immortal, then?" Gariath asked.

"There isn't a word in any clan's tongue for what they are," Mototaru said. "But they are not indestructible. They lose limbs. They lose eyes. Lungs give out, bones break, eventually there is nothing left of them."

"And then where do they go? Where does their Tul go?"

A long period of silence followed. And far from the flippant gesture it should have been, Mototaru's shrug was something heavy and dire.

"It doesn't."

Gariath stared at him for a moment before looking back out the window. Daaru cleared his throat and stepped forward.

"Consider leaving them behind," the young tulwar said. "Give them guard duty. The *malaa* are unstable...unnatural. The other warriors will rest easier if—"

"Go," Gariath interrupted. "Call the clans. Tell them we move soon."

"And what do I tell them about the *malaa*?"

"They come with us," the dragonman said. "Tell them anyone who has a problem with that should grab their sword, come see me, and hope I break it into small enough shards that they can swallow them comfortably."

Daaru stiffened and opened his mouth to say something, but a look from Mototaru silenced him. He merely grunted his acknowledgment and departed, slamming the door behind him.

Mototaru let out a deep hum. "That could cause problems."

"Not as many problems as a clan of unkillable warriors can solve," Gariath replied. "It'd be stupid to leave them behind."

"It'd stupid to bring them along without knowing what they are," the old tulwar said. "The *malaa* are not weapons you can draw and put away so easily. The tulwar are—"

"The next metaphor that comes out of your mouth, I'm shoving it back in along with my fist." Gariath stalked back to the map. "I know what the tulwar are." He stared out over the parchment. "I know *who* they are."

He stared at it, tattered and scarred as it was from his claws, and he could still see them. Every tiny ink smear that would mark another grave. And at the edge of the map, where a jar of ink had spilled over and poured across the paper, he could see the tides of humanity marching over those graves, pounding those tulwar corpses into a road that led all the way to Jalaang.

With *her* at their head.

"But right now," he muttered, "I need weapons."

He turned a scowl toward Mototaru.

"All your traditions, all your problems, all your Tul, they won't mean shit if we don't win this. So forgive me if I don't care to figure out who dies or doesn't die for whatever reason until *after* we've won this." He sneered, baring his teeth at the old tulwar. "Or do you have a better idea?"

And Mototaru stared at him, empty, for a long moment. He took a long inhale on his pipe and looked toward the window, where the sun had already begun to sink out of the sky. And his voice was ash.

"I wish I did."

SIXTEEN

THE SPEAR

The legend told around the fire was that the Howling was one of the few gifts that Riffid gave the shicts before casting them out of the Dark Forest to wander the mortal world. No one had ever disputed this legend, nor did anyone seem to really wonder if there was another reason.

That Kataria had, however, was always just one more reason why she found it hard to fit in with her people.

Riffid was not a vengeful goddess—or at least, it wasn't possible to piss her off more than she already was—so Kataria had come up with several theories of her own as to how her people developed the ability to communicate wordlessly with each other.

Maybe it was just a better way to hunt their prey silently. Maybe they had learned it long ago to find each other in the deep woods and long plains. But Kataria's favorite theory was that the Howling was a rare kindness that made it so that no shict would ever be forced to be alone with her thoughts.

This won't work.

Of course, given that Kataria had no company *but* her thoughts for the past three hours, it was entirely likely that she had been wrong about Riffid not being vengeful.

She's not coming. The map was wrong. You were wrong.

Kataria let out a low growl and folded her ears over themselves, as though either of those would block out the thoughts.

You can't stop her. What made you think you could? Everyone's going to die.

They had always been there, of course. Since she had risen at dawn and ridden hard to the north, she hadn't been able to hear them so clearly.

All because of you.

But here and now, atop a lonely dune beneath a sinking sun, there was nothing to distract her.

The spot had almost been too good to be true. The tulwar's map showed exactly where Shekune would be, exactly when, and her route wound its way through these narrow passes.

Rocks and sand joined cozily here, with the latter piling up around the former in great, hard-packed dunes that never seemed to shift with the wind. The resulting formations of sand and stone rose up like monarchs of the desert, aloof and cold. Each tall, sloping dune wore a crown of stones and desiccated trees and was cloaked in obnoxiously resilient scrub grass.

It made for several ideal positions—like the top of the dune she was currently on, nestled between two tall stones—for an ambush. Surely, Shekune knew that.

But then, it was easy to see why Shekune chose to use this as her patrol. The narrow paths winding through the dunes would prove a challenge for clumsy humans or tulwar and their awkward horses and gaambols. But clever shicts on skulking yijis would find it easy enough.

The hard-packed earth left only a few precious tracks. It had been a miracle that Kataria had found them at all. But from their route through the dunes, she had realized the purpose behind Shekune's long patrols.

Humans had their commanders: kings to bow to, generals to look to, warlords to answer to. Tulwar had their clans: camps to set up, hordes to form, great tides to move.

But shicts? Shicts had no kings. Shicts had no clans. Shicts were ghosts, bad dreams that came in during the night. They moved like shadows, quickly and quietly.

Shekune would keep them in small bands throughout the desert, separated so as to not draw attention from the other races. And she would doubtless be moving between them even now, conferring strategy, issuing orders.

Preparing them for a war.

Even as she led them to a slaughter.

Why could the rest of them not see it? The thought flashed across her skull every other breath now, each time with increasing anger. How could all of them follow Shekune so willingly? How could they all be so blind as to how this would end? How could they all be so...so...

She clenched her teeth, shook her head.

That didn't matter now.

Whatever their reasons, she couldn't afford to think about it. She knew where this led, even if they didn't. And she knew how to stop it.

One arrow. Right through the throat. Shekune would never see it coming. One arrow. And this would all be over. Her people would be saved.

Unless...

The thought came creeping in on soft, spidery legs.

Someone else rises up to take her place.

She wanted to think that wouldn't happen. But then, Shekune hadn't tricked them, hadn't beguiled them. She had merely spoken to them.

And they had listened.

Even Kwar had followed Shekune willingly.

Kwar...

Kataria felt her eyes drift across the dunes, searching for her, even as she knew she'd never see her. Somewhere in all those stones and underbrush, Kwar was hidden, watching the angles Kataria couldn't see. She hadn't seen so much as a flash of the khoshict for hours now.

They had spared so little when they had parted: just a few words, a quick kiss. It had been too swift a good-bye, too full of certainty that they would come out of this all right. And only now, alone with nothing but her thoughts and the lonely murmur of the wind, did Kataria realize she had so much more to say.

Should have run, she told herself. *Should have taken her and run. Shekune couldn't even start this war by herself and you think you can stop it on your own. You can't do it. They're going to die. You're going to lose everything again. You're going to...*

Her ears pricked up, suddenly full of sounds heavier than her thoughts. She shut out the latter, forced herself to focus on the former, and let them fill her ears.

Paws crunching on hard-packed sand.

Quiet murmurs from behind wooden masks.

The excited yowl of a slavering beast.

She's here.

The last thought Kataria allowed herself. Thought was useless now. Now was the time for the hunt and the bow. Now was the time for instinct.

She picked up her bow. An arrow all but leapt to her fingers as she crept as far out from between the rocks as she dared and strung it. She didn't bother drawing it in anticipation; her arm would tire, her heartbeat would betray her. Arrows didn't heed thoughts or hopes. Archery was an instinct.

Patience, though, she had to learn on her own.

They came rounding a dune just a breath later. Four of them, all mounted on yijis. The beasts wound their way through the hardpacked paths carefully, trotting at a light pace, their riders bobbing on their crested backs. Three of them, she didn't know: warriors wearing wooden masks and carrying bows and hatchets on their beasts. But the fourth...

She rode unassumingly, wore the same leathers, the same mask as the rest of them. Her hair was a riot of black feathers, like theirs were. But there was something in the way she held herself, so tall on her yiji's back, her eyes staring at something so far away the rest of them didn't even know it was there, that Kataria recognized her.

Even without the massive saw-toothed spear she carried draped over her shoulder.

Shekune.

She felt her ears twitch involuntarily. That tremor ran down her neck, through her arm, sent her fingers quaking. She forced them still but could feel something raw and animal beneath her skin. It was as though, even without even knowing she was there, Shekune was speaking without words, without Howling, whispering a fear made just for her.

It couldn't be this easy, it whispered. She couldn't succeed, couldn't do it, couldn't save everyone, couldn't—

Enough.

A long, slow breath. A raised bow. A nocked arrow.

Whatever it couldn't be, it had to be now.

Shekune and her retinue continued through the winding passage for another few feet before it happened. The yijis began to growl, yip, and whine excitedly. Their riders spit orders, kicked their flanks in an attempt to make them obey.

But even the most loyal yiji was, at best, only half-domesticated— it was that feral nature that khoshicts said made them so effective at hunting. And a pack of yijis with the scent of dead meat in their nostrils—such as the dead meat that came from the yiji Kwar had killed farther up the chasm and left in the road—would make any one of the beasts excited.

Kataria waited, anticipating that one of the riders should suspect something and look in her direction. But their attentions were focused on calming their mounts down. They whined and muttered but made little movement.

Shekune was right there.

Unmoving.

Eyes straight ahead.

One breath to pull. One breath to aim. One breath to release, Kataria told herself. *You've done this a thousand times. You've killed so much bigger. This is no different.*

Her fingers believed that as her grip tightened on her bow and she drew the arrow back to her cheek. Her eyes believed that as she narrowed her gaze upon Shekune, so far below, and aimed right for her chest. But some part of her, in some dark and empty part of her chest, did not believe that.

And maybe it was that part that Shekune heard.

A half a breath. Right between her second and third. A long pair of dark-skinned ears twitched, went upright. A wooden mask turned to look up the long slope of the dune. A pair of hollow eyes stared across the sands, between the rocks, and within that darkness, Kataria could feel Shekune's stare.

Right at her.

Fuck.

She heard it. Her ears twitched. The tremor ran down her arm, bade her fingers release. The bowstring murmured. The arrow shrieked.

A moment of fear wasn't enough to undo a lifetime of instinct. The arrow flew straight for Shekune. Its song was angry and brief. It ended in the meaty smack of metal cleaving dark flesh and a long, agonized scream.

A body slid to the earth and lay dead.

No.

And it was not Shekune's.

NO!

How had he moved that fast? It was only half a breath! How did he manage to get his yiji under control? How did he see her? How did he know? How?

For all the questions boiling inside her, only one spoke loud enough to be heard.

Why?

She stared at him, this khoshict she didn't know, lying on the earth with her arrow jutting of his chest, staring up at the sky through the hollow eyes of his mask.

Why did you die for her?

A yiji let out a shriek. She turned toward Shekune. And Shekune was gone.

Her yiji was howling, running, charging up the dune. Her spear was glistening, its sawteeth wide in a grin. And her eyes, alive with fury behind her mask, were right on Kataria.

Another arrow leapt to her hand, left the bow, sailed toward her. It struck her yiji and the beast let out a yipe, but she spurred it forward. Kataria drew another and fired; it flew wide. She drew another, and another, even as the sound of the yiji's thunderous charge filled her ears.

It didn't matter if she died.

It didn't matter if they killed her.

So long as Shekune also died here, then everyone else would be safe.

That was what she told herself to keep from running. That was what she told herself to keep her aim steady as she drew back another arrow and stared down Shekune until she drew so close Kataria could hear the sound of her breath.

There would be no missing this time.

Her breath left her in a sudden explosion. She felt the wind break as a massive pair of jaws snapped shut around the air behind her. She felt herself crash against the earth as a heavy weight bore her down.

Kwar.

Without even looking up, she knew.

Mostly by the war cry that followed.

Kwar leapt off her, tore her knife and hatchet free from her belt, and whirled on Shekune. Kataria crawled to her rear and scrambled to snatch up an arrow.

A cloud of dust trailed behind Shekune's yiji as it went rampaging past, carried by the momentum of its charge. But the thrill of slaughter was in its nose now, and when Shekune wheeled the beast around, its snarl was so wide it was almost a grin. The chieftain let out a cry that was echoed by the yiji as she kicked forward into another charge.

And Kwar was not moving.

Hatchet in her right hand, knife in her left, body smeared with earth and sweat, she stood over Kataria. Her roar was loud, loud enough to match the yiji's baying cry. And yet, still not as loud as her Howling.

That Howling found its way into Kataria's ears, louder than any fear, any thought, any instinct. It traveled down her shoulder, into her arm, and bade her draw. She leapt to her feet, pulled the arrow back, and aimed.

And when she fired, she did not miss.

The arrow sailed and struck the yiji square in its eye. The creature's cry turned into a short, shrill scream and turned its charge into a limp crash of suddenly bloodless limbs.

The beast bucked forward as it fell dead to the earth, launching Shekune from its back. But Shekune didn't so much as cry out as she struck the earth in a tumble and came up standing. Her mask had fallen from her face, baring a snarl whose teeth matched the grin of her spear. And it was leveled right at Kataria.

But before she could so much as reach for another arrow, Kwar was there: screaming, charging, slashing. Her hatchet lashed out at Shekune, but found only the thick haft of her spear. It sank into the wood as Shekune brought it up before her and caught the blade in it. With a quick twist of her spear, she tore the hatchet from Kwar's hand.

Not that this seemed to bother Kwar.

Not while she still had a knife.

She lunged at Shekune, lashing out wildly with her blade. She jabbed for Shekune's throat, cut at her legs, tried to leap forward and jam it right in her chest. But every attack was met with Shekune's spear batting away the blade, Shekune's feet dancing away, Shekune's body twisting out of the way.

A dozen times, Kataria saw Kwar overextend herself, make a sloppy move, let her fury leave her open. And a dozen times, Kataria saw Shekune dance away, twist away, letting each opportunity slip away as surely as she slipped away from Kwar's blows.

She's sparing her, Kataria thought. *Why?*

Curiosity turned to concern as a sharp cracking sound filled her ears. Kwar lunged forward, Shekune flipped her spear about, brought the blunt end of it up, and smashed it against Kwar's chin. The khoshict's head snapped backward and she went tumbling to the earth, unmoving.

"Kwar!"

She whirled on Shekune, an arrow drawn and aimed. But it didn't matter.

Shekune was already upon her.

She tackled Kataria about the midriff, brought her low to the ground. Her breath fled her as Shekune's weight dragged her down. The chieftain leapt to her feet and slammed a foot down upon Kataria's chest as she tried to rise. She stared down the length of her spear leveled at Kataria's throat, her blank expression a stark contrast to the saw-toothed grin of her spear's head.

And still, even as she stared death in its grinning metal face, she looked toward the unmoving body not far away.

"Kwar..." she whispered.

"Do not worry." Shekune flipped the spear in her hands. "She will be safe." She raised it high above her head. "I will protect everyone."

The spear came down.

Its butt cracked against Kataria's forehead.

And she fell to the earth and moved no more.

SEVENTEEN

The Tenderness of Flesh

Somewhere, among all the blood and metal he had left behind in the wilds, Lenk had forgotten how to dream.

⊶ ⋅ ⋙✦⋘ ⋅ ⊷

He had memories, of course: quiet nights under an endless sky of stars where he had slept soundly, dreams and nightmares that visited and haunted him alternately, those all-too-rare and gone-forever moments when a breeze would blow over him and a chilly body beside him would growl in her sleep, pull the blanket up around her, and draw closer against his chest so that the tips of her ears brushed against his nose.

But that was a long time ago.

That was many evening ambushes, many long night watches, many cold dawns and tired eyes from sleepless nights ago.

Somewhere between the time he had first picked up a sword and the time he couldn't remember how to put it down, sleep had become a reflex. Just another thing he did, just another thing that happened.

Somehow, he had hoped that when he finally got to put the sword away, the dreams would return.

Not this night, though.

Because this night, as he lay in his tent, his eyes opened from an empty sleep and he sat up in his bedroll for no reason.

No reason but the fact that a small, wordless voice—the same voice that never told him how to put down a sword—whispered something in his ear.

He crawled out of his bedroll and poked his head out of his tent. The night was warm and quiet. They had made their camp at a nearby oasis, and the scarce insects that buzzed around the scarcer greenery were humming a quiet night chorus. Fires burned dimly across the low plain. The Chosen stood around the camp in twos and threes and fours, as they had every night.

It was quiet. A nice night. The sort of night made for shutting out little noises and falling back to dreamless slumber.

But it had been a long time since Lenk had seen a nice night.

How could he have known that he should have gone back to sleep?

He slipped back inside his tent and found his trousers, boots, and shirt in short order. His eyes lingered on his sword for a moment, and an itch crept into his palm.

"No," he whispered to himself.

If he was ever going to learn to put it down, there were times he would have to force himself to. And there was nothing wrong with tonight, he told himself. He was restless. He'd take a walk, clear his head, then return.

The sword wasn't going anywhere.

He walked out of his tent and into the night air. The Chosen didn't look up at his presence, as they usually did. Nor did they really seem to notice him as he walked through them. They weren't talking, weren't reveling, weren't tossing with each other in torrid embrace like they usually did.

They were just ... standing there.

Like freaky bastards.

And normally, that wouldn't bother him—expecting creatures made perfect by a demon's touch to *not* be freaky bastards would be asking too much—but there was something about them, this time. They stood still, silent, staring not at each other but up at the stars or down at their feet or at something so far away Lenk couldn't even see. They used to seem so *alive*.

But now...

Lenk's eyes went across the sands to Shuro's tent, situated at the far end of camp. It hung quiet, with no Chosen even looking at it, let alone lingering near it. Shuro was likely still there, sleeping—after all, where would she go with chains around her wrists?

She's fine, Lenk told himself. *You go over there to check on her, you're just going to hear her cursing at you again, like always.* He glanced at the Chosen. *Besides, what are you worried about? This isn't the first time they've done something insane.*

He stared at them for a long time as they swayed gently in the breeze.

But it's the first time they've done this *insane thing...*

And, without realizing it, he turned and began to walk toward Shuro's tent.

For all of two steps, anyway.

He staggered to a halt as a great shadow rose before him, his hand instinctively leaping to his shoulder for a sword that wasn't there. He tensed, ready to leap backward, before he realized the shadow wasn't moving.

The shadow wasn't even looking at him.

The male Chosen stood over him, arms hanging limp at his sides, swaying just slightly in the breeze. But his glassy eyes stared over Lenk's head, toward some far distant sight, and his mouth hung open, a soft breath escaping through his lips. Lenk hadn't even noticed him, all seven feet of him, so still had he stood.

"Uh, hey," he said.

The Chosen said nothing to him.

"Are you all right?" Lenk squinted at the man for a moment. "Do you need...water? Or...or..." He scratched his head, quite unsure what sort of assistance one offered someone this weird doing something this weird. "Uh, are you all right?"

The Chosen said nothing to him.

Unless one counted a thin trail of saliva oozing out the corner of his mouth as something.

Lenk did not.

Keeping his eyes on the Chosen, he stepped around the looming man and headed toward Shuro's tent with a little more urgency.

Part of him wanted not to. Part of him wanted to spare himself her gaze, her judgment, the painful knowledge that she was right to give him both. But that was the part that wanted empty hands and empty dreams, the part that wanted long nights with someone wearily settling into bed beside him to rise up for a beautifully dull and monotonous job in the morning.

That part of him was getting used to being disappointed.

The other part of him, the part that settled at the back of his neck and kept an eye on every smiling stranger's sword hand, however, was used to being listened to.

And it was for that part's sake that he went toward Shuro's tent, reached for the flap, pulled it back, and—

"It's a pleasant night, isn't it?"

He dropped the flap and whirled around, like a child caught with his hand in a pastry. Mocca stood nearby, hands folded behind his back and eyes on the stars overhead.

"When they cast me down from on high, I resented my station." There was no bitterness in Mocca's voice. His sigh was heavy with sentiment, his eyes dark with memory. "The deserts were barren of life. The jungles were rife with sickness and humidity. I thought it an insult to be sent here to watch over the withered creations that crawled from the muck.

"I don't think I really recognized what I had missed until they cast me into the pit," he said softly. "I never missed the deserts or the jungles, but the nights…" He gestured a hand out toward the sky. "I visited my fellow Aeons in the north once or twice, but I somehow never thought to look up. Is the sky there as full of stars as here?"

Lenk followed the eyes of the man in white toward heaven and the long smears of stars across the midnight sprawl.

"I don't know," he said. "I don't think I remembered to look up, either."

"It's hard, isn't it?" Mocca replied. "When I think back, I can recall a hundred thousand nights like this, but only in the unsleeping hours, the frustrations, the lives lost, and the many, many things I had to do. I can only barely remember the stars."

"You came down from heaven and crawled out of hell," Lenk said. "I mean, the stars are *pretty* and all, but comparatively?"

Mocca shot him an annoyed look. Lenk returned a sneer.

"Oh, come on," he said. "All I'm saying is that someone who went through what you went through should have slightly higher priorities than looking at stars."

"A point." Mocca raised his brows. "But tell me, do *you* not look forward to the night you have no higher priority than looking at stars?"

Lenk fell silent for a moment. A heavy weight settled on his shoulder where his sword should be.

"Yeah," he said. "I do."

"What I went through was long years of blood, of fear, of people weeping and begging and screaming in the night." Mocca held his hands out, helpless. "Just as you went through. I merely had several thousand years longer to experience it." He sighed. "Our priorities are likewise the same. But our work may not be done for a long time. It may be some time before we're able to savor a night like this again."

Lenk looked up at the sky, at all the innumerable stars painted across an endless indigo. And some part of him that he thought had been burned out of him long ago felt an urge to try to count them all.

He didn't say it. But something in the way he tried to lean all the way back to see every last star must have told Mocca he agreed with him.

"May I ask, then…" Mocca's voice was painfully soft, a silk cord tightening around a throat. "Why you would ruin it by going to see that woman?"

And just like that, he snapped back upright.

When he looked at Mocca, the eyes of the man in white were as bright as the night sky. But they were alive with something keen and piercing, something that shined light where light was not meant to shine.

"Do you desire her scorn? Her hatred? Her ignorance?" He gestured toward Shuro's tent. "You will find nothing else beneath her eyes. She doesn't understand. She never will."

"I wanted to check on her," Lenk said. "The Chosen are acting…"

His eyes drifted over Mocca's head, toward the Chosen. The nearest cluster hadn't moved from their spot. But once he laid eyes upon them, their bodies trembled with a sudden shudder. Their necks slowly twisted as, one by one, they looked toward him with those empty eyes.

And smiled.

"The Chosen are…still coming to terms with things," Mocca said, pulling Lenk's attentions back. "It was mere days ago that they were broken, bereft of hope or even a concept of a future. And now, they are alive and vibrant. The world and all its wonders are open to them, all at once. It can be overwhelming."

"Yeah…"

Lenk's eyes drifted back to the Chosen. In the plains beyond, another pair of them looked in his direction, so slowly he could almost hear the vertebrae of their necks cracking. And, in the darkness, he saw the white of their teeth as, one by one, their lips curled into broad smiles.

He forced himself to look away.

"Fine." He glanced back to Shuro's tent. Mocca was right. There was no reason to check on her outside of getting cursed at. "Just tell them to keep away, all right?"

"Of course." Mocca's smile was echoed by a dozen more opening in the darkness as more Chosen looked in his direction, their faces splitting open with the same grin. "They will be certain to respect her space."

"Okay. Good." Lenk frowned out over the field of the camp, with all the Chosen staring at him with their dark eyes and bright smiles. A shudder ran down his body involuntarily, shook a curse out from his lips. "I don't think she'd appreciate waking up and finding these freaky bastards standing over her."

He had barely had a breath behind his words. The closest Chosen was at least thirty feet away. There was no way any of them could have heard him.

And yet, somehow, they did.

One by one, their brows knitted into scowls. One by one, their bodies followed their heads as they turned to face him. One by one, their smiles creaked as they turned upside down and became deep, snarling frowns.

Lenk's blood ran cold. His hand ached for his sword. He took a cautious step back, looking toward Mocca for aid.

And Mocca stared back at him wearing the same scowl as they did.

"They aren't," the man in white whispered.

"What?"

"They aren't." His voice became a hiss. The flesh around his jaw twitched. "After all they've been through, all they'll go through, all they're prepared to sacrifice for, how can you still not understand?"

"Oh, come on." Lenk laughed, but it was a nervous, quavering thing. A dying animal on shaking legs. "I understand you're proud of them, but they're still—"

"They are perfect," Mocca said. "They gave *everything* for me. They forsook family, home, deaf gods, and more to come to me, to believe in me. I gave them much already, but I would give them everything to protect them. I will *not* let you slander them."

A twitch of movement at the corner of his eye. Lenk glanced over the Chosen. They trembled with the last spasms of a motion he had missed. Had he imagined it? Or were they getting closer? He took another step backward.

"Calm down," he said.

"I am calm."

The reply was soft, gentle, perfectly even-tongued. And it wasn't the words, so much, that made Lenk's eyes go wide and his heart go still.

It was the fact that, over Mocca's shoulders, hundreds of lips twitched in echo of his words.

"*I am calm . . .*" the Chosen whispered.

"*. . . am calm . . .*"

"*I am calm . . .*"

"I apologize for alarming you."

Lenk's eyes went back to Mocca. The anger of the man in white ebbed away on a long breath. His eyes returned to a comfortable darkness that failed to warm Lenk's blood.

"They're precious to me, my Chosen," he said. "I will ask so much of them in the coming days. I try to spare them whatever pain I can for now. But I assure you, it won't happen again."

Mocca offered Lenk a smile. A smile that Lenk had seen a thousand times before, one he was sure he had once seen as reassuring, at some point, somewhere. But something had changed. When he looked at Mocca now, the smile didn't look reassuring. It looked like a mess of angles, all painstakingly arranged to show something that wasn't there.

And when he looked over Mocca's shoulder, to the many Chosen staring at him, he saw that same smile.

Carved a hundred times across a hundred perfect faces.

And that little voice at the back of Lenk's head, the one that hadn't let him sleep, the one that told him to get out of his tent, the one that had always been whispering a wordless warning since he had awoken, now spoke a single, perfect word.

Shit.

"Pardon?" Mocca asked.

"You . . ." Lenk's words had not the breath to be accusatory. His arm had not the strength to point at him. He could only think of backing away. "You're controlling them."

He saw the briefest flash of something play across Mocca's face—the beginnings of a soothing reassurance, a honey-sweet denial, a complex explanation, or maybe just the stillbirth of a lie—but these, ultimately, faded in a few breaths.

And a deep, solemn frown creased Mocca's face.

"Not exactly."

"The fuck do you mean?" Lenk said, voice tense as his body. His muscles bunched up instinctively, suddenly aware of all the glassy stares set upon him.

"They aren't controlled," Mocca replied. "Not in the way you're thinking of. It'd be more accurate to say that they're vessels, waiting to be filled. They are bereft of the common maladies of mankind and filled with..."

"*Stop.*"

Lenk found the words hurled from his mouth, a spear sunk into the earth at Mocca's feet. His eyes went hard, bright with fever hotness. He snarled to be heard over the sudden rush of blood in his ears.

"Don't you fucking try to confuse me," he spit. "No more of your fucking fancy speeches, your big fucking words, your trying to show off how smart and wise you think you are. You tell me exactly what's going on with these abominations and you do it right the fuck now."

Lenk had seen Mocca's smiles, those saccharinely sweet curls that looked like what he imagined his grandfather had worn. Lenk had seen Mocca's anger, bright and burning with a passion that he couldn't help but contain. But the expression that smoothed the face of the man in white now, that drained the light from his eyes and the emotion from his face and left behind something cold and dark and terribly, terribly old...

Lenk couldn't remember the nightmare where he had seen that before.

"How can you be confused?" he whispered, his voice soft as skin parting beneath a scalpel. "After so long, so much suffering, how is it you still don't understand?"

The skin around Mocca's chin rippled, split. The heads of vipers peered out with red eyes from beneath his skin. But where Lenk had merely found the beard of serpents unnerving before, with their hissing and snarling, he found their silent attentiveness on him terrifying.

"How is it that you still cry out in the dark?" Mocca whispered. "How is it that you can still scream out for gods who don't listen? You pray, you plead, you fall to your knees and *beg* for someone, for *anyone* to hear you, to listen, to come save you, and the moment I lift so much as a *finger* to do so, you dare call *me* an abomination?"

He held out his hands in a vast gesture. Slowly, the Chosen began to stalk toward him, their eyes glassy stares fixed upon Lenk. He began to back away, glancing back toward his tent, which seemed so impossibly far away now.

"You don't understand. You *never* understood. You think the gift I gave them was their flesh? Their beauty? Mere vanity. I showed them a kindness gods could never bring themselves to."

A smile, just as cold and ancient as his anger, crept across Mocca's face.

"I took away their pain."

"Took away the pain…"

The Chosen burbled in an off-key chorus, whispering in the dark.

"Took away…"

"…the pain…the pain…"

"They're monsters," Lenk whispered, eyes unblinking. "Mindless, vicious demons—"

"Have they harmed anyone?" Mocca asked. "Have they not obeyed? They are not mindless. They simply know no more pain, no more fear, none of the curses that their creators saw fit to burden them with."

"And what *do* they know?" Lenk spit. "Without that, what's left? What else did you take from them? Joy? Love?"

"They don't lack those, Lenk. They have them in abundance. They know everything they need to know, for they share the greatest, most compassionate mind that creation has ever known."

Mocca smiled, raised a finger to his head, and tapped his temple.

And behind him, a hundred bodies mirrored the gesture perfectly.

"Mine."

Fuck.

Lenk hadn't the wit to think of anything greater, hadn't the breath to voice even that. He barely had the energy to stand in the wake of this revelation.

This had been it, the plan all along. Mocca claimed he wanted to save the world, heal its people. And this was how he intended to do it: not by curing the diseases or abolishing the war, but by assuming control. Over everything. Over every body, every mind, every…

A cold fear struck the thought from his head.

He found his eyes drifting to Shuro's tent.

"Lenk," Mocca said, "don't."

But he did.

He bolted to her tent, pulled back the tent, searched for her.

And saw only empty sand.

He turned back to Mocca. The man in white shot him a sad, almost pitiable smile and held his hands out helplessly.

"She doesn't understand, Lenk," he said. "She's too afraid, too wounded to understand. You asked me to spare her." He held out his hand to Lenk. And beneath his smile, a dozen serpents opened their mouths and hissed. "Let me help her."

And the voice at the back of Lenk's head spoke a single, clear word.

Run.

And he obeyed.

Heart in his throat, blood in his ears, stumbling over the sand beneath his boots, he tore across the field. The glassy eyes of the Chosen shone in the dark, each of them a mirror reflecting his flight as he scrambled for his tent, burst through the flap, and emerged inside to see it.

The Chosen, a tall and lanky woman, almost looked surprised to see him as she stood in the center of the tent, his sword clutched in her hands. But the shock slowly slid into a smile that tried to be as warm and reassuring as Mocca's. But it lacked something—some essential lie, some crucial facsimile of compassion—and her wide grin more resembled a scar full of teeth across her face.

"Drop it," Lenk hissed.

"Try to understand," the Chosen said, her voice lilting with a mannerism that wasn't her own. "We are making a world free of pain, of fear. A world where none need gaze upon his neighbor and wonder what plots lurk within. A world where no one needs to worry about disease or filth."

The Chosen's grin almost split her face in half.

"I can create a world for you, Lenk," she said, "a world where you and she can be together. Just you and Kat—"

He couldn't hear the rest of what the Chosen said.

Not over the sound of him screaming.

He couldn't say what it was—maybe all the terror and doubt he had buried in his head to get this far was finally breaking out in one glorious scream, or maybe he just couldn't stand to hear her name spoken from the lips of this monster—but he charged forward, leapt, and tackled the Chosen at the waist.

She toppled to the earth, thrown off balance, and landed with a grunt. He seized the sword, tried to prize it from her grasp. Her long fingers tightened around the scabbard and pulled it back. She was bigger than he was, and stronger, too; she all but hauled him off his feet as she clambered back to hers.

He grabbed the hilt of the blade and pulled it free of its scabbard: sharp and upward. It cracked against the Chosen's jaw with a snapping sound. Her head jerked backward. Her mouth gaped open, a high-pitched shriek tearing itself free from between her teeth.

A shriek echoed outside the tent. A hundred agonies in a hundred voices.

Lenk reeled from the scream, trying to clap his hands over his ears even as he struggled to hold on to the sword. But her pain shot through his skin, shook his bones against his body.

"It hurts!" she screamed in a voice that was her own, almost childlike so shrill it was. *"It HURTS!"* Horror scarred itself across her perfect features as she stared down at her perfect hands, glistening with her own, perfect red life. "You said it wouldn't hurt! You promised ..."

She shut her eyes tight. She took in a long, shuddering breath.

When she opened them again, they were the size of fists and brimming with raw, red veins.

"You *promised*!"

All the instinct fled him—the urge to run drained out of his legs and pooled at his feet, the sword fell from his grasp, there was nothing left in him but the paralyzing terror at what was occurring before him.

Though he hadn't words or prayers or gods to say what that was.

The grin was gone, the crude compassion was gone. The Chosen covered her face with her hand, drawing in wheezing, sobbing breaths that sent her body shaking with each one. And with each shudder of her body, she grew.

She changed.

Her skin quivered, rippled like water, split like paper. The sinew beneath glistened bright red for a moment before it hardened over into thick, coarse scales in a single breath. The tips of her fingers split apart, ebon claws curling over her face. Her hair fell out in thick clumps to fall upon the sand and curl into ash.

From between her fingers, he caught the barest glimpse of the ruin that had been her face: the bulging bloodshot eyes, the lipless mouth gaping open, the brimming rows of fangs from which a guttural, inhuman howl escaped.

"YOU PROMISED!"

She lunged for him, arms stretching longer than could ever be possible. He avoided it more by falling than rolling, the blood leaving his legs and sending him collapsing to the earth.

He found his footing along with his sword as he seized the hilt in both hands. She descended upon him, her mouth stretching open impossibly wide, his fear reflected back at him in the polish of her jagged teeth. He found enough instinct to lash out with the blade, to catch her in the mouth.

A gout of black blood spattered the canvas walls of the tent.

Her roar, in all its monstrous fury, was broken by a sudden sob of agony.

Thick. Wet. And unnervingly human.

She recoiled, clutching the wound that had cloven her face and shrinking back against the wall, weeping through the black blood seeping through her fingers.

Lenk didn't wait to see what she'd do next.

He tore out of the tent. All around him, he could see the faces of the Chosen. The eerie grins and glassy eyes had been replaced with wails of shared agony, with eyes wild with confusion. Those few who could find him through the pain turned toward him, began loping toward him with limbs growing suddenly longer.

Run.

The voice, the instinct, drawing his stare toward the distant desert, the wide-open sands before him. He turned to run, to keep running until he died. Only one thing kept him from doing so.

Soft, meek, barely audible through the animal howls in the night sky.

A scream.

Her voice.

It would have been smarter to flee, he knew. A hundred fights, a hundred scars, a hundred corpses had taught him to listen to that voice that told him to run, to save himself so he could kill again.

The man who wanted to lead a good life wouldn't have turned and run toward the scream, back through the fray of inhuman howls and wide, furious eyes.

But then, those same fights had taught him that doing good meant, more often than not, doing something dumb as fuck.

They bled past him, their screaming, gaping mouths and their red-rimmed stares, as he shot through the crowd of the Chosen. Those claws that reached for him with impossibly long arms, he lashed out at. His blade caught flesh, cut fingers, sent palms back bleeding. And each wound sent a new chorus of pain echoing through the masses.

"*—hurts! Why does it hurt? Why—*"

"*—said it wouldn't, said he could help—*"

"*—lies, lies, lies, everyone lies, everyone lies—*"

He shut his ears to their screams. As much as he could, anyway. Through their wild cries, he focused on that soft mortal scream. He focused on the direction of it, forced himself to run faster as he tore off toward the edge of the sands and to the oasis.

On the shores, by the light of the stars reflected against the water, he could make out their shapes. The two Disciples, their withered old-man bodies on serpentine coils, their great, jutting column heads swaying precarious as they bent over a flat rock formation.

And the slender, silver-haired shape chained to it.

With every step he could see her more clearly: her face twisted in agony, her body writhing in the chains securing her to the stone slab, the silver shimmer of her hair, the clench of her teeth as Shuro tried to bite back a scream.

And failed.

Their claws were in her body, sank into her throat and abdomen. She twitched beneath their touch, pulled against her chains, roared in fury as much as in pain. Whatever they were trying to do, she was resisting. But he could see the tremble in her flesh, the twitch in her muscle. She would give out, sooner or later.

But only if he missed.

A sharp breath. A burst of speed. Two hands wrapped around a thick hilt. The earth left his feet as he leapt.

He landed on the Disciple's back. It let out a groan as it buckled beneath his weight, but only for a moment. In another, he had rammed his sword through its neck, the blade bursting out its throat. Its claws left Shuro's flesh as he bore it to the earth and jerked his sword from its throat.

It stared up at him through its eyes, scribbled black and unreadable. And though whatever humanity it once bore had withered off its ancient face, there was still just enough to show surprise.

"But..." it hissed, "we were going to..."

Lenk didn't bother waiting to hear what it had to say. He whirled to face the other demon, his sword held high and smeared with black ichor.

The remaining Disciple regarded him carefully through its scribble-black eyes, its ancient and withered face set in a hard frown. Slowly, it slid its claws from Shuro's neck. She went limp on the stone.

"Inevitable." When its dust-choked voice escaped its lips, it did so on a long, purple tongue. "After all we have done, you are still so ungrateful."

The creature moved and Lenk tensed, ready to attack. But it simply slid about and slithered away, disappearing into the waters of the oasis and vanishing beneath the water with nary a ripple left behind.

Lenk kept one eye on those waters as he rushed to Shuro's side. She lay still, her breath shallow, unharmed but for the black wounds marking her flesh where the Disciples' claws had punctured her. As to what harm they actually did, he couldn't bear to speculate.

His sword came down in two heavy chops. The chains shattered from her wrists. Her body slid off the stone into his arms and lay there, heavy and still.

"Shuro," he whispered. "Shuro, wake up." He shook her lightly, patted her cheek. But she did not open her eyes, she did not stir. "Shuro, *please*." He felt his eyes grow hot. He forced words between clenched teeth. "You were right. You were right about everything."

"She was not."

Across the sand and water, through the writhing wails of the Chosen, directly into a mind that felt aflame with fever. Lenk heard the voice keenly, viciously close and rife with hate. He felt his eyes drawn across the sands, back toward the camp. And there, amid all that screaming agony, he could feel a pair of eyes set upon him.

"She is not."

At the center of the mass of writhing flesh, a shadow began to grow. Like a long breath drawn in, it rose out of the tangle of wailing bodies. It rose until a crown of serpents scraped the stars, until the earth groaned beneath its weight, until eyes big and white and cold as the moon stared down at Lenk from on high.

"And neither are you."

He raised one colossal foot. It came down with the sound of thunder. Lenk would have felt the shudder of the earth in his very bones if the feeling had not left his body to make room for the fear. He stared up, helpless, as the great form of Khoth-Kapira came striding forward on legs the size of trees.

For a moment, at least.

Then the fear turned to vigor. He took his sword in one hand, Shuro in the other, held them both close as he turned and ran. He hauled her across the sands, through the waters of the oasis, out toward the sprawling desert.

He didn't care that there was nothing out there. He didn't care that they would both die out there. His animal fear wouldn't let him care; it simply told him to run, as fast and far as he could. He didn't care where.

And in another moment, it didn't matter.

Ten great strides. That was all it took. Ten steps of impossibly huge legs, each one making the earth quake and the waters shudder. Ten steps that brought a shadow darker than any night down upon Lenk. And on the eleventh, the earth shook so fiercely that it knocked him from his feet and onto his face.

He scrambled to his rear, gathered Shuro up in his arms, and held her close to him. He raised his sword, holding it out like the barest sliver of a silver star against the endless night looming over him.

"I will not ask you why." Khoth-Kapira's voice, endless and deep as a gorge with no bottom, reached into his flesh. *"I will not ask you to explain your fear, your ignorance."* He knelt down on one tremendous knee. *"Your creators, in their infinite cruelty, sought to ingrain those in your very bones. I will not ask you to apologize for them."* He stared at Lenk through those immense eyes. *"Nor will I forgive them."*

A great hand rose. The air went still.

"I am too close. I have come too far. I cannot let you stop me." Above the writhing serpents that were his hair, his immense hand held. *"May you be the last I fail. I am sorry, Lenk."*

A rush of wind. The stars groaned. Perhaps Lenk cried out. Perhaps he didn't. He couldn't tell over the sound of the great hand that came crashing down, ready to smear him across the earth.

He shut his eyes. He held his sword out. He clenched his teeth and waited for death.

And it did not come.

He did not dare open his eyes, lest he find that the blow had come so swift and so completely that he was already dead and would awake to find himself in hell. But soon, the agony of waiting became too much. He opened his eyes, looked up.

The great hand of Khoth-Kapira hovered over him, shaking slightly. It ached to kill him, to crush him like the insect he was. But it hung there; for a long time, it hung there.

And Lenk could feel Khoth-Kapira's immense eyes on them and he could feel what radiated out of them.

He couldn't do it.

Or he wouldn't do it.

Khoth-Kapira hesitated.

"Lenk..."

A soft whisper. He looked down. A pair of blue eyes, bright and alive, met his. He felt a hand on his own. He felt fingers wrap around his. In his arms, Shuro took a breath and spoke.

"Get down."

She tore from his arms effortlessly as she tore the sword from his hand. She leapt to her feet, then from the earth, lunging at that massive hand hovering over them both. The sword flashed in her hand, cleaved across the dark.

And Khoth-Kapira's scream all but shook the stars from the sky.

He pulled his hand back, whether from shock or pain Lenk didn't know. Nor did he care to find out.

Shuro's hand grabbed him by the collar and pulled him to his feet. And together, they were running. Across the shores, across the sands, out toward the desert.

A howl pierced his ear. Out of the darkness, the Chosen came charging, loping along on all fours like a beast. They lunged out from the darkness, one of them leaping at him.

"Lenk!"

He turned, saw the sword flying toward him as Shuro tossed it to him. He caught it and swung. The blade caught the Chosen in the neck and brought it down to the earth in a wailing heap of black blood and twitching flesh.

The others continued to chase but fell behind. Their howls softened. Or perhaps they were just harder to hear over the anger of Khoth-Kapira chasing them, Shuro and Lenk, as they fled into the night.

How far they went, he didn't know. They ran until the oasis was far behind them. They ran until the sounds of hellish fury died out and left only the thunder of their hearts. They ran until they could run no farther, until their bodies all but collapsed.

At the bottom of a dune, the sole rise in a featureless expanse of sand, they stopped. Lenk doubled over, hands on his knees, as he struggled to catch his breath. When he had enough sense to do so, he turned around.

No Chosen pursued them. No earth shook at the stride of almighty demons. Nothing but their tracks stretched out behind them, and those too seemed to vanish in the wind.

"We made it," Lenk gasped. He turned back to Shuro. "We're safe for—"

She had run just as far as he had, just as fast as he had. Yet where he was ready to collapse, she still seemed to have enough energy to drive a fist into his face.

Her punch cracked against his jaw. The second one knocked what little wind he had from his belly. He fell to his knees, where her foot was waiting to smash against his chin and send him sprawling to the sand.

He cried out something that might have been *Wait* or *I deserved that, I guess*. She didn't seem to care. When he lay there, stunned and breathless and waiting for her to finish it, it never came.

His ears filled with the sound of her feet crunching on the sand as she took off running, leaving him behind. He raised a hand impotently, as if to stop her or beg her to stay. She didn't do either.

Nor could he blame her.

She was right.

The realization settled on him like a stone, pinned him to the earth. Khoth-Kapira was going to do...whatever he had done to the Chosen to everyone he could. And Lenk had helped him to do so. Lenk had believed him. Lenk had killed everyone. Lenk had...had...

He had no strength in him to hate himself. He had no power to drive the sword into his chest out of shame for what he had done.

He lay there, prone and unmoving on the sand. The sun would rise upon him soon. The heat would be unbearable. He had no water, no food, nowhere to go. And maybe that wouldn't even matter. Maybe the Chosen would find him and tear him apart as he lay helpless.

And that was fine.

It wasn't like he didn't deserve that, too.

EIGHTEEN

THE PROPHET AND THE THIEF

D*on't go."*

That had been good advice.

"For fuck's sake, take an escort with you. Ten men. No, twenty. Armed. Eyes on you at all times. At the very least, take me."

That had been good advice, too, if coarse. Dransun was full of gems like that.

"Please, just . . . think about this. Think about how much you mean to us, to this city. You're not just a person anymore. You're the Prophet. Everything we need rests with you. You can't risk everything like this."

And that hadn't been good advice. Aturach had simply stated a fact.

It would have been stupid to be out in the war-torn Souk, alone and at night, in even ordinary circumstances. And the circumstances in Asper's life, of late, had been anything but ordinary.

Those circumstances, at least, had led to friends like Dransun and Aturach. Good men with good wisdom, full of concern for her. She found she had a hard time shaking the sound of their concerned voices from her thoughts.

That seemed unfair.

Despite the years she had spent adventuring, Asper still had a hard time ignoring sensible advice.

How was it, she wondered, that her companions made being stupid look so easy?

Former, she thought, correcting herself. *Former companions.* She let out a sigh. *Can't call them friends anymore, can you?*

A frown pulled itself across her face.

No. I guess you can't.

Lenk and Kataria were gone. By now they either were rotting in shallow graves together or had returned to their bloody old way of life that would see them in one.

Dreadaeleon, if he ever saw her again, was infinitely more likely to kill her than talk to her, unless it was to say something insufferably smug.

Gariath was now a hundred miles away, behind a wall of stone and tulwar, the scent of her blood still in his nostrils and her imminent death on his mind.

And Denaos...

She felt a sudden stab of pain in her chest.

Denaos was why she was out here. Alone. Against all reason.

He had disappeared. Men like him often did. To escape responsibility, blame, or the noose, he had a habit of vanishing. But he had always come back, always made his presence known. She would have liked to have him by her side in these circumstances.

And someone was keen to make that happen.

Should have burned the letter, she told herself. *Shouldn't have even read it.*

But she had.

She reached into her pocket, felt a square of paper damp from all the times she had held it in a sweaty hand and read it over and over. She pulled it out, unfolded it with one hand and her teeth—her broken left arm of little use for it.

The letter was brief, barely two dozen words, having come in the middle of the night. But they were words she had been desperate to read, conveying a message she had been desperate to hear. And they bade her to come alone and unguarded to the dark part of the Souk, in a quest for an answer to a question that had been gnawing at the back of her skull for weeks now. And of all those words, one stood out in a neat, businesslike signature at the bottom of the page.

Rezca.

She knew the letter was genuine. It had said things that only he would know. Not that this soothed her. Meeting with the head of the Jackals would have been idiocy even if they *weren't* desperate. With their war against the Khovura having gone bad, they were little more than starving, frightened dogs backed into a corner. And Rezca was the one with the sharpest teeth.

She had deliberated on it. She had even considered praying on it. But she knew what answer heaven would give—after all, she spoke for it these days—and would not blaspheme by disobeying it.

She had to know. Even if it meant coming out here alone.

Well, she corrected herself again, *not* really *alone*.

Like a cat hearing the wounded cry of something small, weak, and helpless, something stirred at the back of her thoughts.

You rang? Amoch-Tethr's chuckle was black smoke on a stiff breeze. *Oh my. I look away for just a few moments and you go and take us into the nasty part of town.*

She didn't respond. She tried her best not to listen. She didn't need the thing within her to be active, merely awake. Just in case he was needed.

Come, come. Amoch-Tethr chided her. *At the very least, you can make conversation. It's not as though we've anyone else to talk to.*

The darkened houses that rose around her as she went deeper into the Souk were relatively undamaged. They hadn't seen much business even before the war had started. The tenants had fled regardless, but relatively few of the shops were burned out or torn apart by fighting.

Yet their good repair only unnerved Asper more. Windows still held jars of sweets and toys that stared at her with black button eyes. Signs creaked on their posts in a stale breeze. If she didn't look too hard, she could almost trick herself into believing life here was still normal.

And something about that lie caused a pain fiercer than any wound.

"*Fuck.*"

Almost any wound, anyway.

The stab of pain in her chest became an explosion. Breath fled her as her lungs felt like they had just caught ablaze and poured smoke into her throat. She doubled over, clutching her belly. Shards of bone raked something tender inside her. She could feel something wet filling her lungs. Her breath came out in sopping, gurgling gasps.

Had she had breath, she would have screamed. Had she had tears, she would have wept. Had she not been certain it would give Amoch-Tethr so much pleasure, she would have keeled over and died right there.

My, my. Amoch-Tethr made a soft chiding noise. *Are we not feeling well?*

"Shut up," she hissed.

You really don't know how bad it is in here, do you? His laughter was brief and cruel. *Should I tell you of the blood dripping? The splinters of bone? Of all the soft and precious things that are turning black inside you?* She felt his grin twisting in her flesh. *That scaly friend of yours really can hit, can't he? A pity we didn't end him.*

She would have retorted if not for a sudden spike of pain that shot up through her gut. She let out a wet, sopping sob. She shut her eyes and whispered a few harsh words to herself. Her sole retort was her drawing in a sharp breath, biting back the pain, and hauling herself to her feet.

It took much longer than it did two days ago.

She couldn't keep doing this, she knew, as she forced herself deeper into the Souk. Amoch-Tethr was right; things were getting worse. It would have been difficult to recover from these injuries even if she *hadn't* been assembling an army.

But that was all fine, she told herself. If she died, that was fine, so long as everything got done. If she could protect Cier'Djaal, if she could unite the armies, if she could hang on just long enough to see Gariath die...

Well, that'd be a pleasant way to go out, wouldn't it?

"Priestess."

A voice like tepid water. But she whirled around, defensive, all the same.

It wasn't the sight of Rezca that made her freeze up—his burly build was overwhelmed by his bookish demeanor—but the fact that he had appeared behind her without her even noticing.

Moonlight reflected off his spectacles, made his eyes look like discs of pure white as he regarded her. Dressed in a neat outfit, scalp and face clean-shaven, he looked more like an accountant than the leader of the most dangerous gang in Cier'Djaal.

Formerly most dangerous. She corrected herself. But it seemed unwise to point that out.

"You don't look particularly well." Rezca stared at her thoughtfully. "Pardon my bluntness."

She said nothing. Everything she had in her was focused on standing up tall and proud, as a leader should, and trying to ignore the pain stabbing away inside her.

"I heard about the events at Jalaang." Rezca finally broke the silence. "I heard about how you faced down a monster and narrowly survived." His eyes drifted to her broken arm in its sling. "I hadn't heard about how bad the damage was, though."

Inside her flesh, Amoch-Tethr chuckled. She ignored that. She ignored Rezca's comment.

Prophets don't respond to such pettiness, she reminded herself. A surge of pain welled up in her bowels. *And Prophets* damn *well don't shit themselves in front of the enemy, so keep it together.*

"The tulwar could march upon Cier'Djaal any day now." Rezca took a few steps forward, regarding her coolly. "Their armies are thousands strong and the forges of Jalaang are working day and night, belching out swords. Things are grim."

He came to a halt a few feet away from her. A smile, uneven and unnerving, crossed his lips.

"But you've been conducting yourself admirably in Cier'Djaal's defense, haven't you? Uniting the Karnerians and Sainites is no mean feat. Incredible what a few tricks from the couthi can do."

Her pulse quickened. She hid her surprise beneath a scowl. She couldn't show him shock, couldn't give him that advantage.

"Please." He held up his hands in placation. "That's not meant to sound like a threat. I have no intention of telling anyone about your tactics. I admire them." His smile curled a little more upward. "After all, it's not like we're in a position where we can start turning down favors, am I—"

"Stop."

Asper's voice came so forceful it all but slapped the mirth from Rezca's face. His smile faded. His hands fell. In the reflection of his spectacles, she saw her own authoritative glare looking back at her.

"Whatever you think you know, I don't give a shit," she said. "Whatever you're hoping to extort from me, you're not going to get it. I'm not here to play games with you. I'm here for answers."

The pain, as tender and close as a knife in the dark, welled up in her chest again. She spoke through clenched teeth.

"Where is Denaos?"

He held her gaze for a moment longer before turning away from her, as if he were simply going to walk away. A surge of dark anger coursed from her heart into her broken arm. Amoch-Tethr felt it and giggled giddily inside her as she moved toward Rezca.

"Do you know why he took that name?" Rezca spoke suddenly, causing her to stop. "Do you know why he doesn't call himself Ramaniel anymore?"

She stared at his neck, considerate. "I've heard stories."

"Which?"

"The ones he told me."

"Then you heard lies," he said. "Or, at the very least, you didn't hear the best parts. Ramaniel was an excellent liar. He had a storyteller's flair. He knew what ending he had to give people so that they'd be content and never ask questions of him." He glanced over his shoulder. "Which ending did he give you? The one where he settles down and marries an honest woman? Or maybe the one where he finally finds redemption for past crimes. He always liked that one."

Asper's eyes widened at that. The pain inside her chest twisted tenderly.

Careful, darling. Amoch-Tethr hissed inside her. *He's trying to get in your head. There's precious little room for him in here.*

"I told you..." Asper spit her doubts out in a blood-tinged glob on the cobblestones. "I'm not here to play—"

"And I heard you, *Prophet*," he replied, voice thick with spite. "I'd hardly waste your time. But you are a leader of armies and I am just a humble thief. I don't play games. I make deals. I name prices. And mine, right now, is for me to speak and you to listen."

He wasn't lying. He was a thief, and thieves did name prices. But she had known more than a few thieves over the years, some very well. And she knew enough to know that the price they named was never the price they charged.

"You won't believe it," Rezca said softly, "but you found Cier'Djaal in a relatively peaceful time." He glanced at his feet. "Armies are like lovers. They come and go. But thieves are family. You're born with them and you're stuck with them until you die.

"This city used to crawl with them. It was so thick with thieves that you couldn't even call it a profession. It was in the fucking water. Every woman was a murderer. Every man a rapist. Every child a thief. They just didn't all know it yet."

He looked up toward the sky. *Sentimental* was not the right word to describe the expression that crept across his face. Whatever emotion he wore, it was what pulled sentimentality into a dark alley and strangled it.

"This was the world Ramaniel and I found ourselves thrown into."

"Your glory days," Asper remarked, snide.

"I haven't met a poet skilled enough to convince me that such a thing as glory exists. Nor a priest convincing enough to make me believe sin exists, either. Deeds aren't glorious or sinful. They're just scars." He looked down at his hands. "Long, painful things you collect and carry the rest of your life.

"And I have plenty, priestess. Me and every other Jackal. We hung men from bridges and cut their throats over the river. We beat women so badly with wine bottles that their husbands didn't recognize them. We were wicked people. We did wicked things."

"So what?" she asked. "You want absolution?"

"Absolution is poor wine for a man with no taste for sin." He chuckled bitterly. "When my time comes, I'll face the gods with my cock out and fall backward into hell."

"You want me to be intimidated, then," she said. "I've seen worse than you, Rezca. I've killed worse than you."

"I don't want you to be intimidated. I want you to understand." He whirled on her, a scowl knitting his brows. "The Jackals. Ramaniel, Anielle, Fenshi, and Yerk. The Candle and the Scarecrow. Ramaniel and I. Do you know why we did it? Why we never apologized for it?"

"Money. Thrill. Violence." Asper sneered. "Wickedness isn't as unique as you think."

"Mine was, priestess." He held his hands out. "Mine built this city. When we took over, the other gangs fled like roaches. We made rules. We made the game. Those who didn't play weren't welcome here. Murders, thievery, everything played by the rules. *Our* rules. We gave this city order."

"You gave it a gang," she snapped back. "Just a bigger one than they were used to."

"If you've got a better way to describe a government, I'd love to hear it." At her stony silence, he sneered. "The fashas fell into line, too. We set the terms. We made our peace. No one who played by the rules needed to suffer. And things were good, until..."

He hesitated. He wore a shameful look, a blasphemer on hallowed ground. She finished for him.

"The Khovura?"

He shook his head. "Nothing so fancy. Just a girl. A spoiled little fasha's daughter whose dumb bitch of a wet nurse read her too many stories about brave knights before bed."

Asper's eyes went wide. "The Houndmistress."

"You know her."

"Everyone does. She's a legend. She tore this city apart to get rid of your thugs."

"And she would have a thousand more crop up in our wake. The Jackals' heads were scared. Old men who feared nothing more than losing weight. I had bigger concerns. Once she was rid of us, once the rules were broken, this city would slide back into the shit and rot there.

"But nothing we tried worked. Our assassins couldn't kill her. Our archers couldn't shoot her. We couldn't even get a drop of poison in her tea. It was over until the Kissing Game."

Two words. Nothing more. Yet the way he said them was enough to make her cringe. "The what?"

"My idea," he said. "The heads didn't like it. I took initiative." He held up five fingers. "Five Jackals. Five disguises. Start them low: slaves, consultants, tailors, whores. Raise them high: advisers, friends, confidants, lovers. Let them earn their trust, earn *her* trust. Wait one year and then, on the same night..."

His face was cold, empty stone. No joy. No malice. Just another scar he wore across his entire face.

"Ramaniel himself did the deed. Cut her throat as she slept. Saved the whole damn city."

The pain in her chest twisted again. Something foul rose inside her gullet, something so dark and thick that she was thankful it kept her from sobbing.

"We lost a lot of Jackals before it worked out. But it worked. The Houndmistress, her supporting fashas, and Ramaniel...they all died on the same night. Denaos was born the next." He waved a hand. "The riots were a problem, of course. But compared to the violence that would have occurred if we were gone?" He shook his head. "I won't apologize. I won't feel sorry. Not for one drop of blood."

Asper had seen many monsters in her life. So many that, for a few blissful moments in the day, she could convince herself that she wasn't afraid of them anymore. After all, they were all easy to understand, once one thought about it.

Those with crazed grins and dead eyes, they did it just for fun. Those with deep frowns and eyes full of terror, they did it to survive. But the expression on Rezca's face, the way his eyes glinted as they looked upon her, the way he exuded a desperate need for her to understand…

She would never understand. And she was afraid.

"So let me ask you," Rezca said. "Why do you want to know about Ramaniel?"

She recoiled. "What?"

"I was there for the things he did. I held down a screaming man while Ramaniel cut the nose from his face. Ramaniel held a screaming wife's head up, forced her to watch as I beat her husband to death with a hammer. We're wicked people. We're sinful people. And you're not."

He stared at her.

"Why do you care about him?"

She met his stare, held it for a long time. This, too, was a question she had asked herself on many sleepless nights and in many painful moments. Even before she knew all of his past life, she had wondered about it.

And perhaps she had not known the answer until just then.

"Because," she said, "he wanted to be better. He wanted me to help him." She swallowed hard. "And I can't fail him. I can't fail anymore. Not one more person."

Rezca looked at her, his face empty and numb. The desperation faded from his eyes and his look was the cold, quiet appraisal of a hunter. And when his hands went to his sides, she tensed up, half expecting him to pull a knife. Instead, he merely removed a cloth and began to wipe his spectacles clean. A soft smile, tinged with sadness, played across his face.

"Fuck," he sighed. "Why couldn't you have been as awful as she said you were?"

Asper blinked. "What?"

"I was hoping it was true. I was hoping you really *were* just the power-hungry bitch I was told you were. That way, you'd have seen the virtue in it. You'd have played by the rules. But you're not terrible, are you?" He shook his head. "You're so good. And so, so stupid."

"Enough of this shit." She stepped forward, fury leaking from her eyes. "Where is Denaos? Answer or die."

"At the bottom of the harbor," he said plainly. "Dead. For the same reason you're also going to die."

Before she could act, he raised a hand.

And they came.

The shadows stirred. From the alleys and the rooftops, they appeared, slinking out of the dark and climbing down into the streets. Maybe they had been there this whole time. Or maybe they were fiends, spontaneously birthed from darkness.

Jackal thugs approached, their hoods drawn tight over their faces, naked blades glistening brightly.

Khovura cultists slithered toward her, faces shrouded in black veils but for the crazed glint of their eyes locked upon her.

Thief and fanatic, murderer and cultist, sworn enemies approaching her, blades fixed on her, gazes locked on her, ready to kill.

"Rezca," she snarled as she whirled about, trying to take them all in, "you fucking swine."

"I've killed too many people for this city," he replied. "So many I'll gladly rot in a lightless pit for eternity, if that's what it takes to keep it safe. I can't let you ruin that. I can't let you lead us back into chaos. Teneir said—"

"Teneir is *lying*!" She spared a single, desperate look for him. "She's a fanatic! You're smarter than this. You know she's a liar. You know she won't share power! She'll betray you! She'll—"

"Eventually," Rezca said. "But murderers, liars, and traitors have been the only friends I've ever known."

"Listen to me," she shouted. She tried to back up toward a wall but found a Jackal there, a blade fixed on her back. "*Listen to me.* You kill me, this city falls to the tulwar. It can't survive. I can save this city! I can save *everyone*!"

"I wouldn't trust a savior who considers me worthy of salvation, priestess." Rezca turned and began to walk away. "Take comfort that

I'll protect this city from the tulwar, as I've protected it from everything else. Take comfort that this will end better for everyone."

They closed in around her. Asper's world became shadows and steel, unable to see anything but the glint of their blades and the glare of their eyes as they advanced upon her. For a brief moment, before they closed, she saw Rezca pause and look over his shoulder at her.

"For what it's worth," he said, "I am sorry."

And like a bad dream, he was gone.

She thought to try to run after him, to tackle him to the ground and try her damnedest to choke the life out of him with one arm. Or, at the very least, to spit on him a few times before she was killed.

But that urge was overwhelmed by another, more pressing thought.

Fuck.

That word was all she had room in her head for. The rest of her skull was full of the impossibility of trying to figure a way out of this.

A dozen? Two dozen? It was hard to tell how many there were; they seemed to shift in and out of the reaching shadows. She could count them only by the glimmer of their blades.

And they were many.

Panic shot up through her, pounded from her heart to her legs, screamed at her to run. But the pain inside her, that tender ache in her chest, screamed louder, sent a surge of agony twisting inside her belly.

She was wounded from the inside. She had one good arm. She was surrounded by countless blades, all of them fixed on her. Her friends were gone.

I'm going to die.

And the whole of her body was consumed by that thought.

I'm going to die.

Save for one small part of her.

No.

And it reached out to her on a smoke-black voice.

I won't let you.

He sounded softer this time, almost fearful. The arrogance and cruelty were gone, replaced by something painful and sweet. Amoch-Tethr spoke to her, in a voice he had never used before.

Let me save you.

She couldn't answer him.

She didn't have time.

A flash of movement from her right. A shadow swept up behind her. An arm shot out and wrapped around her throat, tried to pull her back. A surge of fear shot through her, bid her to scream.

Fear was a powerful instinct. But it was one of many. And some spoke louder than screams.

Her foot rose up, came down. The hard heel of her boot smashed on the arch of the thug's foot. A snapping sound filled her ears, followed by a sudden shriek. The arm around her neck loosened just enough for her good hand to reach up and snatch it. She swung her shoulder forward, put her body weight behind it, and hurled.

The man—a thin wisp of a fellow in a Jackal hood—came over her shoulder with a cry. She shoved him forward, sent him crashing into a pair of Khovura who rushed her. They fell back in a tangling, snarling mass.

Run.

Instinct. Training. Loud and clear.

Can't.

They were everywhere. Closing in on her. Except for her back.

Wall. Get to a wall.

It was hard to think. Hard to hear that thought. Especially over the voice that screeched inside her on a sharp, painful whine.

Don't be an imbecile, woman! Amoch-Tethr snarled. *There are too many! Let me help you! Let me save you!* LET ME OUT!

She ignored him, focused on the feeling of cold stone on her back, on the shadows surrounding her. They advanced more carefully this time, not keen to repeat their companion's mistake. She could feel their eyes on her, searching for a weakness.

Her hand went to her belt and found a small dagger she kept hidden in it. She whirled it around, a poor answer for the long knives they carried. But it kept them back. It gave her a moment to think.

Listen to me, you foolish girl.

Her heart was thundering in her ears.

We both need to survive. We have so much to do.

Her body was screaming with pain.

Let me help you, for gods' sake!

And Amoch-Tethr was howling.

PLEASE!

Movement on her left. Someone rushed toward her. A blade flashed out. She twisted: right moment, wrong way. The blade caught her in a graze, tore through her sling, and cut through her sleeve, drawing a gout of red. Her left arm, hardly mended from when Gariath had shattered it, fell to her side, numb.

The broken bone inside her twisted.

Her scream tore through the night. Not loud enough.

Not *nearly* loud enough.

I feel it! Amoch-Tethr wailed. He smashed against his prison, sent lances of pain surging up through her arm. *I can feel everything! EVERY-THING! It's torture! It's murder! We'll both die here if you don't let me help you! Asper, listen to me!*

She shut him out.

LISTEN!

Or tried to.

The blade flashed at her again. Her own dagger shot up, but it was too small. It was knocked from her hand, went clattering away. The knife lashed at her again. Her good hand shot out and caught a wrist. The blade quivered a hairbreadth from her face. She snarled, twisted it away, yanked hard on the wrist.

The Khovura let out a grunt as he was hauled, full force, into her knee. She drove it up into his groin, lifting him off the ground. He fell to the stones, gasping for breath as she pulled the long knife from his hand and whirled around as another shadow fell upon her.

A thick sound of carved flesh. A spurt of warm life cooling on the stone. She caught a Jackal in the face with her mad slash, cut her through the hood, through the mouth, through the tongue. The Jackal fell back, hacking up blood, and staggered to her feet, clutching her face.

Three down, she told herself. She held the blade out, hilt slippery with blood. *Three down. Not so many. Not so tough. Stay calm.* She breathed in. *You can do this.* She breathed out. *You can—*

Cold thought.

Cold breath.

Cold metal.

She felt the knife plunge into her back. Just beside her spine, just beneath her left shoulder blade. Her breath left her. Sharp. Sudden. Almost like someone had just slapped her real hard on the back.

She tried to reach for it. She felt a wedge of steel moving against the folds of sinew. She tried to draw in a breath. She felt liquid fill the back of her throat. She tried to walk. She felt herself fall.

And when she collapsed to her knees, she didn't feel anything.

I'm going to die.

"Fuck." A Jackal's voice, distant. "How'd she manage to do that much damage? If it gets out it took us this long to kill a cripple, we're fucking done."

I'm going to die.

"The false prophet's death will resound throughout heaven." A Khovura's hiss, soft and fading. "We must make certain."

"Oh, fuck me, she's still alive? Gods, lady, make it easy on yourself, huh?"

"Deshaa anaca Kapira. We must be certain. We must finish it."

Fingers in her hair, pulling her head back. Darkness rimmed her sight.

I'm going to die.

"Why? Let her bleed out. Who gives a shit?"

"Blasphemy is answered with blood. False faith is answered with death."

A knife at her throat. Cold, maybe. Sharp, maybe. She couldn't tell.

I'm going to die.

"Oooh, so dramatic. Fine. Whatever. Just don't get any on me."

"Kapira, Kapira, Kapira…"

Asper's mouth hung open, breathless, voiceless. She reached up. Someone grabbed her arm and pinned it behind her. Her broken arm fumbled numbly for the blade. Darkness consumed her vision, left her in a lightless pit.

She had seen too much of the world. Too much to believe the priests. She had seen too many bodies, too much blood to believe that gods were kind and heard every prayer. Perhaps she had always known, in the darkest parts of her heart, that no one was listening when she tried to speak to heaven.

Maybe it was just habit, or yet another instinct, that made her whisper one more into the darkness.

"Help me..."

Maybe it was just cruel fate that, this time, someone was listening.

Gladly.

Amoch-Tethr's voice came with a bright, giddy cackle. The darkness fled her eyes in a flash of ugly red light. Angry warmth erupted inside her broken arm. Pain shot through numb fingers as they suddenly curled, of their own volition, around a man's wrist.

A hiss.

A scream.

A knife, falling.

Someone released her other arm, fell away from her, screaming. Someone released her hair, tried to pull away. Someone was pounding at her left hand with a fist, trying to get her to let go. But it wouldn't.

It wasn't hers. Not anymore.

The flesh of her hand glowed with a crimson light that slithered down her wrist into her arm. It split the cloth of her robe. It painted her skin translucent. Within its hellish red glow, she could see the shattered bone of her arm, black and fragile. But she couldn't feel any pain from it. Not as skeletal fingers wrapped tighter around the Khovura's wrist.

Not as black smoke seeped out between the knuckles.

It happened quickly. Skin withered, turned gray, turned to ash. Bones bent, snapped, shrank. Blood boiled, turned to steam. Screams were eaten, turned to choking gasps. Eyes turned skyward and found no kind god to hear the last, desperate words he shouted to heaven before the black smoke came pouring from his mouth.

He was dying. Slowly, painfully, he was dying. She could feel what was left of him turning to ash beneath her fingers. She could hear him screaming. She could feel his agony echo through her bones.

She remembered the screaming. She remembered the pain. But she didn't remember the power.

It coursed through her. As surely as he died, she lived. She found new breath in his screams. She found the chill chased away by a bright, painful heat. She could see her black bones knitting together before her eyes, repairing themselves.

And she could hear him.

Ah. Delicious. Amoch-Tethr purred. *How long has it been since I was allowed more than a fleeting taste?*

Her fingers tightened of their own volition. He let out one last scream as the last of his bones snapped and the last of his skin was swallowed. It lasted a long time. Long after he died. Long after he was nothing more than a handful of dust slipping between her fingers.

She found her feet. She stared down at her arm. It pulsed, alive and hungry. Within it, she could feel Amoch-Tethr writhing in ecstasy.

Did I not tell you, girl? Did I not say I would save you?

"Holy shit!"

She looked up. Jackals and Khovura were backing away, dropping blades, the murder in their eyes replaced by terror.

"What the fuck did she just do? *What the fuck was that?*"

"*Deshaa maa anucca!* Demon! She is a demon!"

"Kill her! *FUCKIN' KILL HER!*"

A Jackal, rushing toward her. Fear tore itself from his throat in a scream. He raised his blade high.

And Amoch-Tethr caught him by the throat and clamped down hard.

Quicker this time. An orgy of sound: a feast of cracking bones and snapping skin and smoke hissing out of what was once a body and was now a sack of meat. For three more breaths, full of screams, he was still a man. After that, he was a mess of broken bones, of unnatural angles, of shriveling skin drawing up over his gums and eyes and peeling off glistening muscle.

And then, he, too, was nothing but dust.

The feeling was incredible. Her breath came back to her, dry and deep. The pain throbbing in her chest faded, replaced by something bright and angry. She felt a spasm of muscle in her back as something was forced out. Steel clattered behind her as the knife fell on the street.

Her skin felt raw, tingling with newborn feeling. Her breath was heavy and ragged and so very alive. Her eyes felt too open. Her body felt too warm.

"Talanas," she whispered, breathless.

Amoch-Tethr chuckled. *Let's leave him out of this, shall we?*

A flash of movement.

It was her. Without knowing it, without feeling it, she was moving.

Her arm was alive, stronger than she was, pulling her forward, pulling her toward them.

She could make them out only by their screams: their threats and their curses and their desperate cries to gods forsaken long ago. They tried to run. She tried to pull back. They tried to beg for mercy. She tried to beg forgiveness.

It didn't matter. None of it mattered.

They couldn't run fast enough. She couldn't stop it from happening, no matter how hard she fought or begged or prayed. The light from her arm was blinding. She couldn't even see their faces when it found a new victim. She couldn't even hear their screams when it fed.

Bones snapped. Skin split. Something deep inside her ate messily and hungrily. Smoke filled her nostrils. Dust filled her hand.

And each time, she felt stronger.

Yes!

Again.

YES!

And again.

"Stop!"

No matter how much she begged.

"STOP IT!"

No matter how fiercely she pounded on her own arm.

It didn't end. Not until the screams had faded. Not until the dust blew away in the wind.

When it was over—if it was over—she stood, breathing heavily, at the center of a ring of dust.

Her body was aflame with pain. Not the sick, rotting pain she had carried since her fight with Gariath. Her skin bristled against the sting of cold wind. Her bones hummed inside her. Her muscles twitched and danced and spasmed of their own accord beneath her flesh.

The pain of the wailing newborn. The pain of the first heartbreak. The pain of living.

Amoch-Tethr had saved her. Just as he'd said he would. Just as only he could.

"Gods..." She wept, her tears painful as they slid down her cheeks. She fell to her knees. She clutched her glowing arm. "Gods forgive me."

"No."

It was his voice. Amoch-Tethr's voice. No longer so distant. No longer in her head.

"Gods didn't save you." He spoke from somewhere horrifically close. "Gods could never save you."

"Tell me . . ." she found the breath to gasp, "tell me what you are."

The light in her flesh went dark. The red glow faded. Nothing remained but skin.

And his voice.

"They don't have a word for what I am. They couldn't think of one when they sealed me away. First in wood, then in stone, finally in flesh."

Her arm trembled. In her palm, something alive and painful wriggled.

"Things of the earth, I could eat," he said. "Wood rots. Stone crumbles. You'd think mortals would be easier, but they are . . . difficult. So much inside you, yet so little of it nourishing. From vessel to vessel, I was passed, fed nothing but hymns and prayers and cries in the night. Until you."

Pain lanced through her arm. Beneath her skin, something writhed, something grew. She screamed out, doubled over in agony.

"But listen to me go on," he laughed, airy and gay. "It'd be ironic if we went through all that just for me to bore us both to death with this prattle. Or would it be poetic? Ah, no matter. To the point, then . . ."

The flesh of her palm twitched. A scream tore itself from her throat. The skin of her hand tore itself apart in a jagged wound. And the frayed edges of her flesh curled upward into a grotesque smile, baring crooked white teeth.

"I'm afraid," the mouth rasped, pouring black smoke, "our time together is at an end."

It wasn't agony she felt. There wasn't a poet, a priest, or a madman who had a word for what she felt.

For the bright red light that burst inside her. For the scream from no mortal source that came out of her. For the horror that followed as she closed her eyes and prayed to gods who weren't there.

Her skin shredded, snapped, and popped. Smoke poured out of her every orifice, choking her and rising in great columns. There was the slurping sound of something heavy and dense hauling itself out of the muck of creation. They joined her symphony of pain, her screams and her prayers and her desperate, terrified sobs.

But it wouldn't end. No matter how raw her throat got, how bright the pain grew, how much she prayed for it, it wouldn't end. The pain wouldn't relent. Her body wouldn't die.

Out of swimming vision, she saw it on the wall: her shadow black by the moon's cold light. Her body was hunched over into a lump of darkness, rocking back and forth. Her skin twitched, bubbled, burst.

An arm not her own reached out of her back. She saw another one join it. From her back, a shadowy shape blossomed.

She had just recognized it as a head when she, mercifully, fell into darkness.

An hour.

A night.

A few breaths.

She didn't know how long she had lain there, unmoving, before she felt warm hands on her cheek and a gentle purring in her ear.

"Apologies. I didn't expect it to take that long."

Her eyelids fluttered open. She wasn't sure how that was possible. She wasn't sure how she was still alive.

She looked down at herself, expecting to find a bloody ruin where a body should be. But aside from tattered clothing and a few red stains, she was whole.

Pain lingered in her, but only in echoes. Slowly, it faded. Slowly, her vision righted itself, and she found herself staring at a woman's feet.

She looked up, past lean legs and narrow waist, past gaunt belly and small breasts, past thin neck and pointed chin to a broad, haughty smile. She didn't recognize the woman standing before her—this skinny creature, steam pealing off glistening skin, a mop of brown hair damp with some unnamed ichor, hazel eyes gleaming maliciously.

But the smile...

She knew Amoch-Tethr's smile.

"You..." She found the breath to whisper. "You're a woman?"

"Am I?" Amoch-Tethr looked himself—*her*self—over. "Ah. Well, I suppose that's to be expected. One does not get as close as we were without rubbing off on each other, hmm?"

"But...I thought you were..."

"Maybe I was, long ago." Amoch-Tethr smiled broadly. "Truth be told, I hardly remember. Everything about that world feels like a pleasant dream." She stretched. Her mouth gaped open just a little too wide to look natural as she yawned. The skin of her body clung to her ribs. "But there was one thing I cannot forget..."

She knelt down beside Asper. Her smile opened unnaturally wide, cleanly bisecting her face. Her eyes turned bright red. The hellish glow engulfed her face, painted her skull black. She spoke with a voice from a dank pit, choked on smoke.

"I cannot forget your pain."

Asper had no strength to struggle. No strength to even scream. Amoch-Tethr seized her by the collar and dragged her close.

"Every prayer, every weeping prayer, I heard. Every doubt, every fear, I felt. You are in such pain, my dear."

She opened her mouth wide, drew Asper close. Inside her gaping maw, Asper saw an eternity of light.

"Permit me to end it for you."

No struggle. No scream. Nothing left for that. Asper simply closed her eyes. And waited.

"Renouncer."

It was not Amoch-Tethr that spoke. Nor Asper. The voice that spoke was so soft that it could barely be heard over the sound of Amoch-Tethr's imminent feast.

And yet that word, whatever it was, was important.

Amoch-Tethr's mouth closed. The light faded from her face, then her eyes. She dropped Asper, unceremoniously, and rose to face the newcomer who had appeared behind her.

A man. Perhaps. It was hard to tell beneath the black rags swaddling his tall frame. They hung from him in tatters, a black cloth wrapped around his head, not a trace of anything remotely resembling a face visible beneath it. Yet as he stood, slightly stooped, there was no doubt he was staring at Amoch-Tethr.

Then again, that might have been because she was stalking toward him angrily.

"I will tolerate any number of profanities," she snarled. "But to speak *that* word to me during my first meal is to invite death." She raised a hand. "May yours be instructional, if messy."

The man made no effort to defend himself. He simply raised a hand.

His fingers held no weapon beyond a rolled-up scroll, neatly sealed with wax, which he proffered to Amoch-Tethr.

And somehow, this was enough to cause her to draw up short and look at it curiously.

"You have a debt to pay," he said.

Amoch-Tethr glared at him before snatching the scroll. She unfurled it hastily, read through it quickly. Asper couldn't make out what it said from where she lay, but it looked like no language she had ever seen. Whatever it said, though, made Amoch-Tethr's anger fade with a smoky sight.

"Qulon…" She rubbed her eyes. "I could ever count on that woman to ruin the mood." She looked over her shoulder, frowning at Asper with a sort of tender lament. "Still…a debt is a debt." She shot her a wink. "Apologies I wasn't able to make it all better, dearest. Try not to miss me too much, hm?"

With a rather obscene spring in her step, naked and glistening as a newborn, the woman, the creature, the curse that Asper had carried inside her for so long went gaily skipping down the street and simply disappeared.

Just like that.

Asper could only stare. Somehow, it didn't feel real. Thinking back on it, it *couldn't* be real. She had felt her skin tear apart. She had seen the shadows. She had seen something…that *thing* crawl out of her own skin.

And yet her flesh was whole. Her wounds were still gone. She could still feel the energy surging through her, the power that had come with devouring those thugs.

She could remember their faces, their screams.

"Prophet."

She looked up. A hand was extended to her, wrapped in black rags. No face looked down at her, yet she knew his eyes were on hers.

Reluctantly, she reached out and took his hand. It felt real enough as he helped her to her feet, as he brushed the dirt from her robes, as he plucked a stray piece of lint from her shoulder.

"You'll be late for your meeting." The man's voice was hollow and distant. "It will work in your favor, though. I expect your entrance will be suitably dramatic. I advise against telling them about this part, though."

"I...don't know what I'd tell them," she said. "I don't know what happened."

"A lot," he replied. "You'll find the words for it, in time. But not now." He gave her a gentle pat on the shoulder. "You have a war to win."

And then, he was gone.

As though he had never even been there.

NINETEEN

THE LAST CHIEFTAIN

*D*oes it ever stop?"

Kataria had asked this, once. Back in the Silesrian forest, where she had lain beneath the bough of an ancient willow that bent low beneath the weight of her rain-slick crown. She had lain there, on a bed of red-stained moss, biting back tears in her eyes as she tied an herb-soaked bandage around her leg.

And someone looked down at her, frowning at the cut in her leg that had been meant for her heart. And someone had said...

"For humans, yes. They go back to their homes and light fires to hide from the night. For tulwar, yes. They go back to their families and huddle together against the cold. But we...we were given the bow and the Howling, nothing else. We were given so little. We have to take the rest. For us, the fight never stops."

She had looked to the corpses of the people lying nearby, her arrows in their throats. The first humans she had ever killed.

"I wish it would."

These were the last words Kataria had ever spoken to her mother.

A few days later, she was dead.

No body to burn. No last words of her own to impart to her child. She simply vanished and the tribe knew she was gone. It was not uncommon; the Silesrian was large and treacherous. The tribe could not wait for her to find peace.

The storms had lasted all month. It had been raining again when someone else had come to find her. And someone had extended her a white feather, for mourning, and told her to weave it into her hair. And someone had said...

"We won't forget her. Or them. The ones who did this to her, we will find them, we will kill them. We will show them that this is our land, that they cannot come here with their fire and axes and stones. We will show them that the shicts take what they need and they will know fear."

She had woven the feather into her hair. She had let it hang there, a weight pulling her head down. The feather she would never take off.

"I don't care about them. I just want her back."

These were the last words Kataria had ever spoken to her father.

Many years later, he was still alive.

And she was gone. She had left the Silesrian not many years after she had spoken those words to him. She was not so stupid as to think that any life, let alone hers, could be free of violence, of bloodshed, of death. But she had wanted something else. Maybe something more. Or perhaps just something different.

And someone had given her the opportunity to do that. And someone had come into the forest. And to someone, she had said...

"Holy shit, how is it you've lived this long, dumb as you are?"

Those weren't the first words she had said to Lenk. Nor even the first time she had said those specific words to him.

And now, not knowing if he was alive or dead, she found she missed him.

If only because it hadn't always been about fighting with him. If only because, once in a while, it did stop.

For a little while, anyway.

She drew in a breath. Against her back, she felt cold rock. Across her skin, a bitter wind slithered. Her head throbbed. Her body ached terribly. Before her, darkness stretched endlessly.

But only for another moment.

She felt fingers across her face. Her head jerked forward as the blindfold was torn from her. She blinked, eyes adjusting to the orange glow of a nearby bonfire. And though the light was dim, it was more than enough for her to see the cold eyes staring down at her from behind a face gaping wide in a scream.

Whoever the poor fucker had been—a father, a merchant, just an unlucky fool who wandered too far into the desert—he was just a decoration now. A dessicated, flayed face nailed into the grinning leer of

Shekune's wooden mask. His open-mouth scream constrated starkly with the toothy smile of the khoshict's mask.

And both were betrayed by the long, cold emptiness of her stare.

Kataria met those eyes, dark and appraising, with her own. For a long moment, the two of them stared at each other in silence.

And then Kataria lunged.

Her teeth bared in a snarl, she leapt forward, as though to seize Shekune by the jugular and start shaking until something red and wet came out. But she hadn't even taken a step before her arms were snapped back, thick ropes biting into her wrists and hauling her back against the rock. Only when her wrists were red and her breath was gone did she fall back, settling into a seething, green-eyed scowl.

And Shekune merely stared back.

"Waiting for me to beg?" Kataria growled between labored breathing.

Shekune said nothing. Kataria drew herself up and snarled again, as fiercely as someone lashed to a rock could.

"Well?" she demanded. "What are you waiting for? Kill me." At Shekune's continued silence, she lunged forward again. *"I SAID KILL—"*

Shekune's hand shot out and clamped around Kataria's throat, crushing her voice beneath her fingers. Kataria froze, all fury drained as she suddenly fought to find breath again.

It came back to her, slowly, as Shekune's fingers slowly eased off from her throat. From behind her mask, her eyes drifted lower, toward Kataria's waist. Her hand followed, sliding from her throat and across her belly before lingering on her belt.

Swifter than her breath, anger returned to Kataria. But before she could make find a voice to go with it, Shekune's fingers flitted. She seized something from Kataria's belt, pulled it away, and held it before her.

The map—the simple hide scroll that she had taken from the tulwar—unfurled before Shekune's face. The khoshict looked it over for a few moments, eyes widening just ever so slightly.

"The tulwar have been tracking us," she murmured. "I didn't think those monkeys were capable of it." She closed her eyes. "They could have ruined everything. I should have paid attention, I should have . . ."

She let that thought trail off and die. Her eyes turned toward Kataria once more. She rolled the map up and held it up before her prisoner.

"This will save many shict lives," she said, "hunters that can feed families, mothers that can raise young, even yijis that can provide for us." She shook her head. "And I wonder, had I never found it, would we ever know? Would you have let them all die?"

She reached up behind her head and tugged at a leather knot. Her riotous braids, all of them laced with black feathers, tumbled around her shoulders. Her mask, with its grin and its scream, fell to the ground and lay in the sand. And when she looked at Kataria again, her long face was full of concern and her eyes were no longer empty.

"Do you hate us that much?"

No hand, no rope, no blade could have rendered Kataria so utterly silent. The question caught her square in the belly, knocked what little wind she had found from her and sent her back against the rock. She stared, openmouthed, at Shekune before shaking her head.

"I don't hate you," she said. "Not the shicts. I'm trying to save them. From *you*."

"Me?" The wrinkles at the corners of her mouth curled as Shekune smiled sadly. "What would you save them from by killing me? Would you send them into the desert, leaderless, to be picked apart by the tulwar clans?"

"No, I—"

"Would you kill me and rob them of any chance of fighting off the humans who encroach into our land?"

"Not that, but—"

"Would you kill me and let one more family starve, one more child be orphaned, one more—"

"*Enough*," Kataria snarled, scowling at her. "If you wanted to convince me of your goodness, you shouldn't have come to me wearing someone else's severed face." She kicked Shekune's mask away. "You know fucking well what your war is going to do. You're going to make the humans retaliate against us a hundredfold. No land will be big enough. No family will be strong enough. No shict will be safe."

She held herself, tense and trembling, as she spit on the ground at Shekune's feet.

"Deny it," she snarled. "Tell me I'm wrong. Give me another one of your bullshit speeches and tell me that you see this ending any other way than thousands of dead shicts."

The smile lingered for a moment longer before it melted off Shekune's face with a sigh. She shook her head.

"You're not wrong."

The curse that Kataria had been brewing died on her lips. She stared at Shekune blankly.

"I know we'll die," the khoshict said. "By the hundreds, by the thousands, maybe. Maybe down to the last shict, we'll die. I can't see an end to this war that doesn't see so many of us dead."

"But...then why..."

"How old were you when you lost your mother?"

Kataria recoiled, as if struck. A hundred different emotions—sorrow, terror, pain—battled to show on her face. Anger won out, as it so often did with her, and she bared her teeth once again.

"Kwar," she growled. "She told you."

"No." Shekune shook her head. "That girl wouldn't speak a single word to me about you."

Kataria stiffened against the rock. "Then how did you know?"

Shekune reached up, tapped her ears. "Your Howling." She turned toward the desert and gestured over the endless sand. "For miles, I can hear every shict. And theirs speaks so clearly to me, tells me everything I need to know. But yours..." She looked at Kataria. "You barely know how to use it. It's always screaming, whining, whimpering. The others can't make sense of it. They shut their ears to it." She smiled. "But it speaks to me."

Over many years, Kataria had been shot at, cut at, poisoned, hunted down, tied up, on her back with blades at her throat, holding back the jaws of vicious beasts with only her boots, nearly burned alive, and wounded.

And only twice before could she ever recall feeling as vulnerable and helpless as she did at that moment.

"I listen to it," Shekune continued. "I hear it. And after a time, it starts to make sense." Her ears twitched, curled at the tips. "It screams out things. Things you don't want to speak, but are desperate to say. You lost your mother." She canted her head to the side. "You lay with a human." She stared at her intently. "You feel alone, betrayed...but you don't hate me, do you? Because you think I've lost someone, too."

"Didn't you?" Kataria asked. "When I think of my mother, when I think of the people who killed her, who failed to save her...only then could I understand."

"My father and mother are still alive. They live on the edge of the desert. My sister takes care of them. My brother hunts for them. They are all very happy."

Kataria shook her head in disbelief. "Then how? How can you want this war?"

"Because I can hear them," Shekune said. "As clearly as I can hear you. All my life, I've been hearing them. Whatever it is about the Howling, it all makes sense to me. I can hear their fears as the humans move in on their lands. I can hear their cries as they remember the ones they've lost. I can hear every terror in the night, every dead hope, every roar of anger, and I can't *stop* hearing them."

She stalked to the nearby fire. Thrust into the earth, her spear stood tall and unyielding. It all but leapt into her hand, its saw-toothed grin gleaming against the firelight as she pulled it free of the earth.

"It's killing them," she said. "The uncertainty, the fear, the *humans*...if we don't fight, if we don't do *something*, we'll all be dead anyway. I can't hear any more pain, any more terror..." She looked over her shoulder at Kataria. "I won't let any more mothers die."

She hefted the spear over her shoulder and walked back toward Kataria. With one swing, she took the weapon in both hands and leveled its grinning head at Kataria's chest. Kataria felt her heart beat a little less quickly, as though afraid doing so would catch the spear's notice, as she stared at her own terror reflected in its metal smile.

"Your turn."

Kataria looked up. Gone was the softness, the sad smile, the gentle curl of her wrinkles. Shekune's face was a hatchet's, all hard lines and hard sneers, dark eyes set in a bleak scowl.

"Look me in the eyes," the khoshict said, "and tell me I'm wrong."

Kataria met the woman's gaze for a long, quiet moment. She could hear the wind howling, the fire crackling, the sound of the ropes creaking as they held her in place. But of the Howling, she could hear nothing.

For so long, she had trouble with it; where other shicts could communicate so effortlessly, she struggled to hear anything through her people's wordless language. She had always considered it a curse, a distance between her and her tribe. Never once had she considered what she might have been spared from, all the pain and fear that the shicts couldn't help but share.

The pain and fear that Shekune couldn't help but hear.

Kataria's mind drifted back to that day, so long ago, when she had woven a white feather into her hair. She could still feel it so keenly: the ache in her chest, the shallow breath, the great cold emptiness beside her where a warm, comforting body should have been.

How many agonies like that had Shekune heard? How many times had she felt that same pain? If Kataria had such a sensitivity, were she capable of even hearing the barest hint of that sorrow…

Would she side with Shekune, like everyone else?

She looked down at the spear leveled at her. There was no terror in the reflection staring back at her. Nothing but a sadness she thought she had put away long ago.

And she sighed deeply. And she looked up at Shekune. And she spoke. "You're wrong."

Shekune offered nothing more than the barest twitch of her mouth, the slightest narrowing of her eyes.

"What?" the khoshict snarled.

"I lost my mother," Kataria replied, firmly. "But I've lost many people. There's always going to be pain for the shicts. For us, the fighting never stops. That's what we do. And the only way it does stop…" She met Shekune's eyes. "Is when we're all dead from your war."

And Shekune's face twitched just a little more. And all the fury behind it seemed to come oozing out between her teeth as she bared overlarge canines in a snarl. The faintest hint of a growl began to boil up in her throat as the spear trembled in her hands, begging for her to sink it into warm flesh.

Kataria held her breath. She tightened her hands into fists. She fought to keep from looking at the grinning spear, fought to keep her eyes on Shekune's.

You kill me, Kataria thought, *you damn well look me in the eyes when you do.*

And as if she could hear even that thought, Shekune shut her eyes suddenly. She swallowed her anger with a long, hot breath. She lowered the spear until it dipped into the sand.

Shekune looked long to the hills. Her ears rose high, the tips trembling. In the back of Kataria's mind, in the quiet parts of her Howling, she could hear a single wordless sound slip from Shekune out into the night.

And Kataria's eyes widened when she recognized it as a command.

A command that was answered but a few moments later by the sound of sand scraping and a snarling voice.

"Let me go! *I said let me go!*" Kwar's roar preceded her appearance over the dune by several feet. And when she came, hands bound behind her back and dragged forward by two khoshicts, she did so kicking, snarling, and biting. "Come closer, you shithead. I can *smell* you pissing yourself and—"

Kwar's attentions were suddenly seized by the scene before her. In an instant, she took it in: Kataria bound to the rock, Shekune's cold stare fixed upon her, the spear dangling from her hand. And in another, she acted.

With a roar, she lunged forward—whether to try to save Kataria or merely to chew Shekune's face off, it was unclear. Nor did it matter, for the two khoshicts seizing her by her bound arms and dragging her to the ground. They forced her to her knees ungently, holding her in place by her hair.

Yet no matter how hard they pulled or pushed, they couldn't keep her from twisting her head up and fixing her dark eyes, alive with anger, on Shekune.

"I've heard every legend about you," Kwar growled. "I know every story about how great you are, and everyone has a different tale about you. But if you touch her, I swear the only story anyone will tell about you is the one where I force-fed you your own intestines."

If the threat shook Shekune, she did not show it. Rather, she turned to Kataria, contempt branded across her face.

"Do you see?" She raised her spear and leveled it at Kataria. "*You* did this to her."

"Drop that spear!" Kwar snarled. "Don't you dare hurt her!"

"I didn't do anything," Kataria echoed her anger. "It's *you* who will kill everyone! She knows that!"

"Do you not know why we call humans a disease?" Shekune shook her head. "This is how it happens. You sympathize with them. You start

thinking they wouldn't kill you if they had the chance. And then..."
She scowled back at Kwar. "It spreads. Do you see what happens..."

She narrowed her mouth, spit her next words out, and let them lie hot and ugly on the sand.

"When you *lie* with a human?"

Kwar's eyes went wide. Her mouth dropped out. And though she valiantly tried to keep it back in, the anger slowly leaked out of her face and left bare only the look of a wounded, frightened beast.

"Or had she not told you that?" Shekune asked. "Did you think she was one of us? Did you think she was worth killing me over? Worth killing *hundreds* of shicts over?"

The fight left Kwar. Her head sank low. "I knew," she said softly.

"And do you still think she's worth it?"

Kwar looked up. There was no defiance on her face, no fury, no coyness, nothing Kataria had grown accustomed to seeing on the khoshict's face. What was there, glistening in her eyes, was something weak and plaintive.

"She is," Kwar said. "I would die for her. I *will* die for her. It was me who planned the attack." She looked at Kataria. "Let her go."

"Kwar..." Kataria whispered, breathless. "Don't..."

"Look at what you have done to her." Shekune turned on Kataria. "She lost everything, too, you know. Her mother, her brother..."

"I know," Kataria replied. "I was there to see it. I was there to see the humans do it because *you—*"

"And now she begs for death to spare you," Shekune interrupted with a hiss. "You, who'd see more of her family dead for the sake of a few humans. You, who'd condemn us all to die by breaths rather than make a stand." She shook her head. "I can't let you do this. Not to one more shict."

The spear came free with a metallic ring. Its sawteeth seemed to curl upward in an ecstatic grin as Shekune took it in both hands and leveled it at Kataria's chest.

"Look away if you will, daughter of Sai-Thuwan," Shekune said. "But know that I do this for you."

"No!" Kwar screamed out, fighting against her captors once more. "Shekune, don't! *Please!*"

"There's no other way," Shekune said. "The humans put this sickness in her. I cannot let it spread."

"Look away, Kwar." Kataria gathered herself up against the rock and stared down Shekune. "Don't listen to her."

Kwar was not listening. But not to the right person.

"Shekune, please!" she screamed. Tears fell down her cheeks. Her voice cracked. "Listen to me! Spare her! I beg you! Let her go!"

"There is nothing to be gained from her living, child," Shekune replied, her voice eerily cold. She raised her spear high, eyes locked on Kataria's chest. "This is for your own good. I promise."

"*LET HER GO!*" Kwar screamed again, pulling so hard against her captors that it looked as though she might break her arms. "Shekune, release her and I'll…I'll swear service to you! I'll vow to help you! I'll do whatever you want! Shekune! *SHEKUNE!*"

Shekune's ears folded over themselves, unhearing. Her eyes narrowed on Kataria's, seeing nothing else but the grim deed that needed to be done.

Kataria met her scowl with one of her own. She drew in a breath, held it so that she would have nothing left to scream with, to beg with, to give Shekune the satisfaction. She gritted her teeth and sent a thought out into the wind.

Kwar. Lenk. I'm sorry.

She stared as Shekune drew back her spear. She stared as Shekune tightened her grip and thrust. She stared as a coy smile tugged at the corners of Shekune's mouth.

Wait. What?

"I'LL SHOW YOU THE WAY INTO THE CITY!"

The spear came to a halt. The tip of it grazed the flesh of Kataria's sternum, forced her to hold her breath. And yet, for all that, all eyes were on Kwar. She stared up, dark eyes desperate, breathing heavily.

"I'll show you the way into the city," Kwar said. "Let her go. Spare her." She swallowed hard. "And I'll show you."

"We know the way already," Shekune said. "Your father told us."

"He knows the old hunting trails into the Green Belt," Kwar said. "But he's never been outside Shicttown. He doesn't know the way into city and its districts."

"We can find them."

"Not into Silktown you can't," Kwar said. "The fashas control the city. You could kill every human but them and they'd still have enough money to bring more people, more humans, more armies. And the moment they hear you coming, they'll call out every last guard they have. *Dragonmen*. You know what happened to the tulwar."

Shekune scowled, but the memory played clear enough on her face.

"I know the ways into Silktown," Kwar said. "I've been there before. I'll show you." She looked to Kataria. "But you have to let her go."

"Kwar, *don't*!" Kataria shouted. "She wants you to do this! She wants—"

She was silenced as Shekune lunged forward, clapping a hand over her mouth. She let out muffled protests, but Shekune's attentions were back on Kwar.

"I can't do that," Shekune said. "She's tried to kill me once already. She's poisoned you against me. If I let her live..."

"Then exile her," Kwar said. "Banish her. Tell every shict not to speak with her. But let her live." She took in a ragged breath. "Swear you'll let her live and I'll show you how to kill the fashas."

Consideration battled scorn on Shekune's face as she looked back to Kataria. "And how do I know she won't try anything else?"

"She won't. I promise you that." Kwar slumped forward. "Please, Shekune." She bowed low, pressed her head to the earth, and let out a soft sob. "Let her go."

There were legends about Shekune. A few of them Kataria had even heard. She had killed five tulwar with one spear strike. She had raced for five days and nights to outrun a mounted human hunting party. She had killed all manner of beasts, birds, and monsters so that the wilds themselves bowed before her. There were countless stories about her courage, her skill, her cunning.

But none of them, not one, ever spoke of how cruel she could be.

And when she turned to her prisoner and flashed her just the briefest glimpse of a broad, self-satisfied smile, Kataria knew why.

"Shekune swears," she said simply.

Her ears twitched, her Howling sending out another command. The two khoshicts responded, pulling knives free. They cut Kwar's bonds loose, backed away from her. But she did not rise. She knelt there, in the sand, her head bowed low and defeated.

"She is more than you deserve." Shekune dropped her spear to the earth. She drew a knife from her belt and cut the ropes from Kataria's wrists. "Her brother, too. They are a good family." She pulled Kataria away from the rock and shoved her forward. "Take comfort that you will bring them no more pain."

Kataria didn't listen to her. She rushed to Kwar, collapsed onto the sand, and grabbed the khoshict by her shoulders.

"Kwar," she whispered, desperate and heated. "Kwar, you can't do this. You can't let her win like this."

"I can," Kwar said, "I have to. She was going to kill you. She was going to—"

"She's going to kill us all." Kataria took Kwar gently by the face and tilted her gaze up. "Look at me, Kwar. *Look at me.*" She saw the khoshict's eyes brimming with the same tears in her own. "Don't let her do this. Not for me."

"Only for you." Kwar's voice was almost serene, despite the tears in her eyes. She smiled softly as she took Kataria's hand. "I have done so much to hurt you. I'm sorry that I have to do it again."

"But she's going to kill so many."

"I know," Kwar said. "I don't care if they die. I don't care if I die. But you..." She pressed her brow against Kataria's and slid a hand around the back of her head. "You have to live, Kataria. Anything else that happens, whoever dies, I don't care. Just promise me you'll live."

Kataria tried to find words: pleas to make, plans to voice, curses to spew. But all that came out of her mouth was a wet shuddering sound. She had nothing but a loose quiver of her lips and a long, mournful sound inside her head.

"Promise me," Kwar said. She shut her eyes as tears fell, squeezed Kataria's hand in her own. "Promise me you'll live."

"I promise."

Weak words. Breathless and soft and frail. They were a brittle blade twisting inside her chest. They hurt to speak, hurt to hear coming from her mouth. But she said them. And she meant them.

Kwar's tears came too rarely for her to waste them.

Kwar forced a smile onto her face. She nodded weakly. She leaned forward and gently kissed Kataria on her brow. Her ears trembled. And inside her head, Kataria could hear a single sound in a wordless language made just for her for just as long as that kiss lasted.

And then it was gone.

A rough hand was on her neck. Shekune tore her away, hauled her from Kwar, and dashed her against the sand. The khoshicts hurried over, tossing at her feet her bow, her quiver, and a single waterskin. Shekune folded her arms, towering over her.

"You are not one of us," she said, "if you ever were. You are not welcome among us anymore. You have no family, you have no tribe, you have no people. You are not a shict, Kataria." She thrust her spear out into the darkness. "Go back to the humans. Or go out and die. It is not our concern anymore."

Kataria wanted to leap up and strangle her, but her body wouldn't will itself to rise. She wanted to snarl and spit and cry and hurl herself on the spear, but she could not find the strength to do so. Failing all of that, any of that, she simply wanted to scream.

But she couldn't.

She couldn't do anything but look past Shekune, past the other khoshicts, to Kwar, kneeling upon the sand with eyes wide and mouth open and ears up and trembling and her Howling wailing in her ears.

You promised.

Somehow, Kataria found her feet.

Somehow, she found her bow.

Somehow, she turned and ran. Into the desert. Into the night. With not a sound but the long, mournful wail of Kwar's Howling in her ears. And the lonely, tired sigh of the wind.

TWENTY

THE KING IN RED

Past the high dunes that formed a barrier around the Green Belt, he could barely see the outline of houses and walls and spires that rose at the edge of the ocean. At night, it was just a collection of shadows huddled in the dark, their lights too dim and too distant to see.

A tiny little city was all it was. A tiny little city full of tiny, stupid people. Cier'Djaal was nothing more than that.

The last time, he told himself. *The next time I look at it, it'll be a pile of ash and rubble.*

And it started tonight.

He glanced back at the gates to Jalaang. Atop the battlements, a trio of tulwar archers glanced back down. He gave them a commanding nod. One of them looked over the other side of the wall and made a gesture.

The great double gates let out a pained, rust-covered moan as they were pushed open. Damage done during the city's seizure had been hastily repaired, and even the best Tho Thu Bhu craftsmen couldn't have done much better than holding the broken gates together with chains.

From the darkness beyond the gates, there was the hush of rattling iron and the tremble of earth. An immense shadow appeared, trudging forward slowly, its huge silhouette painted by the torches burning within. But though the shape was dim from this far away, Gariath could make out the scent well enough.

The bitter reek of resentment was just as keen as ever. But the ashen stink of rage had subsided, burnt itself out, and been doused by a sour odor of fear, which in turn had slowly become a stale smell of exhaustion.

By the time he emerged out into the light of the moon and stars, Kharga did not look much better than he smelled.

Though he was still immense, the colossal dragonman no longer stood quite so tall, nor quite so proud. Chains wrapped his body and secured his arms. His tremendous stride was hobbled by the shackles around his ankles, yet even so, he shook the earth with each step. His head was not quite bowed enough to conceal the glare of his black eyes as he lurched forward.

Beaten though he might have been, his captors didn't seem to believe it. Five nervous-looking tulwar led him by his chains, and they seemed ill-equipped for the task should Kharga decide to make it difficult. Even the ten tulwar surrounding him, following along in a semicircle, pointing thick spears at him, seemed like they would be inadequate if the hulking dragonman put up a fight.

But as he lumbered forward, Kharga made no effort to resist. A few weeks in darkness would dim any fire, no matter how big it might be. And Kharga had been given not nearly enough food, water, or rest to give him the strength to fight back.

"He came willingly enough."

At the head of the tulwar, Daaru came forward. Slung over his shoulder, he carried an immense ax. Despite the security of such a massive weapon, he wore a mask of concern.

"I don't like it, though. He could be plotting something."

"He could," Gariath replied, staring over the defeated dragonman.

"And you still want to do this?" Daaru asked.

Gariath looked at the ax for a long moment. "I do."

Daaru glanced back at Kharga. "It's not a good idea."

"It isn't."

Concern gave way to resignation as Daaru realized this particular line of dialogue wouldn't go further than two words. With a grunt, he hefted the ax off his shoulder and into his hands. He proffered the handle to Gariath, who took it. It was of Chee Chree make, heavy enough to fell thick trees. Suitable for his work.

"Ready?" Daaru asked.

Gariath grunted.

The tulwar turned around and barked a weary order. The other tulwar exchanged nervous glances, fear and confusion plain on their faces, before finally acceding. They dropped the dragonman's chains and backed away, all fifteen of them and Daaru warily stalking back behind the gates of Jalaang.

The last thing Gariath saw before the twin gates groaned closed was Daaru's face, full of pity.

Gariath had spent these last few years surrounded by small things: small humans with their small problems and their small wars. He did not consider himself small, even in the shadow of Kharga.

Yet he wasn't unaware of how the great gray dragonman towered over him. Three feet taller, several hundred pounds heavier, jaws that could break stone topped with a thick, rhinoceros-like horn; Kharga didn't need to be unchained to be threatening. He could simply fall forward and crush Gariath, if he wanted to.

But he didn't. He simply stood there, staring down at Gariath, an empty expression on his face and reeking of a dying scent, as though he had known how this would end.

And Gariath, for his part, simply stared back.

"Nice ax," Kharga finally rumbled, breaking the silence.

"Heavy," Gariath replied.

"Looks it," Kharga said. "I had one like it myself." He sniffed. "It was bigger."

Gariath looked down at the ax. It looked big enough to him.

"You know," Kharga grunted, "for a while, I thought you were going to grant me the dignity of letting me die in a pile of my own shit and be eaten by rats." He sneered. "I can only wonder what I did to deserve being dragged out here."

"It's not about you."

"Fine. Why'd *you* drag me out here?"

"To make a point."

"Oh yeah?" Kharga's sneer turned to a derisive grin. "What? You come up with a little quip you just can't wait until morning to say after you gut me like a coward?" He let out a black, bellowing laugh. "And then what? Go give an inspirational speech to your pet monkeys? Maybe have someone paint your portrait?" His nostrils flared. "I can smell the stink of humans on you. Right down to your bones, *Rhega*."

And suddenly, the ax in his hands did not seem quite nearly big enough.

That thought must have shown itself in the growl rising in his throat and the tremble in his claws as they wrapped tightly around the ax's haft, for Kharga's rumbling laughter grew softer and uglier.

"Not in the mood to trade words?" the bigger dragonman grunted. "Good. Me neither." He stared Gariath down, unwilling to look away or blink. "Do whatever the fuck you need to do and quit wasting my time."

Gariath met his gaze, breathed him in—his anger, his bitterness, the very faint whiff of fear lurking beneath it. He hefted the ax in both hands, took three great strides forward, raised it over his head.

And he did what he had to.

In four great swings. In the rattle of chains and the sound of metal falling to the earth. In the puzzled stare Kharga shot him as his limbs, now free, suddenly stretched out.

"Huh. Didn't expect that." He blinked, then looked at the bright red gash suddenly painting his arm. "Shit. I think you got me."

"Oops." Gariath yawned as he lowered the ax, slick with blood. "If you want, I can take another try at it."

Kharga sneered but didn't move as he stared down at Gariath. "So do I just assume you're stupid? Or should I ask why?"

"Should be obvious, even to you," Gariath growled back. "I want you to go back to your masters in Cier'Djaal. I want you to tell them to make their prayers to their imaginary sky-people. I want you to tell them to make beds out of their gold and hide under them.

"Tell them that I am coming. Tell them that *we* are coming. We come with fire. We come with steel. We'll burn that rotting carcass they crawl over like maggots to ash and force-feed the ashes to whoever's left alive. The day of the humans is over and all the gold they hoard and broken meat they eat won't save them when I come to drive my foot down their throats."

Gariath jammed the ax into the earth. His eyes narrowed to slits. His growl was low and dirty as a knife in the dark.

"Tell them that, *Drokha*. Tell every last one of them, down to the last weeping, screaming, wailing infant."

Granted, Gariath was forced to admit, perhaps he *had* picked up a habit for the occasional speech from his former companions. But in their hands, speeches were long, droning, posturing things. In his, they were short, vicious, necessary to spread the fear he needed the city rife with.

And while Kharga stared at him blankly, he knew that his had had the desired effect. Beneath the odors of ire and resignation, another aroma had began to blossom. A familiar reek, sour and stale in his nose, bitter on his tongue. He had smelled it before. Fear? Terror?

"Oxshit."

Or maybe just regular old contempt.

"I've heard your monkeys talking," Kharga said. "Cier'Djaal's had a week to be afraid of you. You don't need me to do it." His nostrils flared, drew in a deep breath. "And I smell you. I smell your weakness. I smell your doubt."

Gariath was not used to weapons. Humans needed swords, axes, spears to make up for their natural deficiencies; the *Rhega* required only claws and teeth to do what needed doing. And yet the ax in his hand felt decidedly comfortable in weight and heft. He could feel just how easy it was to swing.

Just how easy it would be to plant it in Kharga's face.

"There was a time I would kill you for that," Gariath muttered, more to himself. "Maybe a time I would kill you just for existing. *Drokha* are cowards who traded blood for gold, selling themselves like meat."

"And *Rhega* are—"

"I'M FUCKING TALKING!" Gariath roared. "But that was before I went out into the desert, before I realized how many weak, stupid races there are out there..." He stared at the ax, slick with Kharga's life on it. "And how few of us there are." He snorted. "I still thought about how I'd kill you. I thought I'd boil you down and have you sold by the bowl on the streets by one of those four-armed things..."

"Couthi," Kharga grunted. "You couldn't afford them."

"I wouldn't do it because that's what a monster would do." Gariath stared up at him, eyes hard and black as iron fresh from the dark earth. "I am not a monster. *We* are not monsters."

He hefted the ax in both hands, considered it for a moment, then tossed it aside.

"If you want to die," he said, "I'll be happy to kill you. I'll rip your spine out and choke you with it for good measure." He folded his arms. "But that's your decision."

The lie smelled bitter in his nostrils. But the truth tasted foul on his tongue. How could he look upon a *Drokha* and see anything other than a foe? He saw a tool for spreading fear, and that was true. He saw a beaten enemy, and that was true. But beyond both of those, he saw one of the very last dragonmen in the world. And the thought of killing him no longer made his hands twitch.

It was Kharga's decision what to do next. It had been Gariath's decision to pretend it wasn't his.

Kharga glanced at the ax for a moment, as if he were considering picking it up and putting it to better use. Then he glanced at the chains that had once bound him for a much longer moment.

When his sigh finally came, it was not with the stink of anger, or resentment, or the slightest whiff of fear. All the reek seemed to leave him in one great breath, leaving no scent at all behind. Nothing but a very large, very tired-looking *Drokha*.

" 'We,' " Kharga said.

"What?"

"You said 'we,' " he grunted. "Like you're one of them." He shook his head. "I fought them, *Rhega*. I killed them. By the score, I killed them. I looked into their eyes when they hurled themselves at me. I smelled them as they fled." He waved a massive hand. "You don't want to call them monsters, fine. They aren't monsters. But they aren't us, either. There aren't enough of our kind left for there to *be* an 'us' or a 'we.' "

With a great, hulking stomp, he turned to face Cier'Djaal and began to lumber away.

"There's just you. Nothing else."

Gariath didn't turn to watch him go. He simply listened to the sound of heavy feet shaking the earth as he lumbered away. Over the sound of Kharga's stride, he barely heard himself when he muttered.

"The Uprising."

The shaking stopped. Kharga stopped.

"The tulwar fought their way to the heart of the city," Gariath said, "to the Silken Spire."

"They did," Kharga said. "We arrived hours later to fight them off, when the fashas agreed to pay us."

"They could have destroyed the city before you got there."

"They could have."

"But they didn't," Gariath said. "One of them saw something…and he stopped the attack. What was it?"

Kharga was silent for a breath.

"Same thing I saw when I entered the city," Kharga said. "Same thing I saw when I decided to take their money."

He didn't elaborate. Gariath didn't ask him to. Neither of them said another word as Kharga began to stalk off toward Cier'Djaal and Gariath trudged back to the gates of Jalaang.

They groaned open at his arrival, then slammed shut once he had crossed their threshold. He took ten paces into the city and stopped, staring up through weary eyes at the crowd assembled before him as he sighed deeply.

"What now?"

The tulwar—a hundred? Two hundred? It was late and counting was tiresome—did not smile at his comment. Just as well, he hadn't intended to sound funny. Rather, at his weary annoyance, they met him with faces turned down into snarls, eyes wide with anger and faces painted bright with fury.

And none were angrier or brighter than the tall, rangy tulwar standing before him.

"You let him *go*?" Dekuu, *Humn* of the Chee Chree clan, was almost as tall as Gariath, despite being much scrawnier. And though his body was worn with considerable age, his lean muscles tensed as he snarled, baring yellowed teeth at Gariath. "The murderer? The *butcher*?"

"I called him *Drokha*," Gariath replied.

"Because you weren't there!" Dekuu all but roared, drawing up close to Gariath's face. Though the colors beneath his skin had dulled with age, the *Humn*'s visage was still bright with anger. "I was." He whirled about, swept a hand over the assembled tulwar. "*We* were."

The tulwar said nothing. But they didn't have to. Gariath could see the anger scarred across their eyes, etched in every scowl turned toward him.

"We still remember, *daanaja*," Dekuu said. "We remember the Uprising. We remember those barbarians hacking us apart. We remember the blood of our grandfathers painting our skin. We remember the road they made of our corpses when they trampled us underfoot. That one, the one walking away right now, could have killed a hundred or more of us at that point."

He whirled back to Gariath and thrust a simian finger in his face.

"AND YOU LET HIM GO!"

His howl was taken up by the crowd of tulwar, their roars joined by fists upheld and trembling at Gariath. The dragonman breathed, drawing in a reek of anger so powerful that he got a little dizzy.

"You promised us victory! You promised us vengeance!" Dekuu roared to be heard over the anger of the tulwar. "We gave you command, gave you power, and what have you laid at our feet?"

Dekuu spit on the sand.

"You let *malaa*, the tainted and unclean, walk among us as though they belong here!" Each word was met with a rising roar of angry agreement. "You name the great failure, who led us into disaster so long ago, as your adviser! You give us a city far from our families and at the doorstep of our enemies. And now…" His anger ebbed into contempt as he sneered at Gariath. "You spit on the lives lost in the Uprising, spit on the blood shed there, by turning the dragonman loose."

Gariath took it all in: the stink, the sound, the sneer. He accepted it with unblinking silence, staring at Dekuu quietly. The roars carried on for some time and he let them. When they died low enough for him to be heard, he spoke softly.

"You don't think I can lead," he stated, calmly.

"I do not," Dekuu replied.

"Then is this a challenge?" Gariath asked. "You want to fight me for leadership? Some kind of ancient tulwar tradition?"

Dekuu furrowed his brow. "The tulwar have no such tradition."

"Ah."

Gariath's fist shot out. The sound of Dekuu's jaw cracking echoed louder than any roar could have. The sound of Dekuu's body hitting the ground begat a silence deeper than any death could have.

"Then *that* was just for you being an idiot," Gariath snarled.

Some looked at him with shock. Many more with anger. And just a few with genuine terror. Not one of them moved toward him. He drank in their scents as his lips curled back, baring his teeth.

"And that," he said, "was my speech. It wasn't as dramatic as his was, maybe, but this isn't a time for speeches. This isn't a time to remember the past. This isn't a time to whine about how many of you died long ago." He swept his gaze, hard and slow, across the crowd. "Because if you don't fight now, if you don't follow me now, *all* of you die.

"You want to talk about memories? About families?" He snorted. "You fail now, they kill you and your memories last as long as it takes a bird to eat your corpse. You run now, they chase you back to your families and slaughter the lot of them. You sit here, whining and crying about your revenge, your blood, your Tul over one dragonman you didn't get to kill...then you die in a pile of your own shit."

The fear ebbed away from them. The anger seeped out of them. The stink left behind was stale and old and immovable.

"You think of your past lives, you think of your future lives, but none of you realize that everything hinges on right now." He stomped the earth. "Whatever happened to bring us here, we are here. Whoever died to bring us here, they're dead. We are here. On this earth. On this land. By this time next week, either it is ours or we are all buried in it.

"I don't promise you victory. I don't promise you leadership. I don't promise to honor your stupid ways or your stupid Tul." He shook his head. "But if you don't follow me now...if you don't fight, then I promise you will all be dead. Your families will follow. Then your race. Then your lands. Then everything."

He held his hands out wide, inviting. The tulwar recoiled, as though fearing another attack. He looked down at Dekuu, unconscious and bleeding on the ground, and snorted.

"There are no tulwar. There is no war. There is just you. There is just one choice." He looked out over the tulwar. "Rise up. Or die. There is nothing else."

Not one word was said against him.

Not one fist was raised.

Not one body moved to stand before him as he looked them over then, slowly, stalked through them and headed back to his quarters.

Fear was not a useful emotion. Not for him. Humans needed it to tell them how to survive. *Rhega* knew better. Fear was nothing more than frail twine that held a body together, a scrap of linen bandage over a gushing wound. It was useful to idiots, morons, and cowards, and idiots, morons, and cowards were useful to no one.

Had he smelled fear on the tulwar, who parted to let him through, he would have stopped and stomped it out of the skull of any he had found. An army that followed him out of fear was no army he could use. Warriors afraid of him would not fight as they must for him.

But as he walked through them, as he felt their eyes follow him, he caught not a whiff of that sour reek. Anger still boiled there, to be sure, as did a hundred other unimportant emotions. But burying them all was that same, stale smell that had followed Kharga.

Wariness.

Resignation.

Certainty.

These he could use. These were stronger, older, tested. These were emotions that came to warriors who knew there was only one way fights ended. These were emotions he had given them.

These were emotions he would win this war with.

Huh, he thought as he trudged away. *That wasn't a bad speech.* And, not for the first time and not without contempt, he added: *Maybe you did spend too much time with humans.*

TWENTY-ONE

A Heresy Divine

Left. Then right. One right after the other. One. Two. Just like that.

If nothing else, Asper could still count.

It was hard to walk. Her legs felt like they had never been used before. It was hard to think through the sensation of the cold wind blowing over her and the salt of the sea on it sticking onto her. Her flesh felt raw and tingling with tiny little pains, as though someone had simply peeled her out of her skin and set her, new and raw and glistening meat, upon a world full of terrors.

Left. Right.

But she found the focus to think.

One. Two.

And she found the strength to walk.

Her legs gave out every fifth step, forcing her to lean on the walls of the alleys and empty shops she combed her way through. And every unaided step she took sent her teetering, arms flailing as she tried to keep herself upright. She was unbalanced, her legs too heavy and her head too light, and by the fifth step when she forgot to lean on a wall, she collapsed to the cobblestone road.

She looked up past the eaves and signs swaying in the breeze. In the night sky ahead, the stars were beginning to wink out. The moon had sunk low in the sky, hidden behind clouds. It could only be a few more hours until dawn. Which meant...

One hour, she told herself through ragged breath. *One fucking hour you've been without him and you've already forgotten how to walk.* She shook her head. *Or her. Whatever that thing was.*

She couldn't be too hard on herself, she reasoned. She couldn't remember a time she hadn't carried that curse inside her. Even when it hadn't spoken to her, it had weighed upon her every thought. One simply didn't carry the power to unmake a man in one's left arm without it becoming a part of their life.

And now, without it, she felt...incomplete. Amoch-Tethr had been a part of her for so long, and when the curse had pulled itself out of her skin, it had taken a part of her with her.

Maybe more than she realized.

She had treated patients with rot before, with wounds black and weeping so badly with pus that she had been forced to amputate their limbs. And though many of them went on to live long and happy lives, they often complained of feeling the absence of the foot or arm she had taken from them. They felt pains that they shouldn't have felt, the awareness that something should be there that was *not* there so keen that it caused its own special kind of lonely ache.

She couldn't find a better description for what she felt than that. Only instead of a limb, it was a presence, an entire person that should have been with her. As though someone had been walking behind her all her life and, with them suddenly gone, she was aware of just how terribly big the world that stretched out behind her was.

That thought alone was enough to rob the strength from her and send her back to the street. She let out a gasp as she tried to pull herself down the rest of the street. And, failing that, she simply crawled until she found herself at the corner of an alley.

She collapsed at it, hauling herself up to her rear end and pressing her back against the wall of the building. She was grateful no one was around to see her; this behavior would have looked pathetic on a drunk, let alone the fucking Prophet of Cier'Djaal.

In name only, she reminded herself. *You can't heal the sick with a touch. You can't call down a plague of insects. You're not a Prophet.* She closed her eyes. *But* the Big Fucking Liar of Cier'Djaal *doesn't sound as good, does it?*

She let her eyes stay closed for a moment as she drew in a breath. And, after a while, she found she could not open them again. It didn't seem possible. Or maybe she just couldn't see the point.

Denaos would be proud, she thought. *He'd look at me, lying and cheating and consorting with thieves, all these people eating up the shit I'm feeding them, and he'd applaud and a single tear would go down his cheek and he'd say "Silf, I couldn't be prouder, now let's go pick out a nice whore for you."*

She would have laughed if not for the thought that followed.

But Denaos is dead. He's dead. He's dead and you couldn't help him. You couldn't save him. You couldn't—

"Is it not clear by now that she is not coming?"

The wind died just at the right time to let a voice, a deep and rolling hiss, carry around the corner and slither into Asper's ear.

"Or do you continue to cling to this lie she has birthed and left on the floor?"

She knew the voice of Teneir, the fasha who had demanded she kneel and renounce her faith. Just as she knew the voices that followed.

"It's not a lie." Aturach's. Soft and just slightly worried.

"And she'll be here." Dransun's. Gruff and oh so weary.

They were right there. Just around the corner, exactly where she had begged them to meet—albeit a few hours later. All she needed to do was go around and reveal herself and finish the plan. But that, too, seemed so hard. So pointless.

You couldn't save him.

"Out of gratitude for her service, we shall continue to share company with these pagans." Careus's voice, deep and resonant as a gong. "But it has been hours."

"Don't go acting like you're doing me a fucking favor, scalp." Blacksbarrow. Sharp and flinty as a rough-hewn blade. "You want to scurry back to your nest with the rest of your rats, you go right the fuck ahead."

"Patience, if you would." Haethen. So sweet and so patient and sounding so tired. "I have my reservations about this meeting, as well. But I am curious as to its purpose."

Just get up, she told herself. *Just go out there. You've come so far. You've got—*

A tear slid down her face.

You couldn't save him.

"By the grace of Ancaa, would you listen to yourselves?" Teneir, hissing, furious. "You posture and strut like cocks while at the same time debasing yourselves as you wait for a false prophet? Are you warriors? Are you soldiers?"

"We're believers." Aturach. Forceful as he could be. "And we believe in her."

"And what is *she*?"

A good question, Asper thought.

If she could have saved him . . . she wondered what Denaos would say.

And in the darkness, from somewhere deeper than prayer, deeper than even Amoch-Tethr had dwelled, she got her answer.

You're the fucking Prophet.

Her eyes snapped open.

So fucking act like it.

It was hard to do, but she stood. It took a moment to figure out how, but she walked. She wasn't sure if she could do it, but she put iron in her spine, forced her chin high, her eyes clear, her stride strong as she turned the corner and strode into the square, proud and strong.

As a Prophet should.

Inside the confines of the square, it was as bright as daylight. A hundred torches held by a hundred hands lit up the ruin of what had once been a thriving market. The flickering of the torches threatened to blind her, but she did not so much as squint. She walked, slow and deliberate, into the square until she could see them.

A hundred faces, wide with shock, all fixed on her.

Karnerians on one side, assembled into a tight phalanx, headed by Careus in his black armor, Haethen looking positively tiny at his side. Sainites on the other, in a shifting, unruly gang, staring at her from beneath their tricornes, all gathered behind Blacksbarrow, who wore her shock unabashed. Aturach and Dransun, staring wide-eyed at the woman who stood whole and hale and wondering where their broken, battered, dying friend had gone.

"*Blaspheme.*"

And none was more shocked, more terrified, more furious to see her than Teneir. In a simple azure robe, the fasha scowled at her through yellow eyes, the only thing visible through her veil. But that was more than enough to make her contempt known.

Not that Asper could blame her; doubtless, the fasha had counted on her being dead by now.

"You dare show your face here?" the fasha demanded. "You dare emerge where you do not belong?"

"I *did* call this meeting," Asper replied, coolly. She looked to Dransun. "Did I not?"

The captain, a black hole in his beard where his mouth hung open, merely stared at her. "Son of a bitch," he whispered. He shook his head. "I mean, you did, but..."

"She was fucked up when we last saw her, right?" Blacksbarrow made no particular effort to disguise her shock as she glanced among the Sainites. "You saw her, didn't you?"

"She was barely standing," Haethen whispered, eyes unblinking. "I thought she'd collapse at any moment, but she's..." She shook her head. "That's not possible."

"Daeon has made it possible," Careus replied, the only one who did not appear fazed by her sudden recovery.

Asper said nothing at their shock. She simply stood there, whole and strong and completely undeniable. On their faces, she could see them trying to figure out an explanation for her sudden recovery. And, with satisfaction she was careful to keep off her own, she saw that they had none.

Let them think it another miracle. Let them think the gods did it. Let them never suspect what actually happened.

"How?"

It was Aturach who broke her satisfaction. Beneath his hood, his slender face had drained of color. It was not shock he wore on his face, but terror: the knowledge that she had some secrets that she hadn't even told him.

"How is it possible?" he asked, wounded.

"Is it not obvious?" Teneir thrust a skinny finger at her. "She is a deceiver, a pretender. I have seen opera beggars wear more convincing wounds than she did. She has simply cast them off, as she pleases."

"Bullshit." Blacksbarrow spit on the stones. "I've seen enough dead men to know real pain when I see it. She barely made it through Harbor Road."

"She required ample aid getting around Temple Row," Haethen said. "I thought she might drop dead herself before she could heal Careus, but..." She looked to the towering man at her side. "They are both whole."

"Then you are fools," Teneir snarled. "Or blind. Or both. That she could deceive a handful of *shkainai* is no feat."

"And what of a thousand Djaalics?" Dransun growled, stepping forward. "I was there at Jalaang. I saw that lizard beat seven kinds of shit out of her. You can't fake that. The thousand who came with us will agree with me."

"Then how do you explain it, hm?" Teneir swept around, scowling at the assembled. "How do *any* of you explain it? What was it if not treachery? Magic?"

The derision in Teneir's voice swept through the crowd like venom, sent doubt twisting across their faces. Quietly, they exchanged nervous looks with one another, a few lips twitching as they whispered hushed conspiracies among each other.

Only then did Asper decide to speak.

"Heaven demands a champion."

She barely raised her voice, yet it cut through the crowd like a scalpel, bleeding Teneir's venom dry. The fasha fell silent. The rest followed. Their eyes turned to her, took her in as she held her arms out in a simple gesture.

"Heaven needs us to be strong."

A long silence stretched out between them, as long as the last held breath after a prayer whispered in the dark. But in their faces, she saw no more doubt. And their eyes followed her as she walked through the crowd, into the square. Not a word was said as she bent low and plucked up a fragment of stone dislodged from the road.

"This used to be a market," she said, turning it over in her hands. "I saw it, briefly, when I first came to Cier'Djaal. Children played here, tugged at their mothers' skirts as they haggled with merchants." She dropped the stone and looked out over the rubble and ash. "Not anymore.

"Perhaps you think I'm trying to guilt you by showing you this." She shook her head. "If I wanted to do that, I'd tell you more about the dead. I'd tell you the names I heard uttered on the lips of those that survived the war brought to this city. But I don't want to do that. I want to show you. All of you."

"What is it you wish to show us, priestess?" Careus asked.

"How easily it all falls apart." She turned to them and spread her arms out wide over the ruined square. "Stone, silk, coin; all the petty things you fought over, all the lives lost for it, it all ends up the same."

She kicked. A cloud of black rose up. "Everything becomes ash and dust, no matter who sets the fire."

Across the square, Careus and Blacksbarrow exchanged glowers, as though each one were forming an accusation as to who was to blame for that very cloud of ash. Maybe it was guilt that kept them from voicing it. Asper didn't care, so long as they kept listening.

"I will not try to convince you of the atrocity of what happened here," she said. "I will call it what it is, what heaven condemns it as." She sneered. "A waste. A waste of lives. A waste of warriors. A waste of a war. You fought among yourselves for fleeting things, unaware of the true battle that was yet to come."

She pointed out to the walls of the city, to a sky quickly turning light with dawn.

"Past that wall, through the Green Belt, and just a short few miles, lies the death of every man, woman, and child in Cier'Djaal." She looked hard at the assembled. "You've heard the stories by now. You've seen the faces of those who saw it. You no longer have the luxury of pretending it's all lies, of pretending the true enemy is standing beside you now."

She narrowed her eyes.

"The tulwar are coming. Thousands strong. With swords and with flame and a monster at their head, they are coming. And all the trifling waste you battled over will be more ash and dust beneath their feet if you do not heed the word of heaven."

At this, the crowd finally broke out into hushed, excited murmurs. The soldiers exchanged nervous glances, as though this were the first time they were hearing of such a thing.

"The monkeys?" Blacksbarrow spit. "We had some trouble with them out in the desert, had to withdraw my convoy from them. But it took a whole city of theirs to bloody our nose."

"They have two cities now," Dransun said. "They took Jalaang. Its forges and docks are crawling with the savages now, churning out boats and blades by the score."

"Jalaang was a trading post with no adequate defensiveness," Careus replied. "That the barbarians took it hardly indicates anything more than their own unpreparedness."

Asper gritted her teeth, fought hard to keep the anger out of her scowl. Prophets didn't get angry. Prophets kept their calm. And she did.

"More lies."

But damn if it wasn't hard once Teneir started speaking.

"Even during their so-called Uprising, the tulwar were easily put down," the fasha said. "If they march upon us, there is no chance that they will win." She scowled at Asper. "She merely seeks to coerce you into obedience, as she has plotted from the beginning, with this story of tulwar."

"How can you still…" Dransun growled.

"Have you not heard the people?" Aturach demanded. "Have you not heard the tales?"

"Civvies get excited," Blacksbarrow grunted. "You don't go asking them for advice on war."

"Tales cannot be a part of our strategy in Cier'Djaal," Careus said.

Not now. Asper growled inwardly. *Not fucking now. Not because of this fucking saccarii. Think of something. Don't let them walk away over this. Don't let Gariath win. THINK OF SOMETHING.*

"Tales are for children."

She didn't think of the reply that came, clear and crisp as a bell, but it came anyway.

And so, too, did the wizards.

At the edge of the crowd, they appeared: three figures in long, brown coats, postures perfectly rigid, eyes glowing faintly with magical energy. They stepped forward, the crowd clearing a path for them as though they carried a plague. But if Lector Shinka noticed, her pristinely calm face did not betray it. She merely stared out over the crowd with cold eyes as two Librarians fell into place beside her.

"Do I address children, then?" she asked.

"Guard your tongue, pagan," Careus warned, reaching for the sword at his hip. "Or else I shall—"

"You shall do nothing if you do not heed the priestess—" Shinka caught herself, inclined her head to Asper. "The *Prophet*, that is, for she speaks the truth." She folded her hands behind her back. "The tulwar army is thousands strong and its numbers grow daily. From across the deserts, the savages come flocking to Jalaang to join the battle. They will march on Cier'Djaal before long."

"The word of a godless, bat-shit heathen doesn't mean much," Blacksbarrow replied.

"What of a godless, batshit heathen that can *fly*?" Shinka sneered at the Sainite. "We have seen the savages assembling. We can provide an accurate count to the nearest tenth. We have seen the swords forged and shields hewn. And we have seen their eyes turned toward this city." She narrowed her eyes. "The city where *my* tower is located, thank you, and I'm keen to not see it overrun by monkeys."

"To stand with pagans is one thing." Careus cast a glare to Blacksbarrow, then to Shinka. "But to heed the counsel of the faithless goes against all that Daeon commands of us."

"Heaven does not command." Asper stepped forward. "Heaven demands. Heaven demands champions. Heaven demands those who would defend its creations." She pointed to Careus. "Heaven has delivered you from sickness." She pointed to Blacksbarrow. "And you from strife." She drew in a breath. "And me from death.

"We stand here for a reason," she said. "Amid the graveyard of our sins and our excesses, we stand together. Foes. Pagans. Fanatics. Faithless." She shook her head. "Call yourselves what you will. Heaven would call you champions. Heaven demands your service. Heaven demands a war. Heaven demands a *victory*."

She was aware, then, that she was breathing heavily. She felt sweat on her brow. She felt her heart beating with a fervor that it hadn't beat with in so very long.

"Will you give it one?" she asked.

A hush fell over the crowd. The iron hush of the last man at the last battle falling dead from the last drop of blood. The cold hush of the river icing over for a winter that never ended. The black hush in the falter before every prayer to a deaf god.

And she stood tall. She stood firm. And with her gaze alone, she demanded their answer.

"We have orders…" Blacksbarrow said, looking at her feet.

"Your orders were to save Cier'Djaal," Aturach said. "Will you honor it?"

"Our mission came from the emperor," Haethen whispered. "We can't just…"

"You won't 'just,'" Dransun said. "You'll fight. You'll fight hard. Or else we all die."

"To ask this of us," Careus said, "to ask us to kneel before you and—"

"Emperors ask you to kneel," Asper interrupted. "Sovereigns ask you to bow. Men ask you to lie down and die." She extended a hand. "Heaven demands that you stand. But stand with *me*."

More silence. More looks of doubt. More gazes averted from hers. The fear and doubt was palpable, a fire in her skin. And in its wake, even behind her veil, Asper could sense the smug satisfaction across Teneir's face.

And just as Asper was tempted to leap forward and throttle it off, a flash of movement caught her eye.

From the rigid phalanx of the Karnerians, a soldier stepped forward. He pushed past Haethen and Careus, casting not a look at either of them as he approached Asper. His face was youthful, full of life, and split by a large familiar smile.

What had his name been?

"Pathon," she whispered. "Marcher Pathon."

He smiled. He inclined his head. He stepped beside her and said simply, "I stand with you."

"Marcher," Careus said, a stern warning in his voice.

"The Empire serves Daeon, Speaker. And Daeon stands with heaven." Pathon's eyes snapped open and he added a hasty bow. "With all respect, of course."

"The Venarium, too, stands with you." Shinka stepped forward, inclining her head toward Asper. The Librarians behind her followed suit.

"And now she brazenly consorts with the faithless," Teneir hissed from behind her veil.

Frowns creased the faces of both Blacksbarrow and Careus, clearly ill at ease with this endorsement. But whatever discomfort they felt, they did not give a voice to it.

Not until Haethen stepped forward, anyway.

"*Haethen*," Careus snapped, less in warning and more in surprise.

The woman, though, did not turn back. Not until she stood beside the priestess and stared out over the crowd. "I stand with you."

Maybe it was her reputation that did it, all the "miracles" the people had seen. Or maybe it was latent guilt, the agonies over so many lives lost.

Maybe you're just good at speeches, she told herself.

She didn't care. They came, regardless.

One by one. From the Sainites. From the Karnerians. Standing beside her, standing beside each other. Some bowed reverently, some simply inclined their head, some merely grunted.

But they all said it.

"I stand with you."

With reverence, with a little fear, without hesitation.

"I stand with you."

Soft at first, but growing louder with each repetition.

"I stand with you."

Until only two remained. Neither Careus nor Blacksbarrow had stepped forward, nor had they stopped their soldiers from doing so. Now they stood, facing their own forces, who watched them nervously. Asper, too, felt her heart thunder—moved as their troops might have been, they were still commanders; one defiant word from them could end this whole farce.

And Blacksbarrow, who wore a scowl plainly on her face, looked ready to do just that. She opened her mouth, paused, then glanced sidelong at Careus. She sniffed. Then she snorted. Then she spit a thick glob of phlegm onto the cobblestones.

"Ah, fuck it." She stepped forward, clapped Asper on the back, and grinned. "I'm with you."

A deep sigh and the clamor of iron boots followed as Careus stepped forward. "Our mission remains the same as ever. Do not consider this cessation to be condoning of pagan activity inside Cier'Djaal. We still—"

"Careus." Haethen offered him a single word, a single look, and nothing more.

And this, apparently, was enough to soften the iron in his features. He nodded briefly and turned toward Asper.

"I stand with you, Prophet."

The thunder in her heart slowed. She allowed herself the barest of smiles at this. But she could not call it a victory, not with the sole remaining thorn in her side.

When she looked at Teneir, she had expected to see the fasha trembling with fury. Instead, the eyes that stared at her from past the veil were filled with resignation, almost a deep sadness. As though she had expected this to happen.

Asper couldn't accuse her now, not while this alliance was still so fragile; a fasha could still cause immense damage, even in a city where she no longer held absolute power. And so, while Asper would have liked to throttle her, the Prophet knew she could not.

She extended her hand. And said nothing.

Teneir looked at her hand. Her voice was soft and venomous.

"And what," Teneir said, "will you sing of when you win this great victory, hm? Will you tell tales of how you overcame your petty prejudices to save a city you destroyed? Will you speak of the brave soldiers who died and think nothing of the women and children you slaughtered? Will you shake hands, united at last, as you divide my city up among yourselves?"

She shook her head. She turned away.

"I am a religious woman, *Prophet*," she hissed, "but I am a businesswoman before that. I know a foul deal when I see it. And your bartering in sins and absolutions does not interest me." She waved a hand. "May all you foreign demons find your graves together."

The fasha stalked away from the square. And in her wake, a tense easiness rose. Soldiers exchanged nervous looks with people they had been ready to kill just a few days ago. Excited burble about tulwar and monsters was raised among them. Careus and Blacksbarrow moved to restore order.

When eyes were off her for even a moment, Asper finally let herself breathe. All the tension and fear came flooding out of her in a great, exhausted sigh. Her legs felt like jelly; her heart ached with how fiercely it had beat. But whatever pains she had was nothing compared to the small light of relief, flickering like a candle in a storm, at the back of her head.

She had done it.

"Teneir will be a problem."

She glanced up as Aturach stepped beside her, his eyes fixed on the alley down which the fasha had disappeared. She followed his gaze, sighing wearily.

"You have no idea," she muttered.

When she looked back to Aturach, he wore a look she had not seen before. He was a man of easy emotions, fear and joy painting themselves in broad, vibrant strokes across his face. But the look he gave her now, reserved and scrutinizing...

It moved her to offer an apologetic frown.

"Aturach," she said, "I should tell you. About what happened earlier tonight, I—"

"No." He held up his hand. "I don't want to know. I can never know. Dransun, either."

"But I—"

"You came to the soldiers, broken and wounded. And you emerged to lead them, whole and powerful. Heaven made you well again." He swallowed hard. "That is the truth now. We need that to be the truth. Okay?"

He gave her a smile. But it was a weak and dying thing, small and trembling on his lips. And however slight it might have been, she could see the reality in it.

And she knew he would never trust her again. Not as he once did.

He nodded to her, then walked away, moving to help Dransun in restoring order to the mob. There would be soldiers to rally, tactics to plan, strategies to forge, and backs to watch. But she had done it. She had united them. She had an army to fight Gariath, to save Cier'Djaal.

It felt strange, then, that the pain she felt at that moment was the worst of that evening.

Look at you, she thought. *The lies come so easy now.* She closed her eyes, held back tears. *Gods damn. Denaos would have been so proud.*

TWENTY-TWO

A WORTHY HUNGER

Fuck me, but he's taking his time, isn't he?"

Dreadaeleon's ears still worked.

He could feel his organs shutting down. He could feel his lungs drawing in less air with each breath. He could feel his limbs as leaden weights hanging from him, rendering him an immobile, silent, barely sensate husk on a satin bed.

But his ears worked just fine.

"The Lector said he'd take only a day to die."

His eyes, too. When the Librarian leaned over him—a handsome young man with a sharp face and weathered eyes—he could see the irritation playing across his features.

"Fourteen years," he muttered. "I was selected to become a Librarian fourteen years ago. Fourteen years of reading until my eyes bled, testing until my brains leaked out my ears; I was burned, electrocuted, frozen, and twisted." He sneered down at Dreadaeleon. "All so I could be granted the righteous honor of sitting a corpse."

"He's not dead yet." His associate, a young lady sitting in the corner of the room, thumbing through a book, spoke up. "The Lector says he's had the Decay before. That might account for his resistance this time."

"Does it matter? Decay's decay," the first Librarian said. "Leave him in a ditch and let him rot. You don't need four Librarians to guard him, especially tonight."

Dreadaeleon had seen the other two Librarians only in passing when they had brought him here. But he could hear them still, shuffling around in the living quarters downstairs, apparently as restless and disgruntled as their companions guarding him.

He wasn't sure what everyone was so upset about. True, he was still alive—for reasons even he couldn't account for, given how little life seeped into his numb body—but it wouldn't be for long. And there were certainly more unpleasant places to die.

Shinka's private accommodations were in a well-to-do neighborhood at the border of Silktown and the Souk that had escaped most of the fighting. It was a humble, if elegant, two-story room furnished in pleasant red silks and red furniture. He, in all his numb and lifeless glory, had been laid out on her bed: a sprawling and elegant mattress beneath a tasteful pink canopy, above a tasteful duvet, among a pair of silken red pillows.

The world's cuddliest pyre in desperate want of a torch.

"She wants to be certain," the woman said. "This one, apparently, has a habit of coming back if you don't make certain he's dead."

The male looked him over with a sigh before turning away. "Just so long as she doesn't expect me to clean her fucking sheets if he shits himself."

Dreadaeleon drew in a staggering, rasping breath. And then, with immense regret, drew in another.

It seemed to him that everyone could be happy if they just killed him now. He was, after all, the man who had killed Lector Annis, the most ferocious wizard in Cier'Djaal and their direct superior. They should want him dead as badly as he deserved the dignity of a clean death.

Alas, old man, he thought. *Neither a hero, nor a villain, this all ends with you shitting yourself to death. Just like Gariath said you would.*

"And how are you so calm about this?" the man demanded of his companion. "You trained even longer than I did. How can you be okay with guarding a corpse while the Lector is out there, unprotected?"

"She has Ashimi and Declant with her. She trusts them to protect her, just as she trusts us to handle this. And while I'm not any happier about this...task than you are, I trust her." There was a rather airy, satisfied sigh from the woman. "I hear it's already happened, in fact."

"Really? The whole thing went off okay?"

"Ashimi sent someone over to tell us. You were taking a piss. This 'Prophet' of theirs, apparently, pulled it off."

"No shit?"

"Mm. She gave some speech about gods or heaven or some made-up bullshit."

"And the foreigners bought it?"

"By the pound. The Lector barely had to intervene. They swore fealty right then and there."

"Amazing. I can set a man on fire by snapping my fingers and I don't wield one-tenth of the power of a priestess who spews bullshit to a bunch of morons with swords."

"Life isn't fair, I'm afraid," she giggled.

Priestess?

Did they mean Asper? Was that who they were calling a Prophet? It occurred to him that he had been so consumed by this conspiracy he hadn't even stopped to think what she might have been doing. Was she safe? Was she okay?

Obviously she is, he told himself. *Listen to them. She's...what'd they say? A Prophet? She was always going to be all right. You're the fool who was doomed. That's simply ironic, old man.* He paused. *Or is that poetic? I never can tell.*

"Then that's that?" the man asked. "We did it?"

"The first part, anyway," the woman replied. "There's the tulwar to deal with, before anything else."

"A bunch of savages will be no problem."

"Not with magic, they won't. The Lector is already moving to have us start preparations. But her concerns lie beyond that. Once the tulwar are taken care of, the real work begins."

What?

"That part worries me," the man said. "The barknecks' belief in imaginary gods is enough to unite them. I can't imagine that it'll be easy convincing them to trust us to run things."

Run things? What are they plotting?

"It can't be helped," the woman sighed. "The whole reason we're doing this is that barknecks can't be trusted. The fashas ruined this city for coin. The Lector isn't about to let them ruin it for gods. This Prophet will have to be addressed."

"Addressed." As though she's a debate question. You treasonous swine!

"And you think the Lector can take care of that?"

"I know she can. Whether the Prophet opts to respond to reason or force, Shinka has both in ample."

As though you assholes would ever use reason when you could just kill someone. You shitheads! You fucks! You...you...

His thoughts became formless, wordless rage, a ball of impotent anger that slammed itself against his skull in an attempt to break free. It found no voice to curse, it found no limbs to raise in anger, it found nothing but a creeping numbness that slid a little deeper into his flesh and smothered it into a seething, breathless anger.

They would kill her. They would use her and they would kill her. That was what the Venarium did. They didn't see people, they saw problems and solutions, and people were merely tools to address them. Once Asper outlived her usefulness—and it would be quick—they would kill her. Her. His friend. His companion...

Former companion, he thought, correcting himself. Had he had the breath to do so, he would have sighed. Had he had the strength to do so, he would have closed his eyes. *You ruined that one, didn't you? Or she did. Whichever. Doesn't matter now, does it? Nothing you can do now except die.*

He blinked.

If it's any consolation, old man, your bowels probably won't work enough for you to shit yourself.

There was that, at least.

That and the creeping numbness working its way through him as the rest of him shut itself down, one organ after the other. First his liver, then his bowels, then his—

"Hey!"

A noise from downstairs. One of the Librarians called out.

"The door! Get to—"

His voice was lost in the sound of wood splintering. A scream tore through the house. There was a sharp cracking sound, a scream, something heavy smashing against the wall.

A few words of power spoken. He felt the barest tingle of magical energy expelled, though even that had to be immense for him to feel it through his dead nerves. The temperature dropped inside the room. Frost magic? He couldn't tell. Another shriek, another snap, then two more, and something heavy hit the ground.

"Something's wrong," the female Librarian said, leaping to her feet. "We have to help!"

"What about him?" the man asked, glancing at Dreadaeleon.

"Are you fucking stupid?" She pulled the door to the room open and snarled over her shoulder at her companion. "He's a corpse. Leave him to—"

There was a flash of movement. Something pale appeared in the doorway. A pair of slender arms seized the woman by the throat, choking the scream out of her as they hauled her out of the room.

Dreadaeleon couldn't see anything else. He could only hear it: the rip of flesh, the spatter of blood, the cry of the man as he leapt forward, speaking a magical word that never finished.

There was a brief silence.

There was a blur at his side.

And the room shook as the Librarian's body flew through the air, struck the wall, and fell limp.

"You know, in *my* day, magic was more effective."

A soft and feminine voice reached Dreadaeleon's ears. He heard soft feet padding across the floor, each step accentuated by a squishing sound. A shadow fell over him. With monumental effort, he managed to look up at the person standing beside the bed.

"Things were a little more ... passionate back then."

A woman: short, brown-haired, completely naked, and painfully skinny. Her hands were on her hips, visible through her skin, red-stained fingers smearing blood across her flesh. Her smile looked too big for her thin face as she looked down at him, her lips bright with a smear of blood.

"None of these rules and regulations, just unbridled power." She sighed wistfully, then wiped her mouth with the back of her hand. "I saw the first people try to harness it. I saw them draw it in. I saw them explode." She stared emptily off into the distance. "Such bright flashes they made. They positively lit up the night."

She looked back down at him. He stared back, motionless and silent.

"Ah. You're the one who doesn't believe in gods, hm?" She laid a hand on his cheek, let her fingers slither down his throat. And despite his numbness, she radiated such painful warmth that he could still feel it. "I listened to your little rants so many times. Infuriating. There were times when I wish she had simply laid me against you and let me consume you so that I could show you."

Her voice became a purring rasp as she leaned beside him.

"There are some tortures too exquisite to have been made by mortals." She sighed, letting her hand trail down his chest, sliding inside his shirt and groping at his flesh. Her touch burned him, but he had no voice to scream. "Mm. But I suppose this is just as good, no? Here you are, about to die, and in answer to a prayer, some divine figure descends to save you. I would *love* to linger and see how you explain this. Alas."

She giggled as she stood up, swung one leg over the bed, and straddled him. She leaned down, pressed her skinny frame against him, and took his face in her hands. Her breath was foul, reeking of acrid smoke as she drew closer to him. Behind her lips, past her teeth, at the back of her throat, a red light, vile as a fever, glowed.

"This is only a brief visit," she said, her lips brushing against his. "I've a lot of work to catch up on these days. But before any of that..."

Her tongue flicked out, brushed against his cheek. He smelled flesh burning.

"I have a debt to pay."

And then she seized him forcefully, hauled him up, and kissed him.

Or, at first, he could almost pretend it was a kiss. At first, he could almost pretend it felt human. Her lips were on his. Her tongue was in his mouth. Her fingers were around his cheeks. She tasted him, breathed him in, closed her eyes. She was warm. So very warm.

And then she was ablaze.

She let out a great breath, such that her already tiny body seemed to shrink with it. He felt something enter him, passing from her mouth into his. He could feel it fill him, rushing into numb extremities and setting them ablaze. It felt as though she were breathing black smoke into him, a thousand dancing embers rising inside him, burning him from the inside. The numbness did not leave him. Not completely.

But in the pit of his blackened belly, he could feel something settle and take root. A great emptiness that yawned open inside him. The ashes of an ancient fire that had burned since the beginning.

A hunger. So deep and so painful as to make his dead body ache.

She pulled away from him. She licked her lips. Wisps of steam trailed her tongue. She hopped off him, but the warmth remained. His entire body felt like it was on fire, yet he couldn't move to extinguish it, couldn't find the voice for his pain.

"Do you suppose there'll be a legend about this?" she asked. "As the years go by, will you tell the people you hurt of the mysterious creature who visited you in the night and left you with a terrible gift? Or will you pretend this is all just a bad dream?"

She shrugged and giggled. It was a frightful sound.

"My debt only begged me to give it to you, not to tell you what to do with it. But these kinds of divine interventions always come with a bit of wisdom, don't they?"

She glanced to her side, where the male Librarian lay, trembling and broken against the wall. She reached down, hoisted him—easily one and a half times her size—up with the barest of effort. She poised him, bleeding from his head, eyes full of terror, at the edge of the bed, just a hairbreadth from Dreadaeleon's hand.

"For what it's worth, I can see where you're coming from," she said. "Vile men go unpunished while good men languish. People starve in a world that brims with plenty. Were I to look at the world as you do, I might also doubt the existence of the gods.

"But I've been around. I've seen the beauty of this world. I've seen the abundance of it." She smiled. "And I have tasted it. It exists to sate, just as we exist to hunger for it. One does not truly appreciate this gift, this mortal curse the gods handed down to us, until one embraces it."

She leaned down low. She closed her eyes. She laid a simple kiss on his forehead.

It burned.

"I've given you something very special, Dreadaeleon Arethenes. Use it."

She patted the dying Librarian gently on the head. She offered a decidedly girlish giggle and, with a spry twirl, skipped out the door, her feet squishing in the pools of blood left behind.

Dreadaeleon *would* have called it a bad dream. He dearly wanted to, in fact. He would have liked nothing better than for this to be the last throes of his dying mind before he slipped off into nothingness.

But he couldn't find the mind to do so. He couldn't ignore the painful warmth coursing through his blood on a torrent of embers. He couldn't look away from the shattered bodies around the room. He couldn't ignore the hunger.

It did not so much gnaw at him as devour him from within. He could feel that great gaping void inside him opening wider, consuming more of him with every moment. It was something black and ancient and foul inside him. Something he couldn't ignore.

Just as he couldn't ignore the body, fresh and quivering and bleeding, next to him.

He couldn't say how he knew to do it. Nor could he say where he found the strength to do so. But somewhere, in all that darkness inside him, he clawed up every last bit of energy he had. He forced it all into his hand. And, trembling, he raised it just a few hairbreadths.

And placed them against the Librarian's flesh.

Everything just seemed to happen all at once, without him even trying. The heat inside him all rushed to his hand, poured into his fingertips. He saw the Librarian's face contort in agony. He heard him let out a scream. He smelled the smoke of burning flesh as the skin gave way beneath his fingers.

And something else entered him.

The void inside him contracted, shrank. The hunger eased back, sated. The numbness began to creep away.

He drew a breath.

It was long and deep and pure.

TWENTY-THREE

THE LAST VIRTUE

Being totally honest with yourself, how much of your life have you spent running?

Lenk didn't have the breath or the saliva to ask the question aloud, so he settled for merely thinking it.

It started with Steadbrook, right? Pulled yourself out of the ashes and the corpses you left there and started running away with them. Then you've just been running from one trouble, one kill, one gold coin to the next.

He found that hard to deny. Even if he had the energy to do so, he wouldn't have been able to argue it very effectively.

All right, so admittedly, you're really more just trudging now.

That, he thought between long drags of his feet, was even harder to deny.

But the question remains…

He looked up, stared out over the dawn creeping over the endless dunes ahead.

Where the fuck do you think you're running to?

That was an excellent question. He could tell it was excellent because he didn't have an answer for it and it made him profoundly uncomfortable to think about. And he had spent a very long time running from exactly those kinds of questions.

It was never a question of what he was running from. That was always fairly evident: monsters, *bigger* monsters, armies, angry debtors, angry lovers, a goat one time…

And, most recently, the end of the fucking world.

Likewise, it was easy to answer exactly *why* he was always running from something. It was just simpler to define oneself in relation to how and by what he could be maimed, eviscerated, or devoured. When life was decided by who wanted to end it, it was easy to see where to go.

And, to be fair, it wasn't as though he was lacking for people that wanted to kill him.

He played the events of the previous night over and over in his head, without even closing his eyes, and, somehow, he still couldn't believe they had happened.

Or rather, he couldn't believe he hadn't seen them coming.

Had it been arrogance that made him believe Khoth-Kapira? A belief that he, and only he, could have changed the world by releasing a demon into it? Or maybe it had just been desperation, a desire to save everyone and the fear that he couldn't, that made him think a creature from the pit of hell could have helped him.

But he knew, in some deep and tender part of him, that it hadn't been any of that.

He knew he had set Khoth-Kapira free because he was running, again. Running away from the fact that he couldn't put down his sword, so he freed Khoth-Kapira to do it for him. Running away from his fear of losing Kataria, so he freed Khoth-Kapira to save her. Running, running, running...

All that running, he thought, *and where are you now?*

He looked down at the sand beneath his feet. About seven feet across, two deep furrows cleaved their way through the dunes. He had picked up the wagon's tracks a few miles back and just started following them.

Back then, he told himself he had a plan—find the wagons, recuperate there, figure out what to do next. But that was a lot of running and a lot of thinking in the meantime.

And now, as he trudged up a dune, to where a tall sandy rock jutted from the crest, he found it very hard to do either.

He leaned against the stone, breathing heavily. He wiped sweat out of his eyes and stared long over the horizon. Just beyond the dunes, he could see the wagons. Three of them: the last remnants of merchants, maybe, or just a few people who hadn't heard the desert was a dangerous place yet.

They'll have water, he told himself. *They'll have food. You can get some of both. Somehow. You can take it if you need it.* He looked down at the sword in his hand. *Then, you can stop Khoth-Kapira somehow. Just like you set out to save Cier'Djaal. Just like you tried to stop killing.* He licked his lips. *Water. Food. Maybe a quick nap. Then save the world. Sounds doable, right?*

He nodded to himself. He took a step forward. He collapsed onto the sands.

Or you could lie here and die. That'd be fine, too.

And the longer he lay there, the more it seemed like a good idea.

He looked to his left. He saw the sword lying there beside him, like a lover; the only thing that he hadn't lost, this entire time. The only thing that he hadn't thrown away, hadn't driven away, hadn't ruined. The sword was still there. The sword was always there.

It would have been so nice to lie to himself, to tell himself that these were freak coincidences that had led him to the path he had taken, that cruel fate had guided him back to bloodshed, that he had been deceived and tricked into so much bloodshed, so much chaos.

But the truth was, he was just really good at it.

Everything that had happened so far, happened because he made it happen. Every drop of blood spilled, every life taken, they had been his to claim. He had done it. All of it.

Would it be so bad, then, if he just sat here and let it end?

Not a bad thought. He tried to pull himself up but managed no better than sitting against the sandy stone. *You've tried everything but simply sitting still and doing nothing.* He closed his eyes. He let his head rest against the stone. *That's what you've been doing wrong this whole time.*

Some part of him rebelled at the thought, of course. His sword hand itched. His shoulder ached. The part of him that knew he was at fault and should fix it—a noisy, wretched little part that he had tried to drown, smother, and suffocate at various points in his life—spoke out.

But these were faint and fleeting feelings. His thoughts came more clearly, spoke loudly.

Stopping demons, saving cities, protecting people...that's hero's work. He smiled. *You're no hero, are you? Heroes have things work out. Heroes get happy endings.* His smile faded. *Heroes get the girl.*

A cold wind blew.

You're a killer. No shame in admitting that. You were born that way, right? He nodded. *Right. But the thing about killing is, you never really make things better by doing it. You just end up with more dead bodies, right?* He sighed. *Right. So, the best thing to do is let someone else handle this one. Take one more killer out of the world, save the world a few more dead bodies. It's for the best, right?*

The sun rose higher in the sky.

Right?

A many-legged insect crawled across his hand.

Right?

He shut his eyes tighter. He drew in a breath. He held it.

And he waited.

He lost track of time, of breath, of everything, drifting into something cold and black for a long time.

Until the sound of sand crunching under feet filled his ears.

His eyes opened reluctantly, squinted against the rising light of day. He peered down the dune as someone came trudging up the path his weary footsteps had carved in the sand.

Lenk had heard, from men who found greater meaning in blood than he could, that the dying often experienced visions before the last light left their eyes.

Images of shadows coming to drag them away were common, as were visions of past regrets and accomplishments. But far and away, he had heard, the most common were visions of loved ones.

To that end, he thought, it made sense that he should see her, the scrawny shict in dirty leathers, caked in sweat and grime, stalking wearily toward him. It seemed a little unfair that his dying vision of her should not be at least a little cleaner-looking, but he supposed it was fitting that the last thing he should see was her as he remembered her.

But as she trudged close enough for the stink to hit him, he knew he wasn't dead yet.

And neither was she.

She came up to the stone, without saying a word, without sparing him a glance, and collapsed beside him. Her skin reeked of dried sweat and dust, glowed red from exertion, as she tilted a waterskin up and messily drank of it. After a noisome belch, she passed it to him without looking at him.

He, however, looked at her. Stared at her, in fact, as if to make sure she wasn't actually just a hallucination. But the waterskin felt real as she pressed it against him, and her annoyed growl sounded real enough.

And the water that he poured down his throat left him feeling alive again.

He drank as much as he could before handing it back to her. She drained the rest, tossed it away, leaned against the stone, and closed her eyes.

And, for a very long time, they simply sat there and let a heavy silence blanket them.

And, since he had ruined everything else, Lenk thought he might as well ruin that, too.

"Hey," he said.

"Hey," she replied.

"Thanks for the water."

"Thanks for not having any idea how to cover your tracks." She pointed out toward the desert. "Picked up your trail a while back. Could have followed you in my sleep. How is it you haven't died out here?"

"Just lucky, I guess."

Another silence, not quite so heavy, not quite so long, fell over them.

"So," he said, "how've you been?"

"Not great." She scratched her flank. "You?"

He smacked his lips. "You first."

She rubbed her eyes with the heels of her hand. "I got kidnapped, learned that my people are following a psychotic woman hell-bent on dragging them into war, escaped, watched Shicttown burn, tried to stop her, failed, got captured again, and now I'm basically going to watch my entire race get wiped out because I couldn't stop her."

She shot him a sidelong glance.

"And what have you been up to?"

"About the same," he replied. "I went to an ancient city, betrayed the only person who believed in me and everything I knew to be right, released an ancient demon into the world, and now he's coming up behind me with an army of flesh-changed monsters who are probably going to overrun everything in an attempt to reshape the world into his vision of paradise."

She looked away from him and sniffed.

"It's not a contest," she muttered.

He would have laughed at that, too, if he'd had the energy. As it was, the water had given him just enough strength to sit there with his eyes open, staring out over the endless dunes as the wind blew ghosts of dust across it, with her beside him.

Her, warm and filthy and smelly, just like he remembered her.

And, for a while, it felt good to just let her be there.

"I didn't leave on purpose," she said.

"I know," he replied. "I thought you were dead."

"I wasn't."

"I know." He sighed. "I made some mistakes." He looked down at the earth. "A lot of mistakes, actually. I..." He shook his head. "I don't fucking know what I did. I don't fucking know what I'm doing anymore." He clutched his temples. "I thought you were going to die if I didn't...I thought I was going to be a weapon...I just wanted everything to be normal and—"

"Hey."

He looked up. She was looking at him. Her eyes were bright and shining. Her lips curled up into a smile, softer and gentler than anything she had ever shown him. Her ears drooped slightly against her head, like wilting flowers. She reached down, took his hand. It felt warm.

"Shut up, all right?"

He opened his mouth to take offense, but all he could do was nod.

"All right."

"This all sounds pretty bad, what happened," she said, "what with shicts and demons and..." She squinted at him, searching. "What'd you say? Flesh-something?"

"Flesh-shaped monsters, yeah."

"Whatever. We'll handle it."

"I don't know if I—"

"I do." She yawned. "But I also know I've been running all fucking night, so the end of the world can wait for at least two hours, right?"

"I mean, maybe but..."

She didn't hear him. With the smile still on her face, she closed her eyes and toppled over like a stack of bricks. She lay against his shoulder, her hair, thick with dirt, falling over him and the stink of her sweat in his nose. And she breathed deeply and did not move.

He should shake her awake, he knew. He should tell her that there wasn't time for this, that she didn't understand what he had done, that even two hours was too much time to waste. He should...

But then, it had been a very long time since he had smelled her, had felt her warmth, had heard the sound of her breathing. And it had been a very long time since he remembered feeling like he needed those things.

And so he sat there. He shut his eyes. He laid his head against the stone.

And he waited.

THE CHOIR'S LAST HYMN

Our Fathers,
Long Departed

Thraatu,

I will allow myself to be optimistic for a moment and assume that you did not immediately crumple up this letter, throw it in a fire, or use it to wipe yourself with. Perhaps that is unjustifiably hopeful, but I find myself believing in many strange things these days.

I know we have not spoken in... how long has it been, anyway?

We knew each other first, two lifetimes ago. I have memories of a young woman, proud and tall, the colors in her face bright and her blade stark and shining against the sun. I was a different person back then, with a different name, one better composed to poetry than I am now. It is strange—I can recall the letters I used to describe you, but I cannot recall how they fit together. And I find that, if I focus on them for too long, your face, too, fades and I cannot recall what you look like.

Two lives. One hundred years. So many famines and wars and births and weddings we have seen. It feels odd that the two decades or so since we have spoken should feel like an eternity for people like us.

Yet it does.

Every year, every month, every day that has passed since the Uprising, since I came down and let our people die, I have longed to speak to you. I have longed to tell you why I did what I did. I have longed to beg your forgiveness.

But even now, I cannot tell you why.

And even now, I cannot beg your forgiveness until I beg it of every one of the clans that died because of me.

But I must speak with you.

And you must speak with your clan.

Perhaps you have heard the stories. Perhaps you have heard the songs. The stories are still young and the songs do not quite rhyme, so I do not blame you if you do not believe them. But for all my failings, Thraatu, I have always been honest with you. Even when I could not explain myself, I could not lie. And I do not lie to you now.

The stories are true.

We left Shaab Sahaar, its many clans—Rua Tong, Tho Thu Bhu, Chee Chree, Yengu Thuun, and even Mak Lak Kai—united for the first time in ages. We marched on the human city of Jalaang and took it from its dragonmen protectors. More clans came from the mountains and the hills and joined us. And we marched on Cier'Djaal once more, against its many humans, against its magics and its gold and its monsters.

We rose up, Thraatu. All of us.

We fought. We died. We survived.

And this time, it was different.

You have heard of the daanaja, *I am sure: a great beast that stands taller than any tulwar, his skin painted the color of blood, head like a lizard, wings that block out the sun. They say he tore out the throats of a hundred humans with his teeth and that he broke a dragonman with his bare hands. There are songs about him. They do not rhyme.*

I will not tell you they are true, either. But as far as any tulwar is concerned, they are.

He is a monster. He is a demon. And he led us to a battle we thought we could not win.

And I want you to meet him, Thraatu. I want you to come and see what he has done, as I have. I want you to come and see what he can do, as I wait to. I want you to follow him to the next battle, as you could never follow me.

Perhaps things are still idyllic in your mountains. Perhaps your goats are fat and there is plenty of milk to feed your children. But I do not think so. I think life is hard for you, as it always was. I think life will only get harder.

For all of us.

Whatever else we did at Harmony Road, we bloodied the humans' noses. We rose up, as we always said we would, and showed them that we are not

the backward savages they thought we were. We showed them what the tul-
war were capable of. We spoke. They listened.

And their retort will be bloody.

And should they not kill us, the shicts will. What we witnessed on that
red day, I cannot explain. The tribes have always hated us and wanted us
dead, but never have they tried so hard, committed so much. Humans can
merely kill us. But after what I saw at Harmony Road, I am convinced only
the shicts can truly destroy us.

And this is all beside the . . . how to explain it?

You have heard the story, yes? The one of the day turning dark as night
and the creature that bled serpents? I do not blame you for not believing it.
It is insane. It is ridiculous.

And it, too, is true.

Perhaps your world is still small, Thraatu. Perhaps you still have your
goats and your milk, and your clan is still concerned with things like the
snowmelt and if they will have their children before winter. If so, I envy
you.

And I am sorry, but it will not remain that way for long.

The daanaja *has made us into something more than clans. More than*
tulwar. We are proud. We are ferocious. We are many. And the humans
and the shicts will not ignore us any longer. Not me. Not you. Not our clans.

You asked me why I abandoned the Uprising. I want to show you.

Come to me, Thraatu. Bring your clan. Bring all that you can. Let us
stand together, as we never could.

Rise up with us.

—Mototaru Humn Muusa Gon

TWENTY-FOUR

A CIVILIZED GAME

There were, as far as she could tell, three major roadways into the city.

Through the high dunes and bluffs that surrounded the Green Belt, there was only one natural path. But as trade had boomed and Cier'Djaal needed more room for all the coin and suffering it brought, the Djaalics had dug two more large roads through the earth to accommodate.

A good strategy, Qulon thought. More roads meant more trade, more collections, more means of farmers in the Green Belt to take food to the city itself.

In the dim of the evening, a bright red flash bled across the sky. She glanced southward, toward the southern road—one of the man-made ones—just in time to see it crumble.

The air shimmered around the earth, pulling it down in a landslide. Rocks came groaning down, carried by massive piles of sand. More red flashes erupted in the night and, though it took some time, eventually there was nothing more than a bunch of dirt where a road had once been.

She squinted through her one good eye. It was hard to tell this far away, but she could make out figures in brown coats pulling themselves free of the rubble and walking around, waving their hands and moving earth with a few thoughts.

This was the second roadway the wizards had brought down, leaving only the big one in the middle. This also made sense to Qulon. Cier'Djaal was not a defensible city; the defenders' best bet at keeping the approaching tulwar hordes at bay was to meet them at these dunes and force them into one road, funneling their numbers into something manageable. The other roads could be reexcavated later.

Not a bad strategy. Qulon, in her many years, had certainly seen worse. She had seen mighty generals and kings rise and fall, campaigns rust and crumble, and kingdoms conquered and reconquered. It was exciting at first, but somehow it always seemed to end in a bunch of burly people hitting each other with sticks.

For all the tactics and strategies that could be invented by what passed for their greatest minds, the true secret to victory forever eluded mortals. To win was not a matter of resource, or of positioning, or of numbers.

"To win," she muttered, "one must rewrite the rules."

"Huh?"

Qulon glanced over at her companion across the table. The Scarecrow, as she was so aptly called, glanced up from the game board. Boredly, she fiddled with one of the pieces with one hand, the other pressed against her face. A thin trail of drool leaked out the corner of her mouth.

"I said it's your move," Qulon replied, taking a sip of tea. Another pot boiled on a low fire behind the table and chairs she had brought out. Though she wasn't sure why; Scarecrow continued to refuse all drinks that weren't alcoholic.

"Oh. Right." The tall, rangy woman looked at the board with a sneer. She picked up a Red Regent and moved it forward three spaces. "Uh...here."

"What?" Qulon made a clicking sound. "That will leave your entire flank open to my attack."

"Fine. Here." She moved the piece three spaces to the left.

"That will leave your Blue Prophet open. Has it not occurred to you that the winning move might not be to move your Red Regent?"

"I thought you said he was the most important piece."

"He is. If you lose him, you lose the game."

"Well, if he loses the whole fucking game, he can't be that important, can he?" Scarecrow collapsed in her chair. "Why can't we ever play anything *fun*? Like dice or daggers or skull-thwomp."

Qulon raised one eyebrow. "I am unfamiliar."

"It's a game where you take turns kicking someone in the head and the one to make 'im stop movin' is the one that wins." She grinned.

"One time, we had this prick with a big melon for a skull, I kicked him in the head till he was dead! Hah!"

"How is that a game?"

"It was fun."

"Well, Regents is a more strategic game," Qulon replied. "It was crafted by the finest generals at the dawn of the first mortal empires. Time was, no one could be considered even a novice at strategy unless he had spent hundreds of hours playing. Alas..." She thoughtfully fingered one of the pieces. "One wonders how many boards are left in this world, let alone how many players."

"I'm guessin' interest in it died off right around the time they discovered literally anything else." Scarecrow let out a long moan as she slumped backward in her chair. "Why couldn't youa' asked Sandal to do this shit? I'd be better at scoutin', anyway."

"He's not particularly bad," Qulon said, smirking. "And I only require two scouts and one person to keep me company. That latter position is more difficult to fill with someone whose words I can't even understand."

Footsteps on sand. The faint odor of oil and ash. The familiar, unintelligible cursing drew Qulon's eyes down the dune.

"Speak of carrion and the vultures shall converge," she hummed.

Sandal came trudging up the sand, his stout form bent over from weariness. And though his head was obscured by a greasy wrap, it was evident enough by his posture that he was clearly annoyed. Through his wooden visor, he turned his gaze to Qulon.

"Are you not hot in that?" Qulon asked, quirking a brow at Sandal's choice of attire.

"The Candle ain't never gets hot," Scarecrow grunted. "Be one shitty arsonist if he did." She sniffed. "What's the word?"

"*Thf cfth's rfllhfng, lfkh yfh wfnthd,*" the man spoke—possibly—in reply. "*Frmf's mhvfng fht.*"

Qulon sighed. "I have given you so much, Sandal. I pulled you and your friends out of the smoldering ruin that was your gang. I gave you gifts beyond the ken of mortals. I do not feel I'm asking much when I tell you to remove your headwrap when you speak."

"He says the city's rallying," Scarecrow said. "Like you wanted. The *shkainai* united behind the priestess." She scratched her head. "Or...are *we* supposed to call her the Prophet, too?"

"For all intents and purposes, she is. Get used to the idea." She turned to Sandal again. "What of their forces?"

"Bfnch hf scflps, cfhplf hf bfrds, shft thn hf nfthvfs."

"A mess of Karnerians, a few of them winged things the Sainites ride, a lot of Djaalics backing them up," Scarecrow translated.

"I require more than that," Qulon said, glaring. "I must know if the Prophet can put up a decent fight for the tulwar. Give me numbers. Chains of command. Leaders."

"Fhck, lfdh." Sandal shrugged. *"Cfhplf hfndrfd? Twf? Thrff? Dfdn't gft clfsf hnfgh th tfll. Sfw f fhw bfg mfthfrfhckfrs wflkfng frhfnd."*

"He says maybe a few hundred," Scarecrow said. "But the situation's unstable and security's tight. He saw some scary-lookers walking around, though. Guessin' if they've still got big ones walking, the commanders must be on board with the plan. The Prophet's got backup."

"He said all that?"

"Sort of, yeah."

Qulon narrowed her eyes at Sandal. "Now, do not trifle with me, mortal. Given the plan and your abject eye for detail, do you think their armies will be able to hold off the tulwar?"

Sandal let out a muffled, irate sigh.

"Lfdh, hf F wfs gfnna trhflf wfth yhf, F'd dh ft wfth shx bfttlhs hf fil fnd h shfrt fhckfng fhsf." He stomped the earth. *"Hf yhf hfdn't dfnh fs f shlfd, F'd bf fhckfng dfnh wfth yhf rfght nfw."* He made his hand into a fist, thrusting it forward. *"Hfhr thft? Mf hfnd gfnf rfght hp yfhr fss. Mfkh yhf fnth f fhckfng mfht pfppht. Yfh'rf lfcky F'm sfch f fhckfng gfntlhmfn fr flsh?"* He gestured emphatically to his crotch. *"Bfm! Shfw yhf thf fhckfng gfd hf fhrf, gfrl. F'm f sthllfhn fblhzf, bhtch, rfdf mf fnd yhf gft bhrnfd."*

Scarecrow sniffed.

"He says 'yes.'"

Qulon thought to inquire further but opted not to. While she harbored certain doubts about her choice in servants, they had thus far proven capable at what she had enlisted them to do. And while she might second-guess much about them, she would never doubt their loyalty.

Not after what she had given them.

The wind changed just slightly. She felt a foreboding feeling behind her, like the sensation of a great empty space where something should be.

He had returned.

"This is all I have need of you for, for the moment." She sipped her tea, making a dismissive gesture with her free hand. "Be on your way. I will get in touch with you through the usual means if I have more to discuss."

"Fuckin' finally." Scarecrow groaned, knuckling the small of her back as she got out of her chair. She eyed the many bottles and flasks lining Sandal's belt. "If one of those don't have something I can get shitty on, you and me are gonna have problems."

"Bftch, dfn't fct lfkh F dfn't knfw yhf." Sandal pulled one of the bottles free, gave it a slosh, and tossed it to her.

They trudged down the dune, their conversation devolved into slurred murmurs as they passed the bottle back and forth. Qulon waited until they had vanished before speaking.

— ✦ —

"I hadn't expected you back so soon," she said, without looking over her shoulder. She drained her tea and held out her empty cup. "Kindly refill this for me, won't you?"

She began counting breaths. Three passed, this time, before a pale hand took the cup from her. That was better than last time, she thought, but still not as prompt as she desired. She might have remedied that right this moment, had business not pressed further.

Instead, she let the hand place a warm cup of tea back in her hand. She took a long sip and, staring at the game board, spoke.

"Are they moving?"

A voice, distant and fleeting on a wind that wasn't there. "They are."

"All of them, I trust."

"A small force is being left at Jalaang."

"To keep guard?"

"Perhaps."

She felt her eyelid twitch. "I did not ask you to return to me with 'perhaps.'"

A long pause. And then. "My apologies, mistress."

"What else?"

"The old one is attempting to delay their march."

"I trust there is no hesitation?"

"No. The dragonman is mustering them. They'll be at Cier'Djaal soon, in the thousands. More clans are joining them each day, as well." A moment of hesitation. "There might be perhaps more than the humans can withstand."

"You do not appreciate the virtue of my strategy."

"I admired it. The Candle and the Scarecrow performed as you willed and arranged those little 'miracles' for your Prophet."

"They all performed quite admirably, if predictably."

"And now thousands of tulwar march against them."

"Thanks to you."

There was silence for a moment, long and labored.

"The humans have the advantage of terrain, but thousands to hundreds are still poor odds. They'll eventually be overwhelmed."

"Possibly," Qulon said. "Or possibly, they'll pull through by the power of friendship or something equally stupid. There's really no certainty beyond the fact that there must be a winner."

"A winner."

The word was spoken ponderously, with an emptiness between each letter.

"You ever hear of the term *acceptable losses*?"

"It's used primarily by merchants, isn't it?" Qulon sipped her tea. "I have no particular interest in economics."

"You might want to find one. The idea is that there's only so many accidents, so many poor sales that a merchant can take and still do business. After that, it becomes wiser to simply close up shop."

"I take it you've a point there?"

"Torture only works if you give your victim the possibility of returning to a normal life. Take too much from him and he'll simply lie down and die. Same thing with warfare: Victory might come too steep to convince anyone that any good's come of it."

"Typical mortal shortsightedness," Qulon sighed. "You see things in philosophies and ethics that simply aren't there. Life and death is simply a matter of who is more worthy to carry the former and deal the latter. Victory and defeat, no different."

A pause. "Some victories are losses in disguise."

At this, Qulon rose. She turned to face him, the creature wrapped in black rags that clung to him like a shroud. He stared at her through a hood that hid his features entirely. He had a name that she hadn't bothered to learn, so she simply called him the Shadow—for she required him to be nothing else.

"You sound as if you know from experience." She regarded him carefully through one eye. "Anything you'd like to say?"

The Shadow did not offer his answer, but she heard it all the same. Beneath the black wrap and whatever else was below that, she could hear a heart, faint and weak, begin to beat a little stronger. She could hear blood moving a little quicker. She could hear eyeballs rolling in their sockets as they slid across her body and settled on her jugular.

A smile tugged at the left corner of her mouth. Her eyelid twitched just a moment. She curled her index finger tightly into a hook.

And she heard the heartbeat slow, the blood slow, the eyes freeze in their sockets. She felt, as if in her own skin, a throat closing itself shut, limbs going black, a last breath escaping parched lips.

And it came out of the Shadow's mouth with a single, choked word.

"No."

She released her finger. The heartbeat resumed. Breath returned. The Shadow stood straight and tall before her.

Qulon hated to offer these displays of her power—they struck her as just a tad tacky—but she hated ingratitude more. However little the Shadow might appreciate her gifts, she needed him to perform his tasks more than she needed to appear benevolent.

"Good," she said. "I'd hate for us to—"

There was a flash of black. A blade the color of pitch appeared in his hand. Her eye twisted into a scowl. She stiffened her finger, prepared to snuff his dimming light out for good. But then she heard his eyes rolling in their sockets, his gaze drifting over her shoulder.

She smiled, for there were only two people she knew who could appear behind her without a sound—one stood in front of her now, and the other she was very eager to rub the face in something terribly sweet.

Qulon made a gesture to the Shadow. His blade disappeared into his black wrap and he, too, vanished a moment later.

"Mundas." She turned, her smile as broad and cruel as could be perfected over her many years. "I had hoped to see you. But I really wish you had approached in the normal way."

Mundas's face, dark and empty, was twisted into a noncommittal frown as he stared at her.

"You wasted no time, Qulon," he said. "In but a few days, you have managed to do an immense amount of damage to what took us years to craft."

"Impressed?"

His frown sank a little deeper. "I am not." He shook his head. "You will spend countless lives that we could protect."

"Life spent in service to others is no life," she snapped back. "The answer is not to replace deaf gods with more gods. They must find their own path."

"And what good is a path that kills them all?"

"Not all."

"Then how many?"

"As many as it takes."

He shook his head. "I do not understand, Qulon, how we could have drifted so far apart. We all renounced for the same reasons."

"Renouncers cannot define themselves by what they are not, but by what they must become. *I* renounced because I knew mortals must be free of all gods." She thrust a finger at him. "You merely wished to trade one pair of shackles for another."

Through the many years she had known him—and they had been many, indeed—Qulon had seen the dead-faced emptiness of Mundas's expression betray the mortal he had once been only three times: once when he renounced, once when the Renouncers drifted apart, and now.

Now, as a little color returned to his face and as his frown grew slightly more shallow, something old, tired, and very, very sad pulled itself across his face.

"Do not persist in this, Qulon."

"We swore an oath not to interfere with each other directly," Qulon replied, icily. "It is not in your power to command me."

"I do not command. I request. I plead with you to see the folly in your plan. What we have crafted is too strong to be undone by your recklessness. You will purchase nothing but a patch of blood-soaked sand that will be wiped away in time."

She narrowed her eye. "You speak as though you know something I don't, Mundas. You know I dislike secrets."

"I know mortals, Qulon," Mundas replied. "I know them and their fears and their hopes in a way you never shall. They are not animals to eat or be eaten. The more death you foist upon them, the more they shall seek meaning in it."

"And they shall find it," Qulon replied, "in the living. Do not come to me with empty pleas of emptier morals, Mundas. This is how they came to labor under deaf gods to begin with."

He sighed. Sadness drained from his face, replaced by an emptiness unfathomably deep.

"In time, you will see the wisdom of this, Qulon," he said. "When the time comes, I hope you will admire the good we have done."

In all the many years she had known him, Qulon had felt anger at Mundas many times, but only once could she remember feeling such fury as she did now. Shortly before they renounced, she recalled, when he spoke with such sweeping declaration as he did now. Back then, he had pronounced gods impotent. And now, he was declaring them to be the only way forward.

It seemed unfair now, as it did then, that a man so devoid of emotion could sound so smug.

And she was very ready to tell him such when he disappeared, as he always did, right before she could deliver her retort, the image of his sadness still hanging in the air in his wake.

TWENTY-FIVE

Heroism, But for Assholes

So..." Lenk began to speak through a mouthful of pomegranate, but manners caught up to him in time. He held up a finger, chewed, and swallowed. "Sorry about that." He licked red juice from his lips. "So, the tulwar are attacking Cier'Djaal?"

Nezhi quirked a single eyebrow at him. "That's the rumor, anyway," he said. "You understand, I wasn't keen to stick around to find out. I barely got out of Jalaang in time. My contact wanted to haggle on another bushel of pomegranates. If I had lingered to indulge him, I would be dead, too."

"Yeah, good thing you didn't." Lenk took another bite of the fruit and swallowed. "These things are delicious, by the way. I bet they'll sell fantastic." He pointed to the canteen sitting beside the merchant's feet. "Hey, could you—"

"Oh." Nezhi plucked up the flask and handed it across the doused remains of the fire to Lenk. "There you are."

Lenk nodded his appreciation before draining the canteen dry. He would have felt bad about it, but his days in the desert had left him with a powerful thirst and Nezhi had plenty more. Besides, it was only his second.

Men like Nezhi, a Djaalic man blessed with ample supply and generosity, were the sort of people who rekindled one's faith in the divine. It was good luck that Lenk had found the merchant and his two wagons' tracks and followed them, but the fact that Nezhi happened to have carts full of food and water to trade with the villages along the Lyre River seemed more like divine providence.

"So, they seized Jalaang and now they're on the move?" Lenk asked.

"Not when last heard, but it can't be long now," Nezhi said. "I've met refugees who escaped and were heading south to Karnerian-held lands. They said there were even more tulwar gathering in the city. For what other purpose could they be gathering?"

"Probably not a picnic," Lenk muttered.

"Indeed," Nezhi replied. "I have heard only stories, but it's said a demon leads them. A great horned beast, skin like blood, wings that blot out the sun, and a fiery temperament."

Lenk paused midchew. "Come again?"

"A monster," Nezhi said. "It all but killed the Prophet at the gates of Jalaang. But she has since rallied, calling the armies of Cier'Djaal to her."

"Right," Lenk muttered. "The Prophet. Tall girl, brown hair?"

"Mm. A *shkainai*, like yourself. Perhaps you know her?"

"I should have known better," Lenk muttered. "How long ago was it that you heard this?"

"Mere days. Another merchant I passed on the road informed me. He was chasing rumors of war, hoping to make a few coins off people's desperation."

"Shameful."

Nezhi fixed him with a very severe look. "Indeed."

Lenk pointedly looked away as he finished his pomegranate. He sucked his fingers clean, wiping them off on his trousers before extending his hand across the fire to Nezhi. The merchant warily took it, cringing as he did.

"Nezhi, you've been an absolute blessing to us," Lenk said. "You've given us what we desperately needed and more. I can't ever thank you enough." He stood up, taking his naked sword up with him. "And once again, sorry about this whole..."

He gestured toward the merchant's carts, where Kataria was busy rummaging around in his various goods.

"Robbing you...thing." Lenk cleared his throat.

"For the record," Kataria called out, "*I* said we should just kill him."

"We're not savages," Lenk called back.

"You called me a savage last month."

"Not the point." Lenk looked back to Nezhi. "Listen, I mean it. We really wouldn't do this unless we needed it. But we have a long way to go and there's more at stake than just tulwar attacks." He scratched his head. "See, there's this ancient demon and..."

Nezhi's expression betrayed nothing but contempt. Lenk sighed and waved a hand.

"Forget it. Look, we won't take much. Just enough to get to Cier'Djaal quickly: some food, a few canteens of water, and your horse."

"And these arrows," Kataria called out.

"Right." Lenk smiled sheepishly. "She needs arrows."

"This sword's scabbard I found might fit yours," Kataria added.

"No, not..." He paused, looked at his sword thoughtfully. "All right, I'm getting tired of carrying this around, so—"

"This dagger looks real nice, too."

"*No!*" Lenk snapped. "We're not bandits! No dagger!"

"If you get a scabbard, I should get something nice, too!" Kataria snarled back. "It's not like he's going to—"

"*Take it!*" Nezhi threw up his hands. "Take whatever the hell you want! I don't care! Just leave me alone!"

"Right." Lenk rubbed the back of his neck. "Thanks. Listen, we'll send coins back—"

"I won't!" Kataria interjected.

"Please." Nezhi put his hands together, pleading. "Just go. Run to the tulwar and die, run to your demons and die, run into the desert and die. Just let me be."

"Sure. Thanks again." He began to walk away, paused a moment, then looked back. "So, sorry, I'm usually more certain about this, but Cier'Djaal is..."

"That way." Nezhi pointed west. "*Go.*"

Kataria came scurrying over a moment later, thrusting a quiver, a sword, and a sack full of goods at Lenk. He slung them over his shoulder as she spared a grin and a brief bow for Nezhi. She pulled him by the arm around to the carts.

They found Nezhi's beasts—two oxen and a horse—tied to a nearby stone. The horse whinnied nervously as she approached, but a few whispered words and a stroke on the snout calmed it enough for her to untether it and lead it away, Lenk right beside her.

"You heard all that, I hope," Lenk muttered as they wended their way through the dunes.

"Yeah," she grunted. "The bits about the monster, anyway." She glanced at him. "You don't think that's Gariath?"

"Do I think that Gariath would go out and rally a bunch of tulwar for the sole purpose of killing a lot of humans and destroying all their shit?" He cast her a sour glare.

"Point taken," she sighed. "But what about the other part? With the Prophet? You think—"

"I don't know," Lenk said. "Maybe it's Asper, maybe it isn't. I'll count myself fucking lucky if Dreadaeleon isn't involved in this somehow." He rolled his shoulder, readjusting the load on his back. "Either way, it means we're all dead."

Kataria snorted. "I ever tell you how much I missed these little talks?"

"Khoth-Kapira is on his way to Cier'Djaal," Lenk said. "And he's going to find nothing to stop him."

"What *can* stop him?" Kataria asked. "He's a living god, isn't he?"

"He's a demon." Lenk held his sword up and glanced it over. "We've killed demons before." He hefted it over his shoulder. "But if he comes upon two armies tearing the shit out of each other, it becomes a lot harder to do that. So the first thing we need to do is get to Cier'Djaal and..."

He trailed off as soon as he realized Kataria wasn't walking along-side him anymore. He looked back. She stood there, holding the horse's reins, staring at him. Staring through him, past his skin and bones and into some part of him he worked very hard to pretend didn't exist.

She hadn't done that in a long time.

He hadn't thought she'd do that ever again.

"What?" He knew the answer, but he asked, anyway.

"You never thought I was dead." It almost sounded like an accusation coming from her.

"There were times," he said. "Sometimes, late at night, I would fear—"

"You're lying." She spoke as if she could see the falseness wriggling in his throat. "You never thought I was dead, even after I vanished. If you did, you wouldn't have turned that demon loose to try to save me."

He looked away from her and nodded weakly. "Yeah."

And he could still feel her stare, keen as any arrow in his skin.

"Why?"

"Why what?" he asked.

"Why would you do that? What did you think happened to me?"

He had a few answers to that, a few more lies that he had told himself so many times they *almost* sounded true: that she had been killed, that she had plotted to betray him all along, that she had never really cared for him, that he had been an idiot to trust her. He opened his mouth to say one or two of them.

But it felt like she could see each of them, those wriggling lies, crawling up his gullet. And, bceause he was too ashamed to meet that long, hard stare of hers, they slid back down his throat and disappeared into whatever dark place inside a man where lies were born.

"I thought"—he let the words fall out of his mouth and lie on the sand—"that you were gone." He finally looked up at her. "And that I wanted, very badly, for you to come back."

Kataria was a shict. And though he hadn't known many, he knew they weren't a people prone to softness. Their bodies were lean and hard, their ideas rough and flinty. And the frown that creased her face was nothing tender.

"Everyone tries to do things for me," she said. "The world fucking falls apart around my ears and all anyone can seem to think about is what they can do for me." She shook her head. "And every time they try, I lose more of them."

"All I wanted was—"

"I don't care what you wanted," she interrupted. "I care what you want." The horse snorted at her snarl, and she stroked its muzzle, calming it. "If you want to stop this demon, then I'm with you. I'll stand beside you and keep shooting until my quiver is empty and I have to start stabbing. But..."

She looked away. A great silence, like the held breath of a crowd before the executioner's blade falls, grew between them.

"If you're doing this for me, Lenk," she said, "if you're only doing this because you hope I'll be back with you and everything will go back to the way it was." She frowned again, and though it wasn't soft, it hurt to look at. "I don't...I can't..."

She bit her lip, maybe to hold back whatever she was going to say, maybe to hold back something else. He felt a sudden pain in his chest, sharper and keener than all the new aches and old wounds that riddled his body. And he didn't know what to say to that.

But he said it, anyway.

"I know."

She looked at him. "What?"

"I said I know." He sighed. "I don't know what the fuck I was expecting." He looked at the sword in his hand, naked and bare. "I guess I thought...maybe if I just kept fighting, it'd all work out, somehow."

He set down the sack of supplies, pulled out the sword they had taken from Nezhi. He pulled it free from its scabbard—a dull and lifeless thing, virginal steel and no story to its craft—and tossed it away.

"I've been trying to remember the stories my grandfather told me," he said. "I remember parts of them: the sad beginning, the monsters they slew, the happy endings where they got the girl and the treasure." He sighed. "If there were any stories about heroes who don't know what they're doing, he didn't tell them to me."

He slid his sword into the blade's scabbard. It was a snug fit, but a fit, nonetheless. And when he slung it over his shoulder, he could scarcely tell the difference.

"People like us," he said. "I don't think we get happy endings. I think you and I get through this still standing, we call it a win."

"Lenk..." she said.

"After everything," he sighed, "all the fighting and all the blood, all I have left is this." He patted the sword's hilt. "And you." He shook his head. "If I can't get rid of the sword, let me use it to protect you. So long as you come out of this alive, then you can walk away from this, from me, forever. I won't mind, so long as you get to walk away."

Softness didn't look good on her. Softness was made for gentle ladies and women who had more to laugh about than dirty jokes. She was made for hard times: long hunts, arrows in the sky, and bodies on the earth. Softness, like the kind in her eyes as she looked at him, didn't look good on her.

And it damn near killed him to see her look that way.

But she nodded, like he hoped she wouldn't and like he knew she had to. And he nodded, like it didn't kill him to do so.

And she pulled herself onto the horse, then pulled him on behind her. And with a quick kick, they took off at a gallop into the dunes.

TWENTY-SIX

PAPER GLORY

Smart money says they come in the most straightforward way." Dransun tapped the map. "Right through the front door."

He pointed out over the ridge, toward the long road that clove a clear, straight shot through the high hills. At the very edge of the Green Belt's verdant fields and flooded paddies, the green earth gave way to a steep rise of hard-packed earth. Past that, the dust of the endless desert sprawled out forever.

Asper followed his gaze all the way out to the desert. The dunes crested high there, wearing glittering crowns from the hot afternoon sun: the strange mirages that made it look like liquid was forever on the horizon, just out of reach.

If she squinted, she could almost see the thousands of tulwar that would come pouring over the ridge before she knew it.

But then, that was just another mirage.

Or frazzled nerves.

Or the fact that she had barely slept in days.

"If that's the case, then collapsing the other roads would seem a waste." Haethen hummed, jotting something down on her scroll. "All wars end, eventually. When this one does, having more roads to bring in supplies will be key to keeping the city thriving."

Asper spared a glance for her writings—the Karnerian made no effort to conceal her strategies. But with all the notes and diagrams scrawled with such madness that they seemed to make sense only to Haethen, Asper supposed she didn't have to.

A drop of sweat fell into her eye, sending her mopping her brow for what seemed like the four hundredth time. Had Cier'Djaal always been this hot? Or had she simply not noticed before?

The canvas tent that topped their crude watchtower, hastily crafted from salvaged materials by carpenters with heavy debts, didn't do much to shield them from the sun and wind. But it offered them the best possible view of the battlefield to come.

"I still say that was a good call by her," Dransun grunted. He gestured over his shoulder. "The Green Belt's nothing but open fields and Cier'Djaal wasn't built to defend itself to begin with. We hold the tulwar here, or we don't hold them at all."

Haethen let out a low hum. "If the rumors are even half-true, then they outnumber us greatly. We can't let them run wild." She shook her head, sending her bushy black hair trembling. "The wizards reported back today, at any rate. It's done."

She pointed her quill as though it were a spear, aiming directly for the long road cleaving between the hills.

"Between the last phalanx under our command and what the Sainites have to bring, we'll have enough men to hold the tulwar at the road." She drew two arrows on the map scrawled across the table. "We'll funnel their forces into the cliffs, fight them there."

"I'd like it better if we could build more towers," Dransun said. "Pepper them with arrows until they break down."

"If you can find enough materials and craftsmen to build me some in as little time as we have, I will agree." Haethen clicked her tongue. "After which, I will promptly find you medical attention for having pulled all of them out of your ass." She sniffed haughtily. "Pound for pound, a tulwar is stronger and faster than the average man, but all of our research suggests that they fight in loose coalitions and war bands. They'll falter beneath a true unit."

"And what research do you base that on?" Dransun asked.

She regarded him evenly from behind her spectacles. "The research I have accumulated as chief strategist over six campaigns in service to the largest empire to have ever stretched across the land. Shall I continue?"

Dransun opened his mouth to retort but thought better of it, making a yielding gesture toward her.

"Thank you." She tapped the map again. "The Sainites destroyed most of our veteran companies in the war. But we've got a few left to rally the remaining. I have faith that our phalanx can hold in these spaces, with the Sainites providing backup."

"Worse comes to worst, you've got a few thousand angry Djaalics to fight," Dransun offered.

"With all respect to your kinsmen, Captain, if it comes down to untrained civilians with sharp sticks, we'll be considerably beyond 'worse,' no matter how angry they are. Our best hope lies with those trained to fight."

Asper found her gaze drawn to those very people. The camp that had been set up at the base of the cliffs was small—frighteningly so, if she was honest.

On one side, she could see the black-clad form of Careus, stalking back and forth and barking orders. Responding to each command, she could see the last Karnerian phalanx—a tight square of shields, spears, and flesh—practicing combat maneuvers in iron harmony.

On the other, the remaining Sainites were hard at work fletching arrows for their crossbows, loading up fireflasks, tending to the few remaining winged scraws they had. Blacksbarrow stormed between the tents, snarling commands at them and being met with soldiers hurrying to see them completed.

They weren't working together. But they weren't at each other's throats.

Progress, she supposed.

"The scraws will give us an advantage," Haethen said. "But we'd be fools to think that the tulwar don't know about them. We'll use them tactically, striking where we think the enemy is weak. If we can use them to funnel more forces into the cliffs, so much the better."

"Just send 'em in with their fireflasks and burn the whole shitload down."

"Elegant strategy, Captain. It is a surprise you never saw military service." Haethen rolled her eyes. "Fireflasks gutter out if dropped from too high. And we know that the Sainites took a beating from the tulwar at their city. They are our most precious resource. We must use them conservatively."

Asper stared at the road—seemingly so wide, so massive—and tried to play it out in her head. She saw the phalanx. She saw the Sainites. She saw the fight.

And she saw the bodies.

Through all the strategies they had gone through, all the tactics they had proposed and discarded, it always ended the same way in her head. No matter how conservative or reckless they intended to be, it always ended with everyone dead and the tulwar rampaging through.

How could it not, she wondered? How could heaven look upon the fraud she had committed in its name and still take her side? How could she hope that people who had been at each other's throats just days ago could form together to fight off a horde of that size?

How could she beat Gariath when no man, monster, or demon had so much as slowed him down in all the time she had known him?

"This all hinges, of course," Haethen muttered, "on the idea that the tulwar will have nowhere else to go." She quirked a brow at Dransun. "I hate to harp on the subject, but all our lives rest on the idea that there are no other ways into the Green Belt."

"None," Dransun said. "The Green Belt's farmers have tended this land for generations. There's not a path in that they don't know about." He spit on the floor. "With the other two roads blocked, the only way left is Harmony Road."

Haethen paused in her scribbling, eyeing him for a moment. "What did you call it?"

"Harmony Road," he said. "Kind of nice, isn't it?"

"I've been calling it 'the Godsway' in my correspondence," she said. "Our maps have it labeled as such."

"No, that's the old name."

"Well, what was wrong with it? I thought it sounded impressive."

"Yeah, so did every other ruler with a road and a religion. There's, like, forty different Godsways out there." Dransun jerked a thumb toward the road. "The fashas renamed it Harmony Road a generation ago to encourage more foreign traders to come visit. Sort of a 'come be one with everyone in the spirit of trade' thing, you know?" He shrugged. "It just stuck."

She stared at him flatly for a moment. When she returned her quill to her scroll, it was with a decidedly irate thrust and a less-than-thrilled curl of her lips.

"Fine," Haethen said. "I'll just be Haethen Calderus, chief strategist who oversaw the Battle of Harmony fucking Road. That'll look *amazing* in my record."

"Listen," Dransun said. "Before you go getting upset about that, you might consider the fact that you don't have an end in sight."

"Pardon?"

"Hold off the tulwar for as long as you want, they'll keep coming. And then what? We've got no reinforcements coming. No way to repel them for good. If you ask me, our only way out is—"

"The dragonman."

It was the first time Asper had spoken since rolling out of bed after two hours of sleep and demanding a cup of coffee. And she spoke it without tearing her eyes from the road.

"All we need to do is kill him," she said. "And the rest of them will collapse."

"That's a gamble," Dransun said. "No one knows if that will actually—"

"I do," she said.

She could feel their stares boring into the back of her neck. But she heard no words to go with them.

They had questions for her, she knew—Haethen, especially—about her relation to Gariath, about how she knew so much about him. But after a time, they had stopped asking.

It wasn't that she was intentionally being cagey—she wanted the dragonman dead as much as anyone, if it would save lives. But she was never really sure what to tell them. Because she was still never really sure what Gariath was to her. Or maybe she just wasn't sure how it had all come to this, how she had set out with five other people to become an adventurer and had ended up as a fraud of a prophet facing down a monster that had once been her friend.

In the end, she supposed it wasn't important. Most of their questions weren't, really.

"How are you going to kill him, then?"

Except that one.

"I was there, Asp—" Dransun caught himself. "Prophet. I saw what that monster did to you. You barely laid a finger on him, even without him standing behind a wall of tulwar. How are you going to do it now?"

She stared at the road. She pictured those thousand tulwar streaming down it like a black tide with rivulets of steel. She pictured him at its head, tall and proud and his claws wet with her blood. She pictured all the carcasses in his wake.

She closed her eyes.

"Heaven is watching," she said.

Not a great answer, she knew. But fuck, it seemed to solve pretty much everything else these days.

"Right," Dransun grunted. "I'm going to go check the supplies." He spared a nod for Haethen. "Madam." He spared a stiff bow and stiffer look for Asper. "Prophet."

He trudged down the ladder, his footsteps lingering in her ears longer than they should. A warm breeze blew past. Papers fluttered behind her. Haethen muttered something as she shuffled them back to order and continued scribbling notes in them.

The silence was far too deep and not nearly merciful enough to spare her the sound of her own thoughts.

And so she spoke to drown them out.

"Six campaigns," Asper said. "Really?"

"Indeed," Haethen replied, her voice climbing with a bit of pride. "The speaker and I have proudly served the Empire across many southern continental campaigns, including the Bagwai Forays and the withdrawals from Nivoirian-held territories in—"

"How did they end?"

Haethen paused. "With the completion of the objective, of course."

"No, not that. It's…" Asper sighed. "When you say you completed the campaigns, what happened, then? Were the lands you left peaceful?"

A longer, deeper pause. "Not by the common definition, no. Greenshicts continue to launch raids from the Bagwai jungles. We resumed hostilities with the Nivoirians last summer."

"It never ends, does it?" Asper muttered. "Even if we win here, we'll just have bought a few days. Maybe months. We'll have to fight them again, won't we?"

The silence was punctuated every two breaths by a thoughtful tapping of Haethen's quill to her parchment. After ten of these, she quietly rolled her scroll up and approached to stand beside Asper on the watchtower.

"Approximately one century ago," she said softly, "the disgraced Karnerian philosopher Dadalin Manetheres posited that mankind's doom was inevitable as they saw conflict as points on a line. Your neighbor takes your cow, you kill your neighbor, take back your cow, the injustice is corrected and the conflict is over.

"Manetheres, however, claimed that conflict was a wheel that made a full revolution once every generation. You take your cow back, your neighbor's son avenges his cruelly murdered father by killing you, your family retaliates against him, and so on. Conflict, he theorized, was simply a series of responses that does not end without someone agreeing to not respond."

"There's a lot of sense in that," Asper said. "Why was he disgraced?"

"This theory was famously delivered on the steps of the Imperial War College. When he had finished, Speaker Shondean the Second, Most Revered of His Line, calmly walked out of the crowd, approached Manetheres, and hacked off his head. He then asked the headless corpse to respond to his conflict. As headless corpses tend to not do that, Shondean suggested that the theory had some holes in it."

Asper sighed. "Outstanding."

"Regardless, the theory is still taught to Imperial war scholars today," Haethen said. "However, the lesson tends to be that whoever chooses to end the conflict does so one of two ways: either by being dead or by leaving no one alive to say other—"

Haethen's voice trailed off as her eyes narrowed to slits. Asper glanced at her, curious.

"What is it?"

Haethen didn't respond, rushing to the table and seizing a spyglass. She held it up to her eye, peering out far in the distance. Her face twisted into a grimace that softened with a weary sigh.

"Right on schedule," she muttered as she handed the spyglass to Asper.

With a queer look for her companion, Asper plucked up the glass and peered through it. It took a moment to see, but she found it soon enough.

At the farthest dune, two columns of black smoke rose to stain the blue sky. And at the base of it, she could see the scouts she had sent out into the field mount their horses and go galloping away.

The signal fires had been lit.

Gariath's army was on the move.

Two fires.

They would arrive by dawn.

TWENTY-SEVEN

THE TASTE OF PROGRESS

A rat scurried through a pile of refuse, not ten feet away.

There wasn't anything special about it. Maybe it was fatter than the average rat—there was, after all, a lot to feast on in Cier'Djaal's alleys these days. But it had four legs, a long pink tail, a mess of black fur, and a lot of twitching whiskers as it nosed its way through discarded meat and old scraps of paper.

And when Dreadaeleon raised his hand, made a simple gesture, and the rodent was magically pulled into his grasp, it made the panicked squeaking sound of any other rat.

And when he closed his eyes, squeezed his fingers a little tighter around it, and felt a sudden burst of heat...

The squeaking sound was lost in the hiss of steam. The scent of something acrid filled his nose. And he felt his grasp growing tighter as the rodent's body grew smaller, withered, warped.

When the heat dissipated and the hissing ceased, he looked down at the thing that had once been a rodent in his hand. He unclenched his fingers, dropping the blackened, withered branch at his feet to join all the others.

Rats. Roaches. Seagulls. Vermin—or they had once been, at any rate. Now they were all twisted husks, solidified ash that gathered in a small heap around his boots.

But he could feel it.

Blood rushing through his veins. Heart beating strong and steady in his chest. Skin alive and tingling. Breath deep and clean. Muscles taut, bones solid, even his eyes seemed clearer; he could see every maggot crawling through every scrap of decaying meat in every trash pile at twenty feet.

He felt it. The life. The health. The power.

Well, he admitted to himself. *It's not real power. Not yet, anyway. It's not as though rats are a particularly grand source of magic.*

He smiled to himself. He felt red light burst from behind his eyes, his power all but erupting out of him. He extended his hands to the ground and willed the magic out of his fingers. The air rippled, forcing him off the ground. He raised himself off the ground, hovering three feet above it, and laughed.

All so effortless. He hadn't even needed to speak a word. Just a few flicks of his fingers and the power came leaping to his fingers. He felt stronger, more alive than he had when he had first arrived in this decrepit trash heap of a city. His previous weakness felt almost like a dream. He could scarcely recall the numbness creeping into his limbs, the feel of his organs shutting down, the reeking decay coming from within his body.

And he would have called it a dream, had it not been for the sudden pain in his belly that shot through his bowels and brought him back to the earth.

The hunger.

An endless pain inside him, which no food or drink could soothe. A great gaping pit yawning open, into which everything disappeared. A furnace burning so bright he could feel its fire through his skin.

Whatever it was—whatever that woman had given him—he didn't know, no matter how many canny metaphors he could come up with for it. All he knew was what it could do . . . even if he had no idea how.

It's not possible, of course, he told himself, as he had told himself so many times. *Energy merely changes from form to form. It cannot be . . . eradicated, such as it is. What you're doing here, old man, it's not possible. Not by any law of magic.*

He stared at his hands, felt the heat boiling beneath his palms.

But then, he thought, *what good have any laws done for you lately?*

He called the power to him, willed himself to rise from the ground. He flew higher this time, rising above the alley, above the buildings that formed it. There, his coat flapping in the breeze, he surveilled the city.

Had it always been this small, he wondered? Back when they had arrived, what felt like years ago, the city seemed so massive: a hive, teeming with people who, too, seemed so large with their big coin purses and their big talk and their big powers.

Now, though…

Everything looked so empty from up here. The shops, those few that hadn't been savaged by the war between the Karnerians and Sainites, stood darkened. The harbor was empty of ships but for a few pleasure barges and fishing craft. The streets bore so few people, so very tiny.

They can't even look up and see you, old man.

He turned. Looming large over the city, untouched by war or poverty below, the Silken Spire rose high. Its thousands of silks continued to blow in the breeze, its dozens of giant spiders unmoved by the chaos that had ensued in the city they had made rich. They continued to amble lazily across the silk, spinning as they would.

Enough silk to make a city a jewel.

And even that seemed so pitiful.

He stared down at his hands. Faint wisps of steam rose from his fingertips, lost in the breeze. Beneath his palms, he could feel heat rising and flames stoking. He drew in a breath and felt clean air turn to hot smoke inside him. He seethed with power.

Too much power to be wasted on this petty, tiny hole of a city.

So much of your energy, of your time, of your life poured into this pit. He sneered down at them, those tiny creatures who couldn't even behold the marvel looming over them. *Let us be rid of it, old man.*

Just a thought and he was flying. The wind whipped through his hair, his coat flying behind him like great, leathery wings. High above the fires of little men and their little wars, the air tasted clean up here. He smelled the salt of the sea as it stretched out before him.

What lay beyond it, he wondered? Perhaps now he could finally find out. With this power coursing through him, the gift she had given him, he could do anything. Even flying felt effortless.

He could do it forever.

And he just might have, had the air before him not suddenly turned pitch-black.

A man?

A shadow?

Dreadaeleon would have called it someone's laundry, flown off the line and flying high in the breeze, had it not appeared right before him. He came to an abrupt halt as it hung in the air before him and, from beneath a dark hood, regarded him with a canted head.

"Nice day, isn't it?"

His voice came hollow and fleeting.

His knife, less so.

Dreadaeleon barely managed to twist out of the way as the blade came flashing out from nowhere. The blow missed his throat but caught his cheek, casting his hot blood out on the wind.

He cried out.

It hurt.

How could it still hurt? With this power?

He roared, the power flying from his head to his hands. He hurled his hands out, letting loose a torrent of fire that swallowed the clean air and churned out columns of black smoke.

But the shadow was already gone.

Dreadaeleon snarled, whirling about in the air, searching for his foe through red-tinged vision.

He did not search long before the blade came flying toward him.

Unerringly true, it missed his heart only by a word of power and a flash of his hand. The blade struck rippling air, went spinning into the wind. Dreadaeleon scowled down, toward the roof of a nearby building.

The shadow looked up, raised a hand, and offered a dainty wave.

And, with a howl, Dreadaeleon flew after him.

The shadow vanished in the blink of an eye and reappeared on another roof. Dreadaeleon spun, turned, pursued. His foe disappeared again, emerging on another roof and again, Dreadaeleon altered his course. Across two more roofs, on the streets, through the alleys, he pursued his foe at speeds unheard-of for any wizard, yet the shadow was always ahead of him, stepping in and out of sight.

Dreadaeleon didn't care.

He didn't care that such magic as this was impossible. He didn't care about the power he burned to keep up his pursuit. He didn't care about where the shadow was leading him.

All he cared about was that it still hurt.

After all this power, after being given this gift, people as small and weak and petty as this... this *coward* could still hurt him.

No more, old man, he told himself. *No fucking more.*

He chased, twisting and turning through the alleys and the streets, fire on his hands and the wind at his back and a scream in his throat.

The shadow appeared before him at the mouth of an alley, closer now. So close, he could almost reach out and...

He roared, hands aflame as they thrust out and sought his foe. His fingers barely brushed against the black cloth, drawing the tiniest whisper of smoke, before the shadow vanished.

Dreadaeleon's feet struck the street, skidding to a halt. He whirled around, eyes alight and smoke churning from his hands as he searched for the shadow.

There.

A flitter of movement at the end of the street, a darkness disappearing around a corner. He snarled, stalking forward, pouring everything into the fires in his hands. He rounded the corner and raised his hand, his vision clouded by the power pouring out of his eyes.

The word of power was halfway out of his mouth when he noticed the child.

The fire on his fingers sputtered out. The crimson faded from his eyes. The word died on his lips, along with every other word he might have had for what he saw.

A child, appearing no older than seven, hauling a large bucket full of scraps of wood and nails. She was thin, though she had once been well fed. Her clothes were once nice, now worn and tattered. But if either of these bothered her, she didn't seem to notice as she pulled her burden toward the center of a square.

A square he remembered, once, from very long ago.

It had looked different back then. There had been neatly trimmed bushes around, where there were now squares of dirt. The scent of perfume riding on vents of steam had risen from high and narrow windows, instead of the reek of cooking fires and tar. The people here had been clad in finery and walked with high and noble bearings. Now many people, all of them wearing a shared expression of desperation, milled around the cobblestones toting hammers, saws, and lumber.

But the sign was still there. He remembered it clearly.

Emblazoned across the biggest building at the end of the square was a sleek black cat, curled up with its eyes half-closed in slumber.

"The Sleeping Cat," he whispered. And then, unbidden like a bad dream. "Liaja..."

That was her bathhouse, the one where she worked—he could see from here the window to her room. The same window he had stared out of in those dreamless mornings, watching the sunlight seep in and slide across her naked body tangled in the silken sheets.

He didn't remember the boards over it, though.

Nor did he remember chains across the door. Nor spikes jutting from the front porch. Nor the courtesans—once lovely and fragile and painted—hammering barricades into place beneath the windows, their robes tattered and their once-elegant hairstyles drooping with sweat.

And not just courtesans. There were merchants there, putting more boards over the windows. There were children there, hauling sheafs of arrows and bows into the bathhouse. There were elders, counting potatoes and cooking chickens on makeshift fire pits. There were...

"Liaja."

There. On the roof, with three other women hammering stakes into the eaves. She was thinner than he remembered, her paint replaced by sweat and grime, her hair in ropy, unwashed strands. But that was her.

His empress.

His courtesan.

The woman who called him *northern boy* in such a way that he forgot it wasn't his real name.

It was her.

"Liaja," he said. He stepped forward, hand raised. *"Liaja!"*

"You're not really going to do this to her again, are you?"

He whirled about at the sound of the hollow voice. The shadow was there, sitting on a barrel with more casual haughtiness than a man wrapped in a heap of filthy black rags ought to be capable of.

"You!"

Dreadaeleon roared. The power rushed to his palm. He thrust it out toward the shadow, let the flames burst from his hand. They stoked to a great blaze as he spoke a word of power and—

He let out a cry. A sharp pain opened in his belly. The fire died on his fingers as the word died on his lips. He bent over, clutching his stomach and drawing in a sour breath. He fought to keep off his knees, to keep his eyes on his foe, expecting a dagger in his neck at any moment.

But the shadow merely stared at him from behind his black hood, unmoving but for a simple cant of his head.

"Takes a toll, doesn't it?" he asked. "She didn't tell me about the finer points of the power you were given, but it seems even Amoch-Tethr had limits to what she could do."

Dreadaeleon raised his hand, as if to strike. The shadow raised one in return, though with far less urgency.

"Calm down, boy. I'm not here to fight."

Dreadaeleon mustered the energy for a sneer. "I find that hard to believe."

"Reasonable." The shadow inclined his head. "But I've had ample opportunity to kill you by now and haven't. And it's not as though this is the strangest thing to happen to you even this month."

Dreadaeleon paused. "Reasonable." He narrowed his eyes. "So what the fuck are you talking about?"

"Yes, yes, you're very forceful with your bad language and your labored breathing." The shadow made a gesture. "Calm down. Give yourself a moment. Take a few breaths." He glanced over toward the square. "But make them shallow, hm? I don't think our presence here would make things easier for them."

Dreadaeleon wanted to snarl, to curse, to spit—he managed that last part, at least, while he continued to draw in sour, stale breaths. The great pain inside him let out a soundless moan, a gaping plea to be fed. He fought that pain down for a moment as he looked out toward the square and its construction.

"What are they doing?" he asked.

"Building," the shadow replied. "Fortifying, I suppose you could call it." He pointed to The Sleeping Cat. "Back before bathhouses were legal, the various proprietors of whores would make their places of business sturdy, in case a rival broker would attack. Makes them ideal places of defense."

"Defense," Dreadaeleon gasped, "against what?"

"Haven't you heard?" The shadow chuckled. "Cier'Djaal's about to be burned to the ground." He pointed high over the rooftops, toward the east. "An army of tulwar, a red-skinned demon at their head, is marching against the City of Silk, murder in his eyes and a torch in his hand. Of course, the brave Prophet stands against him, but with a fraction of his numbers, what can she truly do?"

"What?" Dreadaeleon asked. "What does that have to do with anything?"

"These people…" The shadow pointed to the square. "They grew up hearing the same stories that we all did. They know that the ones to survive this battle will be the heroes, the lovers, the brave, and the determined. Common folk like them? The whores, the mongers, the families?" He shook his head. "There's no story for them. They get to look out for themselves."

"So they're digging in," Dreadaeleon muttered, "building a bunker."

"Something like that. The guards can't protect them. The fashas have holed up in Silktown behind their dragonmen. The only thing between the tulwar and them will be however much wood they can put up. Of course, it might not be much. But the ships have left and the tulwar are coming. They've got no other choice."

Dreadaeleon watched her there for a moment, atop the roof. Liaja hadn't noticed him yet. She hadn't even looked in his direction. Her eyes were fixed on her task, her every thought plain on her face: escape, defend, survive.

"You tricked me into chasing you," Dreadaeleon muttered. "Because you wanted me to see this."

"I did," the shadow said.

Dreadaeleon fingered the cut on his cheek, glared at the shadow. "You could have just asked, you know."

"Given what we know about you, wizard, I am almost certain that I couldn't. To get the attention of a man of your talents requires something even more forthright."

He's got you there, old man, he admitted. *What was it you called them? Petty? Small? Weak? You wouldn't have listened to them, would you?* He glanced at the shadow. *Granted, not all of them can do… whatever it is this shithead does. But still…*

He looked out toward the square again, to the people there. They still looked small to him. They still looked weak. But he saw something else in the desperation across their faces and the fear in their movements. Something perhaps not quite so petty, perhaps not quite so weak.

"They need you."

The shadow's voice again, no longer quite so far away. The creature in black had appeared beside him, staring out at the square with him.

"They need someone to protect them," he said.

"Isn't that what they have Asper for?" A note of bitterness crawled into Dreadaeleon's voice. "Their Prophet?"

"Their Prophet will one day sing their glories when she seeks to atone for her failure to save them. I'm sure their deaths will be excellent motivation for her. But, inconveniently, they'd rather live."

"And what do you expect me to do about that?"

"Expect? Me?" The shadow chuckled. "What expectations could I heap upon a man who can fly? I would, instead, implore you to consider what you *can* do for them."

He leaned closer, his whisper like ash on the wind.

"I know what power she gave you, wizard," the shadow said. "I know who died to make you whole."

Dreadaeleon's eyes widened involuntarily. The memory came flooding back to him. The Librarians, lying still and broken upon the floor, barely alive. He could still feel his hands burning, their skin parting as his fingers sank into their flesh with plumes of steam. He could smell the smoke as he broke them down in his hands: flesh to water, water to steam, steam to light. He could feel the strength returning to him, fresh and alive, as he breathed their light in, as he drank them as though they were water.

He could still see the fear etched on their faces...

"Don't presume to threaten me..." Dreadaeleon growled.

"If I can't expect anything of you, I can't expect to threaten you, either," the shadow replied, backing away. "But I can tell you that you alone have a power that can save them. Greater than faith, greater than steel, greater than anything is what you hold inside you, what you can do."

"And why would I want to save them?"

The shadow looked at him for a good, long moment.

"Are you not capable of it?"

Dreadaeleon stared at them. For a much longer moment.

He could see their faces from here: their fears and their desperations and their hungers worn like masks that they didn't dare take off, or couldn't. And they still hadn't even noticed him. They hammered wood, sharpened stakes, cooked chickens like there was nothing else more important than that.

He could destroy it all with a wave of his hand, if he wanted to. Their wood would be turned to ash. He would tear off their doors with lightning. A mere breath of frost would extinguish their fires forever. He could kill them. All of them. With this power inside him, he could turn them all to blackened husks, like so many dead rats.

That thought should have revolted him.

But for some reason, it did not.

This was why they hadn't looked up at him. They probably couldn't even look up anymore. Their entire lives, small and petty though they might be, were in the wood and the chains and the fires. They had nothing else.

Asper could not save them; she was weak, stupid, treacherous.

Gariath would not spare them; he was little more than an animal that had learned how to talk.

But he could. Just as easily as he could take their lives away, he could save them.

He could save her.

And when they finally had enough room to breathe the clean air, when they finally looked up, they would see him. They would finally see him for what he was.

"I am capable," he whispered.

"Capable might not be enough," the shadow replied.

Dreadaeleon turned to him. Red light danced behind his eyes.

"I am invincible."

The shadow inclined his head. "Of course, the Venarium might disagree."

Dreadaeleon's eyes narrowed to thin, burning slits. "The Venarium are nothing. Bookkeepers fussing over their ancient tomes. Pointless. Obsolete."

"Treacherous," the shadow replied. "But, if you think that a few hundred Venarium who were wholly expecting you to be dead and out of the way by now *won't* have a problem with you expending such power to save these people, by all means, ignore them."

A point.

This shadow—whatever he was—was irritatingly full of them. Who was to say Shinka wouldn't go back on her word to not pursue him once they felt capable of doing so? After all, she was already planning on betraying Asper once the priestess served her purpose.

Asper... His lips set into a bitter frown at the memory of her. *As though she would even appreciate you for doing this. As though she would ever think you a hero for doing so.* His fingers tensed. *But if she were to look up*... *to see you over the city, so high above*...

What would she think, then, old man?

Dreadaeleon turned and fixed a glare on the shadow. "Why are you doing this?"

"Is it too hard to believe that I'm a concerned citizen?"

"Concerned citizens don't vanish and reappear like a bad thought. *Nobody* does that."

"Reasonable." The shadow nodded. "I suppose, then, that telling you I am simply acting on behalf of an interested party who has interest in this city remaining safe and has little faith in gods would convince you of my virtue?"

Dreadaeleon's glare did not budge.

"Fine," the shadow sighed. "Whatever our plans might be, it's not as though you simply couldn't incinerate me with a thought once you've got enough power."

At this, Dreadaeleon drew in a breath. He called magic to his hands and thrust them at the street. He rose from the earth, hovering over the shadow and looking down upon him. He inclined his head and grunted.

"Reasonable."

And with that, he spoke a word, hauled himself into the sky, and was gone.

TWENTY-EIGHT

THE RATIONALITY OF VIOLENCE

Gariath quirked an eye ridge and snorted.

"Nak Chamba?"

The tulwar standing before him flashed a grin that was too heinous to be called crooked—gashed, maybe. Naked to the waist, his body littered with scars and the hair on his arms fallen out in patches, he was clad in simple breeches and sandals. A long bandanna was coiled around his head, covering a gaping hole where once an eye had been. The colors on his face had long since faded, and his teeth were worn down.

While he was old, Yuku Humn Nak Chamba was not the sort of creature Gariath would have thought of as a warrior, let alone a leader. But from the way the hundred-odd tulwar behind him knelt in respect, it was hard to deny his authority.

"At your service, *daanaja*," Yuku grunted.

Gariath's nostrils quivered—this tulwar, and all his clan, stank of dirt and death, along with the customary tulwar scent of anger.

He glanced to his side. Mototaru glanced back, shrugged.

"The Nak Chamba are from the north," the old tulwar said. "Mountain clan. Good archers, last I heard." He looked back to Yuku and scratched his chin. "Of course, last I heard, the humans had pushed them off the edge of the map."

"We are all that remain," Yuku replied, gesturing to his clan behind him. "We claw out a living in the far reaches of the Akavali ranges. Yet even as far as we are, word reached us of the great *daanaja*." He fired off a bow toward Gariath. "We heard the stories. Is it true you took Jalaang?"

Gariath stared at him flatly. "If it wasn't, would we be marching from it, moron?"

He stepped back and gestured to the edge of the dune he stood on, and to the river of fire below.

Their thousands-strong lights painted their faces. The hammering beat of drums drove them forward. The thunder of their feet sent them ever onward down the road toward their distant target.

Tulwar.

Of many clans, of many Tuls, of many families. With swords, with bows, with shields. Their faces colored by the reds and yellows and blues that flooded into their scowls.

Tulwar.

Pouring from Jalaang, torches and blades held high, warding off darkness as the sun set over the desert. First as columns, then as packs, and finally as a tide, seeping inevitably forward toward Cier'Djaal.

Tulwar.

Below, one of the warriors looked up and saw him standing high on the ridge. He raised his sword toward Gariath and let loose a roar.

"Rise up!"

Thousands of blades rose in response. Thousands of howls took up the cry, shook the smoke-stained sky.

"RISE UP!"

An army.

His army.

And this dirty vagrant, this Nak Chamba, wanted to join it.

"We are few in number," Yuku growled, "but we are strong. Our arrows are sharp. Our eyes are keen. Let us fight for you, *daanaja*. Let us fight for the clans."

Gariath glanced toward Mototaru. The old tulwar glanced back and made a stiff, short nod.

The dragonman sighed and looked back at the kneeling tulwar. He supposed that once, he would have seen morons: weak, idiot monkeys who didn't know what fighting was. Or perhaps he would have seen warriors, eager to fight and to kill and to win for him.

These days, though, he mostly just saw bodies waiting for graves.

"Sure," he grunted. "Whatever." He waved a hand. "Head to the front of the line, find a man named Daaru Saan Rua Tong. Give him that stupid speech of yours and see if he can't find a place for you."

"At once, *daanaja*!" Yuku turned toward his clan and rose his fist into the air. *"Nak Chamba!"*

"Nak Chamba!" the tulwar roared back, rising to their feet and raising their bows. *"Rise up! Rise up! Rise—"*

"Enough of that shit," Gariath snarled, loud enough to cut them all off. "To the front. Tell Daaru you can yell loud, too."

With a few grunts, Yuku had his clan moving. They hurried off, cheering and hooting, as they slid down the dune and rushed to the front. Gariath was glad to see them go, if only to get their stink out of his snout. Though there wasn't much reprieve to be had, with the reek of steel and smoke everywhere.

"That was a good decision." Mototaru packed his pipe with fresh tobacco and lit it.

"I just wanted them to shut up," Gariath muttered. "If you had told me how much tulwar yell, I wouldn't have bothered with any of this shit."

"I mean accepting them into your army," the old tulwar said. "If word has spread to the Nak Chamba, then it'll have spread to many other clans, as well."

"Word of a fight spreads quick."

"Word of a victory spreads quicker. Win this, you'll have even more warriors answering you."

Gariath snorted. "More yelling."

"More people."

"More fights."

"More tulwar."

"More deaths."

"That is also true." Mototaru puffed on his pipe and shrugged. "Ah, well. Maybe we'll all be massacred and you can be spared the trouble. Think positive, hm?"

Gariath folded his arms and stared out over the river of tulwar. "They're moving quickly."

"They're ready," Mototaru said. "Delaying was wise. They're hungry for battle. We'll march through the night, reach Cier'Djaal by morning, as expected." He exhaled a cloud of smoke. "It'd be wiser if you let them sleep, though. Wait one more day."

"No," Gariath growled. "I've had enough waiting, enough thinking." He drew in a deep breath and swallowed the stink of smoke, of weapon oil, of body odor. "Every moment we're on this road is another moment to—"

He paused.

His nostrils quivered. Through the many base reeks and seething stink of anger, he caught something. Faint, barely there, and fading with every breath. He would have called it nothing and thought nothing of it, if it hadn't smelled exactly like...

"Where are you going?"

He ignored Mototaru's question as he trudged off down the dune. Just as he ignored Mototaru's shout as he stalked away.

"All right, then," the old tulwar called after him. "I'll just be over here. You know, leading *your* army while you stalk off without a word and disappear on the eve of battle. While I'm at it, I'll compose a song about your leadership! What rhymes with *goatfucker*?"

Gariath didn't hear.

Just like he didn't hear the hundreds of roars and blades raised in his wake as he passed through the river of tulwar and emerged on the other side. Sounds were fleeting things—here and gone in an instant—but scent persisted. And the scent he chased now, the faint reek that seemed to grow no stronger even as he followed it up the hill on the other side of the road, was impossible to ignore.

Rainwater and mud caked on boots. Blood on metal and salt on skin. Never by itself, always hidden beneath common scents. He never gave it a name.

But he knew it by the memories that came with it. He smelled it when he emerged from a dark cave and stung his eyes with sunlight. He smelled it when he first extended a hand to a human without the intent of ripping something off. He smelled it when he held two small, still, breathless bodies in his arms and could do nothing for them.

And he smelled it now as he came upon a large rock, where a short, scrawny thing in dirty clothes and wearing a sword on its back looked at him from beneath a mop of silver hair and grinned.

"Hey," Lenk said.

Gariath simply stared for a moment.

This human, too, seemed a hazy and insubstantial thing, like his scent. Gariath barely recognized him—thinner than he was before, dirtier, carrying a few more wounds, and his scars stretched a little longer.

Gariath could hardly remember the last time he had seen him. How long ago had it been? Weeks? Months? The night it happened, he remembered him looking much as he always had: rigid if short, relentless if weak, fierce and always ready to fight, no matter how badly he would lose.

And he had lost badly. Gariath could still remember the sound of his jaw cracking beneath his fist, if nothing else.

This human—this creature—wasn't the strong warrior he remembered. This human wasn't the only one whose name he spoke. And so, for a long time, he said nothing.

But not too long.

"You're not dead," he observed.

"Yeah." Lenk rubbed the back of his neck. "Not so far, anyway. It was close a few times, though." His grin grew a little wider. "I could have used you around."

"You would still have failed," Gariath growled. "No one uses me."

"No, it was just a figure of speech."

"You failed at that, too."

Lenk regarded him carefully for a moment. "I've missed you, Gariath."

Gariath met his eyes before glancing around. "How did my scouts miss you?"

"Your scouts, huh?" Lenk looked long over the dunes, toward the rising sound of drums. "That whole . . . thing belongs to you, then?"

"You sound surprised."

"I do. But I shouldn't." He sighed. "You always said you were going to kill a lot of humans before." He made a gesture to himself. "Well, I'm not running. If you want to start with me, go ahead."

It wouldn't be hard, Gariath knew—it wouldn't be long until one of the tulwar discovered Lenk and then a hundred more did. Or, hell, he could just rip the human apart himself—it looked like it would be even easier than it had been before. And it wasn't like a lot of humans *weren't* about to die.

What was one more?

But Gariath did nothing.

"How did you hide from my scouts?"

"Kat dropped me off a few hours ago," Lenk replied. He pointed off toward Cier'Djaal. "I figured, since this is *your* army, everyone under your command would be pretty eager to get into combat. I just waited out of sight until your scouts got bored and left for the front. Then I came out here and waited for you to show."

"And what made you think I would?"

Lenk shrugged. "We six have always had a way of finding each other, haven't we? I guessed things hadn't changed that much." He stared out over Gariath's army and frowned. "But I've been wrong before."

The dragonman stared at him, this scrawny creature that he had once known. His nostrils quivered, drawing in the faint scent of rain and dry earth. Still so faint, still so fleeting, still so weak.

"We have rear guard scouts, too." Gariath turned away and began to head back toward his army. "They'll be here, soon. If you're stupid as you look, you'll stay."

He had taken perhaps five steps before Lenk proved that, in fact, he was more stupid.

"So how many of them are you planning on killing?" Lenk called after him.

Gariath paused. "Many."

"They aren't all fighters, you know. The city's full of merchants, civilians...children."

Gariath simply began walking again.

"What'd she do?" Lenk asked. "What could she have possibly done to make you do this?"

At that, he stopped.

"What, was it something she said?" the human asked. "Something she did? Or was it...was it us?"

Gariath's hands curled into fists.

"I remember the last night I saw you," Lenk said. "It didn't end well.

I just wanted a new life so badly. If that's what all led to this, I'm sorry and—"

"How is it," Gariath growled, "that things as small as you always think that you're bigger than the world?"

"What?"

"She did nothing." Gariath cast a glare over his shoulder. "There was nothing she *could* do." He whirled on Lenk, teeth bared. "That *any* of you could do. I didn't leave because of you. I didn't find the tulwar because of you. I didn't *survive* because of you." He snarled. "You are small. Weak. Stupid. This is not about you. It never was."

Lenk hopped off the rock and stepped forward. He was short, always had been, but he strode toward Gariath with all the confidence of a man who was *not* about to be pounded into the earth like a stake.

"Oxshit," Lenk spit. "I've fought with you. I've bled with you. I've killed with you. You might have spit out curses the entire time, called me stupid with every breath you could spare, but you stayed. Through all of it, you stayed. And then you left."

"I left," Gariath replied, "because I killed *for* you. I defended you when you were too weak to do it. I saved you when you were too stupid to live. Every drop of blood I spilled and every bone I broke for you, for them, and you all wanted gold."

"We did." Lenk shook his head. "I did. I wanted to stop killing. I wanted . . ." He held his hands out and sighed. "For fuck's sake, Gariath, we've been fighting and killing since we met. Didn't you want it to stop, too?"

Gariath didn't answer.

He had never considered it, really. To humans, he supposed, fighting was something exciting. It sent them coursing with fear, with anger, made them cling to a life that was fast slipping out of their hands with every breath.

To him, fighting was just something he did.

He fought. He won. He survived. And they survived because of him. So long as he kept killing, they lived.

It was simple. It was perfect. Or it had been.

"Gariath, listen," Lenk said. He reached out, as if to touch the dragonman's shoulder, but stopped. "I didn't come here to try to guilt you.

Whatever happened, it doesn't matter. It's what's going to happen that matters. I need you to stop your attack and get ready for—"

Gariath didn't hear the rest of it. He was already turning and walking away.

"Hey! *Hey!*"

Lenk came rushing forward, running in front of him and holding out his hands, as though that would stop Gariath from trampling him outright. Gariath couldn't say why he did stop.

Maybe he was feeling nostalgic that day.

"Listen to me, Gariath!" Lenk said. "It's a long-as-hell story and I'll tell you all about it, I swear, but something's coming. A demon's been unleashed. Khoth-Kapira—you remember, we fought his Disciple in the Souk—is coming to Cier'Djaal. He's coming and he's going to kill—"

Gariath placed a hand on Lenk's shoulder.

Gariath shoved.

Gariath did not remember Lenk flying quite so far the last time he shoved him.

"I *am* tired of it," Gariath said. "I was tired of it when I first met you. I was tired of it when I lost my sons. But it was always easy for me...killing. So if it kept small and weak creatures like you alive, I could do it."

He stared out over the road as the river of tulwar began to thin out, converging farther down as they marched toward their target.

"Gariath, you have to believe me, there's a demon—"

"I believe you," Gariath replied calmly. "But there have always been demons. Or monsters. Or other humans. Whatever needed killing, I killed it. We killed it. And there was always more to kill." He close his eyes. "There will always be demons.

"It doesn't stop. Not for me. Not for you. Maybe the others get to die better—the small one will burn himself alive, the tall female will die on her sword, the rat will drink himself to death. But you and I, we fight until we die. All we do is try to find a good time to do it."

He started walking after the tulwar.

His tulwar.

"I have found mine."

As he walked away, that faint scent persisted, but only barely. It was overwhelmed by baser reeks—fear, anger, the usual cloying odors that followed weak creatures.

They came out of Lenk in great clouds as the human got to his feet, chased after the dragonman, waved his arms in a futile plea. He was screaming something—many things, really, about demons and war and apocalypses. Gariath had no reason to disbelieve them, any of them. He had seen enough strange things to know that Lenk had seen more.

But it didn't matter.

In another few steps, he didn't hear anything. And the faint scent disappeared completely.

TWENTY-NINE

A Last Long Walk

It was said that of all the gifts he gave mortals, the most important thing Talanas ever bestowed upon the world was mercy.

Among the other colder, crueler gods, the Healer alone bore traits shared with the mortals he loved and protected. There were endless hymns and scrolls devoted to describing his capacity for compassion, for sorrow, for joy and for fear.

There were no hymns that suggested he was a passive aggressive asshole who enjoyed watching people's plans fall apart, of course.

But Asper was getting ready to write one.

"FUCK."

And that was going to be a word frequently used in it.

"Fucking fucker and her piece of fucking fucker *fuck*!"

She spit her curses into the air. And when she could think of no better curses, she simply shrieked into the night sky. With a snarl, she hurled the scroll in her hand toward the railing of the watchtower with the intent of throwing it out. It was simply cruel luck—or maybe more of the gods' petty humor—that it struck the railing and bounced back onto the tower's deck again.

It infuriated her that she could still hear the sound of Haethen's steps, perfectly measured and calm as the Karnerian walked over to the fallen scroll, gingerly plucked it up, and unfurled it.

" 'To the attention of the False Prophet,' " she read aloud. "Ah. I can tell this will be interesting. 'In protest of recent blasphemies, the fashas decline to send aid to your movement. While the tulwar form a considerable threat, it would be an utter betrayal of all that this city holds dear to expend wealth that could be better used to—' "

"No dragonmen," Asper interrupted. "They aren't sending any fucking dragonmen. Even a half dozen of them could hold this entire fucking line for a week and they won't send a single piece-of-shit reptile."

"It's signed by the 'Council of Concerned Fashas.'" Haethen hummed. "I didn't know there was a council, let alone that they were concerned."

"There isn't. It's Teneir. That fucking bitch has called back her dragonmen into Silktown to wait this out. I expected her to be treacherous, not brazen." Asper rubbed her face. "Does she not see that we're fighting to defend the *entire* city with her in it?"

"I would say she sees exactly that. When your forces are exhausted, she'll try to use her dragonmen to clean up the tulwar and claim victory. Folly, of course. There will be no containing the enemy should they breach Harmony Road."

"We were counting on those dragonmen," Asper said. "They and the Venarium were going to be our turning point. But I haven't heard shit from Lector Shinka, either. I've sent a dozen runners to their stupid tower and she won't give me a single fucking word in reply beyond assurances that she supports me."

"Her wizards *did* bury the roads for you," Haethen replied. She unfurled a scroll and began writing something down. "Still, the thought is alarming. Our allies' continued silence suggests that there is more behind their support than we know."

"And?"

"And it would be folly to press them on it," the Karnerian added. "Half of strategy is diplomacy, and wizards conform to no etiquette I am familiar with. They could be unreliable allies or very reliable enemies, depending on your words." She sniffed. "Also, you should try to curse less. It's unbecoming of a Prophet."

"Noted." Asper sighed. "Now I have to watch my back around a conniving woman who shits coin and a conniving woman who shits fire. Fucking wonderful."

"Language."

"And how are you so calm about this?" Asper demanded. "No wizards, no dragonmen, a handful of soldiers, and a few scraws to fight off thousands of blood-hungry tulwar."

"A handful of soldiers, a few scraws, and an extremely talented

Foescribe of six campaigns." Haethen rolled up her scroll, tied it off, then took another one, unfurled it, and began writing something else. "I have overseen many defenses, assaults, and supply trains. I am very aware of what I am doing, Prophet."

"I don't doubt your skills," Asper said, frowning. "But I don't doubt what we're up against, either. Gariath's a monster. And he's at the head of thousands of monsters. Even if we had the best warriors in the world, we could all still die horribly."

"I am aware of that, too."

"Then how—"

"Because it is my duty, Prophet." At this, Haethen finally looked up. Her face was firm, the wrinkles exaggerated by recent long, sleepless nights evident in her dark skin. "I swore an oath to the Arda Scriptis, to the emperor, and to Daeon to serve as I must in the capacity I am best suited for. As you have sworn an oath to all who follow you to defend them."

She held Asper's eyes for just a moment longer before returning to her scroll.

"I suggest we both fulfill them."

Asper could do little more than offer a nod before she stepped away from the table, leaving Haethen to her scrolls as she left the watchtower.

The Karnerian was correct, of course—frustratingly so, sometimes. Trying to coerce a wizard into service would have been futile, even in a best-case scenario. After all, she had tried that before.

She paused at the bottom of the watchtower as she realized that, wherever it had gotten her, she wasn't quite sure where she was anymore.

How had it come to the point where she was fighting people she had once called her friends? How had it come to the point that it wasn't just five people, but thousands who were relying on her? How had she gone from a healer to a war leader?

How did it all go so wrong?

She shook her head.

Stop that, she thought, scolding herself. *However it happened, it happened. There'll be time to wonder how when Gariath is dead. Or when you are.* She looked long to Harmony Road, to the forces mustering below. *In the meantime, no sense in making it easy for him.*

A quick trudge down the hill took her to the camps below. The

Karnerians knelt in a perfect square, their helmets doffed and heads bowed toward Careus, who stood in full armor at their head, his voice carrying through the night sky like a gale wind.

"There is no fate but what the Conqueror wills," he bellowed. "There is no cause but what the Conqueror demands. There is no master of man but what he can claim. So says the emperor."

"*So says the emperor*," the Karnerians replied in perfect harmony.

"Let no savage shake you," the speaker continued. "Let no pagan taint you. Let no weak mind, no weak body, no weak spirit infect you. So says the emperor."

"*So says the emperor.*"

"For us, there is no defeat. For us, there is no end. The battle is unending. The conquest is forever. Karneria is eternal."

He caught Asper's look as she walked by. His jaw set. He offered her a nod. And, his voice soft and reverent as a man of his volume could make it, he spoke.

"And heaven is watching."

"*Heaven is watching*," the Karnerians echoed.

She offered Careus a nod of her own before stepping across the road and heading toward the camp on the opposite side.

The Karnerian Empire was, according to some, the birthplace of both warfare and opera. She found it easier to believe after seeing their preparations. Daeon was, after all, a god of war. It made sense that the Karnerians would treat the eve of battle with the reverence and quiet dignity of any religious holiday.

As she approached the Sainite camp across the road, and the sound of a lilting song rose up, she wondered what sort of prayers the Sainites offered on such a solemn evening.

"*Oh, her cunt was slick as honey and his cock was thick and raw…*"

Ah, she thought. *That sort.*

"*And were you to see them nude, your words'd stick in your craw*," the song continued. "*And that's just what happened, one fine and sunny day! When the lady and the lad came strollin' out, naked down the lane.*"

"*DOWN THE LANE!*" a chorus of men and women roared in accompaniment. "*Down the lane! We saw 'em naked and glistenin', strolling down the lane!*"

Where the Karnerians had knelt in uniform lines, perfectly rigid, the

Sainites gathered in a large, rowdy circle around a roaring fire. Where the Karnerians were led in solemn prayer by an armored foe, the Sainites appeared to be taking the lead of a shirtless woman, belting out lyrics in a crass, booming voice. And where the Karnerians fasted and denied themselves, the Sainites ... did not.

"*Well, the Sovereign and the Knight, they both came down to see,*" the half-naked woman said, pausing to take a deep drink from a frothing flagon, foam dribbling onto her chest. "*To gaze upon these two young fucks, walkin' brazen as could be. You'd think the gods would frown upon a love so coarse and odd. But you'd be surprised to see with your eyes the gods stand by and applaud.*"

"*AND APPLAUD!*" the ring boomed out. "*And applaud! The gods smile upon the mortal who walks without a fear of god!*"

Not quite as reverent as a hymn, Asper thought.

But catchier.

"Prophet!"

She turned at the sound of a cry. A Sainite soldier, a young man with a flagon and a broad grin, came rushing forward. His blue coat was dirty, his hair hung about him in unwashed strands, but the crossbow on his back was impeccably cared for.

"May I offer you a drink?" he asked. "It's my only one—W.S.'s orders—but it'd be an honor to offer it to you."

"Er ... and it would be an honor to accept," Asper said, holding up a hand. "But I couldn't deny a soldier his hard-earned—"

"As you say, Prophet!" The Sainite tilted his head and the flagon back, draining it in a few impressive gulps. The belch he let out was a touch crude, but he at least had the shame to cover his mouth after the fact. "Apologies. No drunkenness tonight. W.S.'s orders. One ration tonight, another if we're alive tomorrow. Keeps the edge off."

"Uh-huh." Asper cringed as a particularly crude lyric rose up—she didn't even know there *was* a word that rhymed with *vagina*—and begat a roaring laugh from the crowd. "And ... does that?"

"I suppose it's no hymn," the Sainite said. "But 'The Lady and the Lad' is our regimental battle song."

"And songs about public sex are ... stir you to battle?"

"We're not Karnies, Prophet." The Sainite shook his head. "No man or woman here wants to die and it's a foul song that tries to make us want to. A good battle song reminds us of the life we're going to go back to some day, what we're fighting for."

If that is true, Asper thought, *the civilian life of the average Sainite must be amazing.* But she chose to say something else.

"I need to speak to Blacksbarrow," she said.

"Command tent's at the edge." The Sainite pointed to the far end of the camp. "She's left orders not to be disturbed."

"A Prophet doesn't disturb," Asper replied as she turned and left. "A Prophet delivers."

Perhaps she *should* have had that drink.

But by the time the singing had died down enough for her to think about it, she was already at the far end of the camp. And, as she approached Blacksbarrow's tent, a different song reached her ears.

"*Your voice is ambrosia,*" someone said from behind the tent flaps.

"*Oh yeah?*"

"*I yearn to hear you speak once more, my darling.*" The first voice—a male, deep and lyrical—spoke. "*I feel the ache in my very soul.*"

"*Mm.*" Another voice—female, not nearly so lyrical—replied. "*I've never had a man ache for me before.*"

"*Your eyes glisten like stars. I see the entirety of the night sky within your stare, as vast, as eternal, as deep and as—*"

"*Aw, for fuck's sake, man, what's this? Can't you use your tongue like you did earlier?*"

"*Sorry, it's just... women like it when I talk sweet to them.*"

"*Aye, a few words here and there are nice. I don't need you running a fucking soliloquy to my pussy.*"

Whether it was curiosity or abhorrence that made Asper pull the flap back, she didn't know. But it became pretty fucking clear once she looked inside.

Blacksbarrow, splayed across a straw mat on the ground, looked up with a long and lazy smile across her face. The reason for which was made evident by her clothes lying in a heap beside her and the burly-looking man whose face was buried between her legs.

When Dransun looked up, it was something else entirely that was across his face. And the reason for that, too, was evident.

"Priestess!" he sputtered, his chin glistening with something other than sweat. "I mean...Asper. I mean—"

"I don't want to be accused of insubordination," Blacksbarrow said, "but just because you're the Prophet doesn't mean you don't knock. I could have been doing something sensitive in here."

Asper, for her part, simply stared—she would never be able to sear this image from her mind, anyway.

"I came to see how preparations were going," she said. "Have your scraws reported back with enemy movement?"

"Fuck me, they probably have. Apologies, Prophet." Blacksbarrow sighed and gave Dransun an affectionate scratch behind his ear. "Work to do. Let me up, big man."

The guard tried to sputter out some form of dignity but, failing that, simply scurried away and let her rise. Blacksbarrow rose, gathering her clothes with a yawn and scratching her naked flank. She offered a grin to Asper as she pulled her breeches up around her hips and tightened her belt.

"Forgive the tardiness, Prophet," she said. "I would have gotten the reports to you sooner, but..." She looked over her shoulder and cast a lascivious wink at Dransun. "I got distracted." She fired off a salute and, tugging her coat over her shoulders, slipped out of the tent. "We'll tell you where the tulwar are in a moment. Sit tight."

There were a handful of times where the departure of a mostly naked woman with a drinking problem did not do anything to make a situation less awkward. And, Asper knew, this was one of them.

Dransun pointedly avoided her gaze, and avoided even acknowledging her, as he gathered up his clothes and began to pull them on.

"So, uh..." Asper said, "you and Blacksbarrow are—"

"We are compatriots in battle," Dransun replied, curt and coarse. "We happened to get to talking about our strategy after the meeting. Then we happened to get to sharing a drink. Then we happened to get to..."

He trailed off, clearing his throat as he pulled his belt around him and tucked his shirt into his trousers.

"Okay, so..." Asper rubbed her neck. "Are you..."

"We are a man and a woman on the eve of a battle that could see us both flayed by tulwar blades tomorrow." Dransun looked up long enough to cast her an indignant look as he gathered his boots up. "This may very well be my last night alive."

"No, I get that. Entirely. It's just..." Asper's face screwed up, searching for the words. "You chose to spend it..."

"With my face between the legs of a woman." Dransun offered her a challenging glare as he pulled on his boots. "What of it?"

Asper stared at him for a long, quiet moment.

Slowly, a smile spread across her face. She reached out, touched him on the shoulder, and gave him a gentle, encouraging squeeze.

"You're a good man, Captain Dransun," she said. "The world will be poorer if you die."

Dransun stared at her for a long, quiet moment.

And, with profound unease creasing his face, he hurried out of the tent.

She stared at the tent flap as it fluttered. From the night beyond, the sound of singing could still be heard. There was a new song now, one with a softer tune that not everyone knew the words to. Many of the voices had fallen silent, with a few of them likely having gone to rest for tomorrow.

The Karnerians, too, might have gone to their bedrolls. Those soldiers, regardless of nationality, would lay their heads down on the same uncomfortable blankets. Those who truly believed would whisper a prayer to be reunited with families. Those who doubted would simply close their eyes and wish desperately for it. They would all fight the same fears and doubts before each of them went to a hard sleep, content in the knowledge that the Prophet was with them, and heaven was with the Prophet.

And maybe all of them would be dead by this time tomorrow.

"They're cute," someone said.

"Yeah, it's nice that—"

Asper paused when she realized that the voice had come from behind her.

She whirled around, ready to strike, ready to scream, ready for anything but the sight she saw.

Sitting atop a footlocker, her dusty breeches in a cross-legged position, her pointed ears poking up through a mop of sweaty, dirty blond hair, she looked up at Asper through eyes glittering green in the dark. Overlarge canines flashed as she brought a haunch of meat to her mouth, tore off a piece, and began to chew.

"So you think they're going to get married or what?" Kataria asked through a full mouth, spitting as she did.

"Kataria!"

Asper cried her name and rushed forward. The shict rose up to meet her, grinning, and Asper felt her own face nearly split apart with the force of her own smile at the sight of her.

She was leaner than before. The muscle of her body was more apparent now. And her skin was tinged red. And there was *much* more dirt and grime on her than Asper remembered.

But her ears were still long and pointed. She still wore feathers in her hair. Her canines were unnervingly big. And, as Asper rushed forward and embraced her, she still smelled comfortingly terrible.

It was Kataria.

One of the few friends who didn't want to kill her.

Presumably.

"I thought you were dead," she whispered. "I thought you were lost, I thought..." She pulled back and looked at the shict, amazed. "How'd you get in here? The entire road is being watched."

"Being watched by humans." Kataria half grinned, half sneered. "Which is a little like asking a...stupid thing to...not do something well."

Asper quirked a brow. "Uh..."

"Shut up. I've been riding all day and I'm tired." Kataria glared over the haunch of meat as she took another bite. "I'll say something wittier once I've finished this."

"Clearly." Asper cringed, as lovingly as one could, at the meat. "Where'd you get that, anyway?"

Kataria looked down at the haunch, shrugged, and took another bite.

"You took a long time to get here. I got hungry."

"A long time to..." Asper laughed, breathless. "You didn't have to sneak in. If you had just let me know you were coming, I would have had you welcomed in."

"Yeah, you've got an army now, don't you? What do they call you? The Pratfall?"

"The *Prophet*." Asper drew herself up, unconsciously. "I speak for heaven and—"

"Right, yes, nice." Kataria spit out some gristle before taking another bite. "Anyway, as cuddly as your army of angry humans carrying spears and crossbows looked, I thought it'd be better if I sneaked in. Something tells me they wouldn't like seeing these."

Her ears twitched, folded against her head. Asper winced in response.

"Listen, it's not like that. Tensions are running high, I'll admit, but you've missed a lot since you've been gone. There's an army—"

"Of tulwar," Kataria finished. "I passed them on my way here. They were far behind me when I arrived, but they were moving quick. I think they'll be here—"

"By dawn." Asper's face hardened, the smile fading. "You know, then. Do you also know who leads them?"

Kataria chewed a bit, then swallowed. She tossed the haunch of meat aside and wiped her greasy fingers on her breeches.

"I guess I have missed a lot, haven't I?" She sighed. "Gariath used to threaten to kill us so often, I never thought he'd do it." She paused. "I mean, I never thought he'd get an *army* to do it."

"He did," Asper replied, her voice a stone in her throat, cold and hard. "He killed hundreds at Jalaang. And he's coming with the intent of killing thousands. Every last human in Cier'Djaal, if he can." She shook her head. "He's not what he used to be, Kataria. I don't know what he is anymore."

The weight of her frown pulled Asper's gaze to the earth at her feet.

She had sometimes thought about a moment like this; ever since Gariath had so savagely beaten her, she had wondered what her other friends would have done. She wondered what Lenk would tell her to do, what joke Denaos would make to cheer her up.

And, more than once, she had wondered what Kataria would say. Fierce, relentless, the shict never doubted or compromised; Asper had found herself craving Kataria's voice, urging her to keep fighting, to never give up. Even now, she found herself waiting for those words of encouragement.

What she got, however, was a thick, phlegmy snort as Kataria spit something foul on the sand.

"Well," the shict grunted, "good for him for being ambitious, I guess. But it doesn't matter now. Listen, I'm here to tell you—"

"Doesn't matter?"

Asper all but roared as she looked up. And though Kataria tensed up, keenly aware of how loud that was, Asper didn't care.

"They were people!" the priestess snapped. "*Hundreds* of them. And he just *killed* them! He hung their corpses on the walls!"

"That's not the worst thing he's done with a corpse," Kataria replied, shrugging. "And that's not as many people who are going to die if you don't—"

"Gods damn it, how the fuck can this still be happening?" Asper clutched her hair, gritted her teeth. "How the fuck did I think you'd be any different from him? Than the rest of them? How the fuck is it that, after all of this, I'm *still* the only one who gives a shit about saving lives? How? *HOW?*"

Kataria lunged forward, seizing Asper with one hand, clapping the other over her mouth. She hissed through bared canines, green eyes glowing in the dark as she narrowed them.

"You keep screaming and that's one more life lost," the shict growled, voice low. "*Mine.* And if you'd shut the fuck up for a moment and listen to me, I could tell you that I'm *trying* to help you save lives." She looked intently at Asper. "I'm going to take my hand off now. You scream, it goes on your throat next time. Okay?"

Asper scowled at her but nodded, grudgingly. Kataria let out a breath and removed her hand.

"Listen," Kataria said, her voice growing more urgent, "whatever I've missed, that's not important. It's what you've missed that you need to hear. Something happened in the Forbidden East with Lenk. Something came out of there that shouldn't come out. A demon."

Asper stared at her flatly. "A demon."

"Don't look at me like that, you've seen weirder shit."

"I have," Asper said. "What's this one?"

"I don't...I don't know. I haven't seen it. I just go by what Lenk told me. He's alive, by the way. He says 'hey.'"

Asper's lips pursed. Her eyes narrowed.

"But listen, it's big. It's deadly. It's huge. And it's not the only thing that's coming. There are shicts, too."

"Shicts," Asper said. "How many?"

"I don't know, exactly. Hundreds. Maybe thousands."

"Where are they?"

"I don't know. They scatter around, but—"

"How are they going to attack?"

"*I don't fucking know, okay?* They're *shicts*. You're not supposed to how many of us there are, where we are, or how we're going to attack until you've been dead for an hour. That's how we fight. That's how we ... how *they* will fight when they attack."

Asper stepped back and folded her arms over her chest. Her expression was neither impressed, nor sympathetic, nor exactly believing. But she did not stop Kataria from continuing. And so, the shict sighed deeply.

"Listen," she said, "Lenk is off telling Gariath to stop his attack. I need you to do the same. What's coming next, we're going to need everyone alive and ready to fight. Because what's coming next will make this war you've got brewing with Gariath look like a picnic in comparison. You want to save lives, you start right now by getting ready for something much worse than tulwar."

Kataria met her gaze. She stiffened up, her muscles tensing visibly beneath her skin.

"Asper," she said, "you need to make peace with Gariath."

It sounded crazy, of course. But Kataria was right; Asper *had* seen, and heard, for that matter, weirder than this. Together, they had fought demons, they had fought monsters, they had fought abominations. They had explored the wilds and abandoned civilization together. They had shared bad food, picked parasites off each other, gotten so ill they shat buckets *in* buckets.

Together.

Her, Kataria, Lenk, Dreadaeleon, Denaos, and Gariath.

Once.

And once, she had felt a softness creep into her face, like she did at that moment. Looking at Kataria, her friend, so desperate as to sneak into a camp full of humans to tell her this, she felt something. Something warm, something tender, something she hadn't felt since that day they had all separated.

And when she reached down inside her, took that feeling in her hands, and strangled it until it was dead, it hurt her.

"No," she said.

Kataria's face all but exploded with the shock that painted it. "What?"

"No," Asper said. "I won't. I will never make peace with him."

"Did you not hear me?" Kataria's ears pointed straight up. "Did I not just fucking say—"

"I heard you. I've heard those words a lot," Asper said. "Every fucking time there's a fight that needs to be won, someone comes along and says that the *next* fight will be bigger, worse, bloodier. Maybe that's true. But it doesn't make the one I have to fight any smaller, any better, any less bloody."

"You need to *listen* to me."

"I don't care, Kataria," she said. "You can't tell me what demon is coming. You can't tell me what the shicts are doing. You don't know these things and neither do I. But I do know that Gariath is coming, with an army of tulwar, and he's going to murder everyone. Every man, every woman, every elder, and every child he can get his hands on.

"What am I to tell them? That I can't protect them because something bigger *might* be coming? They'll end up dead, either way, unless I stand up for them." She shook her head. "I'm tired of death, Kataria. But I'm more tired of watching it happen. I'm more tired of failing people. Thousands are depending on me. I can't fail any of them. Not one."

"But Lenk is talking to Gariath right now! He's going to—"

"Kataria…" Her voice softened. "If you can look me in the eye right now, knowing Gariath as well as I do, and tell me that you truly believe anything would make him stop…I'll do what you ask."

Kataria opened her mouth. Kataria looked Asper in the eye. Kataria held her gaze for a long, silent moment that stretched into eternity.

And she could not say a single word.

Asper inclined her head. "Thank you for coming this far to talk to me, Kat. Thank you for telling me Lenk is alive. Thank you for living." She reached down and took the shict's hand in hers. "Go back to him. Go somewhere far away from here. Stay alive."

Kataria stared at her, eyes wide in helpless silence. She smiled, squeezed the shict's hand gently, then let it drop and turned away into a cold and quiet night bereft of fire or song.

"Because tomorrow, I don't think I'll know many people who still are."

THIRTY

HEAVEN IS WATCHING

Shortly before dawn, Marcher Pathon rose.

It was not his choice anymore; he had never slept past this time since he was very young and first entered the legions. And by the time he had been granted the rank of Marcher, his every morning became the same thing, a function so effortless and instinctive he felt more like a machine now.

Not that he minded. Not anymore.

In the first breath, he got out of his bedroll. He ignored the chill breeze blowing across the desert, as he had ignored the weather of every battlefield before.

Five breaths to roll his bedroll up, bind it tightly around the pillow, make certain every sheet was tucked away neatly, as he had been trained.

The next thirty breaths were the most leisurely. He knelt on his bedroll, his head bowed toward the sun that had yet to rise. He closed his eyes. And he recited the same prayer he had recited every morning since he had first joined.

"I am a son of the Empire. I am a disciple of the Conqueror. I am a weapon of my nation and a shield of my people," he spoke to the breeze. "I make no claim, beg no favor, beseech no aid. I go to battle, for I am made for battle. I conquer in your name, for I am made to conquer. Daeon, O Daeon, gaze upon me."

Effortless, like the words barely had any meaning anymore. In truth, he had no real need for the meaning. Just the very practice of saying them every morning was enough to remind him he was what he needed to be. What his empire needed him to be.

Two breaths to stand up. Two more to bow deeply. The next fifty-eight were spent with the armor meticulously stacked beside his bedroll. He had this, too, down to a mechanical process.

Three breaths to pull the long tunic over him. Ten to affix the metal and leather cuirass over his torso. Seven to secure the heavy belt that draped a thick skirt down to his knees. Twenty to tie tightly the metal plates of his shoulder armor. Three to attach his sword. Seven to don his helmet. The last eight spent pulling the heavy-soled boots over his feet and lacing them up.

He stood up.

Two breaths to spare. He was getting better at this.

The rest of his phalanx was still busy drawing up their armor; they had not much time left before the speaker arrived. Whosoever was not in uniform by the time he made his rounds would go without breakfast. This was usually enough to motivate them to be quick about it.

"I am...I am a son of the Emperor. No, I mean...I am a son of the Empire..."

Usually.

He turned to his left and saw another soldier—Dachon, he thought the man's name was—kneeling upon a bedroll not yet rolled up, next to armor that had been placed haphazardly beside him, head bowed and trembling.

"I am a...a disciple. A disciple of the Conqueror. I am a...a..." Dachon shut his eyes tight and let out a fevered whisper. "Fuck."

"A weapon of my nation," Pathon finished for him. "And a shield of my people." He frowned at his fellow soldier. "Those are the most important parts, brother. Daeon does not listen to he who falters."

"Forgive me, brother," Dachon said, averting his gaze. "I'll...I'll finish the prayers later. I should get suited up before the speaker arrives."

"No. Finish the prayers."

"But I won't get breakfast."

"Fast if you must to clear your mind. It is not food, not plunder, not battle that motivates us. It is him. The Conqueror who sends us forward to bring order to this land. Only through him do we win."

"Of course, brother..." Dachon looked up, finally. There was fear in his eyes. "But against tulwar?"

"You've been in Cier'Djaal, brother. You've seen plenty of battle."

"Against Sainites, yes. I can fight Sainites. They're humans. They're not monsters."

"Monsters do not exist outside of fairy tales. What you face are simply flesh and bone, like any other foe."

Dachon nodded, then drew in a breath. "Thank you, brother. I shall pray for Daeon to grant me your confidence."

"Daeon does not grant what a man cannot take on his own." Pathon nodded back. "Finish your prayers. Heaven is watching."

He walked away, leaving his fellow soldier to his routine. In truth, he hadn't intended to sound confident—he had never fought a tulwar, either. Confidence, after all, was simply a mask to hide cowardice. Pathon was a soldier of Karneria. The legion hadn't taught him to be confident. It had taught him to be certain of things.

Things like what to do in the morning. Things like what Daeon expected of him. And, most recently, things like the Prophet's wisdom.

That was why he felt no fear as he walked toward the table where the quartermaster dispensed that morning's rations—unlike some of his brothers who dragged their feet or shook as they walked. Fear was something he was not certain of, so he did not think of it.

The Prophet, he was certain of. Her miracles, he was certain of. How she had emerged before him, healed of all wounds, he was certain could only be proof of what she said.

Heaven had chosen her to lead him. Just as heaven had chosen him to fight for her.

He got in line behind the other soldiers. They moved quickly, each one receiving his rations and hurrying off, rather than loitering around as they ate. He was only confused until he got to the front and the quartermaster thrust a wedge of hard cheese, a heel of bread, and some hot cooked ox meat into his hands.

"Eat quickly," the quartermaster said. "The speaker calls."

He didn't elaborate. He didn't have to. Pathon was already off, eating as he ran in the same direction of his brothers. The speaker rarely called for the legion before they could eat, but not so rarely that Pathon didn't know what to do. He ate not so quickly that he would get sick, but quick enough that he was finished by the time he arrived. He fell into ranks with his legion as they gathered.

The speaker loomed over them all, his black armor drinking what little light had begun creeping over the horizon. His sword, long and heavy in his hand, was not half so sharp as the scrutinizing scowl he swept over the assembled soldiers. Even after so many years under his command, the speaker never failed to cut an imposing figure.

Until that day, anyway.

Pathon found his eyes drawn to the woman beside him. She was clad simply—no longer in her frayed priestess robes, but now in chain mail and leather. It was clearly not new, not resplendent, not some golden armor fit for the great kings from the old legends. But Pathon hadn't expected that.

The Prophet did not need things like that to command attention.

Her brown hair was roughly kempt in a thick braid. She hadn't been able to wash all the grime from her face. The sword she wore hung heavy at her hip, and the shield on her back was round, metal, and simple.

And yet...she glowed. She stood taller than she was. Her eyes were not hard like the speaker's, but they were clear, seeing something far beyond what he could.

He was certain of that.

"Soldiers of Karneria," the speaker said suddenly. "You have been called. The pagan horde has been sighted closing in on us. The time for reflection, for prayer, is over. The time for battle is now."

He nodded to the Prophet, stepping behind her. The Prophet, in turn, looked to the Foescribe beside her. The Foescribe glanced up from the scroll she was writing in to incline her head.

"I know this is the time for a speech," the Prophet said. "This is supposed to be the time where great kings and queens make great words for great wars." She shook her head. "But I have none for you now. Words will not protect this city. Speeches will not save lives. The gods have no ears for the wagging tongues of mortal boasts. They will not care what has been said here.

"But they will be watching. They will see what you did here today. They will see how you stood against thousands. They will see the many lives you saved, even if you laid down your own to save them. And they will smile. This is what they put us here to do. This is why you were chosen."

She raised her hand to them, palm open in benediction.

"Heaven is watching."

And many hands were raised to her, their palms likewise open. And, in one harmonious thunder, hundreds of voices replied.

"Heaven is watching."

She opened her mouth, as though she wanted to say more. And Pathon found himself wanting to hear more, to hear what else heaven had planned for him. So he stayed silent, staring at her, his body tight with a tension he didn't recognize.

But not for long.

Overhead, the shrill warble of a bugle rang out. He looked up, along with the rest of his brothers. One of the scraws—the winged beasts the once-hated Sainites rode—came wheeling overhead. Its rider released three short blasts, over and over.

"The tulwar are in sight," the speaker said. He glared over his soldiers. "To the point, Karnerians. Fist formation. The Sainites will join us. You know what to do." He looked back to the Prophet and the Foescribe. "Heaven is watching."

The Prophet nodded and began to head back to the watchtower. Even as his brothers pushed past, Pathon found himself lingering, staring at the Prophet as she left, keeping as clear an image in his head of her that he could hold on to during the battle.

He felt a heavy gauntlet on his shoulder. He looked up. The speaker glowered at him.

"Marcher," he said. "To the front."

He nodded, turning to go as the speaker hurried with him. They did not go far before a voice called out to him.

"Speaker."

The speaker paused, then turned to face her. The Foescribe stood, the usual inscrutability of her face giving way to something intent and focused.

"Madam?" he asked.

"I have overseen six campaigns with success," she said. "I will not see the Empire disgraced by a pack of savages. I—" She paused, swallowed. "Return victorious. Return alive."

"Madam." He inclined his head.

Pathon didn't dare still be there when the speaker turned. He rushed to catch up to his fellows. They ran through their camp, snatching up their long spears and tower shields. They hurried toward the gap in the hills where Harmony Road wound through.

Across the way, he could see the Sainites mustering. Their crossbow-men were rushing forward, too, in good order, as their scraws wheeled overhead. Their leader, that fearsome Blacksbarrow woman, snarled orders at them as they did.

Pathon found no hate in his heart for them as he gazed upon them—even as he remembered how many of his brothers they had killed. They were here, just as he was here, for a reason.

Heaven had chosen them. Heaven had chosen him. Heaven had chosen this battle.

He fell into the rank, just as he had rehearsed. The second row of the phalanx, Dachon behind him, Apala in front of him. The rows of Karnerians filled the road, just wide enough to form a wall of shields and spears. He held his own closely, staring over the rim of his shield toward the distant horizon, toward the creeping dawn.

Toward the black shadow that stained the horizon, growing ever closer and ever darker.

• ◆ •

Gariath had once thought being too stupid to live as being a confined illness that only that afflicted his former human companions.

Now, from high on the ridge, he could see that it was really more a trait inborn to the race.

"So few of them." Chakaa hummed from beside Gariath, staring out over the desert, painted blue by the desert sun. "Should we have brought less? This won't be fun at all."

Gariath didn't humor her. He was no tactician, but the situation was obvious to him.

The humans—the ones wearing the black armor and carrying the long spears—had settled in a thick square formation in the middle of the road that led through the barrier of hills surrounding the Green Belt. Behind them lay the other humans—the ones wearing blue coats and stupid hats—in a long line. And behind *them* were a rabble of other humans—reserves, maybe. Or maybe just spectators. Who knew.

He looked beyond them all, to the city that had just been a stain on a map until now. Cier'Djaal's walls rose high, but not high enough. Its houses lay silent beyond, a heap of tinder and kindling waiting for a torch. Its gates stood open, mocking him to come and cleanse its filth from the world.

All he needed to do was get through those humans.

"I don't like this," Gariath growled.

"Nor do I." Mototaru plunked himself down beside Gariath. With the stem of his pipe, he idly began to draw shapes in the sand. "It appears they've put aside their differences and united in the face of greater adversity, learning empathy for their foes and, indeed, themselves." He sneered out over the road. "They're always doing this shit."

"There can't be more than a few hundred," Chakaa said. "Against us, what chance do they stand?"

She gestured out below. Beneath the high ridge they had chosen, the tulwar swarmed forward in a tide of black and gray fur, the steel of their weapons like the flashing crests on the crowns of waves. The warriors with stout shields and swords led the rush forward; the bellowing roars of Daaru at their head could be heard, even from here. At their flanks, gaambols shrieked and howled as they scrambled forward, their riders waving spears in the air. And behind them all, upon huge wooden platforms, came the drums. Massive things that took eight tulwar each to lift, bending their backs so they seemed like many-legged insects with leather backs. Two tulwar each stood upon the platforms, pounding out a steady rhythm that drove them forward.

"Plenty," Mototaru said. "We hadn't counted on them closing off the other roads." He shook his head. "I'm still not sure how they did that."

Magic, Gariath knew. The stink of it was still in the air.

"They have the advantage of terrain," the old tulwar murmured as he sketched out a crude map in the sand. "Inside that pass, our numbers mean little."

"Then send my clan in," Chakaa said. "We shall knock politely."

"The other tulwar will not ride with the *malaa*," Mototaru said. "But it's no matter. We can still win this." He sketched two crosses in the sand. "Have our army take up defensive positions here and here. We hold tight until tomorrow. Then, we can make a decisive—"

"No."

Gariath's growl cut through their conversation. He folded his arms across his chest, fixing his black eyes on the square of soldiers.

"The longer we wait, the bolder they become," Gariath snarled. "They will reinforce, they will grow stronger, they will think they can win. We hit now. We hit hard. We break them in one strike."

"A brave strategy," Mototaru muttered. "But brave doesn't beat smart."

Gariath's answer was not for the old tulwar. He stepped forward, to the very edge of the ridge. The sun climbed high behind him, painting his red skin an angry, molten gold color. He spread his wings wide. He threw his head back. He craned his jaws open wide.

His roar carried down the ridge and across the sand. And like a fire, it spread. Into the ears of every warrior, every archer, every rider below. Out of the mouths of every father, every mother, every tulwar. Their mouths opened wide. Their blades went high. Their voices shook the sky to pieces.

"RISE UP!"

"RISE UP!"

Pathon heard them. A thousand voices in a single, endless roar. Heavy drums pounding thunder through a clear sky. Many feet making the sands shudder beneath his. The sound of their fury was strong.

"Stand strong, Sons of Karneria!"

But fury was nothing to faith.

"Daeon's eyes are upon you!"

And a thousand tulwar were nothing to the voice of the speaker.

"You are weapons wrought from iron! Forged in the furnace of the Empire!" The speaker stood at the edge of the phalanx, his sword held high and pointed toward the enemy. *"Every impurity hammered out! There is no room in you for fear, for hate, for anything but your duty!"*

Pathon felt the words course through him. His heartbeat slowed. His breath came out in long exhales. Moisture rimmed the edges of his helmet. Through the visor, he could see them.

They appeared as a stain on the horizon, a spilled bottle of ink rapidly splashing down the hill. The rising sun was behind them, painting their fur black. No formation, no lines, no phalanxes; they came rushing forward as a tide, as strong and formless and unstoppable.

"Battles you have fought! Foes you have slain! All have you led you to this moment! This war! This divine mission! There is no death! There is no failure! There is only this moment and the eternal post that awaits you by the Conqueror's side!"

And as they drew closer, he could see the colors. He had heard of this, their "war paint"—the colors that flooded their faces when their rage was up. And with every step they took, they were more and more color than black. In wild patterns, in brilliant flashes, in yellow and red and blue, he could see them: their war paint, their yellow fangs, their giant eyes. Thousands of burning stars in an endless, encroaching night.

"Humanity's fate is upon your shoulders! Daeon stands with you! And heaven is watching!"

The speaker raised his sword high, screaming to be heard over the thunder of their charge.

"CLOSE THE FIST!"

Shields out. Spears up. Heads low. Every man in the phalanx knew his place. They pressed together. Steel to steel. Shoulder to shoulder. Every soldier a wall for the man on his left, a skewer for the man on his right. They had done this a thousand times.

Never against a foe like this, though.

Through the gaps in the shields, he watched them draw ever closer. A mass of long limbs and painted faces and dirty armor and screaming, fanged mouths. The only way to differentiate them was by the flashes of silver in the tide of darkness. The last thing he saw was the steel of their weapons.

And then, the tulwar were right in front of him.

"RISE UP!"

Their voices were thunder in his ears.

And then, lightning.

The mass of bodies collided with the shields in the first line, thousands of pounds of flesh and fur and hacking steel. Many died, impaling themselves on the long spears. But more stood, plowing past their dead to attack. Their swords lashed out, trying to get past the shields; he could feel blood spatter the sand, splash on his feet. But swords were mere metal. It was the force of their charge that struck the hardest.

The shields in the first line were pushed backward. The man in front collided with his shield. His spear went over his comrade's shoulder, thrust at the tulwar as best he could. Until he, too, was driven back. He felt himself pressed against the shield behind him, felt the spear rise over his shoulder, felt his feet caught in a tangle of legs as he was forced to move back.

The tulwar no longer seemed like a tide. They were too big for that.

They were a storm, sweeping over the shields and spears. Many died, cut down by spear thrusts and falling with shafts broken in their chests. Many were carved apart by stabbing swords that shot between the shields.

But there were many, many more.

Their long, killing blades flashed between the shields and painted deep wounds in the arms and legs of the Karnerians. Their heavy swords hacked gashes in the shields, threatened to splinter them. Those wild few with colors more vivid than the rest climbed over their fellows and leapt into the phalanx, swinging wildly before they were hacked down.

They were pushing. They were slashing. And always, they were screaming.

"Rise up!"

"Rua Tong!"

"Tho Thu Bhu!"

Words he barely understood. Words overwhelmed by the animal screeching in his helmet, the blood pounding in his ears, the sound of sand crunching beneath his feet as he was pressed ever backward. But those weren't the words he needed to hear.

"Stand firm, you faithful!" the speaker bellowed. "Give not a foot that is not soaked with blood! Let no savage threaten you! Let no pagan drive you—"

"Oi!"

A word he didn't know. A voice he didn't expect. The beating of long, feathery wings followed by an avian screech.

"You Karnies look like you're having trouble!"

Overhead, Blacksbarrow flew atop one of the great, winged scraws. The sight used to send Karnerians running for cover. But now Pathon saw what the Sainites did. Blacksbarrow held a spear aloft, the banner of Saine flapping in the wind as she flew over the battle. And she laughed, longer and louder and fiercer than any tulwar could scream.

"Lend these scalps some help, boys and girls!" She wheeled her scraw overhead, flying to the back of the line. "SAINITES! OPEN FIRE!"

Screeching. Whistling. Singing. Bolts flew over his head, over his shield, past his spear. The Sainite crossbows hummed. In swift, elegant arcs, they sent starving birds to seek meat. And the tulwar fell.

Not many, not at first. The ones in front continued to press, not at all tired even as they hacked through wood and metal. But more birds flew, more bolts sang, more bodies fell. And soon, the press of flesh no longer seemed quite so heavy, the sound of their fury not quite so strong.

And he knew the time had come.

"Raise your spears, men of the Empire!" the speaker roared. *"March to glory!"*

He felt the words course through his body, through the phalanx. Their retreat stopped. The men at the back ceased giving ground, started to push into the next line, who started to push into the next. Soon, Pathon felt the shield at his back pushing him forward, and he pushed into the man at his front.

The tulwar redoubled their efforts, screaming louder, hacking swifter. But it didn't matter. Spears shot out, caught them in shoulders and throats and chests. They fell, the fortunate dead and the unlucky dying. And those latter ones, Pathon felt his boots upon.

The Marchers did their job, moving forward slowly. Every step brought a new corpse: a new spear wound, a new sword cut, a new skull crushed beneath iron boots. They pounded blood into the sand, crushed bone into mortar as they pushed their foe back upon a road of skin and screams.

"It's going better than I hoped."

Haethen's voice was clinically flat as she stared through the spyglass. Heedless of Asper's stare boring into her face, her focus was on the battle.

"We lost a few men in their initial rush, but nothing disastrous," the Foescribe said. "The Sainite volley managed to turn the tide." She frowned. "Foolish of Blacksbarrow to fly her scraw in like that. We have no idea where their archers are."

"But it's good, right?" Asper strained to see from the watchtower, but without a spyglass, it all looked like one black blob pushing against a bigger gray blob. "We're doing good?"

"We're doing *well*," Haethen said, correcting her. "Or we would be, if there were such a thing in battle. But there is only victory and defeat. Our line is holding, at least. The tulwar can't bring all their numbers to bear inside the pass. Things are going as we planned."

"That certainly *sounds* well."

"It sounds *good*, yes. If the plan we made is sound." She swept her spyglass over toward the flanks of the army and the great mill of gaambols there. "I don't like the look of their beasts. If those things get into the Green Belt, they could reach the watchtower in twenty breaths."

Only at this did she look over toward Asper. She ran an appraising eye over the dusty chain mail, the stitched leather, the dented shield. She frowned.

"Which wouldn't concern me as much if you wore more armor." She glanced at the scanty few soldiers—a few Djaalics and a pair of Sainites—left to defend the watchtower. "Or if we had more men to spare."

"We need everyone we can get down there," Asper said. She glanced over Haethen. "You're not wearing any armor, either."

"I'm just a strategist. I'm prepared to die. I'm not prepared for what happens if I lose the Prophet, though."

Asper stared down at the melee, frowning. "I should be down there. I should be leading them."

"You speak to heaven, Prophet, not to soldiers. Let Careus and Blacksbarrow do their jobs. Besides, if things go to shit, you'll have plenty of opportunity to—" She paused, held her spyglass up. She grimaced. "Fuck. They're making a move."

"What?" Asper reached for the spyglass. "What's happening?"

"You!" Haethen ignored her, pointing toward one of the Sainites. "They're getting ready to charge with their beasts. Alert Blacksbarrow!"

The Sainite nodded, then rushed to the edge of the watchtower. From his belt, he pulled a pair of brightly colored flags. And, with gestures neither woman understood, he began to make various signals with them. Out in the distance, a scraw screeched and wheeled around in the sky.

"Let me go down there," Asper said. "I can help them."

"You can get killed." Haethen walked to the edge of the watchtower, waved at someone below, then gestured toward the front. "And I can't allow that. Heaven will understand, if it is watching at all."

"It is," Asper said, giving her a hard look. "Believe that it is."

"I believe in heaven, Prophet."

She looked below. Upon the sands, a team of Karnerians in white robes began to haul a massive wheeled platform across the sands. Upon it, a colossal figure shaped of white stone knelt, horned head bowed. A grim look creased Haethen's face.

"But I trust in steel."

＊＊＊

Bones snapping. Skin popping. Blood spattering. The stink of dead meat cooling in the air, then cooking in the sun—was it morning already? Or was it later now?

Pathon had lost track of time somewhere. Had lost track of everything, really.

All he knew now was the march: the endless enemy before him and the road of the dead beneath him.

He pressed on, marching in formation with his brothers. Every step brought the thrusts of spears. Every thrust brought the screams—sometimes the tulwar, sometimes his brothers, sometimes they just seemed to come from nowhere. He didn't have room in his head or his heart to worry about that.

All he knew was the march.

"*Onward, brothers!*" the speaker boomed relentlessly, his voice as steady as any drum. "*To the last body! To the last breath! Heaven is watching!*"

Pathon kept his head down, kept marching, kept moving. Bolts flew overhead as the Sainites followed behind, shooting when they could. Tulwar continued to crash into the phalanx, continued to be cut down. And they kept marching.

Until they stopped.

Something happened. The first line came to a halt suddenly, the men behind them falling into place. Something coursed through the phalanx, a feeling that flowed from brother to brother. First, a mutter. Then, a word. Finally, a scream.

And, somewhere far away, an animal shriek.

Pathon looked up. Between the shields of his brothers, he could see the tulwar thinning out. The warriors melted away, falling back to the flanks. They formed a great, empty corridor of sand before them. And at the end of it, a great cloud of dust came billowing forward.

There were tulwar in it, riding on the shoulders of great creatures that loped on all fours. Hairy monsters with naked, leathery palms, big red eyes, and snouts full of fangs. They were spurred on by tulwar riders, striking their flanks with long spears. They let out animal screeches, their voices frantic with feral intensity as they rushed forward in a massive charge.

"*CLOSE THE FIST!*" There was panic in the speaker's voice, panic as they tightened their ranks together.

Pathon's eyes were on the creatures. How many of them were there? How fast were they coming? How long until they arrived? What were they called? The Foescribe had told them, once. What was the name she used?

"*YENGU THUUN!*" one of the riders roared, a voice right in his ear.

Ah, right.

Gaambols.

One of the beasts spurred itself faster than the rest. It tore ahead of the pack, howling. The Karnerians set their spears, braced for it to come charging and impale itself on their spears.

It didn't.

It ran.

It leapt.

It sailed over their heads, came crashing down in the midst of them like a meteor. It brought its great simian fists down, flailing and shrieking, tossing Karnerians aside like they were sacks of flour. Their screams were added to a chorus of violence, of clanging metal and bodies crashing into bodies. The few who kept their wits about them turned toward the beast, thrust spears into its flanks, tore the rider from her saddle. But the gaambol didn't stop. The sight of blood made it more enraged, caused it to kick out with its legs, grab men, and smash them on the ground.

More men turned to face it. More men turned to fight it. More men died when two more of the beasts came charging forward, crashing into the line.

The ranks fought to keep control of themselves. But the men fought to keep away from the flailing fists, the gnashing fangs, the lashing spears of the riders. The tulwar didn't seem to be in control of their mounts. They simply were along for the ride as the gaambols screamed and thrashed and bit and tore and smashed and painted the ground with blood.

The sounds of the dying were in his ears. And then, there was the sound of his own death coming.

A bellowing roar, deeper and fiercer than the others. Pathon turned and saw it coming: a gaambol half as big as any of the others. It loped more slowly, hauling its massive bulk along. Its teeth were long as spearheads. Its eyes burned like fire. It did not scream, it roared. And behind it, a dozen more gaambols roared with it.

Pathon turned, holding his shield high. If this was what heaven demanded of him, this was how he would die. Fiercely, determinedly, and, he hoped, swiftly.

The massive gaambol drew closer.

The massive gaambol let out a snarl.

The massive gaambol leapt.

There was another screech—not man, not gaambol. There was a flash of movement. Something fell out of the sky; something big as a boulder smashed into the gaambol's side and bore it to the ground.

The beast flailed, its defiance turned to raw panic as it tried to pull for purchase. Pathon could see nothing but fur flying and blood spattering and feathers beating, at first. But as the monster's roars turned to howls of pain and then to whimpers of agony, he saw it.

The scraw lent its savagery to the attack, clawing with its talons and stabbing with its beak, painting the gaambol in a hundred wounds. But it was the lance, its banner soaked in blood and its head thrust deep into the creature's side, that finished it. And, soon, the lance was torn free, blood flowed freely onto the sand, and the beast lay still.

The other gaambols, as if struck by something, suddenly changed. They screamed in what sounded like terror, leaping free of the melee. They dropped their victims, spit out the dead, turned, and ran, with riders cursing commands at them, joining the rest of the beasts who fled back down the lane, leaving a lone scraw and her rider, waving a bloodied lance, after them.

"*That's right, you hairy cocks!*" Blacksbarrow roared. "*Run back to your fucking monkey masters and pick fleas out of their assholes! You think twice before you show your ugly fucking faces on my road again, you pieces of shit!*"

Drums thundered in reply. Something happened. The tulwar massed again and began rushing forward. The gaambols had done what they needed to. The ranks were broken, the Karnerians shattered.

Blacksbarrow spit a curse and spurred her mount into the air, back toward the line.

"Hold on, Karnies! We'll back you up!"

"Save your mercy, Sainite!" The speaker, voice booming once again. *"Daeon's mightiest comes to aid us!"* He pointed his sword to the very back of the line. *"Bring forth the Faithbreaker!"*

The Faithbreaker.

Pathon saw it. Carved from white stone, wrought in the naked and muscular shape of the Conqueror himself, kneeling in contemplation, his horned head bowed. It stood at the back, on the wheeled platform that the Machine Cult had dragged here. That the Machine Cult now climbed on top of.

They in their white robes clambered on the statue's limbs, on its back, onto its shoulders, madly racing to see who would be the one to reach the horns, to see who would be worthy to offer himself to it. Pathon didn't know the names of the two men who reached it first. Their names weren't important. They would be remembered for their sacrifice.

"I have been chosen!" one of them screamed.

He spread his arms wide and flung himself down upon the statue's horn. His fellow followed, impaling himself on the other horn. The white stone burst out of their backs, their blood flowing down the creature's brow, into its face.

Its face that rose, of its own volition, and gazed out over the battlefield.

And spoke.

"Death to pagans."

Booming from a born-deep place, it spoke. It stood up. It walked. Wearing a crown of corpses and a cloak of blood, it stepped from its wheeled platform and made the earth tremble. Twelve feet tall, heavy enough to shake the sky, it thundered forward. Sainites scrambled to get out of its way. Karnerians hauled their wounded out of its path. It didn't look down. It didn't stop. It strode past Pathon, into the fray, repeating over and over:

"Death to pagans."

The tulwar tide drew up short. Those brave few—and they were much fewer now—hurled themselves at it, their war cries lost in the pounding of its steps. They were caught in hand, crushed in a stone grip, or simply buried in the earth as the Faithbreaker walked over them. Those sensible many—and they were many now—turned and ran.

No one knew what divine power fueled the stone from which the Faithbreakers were carved, save the scholars of the Arda Machitorum who cut out their tongues that they might never reveal the secrets. Pathon knew only as much as anyone else: Sacrifice fueled the golem, battle gave it purpose, nothing ever stopped it.

"Brother." A body behind him. Dachon—wounded, cut, but alive— put a hand on his shoulder. "We must re-form the phalanx. Help us."

Pathon did. Or tried to. He hauled the wounded back. He fell into line when the call was made. But his eyes were always on the Faithbreaker.

It swung its arms in massive strokes, tearing tulwar apart. It stomped its feet, grinding them into the earth. It waded forward, its endless droning voice drowning out their terror and rage.

"Death to pagans."

Over and over.

"Death to pagans."

And into the fray.

"Death to—"

"KUDJ!"

A howl. The tremble of earth. The tulwar parted again as three great shapes came charging forward. Loping on all fours, their massive hands carrying tremendous bulks toward the Faithbreaker. The bodies of giant gorillas, their skins the color of the red earth. The horns of rhinoceri, jutting from their brows. They came howling, swinging, bellowing.

Vulgores.

Whatever propelled the Faithbreaker made it aware of their charge. One of them came rushing forward, loping on its knuckles. It lowered its shoulder, barreled into the golem, drove it back. Its massive weight bore the golem to the ground, sent it crashing in a titanic spray of sand.

It roared, looming over the golem. It raised its fists, made to pulverize it. But before it could, a white arm shot out. White fingers grabbed the vulgore's face. Squeezed.

The vulgore's head exploded in a cloud of red mist, chunks of greasy gray matter and bones flying out from it. The Faithbreaker righted itself, shoving the tremendous carcass aside as the other two vulgore came rushing forward.

"Death to pagans."

Dispassionate, droning, endless. It brought a fist forward to meet the first vulgore and caught the brute in its shoulder. There was the popping sound of bones dislocating, but the vulgore seized its arm and pulled it forward. It headbutted the golem, smashing its horn against the stone face. The Faithbreaker staggered but did not relent. It brought forward its fist again, slamming it into the vulgore's chest.

"Death to pagans."

Its fist burst through the brute's rib cage. The vulgore cried out as it toppled over, carrying the Faithbreaker with it. The golem fought to dislodge its arm, struggling to pull it free with a mechanical, single-minded focus.

It never saw the rock coming.

It flew through the air, from the colossal hands of the last vulgore. It smashed against the golem's face, tearing off a massive chunk of stone. The vulgore followed it with a charge, seizing the rock again as it tackled the golem and brought it to the ground.

With one hand still trapped in the vulgore's companion, the Faithbreaker held up its other in a vain attempt to ward off the rock. But the vulgore was powerful, hammering against the arm with its rock, again and again, until great chunks of stone flew through the air.

It hammered its arm to a stump. It hammered its chest to rubble. It hammered its face to a mass of bloodied white bits. And all the while, the Faithbreaker continued to speak.

"Death to pagans."

As its head was rent to rubble.

"Death to pagans."

As its body was pulverized.

"Death...to..."

As it was smashed to pieces.

Pathon had no words for it. No one had said a Faithbreaker could be destroyed. No one knew it could. The golem was Daeon's greatest weapon, sent to his greatest champions.

And now it was rubble.

Pathon simply stood and stared. He had no idea what he was looking at anymore. The image of the pulverized golem was simply not a thing he could understand. He didn't know how long he had been staring at it when he felt a hand on his shoulder.

"Marcher."

The speaker, sword bloodier than his face, looked down at him.

"Come. We retreat back to the pass."

Pathon looked around, suddenly aware that he was alone, suddenly aware that the sun hung high in the sky. He had stared at the rubble for so long, he hadn't noticed that his brothers had fallen back, that the tulwar had retreated, that the battle was over. For now.

"Speaker," he whispered, voice numb on his lips. "The Faithbreaker..."

"The Faithbreaker is a tool of sacrifice, Marcher," the speaker said. "It is fueled by sacrifice. It is awoken by sacrifice. It is only fitting that it ends in sacrifice."

"It is a weapon of Daeon. And we lost it."

"So are you, Marcher. And when you pass, it will be a great sacrifice, as well."

Pathon looked up at him, face empty. "For what, Speaker?"

The speaker turned toward the pass. "For your brothers. For this city. For its people."

"For the Prophet," Pathon whispered. "Heaven is watching."

"Heaven is watching." The speaker nodded.

And together, they returned to the pass, picking their way among the endless dead.

THIRTY-ONE

AN ANGEL FALLS FROM ON HIGH

Lenk found, when he closed his eyes, that he could almost hear them screaming.

That was impossible, of course. His tent was far away from the battle. But he knew that the armies would have met by now. And he knew how it would play out.

They would meet in a clash. They would battle, back and forth, shedding blood and spilling corpses on the ground in great, steaming heaps beneath the sun. Tulwar and human and whatever other poor fools had found their way there. They would fight like they had nothing else to live for, never knowing that there was plenty else to die for.

He played the scenario out over and over in his mind. Sometimes, it changed. Sometimes, the tulwar were victorious and overran the human defenses at the pass. Other times, the humans held firm and drove back the tulwar. Occasionally, shicts showed up and killed everyone.

But it always ended the same. And he could always see it in his head.

The earth quaked. The sun was blotted out by the titanic figure that strode in front of it. Serpents the size of pillars coiled and hissed and shrieked. A pair of great baleful eyes stared down on the battle with pity and contempt. Khoth-Kapira opened his great mouth, spoke a terrible word and...

Then, there were nothing but corpses.

"I failed."

The words had been rattling inside his head for days. Now they had finally grown heavy enough to fall out of his mouth. He lay on the bedroll, stared up at the canvas ceiling of the tent, and said them, again and again.

"I failed," he whispered. "I failed. I failed."

"There was a lot about you I missed."

Lenk leaned up on his elbows. At the entrance to the tent, Kataria sat, cross-legged. She held up an arrow, running fingers over the fletching before she checked it for straightness.

"Your weird little self-loathing monologues, though?" She glanced sidelong at him. "Not so much."

"Well, if you had been around to listen to them, I wouldn't have such a backlog to get through now." Lenk eyed her. "What are you doing?"

"Counting arrows." Kataria held up another one. "I don't just pull them out of nowhere, you know."

"What for?"

"Seventeen." Her ears folded flat against the side of her head. "Seventeen I can use, anyway. I could lose maybe three and still do all right. So these…" She set three arrows aside. "Are for hunting. The rest, I'll keep."

"For what?"

"For whatever we do next," she said. "I don't know what your plan is, but if it's anything like your last ones, I'll probably end up shooting people in it."

He stared at her. "I don't have a plan."

"So you'll make one as you go," she said. "It'll come to you, given the right circumstances."

"No. I mean, there is no plan."

"Fine. I'll just start shooting people and see where the day takes us."

"Do you not get it?" He sat up and pulled his knees to his chest. "Do you not get that this is *beyond* a plan? Do you not understand how thoroughly *fucked* I have made everything? A demon is coming. Not just *a* demon, a fucking *king* of demons. He raised monuments, he built an empire, I've seen it. He's coming here to enslave everything and kill what won't kneel, and I can't do a fucking thing to stop it."

Kataria's ears rose. She didn't look at Lenk. She simply stared at the arrow in her hands. After a moment, she set it aside, picked up another one, and began inspecting it.

"Make it eighteen," she said. "One of them's a little crooked, but crooked arrows can still kill. Sometimes better."

"Your ears are too fucking big to not have heard me," he said. "It's over, Kat. Even the threat of Khoth-Kapira couldn't make Gariath listen to me. He's going to bleed himself dry on the humans and be meat when the demons finally come. I could have stopped it but—"

"How could you have stopped it when you never fucking *shut up*?" Kataria bared her canines at him, eyes flashing angrily. "Yeah. I know what happened. I couldn't get Asper to listen to me, either. Things look bad now, but they've looked worse before."

"They haven't."

"How big did you say this demon was?"

"As tall as a mountain and he makes the earth shake with every step." Kataria sniffed, snorted, spit out onto the sands.

"We've seen bigger." She leaned back, flashing a grin. "Remember back in the wilds? Remember the island with the big squid-lady-thing?"

"She was huge."

"Filled a whole fucking cavern. We got out of that, didn't we?"

"We did. But that was different."

"How was it different?"

Lenk couldn't answer that.

Back then, things had been simpler. It hadn't just been him doing the killing. They fought together, bled together, survived together. That was worth fighting for, worth killing for.

But back then, there had been the promise that whether he won or lost or ran or got knocked flat on his ass, she would be there. With a curse, with an insult, with a bandage sometimes or maybe just with a hand to pull him back up.

But now... things were different.

She hadn't slept in the tent with him, sleeping outside instead. She looked at him in cursory glances now, the same eyes she showed everyone. Even now, she put a deliberate space between them, a space reserved for someone that wasn't him.

Now, win or lose, she wouldn't be there when he got back up.

Those weren't the words she needed right now, though. She needed something shorter.

"Yeah." He rubbed his face. "Yeah, all right. We'll figure something out." He found his boots, shirt, and belt. He tugged them on, plucked up his sword, and got to his feet. "Something with shooting, I guess."

"Food would be nice, first." Kataria shoved her arrows into her quiver and grabbed her bow leaning against the tent. "We ran out of meat this morning."

"There's still some fruit left, I think," Lenk said.

"Excellent. I'll save it for later. Like when I decide to give up on life." She sneered. "Come on. I saw some dead trees farther back with bird nests in them. Eggs are nature's meat."

"That doesn't make any—"

"Who's the fucking outdoorswoman here?"

He sighed and rubbed the back of his head. The wind was slow and hot in his face, plastering hair to his brow with sweat. The days of riding and failing made him feel positively ancient.

Yet to look at her, he would have thought it was just another day.

She was sweaty, still, and grimy, with patches of dirt painting her face, her arms, her belly. Her leathers were coated in dust and her hair hung in damp strands. But through the mask of grime, her eyes were still a bright, vivid green. And her grin, sharp as the knife at her hip, made a white scar through the dirt.

Filthy. Feral. Smiling obnoxiously. Just as she had been when he had first met her. Just as she always was.

Still so gods-damned perfect.

That thought brought him some comfort, at least. Comfort that couldn't be found in elusive sleep, or stale food, or even in the chill breeze that he felt on his back as—

He paused.

Ah.

"You go ahead," he said. "I'm going to check that the horse still has water." He pointed over her, drawing her gaze farther down the dunes. "You said they were back there, right? I'll catch up."

"The horse is fine," Kataria grunted. "Just come on. You can't plan anything if you're hungry."

"I said I'd catch up, didn't I?" he said. "If I start to starve, I'll have some fruit." He waved a hand down the dunes. "You're the fucking outdoorswoman. Go take care of it."

"Yeah, yeah." She hiked her bow up over her shoulder and stalked off down the dunes. "You better come up with something amazing."

"I already did."

He waited until she was out of earshot to say that—and to be out of *her* earshot, she had to be well out of sight. And when she was, he calmly drew his sword from its scabbard, closed his eyes, and whispered into the chill breeze:

"All right. I'm ready."

No answer but the wind.

Growing colder. Stronger. Closer.

The sound of the beating of great wings, like a bloodless heart, filled his ears. When they were too loud to be ignored, he finally opened his eyes. He looked down at the sand.

And saw the great shadow looming over him.

"Thanks for waiting," he said as he turned and beheld the beautiful ruin before him.

And through empty eyes, Oerboros stared back.

In the ugly light of day, the wreck of the Aeon's body seemed even more cruel. His wounds still glistened as though fresh, great holes had been carved in his starved frame. His withered legs hung beneath him as he hovered in the air before Lenk. His branchlike arms looked incapable of wielding the great sword they carried, its metal so twisted and ancient it looked like stone.

One would have thought the Aeon not alive at all, if not for the majesty of his wings.

Brilliant white feathers and emerald scales glittered in the sun, making his wings a sky all their own as they slowly beat behind him, keeping him aloft. His face, an emotionless mask of bronze, looked over Lenk's head toward the direction of Kataria's departure.

"She seems nice," he noted in his bell-rung voice. "Perhaps a tad crude."

"She is," Lenk said, "and she is. But you're here for me, aren't you?"

The Aeon said nothing. Lenk studied his reflection in the bronze of Oerboros's face.

"I was wondering when Khoth-Kapira would send you after me."

"The master has no knowledge of my presence here. In fact, he requested I stay away from you. Or perhaps you did not wonder why I did not pursue you when you and the female escaped."

"Then why are you here?"

The beating of his wings stopped. Oerboros alighted upon the ground. Even earthbound, he towered over Lenk. His ruined skin crinkled as he looked over the desert, face betraying nothing.

"The air is foul down here," he said. "I cannot breathe without the taste of dirt and salt. I have long wondered why he enjoys it as he does. After much contemplation, I believe I have an answer."

He looked down at Lenk. "Up there, we had no concept of love. Whatever you may believe of kind and adoring heavens, they are myth. We knew only what we must know, decided only by what we needed. But here, we were corrupted by mortality. We were so enamored of the diseases that afflicted you, we never once stopped to think of the ones you might spread.

"Everything is so fleeting here, so short and brittle. It makes one desperate to hold on to what little things they can seize. In time, it even drove him to do what he did. He loved mortals, loved the adoration they gave him that heaven would not. It infected him, as it infected me. He could not bear to part with them, just as I could not bear to part with him."

"When I saw you last," Lenk said, "you cursed his name. You called him a manipulator, arrogant and cruel." He cringed at the thought. "I saw Kyrael, your friend. She bled forever into the water, cut open by his hand."

For all of the terrifying emptiness in Oerboros's voice, Lenk had never felt truly unnerved until he heard the Aeon laugh. It was a stilted, halting thing, as though Oerboros were trying to imitate something he had heard long ago.

"She does. He is. And I meant everything I said." The Aeon's laughter died. "It is humorous to me. I recognize all these things about him—his vileness, his wickedness, his terrible needs—and I know that he shall never not be those things. And yet I love him."

"Why?"

"In all sincerity, mortal, I was hoping you might be able to tell me. I am aware of what Khoth-Kapira said to sway you to his cause. Why did you send the female away?"

Lenk felt a pain in his chest, a question he had been avoiding for a long time suddenly clawing its way up into his throat. He would have rather thrown himself on the Aeon's sword right then and there than answer it. But even then, he knew he would have to, eventually.

"Because she's everything I should have fought for to begin with," he said. "She was all I needed and I lost her." He shut his eyes. "But she hasn't lost me. All I know is how to fight. And all I've got left to fight for is keeping her safe, even if I'll never have her again." He let out his breath and his pain with it. He looked up at the Aeon. "And you're here to kill me."

Oerboros inclined his head. "I am."

"For him."

"For him," the Aeon said. "I do remember all his flaws. But I remember, too, the joy he felt at his creations, the brilliance of his mind, and his laughter when he made something new. I wish to see that again. And here, at the dawn of his greatest triumph, I will."

"What?" Lenk narrowed his eyes. "What triumph is that?"

"You could see, if you wanted. You could leave...but you will not."

"And you wouldn't let me live, if I did."

"I would not." He raised his massive sword, the metal groaning as he did. "I confess frustration. I am stricken with your mortal malady and yet I do not understand why I do these things."

"No one does," Lenk said. He hefted his sword. "You just try to get through it as long as you can." He paused. "Whatever happens here...she's got nothing to do with it."

"She is incapable of harming him. No harm shall come to her if she does not interfere."

"She won't." He nodded. "Thanks. For that."

"He will miss you, mortal."

Lenk didn't see the swing.

Just a flash of ancient metal, the sand beneath him, his hair whipping about his face as a great burst of wind followed it.

Oerboros was a little too tall. He was a little too short. All his scars still remembered the hard lessons and had taken him to the ground.

That was all that had saved him from decapitation.

Those same scars told him what to do. They sent him up to his feet, sent his hand clenching around his sword hilt, sent his legs burning as he rushed forward.

He darted to the side as Oerboros's sword came down, bit into the earth. Sand sprayed up in a wave, splashed against his cheek, and clung to the sweat. He felt the shock of the blow in his feet. Frail as he might have looked, the Aeon's sword was still almost as long as Lenk was tall. One cut would be all it took—wouldn't even have to be a good one.

But old pains taught him old tricks.

Get inside. It was the scars talking, not him. *Get close. He can't use that thing close up.*

He didn't know enough about Aeons to know if they could read thoughts. But it seemed Oerboros at least knew enough about fighting to know what Lenk was doing. As the young man rushed forward, he backpedaled, long legs carrying him great strides backward as he tried to maneuver his massive weapon to strike. But Lenk was a short man and short men knew two things: how to fight tall foes and how to fight when it seemed like a bad idea.

He pressed on, kept low, darting beneath the Aeon's swinging sword. Oerboros reached out, trying to seize him. He lashed out with his blade, nicking the Aeon's arm. Blood spattered the sand.

He can bleed, Lenk thought. *Just like a demon.*

Made sense. Demons were Aeons once. And he had killed plenty of demons before.

Few of them had swords *that* big, though.

Oerboros tried backpedaling again, leaping away from Lenk, swinging his sword as he did. Lenk ducked low, hacked up, caught the Aeon at the wrist. The sword wavered and fell, and with it, Oerboros's guard.

Lenk rushed forward, beneath a fist that came crashing down behind him. He leapt low, darting between a pair of long, withered legs. He came up the other side and his blade came with it. He carved a long angry red line up the Aeon's back, sending Oerboros's ruined body twisting with agony.

That's not agony.

Lenk saw the swing this time, but not quick enough. Oerboros's entire body seemed to snap as the massive sword came around in a great backswing. Lenk's sword shot up to catch the blade. The metal groaned as the momentum of the blow carried Lenk off his feet and sent him skidding across the sand.

Shock waves traveled down his arms into his chest, tearing the breath right out of him. He could barely feel his arms as he picked himself up. But the scars wouldn't let him stay down.

Oerboros's great wings were flapping, emerald scales stained with his blood. He was getting ready to fly, take the fight to the air. He wouldn't give Lenk another chance.

And Lenk wasn't about to give him this one.

He tore forward, kicking up sand behind him. He ran straight into the blade as it came down, twisting away only a breath before it hit the earth. He leapt onto the blade, launched off it, and reached out, wrapping an arm around the Aeon's neck. Oerboros let out a brass note of alarm, reaching for him as he wormed his way around, out of the Aeon's grasp. He hung there, one arm wrapped around Oerboros's throat, his heels digging into the fresh wound in the Aeon's back. He saw the meaty joint of Oerboros's wing, the sinewy muscle beneath the feathers twitching as it carried them both off the ground.

Lenk raised his sword.

Steel wailed. Blood sang. Muscle glistened as the wing twitched and fell limp, hanging to the Aeon's shoulder by strings of meat.

Oerboros let out a noise, a freakish rusted trumpet note that made no sense to Lenk. It was as though the Aeon had no idea what it was, this pain he felt, and no idea what to do with it.

But Lenk did.

One more stroke of his sword finished the job, sent them both crashing to the ground. They landed in a spray of sand, Lenk falling clear from the impact to tumble across the earth. He rose to his feet, sword at the ready, but didn't dare approach what was on the ground.

Oerboros spasmed on the earth, making that rusted noise, limbs flailing wildly. Beside him, his severed wing flopped about like a living thing as they spattered each other with red. After a time, and after much screeching, they both fell still. Oerboros's sides moved with soft, labored breathing. The wing moved not at all.

Lenk glanced at the wing and sniffed.

"I'm guessing that doesn't grow back."

He began to approach Oerboros, slowly, cautiously, sword at the ready.

"He's using you," Lenk said. "He used me, too." He gestured to the severed wing. "There's no reason for you to lose more today. Give this up. He doesn't deserve what you're doing for—"

"I am aware of that." Oerboros let out a crinkling gasp. "I have known him for centuries, I know what he does." He rolled onto his side, groping at the stump where his wing had been. "I simply do not know how. How, time and again, he does this to me."

"He knows what people want," Lenk said, taking a step closer. "He offers them what they need. What they *think* they need. He pretends it's real." He shook his head. "I don't know, maybe it is. But he never tells you what he's going to do to make it happen. He never trusts you to understand the whole thing. To him, you and me, we're just...children? Amusements? I don't fucking know."

"No," Oerboros said. "We are animals to him. Rare and beautiful creatures he wishes to protect, but cannot conceive of a way to do it without caging us." He drew in a ragged breath and lay still. "Every time, the bars grow thicker, but harder to see. This time, though...the city would never even know what happened to them."

"The city?" Lenk took a hastier step closer. "Which city? Cier'Djaal?"

"The names are unimportant to me. But he sees how they teem with life, how they cry out for a savior. He craves to be that for them. He already is."

"What do you mean?" Two more steps closer. "Oerboros, tell me. Don't let him get away with it. What's he planning?"

"You suggest he has not already done it." Oerboros's sigh was ancient. "It would not do for a great demon to arrive, heralded by thunder and the wailing of men, and be loved, would it? They had to be waiting for him. They had to know his name."

"No one in Cier'Djaal knows of Khoth-Kapira."

"That is but one of his names. To many others, he was known as the God-King. To a few, he was Mocca. And to them...well, you have been there. You have already heard his name, have you not?"

Lenk's eyes went wide. The realization fell upon him, nearly bore him to the earth.

"Ancaa." He whispered the name. "He made his own fucking religion."

"He has done so before. He merely did so deliberately this time. They have waited for him, the suffering and the weak, without even knowing him. And when he arrives, he shall be welcomed with open arms, no matter what calamity he brings."

Lenk rushed forward. "How will he do it? What's his plan?"

"Already, his prophet works. She gathers the faithful and waits for his arrival. Even she knows not what he'll bring."

"She..." Lenk shook his head. "Teneir. Is it Teneir? The fasha?"

Oerboros said nothing. Lenk knelt beside him.

"Oerboros, tell me," Lenk said. "Tell me how to stop her. Tell me how to stop *him*."

"Would that I knew."

Oerboros's hand shot out and seized Lenk by the throat. He tore Lenk from his feet, the sword falling from his grasp as he rose up, holding the young man aloft.

"There is still so much I do not understand."

He raised his hand, brought it down, and Lenk with it. He slammed the young man onto the earth and held him there. Lenk let out a scream, a curse, a plea—he had neither the sense to tell which nor the breath to let it out. He squirmed, kicking his legs and clawing at Oerboros's hand as the Aeon raised his massive blade.

"Deception, too, is something we did not know. I am sorry to have used it in such a way. I am sorry that I do not know how to stop." His voice was empty, water spilling from a bronze cup. "I am sorry that, even after all this, he will one day hurt me again. But I will be glad that he is alive to do so."

Lenk croaked out a word. He wasn't sure what it was. He couldn't hear his own voice. He could only hear the blood clotting in his ears, the skin tightening around his throat, the groan of the sword's ancient metal.

He never even heard the arrow until it lodged itself in Oerboros's hand.

The Aeon looked at it, the head jutting out between his fingers, as though uncertain what it was. He turned his hollow eyes up, toward the distance.

And, in a breath, another arrow lodged itself in his right eye.

Lenk craned his neck. There she was. Bow drawn. Eyes hard. Staring down the arrow. Lips peeled back in a snarl.

Still so gods-damned perfect.

She loosed. It flew, lodging itself just above the hand that held Lenk to the earth. The head burst out the other side, bloodless. Mortal violence could not harm Aeon or demon, Lenk knew. Only memory could. And while he wasn't sure what exactly that meant, he had a few theories and no other choices.

He reached up. He grabbed the arrow. He pulled it violently out the other way. It came with a spatter of blood. And that long, loud scream that wasn't a scream.

The Aeon's grip loosened, just enough for Lenk to pry himself free. He scrambled away, searched for his sword. He had barely brushed fingers against the hilt when a foot caught him in the side. The kick carried him up off his feet and sailed him breathlessly through the air. He landed hard on the earth, knocking the last breath from him. He rolled limply on the sand, down the dune, before coming to a stop.

Breath gone. Sword gone. A fierce pain in his side. No blood for his legs to stand with. No air in his head to think with.

He had a scar somewhere that would tell him what to do here, he knew. Somewhere on his body, one of the old pains would know how to get out of this. But he couldn't feel it on his body. Not in time, anyway.

Oerboros came crashing down, his one wing carrying him only a few feet before he landed. He advanced upon Lenk, his sword dragging behind him. His bronze face betrayed no pain as he came; his hollow eyes betrayed no pity. He showed nothing.

Not even when she appeared over Lenk, bow drawn, ears aloft, arrow aimed right at Oerboros's throat.

She couldn't hurt him. She had to know that. No arrow she fired would ever harm him. But there she stood, her back to Lenk, her muscles tense, not fleeing, not moving.

She didn't even look back at him.

"I am unconcerned with you," Oerboros said. "I swore no harm would come to you if you did not intervene. And despite that, you still cannot hinder me. Leave now. I will grant him the mercy of sparing you."

"No."

Kataria fired an arrow. It lodged itself in Oerboros's throat. He did not so much as flinch.

"I do not understand," the Aeon said. "He is weak-minded. He is murderous. He has betrayed many to get here, yourself included. Why? Why would you die for him?"

Lenk couldn't see her face. He didn't need to. He could feel her snarl, the sharpness of her canines, the fury in her eyes, just from her voice.

"Because," she said, voice drawn like a blade from flesh, "he's *mine*."

She fired. Once. Twice. Three times. One in the chest. Another in the leg. One more in the eye.

Oerboros didn't care. He didn't stop. He didn't so much as hesitate when he lashed out with a hand, striking her across the face and sending her sprawling.

"Kataria!"

Lenk found his voice. He found his breath. And while he could find no scar to tell him what to do, he did it, anyway.

He scrambled across the sand and threw himself over her protectively. She was still, but she was warm, her blood burning inside her. Her breath was hot and ragged as she groaned. And, so close to her, her pain so sharp in his ears, he knew what to do.

He found her knife.

"I am sorry," Oerboros said. He raised his massive sword high. "I cannot remember if you go to the same place. But you will go together, at the very—"

Lenk whirled around. He lunged. Kataria's knife plunged into Oerboros's withered belly. He snarled, giving it a sharp twist. Red came out in a great wash, pouring over Lenk's hands and staining the earth black.

No sound this time. Oerboros didn't have a noise for this. Oerboros didn't know what this was, what was happening to him. The earth shook as his blade fell from his hands. Sand squished as he slumped to his knees. He looked down at the gaping wound in his abdomen as Lenk tore the knife free.

"Ah." His voice, still so empty, still so calm. "I understand this, at least." He looked up at Lenk. His eyes, still so hollow. "There was no other way to be free of him, was there?"

No answer but the knife. Punching up through Oerboros's jaw, under his chin. Twisting in his flesh, tearing out the last part of him. It held lodged there, a macabre piece of jewelry on the magnificent ruin of his body as he slumped over.

The last Aeon collapsed onto the sullied earth and moved no more.

Another time, that might have weighed more heavily on him. But Oerboros's body was not his concern.

"Kat!" He rushed back to her as she staggered to her hands and knees, coughing. "Easy! Easy." He took her gently by the arm, slowly helping her to her feet. "Slowly. He hit you pretty hard."

In three breaths, she found her legs. In one more, she found her fist. And then, she found his face.

She struck him across the jaw, a wild blow that found him out of luck. He recoiled from the strike, holding his face as he looked at her with a shocked stare.

"What was that for?"

Her only answer was a snarl as she lunged forward, swinging for him again. She missed as he pushed back, but she shoved him harshly, toppling him off his feet and onto the ground. She leapt upon him, throwing wild blows at his face as she snarled through gritted teeth.

"For fuck's sake, *calm down*!" he roared to be heard, trying to block her punches.

"What did I say?" she shrieked. "What the *fuck* did I say?" A fist caught him in the cheek. "No more people saving me. No more people getting hurt for me." A blow caught his ribs. "And what the fuck do you do? You send me off and go rushing off to get killed and leave me fucking alone?"

"I was trying to protect you!"

"How many times have I saved your scrawny ass?" she growled. "Including this time? How many?" She seized him by the collar, slammed his head against the ground. "You don't get to say this was for me. Not any-fucking-more!"

She struck him several times, but he felt no pain. It wasn't force driving those blows, but fear. And the more she screamed at him, the more he realized that wasn't anger in her voice.

But it wasn't until she held still for a moment and took a wet, ragged breath that he was able to look up at her.

And see that she was looking at him.

Her eyes wide and wild and staring through him, drinking him in, seeing more to him than he knew he had. And though her eyes were glistening with wetness now, tears tugging at the corners, he remembered a time when she had looked at him like this. He remembered their first meeting, her eyes so big, so hard to look at, so deep.

But fuck me, he thought, *were they always that green?*

Without realizing it, he reached up. She flinched at his touch for a moment as his hands brushed her cheek, pushed a strand of dirty golden hair from her face. But as his hand took her gently, she leaned into it. He felt her shuddering breath. He felt her tears on his fingertips. He felt her. And she was so warm.

"Sorry," he said. "I'm sorry." He swallowed something hard. "I'm sorry, Kataria."

She cringed, canines bared, looking as though she was about to cry or kill him. She did neither, instead collapsing on top of him, wrapping her arms around him, pulling him close to her. He felt her breath against his neck, her body soften as he touched her, strands of her hair catch in her mouth.

Under the sun falling from its apex, he held her as she held him. He felt the scars on his body fall silent. He closed his eyes.

And remembered the first time she had touched him like this.

THIRTY-TWO

FALLING STARS

The day had died in the dust. But the night was alive with fire.

Pyres littered the tulwar encampment, lighting up the darkness of the valley like earthbound stars. They blotted out the true night sky as they sent the dead traveling skyward on ash-choked columns of smoke. By their lights, tulwar dragging more corpses for more fires could be seen—teams of ten using ropes to haul the great vulgore carcasses to the flames.

Smaller campfires dotted the valley, well away. These were used only to cook whatever food the warriors had brought with them. There was not enough for a prolonged assault.

And farther away from them, almost too far to be seen, was the torch-light of the boats. The barges, laden with green roofs and bow-wielding warriors, plied their way up the Lyre, the light of their torches reflected on the water. They made their way slowly, in full view, intent on drawing attention.

Gariath wondered if they would get it. There was so much fire in the valley, he thought, would the humans even notice just a few more rolling up the river?

"Lucky they held their flying beasts in reserve for as long as they did." Mototaru didn't look up from the map he was drawing in the sand by the light of a torch thrust into the earth. "Just the one might have ruined our gaambols for the rest of the fight."

"The Yengu Thuun haven't found a new chieftain?" Gariath asked.

"Gaambols choose their chieftain. Like everything else, the Yengu Thuun are just along for the ride." Mototaru glanced up at the river. "If they had more of those birds at their disposal, they would have sent them all. Our boats will keep them busy for tomorrow."

"Tomorrow."

The word was almost too big to contemplate after what had happened that morning.

Somewhere along the march, after Gariath had left Lenk behind, he had convinced himself that this was too big to stop. So many tulwar bent on fury, on vengeance; how could anyone have stopped them, let alone someone as weak and stupid as Lenk?

But that was before this morning.

Before the humans and their thick shield walls. Before their many arrows. Before their flying beasts and giant stone golem and the road they had paved by grinding the tulwar—*his* tulwar—into the earth beneath their boots.

They hadn't been able to collect those bodies.

"Tell me again," Gariath said.

"It doesn't matter," Mototaru said. "It won't help anything."

"Tell me."

Mototaru sighed and took a deep puff on his pipe. "Four hundred. Roughly." He exhaled a gray cloud into the night. "Most died in the initial charge, pushing the humans back. Only a few more died from the crossbows. But then they brought that...that..." He gestured out to the desert, where the golem lay in rubble. "That *thing* out and we lost track. There might be even more than we knew dead, including the two vulgore."

Gariath stared down at the valley. Kudj was an immense, unmoving shape in the darkness, sitting and staring with empty eyes and open mouth at the gigantic pyre on which the smoldering remains of his cousins took a very long time to burn away.

"Kudj won't fight again," Gariath said.

"He will if you tell him. He's in shock, but he came through for us. If you just—"

"I said he won't." Gariath snarled. "He's done enough." He looked down at the pyres, too many to count. "Do tulwar burn their dead?"

"Some clans do. Some clans bury. In the north, I hear, they leave them out to be feasted on by scavengers to appease the mountain." Mototaru shook his head. "No one here will care enough. The Tul will take them back; the Tul will spit them out again as new lives. What we do here is make sure they have lives to come back to."

"Four hundred," Gariath muttered. "That's too many for one day."

"It is," Mototaru said. "But you wanted to attack today. There is nothing that could have been done."

"There was." Gariath looked away—far away from the main encampment, to a dark corner of the valley. "And for some reason, we aren't doing it."

There, in the shadow of a great dune without a single fire burning, the Mak Lak Kai clan milled. Their gaambols gnawed at bones and raw meat. The only light was the sparks of warriors sharpening their blades. Their black skin melded with the night, making them invisible but for the bright grins of their teeth and the white paint covering their faces. Every now and then, a coarse laugh would rise from Chakaa, so loud as to reach Gariath on his summit.

And his skin would crawl.

"No," Mototaru said. "Not yet."

"And why not? The Mak Lak Kai could have broken them in a heartbeat."

"Maybe. Or maybe they would have simply been hacked to pieces. Even a *malaa* cannot do anything when he is dismembered. And even if you had, the rest of your army would not follow in their wake."

"They'll have to get over that," Gariath snarled. "Everyone who wants to fight gets to fight."

"But in our ways, not everyone fights together."

Gariath stared long to the mountain pass, where the humans still stood. There was no smoke to mask his sight there. The bones and blood of the fallen tulwar pounded into the earth glistened beneath the moonlight. He narrowed his eyes, snorted.

"Bone and blood, win or die," he muttered, "these are *my* ways."

—— ⊷≣⊶ ——

"Did you know him well?" Dachon asked.

Pathon looked down at the dead man at his feet and frowned. He did not know Apala well. He was one of the newer recruits to the legion, arriving in Cier'Djaal shortly before war with the Sainites had broken out. The liberation of Cier'Djaal was to be his first campaign. He was raw, but disciplined and sturdy, so he had served in the front of the phalanx.

That much, Pathon knew.

Whether he had a family back in the Empire, though? Who would receive the deathscroll, telling of his demise? Whether it would be children or elders or a single woman who wept hot, angry tears at his death? Pathon did not know.

Nor did Pathon know exactly how Apala had died. The Karnerian lay in what remained of his armor on a linen tarp. His cuirass was perforated by spear blows. A deep gash in his side nearly bisected him. One arm was missing, likely wrenched off by those monsters the tulwar rode. It was hard to say which one had killed him.

Pathon hoped the deathscroll wouldn't speculate.

He hoped the deathscroll would instead tell of what Apala had died for. That it would speak of the great sacrifice he had made, not merely for Karneria, nor merely for humanity, but for heaven. He hoped whoever received it would read that, take solace in it, and know that he had served his duty for something greater than even the Empire.

"Heaven is watching," Pathon whispered.

"Heaven watched him get torn apart." Dachon cringed. "Does this not faze you, brother? There was no glory in this death, to be ripped to shreds by animals. One of those beasts might be gnawing on his arm even now. One of their *riders* might, even. Have you ever seen anything like this?"

"I have not." Pathon gestured with his chin to the other end of the tarp. He leaned down and took the tarp by Apala's head; Dachon took the feet. "I have fought many foes but none that have been as savage as this."

"Where is your fear, brother? Daeon says that fearlessness breeds recklessness, that wariness is paramount to the complete conquest."

"I have plenty of fear," Pathon said. "More than you could know."

That was plenty true. Only thirteen men had died that day—most killed when the gaambols had attacked—but when their numbers were already so few, that was a whole line in the phalanx. The tulwar would be able to tear through their ranks that much easier.

And yet his hands weren't shaking as they went about their work. He and Dachon quietly wrapped up Apala's corpse in the tarp, folding it precisely as they had been taught without hesitation, and securing it with twine. It would be sent to the priests of Gevrauch for preservation, then sent back to the Empire for burial. Many more would be going with him.

Assuming they weren't all slaughtered tomorrow.

But this, too, didn't bother Pathon.

"Then share whatever the hell is making you so bold," Dachon said as he tied the twine around the tarp. "I could use some right now."

Pathon blinked. "I'm not sure. I suppose I'm not...really worried about death." He looked up at Dachon. "That's weird, isn't it?"

"The speaker tells us not to fear."

"Yes, and we all listen, but we're trained to listen, trained to believe. For the first time in a long time...I feel like I'd believe even if he wasn't yelling at me. I guess it feels like that, even if I die, it's for something."

"The speaker tells us that, too. Many have died for the Empire."

"But that's conquest. That's to push the borders, to rearrange lines on a map, to secure more gold for the Imperial vaults. This is for..."

He looked out to the mountain pass. The phalanx there was a fraction of what had been there today, a crew to keep watching for if the tulwar returned while their brothers took their rest. They stood, sleepless and rigid, waiting for the day when they would die tomorrow.

"Everyone else." He looked to Dachon again. "We win here, do you know what that means?" His eyes widened. "It means she was right."

"Who?"

"The Prophet. It means that this fight really *is* the will of heaven. Not just Daeon, but *every* god. And not just for the Empire, but for *every* man, woman, and child. It's not just lines on a map this time. It's lives. It's families. It's...different."

Dachon shook his head. He plucked up Apala's bound feet. "You put a lot of trust in the word of a northerner, Pathon."

"I trust not in her words, but in her miracles." Pathon took Apala's head. They carried him over to a waiting wagon laden with three other tarp-covered corpses. "She united us with the hated foes, after all."

"Some are not pleased by that."

"Perhaps. But does it not feel good to have one less enemy in the world?"

Dachon managed a weak smile. "I suppose a little."

"I suppose a lot." Pathon looked upward, to the watchtower looming over them all, the faint light of candles burning within. "And if she can lead us to victory, who knows where else she can take us?"

"So," Asper asked as she stared through the spyglass, "on a scale of one to ten, how fucked are we?"

Haethen took the spyglass. She glanced through it and let out a deep hum.

" 'One' being a perfectly manageable problem and 'ten' being us all getting torn apart, fed to gaambols as our spear-mounted heads watch the rest of the city burn?" She sniffed. "Maybe a six?"

Asper rubbed her eyes. "Fucking great."

"Language."

They had sighted the boats just an hour ago, thanks only to the Sainites. By the time they had flown their scraws back to report, the river barges—each one laden with tulwar warriors—were already half-way down the river.

The morning's victory had made her bold. Harmony Road had been choked with the dead of the tulwar, their gaambol charge broken. The loss of the Faithbreaker was immense, but it had taken down two vulgores that could have easily shattered the phalanx with it. Even Haethen had been encouraged by that, despite the fact that she would have much to explain to her Imperial overseers about losing one of their most treasured weapons.

It seemed almost unfair that, after defeating ape-men, giant baboons, and massive gorilla-rhinoceros-whatever-the-fuck-a-vulgore-was things, she was about to be defeated by a bunch of boats.

"We were idiots not to see this coming," Haethen muttered. "But none of the information we have on tulwar suggests that they know boats." She sighed, setting the spyglass down. "Fortunately, we were lucky that we didn't dedicate the scraws to the defenses today."

"Lucky for those fucking monkeys, maybe."

Blacksbarrow came stomping up the watchtower's steps, her hat tucked under her arm. Her blue coat was stained with black patches where the gaambol's blood had spattered. Red streaked her face, rendering her grin white, stark, and wholly unnerving as she fired off a salute.

"Riders are ready when you are, Prophet," she said. "We'll take care of your river-monkeys for you."

Asper nodded, then studied her intently. "So, uh...you want to take care of..." She gestured around her face. "The whole 'blood' thing?"

"Let them know it was me that sent their gaambols running."

Blacksbarrow snorted. "One fucking lance was all it took." She quirked a brow at Haethen. "Where'd you learn that trick, anyway? Ancient Karnerian secret?"

"Atrepus's Guide to the Meat-Eaters of Bagwai, Volume Two." Haethen sniffed. "Nature book. The gaambols obey a patriarchal structure, following their chieftain. They don't fight without him. Maximum effectiveness with one well-placed blow."

"Like kicking a man in the stones."

Haethen blinked. "I prefer to think of it more like cutting off the head."

"Mine's better." Blacksbarrow turned to Asper. "With your leave, Prophet, we'll get to work."

Asper nodded. "Remember, I want you to slow them down. Sink them if you can, but don't do anything that'll get your soldiers killed. We'll need every scraw if the line breaks."

"If the line breaks, it won't be because of Sainites." Blacksbarrow fired off another salute. "Prophet."

She turned neatly and began to go, when Asper called out:

"Wait!" When Blacksbarrow paused and glanced over her shoulder, Asper took a step forward. "Should you...do you need to see Dransun before you go?"

"No time, Prophet."

"Just to tell him—"

"He's a warrior, Prophet. So am I." Blacksbarrow pulled her tricorne hat on and tucked her hair under it. "Whatever I want to tell him, I'll tell him if I come back. Whatever I need to tell him, he already knows."

She took off, coattails fluttering as she stalked down the watchtower and off toward her riders. The scraws gathered in loose formation below, screeching impatiently as the Sainites mounted them two to a saddle— a jouster in front, a shooter behind.

Impressive beasts. They clawed the earth with their talons, stomped with their hooves, lowered their antlered heads, and made shrill braying sounds. She had no doubt they could kill a good many tulwar.

But there were a lot more than a good many.

And less than thirty scraws to fight them.

"They had to have known."

Asper glanced to Haethen. The Foescribe stood at the watchtower's ledge, the spyglass turned toward the distant tulwar encampment.

"They must have counted on the scraws being here," she murmured. "The boats are there to keep them occupied."

"Our good luck we had the scraws in reserve, right?"

Haethen lowered the spyglass and narrowed her eyes. "Of the many four-letter words I would use to describe our situation, *luck* is not one." She shook her head, sent bushy hair trembling. "I anticipated the tulwar being a pack of savages ruled by strength."

"They are," Asper said. "I know what monster leads them."

"Then either he's smarter than he looks or he has good counsel. Either way, we can't count on the tulwar behaving as we thought they would." She tossed the spyglass aside with less care than usual, then seized a quill and scroll. "I must speak with Careus. I'll be back."

"I'll come, too," Asper said, moving to follow her.

"Stay here. I'll be quicker without you."

"If you're going to discuss strategy, I should be kept apprised."

"You will be, when I return." Haethen pushed past her and began to descend the watchtower. "I have more to tell him than mere tactics."

Asper ran to the railing and called after her as she walked down the ramp. "What else could you possibly have to tell him?"

"He is a warrior," Haethen replied without looking up. "But I am not."

Asper opened her mouth to call out to her again but couldn't find a word that would make her reconsider. She thought to simply follow her, but Haethen's hurried stride told her she'd regret doing so. With a sigh, she resigned herself to stalking to the railing and staring out over the battlefield.

An avian screech raked at her ears. She saw the scraws flap their great wings, taking flight. In a formation of black shadows against the starry sky, they flew off toward the distant Lyre. By dawn, they would either have the boats taken care of or be dead.

And she would still be here.

She looked to the road below. A wagon laden with tarp-covered corpses rattled down, pulled by a weary ox, toward Cier'Djaal. The remaining Karnerians watched it go, their helmets doffed in reverence for their fallen brethren. Tomorrow, there would be more wagons, more corpses. Unless they all died to the last man.

And she would still be here.

She slumped against the railing, her head suddenly very heavy.

When she had performed her "miracles," she had felt many things: deceitful, treacherous, guilty. But at least she had felt in control. It might have been lies that convinced the Sainites and Karnerians that she was the messenger of heaven, but they had been damn cunning lies and they had only happened because she could make them believe.

Now, those lies had become their own truths. It would take more work to convince her soldiers that they *hadn't* happened. As far as any of them were concerned, she was the Prophet. And while Foescribes strategized and wing-sergeants flew and speakers commanded, Prophets sat up in their watchtowers and waited for more people to die.

She had led them to this. And now she was simply watching them give their lives for her.

The moon rose high into the sky. Shadows stretched across the dusty earth and grew in a black garden. The stubborn shrub grass that marked the entrance to the Green Belt became bristling creatures. The cliffs opened wide in a vast yawn, jagged jaws opened wide to swallow the day's suffering. The corpses that remained on the dust sprouted inky blossoms, stiffened limbs sprawling out on the earth in mile-long shadows.

They seemed like living things now, these shadows. They had long limbs and silent voices and empty eyes. And the more she stared at the shadows, the more it felt as though the shadows were staring back at her.

"You are victorious."

A voice echoed behind her. A frail stone dropped into a bottomless chasm. Three bubbles of air escaping a man's mouth and bursting on the surface of the sea. Something intimate and profanely vast, as though the world had just stretched out another hundred miles behind her, made its presence known.

Or rather, his presence known.

Mundas was there when she turned. He stood stark against creation, something that just didn't quite fit. The candle's light flickered away from him. The night sky seemed to slough away from him. He seemed to notice neither of these. Nor even her. He stood at the edge of the watchtower, his hands behind his back and eyes on the river.

"This is what other mortals shall say of today, at any rate." His voice was soft and deep. "Your dead are few. Theirs are many. By your standards, it was a good day."

Asper was barely able to comprehend his presence, let alone his voice. Somehow, he always had that effect on her. And somehow, this time, she found words.

"By my standards, there are no good days," she said, surprised at how rough her voice sounded against his. "We could have avoided this entirely."

"How?"

"People could have listened. I could have tried harder. I don't know." She shook her head. "People are dead. That's never a good day."

"People die every day." He hadn't blinked since he had arrived. "Today, in fact, across the world, many people who do not know your name, your language, or your god died all at once." He closed his mouth, respectful of that fact. "Would it soothe you to know how many?"

"*No.*" She hurled the word at him. "No, it wouldn't. Few things would soothe me today." She narrowed her eyes on him. She had never done that before. "Including your presence here."

Mundas appeared not to have heard her. Or maybe he didn't even care. Or maybe he wasn't even speaking to her but someone far away.

"It appeared so simple when we first thought of it," he whispered. The night shuddered. "We were going to improve on what heaven had done, to remedy the flaws of mortality. But how can it be a flaw when it is by design?"

"What?" Asper shook her head. "I don't understand, and I—"

"The flaw of heaven was to believe that mortality's greatest sin was desire."

Mundas was not there anymore. He was behind her, standing at the map table, looking over the parchment. His eyes seemed to grow wider, as if hoping to take in the entire world in his view.

"But here remains the problem: necessity. To live, they need food. To eat, they need land. To till, they need gold. To buy, they must bleed. It would be too simple to say that gold is the root of it. The problem is thus: Mortality was built to view the world in the concept of exchanges."

She blinked. He was gone. He was on the road, far away, kneeling beside a broken corpse. The Karnerians stationed there did not look at him, for they did not see him. And when he spoke, his voice was still painfully close in her ears.

"We trade lives today for more lives tomorrow. We pay three days of war for three years of peace. Corpses become currency. Budgets are drawn up. Vaults are emptied. Deals are made and they do not satisfy. All this, we do in an attempt to reduce suffering, to exchange it. But we fail to eliminate it."

She blinked. He was gone again. He stood high on the cliff walls, staring down at the earth, frowning at something she couldn't see.

"And in our attempts to reduce, we only add to it. For to exchange, nothing is lost, only more is introduced. The solution, then, is charity: someone to willingly take the suffering and charge nothing. And who could do such a thing? Who could have the capacity to burden themselves with that pain and ask for nothing?"

"Talanas," she whispered. An answer or a curse, she didn't know.

"No. It was his fault—their design—that was responsible for this. We needed a god, but they were distant and uncaring. We could improve on this, as well. Or so we thought. Perhaps it was our own flaw that we believed that those with the capacity did not have their own necessities. Though they demanded no exchange of corpses or suffering, they required something else. Something so precious that mortals have fought and hunted and killed for it since inception, never knowing what it was."

He was beside her now. The entire watchtower seemed to shift, as though the earth were now leery of what stood above it. Though there was no wind, she could feel her breath escaping her.

"Poets called it love. Those more learned might call it acknowledgment. It was our flaw not to realize that he needed it. Our sin not to realize that we had not the capacity to give it."

"Mundas, would you—"

"Consider that, I suppose." His voice robbed hers, smothered it in the sky. "Whatever you do here will be fleeting. An exchange, however fleeting, must always be paid. I pray your debt is not large."

And he was gone.

She could never get used to Mundas. She did not even know of what he spoke half the time, let alone what he was. Whatever laws he obeyed, they were not hers or anyone else's. And into whatever emptiness he disappeared, she knew she should never even look, let alone follow.

But today was too different. Today, there had been too many bodies and too much blood.

"COME BACK HERE, YOU PIECE OF SHIT!"

She hadn't expected to scream that.

She wasn't really sure what to expect as her voice echoed into the night, either. She didn't know what Mundas would do to her for that insult, whether he would kill her, maim her, or simply ignore her.

She hadn't expected him to reappear.

Yet he did. She felt him behind her, his stark unbelonging that made the world a little more uneasy for his presence. And when she whirled on him, she hadn't expected to feel anger boiling up behind her face.

"Every fucking time you show up, it's this shit." She stalked forward, thrusting a finger at him as though he were simply an insubordinate soldier and *not*...whatever he was. "You appear. You say some cryptic shit that I don't understand. You disappear. And then I have corpses to clean up afterward."

He said nothing. He did not scowl or sneer or display the slightest evidence that he could even understand her. Yet his impossibly large eyes opened up to swallow her and she charged right in.

"I'm fighting one friend who's a talking lizard. I've been abandoned by another who shoots fire out of his ass. Together, we've seen so much horrible, evil, and scary shit that this crap that *you* do doesn't impress me anymore."

She stood tall, hands clenched at her sides, jaw set. She resisted the pull of his stare, challenged his profane stance. She snarled.

"So I'm going to give you two options," she said. "If you want to help me, then help me. Give me something I can use. But if you want to spew your gibberish and disappear, then you better stay gone, because I have no fucking use for this anymore."

Whatever Mundas was, she didn't know. What he could really do, she couldn't begin to guess. Yet of all that she was uncertain of about him, she knew, as children know to cry, that no one had ever spoken to him like this before.

Something flashed across his face. No godly rage or terrible vengeance. His eyes did not open up to swallow her and his presence did not engulf her. His lips trembled and curled downward and, with a shudder that told her he hadn't done so in a long time, he sighed.

"I cannot do much for you." He shook his head. "I wish I could. I frequently wish I had not made the oaths I had, broken the vows I did. But this is done. We swore by the same promise, Qulon and I. We are bound to its laws."

"Tell me," Asper said. "Tell me what you can."

He looked at her. His eyes seemed to diminish, become more human. His voice was something she heard once more, rather than felt.

"We were there," he said. "In the earliest days, when heaven was close, we were there. We gazed upon the rancid world we had been set upon and the writhing bodies clawing over each other to escape from the mud. And we looked up to heaven, so close, and saw that no one was looking back upon us.

"We did not give ourselves a name then. We knew only that we could not be a part of it. It was not until after we had decided, those precious few of us, that we wanted nothing from heaven, that we knew what we were." He looked down at his hands, suddenly aware of his flesh. "We called ourselves Renouncers. We denied heaven's authority over us. We denied our part in creation. We have stood apart from them ever since."

"What does that mean?" Asper asked. "What *are* you?"

"It is impossible to say because we have never defined ourselves by what we are, but by what we are not. We are not a part of creation. We are not under the watch of heaven. We do not belong here. And because we do not, we are objective, we are neutral. We can improve on the work of heaven."

Asper's face tightened. "For people who seem to think you're so mysterious, you're pretty fucking common. I've heard a lot of people say they can improve on things. Usually, it means more death."

"As all creation must end in. But we sought to eliminate suffering, to end pain, to end misery. Some of us...disagreed."

"How? Who?"

"Qulon. Azhu-Mahl. Myself. Others still. We agreed, then, that we would not directly interfere with one another. We would permit each other's procedures to carry out to their logical ends and see who was correct."

"You made us into a test," Asper snarled. "All of us, we were nothing but playthings."

"That is...a minimal way of looking at it." He shook his head. "And we did not do anything that others did not already want. The poor and suffering craved vengeance, so we gave them the name Khovura. The fasha craved meaning, so we gave her the name Ancaa. The world cried out for someone who will listen to them, who will guide them, so we gave it the name Khoth-Kapira."

The words made her blood run cold. Her eyes could no longer blink. She no longer had a word for her.

Kataria was right. Lenk was right.

"But I cannot say more without violating the oath. And to violate the oath is to invite people like me, who can do what I can do, to turn to open violence."

He looked at her again. Something changed. The vestiges of humanity that had shown themselves, he shed like a cloak that pooled upon the floor. His eyes grew large. His mouth grew small. His body became a stain on the world that light and darkness avoided.

"This is not feasible. Not without drawing further wrath."

"Wait!" Asper said. "It's not enough. I need you to tell me more. I need—"

"Your necessity is something we will remedy, in time. I cannot tell you what will happen, nor tell you what to do. But I can tell you this..."

He disappeared. He was at the road, among the corpses.

"What we have set in motion cannot be stopped. The war Qulon has engineered will not end what we have created. Who we have summoned shall not turn away."

He disappeared. He was on the cliffs, staring down at her.

"Though the price was heavy, the result was valued. We are guilty, then, of our own exchange. If that is to be the last, then so be it."

He disappeared. He was in the desert, miles away.

"When the time comes, I advise you to recognize it. I advise you to see what can be accomplished, what *he* can accomplish."

He disappeared. He was across the world, his voice still in her ear.

"We have saved this world, priestess. We have done what gods could not. We have listened."

He disappeared.

And she was alone.

THIRTY-THREE

THE LEARNED MAN

I saw my first Librarian when I was about eleven."

Dreadaeleon canted his head to the side as he walked, considerate. His eyes lingered on the orderly hedges of the tower grounds, cut to complement the concentric circles of the stone paths that led up to the tower gates.

"Or was it twelve? Funny, I used to remember it so clearly." He smiled. "I still remember her, though. She was tall, powerful, statuesque. Beautiful, if I'm being thorough." He paused, his mirth turning to a frown. "Oh, don't look at me like that. That she was beautiful does not diminish her power or the respect I had for her."

He paused to kick some ash from his boots. He carefully picked his way across a patch of ice, vapor still rising from the red-stained icicles jutting up like a macabre shrubbery.

"She came to visit my mentor, Lector Vemire. He was on solitary study, took only a few apprentices. Did you know him?" He waved a hand, smoke trailing from his fingertips. "I'm getting off-topic, sorry. The Librarian...she was amazing. I remember the flawless black of her mantle, the perfectly rigid brim of her hat, the way her eyes always seemed to glow just slightly, as though she were perpetually calling up traces of Venarie."

He saw something moving out the corner of his eye. He turned. He inhaled. He spit from his lips a dagger-long icicle. There was a squishing sound. It stopped moving.

"Her poise, her knowledge, the power she had to spare...I wondered if I, one day, would have that kind of strength." He came to a halt before the tower doors and cast his frown downward. "Sometimes, I admit,

I wondered what it would be like to face one in a duel, to fairly pit my skills against theirs."

He knelt down. The man leaning against the doors, breathing heavily, looked up. Blood trickled into his eyes from a gash in his head, yet the hatred burning in his eyes was still quite clear.

"I never imagined it'd be this easy," Dreadaeleon said.

"Fuck..." The Librarian gasped, taking a ragged breath. "You."

Dreadaeleon stood up, frowning. The Librarian had good reason to be angry, the boy supposed. He had just seen three of his comrades cut down by fire, by frost, by lightning. He had lasted only a few breaths against Dreadaeleon before the boy nearly decapitated him with an icicle and used the subsequent distraction to hurl him against the doors. He imagined that most of the Librarian's bones were pulverized now, if the bloodless way his limbs lay around him were any indication.

Of course, that was still no reason for profanity.

"She had a wider vocabulary, too." Ghostly frost vapor coiled from Dreadaeleon's lips with every word. "I won't waste your time by telling you I'll spare you. But I'll give you the opportunity to do the right thing by telling me where Shinka is."

"*Fuck*...you," the Librarian gasped.

Dreadaeleon let out a sigh. The frost condensed on his breath. A frigid blade of ice formed before his lips and hovered expectantly in the air. He raised a single finger.

"Or just be useless."

He pointed his finger at the Librarian. The icicle flew. Red spattered his coat.

"That's fine, too."

He reached down, seized the limp Librarian by his throat, and hoisted him up. The man was a good thirty pounds heavier than him, at least, but the weight felt effortless in his grasp.

So many things felt effortless, these days.

Dreadaeleon felt the hunger open inside him, jaws gaping wide in some dark part of him and inhaling. His fingers slid into the Librarian's throat, puncturing perfect holes in his skin. Wisps of gray smoke coiled from the burning wounds in the man's neck. Blood evaporated. Bones snapped. Skin twisted. What was a man became a cloud of gray mist, dancing and twisting as though alive.

Dreadaeleon took a deep breath. The mist filled his mouth, his nose, his lungs. It flowed through him, settled in his bones, his skin, his muscle. In that dark place inside him, the great hunger quieted. The jaws closed. And he felt stronger.

Quicker that time, old man. He looked down at his hand, clenched it into a fist. He could feel the power surging beneath his flesh. *You're getting better at this. You consume more.*

He looked down at the twisted husk that had been a man, now nothing more than ash-colored limbs twisted like a starved and dead tree.

And leave less. He looked over his shoulder at the other three Librarians who lay cooling in the night air; dead, but whole. *Perhaps you should take the rest, as well. Wouldn't want to be unprepared for—*

He shook his head.

No, no, old man. No need to be greedy. Remember what you're doing this for. The power is only there so you can make this right. Asper is counting on you, even if she doesn't know it. And once she sees how you saved her from the Venarium . . .

He turned to the doors. He thrust out his hand. A great wave of force flew from his palm. The doors burst open with a great smash, their hinges groaning to hold on to the frame. They hung limp and impotent as the forces that had tried to stop him as he came striding into Tower Resolute.

This time, you're *the hero.*

He was expecting heroics when he entered. A battalion of Librarians assembled in a firing line against him, perhaps. An army of apprentices hurling fire and ice at him in sheer walls, attempting to wear him down by numbers. Or maybe even Admiral Tibbles.

Admiral Tibbles would have been nice to see again.

He wasn't expecting to find an empty lobby. The great, circular chamber had always been sparse in aesthetic, bearing nothing more than a few chairs and a desk where the Venarium clerks had received visitors.

The chairs and desk were still there. The Venarium was not.

The chamber was completely bereft of life. There was no defense to be seen. No heroics to engage. To look at the chamber, no one would guess a single soul was here, let alone a cadre of wizards.

That is, if one looked at it with their eyes alone.

Dreadaeleon could feel electricity in the air. He could feel pressure on his temples, the fluctuating temperatures in his body. The traces of spent magic were everywhere, suffused in the very air that he breathed. The hairs on his body stood on end and his eyes burned. A lesser wizard, he suspected, might have passed out from the sheer volume of it all.

A lot of people had used a lot of magic in a very little amount of time.

A battle, he thought. *There's no other explanation. This much magic couldn't have been made without it.* He surveilled the chamber, frowned. *Shinka has been busy.*

He made his way to the back of the chamber, behind the clerk's desk. A pair of double doors hung open, a set of stairs leading to the upper levels. When he had been here last, they had been fastened securely and two concomitants had stood guard.

All that remained here now were scorch marks.

He ascended the spiraling stairs. With every step, the lingering traces of magic grew more oppressive. He could feel pops and sparks in the air. He felt heat and cold running races through him. The pressure on his skull became pounding.

And in another few steps, he found why.

A great hall stretched out before him, forking off at the end into three paths, like a great trident. One led to the libraries, another to a scribing laboratory, a third to dormitories. Not that what it *used* to be mattered anymore.

It was a graveyard now.

Great icicles bloomed from the walls and pillars, in great patches and walls and spikes. Statues and chairs and stones lay strewn about, hurled by massive forces. The floors and tapestries were seared and cut by blackened pockmarks where lightning had struck and great carpets of ash where flame had eaten heartily. The evidence of magical use was everywhere.

And so was the blood.

In greasy streaks that stretched across the floor from one door to the other. In great, red blossoms that spattered the walls. In thick, glistening chunks that painted the stones, the broken pillars, the ceilings. The battle had been fierce and messy, no restraint practiced.

Whatever rules wizards applied to their interactions with the rest of society, it seemed, did not apply to themselves. He would have wondered what could cause such destruction.

"Try to be reasonable."

But that, too, was an answer he was soon to receive.

He followed the sound of the voice to the end of the hall. Around a corner, he spied three wizards. Concomitants, by the look of their coats and spellbooks. One of them lay against the wall, breathing heavily as he clutched a burn wound in his arm. Two others, their hands stretched out and ready to cast should he move, spoke to him.

"There's no need to drag out this violence," one of them, a woman, said. "Wizards fighting wizards is madness. We swore oaths to *avoid* this kind of insanity."

"You seem to have no problem violating oaths these days," the wounded man laughed bitterly.

"*That* was insanity," the other concomitant said. "Do you not see the reason in the Lector's words? We could have spared this city so much suffering with our powers. The Khovura, the Jackals, the foreigners…we could have handled them *all*."

"And do what afterward? Lord over them all?" the wounded man scoffed. "We are wizards. Our calling is higher than even kings. Your Lector would have us violate centuries of protocol for the adoration of the ignorant." He gestured out over the carnage. "And look what's happened."

"It only happened because you refused to see reason," the woman said. "But it's not too late. Let us help you. You can still be a part of something great here."

"I was already part of something great." He sneered. "You and your Lector would seek to use our power to rule over the barknecks. And you'll draw the attention of their armies, their kings, their priests. How long do you suspect you can truly last against the entire world?"

"The Lector has sworn that we'll use our powers only for the good of the world."

"Well, swearing oaths that don't mean anything is rather in style these days, isn't it?" The wounded man's laughter turned to an agonized screech. "Just fucking kill me like you killed the others."

"If you want." The woman sighed. Flames danced along her palm. "Such a fucking waste, though. You're going to—"

She paused. Maybe Dreadaeleon had stepped too close, breathed too hard. She suddenly whirled, along with her fellow concomitant, eyes wide and mouth gaping open.

"*You!*" she gasped. "How in the hell did you—"

"Like this," Dreadaeleon answered.

He flicked his hand. Force rippled across the air and struck her like a brick wall. She flew into her companion, both of them hurtling against the far wall. The rippling force crushed against them, the sound of their bones popping overwhelming the sound of their screams, for the brief moment they lasted. They fell to the earth, broken and unmoving.

He glanced to the wounded man, who slowly staggered to his feet. A sneer was plastered across his face as he looked at Dreadaeleon.

"And so the heretic comes back to feast on the scraps," he said. "It's almost enough to convince me the gods exist. Who else would send us this much trouble?"

"It appears your trouble comes from closer than the gods." He glanced at the carnage. "Things are not going as smoothly as Shinka anticipated."

"She would violate everything we hold dear," the wounded man said. "She wishes to use us to interfere in the affairs of the ignorant, use our powers for meddling." He spit on the floor. "But then, I suppose violations are of no particular concern to you, heretic. I survive her purge only to be finished off by you."

Dreadaeleon blinked. "I take it your mood wouldn't be improved if I told you I have no idea who you are." He sniffed. "Let's spare each other some awkwardness and you can just tell me where Shinka is."

"Obvious, isn't it?" the man asked. "She's the sole Lector in the tower now. She is at the very top."

"That *is* obvious. I suppose I could have thought of that myself." He offered a nod. "But it's nice that we got to chat, at least. Have a good day."

He had taken three steps when he heard the crackle of electricity. He glanced over his shoulder. The wounded man leveled his one good arm at Dreadaeleon, lightning dancing on the tips of his fingers.

"Whatever oaths she violated," he said, "Shinka is a lesser evil than you, heretic. And whatever oaths we have left, I still hold dear. And so long as I still draw breath, I shall not let you defile our—"

"Holy *fuck*, I get it, already." Dreadaeleon whirled about, flicked his hand. "Last good man in a world gone mad, willing to die for his principles. Yes. Fine. Whatever."

Flames roiled from his hand, washing over the man like a tide. He went down screaming, swallowed whole by red, cackling jaws. He fell to the ground in a smoldering heap of embers and ash. Dreadaeleon shook the sparks from his fingers.

"Fucking hell," he muttered. "Everyone's got to be so fucking *dramatic* these days."

Through the halls, up the stairs, on every floor of the tower, it was the same.

Sometimes, the scenarios were slightly different. Occasionally, it was wizards surrendering to wizards, locked in chains with their heads bowed. Now and then, there was an actual battle going on, lightning and rubble hurled through the air. On one floor, Shinka's rebels attempted to break down a door by hurling an immense stone at it while loyalists on the other side tried to reinforce it.

But they all spelled out the same story: Shinka had failed. Her coup had not gone as smoothly as she had hoped. Wizards were killing wizards. And he dealt with them the same way.

Those wise few that had fled from him, he didn't bother pursuing. Those loyal to the Venarium who saw him as a heretic and those loyal to Shinka who saw him as a threat, he made no attempt to tell apart. When he was done with them, they all tended to look the same.

And yet, for all the ash and carcasses he left in his wake, he felt no different. The magic he had expended should have been enough to drain him dry, yet he didn't so much as breathe hard. The power flowed effortlessly from his head to his hands.

And soon enough, as he ascended the tower's stairs to the very top, the sounds of carnage grew faint enough that he could hear something else.

"There are only a few holdouts remaining."

Voices.

"But the purge is nearing its end."

He came before a pair of immense doors. He could envision the meeting chamber beyond it, the circular room he had entered twice before: once as an accused criminal, again as a condemned one. He took his time approaching, savoring the moment he would arrive as a hero.

"Please don't call it that." Shinka's voice was weary but still elegant and proud. "I'd rather not remember this day as anything but a tragedy."

"Inevitable." The first voice, a male, spoke. "We knew some would cling to backward views. It's the entire reason that Annis had to go."

"Most of the bodies have been recovered for harvesting." Another voice, a female's, added. "And only a few Librarians turned against us. It's not ideal, but it's not unsalvageable."

"Then why does it feel like there's a war going on down there?" Shinka let out a long, agitated sigh. "Does no one else feel those fluctuations of magic?"

"I can't feel anything in this shit." Another woman muttered. "The air is so thick with magic I can barely feel my own face."

"That'll pass, too," the first female said. "In the meantime, we've got another problem. We continue to receive requests from the 'Prophet' at the front line for assistance."

"It's worth considering," the man said. "The tulwar numbers are reportedly immense. And we sighted even more coming over the deserts. If we don't aid her, we stand the risk of—"

"I did not pull this city from the clutches of a grasping, ignorant fool just to hand it to another one." Shinka's voice was cold and firm. "It's bad enough that we'll have to deal with Teneir and her cult. I don't relish the idea of contending with two delusional fanatics. To aid the Prophet would be to insult every life we were forced to take here."

"Ordinarily, I'd agree. But the number of tulwar is not insignificant..."

"How many are there?"

"A few thousand, at least."

"And how many Librarians do we have at our call, ready to fight tonight if we were to ask?"

"Perhaps fifty."

"That would mean...what? Perhaps a hundred tulwar killed by every Librarian?" Shinka said. "Upon last observation, the most advanced weapon the tulwar had was a really big spear. Taming them should be well within our abilities."

"That's still a resource stretched," one of the women said. "And there is much work to do in the city."

"I imagine that it will be much more manageable once they finish with the 'Prophet.' Let them break themselves on her. When the last of their ragged assault runs over the remains of her broken army, we shall find them easy to—"

She was interrupted by the sound of metal groaning. A great wall of force blew the doors from their hinges, sent them flying across the room. Dreadaeleon strode into a chamber of wide eyes.

That wasn't how he had wanted to enter.

He had wanted to come in calmly, to hand down his judgment of her insidious plot and then, over the course of a battle laden with perfectly timed witticisms, show her the error of her treasonous ways.

He had savored too long, listened too much. His hands burned. His face felt hot, twisted by the snarl of his lips. His eyes were burning bright as he came stalking into the room, radiating so much power it almost made his own head hurt. And when he spoke, no witticism came out.

"Traitor."

The words they spoke in exchange were those of power. One of the female Librarians leapt forward, exhaling a thick cloud of frost. A patch of ice formed on the floor. She stomped once and a wall of ice grew before her.

He thrust his fingers out. Electricity sang a single, thunderous note as lightning leapt from his hand. It punched through the ice, leaving a smoking hole. In frigid fragments, it shattered and fell apart. The female Librarian stared numbly forward, one hand reaching for the smoldering hole in her chest before collapsing.

Shinka leapt from her chair, speaking a word and thrusting her hands out. The chair behind her—along with every other one in the room—flew at Dreadaeleon in a flurry of wood. He roared, raising his palms and letting the cackle of flames join his anger. Fire washed over the chairs, sent them falling to the ground into cinders.

The male and female Librarians leapt forward, their movements mirrored as their fingers thrust out and shot twin bolts of lightning at him. They converged in the center, forming a great electric serpent that lashed out at Dreadaeleon. He threw a hand up, the air rippling as a shield formed.

The lightning struck him, intensified. He was forced back a step, forced to raise another hand. Inside him, he could feel something begin to burn, a furnace stoked hotter than it should be. He shut his eyes. He roared. He clenched his hands into fists.

The electricity dissipated in a burst of blue sparks. He drew a sharp breath, exhaled a cloud of white. It raced across the floor, coiling around the Librarians' feet. They managed to look down, the beginnings of a spell on their lips, before great spears of ice shot up beneath them. They were pulled off their feet, writhing and screaming on glistening white pikes before they hung limp, slowly sliding downward, their blood freezing upon the ice.

Whatever discipline Shinka had shattered at the sight of it. She took a step back, staring horrified at her impaled minions. When her eyes found Dreadaeleon, when her mind found a spell, his hand was already up.

And closing.

The air rippled around her throat. Her voice died beneath it as a great power suddenly clenched her by the neck and hauled her from her feet. Dreadaeleon whipped his arm across the room, hurling her away. She flew, choking on her shriek, before she struck the wall and tumbled to the floor.

Now's the time, old man. He stalked toward her, eyes ablaze. *She would betray Asper, sentence her to death. But not anymore. She'll see what you've done. She'll see how you saved her. And then she'll* know *she was wrong about you.* He loomed over Shinka. *Now, when you tell her the story of how it happened, make sure you say something witty at this part. Listen to Shinka beg for mercy. Try to say something in response.*

Shinka made a noise as she staggered to her feet.

But it was not begging.

It was laughter. Cold and bleak as the first dead tree of autumn. And though a thick trail of blood marred her face, her grin was unmistakably haughty.

Even as he so easily bested her, she laughed. Even as he lorded over her, she looked down on him.

"I should have known." She coughed. Blood fell from her mouth. "I should have fucking known you'd be back. The moment I found out your body wasn't where it should be..." She shook her head. "I can only guess at what made me think you would be smart enough to stay the fuck away."

"There's a lot of things you should have done," Dreadaeleon said. "You should have decided not to betray my friend."

"Your friend?" Shinka chuckled. "Oh. Are you and the Prophet friends now? All your words against her, all the impotent glares you shot at her back, were merely concealing a beating heart of friendship? How admirable." She spit blood onto the floor. "How fucking admirable."

"She's arrogant, and a fool, but she deserves better than what you were going to do to her."

"Oh?" Shinka's smirk, despite the blood leaking from the corner of her mouth, was insufferably smug. "Whatever did that poor girl do to deserve what *you're* going to do to her?"

Dreadaeleon's hand shot out. He seized her in an invisible grip and hurled her across the room. She struck the floor, skidded across it, and lay still for only a moment. And when she rose up, leaning on her hands, her back turned to him, she was laughing.

"You're stronger, concomitant. It's starting to make me believe in gods. Who else could be so cruel as to give you life again and send you to ruin my plans?"

"It's not the gods. It's *me*, Shinka." Dreadaeleon advanced upon her, his hands smoldering with flame. "I am limitless. I am forever burning. *I* will save Asper. I will save this entire city from all its evils, starting with you."

She wiped her mouth with the back of her hand, still chuckling. His face twisted with rage.

"I will entomb you in ice," he snarled. "I will shake you to pieces with a thought. I will burn the grotesque remains of you to ash and scatter them to every wind. I will wipe you from the earth, Shinka, and tear the very *memory* of you out of the skulls of your minions."

She tried to rise, but fell. Her laughter grew loud and shrieking.

"I will do this, *all* of this"—he roared to be heard over her—"without so much as breaking a *sweat*. Power like you've never seen, that would shatter your mind to simply gaze upon, that I can channel with a thought, and I will use it to make you, your life, your entire *legacy* into *nothing*, Shinka."

She threw her head back. Her smile all but split her face apart. The fires in his hands became infernos. His eyes erupted with red light. His voice shook the chamber.

"SO WHY THE FUCK ARE YOU LAUGHING?"

"All this time, I thought Annis a simple-minded buffoon, out of touch and dedicated to backward laws that helped no one. Now I see how perceptive he was. Why am I laughing?" She looked over her shoulder, grinning. "Why aren't you?"

"Annis was a fool."

"And even a fool could see what you were."

"There are no words that he, that you, that all your fucking libraries in all your fucking towers could find to describe me. I bested a Lector. *Twice.* I came back from death. I hold a power you cannot even comprehend."

"And despite all those things, you are still so frightfully common." She leaned over, her laughter interrupted by a groan of pain. "Obsessed with making loud noises and watching things burn, hungry for the sound of your own voice, taking all the time in the world to lord yourself over a woman..."

She turned on him suddenly. Her arm lashed out. From her hand, an icicle the size of a dagger flew. He blinked, raising a hand just by instinct, with no spell behind it. It was by sheer dumb luck that his flailing caused him to stumble to the side. The icicle tore a deep furrow in his cheek, drawing blood. He let out a scream, shrill and weak.

"Pity," Shinka said, giggling.

He snarled, reaching out for her. The magic pulled her forward, into his grasp. He wrapped his hands around her throat. His eyes burned so brightly she had to squint. And through it all, she smiled, she laughed.

"You *dare*," he snarled. "The powers I hold, the strength I command, and you dare think to—"

"Are you hoping I'll beg?" She laughed in his face. "I don't give enough of a shit, concomitant. You can kill me, you can burn this tower to the ground. You could hold the powers of a god and it doesn't change a damn thing. It'll all be nothing more than bright lights and loud noises to you. And you'll still be nothing more than a tiny, selfish, cruel little *boy*."

She kept laughing. He kept hearing her.

Through the sound of his scream, loud and angry, he heard her. Over the sound of her neck snapping, he heard her. Through the sizzle of flesh and hiss of smoke and the sound of a body breaking itself down into something insubstantial and airy, he could hear her.

"I am not a boy," he said.

When he lowered his hands, nothing but a few traces of ash fell to the ground.

"I am invincible."

What remained of Shinka lingered in a fine gray cloud, roiling in front of him. So proud, so cunning, and now just like the rest of them.

He closed his eyes. He breathed deeply. The great hunger inside him opened itself eagerly, its jaws stretching wide to take what he had consumed. He felt her power coursing through him, filling him to the very brim, like a glass overflowing with rich, red wine. His body felt ablaze with the power. His heart raced. The wound on his cheek sealed itself shut.

His mind suddenly burned with the knowledge of new thoughts, secrets he had never heard, ideas he had never considered.

That's never happened before. He blinked, the sensation uncomfortable, like a centipede crawling across his brain on a thousand skittering legs. *Is this . . . her? Her thoughts? Her ideas?*

He shook his head.

Don't worry about it, old man. You saved Asper, you saved everyone. You destroyed the Venarium. What else could this world offer you? Who else could stand in your . . .

His thoughts continued, of course. But he couldn't feel them anymore. He couldn't hear them.

As he turned and stalked out of the room, down the stairs, through the carnage, all he could hear was the sound of Shinka's laughing.

It followed him out of the tower and into the night.

THIRTY-FOUR

An Echo of Starlight

She had seen him before.

When she had been held prisoner, back at Shekune's camp, he had been there. His ears were aloft and listening when they accused her of lying with a human. The scowl he had given her had been particularly full of hate.

What was his name?

Kenki. The word came to Kataria.

An echo of his Howling hung over his glassy eyes staring skyward, the last thing that had been torn from his skull. It had cried out in the night, reaching out for anyone who could have heard him, who could have helped him.

She stared down at the khoshict's throat, severed almost perfectly in half, and frowned.

Not like he could scream any other way, she thought.

The story of his death was painted across the sand in red, smeared words and broken wood notes.

The fragments of his bow lay three feet away. His quiver was empty—what few arrows could be scavenged, Kataria had taken for hers. Where the rest of them had gone, she didn't have to look far.

The Sainite lay not too far away, facedown in the earth. Three arrows jutted from his back, but it was clear that the fall had been what had done him in—he lay in a shallow grave of his own making, pounded into the earth from when he had fallen.

The battle had been brief. The dying hadn't.

Kenki's chest was smeared with what little blood hadn't spilled out on the sand. His hand, frozen in rigor, forever reached for the fragments of a bow he would never get to. The Sainite had died quicker, but the dust on his hands told her he had still tried to crawl his way out of his grave.

"So, what happened?"

Lenk stood behind her, seeing the same thing. Or rather, the same scene—he could see two dead bodies and a lot of blood, but there were things that he missed.

Things such as the countless tracks of sandaled feet, half-lost to the wind. In death, Kenki had been alone—but he hadn't been that way for long.

Six, maybe seven of them. Though ten would be closer to the average qithband. They had gathered here, at this spot in the dunes between the shore of the Lyre River and the high hills that surrounded the Green Belt. They had lingered for some time before setting out. Kenki had stayed behind.

She stared intently at the tracks in the earth. They all looked the same to her—sandaled feet that had stepped lightly, leaving little behind. But she was tempted to stare, tempted to see if she could tell the difference between them.

Tempted to wonder if one of those tracks belonged to someone she knew.

"Khoshicts." She sighed deeply. "They were here earlier. Probably last night." She looked out over the river; now and then, she could see the shape of a scraw appearing over the dunes and disappearing. "They were spotted, though."

She pointed to the dead Sainite, then to Kenki.

"This one stayed behind to shoot down the pursuer," she said. "He succeeded, but..." She frowned at the gash in Kenki's throat. "I'm guessing the scraw got him."

"And where's the scraw?" Lenk asked.

"Flown off, maybe."

"I see." He paused. "And where are the khoshicts?"

She shut her eyes. It was harder to summon the words than she thought it would be.

"They left toward the Green Belt," she said. "I couldn't be sure if they made it without following them."

Her ears quivered. She could hear his heart beat a little quicker. She could hear his breath catch in his throat. She could almost hear his thoughts.

But in another moment, he voiced them.

"Was Kwar with them?"

She remained silent for a moment. "I don't know."

"Do you think she might have been?"

A shorter moment, this time. "I don't know."

"But if she was, wouldn't you—"

"Lenk." She looked hard at him. "Enough."

He looked back at her with a frown. Something had changed in him. His wrinkles seemed a little deeper. His scars seemed a little softer. It was as though he had melted just a little and re-formed into something a little more brittle; not weak, not slow, just…warmer.

"I know." He shook his head. "I just…back there, I was ready to…"

He didn't have the words to finish that thought. She didn't want to hear them, anyway.

He turned to go. Her hand shot out, caught his. She squeezed him, pulled him closer. He looked at her again. The rest of him might have gotten a bit softer, but his eyes were still clear and cold as winter. They looked into a part of her she wasn't ready to allow to be seen.

But she didn't turn away.

She held his hand in hers. His fingers wrapped around hers. She felt the calluses on his palms. She traced a scar on the heel of his hand with her finger. She smiled softly.

Right where it always was.

"I know," she said. "But there are bigger problems."

He nodded briefly. He managed a smile as she let his hand drop.

"Right." He looked away. "Right." His gaze drifted toward the high hills. "Oerboros said Teneir was up to something in the city." He looked over his shoulder, toward some far-off point. "Something to do with Khoth-Kapira's return. Any chance we have of stopping him comes from stopping her."

"Assuming you can trust Oerboros," she said.

"He wouldn't lie."

"What makes you say that?"

"Because I heard his voice."

"Oh, good. For a moment there, I thought you were going to say something useless and stupid."

Lenk shook his head. "I can't explain it. Not right now. And it's not like we've got any better leads to go off. Gariath and Asper won't help."

"No, they won't," Kataria grunted. "And they won't stop to let us pass the road, either. Which reminds me...how *did* you plan to get back into the city, anyway?"

"Well." He scratched his head, looking out toward the distant Lyre River. "I was hoping to make for the shore. From there, I hoped we could find a fishing boat or something and use it to get into the Green Belt."

She blinked. "You hoped we could find a fishing boat."

"Yeah."

"What, like it would just be lying around? Just waiting for us?"

"Right. Maybe someone abandoned it."

"That doesn't sound a little, I don't know...*convenient* to hinge an entire plan for stopping a demon king on?"

"We've done plenty of shit like this before and I don't remember you complaining then!" Lenk threw his hands up, turning away from her. "Fuck it, though. I don't even know what's happening on the Lyre right now."

They had both seen it earlier that morning when they had reached the shore. Great barges brimming with swords and dark flesh had plied their way down the river, pulled by long oars. Scraws swooped high overhead, painting black shadows and fire on the water. Both were too far away for him to hear.

But she could.

Even now, she could hear traces, ghosts of noises on the breeze. Avian shrieks as the beasts flew through the air. The crack of glass and the roar of flames as fireflasks exploded. The splash of bodies falling into the river and plunging below. The howls of dying men and beasts. The whimpering wail of something wounded.

Wait.

Her ears twitched, rotating on her head as she sought to pick up the sound. It was faint against the distant din of battle, but it was clear, sharp.

Close.

She started to follow it. And Lenk followed her. She waved him back—the sand crunching under his feet was too loud. She could feel his eyes on her, feel his concern, but chose to ignore it.

He had to be used to that by now.

The sound grew louder in her ears as she followed it across the sand—a low, guttural sound, born of some dark and tender place in a body. A pained whimper that slid into a long, slow cooing noise.

She found the blood not long after: spatters of red running down a dune, around a large rock. She followed them closely, eyes locked on the ground, ears full of sound.

And between the two of them, she didn't even notice the claw lashing out.

Instinct—or luck—kept her feet aware, even if her senses weren't. She leapt away, catching a glimpse of the blood-streaked talons as they narrowly missed catching her by the flank. She darted away, drawing an arrow and nocking it as a great head peered around the rock.

A long, black beak ran up to a pair of wide, unblinking eyes. Golden and perfectly round as coins, they looked at Kataria with a predatory intellect. The beast lowered its head and thrust a pair of pronged horns at her threateningly, making that low, guttural noise.

So, she thought, *that's what scraws look like close up.*

Somehow, she'd imagined they'd be filthier.

She lowered her bow. The arrow was ready, but it wasn't what was going to save her. That would be thanks to her slow movements, her averted gaze, and the wide berth she gave the beast as she circled around the rock. She knew the noise it made.

The creature made it again—a low, panicked rumble—as she came into its view, but it did not move toward her. She had surprised it earlier, come in too quick. Faced with her now, moving slowly and cautiously, it didn't think her worth the effort.

Not with that arrow sticking out of it, anyway.

She took the creature in through stolen glimpses, unwilling to meet its eyes and set it off. She saw its long, powerful body—hooves on one end, bloodied talons on the other. That, she assumed, was how Kenki had met his end. A saddle was mounted on its back, behind its wings. Long reins dangled from its head, metal bits clinking as it growled. Its wings were folded tightly against its body, though the left one trembled with the effort, straining against the arrow lodged in its shoulder.

The beast watched her carefully, conserving its energy, gauging her movements. The cleverest beast she had ever met was a horse that could count to five; this was a little out of her depth.

Still, it was a beast, and there were certain laws that all beasts adhered to. No eye contact. No sudden movements. No loud noises.

And if humans can train them, they can't be that *smart.*

She drew closer, keeping the beast's talons in the corner of her eye; if it was going to move, those would move first. She kept herself at its middle, still within eyesight, but too far for it to use its claws easily. Or hooves. Or horns. Or beak.

Really, getting so close to a wounded animal with so many ways to kill her wasn't the best idea. And she wasn't sure what she would accomplish by doing it. Maybe it would fly away. Maybe it would kill her and *then* fly away. She didn't know.

But there was a lot she didn't know lately.

She reached out, holding her breath as she touched the beast's flank. It shuddered and let out a low growl. But it didn't move. And she wasn't dead. She exhaled, let her hand linger there, let it become accustomed to her touch. Her hand slid toward the arrow in its shoulder. She brushed fingers against it. The scraw's growl became a shrill rasp.

She closed her eyes. Absently, she wondered how quickly Kenki had died.

And then she wrapped her fingers around the arrow and pulled.

The rasping sound became a shriek. The beast leapt to all fours, hooves stomping the earth. Kataria backed away but kept her eyes shut. She waited for the feel of hooves cracking her skull or talons slicing open her belly or a beak pecking out her throat.

She felt only the shriek in her ears. The rush of hot air beneath massive wings.

Slowly, she opened her eyes. And met the beast's.

The scraw's head was lowered. Great golden eyes stared down a long beak at her. It let out a low chirruping sound, canting its head as though it expected her to give a reply. The feral panic was gone, replaced by a peculiar sort of intellect playing its in eyes.

But all beasts adhered to certain laws. And, as she slipped a hand into the pouch at her side, she knew it was still a beast.

She produced an egg—hard-baked from that morning before they had broken camp—and held it out in front of the creature. It regarded her with instant attention. She tossed it into the air, stepped back. Its beak snapped up and swallowed it down quickly.

"There," she whispered. "I gave you food. I took an arrow out of you. The way I see it, you owe me." She shot the beast a glare. "You can start by just staying there and not killing me."

She turned her attentions from the scraw to the arrow in her hand. It looked like any other shictish arrow: a long shaft, a barbed head, black feathers. There was nothing particularly special about it.

And yet the sight of it chilled her.

They were here. Khoshicts. So many. So close to Cier'Djaal. They had been in enough of a hurry that they left one of their own behind, unheard-of in hunting parties.

But then, Shekune was not leading a hunt.

She looked to the scraw, idly cleaning away flecks of dried blood from its talons with its beak. This creature had seen them. As clever as shicts were, they couldn't hide from something so high up. That was why they had shot it down. But they had failed to kill it. And if it could find them once...

"Holy fuck, *get back*!"

She looked up at the sound of his voice. Lenk came barreling down the dune, sword in hand. The scraw let out an angry rasp at his approach. She held up a hand to calm him.

"Put that away, moron," she snarled. "Spook it and you'll get me killed."

"Keep away from it," Lenk warned, lowering his sword but slowing his approach. "Those things are dangerous."

"Oh, I'm sure once you look past the giant claws and beak, they're quite cuddly." Her ears flattened against her head. "I know they're dangerous. That's why I keep telling you to put your *fucking sword away*." She let out a breath, looked back to the scraw. "This one's fine. For now, at least."

Lenk glanced from the beast to her. Slowly, he sheathed his blade. She nodded, waved him forward.

"Come here. Slowly."

He eyed the creature warily. "You're sure it's safe?"

"If you keep acting stupid, I can't guarantee you won't die. But I can promise that it won't be the one to kill you." She sneered. "Yes, I'm sure he's safe."

"He?"

"Well, I'm not going to go under there and check." She looked over at the scraw and patted its brow. "If he's a she, I'll apologize to him later. Her later. Whatever. I'll take care of it after we get to Cier'Djaal."

"Cier'Djaal?" He shot her an incredulous look. "You can't mean to fly that thing."

"Why not? That's what they're made to do."

"By Sainites. Sainites who have years of training."

She snorted, waving him off. "Sainites are just humans with fancy hats. And a human is just a monkey wearing clothes. And if a monkey in a fancy hat can ride this thing, I can, too." She put her hands on her hips and looked the beast over. "I mean, I can ride a horse, can't I?"

"This isn't a horse."

"Half of it is." She glanced at its hindquarters, toward its cloven hooves. "I mean, it looks more like a goat, but you get what I'm saying. Besides..."

She approached the creature's flank. It watched her attentively but did not move as she slid a foot into the stirrup and hoisted herself onto its back. It settled easily as she mounted it, held itself attentive as she took its reins in both hands. She shot a grin down at Lenk.

"I don't see you with any good ideas."

There was something in him when he looked up at her; that brittleness in his scars had seeped into the corners of his eyes like tears. She could still remember the last time he had looked at her like that. Right before they had left Cier'Djaal. Right before she had decided to tell him she couldn't go with him. Right before she did, anyway.

She hadn't expected to see that look again. And she hadn't expected to feel what she did when she saw it again.

But ever since yesterday, when she had stood between him and Oerboros, firing arrows into a foe she couldn't kill to protect him, it had been there.

And it wasn't going away.

She reached down. He looked at her hand for a moment, thinking the same thing she was, and knowing the same thing she knew.

He took it. She pulled him up behind her. He drew in close. His hands slid around her waist. And while his eyes were cold and his scars were soft, his hands were warm on her skin and behind her, he felt like a stone. Solid. Immovable. Not going anywhere.

She remembered the last time she had felt this, too, the last time she had felt him. Out there, long before they had come to Cier'Djaal, long before all this, she had felt it every day. Out in the wilds, far from civilization and its problems, that was all she had felt. The feeling that, regardless of how many monsters were out there or how far from help they might have been, he would always be there.

Solid as a stone.

The days up to this moment all felt like fever dreams. The days of endless running, of fears and worries and failures, they were no less real. But only now did she realize how exhausted she was from them. Only now did she realize how much she had missed the feeling of someone else watching her back.

And, with a heavy heart, she realized she wasn't ready to let that go. Not yet.

Shekune couldn't attack an army the size of the tulwar and the humans. No matter how many she had. Whatever plot she was about to launch, it wouldn't be soon.

Khoth-Kapira, though, was much closer, much bigger, and he didn't care about numbers.

Save the world first. Save the shicts once they had a world to live in.

Simple.

She flicked the reins. The scraw chirruped, turned, and started off at a canter. Lenk's hands tightened around her waist.

"Calm the fuck down," she said. "See? It's just like riding a horse."

"We're still on the ground," he replied. "When we're in the sky..."

"I'll handle that, too." She reached down, laid her hand on his. "Trust me."

—◦—✦◦◦—✦◦—

"Try to understand, madam." Aturach attempted to wipe his frustration and sweat alike off his face. He forced his most pleasant smile for the third time. "We have every intention of holding the tulwar at bay. But on the chance that they *do* break through, we can only protect you if you come to the city."

The woman on the stoop of the shack looked back at him with contempt from a face that had been weathered from years of toiling in rice fields. She spared a little more respect for the trio of Djaalic men behind him, with their makeshift spears and shields, but for a finely clothed, soft-fingered priest like him?

He might as well have been trying to convince a dog not to eat its own shit.

"It's *you* that doesn't understand," the farmer grunted. "You had your fancy temple given to you. Your faithful pay for your food and your clothes. *I* had to work all my life." She stomped the deck of her stoop. "And this is all I have for it. And I'll be damned if I'm going to leave it because you said so."

"But madam, the tulwar—"

"I saw the armies heading to Harmony Road," she replied. "I saw those great scraws flying overhead. My grandpa used to tell me tales of them, how they beat back the Karnerians. I can't imagine a force on this dark earth that could stand against them. So long as they're still flying, I'll be just fine."

She settled back on her heels, a smug smile on her face. Aturach's hands clenched into fists as he tried to conceive of a reply that *wasn't* mostly curses.

Before he could even open his mouth, though, he heard the great flap of wings. In the distance, an avian shriek pealed through the sky. And in another breath, it was so close that his ears shook with the force of it.

The great beast came barreling through the sky overhead, jerking wildly through the air and letting out angry screams as it did. It flew so low that the Djaalics threw themselves to the ground. And though Aturach couldn't see its two riders beyond their gold and silver hair, he could certainly hear them—or one of them—screaming as they flew by.

"... *uckfuckfuckfuckFUCKFUCKFUCKFUCKFUCKfuckfuckfuck-fuckfu...*"

When Aturach got to his feet again, the scraw was becoming a speck in the distance. The farmer stared at it disappearing, mouth open and eyes wide. After a very long moment, she looked back at Aturach, sighed, and turned to go inside her shack.

"Fine," she grunted. "Let me just get a few things."

THIRTY-FIVE

THE HERALDING STORM

Even so far away, he was still so big.

On the high ridge, far from battle, she could just barely see Gariath through the spyglass. Yet against the morning sun, he loomed like a scorch mark on the earth. Arms folded over his chest, wings spread, eyes on the battle below. He said nothing, he barely moved.

As he watched hundreds die.

"Rua Tong!"

Asper glanced down. Another wave of tulwar surged forward: steel flashing, roars flying, faces alive with color. Their war cry was just loud enough for her to hear this time as they hurled themselves at the wall of the phalanx, heedless of the barely cold corpses of their comrades to find the Karnerian spears.

That was the fourth one today.

They cared nothing for the crossbow bolts raining down upon them, nor for the wall of spears and shields that met them every time. They barely even seemed to notice the hundreds more that had died before them—and the tiny few humans they managed to kill—each time they ran at the impenetrable wall of Karnerians and Sainites.

There were still thousands of them, to be sure. But so many had died already, having killed so few.

And they just kept coming.

"Something's changed."

Haethen's eyes were locked on the battle below. Sweat fogged her spectacles as she squinted through the morning sun. She nervously chewed at her thumbnail, having already gnawed through the others on that hand, as she watched the tulwar crash into the wall of shields.

"They're charging too frequently," the Foescribe muttered. "It doesn't make sense."

"Trying to wear us down," Asper replied. "See how they keep coming, one after the other? Never letting us rest?"

"Oh, good. I was worried that my years of tactical experience and knowledge wouldn't be enough to deduce a mind-bogglingly simple strategy." Haethen turned an ugly sneer upon her. "Thank the gods I have a peasant inexplicably chosen by heaven to fucking point out the blatantly fucking obvious to me. I wonder what fucking deed I did to earn this fucking blessing from on high."

Asper blinked. "You seem upset."

Haethen shook her head, looked away. "Apologies, Prophet. It's just..." She gestured out to the field. "The numbers they're sending are too small to be an attempt to wear us down. There's too long between each wave. They're just being... sent out. It's a desperation tactic."

"That's good, isn't it? They *should* be worried about us."

"A desperate animal is an animal that can't be controlled," Haethen said. "If they all decide to charge the road at once..."

"Then their losses would be catastrophic."

"And so would ours," Haethen said. "And, at last report, more clans were still trickling in to join the battle."

Asper grimaced as she looked through the spyglass again. A small battalion of tulwar archers, their bows strung and arrows nocked, had ringed Gariath's station. Likely to fend off scraw attacks—not that it mattered, with Blacksbarrow's regiment still at the Lyre holding back the tulwar boats. But Haethen was correct; those archers hadn't been there last night.

"He'd risk his entire army," she said. "But the odds are in his favor." With a suddenness that made Asper start, she slammed her fist on the railing. "Where the *hell* are the Venarium? Shinka said they would be here."

Asper didn't have the heart to answer that, nor the strength to dwell on it. They had sent runners to the tower all day and received no answer. And while that had been the case before today, at least yesterday *those* runners had come back.

"If we need to pull back..." she said.

"Careus is still in control down there. He'd let us know if he wasn't."

Above even the tulwar, the speaker's booming cries thundered. He thrust his sword forward, directing the phalanx in a massive push to crush the tulwar horde once more. Asper tried to ignore the impression that he sounded a little hoarser this time.

"Still," Haethen said, "if the dragonman is losing control, that presents a new scenario. One we must prepare for."

Asper stared at him. From here, he was tiny: a puny thing that she could barely even see if she lowered her spyglass. Yet every time she did, her eye was still drawn to him. And even though he was far away, she knew he could see her, as well.

There had been times before when she would have believed Gariath was out of control. There had been names she had for him, then: *berserker, lunatic, psychotic.* But as time had gone on and he had left more bodies in his wake, she realized she only called him those names because they were more comforting than the truth.

Every bone he had broken, every throat he had ripped open, every corpse he had thrown to the cold earth…

He meant to do them. Each and every one of them. Never once had he lost control.

And he wouldn't, this time, either.

She knew, surely as she knew he was staring at her, that he wouldn't stop until she was dead.

———✦———

There.

Right there, beyond the cliffs. Past the corpses and the blood and the spears and the shields, there she was. He could barely see her. And he might have simply been deluding himself by thinking he could smell her. But the smell of arrogance and hate was in his nostrils, all the same.

Of course, that might just be him.

His snout was full of a thousand reeks—of death, of anger, of fear, of blood—and he couldn't find the thoughts to concentrate on any of them. Ever since dawn, when a rider had come to Daaru, when Daaru had come to Mototaru, when Mototaru had come to him, he had been like this. Too agitated, too angry, too distracted to smell, to fight, even to lead.

"Rua Tong!"

The warriors charged again. Completely unfazed by their earlier failures as they came crashing over their fallen to strike the humans' shields again. But it wasn't bravery that fueled them. Bravery had a different smell than what roiled over him in a wave of stink. Their push was driven by desperation.

Of course, again, that might just be him.

"The clan that came with this information..." Gariath glanced to his right. "What was their name again?"

Daaru looked back at him. His usual reek of anger was overwhelmed by the stink of stale blood. His chest was swaddled in bandages from where a stray bolt had caught him on the last charge. But if the pain slowed him, it didn't show on his face, still bright and vivid with angry color.

"Yanna Jai Janth," Daaru said. "They come from the coast, far to the south."

"What are they renowned for?"

"Fishing, mostly. Boat building. A little gaambol riding."

"Are they stupid?" Gariath asked. "Can they count?"

Daaru's face grew hard. "They can. And they did." He pointed to the south. "More are coming. They will tell us the same thing."

Gariath followed Daaru's finger. Far away, he could see them, trickling in. The Yanna Jai Janth clan came loping toward the tulwar camp, mounted atop gaambols the color of sand, wielding heavy spears. As they had been coming since that morning when they first brought the news.

"Ships," Daaru said. "Black ships with black sails. At least five of them, heading directly for the city. They will be here by the end of the day. We are out of time."

The sound of a dying tulwar's scream rose on the air, carried by the stink of warm blood on sand.

"And this isn't working, *daanaja.*"

Gariath growled. He could see that from the first failed charge. But what else could be done? The cliff gap was too narrow to pour his army into. The humans' shield wall would grind them up, one by one. He had hoped to break their morale with relentless attacks, but it had only earned him more corpses.

And more were coming. More clans continued to trickle in—some as vanguards for larger clans, some as few as tiny villages dotting the desert. More tulwar that had heard of him, of what he was promising. More tulwar that believed he could give them what they so desperately craved.

More tulwar that would be dead once those ships, and their reinforcements, arrived.

Daaru was right. They were out of time. And this wasn't working.

And he was the only one who seemed to give a shit.

He turned, pushed past Daaru, and stalked to the far edge of the ridge. Far from the Nak Chamba clansmen who guarded their vantage, he found his adviser. Mototaru hadn't budged since they had arrived, mopping sweat from his forehead with one hand as he scribbled patterns in the sand with a stick in the other.

"Well?" Gariath snarled.

"Well," Mototaru muttered in reply. "Nice day, isn't it?" He looked up at the sun. A hot breeze whipped his hair about his weathered face. "Warm for this time of year, though. The storms are heading back out to sea and the wind is carrying them. Should have a nice one soon."

"You haven't said a fucking word all morning," Gariath said.

"To be fair, you didn't ask me," Mototaru said. "You just started sending warriors at their shields." He glanced at the dragonman out the corner of his eye. "How's that working out, by the way?"

"The humans have reinforcements," Gariath growled. "More are coming. They'll be here by the end of the day. Hundreds, at least. Thousands, maybe. And we can't even break these few holding a road." He fixed a hard look on the tulwar. "I don't need sarcasm. I need a *plan*."

Mototaru stared at the map he had drawn in the sand. In its crude scribblings, he saw something that Gariath couldn't. And it made the tulwar's lips pull themselves down into a heavy frown.

"The plan," he sighed, "is there is no plan. We came here driven by anger and fear, like we did in the first Uprising. Those carried us all the way to Cier'Djaal, but there were no armies in our path then. They weren't ready for us then." He shook his head, rubbed his face. "Anger and fear can't carry an army. I knew it then, like I know it now, but I still...I thought this time, with you...but we can't...we can't..."

He stared at his drawings in the sand, mouth hanging open, eyes empty. To Gariath, it seemed like nothing more than crosses and circles and arrows drawn in the dirt. But Mototaru saw something vast and hopeless in them, a long story with a hundred endings, all of them unhappy. He stared at them so hard he looked as though he would fall into them, simply fall face-forward into the dirt and simply stop moving, stop speaking, stop everything.

There would come a day, Gariath knew, when he would welcome that kind of silence from the old tulwar.

"No."

But today, he needed a strategist.

His foot came down on Mototaru's drawings. All the strategies and stories and unhappy endings vanished in a cloud of dust.

"There's a way," he said. "We have always had it."

Mototaru opened his mouth to ask, but then the realization dawned on his face. He looked over his shoulder, toward a camp far from the others.

"The other clans will never charge with them," he said. "They are too afraid."

"Fear carried us this far. It can go a little further."

Mototaru shook his head but paused. The wind kicked up, a sudden gust that sent the dust of his former strategies flying across the sky. He watched the grains disappear into the wind, humming.

"Two hours," he said.

"What?"

"Two hours. Make your charge then." Mototaru clambered to his feet. "I will go to Daaru, have him pull our warriors back."

"Back where?"

"Back to the dunes. Back to the sand. I will need them all, every warrior, every archer, every gaambol. I will need them to kick up as much earth as they can."

"For what?"

"You need a plan." Mototaru shuffled off. "I've got one. Just make sure you've got what you need."

Gariath asked nothing more. He had asked for a plan, true, and he had gotten a lot of insane mutterings instead. But, with someone like Mototaru, perhaps they were the same thing.

He made his way down the dune, pausing to roar at warriors lingering in their camps, commanding them to head to the front and heed Mototaru. He counted them as they rushed away—twenty here, fifty or so there—there would be a thousand, maybe, left to fight after all their losses today.

A thousand and however many he could pull from the dingy pit of a camp that loomed before him.

The Mak Lak Kai clan didn't bother with tents or firepits. They slept on the backs of their gaambols beneath the stars. They ate their meat raw and tossed the bones aside. And the stink of both their beds and their meals hit him like a reeking fist, almost bringing him to his knees as he stormed through their camp.

But he forced himself through, ignoring their calls to him, ignoring the shrieking of their gaambols, as he made his way to the center.

And the scarred warrior sitting there.

"Ah, *daanaja*." Chakaa waved idly, lounging against the flank of her snoring gaambol, as he approached. "Is the fight going well? I'd check, but the other clans won't let us near the front. I sometimes hear screams on the wind." She smiled an ugly yellow smile. "Sounds like we're all having fun out there."

"Get up," Gariath snarled. "Ready your clan."

"For what?" Chakaa asked. "Is it lunch?"

"Don't be stupid."

"Chakaa is never stupid, my friend. But she knows what happens when *malaa* try to fight with other good tulwar." Her smile faded. She regarded Gariath coldly. "You asked us to come, we came. You ask us to fight, we'll fight. But it's not us that'll tell you that you ask too much. The other clans—"

"The other clans will learn," Gariath snarled, "that I don't ask."

Chakaa blinked. Slowly, the grin returned to her face as she pulled herself to her feet. She took up her massive beaten-metal sword and hiked it over one shoulder.

"I always knew there was a reason I liked you, *daanaja*."

━━◆━━

Quiet, it was written once, was the soldier's worst foe. Warfare had its own harmony—the rattle of steel, the parting of flesh, the splash of life. It was easy to follow from one note to the next. Silence, however, invited nothing but the cacophony of thought: messy, gibbering things that shouted to be heard over one another. In carnage, there was peace. In quiet, there was madness.

Pathon hadn't believed it at the time. Pathon couldn't even remember the manual he had read that in.

But as the quiet dragged on into its third hour, he was beginning to buy it.

After a morning of near-constant attacks, the tulwar had finally fallen back. Their dead littered the road and their blood painted the shields of his fellow Marchers. He would have called them defeated, but...

There was something about the retreat. It had come too suddenly, with too much disorder. They had fallen back in a mass herd, fleeing over the dunes and disappearing. Like something had happened. Like they knew something he didn't. They were smarter than they seemed, these monkeys. They fought like savages, but they were too clever, too cunning to be so easily written off. They were planning something. They were...

A thick droplet of sweat fell into his eye. He shook his head and, with it, shook those depraved thoughts out of his ears.

It was the wind, he told himself.

The heat in this desert was always oppressive, but over the past few days, the wind had kicked up, buffeting him with hot air. Today, it was blasting in great, burning gusts that flew over his shield and right into his visor, making his helmet feel like an oven strapped to his head.

Too much wind.

Too much heat.

Too much quiet.

Not enough fighting.

He glanced over his shoulder. The speaker stood beside the phalanx, his eyes locked on the distant horizon. Sweat dripped down his face, falling in rivers from beneath his helmet. His black armor must have felt like a furnace, but he did not so much as shift uncomfortably.

He would not move until the enemy was destroyed or the heavens parted so that Daeon might welcome him into the eternal army.

Pathon set his jaw and nodded to himself.

Neither would he.

But just as he had resolved himself, the speaker stirred. He raised the visor of his helmet. Beneath, his eyes were wide as they stared out over the dunes.

Pathon turned and saw it, along with the rest of the phalanx.

A great wave was roiling toward them. A massive cloud of sand and grit, billowing forward like the sails of a mighty ship. It swept forward with such speed that Pathon didn't even have time to appreciate how huge it was until the wind carried it over him and the rest of the phalanx.

If the air had been merely oppressive before, it was an army all its own now. The wind moaned like a war horn. The air became thick and stifling, carrying in sand that plastered itself to their sweaty brows and got into their mouths. The phalanx raised their shields and huddled closer together, but to no effect.

"A whim of nature," the speaker bellowed. "Or pagan trickery. The Empire flinches from neither. Stand together, sons of Daeon."

And so they set their heels, kept their shields raised, and waited.

Pathon was grateful for an end to the silence, at least. The howling of the wind was in his helmet, quieting his thoughts. The sound of grit pelting against his shield was not so unlike the sound of arrows. He could handle this. In the din, he found a kind of peace.

And in that peace, he found another sound.

Soft, muffled shudders, like distant thunder. It carried through the howling of the wind to grow louder, until he could hear it as one continuous rumbling sound.

He squinted. Over the rim of his shield, he could see something in the sheets of sand. Hazy shapes, like bad dreams. They grew into shadows, stark black against the wall of sand. In another hot breath, he could see them take shape. He opened his mouth to cry out a warning, but it went unheard.

In one more breath, they had arrived.

"MAK LAK KAI!"

First as ghosts, voices on the wind. Then as nightmares, black as sin and stained with streaks of chalky white that painted their faces like bleached bones. Then as steel, crude and jagged weapons that grinned with sawteeth and dented edges.

He didn't realize they were tulwar until they crashed into him.

"Stand fast, brothers! Stand—"

The speaker's words were lost in the shrieking of gaambols, cackled war cries torn from fanged mouths, and the groan of wood and steel as the tulwar collided with their lines.

The gaambols plowed through the front shields, howling as spears stuck them. But they did not stop, driven by the kicks of their riders, the black tulwar who swung their massive blades wildly, carving through shield and armor and bone.

Pathon saw his brothers falling in glimpses: seized by gaambols and dragged screaming to disappear into the grit or collapsing without a sound beneath the hacking of great weapons. He heard the hum of crossbow bolts behind him, the Sainites barking orders and firing blindly into the cloud of grit. There was the sound of spears piercing hides, of gaambols screeching, of bolts punching through necks and chests. But of the tulwar themselves, there was no sound of pain. Only their laughter, long and loud and depraved.

"MAK LAK KAI!"

A howl from a beast, rushing through the torn ranks of the phalanx, right for him.

Black as night, its eyes wide and red and its mouth a gaping ring of teeth, the gaambol came rushing toward him. It ignored the spears lashing out at it. Its rider didn't so much as flinch as a crossbow bolt took him in the shoulder. Their eyes, their fangs, their steel were locked on Pathon.

He raised his shield, planted his feet, set his spear into the earth.

And whispered into the wind.

"Heaven is watching."

Steel crunched. Beasts screamed. Earth groaned under his feet as he felt himself sliding backward. The gaambol charged into him with no heed for itself, taking his spear all the way to its collarbone. He felt the hot blast of its breath as it howled, continuing to charge even as his spear burst out the back of its neck.

His shield shuddered as the tulwar rider swung his massive blade in a chop. It cleaved through the rim of his shield, tearing through steel and wood and lodging itself there. He lowered his head, gritted his teeth, and ignored the burning pain as he was driven into the earth by the creature's charge.

But its rage lasted only as long as its howl. It continued only for a few more feet as its shriek of fury became a whimpering gurgle. The beast's momentum turned from charge to stumble as it collapsed into a heap on the earth, taking Pathon's spear with it. The rider went flying from his mount's shoulders, tumbling into the earth.

He twisted away to avoid being buried by the creature, letting it take his weapon. He tossed aside his shield, rent useless by the massive blade lodged in it. He found his sword at his hip, tore it free, and whirled to face the beast.

And the tulwar was there to meet him.

Tall, lanky, his fur the color of pitch and painted with grotesque white chalk, the rider seemed unaware of the carnage unraveling around him as his fellow beasts tore into the fray. His red-rimmed eyes were for Pathon alone. As was his smile, toothy and grotesquely yellow.

And the crude ax that had appeared in his hand.

"MAK LAK KAI!"

He hurled the war cry at Pathon as he leapt forward, clambering over the carcass of his mount to leap at the Karnerian. Pathon ducked away from the savage blow that followed, the ax whistling over his head. He darted away as the tulwar chopped down, cackling as he did.

The blows came fast, each one parting the air with such fury that Pathon had no doubt that even one would be the end of him. But it was simple pagan brutality: the inborn violence granted to all savages. No technique. No foresight. The tulwar's swings grew slower with each strike and Pathon found them easier to turn away.

Fury was a flame: bright and finite and flickering out quickly.

Discipline, though, was as eternal as the Empire.

And by the fifth swing, Pathon saw his opening.

The tulwar's blow went wide, leaving him exposed. Pathon struck, lunging forward and planting his sword into the tulwar's belly. The savage snarled—not screamed—and staggered backward, rasping for breath. Pathon fell back, wary of what fury the tulwar might expel in his death throes.

But no fury ever came. The tulwar paused, looked down at the hilt jutting out of his guts, as though puzzled how it got there. Then he looked up at Pathon, his smile wider than ever. He offered a single wink of a red eye and chuckled in a guttural voice.

"You're adorable."

He howled as he rushed forward, not a drop of blood on his lips or from his wound. Pathon could but stare, wide-eyed, at the tulwar, eyes locked on the useless weapon lodged in his stomach, completely oblivious to the ax coming down upon his head.

"Death to pagans!"

Silver flashed, burning bright through the cloud of grit. A great blade scythed through the tulwar's arm, cleaving down into his shoulder and past his rib cage. The tulwar let out a scream, collapsing to the earth in two twitching, writhing pieces. He stared up at Pathon, mouth twisted in a snarl and eyes wide with fury.

And then there was the sound of crunching bone and a black iron boot where had once been a head.

"Marcher!"

Pathon looked up. The speaker stood over him, black as night against the sand. Sweat poured down his face, the signs of battle clear in his eyes. Yet there was not a drop of blood on his armor, on his sword, on his skin.

"Your sword, Marcher!" the speaker demanded, pointing to the body.

"Speaker," Pathon whispered. "He didn't die...I stabbed him and he didn't...he didn't..."

"Indeed."

The speaker's voice was as grim as the scene around him.

The sands began to give way, illuminating the carnage around him. Gaambols lay dead in heaps, spears and bolts jutting from their hides. Karnerians were cleaved, hacked apart, or torn by massive claws. Sainites waded into the fray, discarding crossbows for swords. The few that still stood wore desperation on their faces as they pushed against their foes.

And the tulwar simply laughed.

The shafts of bolts peppered their bodies. Broken spear hafts dangled from their abdomens like macabre jewelry. Wounds without blood decorated their bodies. They fought without flinching, without falling, their fanged mouths wide and open with shrieking laughter.

"Demons," Pathon whispered. "They're demons. They don't die! They don't—"

"Everything dies, Marcher." The speaker ground his boot onto the tulwar's shattered skull. He reached down and pulled the sword from the now-still carcass. "The Eternal Army awaits even us, should we fall here. But it will be a dark and cold place we send these pagans to." He thrust the sword's hilt at Pathon, pressing it to his chest and closing the Marcher's hand around it. "Every savage has its limit, Marcher. But the

Empire does not." He lowered the visor to his helmet, nodded. "Heaven is watching."

Pathon returned the nod, shakily. "Heaven is—"

"THAT ONE! THAT ONE'S MINE!"

A shriek in the sand. They whirled to see the creature charging forward. A gaambol, huge and hulking against an orange-colored sky, came rampaging toward them, kicking corpses out of the way as it did. Its rider, a female wearing coarse armor and holding an impossibly huge sword over her head, kicked it forward. And over the beast's howl, her laughter was long and loud and black as her.

"With me, Marcher! Get ready!"

The speaker raised his sword, meeting the beast as it came rampaging forward. Pathon joined him, his own weapon looking feeble in comparison. And, as the gaambol approached, he knew what he had to do.

"Now!"

As one, the speaker and he leapt aside. They thrust their blades out, punching through the beast's hide and letting its momentum tear its own entrails out. With a death shriek, it collapsed, skidding across the earth and painting the sand a foul red as it did.

Its rider leapt from its back, expertly twisting through the air to land on her feet as she did. Her eyes were upon the speaker, her blade heavy and ungainly in her hand. Pathon saw her exposed back. He saw his chance.

He rushed forward, taking his blade in both hands and lunging forward, aiming for her spine and—

"No!"

She spoke as if scolding him. Her hand lashed out as though she meant to slap his hand away, chidingly. But instead of slapping, she caught his wrist. She whipped her blade about, bringing the pommel of it down on his elbow.

The sound of his arm snapping echoed in his ears for so long that he couldn't hear himself scream as he fell to the ground.

She cast a sneer at him, fraught more with annoyance than actual hate.

"Chakaa is not here for you, little man."

She turned toward the speaker, thrusting a black, hairy finger at him.

"*You*," she said. "Are you the strongest one here or is your armor simply the shiniest?"

"The Empire is strong, pagan," the speaker replied, raising his blood-slick blade. "I am a vessel of its fury and a speaker of its god. Daeon himself speaks through me."

"Oh!" A smile spread across Chakaa's lips. "Oh, oh, *oh*! That *does* sound very important." She hefted her blade, a massive wedge of metal hammered to roughly look like a sword, in both hands. "I have been looking for you all my life, my friend."

"You have found only your death, savage."

"Does your god give you such witty dialogue? Or did you have to work on that?" She shook her head. "Ah, but hear me prattle. In all this excitement, I almost forgot that I came here to rip your head off."

She swept forward: no sound but her massive blade dragging in the dirt, no emotion but the ax head of a grin plastered across her face. She leapt for the speaker. He was ready, just as he had been for the last. He raised his sword, waited for her momentum to carry her to him, and thrust his sword out for her midsection.

She took the bait.

She leapt.

She spun.

Surprise painted the speaker's face as she twirled out of his sword's path, letting her speed carry her into a wicked spin as she brought her blade up and around, right for his back. He turned, bringing up his own blade to block.

Her blow didn't land neatly, but a weapon that size didn't have to. The mighty blade knocked him aside, slamming his sword against his body and shaking him in his armor.

He recoiled, staggering away from her. The plate of his gauntlet was shattered, exposing a deep red gash in his arm. It was only by the clumsiness of her swing that such a gash wasn't across his throat instead.

That much was clear to Pathon, as it clearly was to Chakaa.

And she moved to remedy it.

She took her blade up in two hands. She rushed forward, hefting it up over her shoulder. She closed the distance in a few strides, twisting away from his sword as he lashed out at her. She moved with her spin, bringing the blade down in a savage blow.

He only narrowly darted away from it, but there was no shock on his face. Strange as her technique was, it no longer surprised him. He waited, he watched.

And when she swung again, he struck.

She spun forward, the momentum carrying her forward. He ducked under her blow, brought his sword up, and aimed for her rib cage. Her spin carried her back, her blade coming up to meet his in a spray of sparks. He was not deterred; his hand shot out and seized her by the throat. His neck snapped forward, the ridge of his helmet smashing against her face.

The sound of bone crunching was loud enough to be heard over the screams of the dying.

She staggered backward. Pathon felt a surge of hope—for he couldn't feel much else in his body—as she reeled. But it wasn't pain or even anger that was on her now visibly dented face. Rather, she looked confused, not quite certain what had happened. It didn't seem to dawn on her until she reached into her mouth with two hairy fingers and pulled out a pair of sharp, yellow teeth.

"Oh." She looked at the speaker with a broad smile. "I *like* you."

She leapt at him, swinging wildly. Rage carried her where momentum no longer could. Her blade, huge as it was, moved like a gale: sweeping in massive arcs and sending the grit in the air wafting away in dusty plumes. The speaker was quick, darting away, parrying where he could, striking where he must.

His sword sang a discordant song across her flesh: a dozen black notes carved across her skin in a jagged harmony. Glancing blows, but more than enough to slow a warrior. Yet she didn't so much as flinch, continuing to wade forward, heedless of the many wounds he carved across her.

The speaker did not panic. He watched. Every wound that failed to kill, he looked for a new opening that would. When he had painted her arms, shoulders, and legs with wounds, it was clear on his face that he knew there was no slowing her.

Only stopping her. In one blow.

Chakaa swung again, spinning in a violent arc, aiming for the speaker's knees. He leapt over her blade, but she was faster this time. As he had watched her, she had watched him. Her blade swung again, caught him against the side of the head.

The helmet fell in metal splinters. He rolled with the blow, tumbling across the sand and leaping to his feet. Sand plastered the side of his head where a great gash wept blood down his temple and into his eyes.

But behind the red and brown smears, his eyes were as calm as ever.

He watched.

He waited.

She was bold now, grinning widely as she lunged forward, swinging to finish it. He did not let her. He lashed forward as she spun, arcing his sword up to thrust up through her armpit. The sword burst out of her shoulder and, for the first time, she screamed.

Not out of pain, but out of frustration. Her momentum came to an awkward and ungainly halt as the sword embedded inside her sinew brought her to a halt. She snarled, flailing impotently to dislodge him as he twisted his blade. He waited for her fury to become a frenzy, a wild twist of limbs and metal until she wasn't even trying to hit him anymore.

He jerked his sword out. He planted his boot against her spine. Her back folded as she launched forward. She scrambled to her feet. She brought her sword up. She whirled about.

She never even saw his blade until it was lodged to the hilt in her chest.

She blinked, not quite sure what was happening. She opened her mouth, as if to protest or curse or simply ask what had happened. But neither words, nor blood, nor breath came out. She made an airy, rasping sound as her body swayed on the blade, her legs shaking.

The speaker's own face betrayed no joy. His eyes were steady, his mouth a hard line across his lips as he pushed the sword forward a little more. She sank to her knees, her heavy blade falling limp in her hand, her fingers still straining to hold on to it even as the light left her eyes.

The speaker held on to his blade as she slumped over. He watched her as her head hung limp, lolling from her neck. He did not relax until she hung, limp and dead upon his blade.

Only then did he allow himself to close his eyes and let out a long, slow sigh.

"CAREUS!"

Only then did Pathon find the voice to scream.

Careus's eyes snapped open.

Chakaa's did, too.

Her body snapped back upright. Her eyes were bright and red. Her mouth was gaping in a wide, wild smile.

"SURPRISE!"

Her arm swung. The speaker's hands fell. Her blade flashed. The speaker's mouth hung open.

"Daeon..."

This was the last sound he made before his head flew from his shoulders.

His blood painted the orange sky, flecked the grit with red. His body fell limp in a clatter of metal. His eyes were still open, still wide with disbelief, as she took his head in one hand and held it up.

Pathon was screaming.

"MAK LAK KAI!"

His brothers were dying.

"MAK LAK KAI!"

Bodies were falling around him.

"MAK LAK KAI!"

And he could hear nothing but the sound of her voice as she, standing tall with Careus's sword through her chest, held his severed head to the sky and laughed wildly until the sound of her joy was just one more horrific noise in the carnage surrounding him.

THIRTY-SIX

THE ASPIRANT, FILTHY AND HOPELESS

It was just a little before sunset when they finally arrived.

It had taken more hours than it should have, he had spewed more curses than he should have known, and he had made more deals with gods than was probably wise, but they had finally made it.

The scraw flapped his wings, letting out a shrill cry as it sailed low over the rooftops of the city and came to an awkward halt, stumbling into a landing in the center of an abandoned square.

The creature clawed the ground anxiously, folding his wings against his body. He cast a glance over his shoulder at his rider, who grunted a few words of encouragement and stroked the feathers of the beast's head. His rider, in turn, cast a glance over her shoulder. This time, though, with a few less encouraging words.

"We landed." Kataria's broad grin told her she was enjoying this a little too much. "But if you want to perfect your impression of a screaming little girl, I can always take him back up."

Lenk looked up at her—crouched low and tight across the scraw's body, his hands wrapped around her waist with his head pressed firmly into her back—and glared.

"Don't even fucking joke," he snarled. "You couldn't control this thing if it was fucking talking to you."

"I think I've just about figured it out." Kataria bunched up the reins in her hand. The scraw raised its head in response. "I mean, we made it, didn't we?"

"After taking the tiles off several roofs, nearly plowing into the Silken

Spire, and that little bit where we were upside down for a few breaths, sure."

"So you admit you're overreacting. Besides, spinning upside down meant you didn't get any of your vomit on Colonel MacSwain's nice coat." She purred, stroking the beast's neck. "And he loves his coat, doesn't he?"

The scraw let out a chirruping noise that might have been described as "cute" in an animal several sizes smaller and possessed of significantly fewer means of evisceration.

"Colonel MacSwain?" Lenk asked, spitefully wiping the last dried flakes from his lips on the back of her shirt.

"He brought us here. I wasn't just going to keep calling him *scraw*."

"No, I get that. But why *that* name?"

"I don't know. Why are you called *Lenk* instead of *General Squealy Baby-Man*?"

"For one, I've never even fought in an army, let alone commanded one. And for two, fuck you." He glowered down at the beast between his legs, the creature stamping its hooves. "I ought to carve him up."

"For you to hurt him, you'd need your hands." She reached down and patted his fingers. "Really, I'm not even sure you can move them by now."

He followed her hand to her midriff, where his arms were—and had been—locked around her in a death grip for the past few hours. She was right—he could barely feel them by now, but he could feel when she patted them. And soon, he could feel other things: the warmth of her skin beneath his forearms, the slow rise and fall of her belly beneath his palms, the way she tensed just slightly as he squeezed his fingers and—

"Yeah, yeah."

He all but tore his hands away, his skin slick with the sweat of hers. He tried to ignore the smell of her body that still clung to them as he slid from the colonel's haunches and landed on bloodless legs.

He leaned hard on the beast, checking to make sure his sword, satchel, and intestines were all where they should be as he tried to find his balance after the flight. After a few moments, he found everything where it should be, and looked up.

And there, he found nothing.

The buildings were still there, of course. Some of the windows had been smashed. Some of the doors had been boarded up. Some of them were shops with signs still swaying and pottery and cookware and rotted sweets in their displays. Some of them looked to have been singed by fire, and some of them had crossbow bolts lodged in the doorframe.

The city was still there, more or less as he had left it.

But the people were gone.

Silence echoed around him. The sounds of bustle and markets were gone; the vocal panic of war and strife was absent. The disaster of their landing should have drawn some attention—or at least a few screams.

"Be good. Stay here," Kataria murmured behind him. There was the snapping sound of the scraw's beak taking something from her hand. "I'll be back soon."

These noises, too, were drowned out. As the moments grew long and the sky turned orange, it was a living silence that descended over the city: not merely the absence of sound, but something vast and unseen that drew in sound and breath and prayer in a great inhale and smothered everything left behind beneath it.

"Where are they?" It felt somehow profane to speak in the presence of this silence, as though doing so might attract its attention. "Where are all the people?"

He turned toward Kataria. The shict shouldered her bow, glanced around at the empty square, and shrugged.

"We've been gone for a long time," she said. "When we left, the city was being torn apart by war. When we came back, it was about to be torn apart by a much bigger war. Maybe everyone's left."

"Cier'Djaal is one of the biggest cities in the world. Even gone as long as we were, they wouldn't all just leave like that."

"They might if they knew their homes were about to be put to the torch."

"They wouldn't." Lenk hiked his sword up and set out toward an alley.

"How do you know?" Kataria called, hurrying to catch up.

"Because you don't give up a home until it actually *is* put to the torch."

Through the alleys, festering with trash and debris. Across squares with the skeletal remains of stalls stripped bare. Around fountains babbling to themselves. Beneath the shadows of homes staring at them through broken-window eyes. Past shrines bereft of long-looted offerings.

It was always the same.

Wide-open streets. Empty buildings. Not a soul in sight. Not a sound to be heard.

He thought he saw flashes of movement from the alleys—shadows that fled when he looked toward them. He thought he heard signs of life over the roofs—banging of hammers or cries in the night. But if he saw anything, he couldn't prove it. And not even Kataria said she heard anything.

"Was this Teneir's plan, then?" she asked as she followed behind Lenk. "To just...remove everyone? Empty the streets so she could have the city all to herself?"

"Don't be stupid. How would she even do that?"

"How should I know? You're the one who swore she was up to something."

"Oerboros said she was."

"Oh, well, if a winged, naked guy said it, it *must* be true."

"Khoth-Kapira's coming. We have to stop him and we have no other leads."

"That's just my point." She sighed. "Khoth-Kapira's coming to do something you don't know. You're going to stop him by coming here and stopping Teneir, who's also doing something you don't know. For world-ending powers, these guys are awfully fucking vague, aren't they?"

"You could have stayed behind," Lenk said as he pressed on through another alley. "You could have let me handle it."

He didn't turn around to look at her. But he could feel the silence in her, as keenly as he felt it in the air around him. He could feel her mouth open, searching for the words. He could feel her look over her shoulder, trying to see how long it would take her to go back. He could feel the tension in her body, the frown on her face, the downcast of her eyes.

"Yeah," she said softly, "I could have."

And when she spoke, he could feel his heart clench.

His thoughts turned to her, her hesitation, her fears that he could feel like a knife in his back. And for a moment, they turned to fleeing; taking her, hopping on the back of that beast and fleeing for as far as they could, and leaving this city to the demons.

But just as quickly, they turned to the day he had awoken and found her gone. And soon, they turned to the day he feared would come. The day she would be gone and, this time, she wouldn't be coming back.

And so he kept his eyes forward, his lips shut, and tried to ignore how much it hurt to drink in the silence and become part of it.

"Ancaa..."

But only for another moment.

"Ancaa..."

Over the rooftops, a windless gale that came wending through the streets.

"Ancaa..."

In great unison, voices raising a formless moan like a banner.

"Ancaa..."

Hundreds of them. Maybe thousands. Loud. Growing louder.

Right around the corner.

He hurried forward, Kataria close behind. His sword came out into his hand. Her bowstring groaned as she nocked an arrow. Together, they pressed through the alley and onto the massive road.

And beheld the tide of flesh before them.

On their hands and knees. On their bellies. Heads bowed, empty eyes upon the cobblestones beneath them. They crawled—weary and tired. They crawled—filthy and torn and ragged. They crawled—sweating and hungry and bleeding and weeping.

They had found the people of Cier'Djaal.

Men and women and elders and children, thousands of them crawling through the road toward a distant destination. Silent, but for the long, low moan that ebbed through them like a river.

"Ancaa...Ancaa...Ancaa..."

Crying out. Sobbing. Screaming. But always moaning. Occasionally, one of their heads would rise long enough to scream to heaven.

"Save us!"

"I am sorry I didn't believe!"

"I swear, whatever you ask of me, I will—"

Always, their heads would bow again. Always, they would return to the river of humanity. Always, their faces would fade and their voices would fade and they would become part of the great, thousand-legged creature that oozed its way through the streets.

"Fuck," Kataria whispered, staring wild-eyed at them. "They were doing this when we first got here. But there weren't this many, were there?" She shook her head. "Gods get a lot more popular when everything's shitty, I guess."

Lenk remembered that, of course: the faithful of Ancaa pulling themselves through the streets on the day they had first set foot into Cier'Djaal. But upon looking at them, he was reminded of something else.

A great, misshapen mass of flesh and cloth. Voices screaming for salvation, becoming a formless moan sent out to nothing. Desperate and broken beasts, begging for someone to help them, anyone to save them. He had seen this before. But their eyes hadn't been on the ground.

Back then, in Rhuul Khaas, they had been on Khoth-Kapira.

"Where are they going?" he whispered to himself.

They watched from the alley, daring to lean out and glance up the road toward their destination. The endless stream of humanity babbled its way in a shrieking, moaning bend through the roads, over the bridges and around the buildings of Cier'Djaal until they finally disappeared, far away.

Behind tall, white walls, pristine and glorious against the red sky.

<hr />

Silktown had never looked exactly welcoming to begin with—he had been there only the one time, and that had ended with him clubbed, drugged, and kidnapped. But compared to the gates that loomed before him today, that was downright hospitable.

The tide of people crawled their way through the great gates, their iron bars thrown open to welcome the moaning, wailing masses. One might have called the sight of the wealthiest town of Cier'Djaal, its doors wide and welcoming to the unwashed and desperate, a little heartening.

If one hadn't seen the dragonmen, anyway.

Two great, gray giants loomed on either side of the gates. Their rhinoceros-like horns swayed back and forth as they watched the crawling people enter with active disinterest. They yawned and talked to each other in booming voices, occasionally pausing to drink wine from massive barrels that they drained in great gulps.

One of them glanced up in his direction. He slid back into the alley, out of sight. Soon enough, the giant returned to drinking.

"Well, all right," Kataria muttered. "That's a little less vague, I'll give you that."

"People crawling toward Teneir's home," Lenk replied, "guarded by giant dragonmen. Whatever she's planning, she's about to do it."

"And what do *you* plan to do about it?" Kataria frowned at the two massive guards. "There's more dragonmen past the walls." Her ears twitched against her head. "I can hear them stomping around back there. You can't charge in."

"No," he said. "But they don't look all that invested in their job." He gestured with his chin toward the tide. "What do you wager I could just put my nose to the ground and crawl in with the rest of them?"

"Nobody ever got rich betting on you to succeed," Kataria muttered. "There's got to be another way we can use."

"We don't have the time it would take to find it."

"Then at least let me come with you," she said. "We stand a better chance at this together."

"Look at those people," Lenk said, gesturing to the crowd. "There's not a sword, a shict, or a scar among them. The dragonmen aren't watching closely, but they'll pick out an adventurer no problem." He shrugged the sword off his shoulder and handed it to her. "The fashas keep regular guards in there, too. I can find another weapon once I'm in, no problem."

He drew a breath and took a step forward. "This will work."

He was stopped suddenly. Usually, he was able to take at least three steps before his plans fell apart. But this time, he saw Kataria's hand wrapped around his wrist. He looked back at her. Her face was hard set in a scowl.

"What the *fuck* did I say back there?" she snarled. "Were you even listening to me?"

"I was, it's just—"

"Just what? Just I wasn't loud enough or you were too stupid to get what I was saying?" She pulled hard on his wrist, jerking him forward. Her canines were in his face, her breath hot and angry. "Every fucking moron around me seems to think that getting killed is the best way to do things, and *everyone* seems to think they can just leave me behind while they go and do it."

Her lips peeled back, baring her teeth.

"No more."

Something glistened in the corners of her eyes.

"Not again."

Her fingers were locked into a claw upon his wrist, her nails digging into his skin. Her ears were rigid and flattened against her skull.

And somehow, for all that, there was something weak and tender in her eyes. Something he hadn't seen often, so rarely that he sometimes forgot she had it.

He stepped closer to her. The muscles of her body went taut as he did. He laid a hand on hers but did not try to pry it off. He swallowed through a dry mouth and nodded.

"I know," he said. "I know. I've felt that way, too. For the past few weeks, I don't think I've felt anything else." He smiled sadly. "And because of that, I made a mistake. And I need to make it right."

"Everyone fucking says that," she snarled. "Every fucking moron thinks there's some reason they know better than I do and that's reason enough to try something dumb like this."

"This time is different."

"How?"

He squeezed her hand and closed his eyes. "This time," he said, "I'm coming back."

Her ears drooped. Her hand fell from his wrist, leaving dark red welts behind. He reached out without realizing he had, his hand rubbing the back of her neck.

"Take my sword," he said. "Cover me. I'm going to get in and find out what's happening, then I'll be back and we'll figure out what to do. Together." He smiled. "Okay?"

She met his eyes for a moment and snorted, hiking his sword up around her shoulder. "You're still a fucking moron."

"I know."

He crept to the mouth of the alley and peered out. The dragonmen were barely paying attention, taking turns hefting the massive wine barrels to their mouths and taking great gulps.

He glanced back at Kataria. She drew an arrow and nodded at him. He nodded back and, before he could think about how stupid this was, slid into line.

He fell to his knees and pushed his way into the crowd of crawling people. No one seemed to notice the inclusion of one more soul. Head bowed like the rest of them, he kept his eyes on the road and the people around him.

He saw only weary faces, aged prematurely by terror and agony— even the children looked one hundred. Some of their clothes were nicer than the others'. Some of them were filthier than the rest. But their faces were the same uniform ancient weariness, so alike in fear and exhaustion that he couldn't tell the difference between them as he crawled alongside them.

Over the stones and toward the gates.

"Bet the others are out of the desert by now," a voice boomed overhead.

"Not this shit again," another replied.

The dragonmen made no effort to disguise their conversation; the humans didn't seem that attentive, anyway. They spoke, loudly and contemptibly, to each other over the tide they guarded.

"The tulwar killed three of us," the first said. "Dran, Geth...Kharga's been missing for ages. The fashas didn't give a shit."

"They knew what they were getting into," the second said. "Seemed happy enough to take the gold when there wasn't fighting to be done."

"There's more on the way, they say. More tulwar."

"We'll kill them like last time. Easy."

"There are fewer of us now. And only one fasha left." He snorted. "Shit, we're not supposed to call her that anymore, are we? What's she want to be called?"

"The True Prophet." The second one spit a glob of phlegm that landed near Lenk's hand. "Humans have got so many of them that they need to differentiate. But this one pays me. And if Kharga and the others want to leave, that's more gold for me." He paused to drink out of a barrel. "Good wine, too. There's even more of this shit in the square."

"For the humans, though. We aren't supposed to touch it."

"A human can't drink that much. There'll be plenty left for us to—"

He paused. There was the sound of a great snout sniffing. Lenk felt his blood go cold.

"What?" the first one asked.

"Smell that?" the second said. "Something stinks."

"They all fucking stink."

"No, this one smells like...metal. And blood. And..."

A long silence passed. Lenk dared to look up.

Bad idea.

A great pair of black eyes glared down a long, horn-tipped snout at him. The dragonman's lips peeled back to reveal vicious teeth.

"There."

The giant took his man-sized ax in two hands. He took a shuddering step forward, sending the earth quaking. Lenk instinctively reached for a sword that wasn't there.

Worse idea.

The giant hefted his weapon overhead. He let out an angry snarl as he took another step forward, kicking a crawling person out of the way and sending them flying. Lenk glanced around the press of bodies, searching for a way out that didn't exist.

He heard the earth shudder. He heard the dragonman roar. He heard the wind whistling, growing into a shriek.

He heard the punch of metal through flesh.

"FUCK!"

The dragonman's weapon dropped, crushing another person. The others moaned louder and tried to scramble out of the way. The dragonman didn't notice; his attentions were for the arrow lodged in his eye.

"MY EYE!" he roared. *"THEY FUCKING GOT MY EYE!"*

"Who did?" the other dragonman asked. He searched the crowd, taking his weapon in hand.

He was roughly the size of a house. An arrow was only as long as half a human's arm. He could be forgiven for not noticing it until it was lodged in his nostril.

Lenk looked over his shoulder. Kataria stood on a nearby pillar, drawing another arrow. She caught his glance and growled just loud enough for him to hear.

"I told you!" she spit. "Didn't I fucking tell you?"

She had told him, it was true. And she would doubtless have told him more if she hadn't needed to turn and go bolting down the street at that moment.

Weapons in hand, earth shaking beneath them, the two dragonmen took off after her, roaring angrily. Lenk threw himself to the ground, forgotten in the wailing scramble of humanity as they tried to get out of the way of the two giants. He felt a great shadow pass over him. He bounced on the stones as a heavy foot came down just beside him. He waited until the thunder of their stride grew faint before he got up and hastily scrambled past the gates.

She'll be fine, he told himself. *She's small and quick. They're big and slow. And big. So big that with just one finger, they could...*

He shook his head, clenched his teeth.

She'll be fine.

Just like you'll be fine.

He put his head down, kept crawling, and tried not to worry about which of those two statements was less believable.

The decadent manors and lawns of Silktown were as the streets of Cier'Djaal proper: as silent, as cold, simply in better condition. The tall houses were quiet, their windows dark and shuttered. The lawns were overgrown, bereft of the furniture and exotic animals that had been present before. Gates were closed shut and locked tight.

Some of the houses looked like they had become fortresses: bars installed over windows, chains secured over the gates, archer barricades set up on rooftops. Others looked like they, and all their fineries, had also been abandoned as easily as the shops and homes in Cier'Djaal.

No spiders walking the street with shepherds. No exotic courtesans and entourages following wealthy men and women. No palanquins borne by burly slaves. Not so much as a servant walked the street.

Just as its people had abandoned Cier'Djaal, so too had the fashas that had built it.

"Your long journey is at an end!"

All but one of them, anyway.

"Through warfare, through bloodshed, beneath the empty promises of false prophets and under the dark eyes of deaf gods have you crawled to reach here."

He hadn't heard her voice much. Only a few words in a life that felt long ago and far away. Yet he knew her voice, her words.

And when he rounded the corner, he knew who it was he was staring at.

"Ancaa asks only that you crawl a little farther."

A massive square opened up in the center of Silktown, dominated by an impressively large fountain. An elegant thing, sculpted to resemble nude women, carrying broad smiles and massive jugs from which they emptied water into a circular basin, it had once been an elegant place for nobles to sit and chat, for merchants to arrange quiet, shady deals.

Today, it was simply a very fancy trough.

The crawling people assembled on their knees around it, fighting and pushing to drink from it. Men shoved women aside, who pushed squealing children away, in their thirst. The laughing stone women seemed to take immense joy in this, the fountain continuously pouring water as if to encourage the ravenous mauling.

"There is no need to fight, my people."

Atop the fountain, perched upon the tallest of the stone women, she stood like a beacon. Dressed in emerald silks, her arms spread wide open and voluminous sleeves cascading like waterfalls, Teneir looked down over her veil and laughed.

"I have brought plenty to all. And Ancaa has brought me to you."

Lenk caught a glimpse of a large hedgerow out the corner of his eye. He quickly rolled into it, disappearing in the underbrush; if the other crawlers noticed, they didn't care. Their eyes were on the square. And as soon as they reached it, they all but broke into a sprint.

Gathered in immense clusters on the road and lawns and any space they could find, they clustered together in tight knots around their feasts. From porcelain plates, they seized grapes, chicken, cheeses, breads and shoveled them into their mouths, pausing only to breathe or laugh in hysteric disbelief at their good fortune.

"Let this gift be the first of many!" Teneir cried out. *"Let my wealth be yours! Let my feast be yours! For under Ancaa's eyes, we are one! One people! One hunger! One salvation!"*

The people, as their hungers were sated, began to take notice. They looked up and laughed, echoing her words through mouths painted by the juice of fruit and grease of meat. They held their food, mashed together in their hands, up to her and cheered wildly.

"Trust not the false prophets who would bring war to your doorsteps! Who collude with the heathens and the brutes who shed the blood of your family in the streets! Their gods have brought you only death and disease! Ancaa has brought your life!"

"Life!" the crowd wailed, holding up their hands. *"Life! Ancaa!"*

No greed in their voices. Theirs were the shrieking, wild cries of men and women who had forgotten anything else. Theirs was the point where joy and desperation were the same thing.

Lenk watched as Teneir's guards, dressed in fineries and wearing swords at their hips, waded through the crowds, dispensing more plates of food with disdain plain on their faces. But the bulk of her force was on the outskirts of the crowd, guarding immense casks of wine lined up around the road, the same as the dragonmen had been drinking from.

People lined up to take cups from them, the many who could find no room at the fountain to drink from. The guards handed them wooden cups brimming with liquid, rudely shoved away those who begged for more, then waved the first one forward. Children who had never tasted it before blanched when parents made them drink. Elders with no taste for it anymore gagged a little but forced it down. None of them knew when they would have this again. If ever.

"*Eat until you have your fill!*" Teneir cried out. "*Drink until you are sated! Rest until you are strong again! A new day is dawning on Cier'Djaal! Free from the tyranny of greed! Free from the misery of war! All will be needed to rebuild! But all will be rewarded, not in some shallow afterlife, but in this one. This mortal paradise is yours. And it has been given to you by…*"

She held her hands out wide. She closed her eyes. And though she was far away and wore a veil, Lenk had seen that look of exultant ecstasy before, and he knew the kind of hungry smile she was wearing.

"*ANCAA!*" the crowd cried. "*ANCAA! ANCAA!*"

Teneir stood there, basking in their chants for what seemed like an age, until she finally lowered her arms and climbed down the fountain. A pair of guards flanked her as she turned and headed out of the square.

Lenk set off, winding his way around the hedgerows and darting between lawns. He found his way into a side street between two manors and hurried to catch up to Teneir.

He had told Kataria that he would only be half an hour. But he had no idea where he would find her after she had lost the dragonmen and only one opportunity to find out what Khoth-Kapira was planning. Teneir would know.

Teneir would talk.

He paused as the ground shuddered under his feet. He darted into an alley as two massive dragonmen came pounding up, hauling more casks of wine. They were laughing, drinking, bellowing, their snouts and mouths full of the liquid as they dragged rolling carts of the barrels through the streets, back toward the square.

When they were gone, Lenk went running out. Wherever Teneir was headed, it was a good bet that she'd have more dragonmen waiting for her there. He needed to find her and take her before she reached it.

Footsteps in his ears. The sight of three bodies walking swiftly, seen through the bars of a fence. He ran ahead, ducked behind a nearby pillar marching down an elegant road, and waited.

He got a chance to catch a glimpse of them as they walked past, their armor dented and well worn. Their faces were old; they wore old scars and moved easily with the weight of the swords at their hips. Teneir, swaddled in silks as she was, looked almost tiny between them. No pretty and ineffective house guards, these were her ugly, her scarred, her real fighters.

But Lenk had fought many things in his life. And some of them had been much uglier than these two.

He waited until they cleared the pillar he hid behind before moving. He rushed out, silent but for the thunder of his boots, as he lowered his body and collided, shoulder first, with the back of one of the guards. The guard let out a shout, staggering forward. Lenk's hand was already on his sword, jerking it free from its scabbard with one swift motion and whirling upon the other guard.

She had just begun to draw her own when Lenk's stolen weapon caught her in the unprotected gap between her breastplate and her helmet. She blinked, straining to look down at the wedge of steel lodged in her throat, before he tore it free.

The other one was already getting up and turning to face Lenk, groping for a weapon that wasn't there. He found it, instead, punching through his armor and bursting out his back. A sputter of exclamation went drowned in the blood bubbling from his lips as he toppled backward, wearing the same look of shock his partner had when she died.

There were no easy kills for men like Lenk. Only thoughtless ones. And his thoughts were not for these two.

Teneir stood, hands folded gingerly before her, making no effort to flee or defend herself or even to look shocked as Lenk approached her, bloodied sword in his hand. Her eyes were steady, yellow serenity locked on Lenk with a decidedly unsurprised look.

"I have been expecting you," she said.

"And I was expecting you to say something like that." He sneered. "Freaky thralls of demons are always saying something dramatic."

"Demons." Teneir sighed, her veil trembling as she did. "How could a blind man tell the difference between a demon and a god? When he feels the warmth of heaven, how could he know it from the inferno?"

"Yeah, see? *That* shit is exactly what I'm talking about." He leveled the sword at her. "I don't have a lot of time, so I'll ask you once before this gets difficult: What are you planning?"

"Planning?"

"With Khoth-Kapira. Ancaa. Whatever you call him. What are you—"

"I know you've come in quest for a power you don't understand. I merely take exception to the term *plan*. A plan is a mortal thing, riddled with flaws and expected to fail. You expect me to have one, yes? Another hand-wringing villain for you to chop down after I lay out my elaborate scheme or some such foolishness?"

"I was planning on getting straight to the chopping, but yeah, something like that."

"Of course. You define your world in bloodshed, one murderer among many, somehow convinced that yours will be seen as righteous when you are called to answer the great question."

There was something heavy in her eyes, an iron weight that settled on Lenk with an uncomfortable certainty.

"It is for you that I was first moved to do this, you know. For the ignorant and the blind, those who saw no end to this ceaseless agony but for the sword. I would beg you to let me continue, to let me find an answer for you…"

She closed her eyes.

"But I am wasting my breath, am I not?"

"You're wasting time." Lenk took the blade up in both hands and stormed toward her. "A lot of people are going to die if you don't tell me what I need to know. So stop your fucking sermons and tell me what you're planning to—"

"I told you, there is no plan."

Her eyes snapped open, a bright and burning and hateful yellow.

"There is only *vision*."

Her silks fluttered. From beneath, a great tendril of scale and sinew shot out toward him. He hardly had time to scream before it slammed into his chest and sent him flying to crash against the pillar. The blade fell from his hands; he rolled to the stones and coughed, straining to find his feet.

"Yes, many will die. Many were dying long before you came here. Many have died under old ways, old gods, old and tired and broken promises. Yet no one seemed to care."

A shadow loomed over him. Through swimming vision, he looked up. Teneir rose up on columns of tendrils, coils of scales that twisted and writhed beneath her. They carried her up on a pedestal of flesh to loom over him, so small and pitiable beneath her baleful gaze.

"Only now, when I have a chance at stopping it, do you care." Her voice became a low and hateful hiss. "Ancaa spoke true. You are driven to bring misery upon yourself, Lenk."

She knew his name.

She knew everything.

And he knew nothing. Not about how she knew it, about what she was planning or even what the hell she was.

He turned to bolt, to hide, to get clear, get Kataria, get another sword, get *away*. But he hadn't taken three steps before he was knocked off his feet by a great sweep of scales. He fell to the ground, felt them entwine around his legs, haul him screaming across the stones.

"It was years ago that I first received her visions," Teneir spoke, unconcerned by his flailing panic as she reeled him toward her. "In my sleep, at first, fleeting dreams of a world of beauty and harmony that I could one day see. But they grew stronger, until I saw it everywhere, in my waking life: a world without poverty, without hardship, where the saccarii could live without fear. It was when I dedicated my fortunes to the realization of this world that I began to...change."

She hauled him off his feet, dangling him before her like a worm on a hook. More coils slipped out from beneath her silks, found their way around his arms, his waist, his throat. He felt them tighten. He felt them squeeze. He felt the breath begin to leave him.

"I have grown stronger these past days. It is Ancaa. She liberates me from my prison of flesh, expands my being. She speaks clearer to me. Her visions come stronger."

She reached up and pulled the veil from her face. Reptilian lips parted in a snarl, baring a long, flickering tongue and daggerlike fangs.

"So tell me...why is it that, where she once showed me visions of a world free from strife, she only speaks your name now?"

He gasped out an answer, unheard as the coils tightened about his throat.

"You. Your face. Your sword. Your terrible thoughts and your terrible lies. You plague her dreams and cloud her thoughts. Why does she obsess over you and leave me without guidance?"

His face betrayed no answer, nothing but primal fear as the last breaths left him. Her eyes almost burst from her head with the force of her snarl.

"WHY?"

The coils tightened closer. He felt something crack inside him. The muscles in his limbs went bloodless and limp in her coils. Darkness crept in at the edges of his vision.

"A test, perhaps? Are you the sole blight on her perfect vision? Or are you simply an object of infatuation she wishes to see in the afterlife? It is no matter, Lenk. For there is no plan. You came here expecting to find something to stop, to destroy."

The last thing he saw was her serpentine lips coiled into a smile.

The last thing he heard was the whisper on her flickering tongue.

"But she arrived an hour ago."

THIRTY-SEVEN

INHERITED SIN

Kataria no longer heard them.

Now she felt them.

The earth shook beneath her feet with every stride they took. Their roars shook the bones in her skin. The wind died around her, the air holding its breath in anticipation.

That was when she knew she had to jump.

There was a great rush of air. She leapt forward, falling into a tumble. The cobblestones quaked as something huge struck the road behind her. Stone splinters flew, raining upon her as she got to her feet and whirled, nocking an arrow.

Why the fuck won't they just give up?

Five feet away, the dragonman pulled its ax out of the road in a spray of dust. Its mouth craned open in a cavernous roar. She drew, fired in one fluid motion. Her arrow flew, found the giant's mouth, sank itself into the soft flesh of its cheek.

The creature let out a surprisingly small yelp of pain.

She hadn't expected that.

She *certainly* hadn't expected it to simply snap its jaws shut, shattering the arrow, no more bothered by it than it would be by a piece of food stuck in its teeth.

And she hadn't expected them to be this persistent, her to be this tired. She had run from creatures like this before, much bigger ones, in fact. She had a plan for situations like this: Run fast, move erratically, get to a place too small for them to get into, and then make a rude gesture at them when they couldn't follow.

She had been planning something particularly coarse for these dragonmen.

But, as it turned out, Cier'Djaal was frustratingly accommodating for its larger residents. This close to Silktown and the Souk, the avenues were wide enough for carriages, wagons, large crowds, and, as it turned out, massive, bloodthirsty dragonmen.

She was quick enough to keep ahead of this one's long strides, but her breath was going ragged, her legs were going numb, and her quiver was going empty. She wasn't sure how much longer she could keep out of the reach of this one.

Or his friends.

Her ears quivered—she could hear them in the distance. One in the next street over. Two in the street behind her. Another one two streets ahead. And this one behind her.

Five dragonmen had come out to hunt her down. Five of them, each one with her scent in their nose, making the earth shake with their feet as they searched for her in the avenues.

They'd find her, sooner or later.

Or she'd trip and fall.

Or she'd just get too tired to keep going.

Really, there were a lot of ways she could die here.

An alley veered into view. Not as narrow as she would have liked, but it was at least narrower than this street. She turned down it, pivoting out of the dragonman's way as it rushed past. It must have been between two shops—she could see crates stacked at the end of it, a tall wall at the end of it.

Perfect.

She heard the dragonman turn about, head for the alley. She scrambled up the crates, swung a leg over the wall, looked back over her shoulder.

The alley was too narrow for the dragonman to move comfortably down. But the dragonman hardly seemed to mind. It roared, charging down the narrow path, its massive shoulders tearing the stone and wood of the walls apart as it charged toward her.

But the wall was too tall for it to mount. There wasn't enough space for it to climb. The crates wouldn't hold its weight. She hopped down off the wall and scrambled into the alley behind it. It went on for a little more before opening out into a bigger road, but she took the moment to lean against a nearby wall and catch her breath.

Her muscles were on fire. Her breath was raw in her throat. Blood was throbbing in her body.

It didn't used to be this hard, she told herself. She used to be able to run all day. Perhaps it was the years of running, of fighting, of surviving that had weighed her down. Or maybe it was the weight of something else.

Finally given a spare thought, she took a moment to think of Lenk. He hadn't followed her. Turned out he could be trusted not to be a complete idiot once in a while. He would have made his way in by now and, if all went according to plan, he would be out by now.

Of course, she thought as she rose up and knuckled a sore spot on her back, *it was* his *plan, so if it all went like he thought it would, he's probably dead by now.*

But if he wasn't, she would handle it. She would protect him. Him and everyone.

She looked down at her bow, ran her fingers over the fletching of her remaining arrows.

She was done losing people.

Her ears trembled at the sound of the dragonman roaring impotently behind the wall. She looked up at it and smirked.

The giant might have been huge. It might have been strong enough to crush her into a fine paste with one well-placed foot. But she was small, nimble, and terribly, terribly clever. She had escaped beyond the beast's reach and there was nothing it could do.

The bricks of the wall exploded as a great horn smashed through. Her smile fell.

Unless it does that.

The wall smashed behind her, exploding into a hail of bricks and dust. The creature's howl filled her ears. She kept running, closed her eyes, lowered her head, and ran for the exit. Its footsteps were in her ears, in her bones, in her blood. Its breath was on her neck. Her skin pricked at the sensation of its claws reaching for her.

She reached the mouth of the alley.

She leapt.

And, for a few glorious moments, things actually seemed like they would be all right.

Before the claw caught her, anyway.

A great hand wrapped around her legs and brought her to the ground. The dragonman was on its belly, wriggling its way out of the alley. She snarled, trying to kick her way free. The creature clambered to its feet, breathing heavily, eyes weary—the chase had taken much out of it, enough that it might not crush her right away.

She couldn't take that chance.

She drew her arrow as the dragonman lifted her up. It scowled down its snout at her, eyes bloodshot and teary. She aimed, she drew, she fired.

The arrow skittered off its scales as its head suddenly dropped. She screamed, anticipating the crushing blow to come.

But it did not come.

What came, instead, was a great torrent of bile as the dragonman's jaws craned open and expelled a wave of vomit onto the stones.

It drew in desperate, ragged breaths as it looked up again. She was quicker, drawing and firing an arrow right into its eye. It let out a shriek, dropping her. She fell and splashed down into the puddle of reeking filth, quickly scrambling away.

But the giant made no move to pursue her. It dropped its ax as it leaned hard against the side of a building, shattering the stones as it did. Its body shook as it struggled to gulp down air. Its flanks shuddered as something came up its gullet.

Kataria kept her bow up, arrow drawn, but did not fire. The dragonman looked as confused as she felt, its fear so desperate as to be plain even on its reptilian features.

It bent low, vomited again. What came out was thick, red, and full of glistening ichor. Its tongue lolled out the side of its mouth as it looked up, wheezing, at Kataria and gasped out a single word.

"Help—"

It couldn't say any more. Its mouth was filled with bile. Liquid came pouring out of its mouth, sluiced between its teeth, until the road was painted with its insides. It clutched its stomach, doubled over in agony, eyes shut tight as it continued to empty itself.

Until there was nothing left.

The great dragonman, tall as a tree, big as a house, strong enough to have killed her in one blow, fell in a puddle of its own puke and lay there, eyes wide and wondering what the fuck had just happened.

She wished she could answer it.

She hadn't *heard* of any god of digestive distress that might have saved her, but she wasn't intending to dwell on it. She hiked up her bow, tried to shake out the pain in her leg, and started to make her way back to Silktown, back to Lenk.

She followed the road sixty paces before her ears twitched.

Elsewhere, there was the sound of something heavy hitting the ground.

One street over, there it was again.

One street behind her, another.

And just ahead, around the corner. She heard a choked, watery scream right before she felt the shock of something huge collapsing and striking the ground.

She approached slowly, peering around the building. The sight of something massive and unmoving greeted her.

Another dragonman. Another puddle of red-flecked vomit. Another pair of eyes, bulging out of their sockets, their last moments of panicked agony forever etched on them.

She left it, moving cautiously through the streets, bow in hand. Not that whatever was happening could necessarily be answered by an arrow, but shooting things in the face had solved most of her problems up to this point.

And the farther she went, the more she saw them.

More dead dragonmen. More corpses in puddles of vomit. More visions of terror and agony across their faces. They had died quickly, they had died painfully, and they had died without having any idea what was going on.

Across every avenue, in every square, the sight was the same.

Except for the last one.

There was a dragonman, again. It was dead, draped over a railing to the river apparently in a vain attempt to get water. Its vomit painted the stones, like the rest of them.

But there was someone else here, sitting solemnly on the beast's massive, breathless shoulders.

Someone she knew.

"Ah."

He looked up as she approached. Age had creased his face but hadn't diminished the strength in it. But stress had given him wrinkles he hadn't had when she saw him last. His hair hadn't been as disheveled. He hadn't looked so skinny and weak. He hadn't worn the eyes of a man ready to die.

"I was wondering what they were chasing," Sai-Thuwan said. He smiled, weakly. "I am glad they didn't catch you."

"Thuwan!" she cried out, rushing toward him. "What are you doing here? I thought your tribe left the city."

"I remember once, when game was lean. The humans and the tulwar had hunted everything for miles. We were starving. Thua's mother and I, we left with a hunting party for the plains far to the south. Bemodons roamed there. Great big things, huge tusks they used to rip trees out of the ground and eat them. Their hooves tore up the land." Sai-Thuwan idly kicked the corpse of the dragonman beneath him. "Bigger, even, than these lizards."

"Are there other shicts here?" Perhaps he hadn't heard her. She drew closer. "Have you come alone?"

"Do you know how we killed them?" He shook his head. "We tracked them for days. We ran them down on yijis, firing arrows at them, keeping them running. We hunted like a pack, attacking and resting in turns, forcing them to run. It took a day of running for them to grow exhausted enough that we could finish them. But they made such a feast. There was more meat than we could carry back, even with the yijis we had brought."

Kataria opened her mouth. The question caught in her throat. She found it hard to ask without wanting to cry. But she had to. She couldn't not ask.

"Is Kwar here?"

"That was a good kill. It fed our families for months. I never regretted any blood spilled for my family." He looked over his shoulder, into the dragonman's last moments of agony bulging from a huge skull. "I thought this..." He gestured to the dragonman, then out over the city. "All of this. I thought it would feel like that kill. That I would feel like I had saved everyone. Someone."

He stared down at the body. His eyes had emptied themselves of tears long ago. His smile had lost every memory it had once had. His face was the night: as vast, as dark, as empty.

"But I don't feel. Anything."

Kataria could not say the same.

At his words, at the realization that followed, something foul and borne on many sharp legs crawled out of the pit of her belly. She tried to speak and, after many choked failures, found a voice for her fear.

"Poison," Kataria said. "Shekune poisoned them."

Visions of days past flashed through her head—of a dark night with fading light, of Karnerian humans doubled over in agony as they spilled their innards out through their mouths, of their friends watching, terrified and helpless, before the khoshicts appeared from the darkness.

Back then, Shekune had poisoned their water. But how had she slain the dragonmen? How could she—

"The wine," Kataria gasped. "She poisoned the wine. How?"

Thuwan stared down at the road, saying nothing. She snarled, reaching out and seizing him by the collar. She shook him until his head flopped in such a way that he was staring at her.

"*How?*" she demanded.

"Shekune asked me to lead her into the Green Belt," he muttered, eyes drifting away. "I knew the old hunting trails. I knew the way. I showed her. But she wanted to go into the city, into the fashas' homes. I did not know. But…"

"Kwar did." Kataria felt her face tighten with the force of her snarl. Her words were desperate, heated. "Tell me she didn't, Thuwan. Tell me she didn't do this."

He fell silent again. She roared, hurling him to the ground. He struck the stones hard, lay upon the floor.

"FUCKING TELL ME!"

"Do not blame her," he said, not looking up. "She did it for me. She did it because she thought it would save us all."

No, Kataria thought. *She did it for me.*

"The wine's already been poisoned," Kataria muttered. "The humans are already drinking it. That was her plan."

"One of them."

Her eyes widened. "What do you mean?"

Thuwan stared vacantly up at the sky. "Kwar and Thua were only three years old when we came back from our hunt. She had been hungry for so long. I remember how her eyes lit up when she ate, and ate."

He smiled. "We thought she would explode, she ate so much. We had to pull her off Thua when she tried to take his food. But her smile...I remember her smile. It was the last time she looked that way and I thought..."

"Thuwan," Kataria said, "tell me."

He sighed. "Shekune knew the tulwar were coming. She saw the humans' defenses and saw a chance to kill them both, slaughter both their armies. It was me who showed her the way up onto the cliffs. It was me who thought that Kwar would see me avenging her mother, at long last. I wanted to..." He shook his head. "I wanted to see her eyes like that again. I wanted to make her happy again."

"By plunging the shicts into a war we can't win?" Kataria loomed over him, hands twitching with the urge to strangle him. "By giving her more death? More corpses?"

He rose on his elbows. He stared at her in a way that made her want to turn away.

"My life," he said softly, "has been nothing but corpses. The truth is, I died with Kwar's mother. All this time, I have simply been waiting for my body to realize it." He sighed, closed his eyes. "Maybe Kwar has, too."

Those words. Of all the things he said, of all the fears and angers he had roused in her, it was those words that made her go cold. Those words that made her hand tighten around her bow and unconsciously reach for an arrow to put in his throat.

"You did die back there," Kataria said. "You went to the Dark Forest with all the other ghosts. Because Kwar is still here, still alive, but you haven't noticed for years, have you?"

"Everything I did, I did for—"

"For yourself. You led Shekune here because you thought it would make Kwar love you. You're going to kill us all for the chance that it might be what she wants."

"She wants vengeance," Thuwan growled. He clambered to his feet. "She wants to give her mother peace!"

"She wants her mother *back*!" Kataria snapped. "But she's never going to get her back. And the reason she's so angry, so violent, so willing to kill anyone is that she looked for her father and he *wasn't there*!"

He recoiled, as if struck. "That's not...She hated me..."

"She did," Kataria said. "Maybe she still does, I don't know. But it's killing her. She doesn't need more ghosts. She doesn't need people who will kill for her. She needs people who will stay alive for her." She spit on the ground. "And you failed her."

Just like I did.

Thuwan's mouth hung open. His eyes did not blink. His limbs hung heavy at his sides. To look at him, one would have called him a corpse, just like the one next to him.

But Kataria did not. For in his empty eyes, she saw something. A rising wetness at the corners of his stare. He swallowed hard. His words were heavy and choked.

"My daughter..." he whispered. "My son...I've lost them both."

"You did." Kataria turned and began to stalk away. "Enjoy fucking dealing with that."

"Wait!" he cried after her. "Where are you going?"

"To clean up your mess," she snarled. "Or to try, anyway. You've already killed us all."

"I haven't!" His voice was brimming now. "I mean, not yet! It's not too late!"

She scowled over her shoulder at him. "Talk."

"Shekune said she would announce her victory when she killed the tulwar and humans. She hasn't yet."

"How do you know?"

Sai-Thuwan's ears twitched. "We would both hear it."

Kataria blinked. "She hasn't launched her attack yet."

"They can be warned. The humans. You know them, don't you?"

She did know them. She knew what had to be done.

And part of it involved ignoring Sai-Thuwan as she took off running.

Asper hadn't listened before, but things were different back then. Now, there was a credible threat, a real ambush. Also, she hadn't tried violence. If Asper wouldn't listen, she would just start hitting her until she—

No. Kataria shook her head. *She'll listen. She has to listen. Worry about what you'll say later. Just get there first. Okay?*

She drew in a breath, closed her eyes.

Okay.

She found a carcass of a dragonman up against a building. She leapt atop the massive creature, using its bulk to scale up the wall, hauling herself onto the roof. She scanned the rooftops and streets, searching for the square where she had left Colonel MacSwain. She squinted, growled.

Who the fuck *made this stupid place so gods-damned* big?

There.

She found the scraw, far away. *Much* farther than she thought he would be. But if she hurried, she could still make it. She just had to fly him to the battle, hope no one shot her down on the way, hope no one *else* shot her down when they saw her flying a Sainite mount, hope no one stabbed her when she got off, hope no one—

She thumped her head with the heel of her palm.

What the fuck did I say about worrying? Get there first.

And she was just about to do that when her ears twitched.

Far away, almost too far to be noticed, she heard a scream. And she would have ignored it—would not have even heard it—if she hadn't recognized the voice that made it.

She rushed to the other edge of the roof. Her ears were aloft, twitching, listening for the sound. A moment passed. She heard nothing.

But she saw . . .

Well, she wasn't quite sure what it was.

A mass of tendrils and coils and scales. A horrible, writhing monstrosity that hauled itself over the wall of Silktown and began to slither on a dozen tails down the street. The faintest image of a head—a face that might have been called almost human, were it not for the broad fangs, sinewy neck, and bristling scales across its cheek—leered out from the mass.

This, too, was something she was ready to ignore for now.

And for the rest of her life, if possible.

And she might have done just that, were it not for the fact that she saw something in the thing's coils.

He was limp, eyes closed, dragged along like a bale of hay. His body was twisted in its scaly clutches, and bruises marred his skin. But even from here, she could see that he drew breath.

Just barely.

And not for long.

"Lenk," she whispered, and then screamed. *"LENK!"*

She moved to take off after him and whatever vile horror had him. But the moment she put her foot on the roof's ledge, she remembered. She looked over her shoulder to the distant square, to the battle she was supposed to stop, to the people she was supposed to save. She looked back, to the man she had sworn not to lose, to the thing that was about to take him from her as it disappeared around a corner.

She stood, paralyzed, cursing her fucking luck, cursing the fucking humans for being so fucking stupid, cursing the fucking shicts for doing this to her, cursing fucking Lenk for not listening to her and always, *always* getting his stupid fucking self in fucking trouble.

She stood. She gritted her teeth. She clenched her hands. She shut her eyes.

She let out a very long, very angry scream.

And then she took off running.

THIRTY-EIGHT

LET THE TRUMPETS SING
HIS RETURN

Before Asper could see it, she knew it.

In the lurch of her gut, the way something deep inside her came unhinged and lodged itself in her throat. In the same way a dog knows its master's grave and a grandmother knows when to say farewell, she knew.

The battle was lost.

And those who had sworn to follow her.

Those who had trusted her to lead them.

They were dead.

The sandstorm had come out of nowhere, sweeping through the cliffs on a hot wind that buffeted the watchtower and made it shake. Though she had tried to peer through it with the spyglass, she had seen nothing more than phantoms—ghosts whose bodies had yet to realize they were dead.

But now, the sands dissipated. Now, the grit fell away and exposed the battlefield. Now she saw the numerous dead.

And Careus.

"No."

Haethen shuddered next to her, body trembling with something she fought to contain with the hand pressed against her mouth. Her eyes trembled, wanting to cry, but she had nothing for them. Sorrow visited later, Asper knew, long after horror had its chance to feast.

"Careus..." the Foescribe whispered.

Asper didn't know who the black tulwar were, with their crude metal and their white-painted flesh. She didn't know how they were still standing with arrows and spears jutting from them. She didn't know how it had happened that one of them stood at the center of the melee, holding Careus's severed head high above and howling with laughter.

Nor did it matter.

Pockets of fighting still raged in the pass. Karnerians and Sainites fought against the black tulwar with spear and blade and shield and crossbow. Despite whatever tenacity they held, a few of the tulwar lay unmoving on the earth. But the watchtower was not so far away that Asper couldn't see the faces of the human dead. Or how many of them were.

But that didn't matter, either.

Through the carnage of the battle below, Asper could hear the sound of distant drums. Far away, they pounded out a message, sending out a call to battle.

A call that was answered.

A tide of ash came flowing out of the dunes. A great gray wave, painted with reds and yellows and blues and bright, flashing steel. The drums drove them forward, calling them to battle in one titanic wave. And soon, the thunder of the drums was drowned out by the roar of their rage.

"The tulwar," Haethen said. "This was their plan ... use those ... those *things* ..." She made a gesture to the black tulwar below. "Break our lines with them, then pull in all at once. They used the sandstorm to do it, they ..." She shook her head. "But how did they know? How did they know it was coming? How come ... *why* didn't I know? How did I not know they could do that?"

She turned, rustling through the scrolls and parchments on the table, picking them up and hurling them aside, one by one, heedless of where they landed.

"It had to be here! It *has* to be here! I missed something! I must have! It was my duty to know them, but I couldn't ... I didn't ..."

Her hands shook as she held a scroll, eyes racing frantically across it. Her face twisted. She let out a scream, tore the scroll in half, and threw it out over the watchtower. She buried her face in her hands, drawing in a ragged breath.

"My fault…" she whispered. "My fault."

The sound of her sob could not be heard through the din of battle below and the roar of the approaching army. But the trembling of her body betrayed her. She stood, shaking, for a long moment. When she spoke, she did so struggling to hide the wetness of her voice.

"I'll sound the retreat," she said softly. "We'll fall back to the city. We'll try to make our stand there."

When Asper said nothing in reply, she dropped her hands. When she saw Asper buckling her sword belt, she dropped her mouth.

"What are you doing?" she asked.

"Everything," Asper replied, cinching the belt up.

"No," Haethen said. Then again, forcefully. "*No.* You're too important to—"

"That doesn't matter anymore," Asper said.

She hefted her broad, round shield and secured it to her arm. She seized the banner—the banner of the three armies, in all its threadbare glory—and held it aloft, inspecting it as though it were a spear.

"You're thinking you're going to go down there and rally them?" Haethen let out a hysterical laugh. "This isn't a fucking storybook, you moron. Even if we *had* the men to do that, you're not going to change anything with a fucking piece of cloth, Prophet or no."

"I don't need to be a Prophet right now," Asper said, hiking it over her shoulder. "I need to be a target."

"What?"

"We have only one way left." She pointed out with the banner, far over the cliffs to the distant dunes. "Gariath. Kill him, this army is left without a leader. We can counterattack when he falls."

"He's a mile away, at least!"

"He won't be for long," Asper said. "Not once he sees me."

"That's insane," Haethen said. "He won't do it. He can't possibly be that—"

"He can. He is. He will." Asper turned and headed for the ramp. "He'll come. I'll kill him. We'll win this. You'll make sure we do."

"Asper, wait!"

"Send the reserves in with me. We just need to hold until he comes," she called out over her shoulder as she charged down the ramp, headed for the pass.

"He won't even see you!" Haethen called after her.

"If heaven can see me, so can he!" she called back, and then was gone.

⊷ ━◆▶◆━ ┼⊶

"It was luck, mostly. Just an old man who happened to be right." Mototaru tapped his pipe against his palm, emptying the ashes onto the sand. "But storms are like birds. They come from the sea, roam around the mainland for a little, and then go back."

He packed new tobacco in his pipe, lit it, and took a few deep puffs.

"Now is the time of year they return to the sea, but any fool who watches the sky long enough could tell you that. And asking gaambols to throw around a lot of sand and make a tremendous mess is like asking rain to be wet."

A smile curled around the stem of his pipe, knowing and ancient.

"But how did I know the wind would be strong enough to carry that much sand? Well, there is the idea that *Humn*'s Tul never diminishes. It is rumored that we remember all our past lives and it is this culmination of lifetimes of wisdom that grants us the authority to lead. I used to think it was all oxshit, of course, but I remembered this storm . . . I remembered this wind, somehow. And somehow, it felt like not so much oxshit and you're not even fucking listening to me anymore, are you?"

Gariath *was* listening, but only barely. Had he been paying a little more attention, he would have found the energy to resent Mototaru's accusation. But as it was, his eyes were locked on the ensuing chaos below.

The humans still stood; their formation had been shattered, their leader had been killed, but there were still more than enough to challenge their foes. The Mak Lak Kai, for their part, continued to fight, even as their gaambols had been slain and their bodies weathered the violence. They would fight to their last breath—and then keep fighting—but Gariath didn't need that.

He just needed them to hold on for a little longer.

The drums continued to thunder, their song filling the sky. The tulwar answered, rushing forward in a great tide. Rua Tong, Chee Chree, Tho Thu Bhu, Yengu Thuun; clans were forgotten, divisions ignored as they swept across the sand in a teeming wave of flesh and steel.

It had been their defeats, Gariath realized. The withering losses they had suffered in the morning had left them hungry for vengeance. And now their need for victory overwhelmed their apprehension about the

Mak Lak Kai. They would not allow the *malaa* to show them up, even if it meant fighting alongside them.

Bloodlines divide. Bloodshed unites, it was once said.

Or maybe he had just made that up.

Someone ought to write that down. It was good.

He didn't care about that, either. His thoughts were for the impending battle. The tulwar would break their last formation, sweep into the Green Belt and right to the city gates. They would have their vengeance. The city would be razed. The world would be free of one more disease.

All it would take was a little more—

A war horn cut through the air, a thin and tinny note barely audible against the bellow of drums. But he caught it all the same.

Just as he caught sight of the humans rushing toward the pass.

Not as many as the tulwar, nor as well armed. Some steel there, but mostly sticks and spears and a few cruder implements. It wasn't warriors they were sending out; rather, the tall human would give him one final insult before he crushed her by sending out farmers and weaklings to die for nothing.

He would have been enraged by that.

Had he not seen something else to be enraged by.

There. At the head of their mad rush. A flash of pale among the dark-skinned humans. A dented and ugly shield. And a big, bold blue piece of cloth, fluttering in the wind like it would do a damn thing.

He could smell her reek from here.

"She's here," he growled.

"Who?" Mototaru asked.

"I need a gaambol." Gariath did not answer as he stormed down the hill. "And a rider. Get me one."

"What?" Mototaru creaked to his feet. "Why? Our warriors will carve them apart in no time. There is no need to risk yourself."

"They couldn't kill me if there were a hundred times more than there are now," he snarled in reply. "There is no risk."

That was half-true.

He knew he could kill her. He knew she could not hurt him. Not in all the time they had traveled together could she ever have hoped to even scratch him. And he knew, too, that she and her rabble could not hope to stand against the tulwar. They would cut her down as surely as he would.

But then, she would have been killed by someone else.

Then, she would die with the smile on her lips as she went to her imaginary god with the belief that he had been too scared to fight her. She would die never knowing why she had to die, why it had to be him to kill her.

She would die never realizing what a moron she and Lenk and *all* of them had been to abandon him.

"I have watched you hurl yourself at monsters that nearly ate you alive!" Mototaru cried, hurrying after him. "You cannot be trusted to not kill yourself!"

"This battle is won, no matter if I survive."

"It's not the battle we have to think of, fool!" Mototaru roared down the hill as he approached the tulwar left behind to guard him. "We are not here simply to kill! This is not simply revenge! It's a murderer that only thinks of the kill! A warrior thinks about what happens afterward!"

That, too, was a good saying. Someone should write that down, too.

Someone else, of course.

He had a prophet to kill.

Pathon wasn't sure what he had been expecting.

Maybe he had hoped that faith would shield him, hold him strong against the tulwar when they attacked. Or perhaps he had thought that the courageous knowledge that the world rested on his shoulders would give him the strength to prevail. Maybe some small part of him, some wide-eyed boy whose grandfather's tales of valor had inspired him to enlist, had expected the skies to open up and Daeon to step down and save Careus and rout the hated pagan.

He had been expecting a miracle. Or at least an advantage.

Yet the sky hung over him, empty and blue and silent. The speaker's corpse lay next to him, cold and unmoving like any of the others strewn across the battlefield. His arm was broken, his body was numb, and he could not find the strength to rise up. The sounds of the tulwar, their bellowing cries, were soft and distant in his head.

The battle was over.

The sky was empty.

Heaven had not been watching.

In the end, it had just been another war. The same bloody and awful mess as all the others he had fought. The stories his grandfather had told him had just been that.

Stories.

Mothers never wept proud tears over swelling breast to hear that their son had died in the dirt far away. The right and the just never swept over the land and won a bloodless rout against cowardly villains. The sky did not open up. Gods did not come down. Prayers were not heard.

People fought.

People died.

This was all it was. Deep down, he had always known that. But some part of him had hoped it wasn't.

A shadow loomed over him. Bright red eyes fixed on him. The tulwar canted his head at him, curious, like he wasn't quite sure what he was looking at. He leaned down, and, satisfied that Pathon was still alive, nodded sagely to himself as he raised his sword and aimed to remedy that.

Pathon drew in a breath. He looked at the patch of orange sky behind the tulwar's shoulder. He watched heaven and waited.

And so, he barely saw it when something came barreling out of the corner of his eye and struck the tulwar, knocking him to the earth.

He craned his neck and saw a dirty man in ill-fitting armor tackling the tulwar to the ground—a Djaalic. The man wrestled with the creature for a minute, stabbing awkwardly with what looked like a crude knife. He held the tulwar down until three more Djaalics came rushing up, jamming their spears into the tulwar and pinning him to the earth.

The reserves. The Djaalic reserves were here.

They were supposed to stand behind and help with the retreat, should it be necessary, or to catch any tulwar that came through. They shouldn't be here, in the real battle. They were farmers, merchants; they'd be killed. They should be running. They should be going back to their families. He opened his mouth to yell at them to flee.

"Are you all right?"

Those weren't his words. That wasn't his voice.

Another shadow fell over him. Dirty armor, clinking mail. An arm

511 GOD'S LAST BREATH

wielding a dented shield. A face smudged with grime, brown hair that
hung in thick, unwashed strands around hazel eyes, deep with concern.
A glimmering pendant of Talanas dangling from her neck as she leaned
over him.

"P-Prophet," he gasped out.

"Easy." She took him gently by the shoulder, easing up him to his
rear end, careful not to touch his shoulder. "Your arm is broken. You
need to fall back."

It was her.

It had been so long since he had seen her up close. From afar, she
looked regal, like someone who really could command heaven. But
here, down in the dirt, she was filthy and sweaty and grimy, like the
rest of them. Her voice was full of concern, not authority. And her eyes
weren't ablaze with divine purpose.

"Did you hear me?" she asked. "You need to go back. Get treated,
Pathon."

She wasn't from heaven.

She was just a woman. A normal woman.

And she was here, in the dirt, fighting. She had stopped to pick him
up, just another soldier. She was just a woman and she was here, standing against so many, fighting with them.

Not like a story.

Something more than that.

He clambered to his feet. She nodded.

"Good," she said. "Try to get to the city, if you can. We'll have to—"

He reached down and picked up his sword with his good hand. She
shook her head.

"No! *No!*" she cried out, rising up and reaching for the blade. "Don't
fight! Your arm is broken! You need to—"

"I need to do my duty," he answered.

"You've done it," she said. "You've done more than enough. Please,
get back and—"

He took up his blade and stormed to the front lines. It was probably
disrespectful to disobey a Prophet. And, truly, maybe she was still a
Prophet. But before that, she was just another person. A person who
would fight to protect this city. A person who would fight to defend
these people. She could have taken her lofty title and grand vision,

demanded riches and power and fled. But she had become a Prophet just to lead them, just to bring them to this fight.

The only fight, of the many he had waged, that really felt like it mattered.

Not for duty. Not for conquest. Not for gods. Just for people.

Perhaps it was simply the agony numbing his mind that made him think these things. Perhaps that dumbshit kid who had listened to too many stories was in control now. Or perhaps his brain was leaking out of his skull from a head wound.

It didn't matter.

As he rushed to the front lines, his sword held high, a wave of gnashing fangs and flashing steel and painted faces rampaging toward him, he was prepared to fight.

Just as she was.

⊹ ▬◆▬ ⊹

"Fucking moron," Asper growled as she waded forward.

A blade shot out at her, screeching across her shield as she brought it up. She shoved out with it and pushed her aggressor back. When the sword went flying high, she lashed her own blade out in a thrust. When she lowered her shield, the tulwar's face was wide with confused fear as he slid off her sword and crumpled to the ground in an unmoving heap.

"Fucking stupid moron."

She leapt over his body, raised her shield, and rushed forward. She slammed the bulk of it into a tulwar engaged in a deadlock with a Sainite. Her momentum carried her forward, into another tulwar, shoving them both to the earth on top of one another. A Karnerian soldier leapt forward and thrust his spear down through the first until it skewered the second.

"Why the *fuck*—"

She caught a swinging blade with her shield.

"—won't *anyone*—"

She shoved the tulwar back.

"—*listen* to me?"

She smashed her shield against the tulwar's jaw and sent it reeling. Her sword followed, hacking down on his neck and sending him to the ground to bleed out on the earth.

She looked up.

There were more.

There were so many more.

In a great flood, they choked the entrance to the pass. Rushing forward in a massive herd, fighting to get over each other, each one of their faces alive and bloody with color, the tulwar howled to reach the fight.

The remnants of the Karnerians and Sainites were doing most of the work still, shooting or stabbing or slashing the tulwar that the Djaalic reserves were managing to keep occupied. Even that moron, Pathon, who refused to head back, seemed like he was holding his own with one sword and a broken arm.

But it was a mess. A mess of people dying. Of people fighting. Of fights breaking out in little, angry pockets of blood and filth.

It was supposed to go easier than this. It had all seemed like it would work.

She looked over her shoulder. Her banner stood, thrust in the earth, whipping in the wind. Bright and blue and beautiful against the gore and dirt splattered across the road in equal measure.

It was supposed to be a line. She was going to plant it, they were going to assume defensive positions, they were going to hold it there until the banner did what it had to do.

But it had all gone to shit.

The Karnerians and Sainites were roaming around, weary and empty looks on their faces, butchers instead of warriors. The tulwar were slavering animals, almost beating each other to get to beating the humans. The Djaalics were flailing and trying and dying with every breath.

And the plan hadn't worked.

He hadn't come.

This had all been for nothing.

These people would die. The tulwar would run rampant, destroy the city, slaughter every last person in it. And that stupid fucking lizard wouldn't even have shown his face this entire time.

It wasn't fair.

It wasn't supposed to be like this.

She wasn't supposed to fail.

"Fuck," she whispered. "Fuck, fuck, fuck." She gritted her teeth. She swallowed down the urge to weep, the urge to scream, the urge to fall to her knees and just let it be over. "Fucking gods-damned fucking—"

"HOLY SHIT!"

That last part hadn't been her.

It had come from a Sainite, far away toward the front of the melee. And in another moment, he was no longer quite so far away. He was screaming, flying through the air, his blue coattails flapping as he sailed screaming away.

And that was when she heard the roar.

Louder than any scream, any horn, any drum. Enough to make the tulwar seem quiet and the Djaalics turn and run. She had heard it a thousand times. Before the screams started, before the bodies fell, before the killing started.

It had made her cringe when she had first heard it, so long ago.

Like it did now.

Something came, rampaging through the melee toward her. The tulwar parted in a great wave to let it through. Brave soldiers rushed to stop it. Smart soldiers ran away when the brave ones fell, broken and screaming. Great spatters of life burst across the orange sky. Bones snapped. Shields shattered. Spears fell.

Two Karnerians ran forward, locked their shields together, readied themselves for what was coming. Something struck them, reached through their shields, seized them by their throats. Like skin flayed by a lash, they went flying through the air, limp and useless.

And like blood from the wound, Gariath burst onto the black earth.

Huge. Horned. Red as life.

--- ❈ ---

Too many bodies.

Pressing in around him. Fighting. Screaming. Bleeding. Dying. Filling his ear-frills with their noise and yelling and terror. Filling his snout with their anger and their hatred and their fear.

Too many bodies.

Victorious or losing. Human or tulwar. Living or dead. Gariath couldn't tell the difference anymore. They were everywhere around him. Pushing into him. Getting in his way. Falling under his feet.

That was fine.

He didn't need to hear. Or smell. Or even see.

He needed to be on the other side of this melee.

His legs needed to be strong to get there, kicking corpses aside and stomping on those who grabbed for him as he waded through the brawl. His arms needed to be long to make a path, swinging wide and knocking the screaming and the dying out of his way. He made his way through. Ankle-deep in carcasses and a wreath of screams settling on him, he made his way through.

But he needed to be faster.

Someone leapt out at him. Human? Dark-skinned? Pale? It didn't matter. It was no longer a human. Just a sword in his face and a sack of meat in his way. He reached out, seized the wrist that held the blade, grabbed the throat from which the war cry came. He squeezed. He pulled.

There was a thick squishing sound. Two pieces fell to the earth.

Someone stood before him. No. Something. Something cowering behind a shield, thrusting a spear at him like it meant anything. He twisted away from the weapon, seized it, tore it from the thing's grip. He pulled down the shield with one hand, smashed the spear against its helmet with the other. It splintered into two. He thrust forward, jamming the splintered haft into the thing's visor, and shoved it aside before it had even stopped twitching.

More fled from him. Tulwar clearing a path for him. Humans running from him. It didn't matter.

There was the whistle of air. Something struck him in the shoulder. He looked down, saw the crossbow bolt lodged in his skin.

He looked up. Three things stood in front of him. Two raised their swords. The third was reloading its weapon.

That didn't matter, either.

He felt the roar tear itself from his throat. He charged forward, kicking up red-soaked earth with each stride.

Their weapons nicked him, grazed against his skin. That was fine. He caught them all at once, spreading his arms out to seize them and drag them forward, barreling all three of them forward at once, like three logs bound together to make a battering ram. They fought, screaming and beating at him with their weapons. He bled. That was fine, too.

Their bodies shuddered as they caught bolts meant for him, swords meant for him, spears meant for him. Their blows grew weaker. Their screams grew louder. They fell from his grip, stabbed and skewered and useless, one by one, until he had only one left.

When he came to a halt, he dropped the corpse, riddled with wounds and unmoving, to the earth. His breath was ragged. His body was bleeding. His eyes were rimmed with red and his body held itself so tense he thought it would snap.

That was all fine.

He was where he needed to be.

She looked different from when he had seen her last. She stood a little taller now, with her shield and her sword, in front of that banner like it meant anything. She was wearing metal instead of cloth. It wasn't the same puny, impotent rage in her eyes this time.

She had changed.

But a human was still a human. Behind the shield, behind the armor, behind all the anger, she was as weak and soft and stupid as she always had been. If she had any sense, she would be running.

But she was not.

Good.

Several humans moved forward around her: small things carrying smaller things. Weapons? He didn't care. He had gone through bigger to get here. He could go through a little more.

"*Get back!*" she cried out. She swept her sword, bidding them to step away. "Let me handle this."

"But Prophet—" one of them said.

"*DO IT.*"

They backed away warily, eyes still locked on him, fear battling relief in their stares. He didn't care. He stepped toward her, rolling his shoulder, rubbing stiffness out from his arm.

"Keep them if you want," he said. "It doesn't matter."

"No one needs to die because of me," she replied, raising her shield.

"They're going to, anyway," he said.

She shook her head. "All this," she whispered, "because you felt abandoned."

"No." He snorted. "Maybe it began that way. I gave up my home to follow you and Lenk and the others. I followed you into your diseased cities and your reeking taverns. I killed for you. I bled for you. I gave up everything for you and you chose to stay and chase coin. That was why I wanted to kill you."

He held his hands out wide to the sprawling melee surrounding them.

"But all *this*," he said, "is for something more. All this…" He glanced at the tulwar, the dying and the bleeding and the howling. "This is for them."

"Bullshit." She spit on the earth. "Whatever you gave up, we gave back to you. We followed you, just as you followed us. We bled with you, fought with you, *stood by you*." Her eyes narrowed to thin slits. "And when we didn't give you everything you wanted, you ran away. Just like you'll run away from them when they don't give you what you want. Because no one will ever be able to give you what you want, Gariath."

She spoke iron. He felt her words sink into his skin.

"No one will ever be your family like we were."

He stared at her flatly. His fists unclenched. He let out a long, slow, hot breath. His nose filled with the smell of sodden earth. He spoke and tasted her name.

"Asper."

Her shield lowered slightly. The anger ebbed out of her face. She looked at him as though she were just now seeing him for the first time. His hands snapped back into fists.

"You still talk too much."

A roar in his throat.

Blood in his snout.

Dirt bursting beneath his feet.

He charged toward her, earth torn apart in his wake. His jaws craned open, his howl his shield even as she raised hers. It would be just like last time. She would try to fight. She would use that little sword. He would catch her arm. He would finish her. He reached out; his claws ached. His lips curled backward, his teeth bared. She raised her blade, so tiny and feeble and puny.

He roared.

He leapt.

She fell.

As he sailed over her, she tilted her shield toward the sky and shot upward. The rim of the metal caught him hard in the stomach, crushing the wind from him in a savage blow. His leap was cut short, sending him crashing to the earth.

He tasted copper on his tongue. He hacked up airless gasps, struggling for breath. Pain coursed through his body as he struggled to find his hands, then his knees, and struggled more to remember how to go further than that.

That wasn't supposed to happen.

He smelled a flash of anger. He heard her boots. He looked up and saw her charging toward him, sword raised and ready to come cleaving down into his skull.

That wasn't supposed to happen, either.

She brought her blade down in a savage arc. He lunged forward, catching her wrist. He snarled, squeezing, ready to twist it off. Before he could, her shield lashed out and smashed against his jaw. He held firm. She lowered it, smashed the rim of it into his side. Agony flared up inside him once more as the little breath he found went screaming out.

He released her arm and swung out with his claw. She ducked away, lashed out with her sword as she did, cut his arm. He roared and brought his fist down toward her head. Her shield was up; his bones rang with the impact. She slashed at him again, her blade finding his shoulder. A flash of pain lanced through his arm.

It hadn't hurt this much last time.

It wasn't *supposed* to hurt this much, was it?

He snarled, reached out, and seized her by the arm. She brought the pommel of her blade down hard on his wrist. His hand went numb and released her. Her blade shot out again, narrowly missing taking his head off before he leapt away from her.

A cold realization settled into him as he landed.

He had retreated from her.

He had never retreated from anyone before.

She didn't press her attack. She was waiting behind her shield, watching him, waiting for his next attack. She had always been hesitant to fight, always waiting too long and acting too slow. But this time, she was waiting with intent, watching him carefully, ready for whatever he might do.

She *had* changed.

"It didn't have to be like this."

The part of her that loved talking, though? That hadn't.

"It still doesn't," she said. "Take your army and go, Gariath. Take them back to their homes. We won't pursue you. Go live your lives elsewhere."

His tongue flicked across his lips. He tasted blood. His nostrils twitched. The smell of his own pain was stronger than the smell of her fear.

"There is no 'elsewhere,'" he growled. "There's nowhere on this earth that's far away enough to keep humans away. If we leave here now, we just die slower."

He lowered his head. He snorted a red mist.

"And I don't have an army."

He let out a roar, rushed toward her.

"I HAVE A FAMILY."

His claws lashed out, catching steel, blade, leather, but no flesh. Her blade answered every swipe, every fist, every grasp. She cut him at his wrist, his elbow, his flank, his knee. Never going for a killing blow, never coming in close where he could put an end to her. She kept back-pedaling, stepping away from his blows, his reaching claws, his gnashing teeth, his lashing tail. And every time he swung, she countered.

The battle wore on him. He became more aware of the stink of his own blood, the pounding of his own heart, the raggedness of his breath. His voice ran hoarse. His blood ran thin.

But his patience ran out before either of them did.

He howled and charged toward her, not caring about the shield, the sword, or what they might do to him. So long as he could wrap his claws around her throat, he could—

She twisted. Her shield caught him in the flank, pushing him away. Her blade followed, whipping about to carve a deep wound in his back. He felt a gout of warm life pour over his flesh. His spine erupted in agony. His legs went out beneath him. He went crashing to the damp earth.

And he did not rise.

He drew breath, still. He bled, still. But he did both of these sparingly. Wounds and pain had been his constants in life before. But the ones he felt now were not the bright, fiery agonies that urged him to rise and keep fighting. Perhaps it was his age. Or perhaps he had been fighting too hard for too long. The pain in him now was something dull and deep and tired. It bid him to lie, to sleep, to let go and join his sons.

"Gariath..."

Even her voice sounded not quite so grating anymore. Distant, soft; perhaps this was what all the other cowards heard when she held their hands before they died. She loomed over him. He could feel his life dripping out on her blade.

"I don't want to kill you," she said. "Don't make me."

He wanted to make her. He wanted to rise up and turn and make her look him right in the eye when she jammed that sword up to the hilt in his chest. She owed him that much.

"It doesn't have to end like this," she pressed. "You can still go home. All of you."

He drew breath that wouldn't come. He willed blood into his arms, but it was bubbling out of his back. He struggled to reach out, to grab the earth, to pull himself up.

"Just see *reason*," she hissed.

And there it was.

Something inside him, harder than blood or bone, suddenly grew red-hot. Maybe it was what she said or just how she said it. He didn't know. He only barely knew what was happening as something surged through him, sent him leaping to his feet to land in a spray of earth.

He roared, whirled on her. She ducked behind her shield, ready to fend him off. He howled, pressed forward, seized the shield by the rim, and pulled her forward. He used the momentum of the pull to bring her up and hurl her over his shoulder, sending her crashing into the dirt.

"Reason? *REASON?*" he bellowed.

He turned on her as she tried to rise. His leg swung out and his foot caught her in the belly, knocked the wind from her, and sent her rolling across the dirt. She scrambled to get up.

"You don't know the fucking meaning of the word," he snarled. "It's one of your shitty human words you made up. You take. And you steal. And you kill. And you call it reason so no one else can call you what you are."

She staggered to her feet and tried to bring her shield up. His fist was there sooner, smashing against her cheek.

"Coward," he snarled.

He struck again. Her shield was up. His claws found the metal and punched through. It screeched as he tore at it.

"Weakling," he roared.

He tore the shield from her arm. He threw it aside. She lashed out with her blade. He took it against his shoulder, slapped it out of her hand, and watched it clatter to the ground. His hands wrapped around her throat and hoisted her off the ground. Her eyes went wide as she pounded at his fists.

"Human."

She fought, with fear and fury that she should have had earlier. She struggled against him, kicking and trying to free herself. He tightened his grip around her throat. She choked out a word. A plea? No. There was no fear in her eyes. Desperation, yes, but no fear.

He strained to hear her.

"Fuck...*you*..." she gasped.

She had changed.

But no matter how much a human might change, they were still just a human. Still so weak. Still so stupid. Still so—

Air whistled. The sky shrieked. There was the sound of flesh punctured.

And suddenly, there was an arrow in his arm.

He glanced at it. It was no crossbow bolt. It was too long. Too dark. Its fletching was of feathers he had seen before.

His nostrils filled with the smell of something strange and alien. Hatred without anger. Murder without fear. Sorrow without sadness.

Another arrow fell from the sky. He dropped Asper as he stepped out of its way. He watched it there, quivering in the ground. And suddenly, he recalled where he had seen it.

And when he looked up, to the high walls of the cliffs, he saw a thousand more aimed at him.

————◆————

In the span of a few last breaths, the battle had fallen silent.

The Djaalics had just broken. The tulwar had just poured through in earnest, five of them for every human on the field. The Karnerians had taken their shields to make their final stands. The Sainites had taken their crossbows to stand behind them. The war cries had been such that he had felt it ringing in his helmet.

But now they were silent.

The clash of steel and the cries of battle and the screaming of the dying, they had all gone quiet, given way to the sound of wind moaning through the pass.

And all around Pathon, the dead lay. The Karnerians who hadn't found their shields in time. The Sainites who hadn't looked up. The Djaalics who had tried to run. The countless tulwar who had been trapped by their own companions' eagerness to attack.

The ones left standing held their breath as they looked up to the cliffs.

And beheld the many empty, wooden smiles looking down at them.

Like ghosts, they had appeared. How they had gotten up there, when they had arrived, how long they had been standing there, he didn't know. He doubted anyone did.

No one had noticed them until the arrows started falling.

But that, Pathon supposed, was what shicts did.

He had never seen them before. Not up close. In Cier'Djaal, they had always kept to their ghetto. He wasn't one of the ones sent to enact retribution on them. Somehow, he always thought they'd be taller.

He had heard stories about them, their hatred of humans. In the stories, they had always been the scheming thieves, the savage warlords with fiery eyes and fanged mouths and long-winded speeches about how they would kill all humans.

But he saw none of that here.

They were short, slender creatures, scantily clad in furs and leathers. Behind their wooden masks, with their hollow eyes and empty grins, he saw no fiery hatred and he heard no dramatic speeches. They, in their thousands, simply stared down at the battle.

And, silently, one by one, they drew their bows back and aimed.

"Not like this..."

A voice to his left. Dachon, his brother, with a wound in his brow and his shield shattered and his spear hanging limply from his hand. The Karnerian stared up at them, the countless shicts and their empty grins, and tears formed in his eyes.

"Not like this..." he whimpered. "Not with no battle."

There were people trying to run, trying to flee the canyon. It wouldn't work. There was no escape. There was no way out.

There was no way for them to survive this.

Pathon looked down the road to a single figure standing there, staring up with wide eyes.

Not all of them, anyway.

And, without really knowing why, he took off running.

Above, a single shict stepped forward.

Pathon charged toward her, a single woman in a single battle, without quite knowing why.

Above, the single shict looked down through a mask with a severed human face tacked to it.

Perhaps it was about ideals. Perhaps it was about duty. He didn't know why he didn't seek cover. But then, he didn't really ask. Faith was like that.

Above, the shict raised a long spear above her head.

And, he thought, *faith is worth dying for, right?*

He leapt forward. He wrapped his arms around someone tightly. He shut his eyes and whispered a prayer to Daeon.

Above, the shict's ears twitched.

A thousand ears twitched in response.

And a thousand bowstrings sang.

───※───

Asper did not know what was happening. Not when Gariath dropped her to the earth. Not when she saw the shadows on the cliffs. Not when Pathon leapt out of nowhere, tackled her to the earth, and wrapped his arms tightly around her.

She didn't know until she felt the shudder of his body as the arrows punched through him.

She didn't find the words until she looked up into his face, twisted in a grimace, his eyes wide and unblinking.

"No..." she whispered.

Pathon stared back into her eyes. He trembled with the effort of it. His face drained of color in a single, halting breath. With monumental effort, he whispered in reply.

"Heaven...is...watching."

His last breath fled his mouth and vanished into the orange sky. He went limp against her body, slumping bonelessly off her and sprawling onto the ground. A dozen arrows bristled from his body.

And around her, a forest of quivering, feathered trees had grown.

Arrows, hundreds of them, seemed to rise out of the earth, growing from a rich soil of flesh and blood. The corpses of men, of tulwar, of beasts, lay still, new gardens for the morbid crop of black and white and red fletching to grow.

Some lay facedown in the dirt, their attempt to cower from the rain of steel having won them only a cloak of arrows jutting from their backs. Some lay on their back, shafts lodged in eyes that had looked dumbfounded to the sky and mouths that still gaped with their last words of surprise. And an unlucky few crawled, moaning and screaming and trying to pull free the arrows that had graciously found only calves and shoulders and arms, leaving hearts and throats free for their brothers.

She couldn't feel herself do it—the feeling had drained from her limbs and pooled into a heavy weight at the back of her neck—but Asper climbed to her feet. She looked around the arrows as the last few stopped quivering. She looked around at the dead.

And, no matter where they were looking, she knew they were staring at her.

The cliffs were rimmed with shadows, empty wooden faces with empty wooden grins staring down at her. Maybe they couldn't see her moving from way up there; maybe they didn't know she was still alive.

Or maybe the shicts just wanted to let her appreciate the deaths she had brought these people before they ended her misery.

Shicts.

Kataria had tried to warn her. She wouldn't listen.

Yet even now, she couldn't find the feeling for guilt. She couldn't even remember the conversation they had. She could barely remember Kataria's face.

It was as though something had simply...broken. Inside her, something important that should be stronger than iron had just snapped and everything inside her—the instincts that would have told her to run, the horror that would have told her to scream, the sorrow that would have told her to grieve—had simply...drained out.

She had seen death before. But never had she seen so many dead bodies born in one single breath. The sensation of so many breaths sucked out, of so many lives bursting like overripe fruits in one moment...she couldn't comprehend it. She didn't know what she was looking at anymore.

No tears to cry. No voice to scream. She had forgotten how to do all that.

She couldn't feel the breath in her throat. Or the thoughts in her head. Or the fingers on her arms, hanging like dead weights at her sides.

She looked up. The shicts stared down at her. Her mouth hung open, trying to remember what it was for, like a crude and fleshy imitation of the empty smiles elegantly carved into their wooden masks.

She could barely comprehend those smiles. She could barely understand that their ears were twitching, all at once. She couldn't remember what it meant as they slowly raised their bows and drew their arrows back and aimed for her.

And in the numb emptiness of her mind, the thick fog where fears and hopes and plans and promises had used to be, a single thought whispered to her.

Do not be afraid.

She heard it clearly, as though it were coming from right beside her, a whisper in her ear right before she fell asleep. It sank into her, settled down on her numb scalp, and breathed with its own life.

You have suffered much at the hands of cruel gods, haven't you? Such terrible violence you've seen and yet, even now, they abandon you.

Every word hung uncomfortably clear in her head, a solid thought forced into her skull. On the cliffs above, she saw some shicts lower their weapons and look around warily, ears aloft and twitching. As though they heard the same thing.

I am so sorry I have come too late to save them. But I will make this right. I will take care of everything.

She found her breath and it came hot and anxious. Her pulse quickened. Somewhere, someone fixated a great eye upon her and saw everything: every thought flashing in her head, every drop of blood rushing through her veins, every bead of sweat on her body. Somewhere, someone was watching her. Watching this pass. Watching everything.

There is no need for fear, for shame, for hatred. Let low the burdens your cruel creators have heaped on your shoulders. Let me lift you up. Let me show you the kindness they withheld.

And she knew, without knowing how, that someone was smiling.

I am here for you.

A scream.

Something sharp and wild and human. It filled her ears. Feeling came rushing back to her in a burst of pain. Colors suddenly seemed too vivid, breath too swift, sounds too loud.

Screams assaulted her, coming from seemingly every direction. From the road, people came running: humans who had escaped the shicts, tulwar who had been left behind. She couldn't tell the difference between them anymore.

The naked terror on their faces made them all look the same.

"DEMONS!"

Over their panicked faces, she could see them coming.

They looked like humans, but far too tall and impossibly beautiful, their skin dark and perfect and their eyes bright like sun. But the way they walked—loping along with such savage enthusiasm, like they had been crawling all their lives and were struggling to remember.

And with each step, they changed.

Their skin twisted. Limbs grew longer. Eyes grew brighter. Their smiles grew wide and bared sharp, glistening teeth. Long tongues flicked out of their mouths. Skin peeled back, became as scales, was left shed on the ground in glistening heaps. Their hair was lost, giving way to naked scalps, and their torsos twisted and became serpentine and their fingers sprouted claws and their mouths gaped open impossibly wide and their voices...

Their voices made her remember what pain was.

Over the humans and the tulwar, she heard them screaming. Theirs was a loud and excited wail, like children running to open presents. They came pursuing the fleeing soldiers, leaping over them and seizing them with their long limbs and dragging them away. They scaled the walls of the cliffs with horrific speed, reaching up to seize those shicts who didn't flee.

Through the wall of scales and sinew and flesh, Asper could see flashes of horror. The hand of a tulwar reaching out as he was crushed under a pair of massive feet. A pair of Karnerian legs flailing as he was shoved, face first, into a gaping toothy maw. A shict screaming as she was bent and snapped and broken like a toy in unnaturally huge hands.

Asper knew she had to run. But the fear that swept through the crowd hadn't yet reached her. And whatever instincts screamed at her to flee, something else spoke louder.

There are no fears here. There are no wars here. There are no gods.

At the back of the pass, something emerged.

There is only me.

The sky turned bloodred. The sun seemed to turn its face away, afraid of what was born on that corpse-choked road. Across creation, a black stain grew from the earth and rose to scrape the sky.

It blossomed in the sky, a dead tree rising out of cold earth. It looked like a man, immensely huge with a crown that touched the sky. His arms unfolded in great, godlike birth, welcoming himself into the world. The beauty of his muscular figure unfurled, a tapestry of sinew and skin forever being woven with his great breaths. His eyes were wide open, two stark white portals that opened up into a world free of pain.

He smiled.

And from his face, serpents.

Growing out of his jaw in a writhing beard. Bursting from his brow in a serpentine, hissing crown. Falling from his cheeks like whiskers. They writhed and snapped and hissed and screeched and laughed with the voices of children and of mothers.

Over the ruin of the battle, he presided. He held his arms open wide and bathed in the screams and the carcasses. He looked down on the morbid feast and smiled gently.

And she knew his name.

"Khoth-Kapira..."

She turned.

"Khoth-Kapira!"

She ran.

"Khoth-Kapira!"

She became part of the flood of people swarming across the pass, fleeing from the monstrous creations that boiled around the demon's ankles. They pursued, wailing and laughing and screaming and begging for the fleeing soldiers to stop and be a part of their beautiful world.

Asper heard them getting closer. She could feel their eyes on her. She could feel his smile leveled down on her. She knew he looked inside her and saw something that he must have. They closed in on her, frothing up behind her and reaching out with their long limbs and their fanged smiles and their wild, excited eyes and—

"Hey."

She stopped.

In front of her, a shadow appeared.

Not a shadow—the Shadow. The one she had seen back in Cier'Djaal. He stood there, pitch-black against the carnage, staring at her with no face.

"How's it going, champ?"

She didn't answer. She didn't have time. He opened his arms wide, seized her, and pulled her into him.

She felt herself falling into a great darkness.

THIRTY-NINE

HIS HOLY VERDICT

Looking at her, it was hard to believe she had ever been human.

Or something like a human, anyway; saccarii, whatever their origins, were not so different. They had two legs, two arms, two eyes. Hearts full of anger, heads full of schemes, tongues full of lies, just like any human.

And they had ambitions.

And as she sat, coiled at the edge of the great wall that supported the Silken Spire, it was hard to understand exactly what Teneir's had been. Or how they had led her to this.

She had no more legs now. Or maybe she did, under the writhing mass of serpentine tails that coiled beneath her waist. Her skin was gone, replaced by sickly gray scales that glistened in the dying sunlight. Her neck was long and coiled, terminating in a head whose eyes were broad and yellow and whose fanged mouth was curled into a tight frown as she stared out over the city.

"It's not a mistake that I am here."

Her voice, at least, was still vaguely normal. It was soft and quiet and full of sadness. For the moment, anyway.

"Grandfather won a spider in a game of dice with a fasha. The fasha tried to cheat him, of course, and Grandfather gutted him in an alley. The spiders bred, made silk, became investments, and our fortunes were made slowly but steadily. Grandfather called it saccarii determination. Father called it luck. Only now, though, do I realize…"

She closed her eyes. A hot wind blew over her.

"It was the divine."

A smile tugged at her lips. A faint image of the person she used to be flashed across her face.

"I do not mean that as a simple means of explaining away circumstances. That would be crude belief. Faith—*true* faith—is a means of discovering why things are as they are.

"I did not realize that until I saw my first dead saccarii. From the window of my room, I saw one beaten to death in the streets. A vagrant, my father said, who had found his way into Silktown and was being punished for transgressing. It was that he was poor, and not saccarii, that he had to die. As though that would set me at ease. Yet somehow, I convinced myself it did."

She looked high into the red sky.

"Until the visions, anyway. They began about two years ago. First, as a voice: a gentle and motherly whisper, telling me that things could be better, that I could fix it. This was when I knew Ancaa was looking over me. All the other gods I prayed to were silent. Only she spoke and told me how to save things.

"So I used my fortunes. I built churches to Ancaa. And yes, I formed the Khovura. I used them to hunt out the rats that infest this city and bring real change." She shook her head. "I lament the violence they caused, but I will not apologize for them. Everything I did brought me closer to Ancaa, made her visions stronger, until just a few months ago."

She swiveled on her coils, casting a sharp-eyed scowl across the wall to the first pillar of the Silken Spire and the battered body hanging from it.

"That is when *you* arrived, am I correct?"

That sounded about right to Lenk. But he had a hard time remembering, what with the shit having been beaten out of him earlier.

He slumped against the pillar, his bound wrists all that were keeping him upright. His attempts at struggle had been brutally suppressed and all he had to show for it was a bleeding forehead and possibly a concussion. The strongest answer he could muster was a flutter of his eyelids as he looked up at the monstrosity slithering toward him.

"The visions became weaker. She spoke to me less. And as time went on, her visions became strange. I began to see your face in my dreams, hear your name whispered in anger, as though she were muttering under her breath. I was uncertain what to make of it. Were you a new prophet? Or were you a vexation that she wished to be rid of?"

She extended a single clawed finger and angled it beneath his chin. He felt blood drip from his skin, gliding down her talon to pool in her palm as she tilted his face up to look at her.

"Or perhaps . . . she was simply spending all her time talking to you, hm?" A long tongue flicked out between her lips, brushing against Lenk's cheek. "To this day, I am unsure what happened."

This wasn't the first time Lenk had found himself in a situation like this. And, despite whatever dramatic stories defiant, smart-mouthed captives told, he knew from many injuries that mouthing off to someone who had him bound and possessed many means of killing him wasn't a good idea.

But maybe he just needed to hear himself say it.

"What happened," he rasped out, "is that your goddess is a depraved demon from hell who has come to twist every living creature into things as horrific as you."

He expected the end to be swift—gutting his throat, maybe, or just strangling him to death. But instead, Teneir merely stared at him, without malice or hatred. Instead, it was a kind of sadness that creased her face.

"I know," she said, softly.

"What?"

"I read many of Sheffu's books back when we were on . . . better terms. I always had my suspicions." She looked down at her scaly flesh and frowned. "This is but confirmation. Though I do not hate my gift, regardless of where it came from."

"It's not a gift," Lenk sputtered. "It's *not*. He doesn't *give* gifts. He—"

"Do you hope to persuade me?" Teneir chuckled. "Do you expect me to fall to the ground and bemoan my choices and beg you to help me make it right?" She shook her head. "I made my choice knowing all that I did. And, if it had to be done, I would do it all again a hundred times more."

"But . . . *why?*"

"How do you view the gods?" she asked. "Do you call on them only in times of need? Do you offer to them only when you think of it? Or are they simply a name you curse when you suffer?" She sighed, running a scaly palm down his cheek. "They are just a word to you, aren't they? Something you simply say, not quite remembering why you said it?"

"And what are they to you? Another rich father to ask for shiny things from?"

"A partner." Teneir seized him by the jaw. "This is what you blasphemers neglect. If gods wrought us in their image, then they must also be in ours. They can be taught. They can learn."

"Taught." He tried to chuckle, as impotent as it seemed. "You think you can control him? He's a demon. He controls *you*."

"Controls me how? Commands me to build for the poor? Commands me to unite the city? Commands me to envision a future in which no girl has to watch a man being beaten to death from her window again? I welcome it. Gods exist to serve a need. Our needs will shape our god."

She released his face, sneered down at him.

"He may enter this city as Khoth-Kapira, demon from hell. But he shall live in it as Ancaa, goddess of Cier'Djaal. Together, we shall cure this city of its ills."

"He doesn't do that." He shook his head. "He makes you think you're the one who wants it, but you're never in control. Everything you do is for him. And whatever you might think you'll do to him, he's thought of it first."

"Enough."

A coiled tail lashed out, caught him against the cheek, and struck with such force as to send him slumping in his bonds. He coughed, spit blood onto the stone. He hung there, staring at the ground as his blood pooled onto it. He sighed and shrugged as best he was able.

"Well," he said, "just fucking kill me, I guess."

He watched as a serpentine tendril crawled toward him. It coiled around his leg and slithered up around him.

"I will," Teneir said, "if you desire it."

Another joined, wrapping about his waist, his ribs, his chest. It squeezed ever so slightly. His body clenched in response.

"If you desire to live," she said, "I can grant that, as well."

A third. And a fourth. The tendrils snaked about him, coiling around his arms, slithering across his stomach, curling into a scaly noose about his neck. They tightened, just so, squeezing the barest air from him.

"Live here in luxury. Be free to wander wherever you please. I can do it all for you, if you desire. All you need is to tell me…"

Her coils tightened. His face was forced up. He met a mouth brimming with fangs and twisted in an angry snarl.

"Why you?"

Her eyes were wide with indignant anger. Her voice was thick with desperation. His eyes, by contrast, bulged and his voice came out in a choking cough.

"What?"

"I have given my life to her," Teneir said. "I have given my fortunes, my reputation, my very *soul* for her and she gives me quiet, gentle visions in reply. But you..." Her eyes narrowed to thin ochre slits. "Your name flashes in my head like fire. She spits it, rather than speaks it. But it is always on her lips, always in her thoughts. What have you given her, hm?"

"Nothing," Lenk hacked. "I gave him nothing."

"LIAR!"

She howled, slamming his head against the pillar. His vision swam. He gulped down breath, but only scant traces of air found their way to his lungs.

"You did something. You said something. And now all she can think of is you." Her coils tightened around him. "Why is your face in her mind so clearly? Why does she think of you so often? Why does she speak of you with such anger and such passion, yet offers me only cold politeness? What did you say to her?"

She snarled, her voice becoming a desperate shriek.

"What did you do to her?"

She was squeezing tighter. Her coils trembled with barely contained fury, just as her eyes trembled with barely contained fear. She searched Lenk's face, looking for any answer. She tilted her ear to his gaping mouth as he strained for breath. Her coils relaxed just enough to allow him the barest, breathless whisper.

"What I did..." he gasped out. He could barely hold on to consciousness, let alone his voice. "What I did...to him..."

"Yes," she hissed. "Tell me. Tell me and I will let you live. I will let you go. Tell me what you did."

"I...didn't..."

He stared her in the eyes. He shook his head. He sighed.

"I didn't love him."

Her face fell. Her lips curled into a frown. Her heart sank in her eyes. For a moment, the monster was gone. All the scales and fangs couldn't obscure the face of the same frightened, sad little girl who had once watched a man die and learned that the world wasn't as she thought it should be.

For a moment, as the despair and disappointment came across her face, she looked truly human.

But sorrow died in an instant and anger came chewing out of its corpse. Her lips curled backward in a fanged snarl.

Her coils tightened around him. Lenk could feel the air shut out of him. His bones groaned inside him. He could feel the blood pooling in his head, his face swelling and turning red, purple, blue. He couldn't so much as squirm against her grasp, and though he strained to find the breath to scream, nothing came out.

From *his* mouth, anyway.

The coils loosened. Teneir's spine snapped as she suddenly reared back, an agonized howl tearing itself from her lips. Her tendrils slipped from Lenk's body as she arched her back, clawed hands groping at something lodged between her shoulders.

Lenk strained to swallow as much air as his crushed throat would allow. His head lolled on its shoulders. Darkness framed his vision. Yet through it, he could faintly make out the struggle of Teneir wildly thrashing.

And the dark-skinned woman jamming the knife into her back.

The shict. The khoshict. Her black braids whipping about as Teneir strained and shrieked and tried to shake her off. Her muscles straining as she clung to the monster's back. Her knife pumping back and forth, bright red plumes bursting out from scaly hide, spattering her arms and belly and face.

Her face. Cold and angry and focused intently on the kill.

What had her name been?

"Kwar..." he gasped.

Even ears like hers couldn't have heard him through Teneir's pain. The monster's shrieks filled the orange skies. She fell to the stone, wailing as Kwar crawled up her back, raised her bloody blade high and aimed for the base of Teneir's skull.

A stray coil lashed up, struck Kwar hard in the back, and knocked her from her perch. She went tumbling, then rolled to her feet as Teneir rose to her full height. Dripping blood down her tendrils, she bared her fangs in a shriek as Kwar stared up at her.

"Fools!" Teneir howled. "Do you not understand? *Does no one understand?* I am doing this for Cier'Djaal! I am doing this for all—"

Kwar didn't believe her, whatever she was about to say.

It was hard to sound convincing with a knife in one's eye.

The khoshict's wrist snapped, sending the weapon flying. It struck Teneir's skull with a meaty thunk. The blow should have killed a woman—but she was no longer a woman, nor a saccarii.

She shrieked, staring at the ground in horror as her coils groped feebly at the knife in her eye. They pulled it free, loosing a red fountain down Teneir's face. She stared at Kwar through the ruin of her eye, the monstrousness of her face unable to hide her horror.

Her tendrils hauled her to the edge of the wall and pulled her over. Her blood painting the stone, her shrieks painting the sky, Teneir disappeared over the wall and vanished from sight.

A swift fight. A brutal finish. Lenk would have said as much, had he the breath to do so. As it was, his head hung down to his chest. The air came too slow, too little. He began to fade into darkness.

Still, it would have been nice to thank her for saving his life.

He heard her footsteps as she approached. He could just barely see her sandaled feet as she stood before him, staring at him.

He watched her as she took up her knife, glistening with blood.

At least it would be quick.

And it came quick. A single stroke. And he fell.

The rope fell from his wrists. He pitched forward, his body too numb to stand. She caught him around the waist, eased him down to his rear, and pressed his back against the pillar. She squatted beside him, studying him intently with her dark eyes.

Her face was calm and placid as a lake at dawn. Her knife dangled in her palm, dancing impatiently as it waited for her decision. His vision faded in and out of darkness and, through the shifting light, the gore spattering her face made her look like a nightmare.

Slowly, her lips opened in a broad, toothy grin.

"Thought I was going to kill you, didn't you?" she asked.

She reached out, smoothed a lock of hair from his face, and stared at him.

"I considered it, if I'm honest."

She frowned.

"And if I didn't know it would make Kataria cry, I'd do it, too." She pressed a pair of fingers to his jugular. "That thing fucked you up good, didn't she? But you'll live, thanks to me." She leveled the tip of her knife at him. A drop of blood fell, stained his pants. "You owe me now. Got that?"

He would have liked to say that he did. Really, he would have liked to say anything. As it was, she was lucky he was conscious enough to understand her.

"So you're going to promise me something, all right?" She leaned close. Her ears were upright and twitching. "Don't tell her I was here. Don't tell her you saw me. Don't tell her I'm here. Don't..." She sighed, then looked away from him. "Just...I don't want her to know what I did, all right?" She looked back. "All right?"

He tried to nod. But that might just have been his head lolling. She seized him, pressed his shoulders against the pillar, and forced him to look at her.

"I saved your life. I could have killed you and I didn't, so I saved your life *twice*. Promise me you won't tell her. *Promise me*."

He gasped out something even he couldn't understand. But whatever it was, it seemed to satisfy her. She sighed, took a moment to make sure he was propped upright, and then stood up and walked away.

Where it had only crept before, darkness now swept into his vision. And by the time Kwar had walked to the edge of the wall, he could see nothing at all.

* * *

"Hey."

Her voice was far away, a dream in a dark and silent sleep. But her touch, her warmth, the smell of her sweat...

Those were close.

He wasn't sure how long he had been out. Nor when she had arrived. When he stirred back to consciousness, his body was stiff and pained, but he could feel. And when he opened his eyes, he stared up at her face. A smile, weak and relieved, found its way onto his face.

Kataria did not return it.

She looped an arm around him and helped him to sit up. She held him tightly, tighter than she ever had before. His body protested, but he did not. He laid a hand weakly on her arm and squeezed her gently. She opened her mouth to say something.

And, instead, she simply stared out over the horizon, toward the distant Green Belt.

He followed her gaze.

And his blood ran cold.

The battle was distant, so far away that he couldn't even see the pass where Asper had made her stand, where Gariath had made his assault. Yet he could see something all the same.

Against the orange sky, Khoth-Kapira rose like a colossus over the cliffs. His beard writhing, his crown coiling, he surveyed the land through empty white eyes.

And though they were miles away, Lenk could see the great demon as he craned his titanic head toward the city of Cier'Djaal. Lenk could see as his lips curled upward in a smile.

And Lenk knew it was meant for him.

HOLDING HANDS AS THE WORLD BURNS

Our Bloodied and Terrible Dream

Rokuda,

You were wrong, old friend.

You were all wrong.

You all swore that the humans were too many. You all swore that our forces were too few. You all resigned yourselves to dying in your forests as your lands shrank away and your families broke.

I do not mean to sound as though I fault you. I once believed the same, as we all did.

But I saw too much. I saw too many families lose their sons and daughters. I saw too many children go hungry when there was not enough game to hunt. I saw too many homes wither and die and be built over by great stone castles.

I had to do something.

There will be cowards who will tell you I did this thoughtlessly. They would see us all rot like fruit fallen to the earth before they would even lift a finger to help. There would have been more deaths, more families lost, had I not acted. And after careful consideration, I knew what I must do.

It was the s'ha shict s'na. The greenshicts, we call them. They drove the humans from their lands with their venoms and their toxins. But they saw only small uses: smearing arrows with venom, killing humans one by one.

I have a grander view.

It had to be war, Rokuda. The humans understand nothing else. Burn their villages, they build cities. Steal from their wagons, they build roads. Kill one of them, a hundred more come looking for revenge. These petty raids and assassinations would only bring us more despair.

You were not old enough to remember the war with the couthi, were you?

The bugs were relentless foes. They had numbers, they had weapons we didn't understand, and they were keen on hunting us down. We knew that we would be fighting our war with them forever if we did not act decisively.

But even if you don't remember it, you know what happened, don't you?

We lured them out into the forests. We let them chase us. We let them think they had us on the run. All the while, more of us circled around and struck at their city. We burned their children alive. We flayed their precious maidens. We left their homes in rubble.

And that war was over. And many shicts lived.

This is our way, Rokuda. Anyone who tells you differently is lying. Anyone who pretends this is a war we can win through conventional means is an idiot. And anyone who says we shouldn't fight would watch us die and do nothing.

The events at Harmony Road and Shaab Sahaar should provide proof of what I tell you. The desert is ours once again. The tulwar are simple-minded imbeciles who cringe at shadows. The humans are pathetic cowards who kill each other to flee from us.

The incident...I have no explanation for. Not now. Not while I must win this war.

Your daughter's fate is a shame. I am sorry that you will feel the pain of that loss. But I will not apologize for doing it. I cannot let one more shict die because I failed to act.

I am a chieftain.

As are you.

And this responsibility extends to you, as well. Join with my tribes. Join with the khoshicts. The greenshicts are on their way and we are reaching out to our cousins in the north. We will become a great beast, long of tooth and silent as the grave. And we shall hunt.

And we shall feed.

Be swift about your response.

—Shekune

FORTY

FAREWELL TO FLESH AND BONE

Where are they coming from? What are they?"

Asper could still hear them.

"They're too fast! I can't see them! No one is helping me! Someone help!"

So far away and in such a dark place, she heard their screams. Before, though, they had simply been one incomprehensible mass: a stew of agony and fear through which individual words sometimes bubbled up to the surface and popped.

"I'm not supposed to be here. I'm not saan! *I'm* duwun! *I should be back home! I want to go home!"*

Now she heard all of them. Each and every word they last uttered, every corpse that had walked that cursed road. Tulwar, human; it didn't matter. They spoke as though they were right next to her.

"I was an idiot to believe her. She had us working with Karnies, for Sovereign's sake. Where's this Prophet bitch now? Where are you now?"

She couldn't see them, at least. Darkness stretched out around her, so deep and thick she wasn't sure if she was in it or a part of it. Maybe this was hell. Maybe her soul had simply fused with this cold void and her punishment was to be one more voice in the blackness, screaming to no one that would hear her, asking questions that no one would listen to.

"Heaven is watching…"

That would be fitting.

"Heaven is watching…"

She had spent all her life doing that.

"Heaven is watching, Prophet."

And what was hell but living?

"I didn't fail you. Don't you fail us."

The next thing she heard was her own cry.

Asper shot up, sweat dripping, heart pounding. Pathon's voice still echoed in her head. Those hadn't been his last words, though. Had that been a vision? A message from beyond?

Or have you, quite understandably, finally gone crazy as shit?

She got no answer for that thought. Pathon's voice faded, along with the darkness. Around her, she made out the shapes of simple furniture—a chair, a table, a dresser, a bed with sweat-soaked sheets. She couldn't tell where she was, but the darkness around her was the shadowy softness of nightfall through a cracked window. Not the vast, endless blackness from where she had just been.

Unless this was all part of that, she wondered. Perhaps this, this seeming normalcy, was just one more part of hell: a moment of relative pleasantness to be snatched away in another moment and replaced with more screaming.

But as she eased out of the bed and put her feet to the floor, she quickly discounted that.

Even hell couldn't provide the kind of pain she was in.

Her head hurt. Her skin hurt. Her bones hurt. It was the kind of new pain of a body remembering how it was supposed to work. She hadn't felt anything like it. Not since Amoch-Tethr had left her, anyway.

She looked down at her left arm, fleshy, mortal, useless.

Would things have been different, she wondered, if Amoch-Tethr were still with her? Could she have simply lured Gariath out and destroyed him—utterly consumed him, as the fiend had done to so many others—and had her armies ready for the demons? Could she have simply done that to the demons, as well?

Maybe it would have been worth bearing that curse, then, if it would have saved others.

Or maybe she'd be free and even stronger.

In the end, it seemed anything she did lately meant people were going to die.

In hindsight, she preferred it when she simply felt helpless to stop deaths, rather than actively causing them.

She made her way across the floor, clad in a sweat-soaked undershirt and drawers, finding her way to a decrepit staircase. She made her way down, wincing as a splinter lodged itself in her big toe. The decrepit house was a match for her aching body.

In a tiny little room, consisting of little more than a few cupboards, a few chairs, and a fireplace, he sat, one more shadow among many. A meager fire burned quietly in the hearth, but whatever light it shed wasn't enough to make him look any warmer. He was stark and black against the night, a darkness so deep that the lesser shades seemed to reach out enviously for him.

The Shadow leaned forward, elbows on his knees, staring intently into the fire. Yet even then, she couldn't see any sign of a face within his hood. And when he spoke, his voice was soft and distant.

"I can't even feel it." He held out his dark hand, moved it back and forth in front of the fire. "It doesn't feel hot. Not cold. Just...nothing. Above all else, it's the warmth of a fire I miss the most."

He paused, as if considering that statement. Then he held up a finger.

"Actually, no. I miss whiskey more than I miss fire. And wine. And beer. Liquor altogether, really." He snapped his fingers. "Oh, and sex. I miss sex a *whole* lot."

She approached the fire carefully, one eye always kept on him. Yet if he looked at her, she couldn't tell. She took a seat next to him and stared into the fire.

"You saved me," she said, after a time.

"I did."

After a longer, more awkward time, she added: "You also undressed me."

"You looked hot."

She looked at him. "Can I ask how you did it?"

He didn't look at her. "You can."

"Should I?"

"You shouldn't." He looked down at his hand and flexed his fingers. "What did you see?"

"When?"

"When we jumped. Disappeared. Whatever you want to call what I did. What did you see?"

She shook her head. "Nothing. Just...darkness."

"Eerie, isn't it?"

"The voices were worse."

"Voices?"

"Are those not a part of it?"

"I haven't heard any. You must just be special." He chuckled. It wasn't a pleasant sound. "Lucky, lucky you."

A long moment passed as they stared into the fire. She found it difficult to look at him but harder to hear his voice.

"We're in Cier'Djaal, if you hadn't guessed," he said, finally. "On the border of the Sumps. The remnants of your army are still filtering in, those that survived."

"There were survivors?"

"Not many. They ran away in one direction. The tulwar ran in the other. The Chosen—the scaly guys—sort of milled around. Khoth-Kapira permitted the ones that still could to flee. The ones that couldn't, well...I mean, you saw."

She stared down at her hands. "Yeah. I did."

The silence stretched out, put miles between them. She told herself it was because she didn't want to relive her failure, to have the images of the dead put back in her head so quickly. But she knew that was a lie. They were already in her head, their voices still in her ears. And she would have taken them gladly.

Because when he spoke again, she felt as though she might cry.

"Ask me," he said.

It came suddenly, a well of tears behind her eyes, something heavy caught in her throat. She spoke through it. "Where are the survivors gathering?"

"Not that."

They came slowly, all but creeping out the corners of her eyes. She sniffed them back. "Are they safe? Are they well?"

"No."

She shut her eyes tight to hold them back. "Did Gariath's forces—"

"Asper."

She looked at him. His face was just an empty void in a hood. But she knew he was looking straight at her.

"Ask me," he said.

"No." She shook her head. "No. I already know. Don't make me. Don't make me look."

He didn't say anything. He didn't have to. Because he knew she couldn't not acknowledge it, because he knew she had to ask.

Because he knew her. As she knew him.

Somehow, she had always known.

"I'm not going to ask." She forced her jaw firm, stared into the darkness of his hood. "Just show me."

He waited a long moment, a black pit staring at her. Then, slowly, he inclined his head. His hands went up to his hood. His fingers tugged it back. She held her breath.

He looked much as he had. Paler, of course, but she had been expecting that. But he was still handsome, his jawline still strong, his smile still easy. But his eyes didn't gleam as they used to. The mischief and the malice and all the secrets they had hidden were gone, and left behind was something dark, something so dark it swallowed the light.

And so, so sad.

"Hey," Denaos said.

"Hey." She did not try to weep, yet the tears came all the same, sliding down her cheeks. "You look...you look good."

"Oh yeah? You think so?" He gestured to his face. "Well, you know, the gods give you a gift, you do your best to take care of it."

He cracked a grin. And it looked just like the countless ones he had given her. His lips were pale, but other than that? It was just like him, only...not.

It would have been easier if he were a monster, some rotting thing with the bones of his cheeks exposed and hollow eyes. But it looked just like him. Like he had never left. Like she had never left him.

"Yeah." She nodded shakily. "You're...you look..." She stared at him. She bit her lower lip. She shook her head. "You look great."

He reached a hand out to her. "Asper..."

"*FUCK!*" she screamed. She buried her face in her hands. She clutched her hair and tried to tear it out. "I can't! I can't fucking do this! I can't pretend like you aren't...you aren't..." She looked at him with desperate, tear-streaked eyes. "*What the fuck are you?*"

He blinked. If her tone bothered him, he didn't show it. He stared into the fire. His eyes did not reflect its light.

"Dead," he said, softly. "I don't have a fancy title for it or anything. I'm just...dead. I went into the river. I went somewhere dark. And when I came out, I was like…" He held up a hand, tugged free a glove. Four pale stumps where fingers should have been wriggled. "You'd think she'd at least give me back my fingers, but beggars, choosers, you know how it goes."

"She? Who is she? Who did this to you?"

"Don't worry about it," he said, tugging his glove back on.

"What do you mean, 'don't worry about it'? How do I not worry about this? Why should I—"

"Because you have bigger problems," he replied, terse. "*Fuck*, you always did this. Go around talking about faith, about trusting a higher power, but you have to go and demand an explanation for everything. I'd expect this shit from Dread, but not…"

He saw the tears running freely down her face. His voice trailed off. He sighed, then lowered his head.

"How is Dread, anyway?"

"He's…he's bad." She shook her head. "He's gone. I don't know where. I don't know where Kataria or Lenk are, either. Or…or…"

She all but toppled forward with how her head came crashing into her hands. Tears fell through her fingers, pattered on the floor. The sound that came from her was something that had been born long ago, feeding for months, growing fatter every time she tried to deny it. A long and ugly sound that she was ashamed to make in front of him, in front of anyone.

And through it, she could but make a shuddering whisper.

"I'm sorry."

"What?"

"I'm sorry, Denaos," she sobbed. "I'm so sorry."

"Don't fucking—"

"I should have saved you. I should have helped you. I should have listened to you. I'm sorry for failing you, like I failed Dreadaeleon. Like I failed this city. Like I failed Gariath and…and…"

Something cold slid around her wrist. His hand slowly took hold of hers. He gently pulled it away from her face. With his other, and all his missing fingers, he tilted her chin up. His smile was colorless. His smile was cold.

But it was his smile.

"You always do this shit, too, you know?"

"What?" she asked.

"Dreadaeleon was a shithead. He was our friend, but he was a shithead. This city treated you like garbage. Gariath tried to kill you and I never once listened to you. And somehow, you take all these facts and pretend like they're your fault."

"They are!" she insisted. "I could have done something!"

"How?"

"I don't know. I could have thought of something. I could have fought harder, I could—"

"What would that have done?"

"It'd . . . it'd work out, somehow, I don't know! But I could have done something. I *should* have done something."

"Why?"

"BECAUSE I'M THE ONLY ONE WHO TRIES, GODS DAMN IT!"

It all but tore itself from her throat. She hadn't been thinking it. She barely realized that she had said it. But it came, all the same, and it hung in the air between them.

She was the one who tried. She was always the one who had struggled for something bigger. She was the one who had fought the hardest for the smallest stakes. She had always tried.

And she had always failed.

And that realization, even as it felt like an iron coming off her chest, felt like a dagger being driven into her breast. She felt the urge to cry again, or simply to lie down and not move for a long time.

But Denaos simply squeezed her hand. His smile didn't falter.

"I wonder what you did to piss off Talanas so that he stuck you with a bunch of fuckers like us," he said.

"I didn't mean it like that."

"You did. Because you're right. You are the one who tries. You're the one who always wanted to do things differently, even if we didn't." He shrugged. "You're also kind of a smug asshole about it, but that's besides the point."

"This isn't making me feel better."

"If I wanted to make you feel better, I'd tell you about the times I *almost* showed you why they called me Silky Digits back in Redgate."

"How was that—"

"What you need is to hear the truth," he interrupted. "Gariath, Dreadaeleon, Lenk…they were all going to do whatever they were going to do. And me…" He smiled sadly. "Everyone pays their debts, eventually. You can't do anything for us now, no matter how hard you try. But because you're you, you're going to keep trying. So try for someone that needs it."

He gestured to the window with his chin.

"It's a little before midnight right now. Khoth-Kapira won't come now, she said. He wants to give the city time to appreciate his presence, to savor him. He'll be here soon, though. Tomorrow."

She nodded. "I'll be ready." She sniffed. "I'll fight harder this time. I'll—"

"You don't have the soldiers to fight him. What you have is a city full of people who you said you'd protect."

She shook her head. "How do I do that?"

He smiled. "That's where you try."

The tears had stopped without her noticing. The pains had abated. She stared at his hand, fingerless and maimed, and frowned.

Could she have truly stopped that from happening? Any of this? Maybe Denaos was always going to end up carved up like dinner. Maybe Gariath was always going to one day turn against her. But if that was the case, why did she even try with any of them?

And, without knowing, a smile tugged at her face.

Because he knows me, she thought. *And I'm the one who tries.*

And without quite realizing it, she whispered, "I can do this."

FORTY-ONE

THE DEMON REPENTANT

When they had just been ink stains on a map, they had been easier to handle.

Their scent had been pungent, but only slightly. They had been easy to count, easy to track. They hadn't even been real: just a few black blots on a ratty old parchment.

But now the smell of their rotting bodies was overwhelming. The sight of them was too many to count. And no matter how many times he tried to envision them as ink stains on a map, they were still corpses.

Corpses that had been warriors.

Corpses that had followed him into battle.

Corpses that had cheered his name just moments before they had died.

Gariath couldn't even see them all from the top of the rock, but he knew they were there: impaled on spears, ripped limb from limb, ground into the earth. They had given their lives.

All so he could face a single human he hadn't even been able to kill.

That was the part that stuck in his hide like an arrow—or another arrow, at least. He felt no guilt for leading the tulwar to their deaths. Neither they nor he had ever pretended they wouldn't die. But he had promised them good deaths, deaths at the hands of warriors, deaths that would mean their children wouldn't have to fight so hard.

And instead he had given them a meat grinder. Instead he had led them into the jaws of the shicts and their thousands of arrows for teeth. Instead he had led them into...into...

Whatever the fuck he was looking at.

Gariath had seen demons before. And before, the word had always seemed like a fancy way to say *big thing that takes slightly longer to kill*. But the great shadow that loomed over the pass, the titanic creature that looked down over creation through baleful white eyes as a crown of serpents coiled upon his brow...

It would take a great long time to kill that thing.

He was miles away, yet Gariath could still see him clearly, so huge did Khoth-Kapira stand. The great demon could rampage across the Green Belt, if he chose, be at Cier'Djaal in a few great strides and topple the entire city in just a few more. Yet, for a reason known only to the demon, he seemed to be concerned primarily with surveying the ruin of the battle that had been, the madness he had ruined good deaths with.

But, Gariath supposed, if the demons hadn't killed them, it would have been the shicts. And if it hadn't been the shicts, they would have broken on the humans.

In a moment of quiet, a single thought echoed through his mind.

It was all for nothing.

Suddenly, Khoth-Kapira swept his gaze toward Gariath's perch. There was a temptation to call out to the demon, to challenge him to come and finish the job he'd started.

But what would be the point?

It was a weariness, bone-deep and etched in every wound, that dragged him to the edge of the dune, down its face, and made him trudge to a small clearing nearby. And every step he took, he felt more tired. By the time he reached it, and the two shadowy shapes sitting in the shadow of an abandoned shack, he had forgotten how his legs worked and simply collapsed, seeing no particular need to rise up again.

Chakaa didn't seem to notice. She was busy reaching around her back, tongue stuck out and one eye shut in concentration as she groped for something she couldn't quite reach. After a moment, her face lit up.

"Hah!"

There was the sound of something tearing. She jerked free an arrow, a tuft of her black fur hanging from its head, and held it up proudly.

"I thought I would never get that out." She glanced to the much larger shape sitting beside her. "Not that *you* were any help."

Her gaambol, some great black-furred thing, opened a single yellow eye and regarded her with keen distaste before returning to resting. She snorted and glanced over at Gariath, who was sprawled out with considerably less grace than a gigantic, smelly monkey.

"Or you," she added.

Gariath didn't see the point in responding.

Chakaa looked up over him. She squinted into the night and frowned.

"It hasn't moved," she said. "Why does it just sit there, staring at the dead? Does it admire our work?"

Gariath had known demons to be many twisted things, including macabre. It wouldn't surprise him if Khoth-Kapira *was* simply taking in the grandness of the slaughter. But he had expected cackling, depraved smiles, wild-eyed glee.

All he could recall on the demon's face was a very long frown.

But he didn't see the point in telling her that, either.

"It's not chasing the clans, then." The sigh she let out was not a sound he thought he had ever heard from her. "That is some small fortune, at least. The clans escaped. The ones that were left, anyway."

Left?

Had there been any left? When Gariath had looked out on the devastation, the road of corpses, it seemed all he had seen was tulwar bodies, mangled and broken and ground into the earth. He found it hard to remember what a living tulwar looked like. When he pictured the faces of Daaru and Mototaru, he saw only the same wide-eyed, openmouthed mask, all features twisted away in agony, repeated over and over.

"And there will be more clans," Chakaa said. "Reinforcements must have reached our camp by now. Soon, we will be strong enough to fight again. Soon, we will have the steel to bring this beast low. And what a crash it shall make when it is! We shall—"

"Would you shut the fuck up already?"

The words oozed out of his mouth like spittle. He flung an arm over his eyes and growled into the night.

"It's over. If the clans ran, they should keep running. They should forget the people who died here. And the ones who did should wait until their Tul spits them out into a new body or however the fuck this works and pray they don't remember anything about this mess."

He flashed a sneer at her. Behind her white paint and the spatters of blood, her face was empty.

"Big dramatic speeches are something humans puke out when they know they've lost. They make big words to hide behind and pretend they're not small and stupid. Don't pretend to be as small and stupid as they are. This wasn't a fight. There was never a fight. There's not going to be another one."

That was that. He'd finally said it. And now he waited for her to go away and leave him to die.

Chakaa was crazy, but she wasn't stupid. Even a mind as damaged as hers could see that he was right. And if she couldn't, all she had to do was go out over the ridge and look at the corpses. Then she would leave, go back to wherever the Mak Lak Kai festered, and he could get on with the business of joining the dead.

"You're wrong."

The voice wasn't hers. It was so soft and so gentle that it had no business being in a mouth that spit blood and hurled war cries like they were spears. So he simply snorted.

"I'm never wrong," he growled.

"You are about this one," she said. "There will be another fight."

"There won't. This is over."

"Then there'll be another one without you. There will never be an *end* to fighting because that is what tulwar do. We are born, we fight for what little we get, we die, and then we come back and do it again. This is why the Tul brings us back, because the fighting is never done. Stay here, the clans will still fight. Die here, the clans will still fight. This demon-thing burns the world to cinders, the clans will fight for the ashes, the Tul sending them back over and over."

"Except you," Gariath replied. He eyed her sidelong. "Daaru told me that the *malaa* don't come back."

She pressed her lips together and nodded. "That is true."

"Then you don't need to fight," he said. "You can let go. Or you can fuck off and go do whatever you want. You don't need to fight for them, either."

"That is also true."

"They fear you."

"And that."

"They hate you."

"And that, as well. You have a point somewhere, maybe?"

"That *is* the point, idiot!" He roared to his feet, baring teeth at her. "This whole thing, all this death, it's been for *nothing*! We came here to break the humans, we didn't. They didn't die well, they just *died*! Shicts shot them, humans stomped them, demons tore them apart, and we have nothing to show for it but a chunk of wet earth."

He stormed toward her, thrust a claw in her face.

"And *you*, the one whose name they spit on, want to go back and fight again? For what? Do you like the taste of their spit?"

"No."

"Then don't be an idiot," he snarled. "Leave them. Go fight for yourself."

She shook her head. "I can't do that."

"Why?"

She looked down at the arrow in her hands, wrenched from her own body, bloodless. She rolled it around in her fingers, toying with it.

"Because if I do…" She looked up at him. "If *you* do, they go back to fighting over nothing. They go back to fighting over too little food to eat and too little land to rest on." She shrugged. "And what do they care? When they die, the Tul takes them, and they are born again somewhere else. Maybe somewhere better. Maybe worse. And if it is, they just die again and the cycle repeats."

She tapped the arrow to her arm, to her leg, to her torso. To the dozens of knotted scars across her flesh, to the wounds she had earned that day that refused to bleed.

"But not the *malaa*," she said. "We get only what we have now. And what we have now is clans that hate us, *Humn* that fear us, land that is not ours." She regarded him thoughtfully. "But with you…we had something more."

"We had death," he spit. "That's all I gave them."

"They were going to get that, anyway. Do not be so arrogant to assume you're the only one who can kill people. I do it all the time." She hummed thoughtfully. "When you told the Mak Lak Kai to lead the charge, they did so eagerly. We were pleased for the opportunity."

"The honor."

"I didn't say that. I said 'opportunity.' We wanted to show the other clans. We wanted to protect them. But mostly, we wanted to push forward to this land you were leading us to."

"The city?"

"I didn't say that, either. Don't interrupt, it's rude." She shook her head. "No. It was never just war with you, *daanaja*. It was never just revenge. It was land. It was food. It was homes. It was people. It was fighting now so we wouldn't have to fight one day. With you, there was a chance that things might get better, that the tulwar might have more than just fighting. That eventually, there would be enough food and enough land that they might forget they hated us. Just a little."

She rose to her feet. She looked to the arrow in her hand, frowned a little, and tossed it to the side.

"The other clans don't know it, of course. Neither do you, *daanaja*. No one but the *malaa* know to look this far ahead. It's other clans, other races, that get the luxury of dying peacefully. They fight to die. We fight to live."

Chakaa was crazy.

And Chakaa probably *was* stupid.

What she said made not a lot of sense to Gariath, which was probably to be expected. Someone who had been stabbed as many times as she had probably hadn't walked away from it with her mind intact. And her words were stupid. And her ideas were stupid. And that whole dramatic speech sounded as stupid coming out of her mouth as it did coming out of any human's mouth.

But...

There was something she had said in the middle of all that mess. Something about fighting so that there would one day be no more fighting.

Something about that, he didn't know what, made him feel lighter.

She walked to her gaambol and kicked it awake. The beast shrieked but clambered to its feet. She grabbed its harness to mount it.

"Wait."

She turned, regarded him. He stood, taller than he felt like he could.

"I need you to do something for me."

And, as a big yellow smile split apart her face, she looked like the Chakaa he knew. "Of course, *daanaja*."

"I need you to take a message to the clans," he said. "An important one."

"They shall have it."

"And I need your gaambol." He looked over the ridge. "Can you get past the demons on foot?"

"Well, obviously." She slapped her chest. "I am Chakaa Humn Mak Lak Kai. They are simply demons. What can they possibly do? Kill me?"

"Tear you apart, eat you, digest you, and maybe shit you out."

"Ah."

Chakaa paused, looked thoughtful. Then she shrugged.

"Eh. I'll do it, anyway."

FORTY-TWO

A COMFORTING SIN

They *failed*? How?"

A woman. Middle-aged mother, if the husky weariness of her voice was any indication. She was breathless in a way she hadn't had the energy to be in quite some time.

"It was an ambush. The tulwar, they pushed into the pass. The Prophet's army fought back, but..."

A man. A little younger than her, with a shrill, weedy voice used to haggling and complaining. Though today, the snide edge was tempered by fear.

"But what?" the woman demanded. "My son was in the reserves! *But what?*"

"Shicts," the man said. "They appeared on the cliffs, like ghosts. They filled both armies with arrows. There was not a man alive after they were done."

Silence. A wet, choked breath. Then a sobbing shriek.

"Lying," the woman said. "You're *lying!*"

"I am not, woman. The scouts just got back, you can ask them yourselves. They were raving about demons and monsters. But I heard the word, over and over. '*Shict! Shict! Shict!*'"

"No...those animals. Why would they?"

"Because they are animals," the man said. The sneering anger returned to his voice. "Because they are beasts. They hate us and always have. Why *wouldn't* they attack the Prophet?" He made an ugly retching noise. "A false Prophet. It is as the fasha said. Our only hope lies in Ancaa, now. We must go to Silktown with the others."

"But...my son..."

"He is dead. They are all dead."

There was more that followed—the usual sobbing and weeping and the predictable ensuing pleas for calm and insisting that they must do what he said. Humans tended to follow the same routines, after all.

But Kataria had heard enough.

Her ears folded over themselves as she slipped away from the edge of the roof and made her way back down into the alley. She stole down the side streets, making her way back to the abandoned buildings at the edge of the Souk.

She wasn't quite sure why she was being so stealthy, though. It wasn't like anyone was left to see her, anyway. The streets remained silent as they ever had been. So silent that, even through her folded ears, she could hear the mutter of the wind, the creak of houses...

You could have stopped it.

The whisper of her thoughts.

You could have warned Asper.

Step after step.

You could have killed Shekune. You knew where she'd be.

Breath after breath.

But you didn't.

All the way through the alleys, down the streets, through the door of the abandoned shop she had found and up the stairs to the bedroom on the second floor.

You saved him, instead.

He was there when she entered, sitting on the edge of the bed instead of lying down. Waiting for her instead of resting. The bread and cheese she had found sat untouched next to the jug of water, still full.

He hadn't eaten. He hadn't rested.

She had let her people die to save him and he couldn't even take care of himself.

"What's going on out there?" Lenk stood up and rushed to her. "What's happened?"

"Sit down," she said.

"There's no time for that, I've got to—"

"*Sit down.*"

She hadn't raised her voice. She merely met his eyes. His, full of panic and fear. Hers, steady as a river. She placed her hand on his chest, felt his heart pounding in her fingertips as she eased him back onto the bed. She took the plate of food from the table beside it and thrust it into his hands.

"Eat."

He looked as though he might protest but only until he met her eyes again. And under her gaze, he seemed to steady. He let out a sigh and began to eat.

"It was a failure," Kataria said. "Asper and Gariath, both their armies were wiped out."

"By demons."

Kataria shook her head. She opened her mouth, but found that the word would not come. She clenched her jaw and forced it out from behind her teeth.

"Shicts."

Lenk blinked. "Shicts?"

"Yeah."

"How? Shicts are just—"

"Shicts are shicts." Kataria interrupted him with a harsh bark. "We don't fight, we hunt. We *kill*." She felt a cold feeling welling up in her belly. "Sai-Thu—" She caught herself. "Someone showed them a way into the cliffs above the armies. They rained arrows down on both of them, killed most of them. The demons just came in and ate the scraps."

"What?" He looked incredulous.

"I heard dozens of people talking," Kataria snapped back. "It's not demons they're cursing out there."

With his mouth full of food, he simply stared down at his plate. And she stared at him, only barely aware of how her hands were curling into fists at her sides.

She had said those words a hundred times in her head and had seen this situation just as many. She thought of everything he would do. He would tell her to think of the greater threat and forget about how her people had just damned themselves. He would moan about there being yet another thing out there to kill him. He would sigh wistfully about how he should have put his sword down long ago—yet again—and why couldn't he give this up and why couldn't anyone just let him be.

And then she would hit him.

Maybe hard. Maybe really hard. Maybe enough to knock him out, entirely, or even break some teeth loose.

But she would hit him. She would show him that she could still hurt him, that even if she had saved his life and let everyone else die because of it, she could still do that to him.

She would hit him.

She would prove she could still hurt him.

And it wouldn't feel good. But it would be necessary.

"I'm sorry."

Of course, he had to go and fuck that up, as well.

He put the plate down. He stood up. He met her gaze again. And the fear was gone from his eyes.

"How..." He paused and laid a hand on her shoulder. "Do you feel all right?"

She didn't know how to answer that. Her head felt like someone had lined her skull with iron. Her heart felt like it had turned to a stone and sunk into her belly. She felt like she was going to vomit out something she needed to live.

"Fine," she said. "I feel fine."

She didn't feel fine. But what else could she have felt? What else could she have done, she asked herself?

It was an entire tribe, an entire people, an entire war she had stood against.

She couldn't have stopped any of it.

And now, she thought, *you can't even punch one fucking human.*

Her arms felt numb, like the rest of her. No urge to hit, no urge to kill, no urge to do anything that would make this better. She simply stood there, staring at him, as he stared at her with his punchable face that she couldn't even fucking hit, she was that fucking powerless.

And he saw her mouth hanging open, her hands hanging limp. And he frowned.

"You're not fine," he said.

"I am."

"But you—"

"I said I was." Her teeth were out, her ears flat against her head, eyes twisted in a scowl. "You think I'm lying or something?"

He didn't run. He didn't flinch. He didn't even blink as he whispered. "No."

"Then shut your fucking face."

She met his eyes with her scowl, her body tense, jaw clenched, daring him to press the issue, to give her a reason.

But him, with his blue eyes that didn't turn into a scowl and his old scars that didn't bunch up into muscles to fight her and his body that just stood there and waited for her and didn't even have the decency to give her a reason to hit him...

"Useless," she muttered.

Her eyes drifted far to the edge of the city, toward the wooden walls of Shicttown. The smoke of campfires did not rise from behind its walls anymore. She could not hear the Howling of the people there. It stood, as empty and dead as the rest of the city.

And as her eyes drifted, so, too, did her thoughts. Back to the day when that ghetto had burned as Karnerians had stalked its streets in search of shicts to kill in revenge. Shekune had led the attack that spurred them. The shicts had followed precisely because they knew the humans were simply looking for an excuse to kill them. There were generations upon generations of grudges, vengeances, and sins that they wanted answered. Thousands of years of hatred.

What made you think you could have stopped all that?

Her legs felt weak. She fell forward, pressed her head against the window. The glass was cool on her brow as the night deepened. But she could barely tell; all of her felt cold at that moment.

Behind her, she heard Lenk moving toward the door. Maybe running away. Maybe giving her some space.

She didn't know.

Or care.

She heard him walk to the door. She heard him stop. She heard him open his big stupid mouth.

"Kwar saved me."

A surge of heat coursed through her. Uncomfortable, almost painful, like a scar opening again and warm blood hitting cold air.

"From Teneir," Lenk said. "She was there. She jumped on Teneir, stabbed her a bunch of times, and then...just left." He paused. "She made me swear not to tell you, but I was a little dead at the time, so I don't think it counts. But...yeah. She was there. And I'd be dead if she hadn't been."

Those weren't words she was ready to hear. That wasn't a name she had expected to hear again, not from him. He didn't spit it. He didn't curse it. He could have not told her. He could have lied. He could have been as horrible and shitty and awful as everyone else.

But, she thought, *he fucked that up, too. And so did Kwar.*

"Thank you."

His hand was on her shoulder. She hadn't heard him approach. When had he ever been able to sneak up on her? She could feel the calluses on his hand, warm against the bare skin of her shoulder.

"For everything," he said.

His hand lingered there for another moment. She heard the wood grind beneath the heels of his boots as he turned to leave. His hand began to slip away.

Until she reached out and caught it.

She didn't know why—not in her head, at least. Something deeper inside her knew why she took his hand, why she squeezed it. Something that had lain quiet for a long time in a very cold place and now craved something warm. That part of her knew why she pulled his hand lower, pressed it against her naked side.

The warmth—his warmth, old and familiar and in every one of his scars—flowed into her. His hand squeezed her side gently. And then harder.

Her arm snaked up, found his neck, found his hair, wrapped fingers around it. She pulled him close to her, felt his body press against hers, felt the beating of his heart through her back.

She pulled his head toward her. His lips found her neck, brushed across the tender skin of her throat. She could feel the cold slipping away, feel her blood rushing up to her skull, into her ears as he whispered.

"Kataria..." he said, "if you're feeling...confused..."

"I'm not," she replied.

"But if you are—"

"Lenk."

She looked to the window. By the moonlight, she caught the barest glimpse of his reflection as he looked at her, the barest glimpse of her canines as she smiled in a way she hadn't smiled in a long time.

"Shut the fuck up."

Her hand slipped from his hair, down his chest, to the the leather of his belt and down to between his legs. She found him ready beneath her hand as she gave him a squeeze, as she pulled at the buckle of his belt, as she let his trousers fall around his ankles.

She pressed herself against him, felt him pushing at her breeches as she fumbled at her own garment. She hooked her fingers into the waist of her breeches, pulled them down, bending low. She took his hands in hers, she guided them to her hips, she squeezed his fingers.

And, slowly, she slid herself onto him.

He met her. Her body tensed as his hands tightened around her. Her forearms pressed against the cold window, her breath fogging the glass as he pressed into her. Her ears drooped low, the blood leaving them, her head, her neck, rushing down to her belly, her hips, her legs.

He began to rock against her, a slow rhythm that steadily picked up. She could feel him behind her, feel the coil of his muscles, growing taut in the way she knew they did. She could feel the roughness of his scars upon her, the familiar lines that told her everything she needed to knew about him. She could feel his breath on the back of her neck, his thighs pressed against hers, his teeth clenched.

And it all felt so easy.

She pushed back against him, forced him to give a step. She arched her back. She pressed her brow against the glass. She pushed herself against him, pushed him deeper inside her, pushed until he pushed back.

He pressed her against the window. She felt the cold glass against her belly. She felt her hair falling across her back, trailing down to brush against his hips. She felt herself growing more numb, pushing against him, her hips pressing hard until she forced him back again.

And this time, he yielded. He held on to her, his breath coming out in harsh gasps as she thrust herself against him. A growl escaped between her clenched teeth as his hands tightened around her hips, as she tightened around him. She felt him respond to her, felt the blood rush down to his hips, felt his grip go tight and numb.

She needed this. This moment, this breath, this lightheaded feeling of a wide open sky beneath her and a solid rock behind her. She needed this moment where she acted and he followed, where he was strong and solid and unyielding as she needed him to be. She needed to control this moment, as she could control nothing else.

The blood left her head, left her arms, left everything to rush to between her legs, to feel him with everything she had. And there, she could feel everything inside her, inside him, come together into one singular warmth.

As though this moment, and him and her in it, shared one heartbeat.

Her cry came loud and long, a noise from somewhere deep inside her that she hadn't let out in a long time. His followed, a grunting, snarling noise she had missed too much. And when it was over, she leaned against the window and let herself go limp in his arms. She let him guide her to the bed. She let her head fall against his chest, let the blood return to her ears, let the sound of his heartbeat fill her ears.

He was safe, at least. He was alive, at least. Even as the rest of the world burned, he was still here.

If this was all she could save, that was fine with her. If the people she loved were all she could protect, then she would protect them.

If armies burned down the world and demons choked on the ashes, she would not let them die.

Even if everything else did.

That thought, she suspected, should not have made her feel as warm as it did.

But, as she felt his breath in time with hers and the heartbeat of this moment continued, she found she did not care.

FORTY-THREE

A CALL BETTER LEFT QUIET

After a long moment of surveying the Souk—or what had been the Souk—Lenk nodded to himself. He put his hands on his hips, stared down at the great skeletonized bazaar, and spoke.

"Here."

Kataria, shooting him a sidelong glance, seemed less than convinced. "Why here?"

"Space, mostly."

He stretched his arms out wide over the great circle that had been Cier'Djaal's biggest market, turned into Cier'Djaal's biggest battlefield, and was now Cier'Djaal's biggest graveyard.

Civilization hadn't been so different from the wilds, really. Whether it be coin or blood, everything obeyed the food chain. The great merchants had been laid low by predators: first thugs, then soldiers. The looters and thieves had swept through to scavenge the remains.

Some buildings remained, those that hadn't been scarred and gutted by fire. A few noble stalls still tried to hold tall, surrounded as they were by those that had been collapsed or trampled. The debris of smashed pottery, dented metal, and those scraps unworthy of Cier'Djaal's high standard of thievery remained behind.

"There's room to maneuver here," he said. He pointed to a cluster of buildings. "He's huge, so we'll need high places to attack from. If worse comes to worst, we can use that."

He pointed to the Silken Spire, looming large over the Souk. Whether by reverence or by the fact that sheer size prevented any meaningful action from being taken, the Spire was untouched by war, by looting, by any of the city's ills. It fluttered and flapped in the morning breeze, as bright and glimmering as it had been on the day he had arrived. The spiders crawling across it seemed no more perturbed by a giant demon's approach than they had been by gang violence or warfare.

"And it probably will come to worst," he sighed. He looked at Kataria. "What do you think?"

The shict stared out from their perch atop the building at the edge of the Souk. A frown creased her face, her ears drooping.

"I think I see a lot of wide open space and not a lot of places to hide if a gigantic demon decides to step on us," she said.

"Can't risk getting cornered in the proper city. He could bring a building on top of us if he wanted. This way, he at least has to aim for us."

"Uh-huh. I also think I see a lot of high places that work if he decides to get close enough." She shook her bow in her hand. "I can't hurt him, remember. Only you can." She eyed his silver hair. "For whatever reason."

"But he'll have to get close if he wants us," Lenk replied. "We'll have an opportunity, then."

"Will we? What if he decides he doesn't want to get close? What if he decides to spit poison or vomit snakes on us or use some kind of demon death ray?"

"Don't be—" Lenk paused. "Can he do that?"

"*Can* he?" Kataria shook her head. "We don't even know what he can or can't do."

"Yeah...yeah." Lenk sighed and looked out over the Souk. "Let me ask you this: Do you think you see any better ideas?"

Kataria looked around: at the ruined Souk before them, at the maze-like city behind them, at the looming Spire above them. Slowly, she looked back at him and shook her head.

"Me neither," he said. "This is our best chance."

"If he comes," Kataria said.

Lenk looked toward the city walls. And somewhere far away, someone was looking back at him.

"He'll come," he said.

<hr />

They made their way down from the building, picked their way through the debris of the Souk, and found a spot that would allow them to see whatever was coming. Not that Lenk anticipated this last part to be a huge problem, what with their enemy being roughly the size of three or four houses. But it helped soothe him.

He stared at the gate leading into the city.

There, he said. *If Khoth-Kapira comes from there, he'll come straight for me. I just have to lead him toward a tall building I can fight from. Get up on him. Get in his eyes. Carve them out and finish him off.* He nodded. *Assuming I don't get stepped on, crushed, or eaten, that should work. Unless...*

He cast a glance over his shoulder, toward the distant Sumps.

If he comes from the Sumps, he'll plow through the city. The houses there won't stop him any more than tall grass would. He might try to force me to come to him, keep destroying and killing until I do. He sniffed. *Should just let him kill them. That'll show him. Of course...*

He looked up toward the sky.

What if he just comes plummeting down from above and crushes me? What if I just see a big shadow and hear a faint whistling sound and then BOOM? Can he do that? He cringed. *No, that's insane. He can't do that.*

Yeah, you're right, he told himself. *He can turn into a gigantic monster with snakes for a beard who can appear anywhere he wants, but* flying? *That's just ridiculous. Listen to yourself, you stupid bastard. If you're not considering every possible angle, every possible outcome, every* possible *attack...*

He paused. The last thought sank into his head like a hatchet.

Then you're not realizing how completely fucked you are.

He saw Kataria moving. Her ears twitched and went rigid. She turned toward the eastern gate, drawing an arrow from her quiver. He followed suit, sliding his sword out, waiting.

In another three breaths, he heard it, too: boots crunching on grit, metal dragged across stone, heavy breathing. Desperate soldiers deserting, Khovura skulking, some other manner of demon he hadn't seen yet; he didn't know what it was, but he hadn't met anything yet that couldn't be solved by putting a sword in it.

Whatever it was, he was ready for it.

Or so he thought.

Not that he *wasn't* ready for the woman who came trudging out of the rubble toward him, but he certainly hadn't expected to see her alive again, even if she looked even just barely alive.

She was more tired than he remembered her looking, bruised around the face and neck. She had worn robes instead of dirty armor, carrying a medicine bag instead of dragging a shield and sword. But the pendant of the Healer's Phoenix around her neck was the same. And the smile—the weary smile she gave when she didn't know what else to give—was exactly as he remembered.

They lowered their weapons. Asper came to a slow, weary halt before them. She stared at them for a moment before looking back over her shoulder.

"It was shicts, at first," she said. "They got around us somehow, got up on the cliffs. We were attacked from above. And then..." She paused, staring into the distance. "Then the demons came. I didn't listen to you." She looked at them. "Either of you."

She neither made nor demanded an apology—for her not listening, for them not doing more. She fumbled for no explanations and made no prayers. This woman, dusty and tired and hard, was not the same priestess he had left behind.

Which was fine by him. This woman looked a little more useful in a fight.

"That thing..." Asper said. "That demon...it's coming here, isn't it?"

Lenk nodded. "He is."

"And it's not going to stop."

"Not unless we kill it."

She looked at him meaningfully. "And...can you?"

He glanced at Kataria. The shict looked to him, frowned, and shrugged. He sighed, turned to Asper, and smacked his lips.

"Kind of? Maybe?"

Asper's face drained of emotion. "Outstanding," she said. She rolled her shoulder. "I'm in."

"Asper," he said, "you don't have to."

"I know," she replied.

"This isn't some ordinary demon."

"I know that, too."

"This is Khoth-Kapira. The God-King. This foe is beyond anything we've ever—"

"Holy shit, I *get it*, all right?" she snapped. "I know it's huge. I know it's a demon. I know we probably can't win. We've survived things like this before, right?"

He shook his head. "Not like this."

"It doesn't matter," she said. "I've lost everything so far. Every battle that counted, every life that I needed to save. If I have to keep losing...then let me do it trying my damnedest." She forced a weak smile. "Okay?"

He sighed. "Yeah. Okay." He rubbed the back of his head. "If it'll make you happy, you can come die horribly with us."

She didn't seem happy with that—though it was hard to imagine how this situation could ever be happy—but she seemed satisfied, at least.

"That's fine and all," Kataria grunted. "But what's she even going to *do*? As far as we know, only Lenk can hurt the damn thing. We're going to need her to bring more than just hacking at its ankles."

"I brought more." Asper looked over their heads. "And he's right here."

Lenk whirled and, at the sight of the shadow looming out of the ruins of the Souk, raised his sword. It stood stark as night in the morning, an inky void shaped like a man. One of Khoth-Kapira's tricks? Some other sorcery? He would have charged it right then and there, regardless, had it not spoken.

"What the hell is *that* supposed to do?" A black hand reached out and pointed to Lenk's blade. "You see a creepy thing made out of darkness incarnate and your first thought is to whack it with a big metal stick?"

The voice rang familiar enough for Lenk to lower his blade. "Who are you?"

And though the thing had no face beneath its hood, Lenk could have sworn it was smiling at him.

"Fine," it said, "but promise you won't say anything stupid."

A hand went up to the hood and peeled it back. A face, colorless, and two dark eyes stared back at Lenk. And though the grin he shot them was familiar, Denaos's smile had never been so unnerving.

"Denaos," he whispered, breathless. "By all that's holy—"

The rogue held up a finger. "So I know you didn't promise, but let's not go compounding stupidity with blasphemy. I know what I look like."

"Shit," Kataria whispered. "Are you...dead?"

"I am." He stood tall and resolute, hands on his hips. "And I am here to help. In your darkest hour, I've—"

"But how, though?" she interrupted. "Dead people are supposed to stay dead."

"That's not important right now. What *is*—"

"The hell it's not important!" she snapped. "You're fucking *dead*! How is that possible? Do you crave flesh? Blood?" She quirked a brow. "Virgins? Is that how this is supposed to—"

"For fuck's sake, woman, I *just* got done explaining this whole shitty thing to Asper. I can't very well be mysterious and dramatic every time I have to open my mouth." He waved a fingerless hand at her. "I'll explain this whole...*thing* later."

"I think I'd rather know now," Lenk said.

"Oh, would you?" Denaos replied. "Can you afford to be choosy about who helps you or am I mistaken and that's some *other* gargantuan demon king marching toward us?"

Kataria glanced toward Lenk and muttered, "I mean, whatever happened to him, he's still a gigantic asshole, so it couldn't have been *that* bad."

"I heard that," Denaos said.

"*Good*," she snapped back.

"Look," Lenk said, holding up a hand. "Whatever happened, whatever's *going* to happen, it's not your responsibility. Heroism isn't going to save us."

"No," a voice from above echoed. "But power will."

Eyes drifted up to the eyes looking down upon them. Hanging there like a ghost, the tails of his dirty coat swaying beneath him, Dreadaeleon hovered in the middle of the air. His hands were outstretched, the air shimmering around his fingertips with whatever power was keeping him aloft. Though his hair still hung in greasy strands and he looked as scrawny as ever beneath his coat, there was something off about him. There was something in his eyes, an intensity that hadn't been there before.

Also, Lenk noted, *his eyes are on fire. That's new.*

The wizard slowly let himself down to the ground. The fires in his eyes, bright crimson, should have dissipated as soon as the spell was released. Yet they merely dimmed to embers, glowing in the morning gray.

Lenk swept his eyes about, glancing from Dreadaeleon's burning stare to Denaos's colorless face to Asper's dirty armor.

"So," he said. "Looks like we've all been busy."

"There are few words that could describe what happened to me," Dreadaeleon said. "And those that exist are beyond the grasp of your mind. Suffice to say..." He flexed his fingers. Cobalt sparks danced across his knuckles. "I have become...something more than the boy you left behind." He clenched his hand into a fist. A burst of bright electricity blossomed. "And what I have become, you cannot afford to deny."

A silence fell over them, their eyes fixated on the boy—or whatever he was now. And when the quiet was broken, it was Denaos who spoke.

"Did you come up with that just now?"

"Yes." Dreadaeleon coughed. "I mean, I thought about it a little on the way over. It sounded good, though, right?"

"Was a gods-damned letter sent out or something?" Lenk asked. "Why have you all decided to show up now?"

"What'd we come together for in the first place?" Denaos asked. "I thought it was gold, back then. Or maybe running away from the guard. Something like that. It didn't become clear to me until this happened to me." He sighed. "Some are born with money sense, some are born with excellent taste in wine..."

The smile he offered Lenk was soft, small, and terribly sad.

"And some are just born to troubles."

Lenk found it hard to dispute that. After all, it had been...what? A month? Two months? And in that time, Asper had formed and lost a holy army, Dreadaeleon had found power that he clearly shouldn't have, and he didn't have words for whatever the fuck had happened to Denaos.

And him? He had released the demon that would end a thousand lives, a thousand cities, an entire world.

All in two months.

It had taken the gods centuries to create it and, in maybe one more day, they'd destroy it all.

Born to troubles, he thought. *Isn't that the gods-damned truth.* He sighed, looking over his companions—the men and woman he barely recognized. *Still, I guess it could be worse.*

And, in another moment, it was.

It was Asper who noticed first. She glanced up, tensed, drew her sword and shield in one fluid motion, and made ready. Their glances followed and, while they might not have had *exactly* as severe a reaction, Lenk could feel every cheek of every ass collectively tense at the creature approaching.

Even after all this time, there were some things that just didn't change.

And the sight of Gariath was one of them.

From a distance, he looked huge, imposing, unstoppable. And as he drew closer...well, he still looked all those things. But Lenk could only now see the fresh wounds, the old scars that were a little too apparent on him, the hint of stiffness in his limbs. And his eyes, so often unfathomably reptilian and dark, reflected a weariness that Lenk had never seen in him before.

Gariath came to a halt a few feet away. Perhaps he noticed their collective tension and was being cautious. Or perhaps he simply wanted to be respectful, given the circumstance.

"You all smell awful," he growled.

Or maybe it was that.

"I caught your scent at the city gates," he said, sweeping his eyes from one of them to the other. "I didn't expect to find you all here." His gaze settled on Asper. "I am not here to fight."

"Then consider this to be a fucking bonus," Asper roared.

She took a leap toward him, only to find herself suspended in mid-air. She glared over her shoulder toward Dreadaeleon, the air trembling around his hand. She snarled.

"*You!*" she snapped. "You would help him, wouldn't you?"

"Only because we need both of you," Dreadaeleon said. "Asper, I—"

"*No!*" she roared. "Put me down. Let me fight him! Let me die or kill him, I don't fucking care anymore! If you knew what he did, what his army did, you'd—"

"My army is dead."

It was the way he said it that made her, and the rest of them, pause. His was a voice made for hard statements and unflinching words. To hear him speak with a damp voice, creaking at the edges, was unsettling enough to cause them to stop.

"I led them to their deaths," he said. "Even before the shicts, the demons, they were dead." He stared at the ground. "I promised them new lives, a new home, free from fears. All I could give them was death."

He looked toward the city walls and snorted.

"And if all I can give them is death, then I shall give them the biggest one there is." He looked back to them and spit the next words. "The demon."

Asper slowly slid to the ground as Dreadaeleon's magic faded. And though she no longer looked eager to fight, she regarded Gariath with a glare.

"If you think I'm going to fight alongside him ..."

"I don't care," Gariath growled. "I sent the rest of the tulwar away. They'll go back to their homes, back to their families, try to forget this day. But I'm here to fight, to kill or to die. One way or another, their deaths will be answered. Whether you're here for that or not, I don't care."

Dreadaeleon cast a burning glance toward him. "He's here. We might as well use him. I've seen the demon from on high. Even *I* can't stop him alone. We'll need every—"

"Oh, not even you?" Asper snapped. "Not even the great and mighty Dreadaeleon, whose power of magic is matched only by the amount of awkward erections he suffers, can stop it? Spare me. You want him around because he's like you. Neither of you can take responsibility for what you've done. If you knew what he—"

"I don't know and I don't care," Dreadaeleon snapped. "Your problems and all your invisible sky people and delusions of heaven were trivial before, and they've only grown more trivial now. Your losses are nothing compared to—"

"Yours?" Denaos interjected. "What losses would those be? The people you killed to get your power? The oaths you broke? The buildings you've burned? You don't know loss." He sneered. "You only break everything you touch."

"That's probably true." Kataria sniffed. "But, as a counterpoint, may I point out that you're fucking *dead*?"

"That doesn't mean—"

"Like fuck it doesn't," she snarled. "All of you are bickering and whining about which one of you is the dumbest, but none of you are going to be worth shit when the fighting happens. I've had *enough* of trusting everyone else not to fuck things up and—"

"Oh, don't act like you're—"

"—*you're* the one who should be—"

"—you can't be serious, you'll just make things—"

Expletives assaulted his ears. Words he hadn't heard in a long time felt like salt on wounds. From cursing to invitations to suck one thing or another and back to cursing they went, bickering and yelling.

And somehow, Lenk started laughing.

He wasn't sure why. It wasn't funny. But somehow, the idea that this, at the eve of destruction, should be just like none of them had ever left each other and they should all be close to strangling each other and leaving nothing for Khoth-Kapira to kill…

Well, what else could he do?

The others, though, perhaps resenting his intrusion on their anger, turned their glares on him. He held his hands up, smiling.

"Sorry, sorry." He shook his head. "I don't mean to laugh, but…" He rubbed his neck. "I mean, you're all right. Gariath's a murderer, Denaos is dead, Dreadaeleon's…. Dreadaeleon, and we're all fucked. But it's you"—he pointed to Denaos—"you're the one who's most right."

"So you agree with me that Kataria *does* smell like—"

"No, not that. The other part, about being born to trouble." He looked around his companions, dirty and beaten and half or fully dead. "All this time, I've been trying to put this down." He patted the hilt of his sword. "And every single time I try, everything gets worse. I just keep making more corpses, more blood, more trouble.

"And maybe that's all we've got to give, anyway." He stared at his feet as though they were going to give him an answer that everything else had failed. "Maybe, for all we do, more corpses is just what we make. Seems a little fucking late to go trying to deny it now, doesn't it?"

He looked up at his companions.

"Doesn't it?"

Denaos pointedly looked away. Dreadaeleon opened his mouth like he had an answer but said nothing. Asper simply gritted her teeth and glared at Gariath, who stared off somewhere different. And Kataria...

She looked at him. Right through his skin, like she was watching this realization crawl its way out of him.

"Yeah," he said. "The time to pretend is over, isn't it? We can't go acting like we weren't made for situations like this, like we don't go looking for them. Otherwise, we'd put down our weapons right now and leave, like anyone sane would."

He inhaled, held a sour breath in his mouth.

"I'm not leaving." He spoke more to himself than to them. "I've tried that already. It always ends in fighting, anyway. So... I'll fight. I'm not leaving." He looked to his companions. "But you can. I made this problem. I don't quite know what I'm going to do to try to solve this. I don't have a clue what *you* could do to solve it, either. I barely know that I can hurt him and I know you can't."

He gestured toward the direction of the city gates.

"If you're staying, you're stupid. But if you're going, you should go now. When the time comes... when Khoth-Kapira comes... I'll be waiting right in this spot for him." He held out his hands. "And either you'll be here or you won't."

Not his best speech.

But when had he ever had a good one?

Speeches were for heroes, after all: brave generals addressing great troops, prophets making declarations to the faithful, the right people at the right moment saying exactly the right thing.

His moment had come and gone and he had done exactly the wrong thing in it. He was no hero. He was just a man with a sword.

He thought his speech, at least, got that much across. He thought his speech, at least, would convince them to run.

But he was their leader, once. And if he was a moron for staying, they were fools for following him. So he was a little shocked that they didn't leave.

"I'll be here," Asper said.

He was a little shocked that they spoke.

"I'll be here," Dreadaeleon said.

And he was very shocked that he found himself smiling at it.

"I'll be here," Gariath growled.

And when he felt a hand on his, when he looked to his side and saw her there, somehow things didn't feel quite as hopeless as he'd said they would be.

"I'll be here," Kataria said.

Denaos glanced around them. His smile came so easy that Lenk almost could believe he wasn't dead. He shrugged.

"Well," he said. "I had nothing better to do, anyway."

"Then we'll stand together," Lenk said. "One last time, like we used to. And when Khoth-Kapira comes, we'll be ready."

Asper nodded grimly. A morbid smile creased Gariath's lips. Dreadaeleon's eyes flared in anticipation. Kataria's ears twitched excitedly. Denaos cleared his throat.

"Great..." he said. "So, uh...what do you want to do until then?"

Lenk opened his mouth, but found no answer. He exchanged various dumbfounded glances with the others as a long, awkward silence passed. When it was broken, it was by the uncouth sound of Kataria's belly growling as she scratched herself, sniffed, and looked to Lenk.

"Get some curry?"

FORTY-FOUR

A Feast for the Damned

It wasn't when the gods answered no prayers that Asper got irritated. If they were just totally silent, she could simply dismiss them and get on with her life.

It was when they answered *just* enough to make her doubt their un-existence that she got irritated. When they didn't answer the big prayers but answered just a few of the little ones.

Such as finding a functioning curry shop in the middle of a down-trodden, war-torn city like Savadan's Spicy Dishes.

"Don't get me wrong," Asper said as she watched the man ladle a hot mixture of spiced chicken and thick red sauce over a bowl of rice. "I'm pleased you're here and I applaud your entrepreneurial spirit, but...you know...there *is* a gigantic demon-god-king approaching the city, intent on destroying or enslaving all life as we know it, even as we speak."

Savadi—Savadan's great-grandson, as he introduced himself—looked up from his bowl. "How gigantic?" he asked.

"Colossal," Asper said. "Big enough to flatten your store with one foot."

"That's pretty big," Savadi said, returning to the task of arranging the bowl.

"Yes." Asper blinked. "Yes, it is. It would be smarter to leave now."

"It would be."

"Like *right now*."

"I know."

"So...can I ask?" Asper didn't wait for an answer before slamming her hands down on the counter. "Why are you still here?"

Savadi looked at her like she had just spoken another language. "It's my great-grandpa's shop."

"Yes, and it's about to be stomped on."

"My father left it to me, as his did to him, since Savadan opened it. I can't just leave it. Where would I go?"

"Muraska? Karneria? Somewhere not about to be destroyed?"

He shook his head. "This shop has seen the fashas, the Jackals, the Uprising, the Khovura, and outlasted them all. I am certain that this demon is not so big as you are describing."

"There isn't a word in *any* description for how big he is! You *need* to leave."

"I cannot take four generations with me. I cannot take the promise I made with me. If I am to die here, then I will die where my fathers have and be buried, as well, even if I am simply a greasy smear on the street." Savadi smiled, offering her the bowl. "One bowl. Extra raisins. That will be five zan."

Once payment was made and customary curses had been offered, Asper stalked toward the only table remaining in the shop—the others, along with much crockery and iron, had been looted ages ago. Her rage was such that she hardly noticed who else was sitting there until she slammed herself down into the chair, dropped the bowl onto the table, and began to angrily shovel food into her mouth.

Dreadaeleon's burning eyes did not leave much room for distaste, yet he managed it, anyway.

"Something on your mind?" he asked, wincing.

She shot him an angry glare, thrusting her fork at him. "Don't. Don't you fucking start."

He opened his mouth to reply but—perhaps for the first time—seemed to think better of it. He fell silent, his eyes dropping to the curry bowl before him. Asper was grateful for this. At least, until her thoughts started kicking in.

Just one, she thought to herself. *Just one stupid motherfucking curry-monger and I couldn't even save him. The gods-damned Prophet can't even convince one guy to save himself.*

She ate, though she could barely taste the food. And when she looked down at the remains of her curry, she found she wasn't hungry anymore. She merely pushed a bit of chicken around with her fork.

Just one thing, she said. *Just one little fucking thing is all I want to go right. Okay, maybe not always little. But aren't I entitled to something good happening?*

"You shouldn't have stopped me."

The words came out before she knew them. But when she looked up at Dreadaeleon, she knew she meant them. And, by the look of his frown, he did, too.

"You should have let me kill Gariath," she said. "The people he killed are owed that much."

She waited for him to give her an excuse—to say something smarmy and smug, to say something stupid—anything to give her the chance to punch him in his greasy face. She waited a long time before he answered.

"I know."

Not what she had been expecting, but it didn't rule out the opportunity of punching him.

"He's killed hundreds and will kill hundreds more, given the chance," the boy said. "He's dangerously unhinged on his best days and he hasn't had a good day in a long time. It would make sense to kill him now."

"Then why?" she roared, shooting to her feet. "Why did you stop me? Why couldn't you let me have done just *one* good thing?"

Dreadaeleon looked up at her. "I could do it for you, if you'd like."

She narrowed her eyes. "What?"

"He's just outside the door." He gestured toward the shop's exit. "I could do it without even getting up." He held up a single finger. "One finger, I can crush him like an insect."

"That would be—"

"Two fingers..." He held up another digit. "And I can level this entire street. I'd leave nothing behind but bone and ash, if you wished." He held up one more finger. "Or how about three? I could wipe out the next six streets, too, if you wanted to be extra certain he's dead."

Dreadaeleon had only ever been as complicated a man as a boy could be. That was, he wore his expressions plainly, made his intentions obvious, and was never more apparent than when he was trying to sound mysterious.

And perhaps it was just the ever-burning fire in his eyes that made it seem so, but Asper found him impossible to read now. He stared at her, completely expressionless, as though he were seriously awaiting an answer.

The only one she gave was a steady stare and a few soft words.

"Dread," she whispered. "What happened to you?"

He lowered his hand and turned away. "Nothing I can tell you. Not in any way that would make you understand. Suffice to say, I have come to understand the price of power. No action can be taken without proportionate reaction, and the greater the action taken, the greater the response until..."

He wiggled five fingers. Flames danced across the tips.

"I'm fairly sure that was the first lesson my old Lector ever taught me. I wonder why I never remembered it."

He looked up at Asper and smiled wearily.

"I could still do it, mind you. But it would have a repercussion. I don't know what that would be, but it would be big. So big that you might not even begin to see it happening until it's already there. Still... if you really want, I'll do it right now, if you can answer me one question."

She folded her arms and stared at him evenly.

"Do you remember what I asked you?" he asked. "The last time we saw each other? I spoke of a girl in a bathhouse. Do you remember her name?"

Asper squinted, searched her memory before it surfaced.

"Liaja."

"She's still in the city, in the square on the western edge of the Souk. I want her to..." He paused, staring down at his hands. "I would like it if you could get her out of here. Assuming the impossible happens and we win. Or the predictable happens and we lose. Just... promise me you'll do your best to save her."

He looked back at her. His face was empty.

"And I will kill anyone you want."

Asper had never studied the finer points of wizardry, save that she knew that all the power it offered came with a price. Magic altered the body, the blood, burned these as fuel until it left behind only withered husks that had once been wizards.

Nothing she had heard of had ever said what it did to the soul.

Whatever Dreadaeleon had given up to achieve whatever it was that he was now, it had been something important, something so crucial that he hadn't even known how badly he needed it. But it was plain in the emptiness on his face, the sincerity in his voice.

He really would burn this whole city down just for one woman.

Perhaps he knew the insanity of that thought. And perhaps that was why he'd requested that she go and deliver this woman, Liaja, to safety rather than doing it himself.

Perhaps he feared what she would say if she could see the face Asper was seeing now.

And perhaps, then, sparing her that horror, saving her from this hell of a city, would be the one good thing the gods would allow Asper to do.

"Forget it." She sighed, sitting back down. "I'll find her." She met Dreadaeleon's stare. "I promise."

He nodded as she dug into her curry again, pausing to glance suspiciously at him and his untouched bowl. "Aren't you going to eat?"

"No." He smiled. "I did before I got here."

<hr />

When Kataria had first seen Gariath, the dragonman had his claws around Lenk's throat. She was ready to put an arrow in him right then, but two things had stopped her. The first being that she wagered an arrow probably wouldn't stop him and the second...

It had been hard to describe, at the time, but there was a moment's hesitation that came from seeing him. He had been snarling about human cruelties, human crimes. And at that time, she hadn't known Lenk long enough to know him from any other human.

It had been a fleeting and peculiar feeling, but for a moment, there was a sort of kinship with the dragonman.

They had nurtured this, quietly and without words, over the months; the two nonhumans in a group of round-ears. There was unspoken trust between them.

That had been long ago. He had been different back then, as had she. And while some things had changed, others stayed the same. As she squatted down beside the curry shop door, absently shoveling her food into her mouth, he loomed beside her, staring out into nothing, saying nothing.

These were nice moments with him.

Moments when he didn't open his big, stupid mouth.

"I can smell your shame."

Those moments didn't come around so much anymore.

"You reek of it."

She didn't bother looking up at him. She could already feel his black gaze upon her, hard and sharp like a stone knife, even when he wasn't trying to be cruel. She merely chewed on another chunk of chicken and spoke through a full mouth.

"What's it smell like?" she asked.

"Stale water, salt drying on stone," he said. "It pours off you."

She shut one eye. She raised one leg. She let out a long, loud fart.

"How about now?" she asked.

This time, she did look at him. And it was with morbid pride that she noted the curl of his nostrils and his lips.

"You disgust me," he growled.

"Don't inhale next time."

"I have known you were a coward for a long time now, sitting away and firing sticks while I do the true fighting. I had thought it a symptom of your own stupidity, a quirk." He snorted. "And now I discover your whole people are like that."

She sniffed, looked away. "That's awfully judgy coming from a guy who just got his army killed."

"Because of you." He slammed a fist against the shop's wall. When he pulled it away, splinters were lodged in his skin. "A handful of shicts, scrawny and puny, and hundreds died." He snarled. "And you did nothing to stop it."

Kataria chewed her curry, swallowed, and licked her lips before answering. "What should I have done, then, if you're so smart?"

"Stop them."

"How?"

"Kill them."

"All of them?"

"As many as it took." He shook his head, snarling. "You knew, didn't you? You knew they were coming."

"I did," she said.

"And you didn't warn me. You didn't—"

"No, I didn't." She shot him a glare. "Would you have listened?"

"I would have known."

"You would have. And you'd still have charged in, dumb as a fucking post. Everyone would *still* be dead." She tossed her bowl away, rice and chicken spattering across the stones. "You think I haven't run this over a thousand times in my head already? You think I *don't* wonder what would have happened if I *had* tried?"

"Why didn't you?" he snared.

"Because of *him*, you moron!"

She all but exploded to her feet. Despite him standing feet taller, she rose up to him. Despite him outweighing her by hundreds, she shoved him. Despite his teeth being so much bigger, she bared her canines at him and she snarled.

"Because I *always* choose him. Every single fucking time. I always do it, I always feel like shit for doing it, and then I always do it again. And I'm fucking *tired* of that middle part."

She spit onto the ground. Her ears flattened against her head. She scowled down at her feet.

"Yeah, I did it. I let your army die. I let Asper's army die. I let my people go make themselves into murderers. And I did it for him."

She stared up at him, right into those stone-knife eyes.

"And because I did, he's alive. I chose him. I chose to save him. And at least one person is alive because of me." She met his stare and she did not blink. "How many are alive because of you, Gariath?"

She expected him to strangle her right there. Or maybe snap her like a branch and toss either half of her aside. Or perhaps he'd just open his mouth a little wider and bite out her throat right then and there.

That would all be fine, she thought.

If he killed her right now, she would die as the only shict, the only woman, the only person on this dark earth who had ever struck Gariath, killer of monsters and men, totally speechless.

And for a moment, as his body tensed and his hands curled up into fists, she thought that was just what he was about to do. She gritted her teeth, she met his scowl, and she did not turn away.

The blow came.

Again and again, his fist rose and fell.

And with each blow, red smears blossomed.

He continued to hit the side of the shop, until there was a deep dent in the wood and splinters were lodged in his skin and his blood painted the wall. And when he could hit no more, he snarled, he roared, he cursed the shop for not falling down when he needed it to.

And when his voice had been exhausted, he let loose a great, heavy breath and slumped to the stones.

"There was someone I could have killed." His voice came out on a ragged breath. "Someone I could have broken. I could have killed someone and stopped this."

"That's not how it works."

"That's *always* how it works."

"Not this time, you dumbshit," she grunted. "It never did work. We've just been killing this whole time hoping it was going to get better and lead to something else, but it hasn't. And if all I get to walk away from this with is just one person, just…" She winced, as though it hurt to say. "Just him. Then that's what I'll take."

She stalked to where she had left her bow and quiver and snatched them up. She walked back to him and looked down at him. He hadn't looked this small before.

"There's going to be a lot of dead bodies when this is all done," she said. "You're welcome to all of them, if you want. But me?" She looked at her bow in her hand and frowned. "I'm either walking out of here alive with him…or we're both going to be two more corpses out there."

Gariath stared down at his hands, bloody and laden with splinters. He unfurled his fists and looked at his claws.

"And I," he whispered, "I will—"

"I don't give a shit what you do," she said, interrupting him. She reached down and snatched up the wooden bowl in front of him. "And give me your curry."

With that, she stalked away.

The first time she had met Gariath, she had thought an arrow, maybe even a hundred arrows, wouldn't stop him. And now, the last time she thought she would ever see him, she could hardly believe he had been stopped by just a few words.

They were different now.

But that was a worry for a woman with more shits to give and less curry to eat.

——◆——

It had started simply enough: just two men eating curry silently. Lenk wasn't sure at what point he had started staring at his companion. But it was fairly evident when his staring became noticed.

Denaos sighed. He speared a forkful of curry and spoke through a full mouth.

"Go ahead and ask."

"Can you even *taste* that?" Lenk asked.

"Eh." Denaos shrugged. "Not really."

"So, why do it?"

"It's nice to pretend to be normal sometimes." Denaos stared down at his bowl of curry. A sad smile crept across his features. "You know the worst part?"

Lenk had never really found Denaos's grin unsettling before that moment.

"I can remember it." Denaos ran his finger along the inside of the bowl. "I remember the thickness of it, the way it feels going down, the spiciness of it. I remember the first time I had it, when I was fresh off the boat from Muraska. Thought I'd shit my innards out the first time, but after that, I couldn't get enough. I ate it as often as I could. But now?"

He pulled back a finger stained with red sauce. He put it in his mouth, sucked it clean. He smacked his lips, staring out to somewhere far away.

"Nothing." He swirled the curry and rice about in his bowl, watching it thoughtfully. "It's like I'm always halfway there, but I can't quite make it all the way. I remember how everything's *supposed* to work, but no matter how hard I try to make it, it just…doesn't."

Denaos was a man who had routinely slit throats, poisoned drinks, tortured people for information, and spun lies as easily as spiders spin silk for as long as Lenk had known him. Yet all that grisly business was not half so uncomfortable to watch as Denaos being serious. The rogue had a face ill-suited for frowns and sorrow, and its colorless pallor made him look even worse.

"I'm sorry," Lenk whispered. "I should have done something, I should—"

"Don't." Denaos fixed him with a dark-eyed glare. "I believe Asper when she says it because she means it. You're just trying to make yourself feel better."

"That's not true."

"Relax." Denaos waved a hand. "That's what she does. She saves people, bleeds for the poor and the sick, always thinks of others. You know." He took another bite of curry. "Like a moron. But you and me, we're not like that."

"Bullshit," Lenk said. "I've saved plenty of people."

"So have I. But you and I both know that it's simply incidental. You and I, we kill monsters. If someone gets saved, then hey great, that's a bonus. But our talents have always lain in putting pointy bits into soft bits." He grinned at Lenk. "Haven't they?"

Lenk thought to protest that, to insist he had always tried his hardest. But his mouth was too full of curry to allow room for that much bullshit. He merely swallowed and sighed.

"Yeah..." He looked down from their perch atop the curry shop's roof. "Yeah."

The streets lay empty and broken. This neighborhood had seen some of the worst fighting, with its roads scarred by fire and its windows shattered. The curry shop seemed to be the only person, let alone business, still around.

For this, you're going to die tomorrow, he told himself. *Is it worth it?*

He looked down at the bowl in his hands and considered.

It *was* pretty good curry.

"If it will soothe you..." Denaos's whisper returned him from his reverie. "You could have had all the gods on your side and a magic wand that shot fire from one end and pissed whiskey from the other and it wouldn't have made a difference."

Denaos held out his fingerless hand and wriggled the stumps.

"This...was a long time coming."

"This?"

"Well, maybe not *this*, exactly, but I knew I wasn't going to end up somewhere nice when this was all over. Fuck, I knew it after the first throat I cut." He leaned back onto his elbows, stared out over the city, and frowned. "But I didn't stop, then, either."

There were moments in a man's life, Lenk's grandfather had once told him, where one simply knew something was a bad idea. To open a door when one heard a knock late at night, to follow a shadow out into a storm, to turn down an alley one had just heard a scream from; these were things it was safer not to do.

And what separated wise men from foolish men was the wisdom not to do them.

Lenk's grandfather had taken a puff on his pipe, contemplative, and spoken once more.

"And what separates men like us from both of them is that we do them, anyway."

And so, even though he knew he shouldn't, Lenk asked.

"What did you see?"

Denaos's face, already colorless, simply seemed to fade away. The ghosts of his grins and his frowns vanished and left behind something white and empty as a field of salt. He stared at something far away, something he would always be able to see, no matter how hard he shut his eyes.

"It's funny," the rogue whispered. "It was always said that, when you go, if you've paid your debts and didn't squeal on anyone on your way out, Silf opens his hall to you and you're awash in wine and whores for eternity. That sounded nice and all, but I liked the Talanite version."

"What's that?"

"Asper told me once..." He closed his eyes. "It's a very big, very blue sky. Your worries about coins, about the bad things you've done, about the people you've let down, simply slide off you and you start to float there."

Lenk nodded. "That does sound nice."

"But when I went under..." Denaos's voice grew so hushed that Lenk had to strain to hear it over the murmur of the breeze. "I saw Asper. And you. And the others. I saw all the things we had done and all the people we killed and all the ale we drank and times we cursed each other out and the jokes I told and the times you laughed. And I saw them..." He reached out with his fingerless hand, as if to grab something that wasn't there. "Just getting smaller. And smaller. And smaller."

He dropped his hand, still staring.

"And the last thing I saw was her face...and then she got so small, I couldn't see her anymore."

Lenk stared at him for a moment. "And then?"

"And then...nothing."

"Darkness?"

"Did I say darkness?"

"You said nothing."

"And I meant nothing." Denaos shook his head. "What do Khetashe-ans say happens when you die?"

"My grandfather had two different answers, depending on how much he'd had to drink," Lenk replied. "In one, we waited in the earth until the Wanderer passed our graves and then we rose to follow him across the world. In the other, we got stuck in a hole in the ground and stayed there until we were wormshit."

Denaos lofted his brows. "Huh. Which was the one where he was sober?"

"I can't remember."

The two men remained silent for a long time, quietly eating their curry. When there was no more curry, Lenk scraped the last few traces of sauce from his bowl. When there was no more sauce, he simply kept scraping.

He looked up at Denaos and opened his mouth to speak but found his heart lodged in his throat. Even trying to find the words caused a deep pain to resonate in his chest. And this time, Lenk did not think he had to strength to overcome them and ask.

"I don't know if that's what'll happen to you when you die."

Denaos, however, answered anyway.

"Maybe that's what happens to men like us," the rogue said. "Maybe that's hell for us. We spend all our lives making a big, bloody mess so the gods will notice us and then ... nothing." He sniffed. "Still ..."

He turned his eyes toward Lenk. And in them, Lenk saw a vast, yawning nothingness that he dared not meet for too long.

"If you're worried," he said, "it's never too late to run."

The thought was tempting. He had tried fighting. He had tried not fighting. He had never tried simply running. Turning, dropping every-thing, running for the gate and continuing to run until this all seemed like a terrible dream.

Khoth-Kapira could take this wretched city; it was a hellhole, any-way. The world could rot and wither under endless war; there was more earth than people and they couldn't be everywhere. He could find a place where he would be safe, where he could live in peace.

But that thought, tempting as it was, sat ill with him.

Because, he realized, it wasn't his peace he was concerned with.

Not anymore.

"It is," Lenk sighed. He looked out over Cier'Djaal, to the distant gate. "Maybe it always was." He set a hand down on the sword at his side. "It was me who couldn't put down the sword, me who couldn't stop killing, me who made this whole shitty mess we're in. I can't run away from myself."

"Yeah." Denaos echoed his sigh. "I guess you can't."

"In the end . . ." Lenk turned to his friend and offered him a smile, as warm as he could make it. "If we die for each other, then that's something, isn't it?"

Denaos looked back at him, blank. "Something shitty, maybe."

Lenk frowned. "But you said—"

"Yeah, you clod, I was brutally murdered and returned to a nightmarish hell of an unliving existence so I could teach you about the magic of friendship."

"Well, don't fucking yell at me, I was trying to make this nice for both of us."

They fell into another silence. Lenk glanced at Denaos's curry. The rogue grunted and handed the bowl over to him. He stirred the dish around with his fork for a moment.

"So," he said, "you say the last thing you saw was her face?"

Denaos nodded. "Yeah."

Lenk speared a forkful of chicken and chewed it. He stared out over the city that he had destroyed and was about to die to try to save what was left. He nodded, sniffed.

"That doesn't sound too bad."

FORTY-FIVE

His Word

No speeches. No grand armies marching to war. No fire raining from the sky.

The end of the world began with one weary man with an unpolished sword walking out of a dark corner.

Beneath the endless gray clouds of the sky that slid overhead like ink from a spilled bottle, he walked into the graveyard where civilization had been buried. With the shattered stone crunching beneath his feet, Lenk counted his steps.

One...

Two...

Three...

And all the way to fifty-three, which took him to the center of the ruined market.

And there he stood. As the sunset's orange glow veiled itself behind the gray sheets, he stared out over the horizon of the city. He slid his sword out from its scabbard and tossed the leather to the ground. He sat down on the shattered stone. He laid the sword naked in his lap. He closed his eyes.

And Lenk began to wait.

An hour, perhaps. Or maybe just a few breaths. Too weary for fear, too nervous for courage, his thoughts were empty as he sat, hands on the steel of his weapon, and waited.

Until it happened.

Somewhere in the distance, a great sound of thunder. But it came not from the sky. The noise came from the earth. He felt its shudder in the stones beneath him, shaking his bones in his body.

One.

Stones shattered. The skeletons of burnt-out buildings toppled into ash. The last panes of glass cracked and broke and made glistening graveyards on the streets.

Two.

Rats fled across the roads in tides, swarming out toward the sea. The last gulls and ravens and carrion birds flew from their rookeries and disappeared into the great gray sky.

Three.

The sky let out a long and breathless moan. The clouds settled and grew dark overhead. A night bereft of stars or moon spread over the city as the wind groaned and clawed itself across the sky.

Three steps. That's all it took.

Lenk opened his eyes.

And Lenk looked up at the great darkness that spread across the sky.

Blacker than the night. Eyes empty and pale. A crown of serpents writhing, flashing ivory fangs with every excited hiss as they burst from his skull, his jaw, his neck. He stretched tall enough to scrape the heavens.

Though Lenk wondered if he had not seemed much bigger before.

Amid the rubble of the city and the destroyed buildings, Lenk thought he must have looked like one more piece of dirt: gray and grimy, run-down and broken. He would have felt it, too.

Were it not for Khoth-Kapira's great eyes focused intently on him.

The demon stared at him for a time. Then he looked up and cast his gaze out over the city. His serpents schooled after him, turning their bloodred gazes out toward the distant buildings.

"Listen."

His voice spoke not to Lenk. His voice spoke to the bones in Lenk's body, the blood in Lenk's veins, the skin drawn across Lenk's sinew. And Lenk could feel them respond.

"Can you hear them?" Khoth-Kapira boomed. *"Their prayers? Their cries?"*

Lenk looked up at the great demon without rising.

"What do they say?" he asked.

"They weep for their loved ones. They weep for the tragedies they have seen." He closed his eyes, content. *"They look to me and beg me to save them."*

Lenk nodded, slowly.

"I believe that. I did the same thing, once."

"And did I not give you what you asked for? Did I not give you the peace you craved? Would I not have given you everything, had you not been so ungrateful?"

"I believed that, too."

Khoth-Kapira stared down at him, his baleful eyes growing so wide that they almost drank the night. Lenk had to squint to see past them, to the dark creature they belonged to. To remember he was here to kill this thing.

"So much potential," the demon bellowed. *"You could have been there, at the start of this new world. I would have given you everything you would want and things you did not even know you needed."*

"You still would." He rose to his feet and took his sword up in his hands. "Am I right? If I asked you right now to give me those things, you would."

The silence of Khoth-Kapira's response was deafening.

"But you can't. Now I know what you're really offering. And what you give isn't for me. It's for you. It's always been for you."

"And because of this... this horrid blasphemy you believe, now, you have come to battle me?"

"No." Lenk shook his head. "I've come to kill you."

In the stories, the great villains would bellow at such a threat. They would laugh and gloat and spew dramatic lines denying how any creature so small could ever hurt them, thus setting the stage for their inevitable defeat.

But Khoth-Kapira was ancient. He had read those stories. He was something greater than those demons.

And at Lenk's words, something trembled in the darkness of his features. Something too young and too tender to belong on a demon so old. His frown was bare, but on a creature so massive, it spoke magnitudes.

For he did not look upon a creature so small. He looked upon a man who had so many sorrows to be soothed, so many agonies to be healed. A man who would believe any lie, any tale, any promise, so long as it answered his problem. A man who, even with all this, still denied him.

Khoth-Kapira stared down at his tiny, greatest failure.

And, with a sorrowful sort of reverence, he raised his foot and prepared to crush him.

"*I am sorry,*" he said. "*For everything.*"

"As am I," Lenk said. "But just for this."

The screams came as one: the great avian shriek and the howl accompanying it. The scraw followed, dark wings across the dark sky as the beast came shooting out from the ruins and swooping toward the demon.

Khoth-Kapira looked up and beheld a great fire flying across the sky.

Flame erupted across the demon's face in sheets, licking at his eyes with red tongues. Khoth-Kapira roared and staggered, his colossal foot coming down as Lenk ran for cover. The impact of his stomp shook Lenk from his feet and buried him beneath a wave of dust.

He rolled to his back, looked up, and saw that Khoth-Kapira's eyes were no longer on him. The demon snarled, trying to swat away Colonel MacSwain as the creature flew in circles around him. Dreadaeleon's coattails flapped in the wind as he hurled fire at the demon. And at the beast's reins, her eyes bright and ferocious in the gloom, Kataria spurred the scraw around the demon's head as his crown of serpents lashed out with gaping jaws.

Khoth-Kapira bellowed, "*Do not bring them into this. Their deaths will be on your hands.*"

That was only half-true, Lenk knew. He shouldn't have brought them into this.

"Get up," a voice rumbled behind him.

But they had been insistent.

A red claw grabbed him by the shoulder, hoisting him up and off his feet. Gariath glanced over him, dangling from his grasp, and, seeing that he wasn't quite dead yet, snorted.

"Ready?" the dragonman asked.

Lenk nodded, gripped his sword.

"Ready."

"Good."

Gariath swung the young man around to his back. Lenk wrapped his arms about the dragonman's neck as Gariath fell to all fours and took off at a run. They charged together through the clouds of dust roiling out as Khoth-Kapira raised a massive foot. He picked up speed, rushing beneath a great shadow as the demon brought it down again. The earth shook as shards of stone rained down upon them, but Gariath did not falter.

Their goal was in sight. Khoth-Kapira's ankle loomed tremendous before them.

The dragonman snarled, leapt, found purchase on the demon's heel. As blasts of fire lit up the night sky overhead, he clawed his way up, hand over hand, across the demon's flesh.

Khoth-Kapira did not seem to notice. Why would he, Lenk thought? It wasn't as though Gariath could have hurt him with claws ten feet long. Nor was it likely that Dreadaeleon's flames did anything more than annoy him. A distraction was all this was, and a fleeting one at that; Khoth-Kapira already was starting to study the scraw's flight. It wouldn't be long before he intercepted the beast, Kataria, and Dreadaeleon and crushed them all in a breath.

But a breath was all Lenk needed.

Gariath clawed his way up to the demon's knee and gripped firmly. The great tendons of Khoth-Kapira's leg bulged. One blow to sever them, one more to send him toppling over, and this colossal immortal demon would be merely immortal. Lenk raised his sword.

Aimed.

Thrust.

Khoth-Kapira staggered, roaring as a blaze struck his eyes. Gariath was shifted from his grip and slid down the demon's calf. Lenk jammed his sword into the flesh for purchase, finding only thick muscle instead of sinew.

But if the scream that followed—along with the great gout of black blood—was any indication, it didn't tickle.

"VERMIN!"

Khoth-Kapira's hand followed his bellow. Lenk looked up to see the dark shape descending upon them. He swung, feebly, as the great palm enveloped him and Gariath both. There was a sudden lurching sensation as he was swept up into the air, miles high.

When Khoth-Kapira's hand opened, his eyes loomed large as moons as they narrowed on Lenk. His serpents hissed in irritation, both them and their master no longer paying attention to the fire raining down upon them.

"*Ingratitude,*" he roared. "*Ignorance. Be free of them both.*"

And, with a sound like stone groaning, his great hand began to close.

Shadow fell over Lenk as the fingers curled over onto him. He crouched, looking desperately around as they crushed down upon him. He shut his eyes tight, gripped his sword, and waited for the end.

It did not come.

"*Fucking... move...*"

A curse did, though.

Behind him, Gariath loomed. His back was pressed against Khoth-Kapira's colossal thumb, his feet on the demon's largest two fingers, his legs trembling as he fought to keep them from closing in. His eyes strained with the effort, teeth clenched as he spit out a word.

"*GO.*"

Lenk took up his sword and took off, sliding down Khoth-Kapira's palm. He ducked beneath the demon's smaller two fingers as they came closing down upon him. He slid to the heel of the demon's palm, then glanced up as a pair of eyes burst bright red in the darkness.

A serpent, its jaws half as big as he was, lashed out, fangs flashing ivory. He swung, catching it by its cheek and drawing forth a gout of black blood. Even as it recoiled with a shriek, another launched itself forward, and another and another as he swung wildly to keep them at bay.

"*NOW!*" Gariath roared behind him. There was the sound of a bone popping.

No more time. Lenk took up his sword in both hands and jammed it down between his legs. He found a thick vein in Khoth-Kapira's wrist and twisted the blade.

Khoth-Kapira's scream shook creation.

His arm went flailing. Gariath flew from the demon's grip with a howl. Lenk only barely noticed as the dragonman disappeared into the dust and darkness below. He was busy holding on to his sword to keep from following his companion.

Yet it wasn't enough. Khoth-Kapira's hand snapped forward, tearing the sword free from his vein and dislodging Lenk. The young man was sure he was screaming, but he couldn't hear it over the sound of wind howling as he went plummeting headfirst toward the earth below.

He came to a sudden halt with the distinct feeling of his guts ramming against his skull. Yet as those guts didn't then explode *out* of that skull, he was fairly sure something had gone right.

The air shimmered around him. He was yanked out of the sky by an invisible force, twisted upright, and pulled onto a hairy back. Dreadaeleon's eyes burned in the darkness behind him as Kataria's hair whipped into his face. Colonel MacSwain grunted at the sudden addition of weight but didn't protest.

"What the fuck just happened?" he screamed.

"You're welcome," Dreadaeleon replied.

"Gariath," he cried out. "He fell! Did you get him?"

"I didn't see him," Kataria shouted to be heard over the wind as she wheeled the scraw around. "What did you do to the demon?"

"Stabbed him," he shouted back.

"Did it work?"

Khoth-Kapira let out another scream. The great demon stared at the wound in his wrist, the blood gushing forth. In truth, it was not so great a wound as to be fatal, nor even injurious. Yet the terror shone plainly even in eyes as empty as his.

The God-King had not thought he could even feel pain anymore.

"I'd say so." Lenk's eyes drifted down to the city streets. His blood ran cold. "Too well."

Even through the darkness, he could see them. Pouring like a river of flesh, gushing out of the alleys, and trickling down the streets. Twisted and malformed, loping on elongated limbs, fanged mouths craned open in terrified screams, and desperate, yellow eyes turned skyward for their wounded master.

The Chosen, in all their abhorrent panic, were rushing to their master's aid.

"You didn't say he had those!" Kataria snarled. "Did you not think it would come up or what?"

"I will handle it."

Dreadaeleon, by contrast, spoke calmly. And, just as calmly, he stood up on the scraw's back and let himself drop from the beast to plummet into the darkness before Lenk could even say a word.

Not that there was much he could say. Or do. Dreadaeleon had made his choice as clearly as Gariath had. They were beyond his reach, as was everything except the sword in his hand and the demon looming before him.

He moved forward on the scraw's back. He wrapped an arm around Kataria's waist and shouted.

"Bring me as close to the eyes as you can. We end this quick."

She grunted. One hand took her bow, another drew an arrow, and neither, Lenk noticed, was on the colonel's reins.

But he was beyond questioning her. She kicked the beast's flanks, spurring him faster. Khoth-Kapira's agony was short-lived. He looked up at the sight of the great, shrieking beast flying toward him, his eyes wide and bright.

There was no way Kataria could have missed.

Her arrows did not sing so much as curse. They spit hateful, angry slurs at the demon as they flew, one after the other, toward his eye. Even with the wind whipping and the scraw's erratic flight, more of them landed than missed. And though the arrows could never truly harm him, they did what they had to.

Khoth-Kapira snarled, turned away, and shut his eyes. His throat, a massive column of muscle and tendons, was exposed. Lenk hopped to his haunches on the scraw, ready to leap, his eyes locked intently on his target as Kataria kept her bow ready for the demon to show his face again.

Neither of them saw the hand coming.

In a great flood of air, Khoth-Kapira's palm came down. Lenk managed to look up just in time to scream a word of warning. Kataria, too absorbed in her aim, looked up too late.

The hand came down upon them. Colonel MacSwain shrieked as he was knocked from the sky. Lenk managed to grab onto one massive finger by pure luck and held on by pure grit. He clenched his teeth and held his eyes shut.

And when he opened them, Kataria was gone.

No.

He didn't have the breath to whisper the word, let alone scream it. He searched the darkness, the roiling clouds of dust and grime for anything, a flash of gold or of green or of...of...

Darkness.

Dust.

Nothing.

His voice left him. His body went numb. His mind followed. He had known the risks, as had she. They both agreed to them and yet...

Somehow, he never thought this would actually happen.

His grip slipped. He began to fall from the demon's finger. And, for a moment, he couldn't think of a reason not to let go.

And so he did.

And when he didn't plummet to join her, he became aware of a cold hand on his wrist. He looked up. Clinging to Khoth-Kapira's hand like a spider, Denaos looked down at him. His colorless face was set in a gentle smile he couldn't have managed in life.

"Not yet," he said. "Later. Okay?"

Lenk looked at the sword in his hand, stained with black blood. He looked back at his companion. He swallowed what felt like a rusty blade and nodded, stiffly.

"Okay."

"Great." Denaos shut his eyes. "Hang on."

"For wh—"

Lenk didn't finish it before he disappeared.

Darkness enveloped him, sweeping in from the corners of his vision like a shroud, so fast he didn't have time to scream. And when he did, no sound came out. Not until the darkness swept away.

And when it did, they were on Khoth-Kapira's arm, bent at the elbow. The great demon scowled down at them as though they were ants. His serpents hissed hungrily.

"There you are."

His other hand came down to crush them. Its great shadow drowned Lenk in darkness. But before it could, something darker still swept over him.

Silence. Emptiness. Nothingness.

Then it retreated and he was on the back of the demon's hand, Denaos still holding his wrist firmly. Khoth-Kapira snarled and brought his hand up. His serpents lashed out, jaws agape.

And they vanished again.

Darkness.

Light.

First on the hand.

Then the wrist.

Over and over, they leapt in and out of the gloom, disappearing and reappearing somewhere else each time. Khoth-Kapira's hands moved too slowly to catch him, his serpents too sluggish to keep up as they slipped further and further up the demon's body.

Until they finally appeared on his shoulder.

And Khoth-Kapira finally caught them.

The demon's hand was already crashing down by the time they reappeared; he had figured out where they were heading. The two men broke into a sprint, Denaos releasing Lenk's wrist as they tore across the great shoulder. Khoth-Kapira's hand came down. Lenk leapt, tumbled, scrambled back to his feet for purchase.

Denaos was nowhere to be seen. Had he disappeared? Been crushed? He couldn't know. He couldn't afford to think about him, or Kataria, or Gariath, or any of the people who were dead because of him.

No, he told himself. *Not because of you. For you. They did it for you.* He took his sword up in both hands. *Don't disappoint them.*

He charged up the demon's shoulder, intent on Khoth-Kapira's throat. He watched as the great column of flesh twisted. He saw the great baleful eyes narrow. He saw a massive mouth crane open, a maw full of teeth glisten, a long forked tongue lash out.

It shot against him. Barbs from the spongy flesh raked him, pierced through his clothes, sank into his flesh. He let out a cry, short-lived as the tongue immediately retracted and pulled Lenk toward the great, dark maw.

The sound of thunder behind him. Teeth slammed shut. Everything went black. He could feel his feet slipping beneath him on something slick and glistening. He could hear the sound of something ancient groaning from somewhere very deep. He felt the tongue tilt up beneath him, his feet sliding.

No time to think. He could only choose a direction, run.

And start cutting.

He thrust his sword into something thick and sinewy. He felt it resist, growing taut against his blade, until he finally felt it give. Black, cold ichor washed over him as his blade burst free on the other side. The great mouth opened, wind whipping around him as a scream tore itself free from Khoth-Kapira's throat.

His ears rang with the sound. His skin sizzled with the sensation of the blood washing over him. His grip was slippery. But he didn't care. He couldn't. He pushed forward, he pushed down, he cut his way out.

And pulled himself free out of the demon's cheek.

Grip slippery with blood, he skin and clothes torn, he pulled himself out of the jagged wound and looked up toward something big and white. Ignoring the pain, the foulness, he clawed his way up the demon's cheek, hooked a hand under his eyelid, and pulled himself up to the great white orb that widened as it beheld him.

And his terrible blade.

He jammed the sword deep into Khoth-Kapira's eye. The demon's head shot back with a scream that sent the clouds roiling. Lenk tumbled down his face, his lips, across the fanged mouth that snapped shut as he cleared it until he found a grip on one of the writhing serpents of his beard.

Lenk hung from it and saw his last target.

As agony pulled itself free from Khoth-Kapira's throat, the great muscles of the demon's neck tensed and fluctuated. And there, black and throbbing, he saw the creature's jugular.

The serpents slithered toward him, jaws gaping. He leapt from his perch, sword in hand. He fell upon Khoth-Kapira's throat. He raised his sword high, he gritted his teeth, he spit a curse.

He thrust.

He cut.

He tore a great hole in Khoth-Kapira's throat. The blood burst from it in gouts. And with it, the wind from Khoth-Kapira's screams. The demon's agony reverberated through his flesh, into his bones, threatened to shake him to pieces.

But he didn't stop.

He couldn't stop.

Gariath hadn't stopped. Denaos hadn't stopped. Dreadaeleon and Asper hadn't stopped.

Kataria...

If he could give the world only corpses, he would give her the biggest one he could.

But before he could finish the job, he felt a hand wrap around him. The sword was torn from his grasp and fell from his hands to join everyone else in the darkness below.

As if Lenk were simply some foul and dirty thing that Khoth-Kapira just wanted gone, the demon hurled him.

And he flew.

And disappeared into the endless dark.

FORTY-SIX

INVINCIBLE

Fire," he whispered.

And it was there. It flowed from Dreadaeleon's hands and washed over the malformed monstrosities pouring from the alleys and streets. They fell beneath its shrieking sheaves, their skin glistening and melting beneath its heat.

He turned and held a finger out.

"Lightning."

And it came to him. Dancing and cackling in a bolt that leapt from his finger to strike the nearest serpentine face. It leapt, branching off like a bright blue tree, to reach with crackling spears and impale more of the abominations, over and over, until ten of them collapsed, their eyes bulging from their sockets, steam pouring out of fanged maws pouring wide.

"Frost."

And there were clouds of white and red-stained icicles.

"Force."

And there were bones snapped with the flick of a wrist.

"Fly."

And there were bodies sent shrieking into the sky, flung far and wide.

There was no barrier between thought and power, no language of magic, no toll of body and mind. It flowed as cleanly through him as rain fell from the sky. And with each wave of his hand, each whisper from his lips, more came. More flame, more ice, more thunder.

The power was limitless.

"Fucking shit, would you *stop* showing off?"

Their numbers, however, were not.

Asper stood before him, her shield upraised and shaking as one of the monstrosities raked a long claw down its metal face. She lashed out with her blade, hewing its hand from its wrist. It let out a shriek and recoiled, only to be replaced by another mad-eyed creature clawing over its wounded companion to get at her.

She took a step back, holding the creature at bay with her shield as its long limbs tried to reach around it. She cast a furious, wide-eyed snarl over her shoulder.

"Anytime now."

Funny, he thought. That look used to bother him quite a bit.

But now, he barely even noticed it. He simply raised a hand, leveled a finger at the creature, and whispered.

"Li—"

Boy.

The thought struck him like a glass bottle, left a shard lodged in his mind. It threw him off. He blinked, suddenly not quite remembering how the word was spoken, how the power flowed.

"DREAD!"

"Light... *LIGHTNING!*"

He stammered the word, spit the spell. The bolt of electricity burst from his hand with such force that it knocked him to his rear. It almost sheared off Asper's head, her hair standing on end as it tore across the sky and struck the monstrosity clawing over her shield square in the jaw.

The beast fell. The others recoiled, shrieking back into the darkness. Asper, however, looked no more impressed.

"If you're going to kill me, next time do it faster," she snarled. "That way, you'll at least only disappoint me once."

"I... I'm sorry..." The power had come easily, but now he struggled for the words. "I thought I was going to..."

To what? To simply wave your hand and make it all better? Or to make a very loud noise?

A laugh rang out inside his head. He knew it.

Or can you even tell the difference anymore?

"No time." Asper was already moving past him, rushing into the darkness. "Come on. They'll be back at it before long."

He staggered to his feet and hurried after her. The things had emerged suddenly, pouring out from every shadow, their yellow eyes lighting up the darkness like stars in the night, their claws pulling their emaciated, gangly bodies along like hounds. He didn't even have a name for them before he had a fear of them.

They were mortal—or at least, fire and lightning killed them as surely as a mortal. But they were everywhere. And even now, he could hear them in the gloom surrounding them: shrieking, screaming, wailing inconsolably a name he didn't know.

"Up ahead!" Asper shouted. "The gate!"

An archway loomed, leading into the Souk. Narrow and cramped, it was defensible enough, but it would offer no escape should the monstrosities overwhelm them.

One of the beasts leapt out from the alley nearby, reaching for him with impossibly long arms. He snapped his fingers. The air shimmered and the thing went flying, shrieking into the air.

Come, then, old man, he told himself. *Being overwhelmed seems a little unlikely, doesn't it?*

"Old man?" Is that what you call yourself?

The voice. That glass shard of a thought. Not his.

Is that supposed to be funny? Or just—

"Over here!"

Asper was at the gate, her shield up and bright even in the night, her sword flashing. She stood firm as he rushed behind her, a bulwark against the darkness, which even now began to light up with a hundred unblinking yellow eyes.

"If they get past us," she said, "that's it for Lenk. We hold them off until he finishes what he's going to do."

"Keep them back," Dreadaeleon said, nodding. "I'll handle the rest."

"Me doing the hard part while you make a bunch of loud noises and flashy lights?" She looked over her shoulder. Through the grime covering her face, her smile was white and big. "Just like old times, eh?"

And despite all that had happened before—her many insults, all the things she had said, all the things he had thought—and the very imminent doom lingering around them, he found that he couldn't help but smile back.

It *was* like old times.

Back when all this was simple.

He had wanted to impress her back then, too. He had wanted her to respect him, his power, all he could do. The only difference was now he actually could.

"MASTER!"

They came again, pouring out of the shadows. Crawling over each other, slavering, reaching and shrieking and stumbling in their desperation to reach them. They didn't even seem to appear to notice the woman and wizard standing in their path. Their eyes were locked on the Souk and the great demon looming over it.

Dreadaeleon drew in a deep breath. He held out his hands. The power flowed, his fingers erupting into flame almost immediately.

"Get back," he whispered.

Asper slipped behind him. The flames leapt out, great jaws of fire that opened wide to swallow the monstrosities. Like flowers of flesh, they wilted before the flame, their skin bubbling and blistering beneath the heat as their glistening bodies curled around themselves, becoming blackened husks in the span of the breath that was robbed from them.

Just like that, old man, he told himself. *Hold them back. Everything's counting on you now.*

Oh, yes. The glass shard twisted in his skull. *You've turned everything to shit before, but I'm sure you'll do better now.*

Without you, Lenk dies. Without you, Asper dies. He gritted his teeth and forced that thought away. *Without you, this city, these people, this* world *burns to cinders.*

Ah, it would be a shame if it all burned down before you got the chance to do it yourself, wouldn't it?

No, no, NO.

He shut his eyes tight. He threw lightning into the darkness. In bright blue flashes, the monstrosities' twisted bodies were revealed for but a moment before disappearing into blackness. Each time, they drew closer, their mouths gaped wider, their eyes burned brighter.

Don't lose focus now, old man. Ignore that. Ignore everything. You need to fight! You need to save this city! You need to save Liaja!

Liaja? The glass shard thought purred, wedging itself a little deeper in his skull. *All this effort for a common whore? And yet all you give a proper lady is death? Priorities, I suppose.*

His hands fell. His eyes widened.

He recognized the voice.

"Shinka…" he whispered.

That took long enough. I've been devoured by a moron. Outstanding.

"How are you…"

How? You can barely understand the magic you already hold, let alone the kind that permits you to pervert life like this.

"No, you're not real." He shook his head. "You're a side effect, just…"

"Dread." Asper's voice was low in a warning growl as she stepped in front of him. "If this is you being dramatic, it's poorly timed."

You always were a fool. It's suitably poetic that an imbecile like you should have such power, isn't it? Perhaps they'll write an opera about it.

"No." He clutched his head. *"No."*

Perhaps your whore can act it out…

"Don't you talk about her."

"Dread," Asper snapped. She looked up as the beasts came roiling forward out of the darkness. "Dread, get *up!*"

I can see everything about her in here, you know. I hear her voice. I remember her smell. I can see that sad little smile on her face when you couldn't satisfy her but she was too kind to hurt you.

"Stop!" He screamed into the darkness. *"STOP!"*

"Gods fucking damn it," Asper snarled, "does *everyone* just start talking to themselves these days?"

I can hear her, that little name she calls you… what was it?

"No…" he whimpered, "please no."

"Northern boy."

He collapsed. The pain was too much, that shard of a thought twisting itself over and over in his skull. He could feel memories bleed out of it. His mind flooded with images of her: Liaja's smile, Liaja's hair, Liaja's eyes…

And slowly, they twisted. The memories grew darker in his mind, the color seeping out of them, the life leaking out of her. And when he thought of her again, all he could see was the last way she had looked at him.

Mouth twisted into a frown.

Hair hanging dirty around a sullen face.

Eyes wide and full of fear for him. What he could do, how easily he could kill. He couldn't get the thought out of his head. And neither could he get the voice.

What would she say if she could see you now, "old man"? Would she know what you do to people now? Would it even matter? Or do you think she already knew what a monster you were?

He couldn't move. He felt his jaw lock, his teeth set on edge. His fingers dug so deeply into his skull he could feel their pain, as though he might claw the thought out of the bone. He could barely hear anything but Shinka's words, her morbid cackle.

Yet even still, the sound of battle was too loud to ignore.

Asper had given up talking to him. Her sword lashed out in silver arcs, pulling back crimson each time. The beasts came surging forward, reaching and shrieking and groping for a way to get over her.

She cut deep gashes in their limbs. She carved scars into their faces. She snatched bulging eyeballs with stray strokes and hewed hands from limbs when they reached too close. Each time, they would shrink back from her blows. Each time, another would surge forward to take its place.

She was retreating, step by step, giving more ground even as the ground before her became littered with severed flesh and spatters of blood. It wouldn't be long before she was overrun, before she died cursing his ineptitude, his weakness.

Shinka hissed in his skull. *This is how it ends, "old man." You pretended to be a great man when you couldn't even manage an average one.*

He tried to simper out a reply, to gasp some protest. His mind was numb, his body followed, and his mouth managed nothing more than a sucking gasp. Long shadows of long limbs descended on him.

For all this, you are still just a boy.

He opened his eyes. He saw the great, gaping jaws. He felt a long claw brush across his cheek, drawing a thin line of blood.

And then he heard the roar.

Even through the numbness in his body, he could feel his bones shake. Even through the laughter echoing in his skull, the sound of fury split apart his thoughts like an ax through stone. Even against the darkness, the flash of bloodred skin burned brightly.

Gariath just had that kind of effect.

Just like old times.

The dragonman came howling out of the blackness. His claw shot out, seized the monstrosity looming over Dreadaeleon by the throat, and slammed it to the stones. His foot followed, heel coming down hard on the creature's skull. Dreadaeleon flinched as wet, glistening matter splattered against his face.

He looked up. The dragonman stood over him, scarred and bloodied and bruised. His left arm hung dislocated and limp from his shoulder. For the first time in a long time, the dragonman appeared covered in blood that was mostly his own. And yet for all the hell he had been through, he still looked down on Dreadaeleon with a sneer.

"Die useful," Gariath growled, "or die quickly."

"On that, at least, we agree."

Asper stepped forward, the sound of droplets of blood falling from her sword heralding her footsteps. She approached Gariath and exchanged a long, hard scowl with him. He met her with a pair of empty black eyes, unflinching and unapologetic. And whatever wordless conversation was exchanged between them was brief and harsh.

And yet they turned as one.

They strode out as one.

And, as one, they began to kill.

Claw and blade. Jaws and shield. Flesh rent. Bones broke. Metal rang as roars shook the night. Asper led the charge, smashing aside monstrosities for Gariath to bring his foot down on. Gariath caught them by limb and by throat, hurling them toward Asper to stagger themselves upon her blade and fall lifeless to the ground. Without a word but the sound of their anger, they fought together, cutting down foe after foe.

As Dreadaeleon, paralyzed, watched from the gate.

Oh, this is familiar, isn't it? Shinka's voice chuckled. *How many times has this happened before, boy? You, the great and powerful wizard, shitting yourself helpless on the ground as your friends do the work?*

He struggled to find his breath, long and slow and heavy. He drew in shallow breaths, growing deeper. He closed his eyes.

Yes, I can see them all. So many memories of uselessness. The mind boggles to understand how so much power can accomplish so little. But then, you do think you're quite special, don't you?

He gritted his teeth, pushed blood back into his limbs. He forced one foot to rise and find ground. Then another. Then he pushed himself up to his feet. With every step, the glass shard in his skull twisted.

I owe you an apology, old man. It's not a monster your whore will see. When she looks upon you, all she'll see is a useless...

He opened his eyes, let the fire burn bright.

...weak...

He called to mind a word.

...pitiful...

And then...

...boy.

He shouted it.

"FLY."

The air shimmered beneath him and shot him up into the sky. It radiated out from him, an invisible wave of force that roiled along the ground like a shook carpet. And every monstrosity it touched flew as he did. With bursts of magic beneath them, the beasts were hurled shrieking into the air. One after the other, flailing and screaming and reaching, they tumbled helplessly into the sky as a twisted mass of limbs and panic.

He held his arms out and closed his hands. He felt more of them out there in the shadows. And, as though he were picking berries, he simply reached out and plucked them up. Soon he hung in the air, haloed by a ring of shrieking monstrosities. The power strain was immense; he could feel himself burning from within.

But there was simply no other way.

No other way to prove he was powerful. No other way to save this city, the people within it. No other way to make this world safe for Liaja. And...

What are you doing?

Most importantly...

Stop! The power is too much!

No other way to make her shut up.

"DIE!"

His shout shook the sky and the creatures trapped within it. Power burst out of him in a massive ring of shimmering, twisting wind. It flew in a great circle, coursing through the ring of monstrosities hovering in the air with him. The force of the gale, thick and fast, struck them like a wall of iron.

And, like a wall of iron, unmade them.

Magic flashed in bright crimson blasts. They burst like overripe berries. They cracked like dry tinder. Some erupted in ways that defied explanation, let alone metaphor.

And in the pervasive darkness, for one glorious moment, the sky was alight with bright red life as hundreds of monstrosities became mere flecks of gore.

He opened his eyes.

Fragments of bone and scraps of sinew hovered in place around him. A broken tibia tumbled lazily through the air. The collapsed remains of a fanged jawbone floated past him. Droplets of blood hung glistening in the sky and quivered at the slightest sigh of wind.

And everything, even his own head, was silent.

"Nothing now?" he whispered into the darkness. "Have you nothing else to say to me, you vile shrew? Where are your insults now? Where is your laughter?" His chuckle echoed off the wall of gore. "I have won. I beat you, as I beat Annis, as I beat *everyone* who opposed me and—"

And everyone was dead.

This was it, then. This was how he found peace. Only when everything else was dead and quiet.

The limitless power he had, and all he had done was kill.

And for whatever Liaja might see when he came to her, that was all he would ever have. And that was all he would ever be able to—

A surge of pain flooded his thoughts. He felt his body go bloodless, the air quivering around him.

It had been too much power. All that magic, all at once, to kill so many. Shinka had been right.

No, no, NO. He roared inside his skull. *She was* not *right. She wasn't right about you being a boy, she wasn't right about you being a monster, she wasn't right about how she thought she could use you. She's been wrong this whole time. You're better than that, right, old man?*

A long moment passed.

Right?

And his thoughts were silent.

And the sky was dark.

His eyes drifted long over the ruined buildings and blackened city, far out to the desert and the Green Belt. And in the gloom beyond the city, like a night unto itself, he could see a thousand tiny lights dancing far beyond. He could not see so far as to make out what, exactly, they were. Yet from here, he could feel them: the heat of their torches, the beating of their hearts, the thunder of their footsteps.

An army.

An army was approaching, coming from the pass and flooding into the Green Belt. They would be here soon.

And they would find no demons to slay, no monsters to threaten them. All because of him. He had saved everyone. And now, they would all have to realize it and acknowledge that he—

A surge of pain shot through him. He felt the power ebb out of him, the fire in his eyes dim. Slowly, he began to sink to the ground. Gariath and Asper stared up at him, agog, as he descended. And even when his feet touched the cobblestones and he found that his legs couldn't support him, they still stared at him in awe.

"Dread," Asper whispered. "You killed them . . ."

"I did," he wheezed in reply, his voice a ragged gasp.

"Hundreds," Gariath muttered. "There had to be hundreds."

"Four hundred fifty three." Dreadaeleon stared at the ground, slick with gore. "And I felt them all die."

"Are you . . ." Asper winced. "Are you all right?"

"I will be fine," he said. He lied, rather. Drawing in a breath, he knew he had spent too much. He would have to get more. Someone else would have to die. "*We* will be fine." He looked up and managed a weary smile. "I saw them, Asper. They're coming."

The priestess's eyes widened. Gariath's, however, betrayed nothing.

"An army," he said. "I saw torches. Hundreds. Thousands, maybe. They just entered the Green Belt. They were marching for Cier'Djaal."

"That's not . . ." She shook her head. "That doesn't—"

"It does!" Dreadaeleon nodded vigorously. "Someone has come to help, Asper! This city is going to be safe! Everyone will be saved!"

Perhaps he had missed something—some crucial point of information or important conversation. Or maybe he had said something the wrong way—too enthusiastic, not sensitive enough. Something, surely, had to explain why she looked at him with such alarm and sorrow painted on her face.

"Dread," she said, "my army was destroyed. Totally. There were no survivors."

He felt the frown weigh on his face. "Then who—".

"Mine."

Their eyes both turned to Gariath. His voice came without passion. His eyes were dark and empty. He did not even blink as he spoke.

"It is my army," he said. "My tulwar. They are coming."

"To help?" Dreadaeleon asked. "To make the city safe?"

Gariath simply stared at him. And his silence filled the night sky.

"You..." Asper stared at the dragonman, breathless, trying to summon the words. "You...you..." And eventually, she found an old favorite. *"PIECE OF SHIT!"*

She leapt at him, her sword coming down in a shining arc. His arm went up, catching the blade on his bracer. Yet whether he was that wounded or she was that furious, he staggered under her blow.

"You said your army was broken!"

She pressed her blade against him. Sparks flew from the kiss of their metal. She drove him back a step, then another, then another. Her shield lashed out, caught him in the chin, and sent him reeling.

"You said they had gone home!"

He brought up his hand to defend himself as she drove forward. But he could not raise his arm high enough and she could not stop her charge. Her blade stabbed past his arm, found his flank, and dug deep into it. His howl was long and loud, ending only as she slammed her boot into his gut and sent him sprawling, rolling along the stones.

"You said fighting me was a mistake!"

He staggered to one knee. He spit blood onto the ground. And even through all the wounds he bore, his face betrayed not a hint of rage or sorrow as he looked at her with empty black eyes and spoke, painfully softly.

"I lied."

Shock battled horror on her face. In the end, fury strangled them both. The scream she let out was not her own. It belonged to the dead. It belonged to the survivors. It belonged to the weak and the sick and the dying. And it carried her forward in a savage charge, her sword flashing red over her head, ready to cleave Gariath's skull in two.

And it would have.

Had a wall of flames not leapt up between them.

She skidded to a halt and let out a scream. She sought a way through the blaze with wild eyes, but the flames only grew hotter as she did.

Through a veil of orange and red, Gariath rose on shaking feet. His blood pooling on the stones, his arm hanging limp at his side, he regarded her with a stare that was not mocking, not scornful, not even irritated. Eyes like his, obsidian hard and black, could only scarcely betray it, but for a brief moment, Gariath looked almost apologetic.

As he turned his back to her.

As he limped away.

As he disappeared into the darkness.

"You!" She whirled about and saw Dreadaeleon on his hands and knees, one arm outstretched, controlling the flames. "How could you? You little, vile—"

She couldn't find a word foul enough to finish. And if her snarl was any indication, the kick she settled on delivering to his ribs was not sufficient, either. He rolled away, gasping for breath, unable to lift a finger to defend himself as she seized him by the collar, as she hauled him to his feet, as she leveled her sword at his throat.

"You…" he gasped, "you…"

"Don't fucking say it," she snarled. "Don't fucking try to explain yourself. I have fucking *had* it with letting people do this to me. I have lost everything! And I have been betrayed by *everyone* and—"

"Not by yourself."

He hung limp in her hands. He was having a hard time breathing. But while she hadn't moved the blade from his throat, she at least hadn't driven it through, either.

Not the worst start.

"You can't stop them, Asper," he said. "I saw them. They are thousands. They will be here by morning, too." He swallowed hard. "Kill Gariath, you change nothing except maybe getting killed yourself. And then no one can save these people."

"How?" she demanded. "Dread, how the *fuck* am I supposed to do that? How was saving him going to change anything? How the hell do you think I'm going to do it?"

"I know you can."

"How?"

"Because," he gasped, "you promised."

And she lowered the blade.

And the fury ebbed from her face.

And while it wasn't kindness or softness or anything gentle that remained behind, there was something in her eyes. Something hard, something unyielding, something that had been there every time she had struck him, every time she had hurled abuse at him. Something that could get things done.

And she dropped him to the ground.

And she sheathed her sword. And shouldered her shield. And she walked off into the darkness, as he knew she would, to uphold her promise, leaving him limp and exhausted on the ground.

He might die here, of course. The tulwar might find him, the magic might burn out in his veins. But this city would be safe because of her. And she would be safe because of him.

And that was reason enough to smile, had he the energy to do so.

FORTY-SEVEN

A STILL AND SILENT HELL

The moment the knife slid into his side, Lenk knew he wasn't dead.

His scream tore him out of his unconsciousness. His eyes opened to a blurry red haze. But whatever instinct told him not to die just then also told him to seize the blade. His fingers found the knife, tore it from the hand that drove it in, and pulled it from his side. He slashed wildly with it, aiming for an indistinct blob of red and black in front of him.

"Ah." Through the pain, the sound of a feminine voice was sharp and fresh. "Not as dead as we thought."

His hand went to his side. He felt blood, but not the kind of thick gush that would indicate a fatal wound. Had he woken up just a moment later...

He held the blade out before him, slashing blindly as he sought to recover the feeling in his body. He could remember falling from a great height, plummeting into the earth. He did not remember the impact. Though he could feel and smell something soft and musty beneath him: old silks, long since moth-eaten and rotted, but enough to spare him a grisly end.

Sight returned to him last of all and, as the red haze blurred and was replaced by darkness, the shadows standing before him took shape.

Short. Lean. Dark of skin and hair. Their ears were pointed up and quivering like spears. Their faces were empty eyes and hollow smiles. Six of them—maybe seven, it was hard to tell. And at their lead, as tall and rigid as the spear in her hand, a woman wearing the face of a man.

"A pity." Shekune spoke in long, languid tones. "You survived the fall. It does not seem fair."

Khoshicts.

Armed with short blades and dressed in dark leathers, they observed him through the vacant grins of their wooden masks.

Get up.

His mind urged him to move, but the rest of him was not listening. He might have survived the fall, but his body didn't believe it. His leg felt twisted. His ribs were bruised. His head was swimming and he was bleeding from more than a few cuts.

He managed to claw his way to his rear, then to his knees, all the while flailing with the knife in a desperate bid to hold the khoshicts off. Yet they made no move to attack him. Indeed, they seemed amused to watch him struggle.

"Stay back," he gasped as he struggled to one foot. "I didn't ... I didn't kill him. I have to finish it. I have to ..."

"Finish what?" Shekune chuckled. "The demon?" She shook her head. The flayed skin nailed to her mask quivered. "He looked quite bloody when you left him. I am impressed, *kou'ru*."

"He's still alive." His leg was wrenched, and it screamed out in agony as he forced himself to stand. But he forced himself, nonetheless. "I have to stop him. He'll kill us all."

"Will he?" Shekune sounded mildly bemused.

"Yes! Everyone in the city!"

He made a move to push past them, to head back toward the Souk. He found her grinning spearhead leveled at his throat.

"And who," she asked, "is in this city beyond humans?"

He stared down at the spearhead before looking up into the desiccated flesh of her mask. His thoughts crystallized through the pain and his eyes widened at the realization.

"You can't be serious," he said. "You saw that thing. Anything he doesn't rule, he'll kill. You, me, *everyone*. If I don't stop him—"

"Then he reigns over the land with an iron fist. All who gaze upon him bow before him or die in vain." Shekune's growl rumble out of her mask. "My people have lived in these deserts since before yours learned to walk upright, round-ear. I have heard the legends."

She thrust the spear a little closer, forcing him back a step. He saw the fear in his eyes reflected as its grinning head brushed against the skin of his throat.

"I know what happens if you do not kill him," she said. "And I know

what happens if you do. If you do not stop him, this desert and everywhere
else shall be turned upside down and everything changes. And if you do..."

From the eyes carved into her mask, he could feel her scowl.

"Nothing changes. Your people have a celebration, build a statue of
you, forget you, go back to making money, and everything goes on like
it always has. And my people?"

She spun the spear suddenly. The haft of it struck him hard against
the side of his head and sent him to the ground.

"*My* people die. *My* people are pushed back into the dark places. *My*
people lose land to your cities, lose lives to your greed, lose family to
your wars. You seek to save a world that would kill us. You are a hero to
those who would murder us."

She took her spear in both hands. In the dim and dying light, its saw-
toothed grin seemed to grow anticipatorily broader.

"My people need your blood."

Lenk tried to back away as she approached, holding his knife out,
puny against her spear. Fear played in his pain. Pain racked his body.
He drew in deep, ragged breaths.

"You're insane," he said. "He'll come for you! Those who don't serve
him—"

"We will hide. We will let him gorge himself on your people."

"But he'll come for you, eventually! He's a demon! If I don't kill him
here—"

"We will find a way. The legends are long. We will do it."

"But how?" Lenk's eyes widened as he screamed. "How are you going
to survive?"

From beneath her mask, he could see her lips curl into a soft and
cruel smile.

"We survived humanity. A demon will not be so hard."

She raised the spear over her head. She aimed for his chest. She tightened her grip. She thrust.

And a hand shot out.

Both her eyes and his went to the woman who had appeared beside
her. Another khoshict, yet this one wore no mask. Her hair hung in
thick, sweat-slick strands. Her dark scowl smoldered. And her canines
were a stark white in the dark as her lips curled back in a snarl.

"Let go, Kwar," Shekune commanded.

"I did not want to believe it," Kwar whispered in reply. "I did not want her to be right. But she was, wasn't she?"

"She is not one of us. She never was."

"You would kill us all. By war, by demons, it does not matter." Kwar shook her head. "You want vengeance so badly that you don't care if we all die to get it."

"Perhaps she is right…"

Another voice. One of the khoshicts approached. He removed his mask, revealing an older man beneath, face weathered by wrinkles and eyes heavy with sorrow.

"Perhaps there can be another way," the older shict said.

"Sai-Thuwan," Shekune replied. "You cannot believe that."

"I…I do not know." He shook his head. "There has been so much death already, and if vengeance will only bring more…how many must die before we have achieved our goal?"

"I do not want vengeance." Shekune spoke softly. "I want to protect our people. I want to make sure no shict ever meets a fate like your wife. Like your son."

"Do not speak of them!"

Kwar roared and tried to tear the spear from Shekune's grasp. But Shekune was older, stronger. She pulled back, drove her knee into Kwar's side, and threw her to the ground. She snarled, hefting her spear over her head.

"It is a disease," she hissed. "*They* are a disease. Kataria had it and now it has spread to you. You linger around humans and this is what they do to you." She growled and drew her grip tight. "This will be kinder, Kwar. You will see."

"NO!"

Sai-Thuwan hurled himself at the woman. She was swift, swinging her spear about to meet him. And he was slow. The head's sawteeth caught him in the side and tore a great burst of blood from his flank. He let out a gurgling shriek as he fell. Kwar screamed out something dark and deep. The other khoshicts fell back, agog.

And Lenk saw his chance.

While the spear was tangled with Sai-Thuwan, he lunged forward. The knife found a way between the woman's arms, into her chest. She let out a scream as he sank it to the hilt.

Her foot lashed out, caught him in the belly, and sent him barreling backward. He fell to the ground and just as quickly began scrambling to get back up, ready for the blades that would follow.

But the other khoshicts were concerned for their chieftain. They swarmed around her, seizing her by her arms and legs and hoisting her up. Shouting among themselves in their own language, they pulled her into the darkness, disappearing with her.

And Lenk was left with a pair of bodies.

"Father..." Kwar cradled Sai-Thuwan's body in her arms. The old khoshict was rasping, his eyes glazed, his face twisted in pain. "Father, why did you..." She forced words out of a snarl. "Why are you so *stupid*?"

Huh, Lenk thought. *I guess all shicts are like that.*

Sai-Thuwan let out only a pained groan in response. Lenk approached warily.

"Here," he said. "Let me help."

Kwar held up a hand, slick with her father's blood. "He will live. But *I* will help him." She looked at him with hard eyes. "Is it true what you said? Can only you kill the demon?"

Lenk met her eyes and nodded. "As far as I know."

She grunted. "Then do that."

She hoisted Sai-Thuwan to his feet, whispering to him in their own language as she did. He was limp, groaning in agony, but his ears were aloft and quivering. Together, they began to make their way away, slipping into the darkness.

They had almost disappeared entirely before Lenk called out.

"Thank you."

Kwar paused. "It wasn't for you that I did it."

"I mean, that makes twice now. Whether it's for me or not...I still owe you."

Kwar's eyes dropped to the ground. A heavy sorrow painted her face.

"Shekune is not dead. I can hear her still." She shook her head. "I showed her the way into the city. And now she has killed us all." She shut her eyes. "Everything Kataria tried to stop...I betrayed it all."

She looked over her shoulder at him.

"I can never face her. She hates me for what I did. And I deserve it. But if you owe me..." Her words became a whispered choke. "Then tell her I am sorry. Tell her I cannot undo it. But...if it would still mean she is still alive to hate me..."

Tears formed at the corners of her eyes and slid down her cheeks.

"Tell her I would do it again. Every time."

They began to disappear.

And Lenk began to watch them.

And before they vanished entirely, Lenk found his hand reaching out. He found himself touching her shoulder. He felt her grow tense under his touch. He saw her ears twitch as he spoke.

"She would want you to tell her yourself."

Kwar stared at him, searched his face, as though searching for a lie or a trick or a mental illness that would have made him say such a thing. But all he offered her was a weary smile.

"Take care of him," he said. "Then, find us. Find her."

"But you..."

"It's not about me."

She stared at him for a moment longer. Then she nodded. And with her father, they slid into the darkness.

Lenk didn't have the heart to tell her that, for all he knew, Kataria might be dead.

But it didn't really matter, did it?

After all, as he turned and started hurrying back toward the Souk, it wouldn't be too long before he was dead, too.

FORTY-EIGHT

Heaven's Throne
Stands Empty

The stones were silent.

And there were no birds to sing, nor beasts to cry, nor wind to moan.

And the skies grew still and dark and the distant ocean held its breath.

As all the world fell into a respectful silence as it waited for a god to die.

Lenk limped through the gate to the Souk expecting to find his death. He expected a bellowing, wrathful demon, recovered from his wounds and ready for more battle. He expected the heavens to part and bare a bloodred sky. Failing all that, he expected a tremendous foot to simply come down and crush him.

But he found none of those.

The clouds overhead had formed a ceiling of gloom, starless and black. The shattered streets were caked in thick black blood that drank what little light there was. It was as though Lenk walked into a void, not so unlike the cold dark that Denaos had described.

Perhaps this was what hell was like.

It was, after all, where he found demons.

Far from the wrathful titan he expected to find, Khoth-Kapira loomed over the Souk, bent and broken. He leaned heavily on the Silken Spire, the sinew of his back shuddering with a hacking cough. A hand was clutched to his opened throat. Streams of ichor poured out between his fingers to spatter on the ground in thick black stains. They congealed into serpents and slithered away into the dark.

It was not with a great, bellowing rage nor a dying speech to heaven that Khoth-Kapira, the God-King, He Who Held the Light, was unmade. It was in drops. It was in ragged, whispering breaths.

Eyes that had scowled enviously at heaven now rolled back to search an empty sky for something that was not looking back.

Lips that had spewed curses to the gods and sung music to mortals now opened in a desperate bid to say something, to plead something, to be heard.

But all that came out was a long, ragged sigh.

And as his breath left him, so too did he diminish. The crown that scraped the sky shrank to the earth. The serpents that writhed and hissed became withered and disappeared. The eyes that held the world in their baleful gaze dimmed and became dark.

And when Khoth-Kapira's knees finally hit the stones, it was not with the earth-shaking crash of a titan, but with the tired groan of a broken, bleeding man.

Khoth-Kapira was dead.

And Mocca was soon to follow.

Lenk limped toward the man, who hunched over on his hands and knees, coughing up blood. He glanced out to the side and caught a glimpse of silver, the last light in the endless dark.

His sword. There, as if it had been waiting for him. As it always would.

He picked it up without ceremony. He dragged it behind him, barely enough strength to hold it, let alone lift it. He had enough in him to walk to Mocca. He had enough in him to strike him down.

And past that, it didn't matter.

"Just a few cuts..." Mocca's voice was thin and rasping through the hole in his throat, yet he managed. "A few cuts with a big knife. And I, who could have saved this world, am unmade." He forced out a chuckle. Blood wept between his fingers. "You must feel so underwhelmed."

"No," Lenk said. "I set out to kill you."

"And you did. Did you expect a better fight?"

Lenk shook his head.

"Did you expect to die?"

Lenk nodded.

"I am sorry, then. For everything. But my power never lay in brute force."

Mocca stared at his life leaking out onto the street. His lips twitched, numb as they spoke.

"Covetous Ulbecetonth had a brood that numbered the thousands. Cruel Avictus could level cities with one great swing of his blade. Yet of all of us they cast into hell, it was Khoth-Kapira that the gods feared and it was he for whom their most painful torments were reserved."

He looked up at Lenk.

"Do you know why?"

Lenk stared back for a long moment before speaking.

"Because you did what they couldn't," he said. "Because when someone whispered a prayer to the night, it was you who heard it. It was you who built them homes, you who healed them, you who answered their prayers."

"All I ever wanted to do. And you would take that. You would cast them back into a dark and silent world under a cold heaven."

"I would not." Lenk hefted his sword in both hands. "Gods don't give. But neither do you. And what you want, you'll take from everyone."

"Ah," Mocca replied. "So it's *you* who are the savior of mortality, then. You would speak for all of them, then? You would rob the dying and the ill and the poor of my blessings?"

"I would spare them the day they displease you."

Mocca sneered. His face was paling quickly. His cheeks had gone gaunt. And his eyes were hollow of all but scorn.

"No," he snarled. "Lie to yourself if it will soothe you, but do not tell me you do this for a sense of righteousness. Even when you were doing the right thing, you did so only because I promised you I could save her." His lips peeled back. His teeth were stained black. "But your fragile lusts and desires are still no match for your nature."

Lenk lowered his sword. Mocca spit his blood onto the ground.

"Do you know why the gods cursed your kind and cast you and your silver-haired miscreants out? Because you do not exist. Not truly. For as vile as they claimed us to be, the gods knew the Aeons could nourish, could encourage, could *create*. For all our sins, we still managed to change this world. But you? You know nothing of this. You were made to destroy. You were born to kill. You were created for no other purpose than slaughter. And so you have fulfilled that purpose."

He stared at Lenk, hollow and empty.

"And perhaps if I had seen you as the weapon you were all along, I would have been wise enough to leave you where you could hurt no one else."

Mocca rose to his knees. He held his hands out wide. His chest, naked and painted with his own blood, rose and fell with each ragged breath.

"Do it, then. Prove the gods right. But when you doom this world, just remember..."

He narrowed his eyes. He smiled a black smile.

"I could have stopped it."

Mocca was right.

Mocca was always right.

Lenk was a weapon. He was fit to kill. It was all he had ever been good at and, as hard as he tried to stop, he found himself here again.

In a dark place.

With a sword in his hand.

And blood on his feet.

To do it now, to strike Mocca down, would prove them right. The gods, the demons, himself; everyone who had always suspected he couldn't do it. To kill him now, even if it was the right thing—*if* it was the right thing—would prove himself the weapon he'd always feared he would be.

There was only one thing a man could do with a sword.

But there were many reasons to do that one thing.

Some of them were right. Some, maybe not so much. But men like him, men of scars and regrets and so many empty and broken things, never got to decide which were which.

They merely took up the sword.

And let it decide what happened next.

He took up his blade again. He clenched his jaw. He looked Mocca in his eyes.

And he thrust.

Not a scream but an agonized moan. Not a flash of light but a burst of blood. The sword entered Mocca's chest, sank past his rib cage and up into his heart. The man's eyes went bright for a moment. His body stiffened.

And, with blood leaking from the corner of his mouth, he smiled.

From the wound, it slithered out. Mocca's blood, black as night, crept out in glistening tendrils. They coiled over the steel of the sword. They coiled up the hilt. They wrapped around Lenk's fingers, Lenk's hands, Lenk's wrists.

He stared, his mouth hanging open, his eyes unblinking. He struggled violently, pulling against the coiling tendrils, but found no release. They tightened at his struggles, constricting across his wrists.

Panic seized him. Was this some last, spiteful act? Or had Mocca planned this all along? Was this the entire idea? To return to hell once more, only not alone? It wasn't fair. He had given everything. He had fought. He had won. It wasn't fair. *It wasn't—*

"Lenk."

Her hand was on his shoulder. Her arm was around his waist. Her voice was in his ear as she leaned forward and placed her head on his shoulder.

"Just let go," Kataria said.

He looked at the sword in his hands. He closed his eyes.

He let go.

She pulled on him, letting out a grunt of exertion. The black tendrils reached for him, sought to hold on to him. But as he dug his heels in and she hauled at him, they finally released.

The two of them tumbled backward as Mocca's body snapped backward. The demon's spine bent. His head arched backward, his eyes staring emptily toward heaven. His mouth opened, twitched in a last whisper.

"I could have stopped it…"

His blood coated his body. His skin was cloaked in black. It hardened over his flesh, became as twisted and jagged as obsidian, until Lenk could recognize neither the demon nor the man.

Overhead, the clouds began to dissipate.

The stars began to shine.

And below, the sword's hilt drank its light and it did not shine.

FORTY-NINE

THE GOLDEN GOD

Asper clasped her hands together. Her eyes closed, she respectfully bowed her head.

"I know we haven't talked much."

The words came hesitantly. She had to pick each one out of her mouth and set it on the table. She had gone over words just like this a million times in her head, yet somehow it was never as easy as actually saying them.

"And I know...the last time we did, I was not as respectful as I might have been."

She stared at her hands, clasped together as they were, and felt the sudden urge to stop talking and simply walk away. What good would this do, anyway? It hadn't helped so far. And yet, she continued.

"Maybe you'll think this is just opportunism. We only ever seem to talk in a crisis, anyway. Maybe you'll think I'm just looking out for my own skin. And I guess—"

She paused. This felt so stupid. So forced. It wasn't going to do anything. It never did. And still...

"And I guess I can't blame you for that. And I wouldn't blame you for not believing me. Hell, I wouldn't even be asking—I don't even know if you *do* answer—but it's not about me. It's not about my problems."

She looked up. She forced iron into her stare. She forced the words to come out.

"It's about the people. However many thousands are still left in this city after all the war and the murders. So many have fled, many more are dead...but there are still so many who could be killed when the tulwar arrive tomorrow. I can't..."

She grimaced and buried her face in her hands. She bit back a sob, wrenched her hair. She told herself she wouldn't do this. She knew it wouldn't help anything. As it was, she managed to fight back tears and just let all the anger show on her face.

"I can't fail them. I know I've said that before, time and time again, and I keep failing them. But I have to keep trying. I have to fight for them. Until my very last breath, I have to fight. But I can't do it alone."

She took in a breath. She placed her hands on the table. She looked up.

"Will you help?"

A trio of tasteful portraits stared back at her: an elegant lady in repose upon a bed of silks, a still life of a bowl of fruit, a rolling landscape of sunny hills. The idyllic scenes offered no answers to her.

Yet, despite the fact that she could see none of their faces, Asper knew that behind each of the paintings, the couthi were smiling at her.

"This one expresses sympathies to your conundrum." Man-Shii Kree, behind the elegant lady, leaned forward. He clasped all four hands on the table, the sleeves of his voluminous red robe pooling around his wrists. "Sincere expressions of gratitude are heaped upon your face, *shkainai*, as this one equates your honored and tragic torments to his own life."

"This one adheres to strict agreement of the previous assessment," Man-Khoo Yun added in an identically chilling monotone. His portrait of a bowl of fruit inclined toward her. "Inquiries into events undergone in the previous two days have been processed. This one has arrived at sufficient empathy to express sincere hopes as to the honored Prophet's recovery."

"Proficiency in understanding was employed with imminence," the third, yet-unnamed couthi, clad in violet robes and wearing the rolling landscape portrait, added in a voice identical to theirs. "This one adds emphasis to all above statements and directs and thrusts queries of well-being directly at the honored Prophet."

Asper quirked a brow at this latter one. Man-Shii Kree was quick to interject, gesturing with two of his hands toward his fellow couthi.

"May this one be burdened with the special task of introducing associate and captain of the merchant fleet, Man-Leng Qij," he said. "The esteemed member arrived insignificant days ago to collect what remains of the Brotherhood's investments in Cier'Djaal before we evacuate to kinder quarters. But please..."

All three couthi leaned forward in eerie synchronicity.

"These ones express polite inquiry as to the state of your health."

"I'm fine," Asper said. "We're all..." She shook her head. "The demon is dead. His followers are dead. But Cier'Djaal is destroyed. I don't have men or fortifications to hold this city. All I can do is try to save who I can."

The three couthi exchanged pointed glances toward each other. Or at least, Asper assumed they were pointed. It was impossible to tell. Man-Shii Kree inclined his portrait toward her. The other two followed.

"This one struggles to find the capacity for the awe expressed at such an undertaking," he said. "May assurances be heaped upon the honored Prophet's face that all available members express profound and illuminative admiration for her cause."

"This one risks redundancy by concurring, once again," Man-Khoo Yun added. "All expressions of immense truth emit from this one's oral orifice when this one commends and congratulates the honored Prophet in her resolve."

"This one apologizes greatly for adding a third redundant approval," Man-Leng Qij said. "But this one finds all imperatives to remain silent overwhelmed by lust for—"

"Oh, would you just *fuck off* with this?"

Asper hadn't meant to sound quite so incensed. And she certainly hadn't meant to slam both fists on the table, causing all three couthi to recoil. But if she wasn't above cursing at her friends or her deities, she wasn't going to put on airs for three bug-fuckers.

"No more," she snarled. "This isn't the Souk. I'm not a customer. You're not trying to sell me porcelain dogs. The city is destroyed and I've got countless lives to save. I've seen behind your paintings and I've heard your real voices and I *know* what you really want. I'm not here for platitudes."

She stiffened up in her chair. By the light of the single oil lamp hanging overhead in the basement room, her face was creased with shadows.

"I'm here to negotiate."

The three couthi fell silent. All twelve of their limbs disappeared behind the table. They stared at her through their paintings, each one of them so still she wasn't sure they were even breathing. And as long, silent moments passed, she realized that, for the first time since she had met them, she had absolutely no idea what the couthi were thinking.

And she hadn't realized how terrifying that was until this moment.

"Very well."

Man-Shii Kree spoke. *Truly* spoke. His voice was guttural and clicking, a many-legged thing crawling out of his throat.

"Let us negotiate, *shkainai*."

"We have heard of your dead demon," Man-Khoo Yun rasped out, leaning forward. "We undertook considerable risk remaining in the city. Our fleet possesses five ships, each of them capable of carrying a considerable number of humans. We will connect with an additional three ships farther up the coast on the way to Muraska. We have supplies enough to feed and care for as many humans as you need on the trip to Muraska."

"Understand that, while the city is unsalvageable, our assets here are not inconsiderable." Man-Leng Qij's voice was drier, harsher, perhaps older than the other two. "We possess caches of matériel, silks, and other treasures that we value at immense profit. There is not room upon our ships for both your humans and our investments, though."

"So you want something in exchange," Asper said. "Name it."

"Of course... Prophet." Man-Shii Kree's voice carried a particular menace on that last word. "We have followed your rapid ascension with great interest. No doubt, exploits of your heroic last stand at the Green Belt will be reaching far and wide."

"But I lost that battle," she said. "I lost everything there."

"You *sacrificed* everything," Man-Khoo Yun offered, holding up one monstrous, clawed finger. "Bravely, outnumbered and defiant against the savage horde, you fought to your last and ultimately broke the beasts. It took an act from hell to give them the advantage to best you, and though you might have lost the city, you saved so many lives."

"That's not what happened, though."

"It doesn't matter," Man-Leng Qij spoke. "Humans love these stories. They will fill in the parts that don't make sense with what they wish had happened. Your legend will grow swiftly. When you arrive at Muraska, you will find their leaders receptive to your plight." He steepled all four of his hands. "We would like to benefit from this."

"Of course," she muttered. "And how do you aim to do that?"

"Nothing the Prophet cannot give us," Man-Shii Kree said. "Favorable trade agreements, exclusive rights for mercantile properties, further—"

"Bullshit," she interrupted.

"You are not in a position to refuse so easily," Man-Leng Qij hissed.

"No, not that." Asper leaned forward. "This isn't what you really want. Your Brotherhood has been operating for longer than Muraska's been a country. You can get all the agreements you want. And even if you couldn't, something about your story doesn't make sense.

"No matter how considerable your assets are, you can't use them if you're all dead. Yet even now, you stayed through the demon attack. And you have supplies to feed all the people of Cier'Djaal?"

She narrowed her eyes and folded her arms.

"You were waiting for this," she said. "You knew I'd come to you. So tell me what you're *really* after."

The three exchanged glances. It was evident, at least, by the shakiness of their portraits that they hadn't expected her to see through them this quickly. Yet it was also evident by how quickly they composed themselves that they were ready to proceed. One by one, they turned to her. And when Man-Shii Kree spoke again, his voice was thick with hatred.

"Revenge."

"What?" Asper asked.

"You don't know what we're talking about? They almost went unnoticed, didn't they? Between the tulwar and the demons, you forgot all about them. That's their way." Man-Shii Kree's voice sank to an angry, bitter snarls. "Shicts. They are vile."

"It is clear to us that you will be powerful in the days to come, Prophet," Man-Khoo Yun said. "With or without us, humans shall look to you for leadership, for guidance. We merely desire that an additional verse be added to the song of your legend."

"A verse of the treachery of the shicts," Man-Leng Qij rasped. "A mere few lines telling the tale of their vicious ambush, their cowardly retreat, their vile methods. That the world may know, as the couthi have known, their cruelty and their hatred. And that the shicts may know the vengeance of the couthi."

"We are too few, too scattered to fight the tribes. But we can give you ships," Man-Shii Kree said. "We can give you gold. We can give you a tale that will have the world of men rally every spear to you to fight the tulwar, to reclaim your city, to save every life you desire. All you need to give us is a promise."

"A promise of vengeance," Man-Khoo Yun growled.

"A promise of retribution," Man-Leng Qij added.

"A promise of war," Man-Shii Kree said. "No contracts. No signed papers. The arrangement shall go deeper than that. Give us our war against the shicts, and we shall give you an army to do it."

Asper stared at her hands. She had been prepared for exorbitant prices; she had been prepared to be asked to do the unthinkable. But she hadn't been prepared for this.

It had been only a few weeks since fraud and treachery had made her a Prophet, and now she was asked to lead more men than she had even thought possible, and lead them into a war bigger than she had ever considered.

This had all started as a means to fight Gariath, to defend Cier'Djaal, nothing more. And she hadn't even done that. Gariath would have this city.

And every other city . . .

The thought came unbidden, from a dark part of her mind that spoke no lies.

He won't stop with Cier'Djaal. He won't stop until everyone is dead. You know this. And so do the tulwar.

But still . . .

"To fight shicts," she whispered to herself. "What would Kataria say if—"

"Keep your pet, if you wish," Man-Shii Kree said, making a flippant gesture. "We brook no grudge with her. We shall not bar her from the ships. Take her with you, wherever you want. But consider this . . ."

"She is but one life," Man-Khoo Yun said. "Against thousands. Against *tens* of thousands. If the shicts would attack Cier'Djaal, where will they strike next? Who will die if they are not stopped?"

"The lives of more than Cier'Djaal hang in the balance," Man-Leng Qij said. "What has been set in motion, you cannot stop, even if your gods were listening."

"You can only save who you can," Man-Shii Kree said. "And you can save many."

They fell silent and waited for her answer.

And Asper realized she did not have one. There was too much to consider, too many lives to save, too much war to wage. Her head couldn't hold it all. Everything she even tried to consider, every possible negotiation, every rebuttal, all came up blank.

And through that emptiness of thought, her answer emerged, in an unbidden whisper.

"I can't fail."

She had become a priestess to help people.

She had joined Lenk and the others because she thought she could find more injured, more sick, more wounded to aid.

She had taken up the mantle of the Prophet, indulged in this depraved charade, because she thought it was the only way to help people.

Never once had she thought about fame or glory.

Yet the idea of her legend was heavy on her head as she walked out of that building and into the dark streets of Cier'Djaal.

This is the tale of Asper, the Prophet, Savior of Cier'Djaal.

So heavy that it bore her head lower and lower with every step.

The woman who came to the city to help people and sat by, helpless, as war between four different armies ravaged the streets and she couldn't count the dead.

She felt nauseous as she walked. The air was too thick.

The woman who deceived three nations into thinking she was the voice of the gods and led them into a war that became a bloodbath.

She had to stop and lean against a wall. She rubbed her face, suddenly feeling feverish.

The woman who swore a dozen oaths, made a hundred promises, asked a thousand prayers, and sold them all. This is the tale of Asper, the Prophet, the woman who fucking ruined everything.

She snorted, spit onto the ground.

If they can set all that to music, then we're set.

She heard boots on the stones behind her, moving silently and carefully. An assassin from the Khovura or Jackal holdouts come to kill her, maybe. Or an advance scout from the tulwar. Or simply a disgruntled citizen, knife in hand and murder in his eyes, who had watched his city collapse since she had come.

Any one of those would be nice, really.

But no killing blow, nice and neat, came. And after a long moment of nothing happening, she turned and faced her new company. And, almost instantly, wished it had been a knife she were looking at instead.

What had Aturach looked like when she first met him, she wondered? Tired, frazzled, overworked, certainly. But he had still been handsome, vibrant, burning with energy that could not be doused. The man standing before her now was haggard and gaunt, looking as though he had gone a hundred days without food and a hundred years without sleep.

"You're alive," she observed.

You don't look it, though, she chose not to add.

Aturach merely nodded, saying nothing else. The silence drew out like a knife between them. And when she spoke, Asper could feel its edge.

"I couldn't stop it, Aturach." She stared at her feet. "Any of it. All that we tried to do, all the people we tried to save, and I just..." She shook her head. "They're all dead. I couldn't—"

"Not everyone is dead."

He spoke softly. His voice was hoarse. But it was enough to make her look up. His smile was short and weary.

"And more would have been dead without you," he said. "This city has been bleeding for years, Asper. You tried to stanch the wound, but it was always going to die."

"You don't mean that."

"He does."

Hard boots on hard stones. Dransun came walking forward, a bundle tucked under his arm. He was dirty, weary; dried blood ran down the side of his face and stained his beard.

"You never saw it," he said. "But we did. We've lived here all our lives. We saw the fashas drink us dry. We saw the Jackals tear people apart. We saw the saccarii swear revenge, over and over. But you're just a *shkainai*. You thought you could fix it."

"I did." Asper shook her head. "I was wrong."

"You weren't," Aturach said. "Maybe you couldn't fix everything, but you've given us something."

He looked to Dransun. The old guard took the bundle in his hand

and unfurled it, holding it up. Tattered and torn, stained with earth and blood, the banner sailed. The sigils of Karneria and Saine were barely visible, the sigil of Talanas all but worn away.

Asper furrowed her brow. "How did you get that?"

"We went back for it."

From the shadows, they emerged. Beaten and limping, dirty and caked in sweat, bruised and bleeding and ragged and barely upright. But they were alive. And they were here.

Haethen came, her spectacles cracked and her robes torn. Blacksbarrow came, her sword broken and her hat gone and a new cut on her face. Their troops followed: the remnants of the Karnerians and Sainites, their armor torn and shields shattered. They all came back to her.

"Specifically," Haethen said, gesturing to one of the Karnerians, "he did."

The young man looked around as eyes suddenly turned to him. He saluted, pressing a bandaged fist to a blood-soaked tunic. He made a brief bow toward her.

"Marcher Dachon, Prophet."

"Why?" Asper asked. "Why did you go back for it?"

To her, it had been a lie, just one more on top of all the other frauds she had committed. It had just been a pretty piece of cloth. And now, it was just a ragged scrap caked in filth.

"Pathon..." Dachon hesitated before continuing. "My brother died for that banner, madam. Many of my brothers did."

"And mine," Blacksbarrow grunted. "And my sisters. And my cousins. And my birds."

"Then you should go back to them," Asper said. "While you still can."

"We were going to," Haethen replied. "We were scattered and lost. But we were asked to return here."

And she didn't have to ask to know.

There, at the back of the crowd, bloodier and more beaten than anyone, they stared at her. Kataria smiled at her, waved wearily. Lenk looked like doing even that much might make him faint. He merely nodded at her.

"Too many have died for us to give up," Haethen said. "I shall not return to the Empire without doing everything I can."

"We swore to follow you," Blacksbarrow added. "No man or woman of Saine is an oathbreaker."

"For all this to mean something..." Dransun gestured to the broken, the weary, the bloodied remnants of her army. "*This* has to mean something."

And he held the banner, ruined and ragged. It hung limp in a sky without wind, the last flayed remains of her cause.

And yet someone had gone back for it. Back into a field crawling with demons and the dead, they had gone to find it. And they, her army, a perfect match for its shabbiness, had rallied to it, still.

Whatever oaths she had broken, they had not.

Whatever promises she made, they had kept.

And whatever prayers she had offered...

They would expect her to answer.

"There's no saving the city," Asper said. "There are too many tulwar and too few of us. But there are ships. We can get people out of here."

They listened, nodding attentively, as she told them her plan. They ran off to enact it, to find the survivors, to bring them back. Still alive, still fighting, they went about their work.

And Cier'Djaal held its last, dying breath.

FIFTY

From on High

It was not as easy as it used to be.

There was a time—not so long ago, in fact—when Gariath could remember scaling trees with ease and nearly sprinting up sheer rock walls. His claws made grip where there was none and his muscle took him the rest of the way.

Now? Now, he could barely climb up a simple, shoddy wall without stopping to breathe heavily every few moments.

He supposed that stood to reason. His arm—dislocated in the fall he had taken—was set in a splint and wrapped with bandages. His severest wounds had barely been dressed and the lighter ones hadn't even been looked at. He had almost died last night. He had no business climbing anything, let alone something like this.

But he had to climb.

He had to see.

Hand over hand, foot over foot, claw by claw, and breath by breath, he hauled himself up the wall of the Souk. The day was gone by the time he made it to the top. And in the light of the setting sun, the Silken Spire's namesake fluttered gossamer, the last twitch of a butterfly's wings before it died.

On the edge of the Spire, Gariath stared out over Cier'Djaal.

The city stood empty now. Its homes were silent and its shops were darkened. Its squares were populated only by rubble, and the sole living things were the occasional abandoned livestock, wandering blissfully empty streets. Row after row, the buildings stretched like gravestones, monuments in the world's largest tomb for all its silent ghosts.

Just as it had been when they had arrived.

There had been no battle when his army had finally arrived. Asper had not met him at the head of a ragged band of spirited misfits, ready for a heroic last stand. Lenk had not stood there, ready to go down fighting. Not so much as a stone had been thrown in defiance when the tulwar had finally entered.

He knew that would happen. The tulwar's march had been slow, his army still ragged and worn from the atrocities at the pass, and many had been reluctant to heed the call to return to the demon-plagued city. But Chakaa had carried his message, Daaru had delivered it, and Mototaru had seen it through.

And on a pale morning, the tulwar conquered the skeleton of the greatest human city on the face of the world.

He watched his warriors wend their way through the streets in small knots, scouring the city for survivors or salvage. They were thousands, their numbers augmented by late reinforcements to the battle. But from up here, they seemed tiny and thin, simple stains of ink moving across a long, empty parchment.

Some of them would find a few handfuls of humans—maybe a few dozen, maybe a few hundred. Most of them had disappeared on the black ships. More had fled into the surrounding deserts. The tulwar were in no shape to pursue them. But the humans were in no condition to fight.

Only broken windows and empty bedrooms and abandoned toys were left to oppose him.

Was this it, then?

His thoughts were soft and fading in the morning light.

Was this what you saw, Mototaru? A bunch of houses and streets scared you away from conquering Cier'Djaal? Was it different back then?

He narrowed his eyes and swept them over the city.

What did you see?

He tried to picture it as it once was, brimming with humans ready to fight. He tried to picture it with *Drokha* mercenaries lining the streets. He tried to picture it with ballistae and catapults and great beasts of war. Anything that would have made Mototaru come down and abandon the Uprising as he had done.

But all he could see was houses.

Houses and shops.

Houses and smithies.

Houses and docks and empty taverns and lonely streets and old walls and…and…

And then he saw it.

Just like that. As if he only needed to see it from here, so high up.

He saw it.

And he suddenly felt very tired. He fell to his rear, letting his legs dangle out over the edge of the Spire. He leaned forward, breathless, and stared at it for a very long time.

A long time passed. The sky grew to a weary red. Night grew on the horizon. And he had not moved by the time he heard a grunt of exertion as someone else came clawing up the side of the wall.

"It was easier when I was younger." Mototaru hauled his considerable weight up over the ledge. He lay there, breathing heavily. "But I thought that having taken the city, I would find the strength to…to…"

He waved a hand, snorting. Slowly, he rolled to his side and got to his feet. Sweating profusely, he hobbled to the edge of the Spire. Gariath did not look away from the city.

"The Rua Tong have swept the city. The Mak Lak Kai have scoured the Green Belt. There is no enemy to fight and no reinforcements behind us." Mototaru, despite his labored breathing, pulled his pipe out and began to pack it. "Despite all its worth, Cier'Djaal was without friends at its moment of need. Poetic, no?

"We cannot count on that to last, though. Too many humans escaped. Word of what happened here will spread. Others will come seeking us. We must make preparations to defend ourselves." Mototaru lit his pipe, noting the one-sidedness of the conversation. "Are you listening to me? I said—"

He paused. He observed Gariath staring out over the city.

"Tell me, *Rhega*," Mototaru spoke softly through the smoke of his pipe. "What do you see?"

"Houses." Gariath's voice was numb. "I see houses. And shops. And streets. And smithies. I see homes. I see a city. And it's huge."

Before, it had only been fragments. Knots of people, clusters of houses, walls in his way and smells he was eager to put behind him. It had been only a series of annoyances. And perhaps that was what led him to look at it as something he could destroy.

As he looked at it now, he saw the house built with the lumber from that warehouse at the edge of the city. And he saw the street built from stone carried to those docks by a ship. He saw a shop made with glass from a glassblower. He saw mansions carved from marble brought from far away. He saw silks spun and sent out. He saw it not as fragments of a dying thing, but as one immense, living, breathing thing. Connected, from every home to every street.

And it was terrifying.

"Is this what you saw?" He looked to Mototaru. "This huge thing?"

Mototaru considered the question. "I saw years. Years that had been spent building while my people fought and scavenged. And I wondered, in all those years, how many other cities had been built? How many more humans were there? How big was their empire?"

He stared grimly over the city through a veil of pipe smoke.

"And I knew we could not fight them. We could kill them. We could kill thousands of them. And we would go on fighting and killing until all of us died out. And when we were gone, there would be nothing but dust."

He swept a hand over Cier'Djaal.

"And they would still be here."

In silence and smoke, they sat, staring out over the foe that neither of them, with all their armies and fury, had been able to kill. Gariath watched the tulwar pick their way through the streets below. He had thought them alternately brave and stupid. But never before now had he looked at them and realized how very small they were. How very few.

How very insignificant.

"The reinforcements that came," Gariath said. "Daaru didn't tell me where they came from."

Mototaru was silent for a long time. "Shaab Sahaar is gone."

Gariath thought he should express outrage over that. He wasn't sure why it didn't surprise him.

"It was shicts," the old tulwar said. "They circled around us as we marched to Cier'Djaal. And more emerged from the forests. They crept in, set the city ablaze. Those warriors that survived came to join us."

"And those who weren't warriors?"

Mototaru was silent for a longer time. "We are all warriors now."

This was what he had given them.

He had promised them war; he had given them death. He had promised them vengeance; he had given them corpses. He had promised them a city, and he had lost their home. And at the end of their long struggles, all he had to offer them was empty houses and broken streets.

They had given everything to him.

He pulled his battered body to its feet. He cast one final look out over the city they had taken. He let out a snort and began to remove the splint from his arm.

He would spend a very long time repaying them.

"What are you doing?" Mototaru asked, quirking a brow. "The healer said—"

"Tell the healer I will need a new sling," Gariath interrupted. "Tell the warriors to begin searching the city. Tell them we need food and steel. Any beast that cannot carry a load should be slaughtered for meat. Any human..."

He finished tying the bandages around his splint. He snorted.

"Kill any who try to fight. The others... let them go."

"That is not wise," Mototaru said. "We are weak right now. We should limit the humans who know it."

"Let every human know it. Let every shict know it. And every tulwar must hear that we are not weak." He reached down and plucked the pipe from Mototaru's lips. "We survived the demons. We will have vengeance on the shicts. And now..."

He pressed the pipe to his splint. The embers caught the bandages. A makeshift torch blossomed in his hand.

"We will do what we should have done during the first Uprising."

He looked to the Silken Spire above. He looked to its fluttering silken sails. He looked to its skittering, lazy spiders. He narrowed his eyes.

"The humans are not the only ones who can build. We will take what we need. We will build our own empire. They have given me everything." He growled. "I will give them their home."

"This city is too big for us to defend properly," Mototaru mused. "Still, there is much for us to take here. The silk stores alone could—"

"No." Gariath stalked to the Spire. "I will not build on human weakness. Take stone, take steel, take meat and wood and solid things. Leave the gold and the silk."

"And everything else?"

Gariath stared at the torch in his hand and spit three words.

"Burn it down."

He raised the torch to the silk. In the breeze, it caught slowly. But from just one spark, a fire spread. It nibbled at the silk in timid orange jaws. It found the taste to its liking and spread to a cackling gape. And then, as it swept up the great silken sheet, it began to feed in earnest.

The spiders barely knew it was happening. Those that saw it coming made a halfhearted effort to escape the flames. But all were consumed, disappearing soundlessly beneath the roar of the flames to be devoured.

And as night fell, Cier'Djaal's last moments were of glorious brightness.

FIFTY-ONE

Respite for the Lost

The bells are tolling, my children!"

Teneir's voice was loud and gay as she walked among the white square of Silktown. Her arms were thrust out wide and inviting, her mouth full of songlike laughter, and though she had but one eye left, it offered a brightness the like of which could only be matched by her smile.

"Can you not hear them?" she asked the assembled. "They are singing to us! They are the voice of Ancaa! She has come to give us that which we deserve!"

The people of the square were rapt in attention. Their eyes, unblinking, were fixed on her, save for those who were watching heaven. Their mouths hung open in awe as she twirled and danced through the square. Not a soul moved as she made her way between them.

"Rise up, my children!" Her voice shuddered with laughter. "Rise up and hear the bells! Come and be adored! Come and let her love you!"

She turned to a child upon the lawns surrounding the square. She leaned down and took his face gently in her hands. She smiled widely at him, at the empty wonder in his eyes, at the red smear around his mouth.

"Child...child..." she whispered. "It is as I promised. Ancaa has come, child. Rise up and greet her!"

The child's mouth hung open, silent. A fly buzzed around his head, landed on his bloodshot eye, and crawled across it.

"Child...child!" Teneir whispered. "Rise up!"

From the edges of the lawn, Dreadaeleon watched. It had not been long since he had arrived in Silktown, even less since he had seen this creature.

He did not know what else to call her. The fasha, noble and draped in silks, was gone. So, too, was the monstrosity that Lenk had described. The woman here now, bereft of Khoth-Kapira's influence, was wounded from many cuts, including a great hole where an eye should be. Her nude flesh was scabbed over with scaly patches, her hair gone and left with thick hide. Her remaining ochre eye shone brightly and her mouth was wide with fangs.

But he could not call her a monster.

"Ah, their song is beautiful! You glorious few who believed in her, she has come to reward you!"

What mind, however fiendish, *could* keep their sanity in the wake of this?

The lawns were scattered with their corpses. The square was stained red with their bloody vomit. The sky was alive with the flies that fed on them and the few enterprising carrion birds that had returned to feast in their wake.

Young and old. Men and women and children. A few hulking dragonmen sprawled on the ground, a number of slain saccarii strewn across the square. Each one wearing the last moments of horror when the thick slop that had been their entrails had spilled out onto the stones.

Thus was the fury of the shicts.

He had deduced it from what Kataria had told him. But it only came together once he found the barrels of wine. The remnants of the poison still clung to the wood in a thick green sheen.

With just a few barrels of wine and just a few drops of poison, the shicts had accomplished more carnage than a colossal demon could with an army of abominations.

Faced with the scope of such hatred...

"Brothers! Sisters! Sing with me! Rise up and be heard!"

What mind would *not* simply break?

It would be better to leave her, he supposed. Whatever madness had claimed her had given her more bliss than the sane world ever had. Perhaps it would be kinder to simply let her live out whatever remaining fantasy she had.

But then his eyes drifted to the Souk and the burning pillars of the Silken Spire.

He had been too weak to take on the entire tulwar army. But even weakened, the threat of him had been enough to convince them to slow their march long enough for Asper's plan to evacuate.

He had...opted not to aid the evacuation in a way that would put him at the fore. Better that he not be seen, he thought. Better that he remain behind, to further warn the tulwar. Even now, as they prowled the city, he had no fear of them.

But they would not know what to do with this woman. She was no threat to them, clearly. But they would not leave her in peace. This was Gariath's army, after all.

A familiar urge crept into his gullet. An unfamiliar voice crept into his head.

Perhaps it would be kinder, it whispered, *to make better use of her.* His fingertips ached. Wisps of smoke peeled from them. *You are still weak. You must eat something soon. Why not ease her agony? Why not use her strength? You could protect so many...*

He shook his head.

"Prophet," he said. "Prophet...they have heard you."

Teneir looked up toward him. Her eye lit up brightly, her smile wide at him. She came rushing up to him and took his hand in her own. He could feel the warmth racing through her fingers, the pulse of her blood in her palm.

"Brother!" she whispered, reverent. "You have heard! You have risen!"

"I have." He nodded and smiled softly as he reached up and laid a hand on her cheek. "But it is these mortal distractions that cloud my mind so. I can only hear her clearly when I shut them out." He looked skyward and closed his eyes. "They are so much clearer now, sister."

"Are they?" Teneir followed his gaze. Her eyes fell shut. Her smile grew broader, almost tranquil. "Yes...*yes*, I can hear her! Tell me, brother, do you think she is pleased with all I have done?"

"She is. Rest easy, sister."

Bright electricity flashed from his fingers into her skull. She stiffened in his grip for a moment. Her hand slipped from his.

"Your work is done," he whispered.

It had been a kind death, he told himself, even if she had not been a kind woman. Perhaps Asper would have made her suffer more—or at least *wanted* her to suffer more. But he had a grander view of death these days; its scale, its scope, its intimacy. Perhaps in these, he had learned compassion.

Yes, another voice whispered. *What with blowing people to bits. You positively ooze compassion.*

He ignored that.

Or tried to.

"I would have let her suffer."

He looked up at the sound of a voice. Sitting on a bench beside a fountain, perhaps the last living man—or the last living *mere* man—stared at Dreadaeleon.

One wouldn't guess it to look at him, though. His spectacles were cracked. A gash streaked his shaven head with red. His clothes were in tatters. He was the pale color of a northerner, though, not the dark Djaalic color. Pity to have come all this way to visit on this day.

"She deserved it," the northerner said, "for what she did to this city."

Dreadaeleon looked down to the many corpses strewn about the square. "And them?"

The man looked at them, sniffed. "Them, I tried to save."

"You didn't do a very good job."

"No. I did not." The man sighed, stood up, and knuckled the small of his back. "I would argue that my intentions were good in the long term. But..." He looked up to the burning Spire. "This was my city, you know."

"This city seemed to have many masters."

"This city had no masters," the man said. "And few friends. Many thought they were the former, of course, that they could just push the city to do what they want. Only a few of us knew the truth."

"That being?"

"The city makes silk. Silk makes gold. Gold makes fashas. Fashas make thieves. Thieves make corpses." He shook his head. "The city does what it wants. It humors tyrants until it's done. It indulges thieves until it doesn't. Best you can do is just try to be in a spot where you benefit."

"You were a thief, then."

"Me?" The man shook his head again. "No. I was a friend." He grinned. "Not a very good one, I suppose. But I tried to do right." He glanced at Teneir's corpse. "She and I...we both did, I suppose."

Dreadaeleon followed his gaze. "Seems you failed each other."

"Seems so." The man sighed. "Understand, though, this city...it doesn't have room for ideals. Hers or the Prophet's."

Dreadaeleon felt his eyes narrow at the last word.

"But hers? She wanted a god that would never come. Dreams, we could make room for. The Prophet, though, wanted change." He shrugged. "And the city...well, she got in its way, anyway."

"What did you say your name was?" Dreadaeleon asked.

"No need. I died here today, friend. Along with all of Cier'Djaal's friends." He turned and began to trudge away. "But it wouldn't be the first time. Someday I'll be back with a new name." He threw up a half-hearted wave. "Maybe I'll see you around then, friend."

The man froze suddenly.

His body stiffened and went straight as a spear. His jaw clenched itself shut. His eyes bulged from his skull, made the spectacles fall from his face and shatter on the ground. He let out a thick, wet choking noise as he tried to turn to face Dreadaeleon.

The wizard held his hand out, the air shimmering about his finger-tips. He felt the man's rib cage in his grip, felt it resist as he began to curl his fingers.

"Yeah," Dreadaeleon said.

He closed his hand into a fist. There was a loud, cracking sound.

"Maybe you will."

The man flopped over, still. Dreadaeleon walked to his body and stared at him.

A kind death, in its own way. This was a day when cruel people received such, anyway. He supposed, if they were still alive to do so, they might ask him who he was to mete out such judgment.

He might reply, if he felt like it, that it was for the same reason he did not go to see the ships off when they left. Mere men, they had such a tiny view of death: Either a thing was alive or it wasn't. But him? He had a grander view of such things now.

And he was no mere man.

Not anymore.

He closed his eyes. He pressed his fingers to the man's scalp. He felt the smoke peel off his fingers.

And beneath the burning Spire, he fed.

FIFTY-TWO

THE PARTING WORD

It had been a long time since Mundas had last smiled.

It hadn't been sudden. He remembered the joy he had felt when he had first renounced. But over the years, he slowly gave up his capacity for it. There was no real point in it. There was no pleasure to be had in seeing the necessary done, no satisfaction in seeing the inevitable occur as it should; the outcome was the same, regardless. Mirth was simply a momentary lapse of concentration he could ill afford.

To that end, Mundas thought he had also lost the capacity to despair.

But as he stared at the great column of fire as the Silken Spire burned brightly into the night, he began to doubt that.

Decades of planning. Years of implementation. Months of execution. Undone in a few days. Destroyed with a single spark.

A savior slain. A civilization destroyed. A world doomed.

He paused, allowing himself to search for sorrow.

He found nothing.

Across the long verdant fields of the Green Belt, he felt something. Miles away, a pair of eyes were set upon him. A single breath later, someone was behind him. He turned. He regarded his new company.

A man made of threads stared back at him.

He supposed others must see something else when they looked at the dark figure that stood before him. Most might see a shadow in the shape of a human. A select few might see the colorless husk beneath. But for someone like Mundas, who no longer perceived flesh or breath as others did, he could see but the few thin threads by which this unliving thing clung to this dark earth.

Qulon had employed things like these before; hers was to challenge the flesh, after all, and death held no more mystery than life for her. This thread-man was but the latest of her private army of killers. No doubt, this one had taken many for her.

Yet he hesitated.

"You seem nervous," Mundas observed. "Generous of Qulon to leave you that quality." He stared at the shadow for a long moment. "Do you wish to introduce yourself?"

The shadow did not. But he did not need to. Mundas knew this one's name, for he had heard it once, in a time not here, in a place not here.

"Perhaps you believe I will react with violence to you for your part in this?" He glanced back to the burning Spire and shook his head. "That is forbidden by our agreement. Speak whatever message you were commanded to deliver."

"Qulon wishes you to know that she will be moving on," Denaos said. "She feels her time will be better spent preparing for what is to come."

Mundas accepted that with a quirked brow. Qulon rarely considered other activities more worthy than gloating. But, then, this was a rare victory for her. Perhaps she simply didn't know what to do with it.

"She advises you not to worry. What is coming will ultimately result in a stronger world, after weakness and corruption have been forcibly shed."

Mundas did not worry. Nor did he respond to that. Whatever mistakes Qulon labored under, he would correct, eventually. Though it would be many lives before he could.

He turned away from Denaos, the thread-man, and looked back to the burning Spire to contemplate this. But the thread-man did not leave.

"And people are free now," he said, his voice hesitant. "Whatever else happens, there'll be no demons to lord over mortality. Everything else, it almost doesn't matter."

Mundas did not bother looking over his shoulder. He almost didn't bother answering. But something in Denaos's voice compelled him to. Bereft of joy or despair, perhaps he still had a fragment of pity left in him.

"Qulon did not instruct you to say that," he said. "Nor do you believe I will heed you. You are speaking to soothe yourself."

"And?" Denaos asked. "It doesn't make it any less true. Khoth-Kapira is dead."

"He is."

"The demons are gone."

"They are."

"Mortals are free."

"To kill each other, destroy their homes, and eat their children, yes." Mundas sighed. "And you think that this virtue, however small, justifies what happened to you? What she made you?"

Denaos was silent for a moment. "I have to."

Mundas was silent for a longer moment. "You do."

Whatever allowed Qulon to create as she did, he had no desire to know—this was the truth she had discovered when she had renounced, just as he had found his own. But there was something different about this one. She had returned his flesh but had not spared him the fears and worries that had come with them. Cruel of her, he thought. Or perhaps her truth was deeper than mere cruelty.

"It will not soothe you to know this," Mundas said, "but truth does not soothe, it merely solidifies. The objective was never to give mortals a master. Their fickleness and violence precludes that. Rather, we sought to provide a bulwark on which their greeds and fears and furies could break, something that could burden itself with their sins and allow them to fulfill other requirements."

"Khoth-Kapira wouldn't do that," Denaos said. "He was a monster."

"There are no such things as monsters. There are merely different purposes and different things to fulfill them."

Mundas closed his eyes. Far away, he could feel ships on the sea. Hours from now, he could hear prayers whispered in the dark. Years from now, he could feel flames licking his face as the world burned.

But that was far away.

He felt a fleeting urge to disappear, to vanish from this world, this moment, and find somewhere and sometime new. But that would accomplish nothing. He had much to contemplate and the night was, for this moment, cool.

He turned and began to walk down the hill, deeper into the Green Belt.

Denaos watched him go from beneath his hood. "What now, then? War?"

"That was Qulon's aim, yes," Mundas replied as he walked farther down the hill. "War. Strife. Suffering. And from these, truth."

"She said we would find an answer there. But she didn't say which," Denaos said, "except that it would be without gods."

"Then she is mistaken."

"No, she isn't. Because of her, Khoth-Kapira is dead."

"Indeed. She thought to kill one god." Mundas sighed as he trekked into the night and disappeared into the dark. "And instead, she created two."

FIFTY-THREE

TEN THOUSAND
HEARTBEATS AWAY

Can you hear them, daughter?"

Sai-Thuwan lay still—his breathing had calmed and his limbs no longer twitched in agony. His hand was pressed firmly to the bandage at his side, holding it close to him. His eyes were cast skyward and he did not blink.

But his ears were twitching, trembling, shifting every which way as he listened.

"There are not many still in the city," he said, his voice weak. "But they are so loud." His ears went erect, trembling and leaning toward the left. "Shaab Sahaar is dead, they say. The tulwar have been driven from their city. Cier'Djaal is dead, they say. Their people have fled and the richest lie dead from poison." His ears twitched, then drooped. "Shekune is here. She calls this a great victory."

He settled on the mat of straw, a funerary shroud of skin and bone draped over a spirit that had died.

"And I have helped her."

It was not that Kwar did not care. The sorrow that hung heavy in his voice settled on her heart like iron. But his were not the only ears that were aloft and listening.

In truth, she could not hear what he heard. She knew the khoshicts were still out there—Shekune would want them to monitor the tulwar's movements, watch for weaknesses. Their new leader, the red thing with the claws and horns, would be of great interest to her.

Him, she could hear.

Far away, beside the burning columns of the Silken Spire, she could hear his growl, his roar, his anger. She could see him, a bloodred stain beside the inferno, the stray spark that would burn the city down.

The tulwar, she could hear, too. They roamed the streets in packs, checking from house to house. Many were growling, snarling as they tore apart the homes for anything useful. A few let out quiet sobs at the memory of what had happened to their city as they fought for this one. But most of them simply let out long, weary breaths—after all that had happened, this was all they remembered how to do.

But of the khoshicts? She heard nothing.

She knew they wouldn't find her. Even with her father's unguarded voice, their position high up in the attic of an empty sweetshop was too far removed from the searches of anyone. The tulwar were looking for food and steel. The khoshicts were looking for tulwar. No one was looking for melted chocolates or stale pastries or a dying shict and his daughter.

No one, except for one.

And that was what Kwar heard.

Through the alleys and streets crawling with the tulwar. Over a sky lit up by laughing flame. Across the stones painted black with demon blood. Upon miles of a dark and sparkling sea.

A single word. In a language made just for her. A long and lonely word stretched out over many miles and reached her ears through the Howling.

And Kwar's heart sank.

She didn't wait for me.

A pang of guilt struck her. Of course, she couldn't have waited. The tulwar had come quickly. The khoshicts prowled the city, still. The evacuation out of Cier'Djaal had been swift. To have waited for her would have been to die, and Kwar would never have forgiven herself for it.

She had to leave. It was the only way.

And yet, as logic and reason so often failed to prevent, her heart did not hurt any less.

"You should have left me."

She looked over her shoulder to the mat on which her father lay.

Sai-Thuwan's eyes were shut tight, his body still. His ears were flat against his head and a deep frown was carved across his face.

"You should have gone with her," her father said. "I was so foolish, daughter. Since your mother died, I listened to everyone but you. And it has cost our family everything." He let out a groan. "The pale shict was right. Shekune will lead us to a war we cannot win. You should have gone with her. Left me."

And it hurt Kwar to admit to herself that, in some dark and angry part of herself, she wanted that to be true.

Her mother had died and he had done nothing. Thua was gone because he had believed in him. War had come to her people and he had helped it. All her sorrows, she wanted to be his fault. She wanted it to be that easy, that she could have simply left him and all her pain behind to bleed out in that dark alley, while she disappeared with someone who loved her.

But it was not that easy. And it had never been.

Her thoughts drifted back to the human and his blue eyes that should have been empty and his words that should have been foul. She remembered the way he had reached out to her with a hand instead of a sword. She remembered his last words to her.

"Find us."

After everything, he hadn't wanted her dead. And whatever pains she had given him, he did not give back. She wanted to return with him to Kataria.

Because, she knew, Kataria loved her.

As he loved Kataria.

And if Kwar had gone back with him, that love would have still been there, a blade wedge between them. And every time they looked at each other, it would cut a little deeper. And it would linger there, in cold doubt, for a long time.

And, one way or another, she would be alone again.

A groan came from behind her.

She turned and saw her father lying there, wounded and still, but alive. She hadn't realized how strong he was until now, to take a wound such as he had and still draw breath. And though he made noises of such pain, it wasn't that which she heard.

It was a soft noise she hadn't heard for a long time. It was a long, slow word in a language spoken only between her family. It was a voice without sound, a whisper without breath.

A Howling she had not heard for a long time.

And she did not feel so alone right now.

"Can you walk?" she asked.

"I cannot," he replied.

Her ears twitched. She heard his Howling. She knew he was lying.

"We will move soon," she said. "I will help you up and we will make for the desert. There are yijis that will take us to a camp where you can recover. We must go before the tulwar settle in here."

"It's too dangerous."

"I know."

"You must go on, save yourself."

"That would be wise."

"Leave me."

She looked at him. She smiled.

"No. Never again."

And her ears twitched. She spoke a short, terse word without a voice. His ears trembled in response as he heard it. And, realizing he could not argue with her, he settled back down on the mat.

"Give me an hour," he said. "And some water. And I will be all right to move."

"I can manage an hour."

She looked out the window, across the dead city of Cier'Djaal, across the long sea and the black ships fading on the horizon. Her ears rose and listened to that sound made just for her. And she held it as long as she could.

"You will see her again," Sai-Thuwan said. "One day."

She pressed a hand to the glass. "Maybe."

"A girl like that makes trouble. You love trouble."

She smiled. His Howling reached out to her and told her a truth she could not deny.

"After all," he muttered, "you are terribly clever like that."

FIFTY-FOUR

A Prophecy of War

Perhaps a poet would have been able to put Asper's thoughts into words.

As she stared out over the burning Spire, its flames lighting up the night sky, she felt many things. Despair, of course, and its companion, guilt. Anger and rage she wore like scars these days. Emotions swirled inside her, endlessly churning as she watched the funeral pyre for civilization burn itself out.

A poet could have done something great with that image, she thought.

But most of the poets were dead now—slain in wars or in Silktown. And aboard the couthi ships, no one had a profession. Or a home. Or a name. They were all simply refugees.

And as the ships pulled farther away from the dead city, and as the burning Spire grew fainter and fainter on the horizon, Asper had no words for the emotions inside her.

Instead, her head was full of numbers.

Seven thousand.

Aturach had done the count as best as he was able, kept track of everyone he could. The evacuation had gone as smoothly as it could, but there had been problems. Many had fled on foot. Some had stayed behind. Some had sobbed and begged and fought to get on. Some had been trampled over in the mad rush to get on. Some had fought when the meager belongings they had held were discarded to make room for another life, another soul.

And in the end, they had managed to save seven thousand.

The conditions on the ships were cramped. Intolerable, really. But it needed to last only another two days. Man-Shii Kree had told her that their fleet would meet with more farther up the coast, which would relieve some of the burden on the way to Muraska, where she would meet with the eight Gray Lords.

Eight. Four men. Four women. Each one to convince to take seven thousand people with no coin and many problems into their city.

The couthi would help, of course. The Bloodwise Brotherhood had pull in the city. But their aid was reliant on Asper fulfilling her end of the bargain. In addition to convincing Muraska to take the refugees, she would have to persuade them to go to war with the shicts.

All the shicts.

Twelve tribes of shicts. Each tribe containing several thousand over the span of thousands of miles. The Silesrian tribes alone number in the millions. Four men. Four women. One of me. Three couthi. Somehow, an army to attack millions of shicts has to come out of that while they also take in seven thousand people.

If they did.

If it came down to it, she might only be able to convince them of one of those. And if it came down to throwing their weight behind waging war on the shicts or pushing to resettle the refugees, she knew what the couthi would choose.

But it wasn't like she had to have the answer now.

After all, she thought as she leaned on the railing, *you're the Prophet now. You're going to be doing this shit until you die.*

The ship was silent behind her. The refugees had been crowded so tightly that they sprawled out on the deck, trying their best to sleep through the chill wind and the rocking waves and the children crying for their pets left behind and the soft moaning of mothers who had only made it with one of their daughters and the . . .

She let out a long sigh. She leaned so hard on the ship's railing that she thought she might break it and go plunging into the oceans below.

And, as she stared at her twisted reflection in the rippling salt water below, she thought that might not be so bad.

"Excuse me . . . Prophet?"

She wasn't sure how long she had been staring when she heard the voice behind her. Nor was she sure who the woman was that had appeared there.

A Djaalic woman, and very beautiful. The grime did nothing to obscure her grace. Her dark hair was no less gorgeous when it was plastered to her face by dried sweat. And the drab, workmanlike garb she wore only barely hid her curves.

Yet these were things Asper noticed only because of how little beauty there had been lately. And it was the woman's eyes—the first eyes Asper had seen in a long time that were not overwhelmed by fear—that held her attention.

"I am sorry to disturb your meditations," the woman said, inclining her head in a properly rehearsed manner. "Shall I come back?"

Asper blinked, unsure as to what she had just said. But it slowly came to her.

Right, she told herself. *You weren't sitting here about to shit yourself out of sheer terror. You were "meditating." Prophets have meditations.*

"It's fine," Asper said. "What can I do for you?"

"There are three children." The woman pointed to the end of the deck. "They're cold, Prophet. I was hoping there might be more blankets for them? Two of them are small, they could share one."

Asper stared at her.

Two blankets.

Millions of shicts to kill. Eight Gray Lords to persuade. Three couthi to appease. Seven thousand refugees to settle. And it was the thought of a few blankets that sent her mind blank.

Where was she going to get blankets? Supplies were stretched so thin they would snap like a thread in another day.

Where was she going to get the influence to tell the Gray Lords to take in seven thousand people?

Where was she going to find the men to staff an army to kill millions of shicts? And millions upon millions of tulwar? And one dragonman? Where would she get the armor? Where would she get the weapons? Where would she get the money?

How the *fuck* was she going to do any of this?

"Prophet, I hope you won't…"

The woman's voice snapped her back to attention. She was looking at her feet, her hands curled into fists.

"I don't know how to say it," she said. "I didn't think I was going to escape that city. We turned our bathhouse into a bunker to survive the tulwar. Then that...that *thing* came. But even before that, I was..."

She looked up at Asper. The smile on her face was a meek and trembling thing, but she couldn't keep it hidden. And the tears at the corners of her eyes glistened like stars.

"I was never ashamed of what I did, Prophet. But it wasn't my choice to do it, to be in that bathhouse. And there were times when I thought I would die there." She shook her head. "Thank you, Prophet. Thank you for this."

Asper did not know what to say. Her mind empty, her lips numb, the words simply came tumbling out.

"For this?" She gestured out to the deck. "For open skies and uncertain fates? For cold winds and too few blankets? For sobbing mothers and hungry children?" She shook her head, mouth hanging open. "I don't deserve your thanks. I couldn't protect the city. I lost you your home."

"Cier'Djaal was just a city," the woman said. "It was never my home." She looked over the refugees. "Maybe it was never any of ours." Her smile grew firmer as she turned back to Asper. "If Cier'Djaal is gone, we are still Djaalics. We build. We create. We work."

"What did you do?" Asper asked. "Before this?"

"I worked in a bathhouse, Prophet," she said. "I was a courtesan."

Asper stared at her. "What is your name?"

The woman brushed a lock of hair from her eyes. "Before I came to the city, my name was Rishia. But in the bathhouse, some called me Liaja."

Asper stared at her again. And, after a moment, she nodded stiffly.

"Go back to the children, Rishia," she said. "I'll bring you some blankets."

"Thank you, Prophet."

The woman turned and left, bowing profusely. And it was only after she turned away that Asper allowed herself to lean on the railing, suddenly weak in the knees.

Three children.

Two blankets.

One woman.

She had saved that many. And six thousand, nine hundred ninety-seven others.

She drew herself up and held her breath. She picked her way across the deck, toward the gangway leading down to the ship's hold.

She would find Haethen down there. Together, they would put together a plan to make an army to fight a million shicts.

She would find Dransun and Aturach down there. With them, she would make a plan to persuade Muraska to take seven thousand people.

She would find the couthi down there. And with them, she would save many more.

Tomorrow, there would be war. Tomorrow, there would be suffering. Tomorrow, she would build this world anew.

But right now, she had to find blankets.

FIFTY-FIVE

Somewhere Warm

Somewhere, far away, a fire was burning brightly. And with every breath, its brightness grew dimmer until it was just one more star in the sky, burning itself out quietly.

And, her eyes closed and her heart silent, Kataria's ears were full of the night.

There. Miles away. Across ocean and stone and sand. There was the sound she had searched for, shouting out into the Howling for so long.

A heartbeat, faint and warm. A weary sigh cast into the night to disappear among the stars. A single word spoken in a single language that spanned a thousand breaths.

And it sounded like good-bye.

A numbness set into Kataria's bones. And, in its wake, a sick and sour feeling in her belly.

Kataria tried to reach out, to hold on to that word, to strangle it until it would stay so she could explain and apologize and plead. But with each moment she held it, with every breath it echoed in her head, she could feel the pain in her stomach crawl up into her chest and twist her heart.

And still, she clung to it, that last word. She held it tightly and tried to tell it all the things she desperately wanted to, until the pain was so sharp and so intense that she almost collapsed on the deck.

Her ears fell. Wet eyes opened. Her mouth fell, but no word came out.

And she let Kwar go.

Silence. Nothing but the night breeze and the sound of water lapping against the ship's hull. Neither of them was loud enough to drown out the great, empty sound in Kataria's mind. And their plain ugliness felt like a knife in her skull in the wake of that singular sound.

Stupid, she thought, cursing herself. *It's better this way. How was it ever going to work? It wasn't. You hurt Lenk for her. You owe it to him to . . . to . . .*

She drew in a breath. It hurt.

And she betrayed you, didn't she? She helped Shekune. She betrayed you . . . to save your life, she betrayed you. She saved you and . . .

Something lurched into her throat. She snapped her teeth down, as though she could decapitate it and send it back down.

There's a war. Shekune started a war. You've got bigger shit to worry about. You've got tribes to save. You've got to help them.

Wetness stung at the corners of her eyes. That sick feeling in her belly spread to her body. The blood rushed from her head. She clung to the railing to keep from falling over, bit her lower lip.

Don't you cry, stupid. Don't you fucking cry. Not now. Not here. There'll be time for tears later . . . there will . . . there . . .

Maybe that was true.

Maybe there would be time for tears later. Maybe there would come a time when she could bury these feelings, this pain in her chest. And maybe, one day, it wouldn't hurt quite as bad.

But now, in the night, as fires faded and stars were mercilessly quiet, they came anyway. And here, on the deck of a ship taking her far away, it hurt.

And she couldn't help it, no matter how many times she cursed herself for doing it.

Kataria leaned over the railing, buried her face in her hands, and cried.

He could hear her.

Above the coughing and the restless moaning on the ship's deck, Lenk could hear the sounds of her tears.

It was an odd feeling, really. She was always the one to hear him approaching. She was always the one to hear his breathing. Sometimes, he swore she could hear his thoughts. He had never really heard her, as he did now, the sound so sharp it felt like it could cut right through him.

Was this, he wondered, what she felt like when she heard him?

A great shape shifted next to him. He turned and saw a pair of great avian eyes glittering in the dark, an almost accusatory glare locked on him.

"Don't give me that look," he muttered. "Don't you think I want to go to her?" He shook his head. "She'd hate that. Trust me." He looked long to the railing where she leaned. "This"—it hurt to say it—"this is something she wants to do alone."

Colonel MacSwain's horned head swiveled toward Kataria. After a moment, he lowered his head sullenly onto his forelegs, content only to watch. Lenk sighed and leaned against the scraw's great bulk.

They had been given a wide berth by the ship's crew and her refugee passengers. The Djaalics had chosen to sleep in even more cramped conditions rather than risk getting near the great beast. Just as well; he had been injured in his fall. He would need time to recover.

"It's funny," Lenk said. "I'm sure there have been some problems I've solved without the sword." He looked at his empty hands before him. "But honestly, I can't think of any. And right now, I feel like...if there were a way I could stab it and make it all better..."

He stared at his hands for a long time, his callused fingers and scarred palms. Hundreds of battles, dozens of bodies, and they couldn't do a damn thing but sit here on his lap and wait. And even if violence could have solved this...

His sword was gone.

Along with everything else.

Shuro had disappeared, of course, and if he ever saw her again, she would kill him. His companions had been scattered—to conquest, to war, to hungers and curses he couldn't understand. And Cier'Djaal, his new life, any life, was gone.

He hadn't even been able to call the city his before he had lost it forever.

Really, the loss of a sword—a piece of metal he had been trying to drop ever since he picked it up—shouldn't have made him feel as he did right then. He shouldn't have felt so weak, his empty hands shouldn't have felt so heavy, he shouldn't have felt like he couldn't help her.

But he did.

Because it had been his sword. And through everything, it had been the one thing he had been able to hold on to. Until now.

A long moment of silence passed. Lenk looked around him. Nothing but the still night air and a sky full of stars greeted him. And yet, even though he had struck the fiend down himself, he somehow expected Mocca to show up any moment with that enigmatic smile of his and tell him exactly what to do.

Find another sword, he would say. *The steel is not the weapon. You are. Take it up and be strong once more.*

And maybe he could do that.

Maybe.

His ears pricked up. Footsteps on wood. Soft breath. A pair of eyes locked on him.

He looked up.

And there she was. Dirty with dried sweat and grime. Her clothes torn and tattered. Her eyes were dark and exhausted and still wet.

But she was here. And so was he.

"Hey," she said.

"Hey," he replied.

Colonel MacSwain looked up as she approached. He raised one of his wings, making a space for her. She settled against his side next to Lenk, leaned against the beast, and patted his flank. The scraw let out a contented purring sound.

Lenk felt the rise and fall of the beast's side as it breathed quietly, settling back down to sleep.

"The Sainites came by," he said. "They'll want him back, eventually."

She sniffed. "He likes me better."

"Still…"

"He'll be ready to fly in a day or two," she said. "We'll be gone. If they still want him, they can come fight me for him."

He smiled at that. The very mention of the word *fight* made him weary, as he could tell it did her. Yet he knew she'd beat every last one of them into the earth. Hopefully, it wouldn't come to that. Hopefully, they would be gone before long.

Asper wouldn't need them. In fact, it would be easier if they were gone. She would have a hard enough time dealing with Muraska without them wanting to know about demons.

They couldn't go to Gariath. He was still a bloodthirsty brute. But he was no longer their bloodthirsty brute. And whoever he was—and whoever called him their leader—they wouldn't be safe around any of them.

Dreadaeleon had vanished after the evacuation. Perhaps he had turned invisible. Or maybe disappeared into another world entirely. Nothing seemed impossible for him anymore. Lenk didn't know who or what he was anymore.

And Denaos…

Well, maybe he just couldn't bear to see Denaos again.

"We could go back." He almost didn't realize he was speaking until he had said the words. "We could fly back to Cier'Djaal and find her."

Kataria shook her head.

"We can't," she said. "The city will be crawling with tulwar by then. The desert will be full of shicts. She'll be silent. Even if she wasn't…she…" She closed her eyes. "We can't."

Lenk turned back to his hands. His empty hands that couldn't fix this. He stared at them.

"I just thought…"

Her hand appeared in his. Her fingers wrapped around his. She squeezed them tightly. And when he looked up, her smile was soft and warm.

"I know you did." She slumped over onto him. She laid her head on his chest. Her ears twitched against his chin and she pulled his arm around her. "And I knew you would."

He felt her breath on his chest, he felt his heartbeat in her ears. She was warm and tired and filthy and beautiful in his arms. And with everything else gone and all the battles behind him, he found nothing hurt quite so much anymore.

He looked to the sky, held her closer. "Where do we go, then?"

"I want to go someplace warm. With less people." She looked up at him. "Where do you want to go?"

He looked down at her. "I want to go home."

"Where is that?"

A fair question. His childhood home was gone. Shuro was gone. Cier'Djaal was gone. She could never return to her home, either, after what Shekune had done. They had no money. They had no weapons. They had no food.

But they had a scraw.

And they had the night sky.

And they had the sound of his heartbeat in her ears and the feel of her warm hands on his scars and the way she looked right into him sometimes.

"I guess," he said, "home could be anywhere."

"Anywhere." She yawned, exposing her canines. "That sounds good. Let's start there."

She fell against his chest. Her breath was hot on his skin as she fell asleep. He leaned back against the scraw and closed his eyes. His body, with all its scars and its aches, settled into a weary groan. But it was a comfortable pain, a familiar pain.

And it did not hurt quite so bad anymore.